PENGUIN  CLASSICS

THE MAN WHO WOULD BE KING: SELECTED STORIES OF RUDYARD KIPLING

SERIES EDITOR: JAN MONTEFIORE

RUDYARD KIPLING, born in December 1865 in Bombay (now Mumbai), was taken to England in 1871 with his younger sister Alice and left for five years with an abusive foster-family in Southsea, after which he was sent to the United Services College in Devon, the public school affectionately recalled in *Stalky & Co.* (1899). He returned to India in the autumn of 1882 to work as a reporter. The poems, sketches and stories which he wrote during his 'Seven Years' Hard' in India, especially the series 'Plain Tales from the Hills', published as a book in 1888, won him immediate acclaim and, from his arrival in London in 1889, worldwide literary celebrity. This was increased by the powerful stories collected in *Life's Handicap* and the originality of *Barrack-Room Ballads* (1892), whose poems 'Mandalay', 'Tommy' and 'Gunga Din' became immensely popular performance items in music-halls – which, like hymns and ballads, were a lasting influence on Kipling's verse.

In 1892 Kipling married the American Caroline Balestier and lived with her in Vermont for four happy years, during which their daughters Josephine and Elsie were born and Kipling wrote some of his best work, including the two *Jungle Books* (1894, 1895). They moved to England in 1896, settling in Rottingdean, East Sussex, where their son John was born, and eventually at the house Batemans, at Burwash. Kipling continued to travel widely with his family, spending nearly all the winters from 1898 to 1908 in South Africa. On a trip to New York in 1899, his 6-year-old daughter Josephine died of pneumonia, which Kipling himself narrowly survived.

Kipling published his masterpiece, *Kim*, in 1901, and the *Just So Stories* in 1902. He turned to the theme of Englishness and history in his children's books *Puck of Pook's Hill* (1906) and *Rewards and Fairies* (1910), interweaving poems and stories to subtle intertextual effect. His stories for adults after 1900 focus on the lives of ordinary people, uniquely combining a creative response to the new twentieth-century technologies of communication with a strong imaginative feeling for the strange and the numinous, intensified by his pared-down, understated style. His public poems, including 'Recessional', 'The White Man's Burden' and 'The Islanders', all printed in *The Times*, preached the virtues of patriotism and duty.

From the outset Kipling identified with the rulers and officials of the British Empire, although he was never their servant (he refused both a knighthood and the Order of Merit). Yet he sympathized deeply with children, outlaws and outsiders, who often engaged his best energies as a writer, as witnessed by the vitality and subtlety of the *Jungle Books* and *Kim*. He was a strong supporter of the Boer War, for which he wrote journalism and propaganda; this, together with the hardening of his conservative political views after 1900, made him increasingly unpopular with liberals and anti-imperialists. Kipling returned their dislike. His books continued to sell and to be read widely and he was awarded honorary doctorates by many universities and the Nobel Prize in 1907, but he never again enjoyed the brilliant reputation which he had held in the 1890s.

In the First World War Kipling remained a strongly patriotic writer, but after the blow of losing his son John at the Battle of Loos in 1915 he became a more private man. He nonetheless played a major role in the War Graves Commission, arguing successfully for equality of treatment for all ranks and choosing the inscriptions for the memorial stones. He commemorated the dead in his own moving 'Epitaphs of the War' and his *History of the Irish Guards in the Great War* (1923), an account of his son's regiment. His late stories of loss and bereavement are written with an acuteness and subtlety not always perceived by their contemporary readers.

Kipling died in 1936.

JAN MONTEFIORE is Professor of Twentieth-Century English Literature in the University of Kent at Canterbury, where she has taught in the School of English and American Literature since 1978. Her books include *Rudyard Kipling* (2007), *Arguments of Heart and Mind* (2002) and *Feminism and Poetry* (1987). She is married to the war correspondent Patrick Cockburn.

RUDYARD KIPLING

The Man Who Would Be King

Edited with an Introduction and Notes by
JAN MONTEFIORE

PENGUIN BOOKS

PENGUIN CLASSICS

Published by the Penguin Group
Penguin Books Ltd, 80 Strand, London WC2R ORL, England
Penguin Group (USA) Inc., 375 Hudson Street, New York, New York 10014, USA
Penguin Group (Canada), 90 Eglinton Avenue East, Suite 700, Toronto, Ontario, Canada M4P 2Y3
(a division of Pearson Penguin Canada Inc.)
Penguin Ireland, 25 St Stephen's Green, Dublin 2, Ireland (a division of Penguin Books Ltd)
Penguin Group (Australia), 250 Camberwell Road, Camberwell, Victoria 3124, Australia
(a division of Pearson Australia Group Pty Ltd)
Penguin Books India Pvt Ltd, 11 Community Centre, Panchsheel Park, New Delhi – 110 017, India
Penguin Group (NZ), 67 Apollo Drive, Rosedale, Auckland 0632, New Zealand
(a division of Pearson New Zealand Ltd)
Penguin Books (South Africa) (Pty) Ltd, 24 Sturdee Avenue, Rosebank, Johannesburg 2196, South Africa

Penguin Books Ltd, Registered Offices: 80 Strand, London WC2R ORL, England

www.penguin.com

This selection first published in Penguin Classics 2011
004

Introduction and editorial material copyright © Jan Montefiore, 2011
All rights reserved

The moral right of the editor has been asserted

Set in 10.25/12.25pt Postscript Adobe Sabon
Typeset by Ellipsis Books Limited, Glasgow
Printed in England by Clays Ltd, St Ives plc

ISBN: 978-0-141-44235-8

www.greenpenguin.co.uk

MIX
Paper from
responsible sources
FSC™ C018179

Penguin Books is committed to a sustainable
future for our business, our readers and our planet.
This book is made from Forest Stewardship
Council™ certified paper.

ALWAYS LEARNING   **PEARSON**

Contents

Chronology

1865 Joseph Rudyard Kipling born 30 December in Bombay, India, to Alice and John Lockwood Kipling, teacher of Art and Crafts at the Sir Jamsetjee Jejeebhoy School of Art and Industry.

1868 Sister Alice ('Trix') born.

1871–7 Rudyard and Alice taken to England and left in the care of the Holloway family in Lorne Lodge, Southsea (the 'House of Desolation').

1878–82 Attends United Services College at Westward Ho!, Devon.

1880 Falls in love with Florence ('Flo') Garrard and corresponds with her for four years.

1881 *Schoolboy Lyrics* privately printed in Lahore, India, by Alice Kipling.

1882 Leaves school to join his family in Lahore (where Lockwood Kipling has been Principal of the Lahore School of Art and Curator of the Lahore Museum since 1875); 'unofficially' engaged to Flo Garrard.

1882–7 Junior reporter on *Civil and Military Gazette* in Lahore at a starting salary of 150 rupees a month, rising to 200 after six months and 400 after a year.

1884 Indian National Congress founded. Flo Garrard breaks off their connection. *Echoes*, a book of parodies and spoof poems written jointly with his sister, privately printed and published.

1885 In Lahore, publishes *Departmental Ditties* and *Quartette*, a supplement to the *Civil and Military Gazette* written by the Kipling family, including 'The Phantom 'Rickshaw' and 'The Strange Ride of Morrowbie Jukes'.

1886 *Departmental Ditties* published in London. November 1886–June 1887: 'Plain Tales from the Hills' appear as 'turnovers' in the *Civil and Military Gazette*; negotiates with Thacker Spink in Bombay about publishing them as a book.

1887 Moves to Allahabad to write for the *Pioneer* newspaper, with increased salary of 600 rupees a month. Writes travel sketches of

Native States entitled 'Letters of Marque' (later reprinted in *From Sea to Sea*, 1899).

1888 Thacker Spink publish *Plain Tales from the Hills*, revised and enlarged, in Bombay and England. *Soldiers Three, Wee Willie Winkie, Under the Deodars, The Phantom 'Rickshaw, In Black and White* and *The Story of the Gadsbys* published by A. D. Wheeler in the Indian Railway Library series.

1889 Leaves India to become a full-time freelance writer, travelling through China, Japan and the USA, as described in *From Sea to Sea*. Arrives in England, settles in London near Charing Cross, and achieves spectacular early literary success. Macmillan become his London publisher, publishing all his works apart from his poetry.

1890 Elected to Savile Club. Publishes 'Barrack-Room Ballads' in *Scots Observer*, and many poems and short stories in *Macmillan's Magazine, St James's Gazette* and *Lippincott's Monthly Magazine* in New York. Suffers a breakdown and recovers; meets Flo Garrard, again falls in love and is again rejected, fictionalizing the experience in *The Light That Failed*. Becomes a close friend of Wolcott Balestier, American literary agent, and with him begins their joint novel, *The Naulahka*.

1891 *The Light That Failed* and *Life's Handicap: Stories of Mine Own People* published. In October sets out by ship for South Africa, New Zealand and Australia, revisiting India for what proves to be the last time. On 7 December learns by telegram from Caroline (Carrie) Balestier of her brother Wolcott Balestier's death and on 27 December leaves Lahore for England.

1892 10 January: marries Carrie Balestier at All Souls, Langham Place, London. 3 February: the couple set out for Brattleboro, Vermont, to meet the Balestier family. March: they continue their honeymoon journey via Vancouver to Japan. 9 June: Kipling loses his savings of nearly £2,000 when his bank (New Oriental Banking Co.) goes broke; they return to the USA, and settle in Brattleboro, in Bliss Cottage. 29 December: their daughter Josephine ('Best Beloved') is born. *The Naulahka* published. *Barrack-Room Ballads* (Methuen) sells 7,000 copies in its first year.

1893 The Kiplings move into their own house, Naulakha. *Many Inventions* published.

1894 *The Jungle Book* published. Lockwood and Alice Kipling leave India, retiring to Tisbury, Wiltshire.

1895 *The Second Jungle Book, Soldiers Three and Other Stories, Wee Willie Winkie and Other Stories* published. Anti-English feeling between the USA and Great Britain over Venezuela makes Kipling uncomfortable. He is approached about becoming Poet Laureate on the death of Tennyson and indicates refusal.

1896 A second daughter, Elsie, born 3 February. Quarrel with Carrie's brother Beatty Balestier, followed by an embarrassing court action, decides Kipling to return to England. In September they take a house in Torquay, Devon.

1897 Family moves to Rottingdean, East Sussex. In June, Queen Victoria's Diamond Jubilee celebrated; Kipling writes the admonitory 'Recessional', which appears in *The Times* 17 July. Son John Kipling born 17 August. *Captain Courageous* and *The Seven Seas* (poems) published.

1898 Kitchener killed at Omdurman. *The Day's Work* published. The Kipling family visits Cape Town, South Africa, from January to April. Kipling becomes a friend of Cecil Rhodes and Alfred Milner.

1899 *Stalky & Co.* published. February: 'The White Man's Burden', encouraging US annexation of the Philippines, appears in *The Times* and in *McClure's Journal* in the USA. Kipling and his family set out on a disastrous visit to the USA. Arriving in New York, Kipling becomes critically ill with pneumonia; his near-death and recovery is global headline news. 6 March: his daughter Josephine dies. His sister 'Trix' suffers her first mental breakdown. Travel writings collected *From Sea to Sea* (2 vols.) published. 11 October: Boer War begins. Kipling, a strong supporter of the Government, writes 'The Absent-minded Beggar' which, set to music by Arthur Sullivan for the Soldiers' Families Fund, nets £300,000.

1900 January–April: Kipling and family visit South Africa, staying in Cape Town; Kipling visits the army to raise morale. Later he works on *Kim*, discussing its progress with his father. From 1900 to 1908 Kipling and his family spend their winters in Cape Town at The Woolsack, a house built specially for them by Cecil Rhodes.

1901 *Kim* published.

1902 Cecil Rhodes dies. Treaty of Vereeniging ends the Boer War. 2 January: *The Times* publishes Kipling's 'The Islanders', a poem rebuking the British for military unpreparedness. Kipling purchases his house Batemans in Burwash, East Sussex, and moves in on 3 September. *Just So Stories* published.

1903 *The Five Nations* (poems) published.

1904 *Traffics and Discoveries* published.

1906 *Puck of Pook's Hill* published.

1907 Kipling awarded Nobel Prize for literature and Hon. D.Litt. by Oxford and Durham universities.

1909 *Actions and Reactions* published.

1910 *Rewards and Fairies* published. Death of Edward VII. Union of
    South Africa created, to Kipling's disgust. 23 November: Alice
    Kipling dies.

1911 26 January: Lockwood Kipling dies. C. R. L. Fletcher's *History
    of England*, with poems by Kipling, published. Public agitation for
    women's suffrage; Kipling publishes 'The Female of the Species' in
    hostile response.

1912 'Marconi scandal' of insider dealing by Liberal Cabinet members,
    including Rufus Isaacs, outrages Kipling. *Songs from Books* (poems)
    published.

1913 Rufus Isaacs appointed Attorney General: Kipling writes and
    privately circulates the anti-Semitic poem 'Gehazi', attacking him.
    Home Rule Bill for Ireland passes the Commons twice, to be rejected
    by the Lords. Edward Carson foments rebellion in Ulster, supported
    by Kipling in speeches.

1914 Home Rule Bill for Ireland passes its third reading in the House
    of Commons, infuriating Ulster Protestants. April: Kipling's poem
    'Ulster' supporting Edward Carson's sedition published in the *Morn-
    ing Post*; he makes a speech in Tunbridge Wells attacking Liberals
    and Home Rule. 4 August: Britain declares war on Germany.
    1 September: Kipling's call to arms, 'For All We Have and Are',
    published in *The Times*. 10 September: Kipling's son John joins the
    Irish Guards.

1915 Kipling writes war stories, including 'Mary Postgate'. John
    Kipling's battalion moves to France to take part in Battle of Loos
    (25–8 September). 27 September: Second Lieutenant John Kipling
    is reported 'wounded and missing'. Kipling begins to suffer the
    serious stomach pains that will trouble him for the next nineteen
    years. Writes naval sketches and poems published as *The Fringes of
    the Fleet*; four of the poems are set to music by Edward Elgar.

1916 Easter Rising in Dublin quashed by British Army; execution
    of its leaders. *Sea Warfare*, including the poem 'My Boy Jack';
    published.

1917 Kipling is asked to write the regimental history of the Irish Guards,
    and agrees. *A Diversity of Creatures* published. His poem 'Mesopotamia',
    protesting at the losses in the mishandled Mesopotamian campaign,
    published in the *Morning Post*. September: Kipling is appointed to War
    Graves Commission. Begins writing 'Epitaphs of the War'.

1918 End of the First World War.

1919 Election of Sinn Fein in Ireland, leading to unrest suppressed by
    British troops ('Black and Tans'). Kipling writes the poem 'Gods of

the Copybook Headings'. *The Years Between*, a book of poems including 'Epitaphs of the War', published.

1921 Irish Free State established.

1922 Kipling falls ill with stomach pains, wrongly thought to be cancer.

1923 Elected Rector of St Andrews University. *History of the Irish Guards in the Great War* and *Land and Sea Tales for Scouts and Guides* published.

1924 Elsie Kipling marries Captain George Bambridge.

1926 *Debits and Credits* published.

1930 *Thy Servant a Dog* published, becoming an instant best-seller.

1932 *Limits and Renewals* published. Kipling writes the text of the first royal Christmas message to the Empire, broadcast by King George V.

1934 Kipling's stomach pain finally diagnosed as a duodenal ulcer and properly treated. His health improves.

1935 August: Kipling begins writing *Something of Myself*.

1936 12 January: Kipling falls ill with a perforated duodenal ulcer. 16 January: dies. He is cremated at Golders Green. 23 January: his ashes are interred in Poets' Corner, Westminster Abbey; pall-bearers include the Prime Minister, his cousin Stanley Baldwin.

1937 *Something of Myself* published.

1937–9 Sussex Edition of Kipling's works in 35 volumes issued.

Jan Montefiore 2011

General Preface

Rudyard Kipling (1865–1936) was a Victorian and an early modernist, a preacher of the imperialist virtues of discipline and duty whose imaginative sympathies lay with children and outlaws, and a lover of the stability of 'Old England' who much enjoyed travelling outside it. He was a world-famous author, the most genuinely popular English writer since Dickens, and his poem 'If –' is to this day read and admired by people who do not otherwise read poetry; yet when his ashes were interred in Westminster Abbey he was considered by many intellectuals as barely worth serious reading, even though he was admired by T. S. Eliot, Bertolt Brecht, W. H. Auden and André Gide. The 35-volume Sussex Edition of his work represents an extraordinary diversity: *Kim* and three other long prose fictions including *The Light That Failed*; eleven collections of stories, from *Plain Tales from the Hills* (1888) to *Limits and Renewals* (1932); seven books for children (the two *Jungle Books,* the *Just So Stories,* the two *Puck* books, *Stalky & Co.* and *Land and Sea Tales for Scouts and Guides*); journalism, propaganda, public speeches and travel writing, the little-read classic *History of the Irish Guards in the Great War*, a great deal of verse and the posthumous memoir *Something of Myself*. A virtuoso of the short story, he wrote ironic comedies and tragic dramas, tales of adventure and of work, ghost stories, revenge farces, psychological studies, animal fables and machine fables. D. H. Lawrence is the only English writer of the twentieth century who can match his record for brilliant and diverse writing which escapes conventional classifications, and as a storyteller he has no contemporary English rival.

Kipling's work is as much energized as fissured by these contradictions, the roots of which lie in his own childhood experiences of dislocation and exile. Born in Bombay, where his first language was the 'vernacular' Hindi spoken by the servants, who would remind him on visits to the drawing room to 'Speak English to Papa and Mamma', he was as a small child taken to England with his sister and left with a foster-family in Southsea, to endure six years of bullying and abuse culminating in near-blindness and 'some sort of nervous breakdown'. After four years at a tough public school which he came to enjoy, he returned to his family and a gruelling job as reporter, which reintroduced him both to India's rich glamour and to a colonial world where life was cheap and death common. He insisted that his harsh childhood had proved an asset to his career in that it taught him to survive by inventing stories and entering other imaginative worlds, while observing others' behaviour with due wariness and maintaining his independence. But the unforgotten rage, hatred and despair of the dark years in the 'House of Desolation', mitigated by a delight in imaginative play, continued to shadow his work in his identification with the stern wisdom of just authority, and in his fascination by the strange worlds beyond its understanding.

After Kipling's initial enthusiastic reception in London as the young genius from India, responses to his work became divided. In the 1890s Mrs Oliphant praised him for showing how the Indian Empire was 'defended and fought for every day against the Powers of Darkness', while Robert Buchanan condemned him as a jingo who spoke for 'all that is ignorant, selfish, base and brutal in the instincts of humanity'. Both writers defined Kipling in terms of a politicized split between defence of order and a daemonic abyss, one identifying him with the civilized side of the barrier, the other with the powers of darkness. This opposition is itself obviously conditioned by imperialist forms of thought, yet these writers correctly sense a connection between Kipling's political allegiance with Authority and the potentially anarchic energies of his work. The knowing young writer's ironic stories and poems insisted on the frustration, danger and misunderstanding that formed the conditions of colonial life, where 'two thousand pounds of education / Drops to a ten-rupee *jezail*' and British soldiers in barracks endured a monotonous life relieved by comradeship and the occasional prospect of action. Yet he was also fascinated by the unknowable strangeness of the 'life of the peoples of the land, a life as full of impossibilities and wonders as the Arabian Nights' just as he loved the idea of the sea, whose uncontrollable turbulence and endless horizons can be challenged but never subdued by human courage and skill.

But to take the sea as social metaphor meant identifying imperialism with the natural world; and this raises the problem of Kipling's politics. Despite his genuine respect for the humanity as well as the 'otherness' of Indian Muslims, Sikhs and Hindus, his 'anthropological' insistence on cultural difference as a social fact, and his fellow-feeling for private soldiers, Kipling's wide-ranging sympathies are based on the assumption of an unbreakable class, race and gender hierarchy. Defiance of the property-owning class by socialists, of all-male rule by feminists, and above all of the British Empire by nationalist subjects, whether Boers, Irish or Indian, all provoked him to splenetic writing, while his patronizing, uneasy or downright contemptuous attitudes to the Irish, to Jews and to Africans are no more defensible than those of his Victorian and Edwardian contemporaries. These opinions, articulated with his characteristic candour and vividness, have made Kipling's work a mine for post-colonial historians of imperialist thought from Edward Said's *Orientalism* onwards.

Yet although Kipling's writing is certainly informed, and sometimes deformed, by his political views, it is by no means reducible to these. This can be seen in his masterpiece *Kim* (1901) and to a lesser extent in the two *Jungle Books*, colonial fictions in which 'otherness' is regarded with pleasure, not anxiety, just as the *Just So Stories* deal with the 'other' world of the animal fable and the *Puck* books with the differences as well as the continuity of English history. The orphaned heroes Kim and Mowgli, never disciplined to the life of labour and duty whose virtues Kipling so often preached, are made free of the Jungle and the street-life of Lahore, apparently threatening places which are really magical worlds and whose citizens, whether human or animal, speak the richly rhetorical, archaized idiom that Kipling invented for Indian 'vernacular' speakers. This 'vernacular' equivalent signals its own difference by its obvious distance from the narrator's modern English, and yet is equally intelligible, and on the printed page indistinguishable from it, unlike cockney or Irish dialect with their dropped gs and aitches. These enchanted Indian worlds have their own cultures; the Jungle, far from being a place of raw terror, is ruled by a Law 'which never forbids anything without a good reason', while Akela the wolf and Bagheera the panther are models of nobility, unlike the cruel and superstitious villagers. The enchantment of *Kim* lies in the way the hero's double story, as spy in the Government's 'Great Game' and *chela* (disciple) to a Buddhist priest in quest of salvation, is lived through a rich variety of lovingly recreated and sensuously evoked Indian social worlds. Colonial racism is mocked in the persons of the fat drummer-boy who calls all natives 'niggers' and the parson who observes the holy and innocent Teshoo Lama 'with the triple-ringed uninterest of the creed that lumps nine-tenths of the world under the title "heathen"' while *Kim*'s Indian characters are far more complex and interesting than the English. Colonel Creighton may be significant for his joint role as ethnologist and intelligence boss, but as a character he barely exists compared with his agents Mahbub Ali and Hurree Babu. That said, Kipling's conservative imperialism is obvious, not just in Kim's work as a spy or in the stereotyping of 'Orientals' as lazy or untruthful, but more subtly in the vividly realized and sympathetic Indian characters whose assumptions about the benevolence and legitimacy of British rule match Kipling's own, like the loyalist old soldier recalling the 'madness' of the Mutiny, or Hurree Babu deceiving the Russian spies by pretending to resent the British Government for having given him an education which he is not allowed to use. It is unthinkable in the world of *Kim* that nationalist claims or grievances might be justified.

But Kipling's achievement goes far beyond his 'Indian writings' and his books for children. His later stories and poems represent a substantial contribution to modernist literature, partly in the deep intuition of chaos underlying the 'Law', which Kipling shares with Eliot and Conrad, and partly in his response to the possibilities of modern communications technology, to which the stories 'Mrs Bathurst' and 'Wireless' are among the first and strongest creative responses in the twentieth century. Moreover, the scope and versatility of the early stories, written in styles ranging from understated irony to demotic dialect and the flowery archaized idiom of his 'vernacular' equivalent, developed in his later work into an irony and indeterminacy which are characteristically modernist. A similar modernist indeterminacy is discernible in Kipling's poetry, not just in the rare but very successful free verse poems like the 'Song of the Galley-Slaves', but in what look like obviously 'traditional' forms; the cockney language and self-invented elaborate stanzas of *Barrack Room Ballads*, admired by Eliot and Brecht, are instantly identifiable as 'Kiplingesque' yet not identifiable with Kipling's own voice. His poems are rarely or never spoken in his own person, just as the knowing 'I' who narrates so many of his stories is not identifiable with Kipling himself. Even the elegy for his son John, 'My Boy Jack', takes the form of a dialogue in which an anxious mother is repeatedly told that her son is lost to 'this wind blowing and this tide', a refrain suggesting the blast of trench mortars and the waves of troops advancing in battle while locating Kipling's own unspoken loss in that figurative ocean. Through the use of the monologue form which he learned from Browning, his use of 'impure' demotic language and his skill as a parodist (evident from the 1884 'Echoes' written with his sister to the 1904 'Muse among the Motors'), the modernity of Kipling's poems lies in the interpretative uncertainty generated by the multiple voices and registers that speak his poems.

There is evident traditionalism in Kipling's contributions both during and after the First World War to the literature of mourning, such as the motto he contributed to the war cemeteries, 'Their Name Liveth For Evermore', and the formal sequence 'Epitaphs of the War' – and yet the famous couplet 'Common Form' ('If any question why we died / Tell them, because our fathers lied') bitterly mocks its own mode of heroic elegy. His pared-down, understated stories of mourning deploy a characteristically modernist irony, especially his tales of bereaved women. 'Mary Postgate' is as ambiguously open to interpretation as Henry James's *The Turn of the Screw*, and like that story turns on perverse sexuality and death. In both this story and 'The Gardener', the drily matter-of-fact narrative participates in the bad faith revealed in the protagonist, achieving both deep feeling and ironic ambiguity.

Kipling continued to break ground in his late stories. Their varied subject matter, which includes psychosomatic illness, forgery and the journeys of St Paul, their length, complexity and unobtrusive use of motif and symbol, allowed him a new depth and range in his treatment of men and women. His writing had always insisted on gender difference, partly through its emphasis on the homosocial masculinity of soldiers in barracks, officers in their mess and experts talking in their clubs; but his dwelling on masculine solidarity becomes even more marked in the late stories of war veterans coping with their scars through the ritual and comradeship of freemasonry, or first-century Roman sailors talking shop over their wine. His women, conversely, are defined by sexuality and motherhood and are often associated in more or less complex ways with the numinous – like the Woman in the tale of 'The Cat that Walked' who domesticates Man and animals by her magic, and yet is responsible for letting in the untameable Cat. His late treatments of women, like the fiercely possessive yet selfless Grace Ashcroft in 'The Wish House', achieve a new psychological depth. As with the short-story form which he practised with such brilliance, Kipling is a writer whose limitations paradoxically allowed him an unsurpassed range.

Jan Montefiore 2011

Introduction

Rudyard Kipling is a magical storyteller, about whose powers people have disagreed passionately for over a hundred years. Virginia Woolf mocked him; Brecht admired him; Borges revered him; T. S. Eliot anthologized his poetry and in 'Burnt Norton' drew inspiration from the elusive children in 'They' (as, I think, the over-decorated bedroom in *The Waste Land* draws on the garish interior of the chemist's shop in 'Wireless').[1] His prose has been described as a delicate precision tool and as a monument of crudeness.[2] Enemies have dismissed his stories for jingo patriotism and/or racist reaction; admirers have praised their compassionate humanity. More recently, his Indian tales have been read both as political allegories prefiguring post-colonial perceptions of the intellectual and political limitations of Empire, and as elaborated symptoms of an anxiety-ridden desire to contain colonial lands and people by subjecting them to imperialist fantasies of knowledge.[3]

Kipling's public reputation has varied equally widely. The 24-year-old from India who was the sensation of literary London in the 1890s was the first brilliant young writer to become, not just a national figure like Dickens, but a global celebrity (which is partly, no doubt, why Kipling would become so fiercely protective of his own privacy). The advent of mass-produced newspapers and magazines, circulated by sea and railway, which 'boomed' the new author meant that, as his father Lockwood Kipling observed in 1891, 'in one year this youngster will have had more said about his work, over a greater extent of the earth's surface, than some of the greatest of England's writers in their whole lives'.[4] When Kipling nearly died of pneumonia in March 1899, his illness was headline news throughout the world, and the congratulations on his recovery included a telegram from Kaiser Wilhelm II of Germany. Yet in the wake of his public contribution to the Boer War as journalist and pro-militarist propagandist, and despite public honours, including the Nobel Prize in 1907, his literary reputation after 1900 went into a decline that was to make him so deeply unfashionable amongst liberals and intellectuals that Edmund Wilson called him in 1941 'The Kipling That Nobody Read.'[5]

Yet Kipling was still read with excitement by other writers in England and abroad: Alain-Fournier drew on Kipling's 'They' in *Le Grand Meaulnes*, Isaac Babel turned up at an Odessa newspaper office in 1921 with a book of Kipling stories under his arm,[6] and the list of those who published significant criticism of his work includes George Orwell, W. H. Auden, T. S. Eliot, Randall Jarrell, Frank O'Connor and the poet Craig Raine. More recently, his work has been central to critiques of empire by the post-colonial critics Edward Said and Sara Suleri.

Kipling's tales tend to escape any single definition, however sophisticated. Even by the sparing standards of the short-story form, Kipling's are remarkable for their extreme verbal economy, leaving out everything except the essentials so that readers must put together the stories' significance from their language, point of view and incidents. (He explained this method in *Something of Myself*: you delete everything superfluous from a 'final' draft, brushing the redundancies out with Indian ink, let it 'drain' for days or months, and repeat the process twice.[7]) One aspect of a story may well contradict another. The description of Findlayson the engineer surveying his almost-completed great Kashi Bridge at the start of 'The Bridge-Builders' seems a classic example of 'magical art' written to arouse the socially useful emotions of patriotism and pride in work well done;[8] yet loyal English readers inspired by Findlayson's dedicated, unthanked skill must be disconcerted when his working day turns to a night of 'long silence' while the Hindu Gods debate whether his bridge is even worth the bother of destroying it: 'Let the dirt dig in the dirt if it pleases the dirt.' A puzzling and exhilarating diversity is likewise manifest between tales: the delighted Hindu child giggling when the money-lender is trapped in 'The Finances of the Gods', versus Gurkhas using their *kukri* knives on Afghans 'with a nasty noise as of beef being cut on the block' in 'The Drums of the Fore and Aft'; British soldiers in 'On the City Wall', forbidden to shoot rioters, 'banging the bare toes of the mob', versus a former artilleryman in 'The Janeites' feeling nostalgia for the companionship of trench warfare where mess-steward and officers met in the unlikely common ground of Austen's novels. Despite – or because of – the preoccupation with those administering practical law and order in these stories, ghosts, madness and the supernatural are never far away, a paradox exemplified by Morrowbie Jukes making his vainly exact measurements of the nightmarish pit of the living dead. And for all his emphasis on discipline and order, Kipling has a strong sympathy with outlaws, children and outsiders in stories that give literary voices to, among others, a furious 'honour' killer, an expert polo-pony and the rivets in a steamship. The harrowing autobiographical 'Baa Baa, Black Sheep', in which the spoilt, beloved *Punch-baba* finds himself inexplicably taken to England to be abandoned to the loneliness and cruelty of Aunty Rosa's bullying Calvinist regime, becoming the outcast 'Black Sheep' who tries to knife his tormentor and poison himself, shows how Kipling in his vulnerable childhood became acquainted with the dark places 'where the injured / lead the ugly life of the rejected'.[9] Punch's parents are of course never blamed; but in choosing to publish this bitter story in an Allahabad newspaper's Christmas supplement, whose Anglo-Indian audience certainly included his parents, Kipling allowed himself, consciously or not, his writer's revenge.

What value you put on Kipling's stories rests both on which ones you choose to read (post-colonial critics, though persuasive in many respects, tend to edit Kipling's *oeuvre* down to his 'Indian' fictions, leaving out the post-war tales altogether) and on how you read him. For despite their frequent opinionated asides about imperialist virtues or the greatness of the British Empire, the final meaning of these tales is, right from the start, remarkably hard to pin down. They offer not a total vision but a multitude of intensely perceived provisional truths and local effects in a way that makes Kipling as much or more modernist than Victorian.[10] And the ambiguities increase in his post-1900 works – most notably in 'Mary Postgate', the significance of whose horrible denouement rests, quite as ambiguously as in Henry James's *The Turn of the Screw*, on the reader's interpretation. 'The Wish House' and 'The Gardener' are also heavy with unanswered questions. This selection of his stories, following the development of his work over fifty years, balances substantial selections of the 'Indian' tales by which he first made his name with the pioneering modernist 'middle' Kipling and the highly wrought subtleties of the later work. Selecting from the works of such a wonderful and prolific storyteller inevitably entails omissions, most notably of his children's classics. Giving the *Jungle Books*, the *Just So Stories*, *Stalky* and the 'Puck' tales a fair showing would have made it impossible to represent the richness and variety of the stories that inspired his young Russian-Jewish contemporary Isaac Babel to claim that 'everyone should write his kind of steely prose'.[11]

But an introduction to Kipling's stories necessarily begins with the early 'Indian' tales which made him famous, written by a very young man in love with India, who as he declared 'would sooner write about her than anything else . . . [the] heat and smells of oil and spices, and puffs of temple incense, and sweat, and darkness, and dirt and lust and cruelty, and above all, things wonderful and fascinating innumerable'.[12] The nature of that fascination can be glimpsed by summarizing the first few stories:

An addict tells of the opium house in Lahore where he is placidly dying. A Lahore con man who exploits an old miser's credulity in a *séance* is about to be poisoned by his prostitute lodger. An English engineer falls into a pit of pariah Indians and barely escapes. A Kashmiri girl's life is ruined by an Englishman who flirts with her. An Englishman has a secret affair with a lovely Hindu widow, for which both are terribly punished. A cuckolded Afghan who has murdered his wife obsessively pursues her lover. An English adulterer falls to his death in front of his mistress.

The harshness of this world is obvious, as is the unusually wide social range it owes to Kipling's experiences as a young reporter in Lahore (which included reporting a disaster as grim as his own stories when the roof of Lahore High School collapsed at midnight, killing three boys whose sheeted corpses he saw amongst the debris[13]). In 'The Man Who Would Be King' he describes with relish and gaiety the endless visitors to a newspaper office – disgruntled colonels, missionaries who want to abuse their colleagues, theatrical companies which are unable to pay for their advertisements, dubious inventors of unbreakable swords, and 'every dissolute ruffian that ever tramped the Grand Trunk Road' wanting the job of proof-reader. These early stories take in not only army officers and their wives, civilian officials, femmes fatales and missionaries but Indian opium addicts, beggars, con men, horse-dealers, but no 'ordinary' Indians. There are none of the farmers, village priests, grooms, letter-writers or shopkeepers whose alms and kindness support the hero of *Kim*, let alone the English cooks, hairdressers, fur-dealers, chemists, solicitors and sailors whose passions and tragedies preoccupy the later stories. With the dubious exception of the men in 'The City of Dreadful Night' sleeping by the roadside like corpses, 'Some shrouded all in white with bound-up mouths; some naked and black as ebony', almost all Kipling's early Indian characters either come from a criminal underworld or end up somewhere worse, decayed by drink, punished with mutilation, condemned to the pit of the living dead, or bound to madness and death, as in 'Dray Wara Yow Dee'.

This story, which begins in a happier world of horse-dealers cheerfully selling useless nags to 'the Officer-fools', is also a splendid instance of Kipling's unique invention of the archaized English exploiting the language of the King James Bible, by which he rendered the 'vernacular' speech of native Indians. This invented formal dialect, at once readily comprehensible and distant enough from English conversational idiom to suggest the 'otherness' of a different language and society, is capable of a lyrical directness which narrative and social convention deny to the English – as when the speaker longs for Afghanistan: '*Here* is only dust and a great stink. There is a pleasant wind among the mulberry trees, and the streams are bright with snow-water, and the caravans go up and the caravans go down, and a hundred fires sparkle in the gut of the Pass, and tent-peg answers hammer-nose, and pack-horse squeals to pack-horse across the drift-smoke of the evening.' But this paradise turns out to be a place of adultery and savage murder, leading to the haunted quest which has brought the narrator to British India and perhaps beyond: 'If my vengeance failed, I would splinter the Gates of Paradise with the butt of my gun, or I would cut my way into Hell with my knife, and I would call upon Those who Govern there for the body of Daoud Shah. What love so deep as hate?'

In 'A Wayside Comedy', a handful of isolated English officers and their wives make a similar discovery, though without the Afghan's stylish savagery. In the dreary hell-hole of Kashima where there is not enough 'public opinion' to keep sexual behaviour in line, a bitter farce of frustrated desires and affairs gone sour leaves everyone except the blissfully ignorant Major Vansuythen prey to 'jealousy and dull hatred'. The squalor of the quarrels is matched by their tired language: '"Oh, you liar!" Kurrell's face changed. "What's that?" he asked quickly. "Nothing much," said Boulte. "Has my wife told you that you two are free to go off whenever you please?"' The worst of the situation is that the civility of the English officers and their wives is not a pretence: simmering with lust and resentment, they only know to live by the rules they have broken. And in all the stories, there is a striking and very un-Victorian absence of moralizing: people from different societies work out their own damnation without moral comment beyond 'you dare not blame them', and with little political commentary apart from some wry remarks about officials' loneliness and boredom and the need to keep graves dug for 'incidental wear and tear' among the English in 'At the Pit's Mouth'. Written for Anglo-Indian readers, these early stories take their own assumption of English racial superiority for granted in the horror of Morrowbie Jukes finding himself powerless in a pit of stinking pariahs, or in the comedy of competing illegalities among delinquent rajahs and blackmailing white freebooters in 'The Man Who Would Be King' (where the hero's hubris also implies a disquieting parallel to the British Empire[14]) rather than in explicit preaching. Even in 'On the City Wall', the narrator's knowing grumbles about Englishmen doing work for which educated Indians will take the credit is less telling than the ingenious conspiracy which makes a fool of him but never seriously worries the imperturbable officers in charge of Lahore.

Apart from Punch in 'Baa Baa, Black Sheep' demanding the tale of 'the Ranee that was turned into a tiger', and Daniel Dravot in 'The

Man Who Would Be King' crossing the border to Afghanistan disguised as a crazy priest, there is little interchange in these early stories between the peoples of these different races and societies. Kipling's English and his Indians do not speak one another's idiom, their only common denominator being the knowledgeable writer who creates the worlds of low-life Indians, respectable officers and civilians, and the British Army's private soldiers. But in the longer, more highly wrought stories of the 1890s, Kipling develops the complex possibilities of different speech styles in sophisticated ways. Instead of the earlier monologues, we are given storytellers engaged with responsive audiences, like the delighted child in 'The Finances of the Gods' listening to Gobind, or the listening women too well acquainted with famine and insecurity, murmuring their chorus of sympathy as Little Tobrah recounts his terrible history, of which his English saviour, shocked at the boy eating oats wetted with horse-saliva out of a used nose-bag, will remain happily ignorant. Stories that feature English characters who, unlike the monoglot Morrowbie Jukes, are fluent in Indian vernacular, set up a productive tension between the cultures of colonial 'Sahibs' and native speakers. Hummil's personal servant in 'At the End of the Passage' voices a sympathetic yet eerie knowledge of the agonies that destroyed 'this that was my master', thereby disconcerting the bluff Dr Spurstow who snubs him – 'Chuma, you're a mud-head' – but can offer no better explanation. John Holden in 'Without Benefit of Clergy' converses with his Muslim 'wife' Ameera in exchanges full of tenderness, momentary jealousy, teasing, pride, sorrow and consolation, and then goes back to talking administrative shop at the 'Club', whose wry, stoical idiom will be all that is left him when Ameera is dead (though the last elegiac words are appropriately given to Holden's vernacular-speaking land-lord). Findlayson in 'The Bridge-Builders', that ideal administrator full of close attention to technical details, pride in his work and smug amusement at his foreman Peroo's superstitious anxiety about the river's anger 'now we have . . . run her between stone sills', disappears as a centre of consciousness once the Hindu Gods appear, speaking in the 'vernacular' style of formal yet flexible archaism, to debate the bridge's future. This layering of speech styles gives the illusion of undoing humanity's curse of Babel whereby speakers of different languages are unintelligible to one another, so that in Kipling's stories, English-speaking readers are made free of linguistic and cultural worlds which in real life are closed to them.

   The world of these Indian tales remains harsh. The lovers' fragile happiness in 'Without Benefit of Clergy' is vulnerable to 'the old pro-gramme . . . famine, fever, and cholera'; an official in 'At the End of the

Passage' coping alone with a heavy workload in the murkily stifling hot weather dies of insomnia; and we know from 'The Story of Muhammad Din' and 'Little Tobrah' that the bright-eyed child in 'The Finances of the Gods', weary from carrying dung-cakes to market, may be vulnerable to fever or smallpox. Meanwhile Kipling's imperialist politics, now he is addressing an English audience, become both more emphatic and more central to the stories' actions. Hardly a tale lacks a reminder that Englishmen are sacrificed for the Empire: English soldiers, helped by Gurkha regiments, hold back Afghan tribesmen in 'The Drums of the Fore and Aft' and 'With the Main Guard', while English administrators cope efficiently with natural disasters in 'Without Benefit of Clergy' and 'The Bridge-Builders', work unrewarded and unthanked in 'On the City Wall', and suffer misery and death in their lonely labours in 'At the End of the Passage'. No wonder that Margaret Oliphant suggested in an 1891 review that Queen Victoria might learn from these stories 'how her Indian Empire . . . is ruled and defended and fought for every day against the Powers of Darkness'.[15]

At the same time, these tales show Kipling's great and increasing fascination with labour and its techniques, classically manifested in the virtuoso description of the Kashi Bridge under construction by the ass-drivers, riveters, crane-men and train-drivers who make up a 'humming village of five thousand workmen', and their skilled, dedicated labour to save the great work from the coming flood in 'The Bridge-Builders'. Like no other writer, Kipling communicates the feel of action – the foreman inventing a tackle for heavy weights 'loose-ended, sagging . . . but perfectly equal to the work in hand' and the engineer feverishly calculating the strength of his work threatened by the water 'plucking and fingering along the revetments'; or the discomfort of a sweaty polo pony 'stiffening up to get all the tickle out of the big vulcanite scraper' before being hemmed in by people crowding too close to his playing-field's boundaries in 'The Maltese Cat'; or how when galley-slaves mutinied they 'choked [the overseer] to death against the side of the ship with their chained hands quite quietly, and . . . fought their way up deck by deck, with the pieces of the broken benches banging behind 'em' in 'The Finest Story in the World'.

Kipling's fascination with the minutiae of action gives his tales of battle a savage vividness combined with a clear if sometimes idealized perception of battle-strategy. Thus Mulvaney in 'With the Main Guard' cheerily recalls the experience of hand-to-hand fighting, when his troop was so jammed against the enemy that when one man's throat was cut, the colonel 'wint forward by the thickness av a man's body, havin' turned the Paythan under him. The man bit the heel off Crook's boot in his death-bite', and when the battle moved on, 'we opind out an' fair danced down the valley, dhrivin' thim before us. Oh, 'twas lovely, an' stiddy too!' Still more vivid is the terror of the novice troops in 'The Drums of the Fore and Aft' lying prone and firing 'for the sake of the comfort of the noise' only to plough up the ground ahead of them, and turning tail when charged by knife-wielding Ghazi berserkers while their officers try with curses and blows from sword-hilts to drive them back to the battle. This is finally won by the coolly intelligent Brigadier who knows both how to plan and where necessary to take a chance – or, say the witnesses, by the gallantry of the two youths who played 'The British Grenadiers' to a deserted battlefield, and 'whose little bodies were borne up just in time to fit two gaps' in a common ditch-grave (the corpses filling convenient gaps in a heap are a characteristically telling detail). And 'On Greenhow Hill' makes it very clear that the price of the soldiers' courage and comradeship is an emotional impoverishment that limits Ortheris to finding pleasure in his deadly marksmanship, and leaves Learoyd for ever haunted by the dying Liza Roantree, 'And I've been forgettin' her ever since.'

Kipling's later stories move away from colonial scenes, apart from the stories of the Boer War (which, since I find them relatively weak, I have not included here), and 'Mrs Bathurst', where the South African railway siding represents one point in the global triangle of Cape Town, Auckland and Paddington Station in London. Outside the children's books, children feature only as the elusive wraiths of 'They'. Scenes of action and adventure change to an informed interest in the means of communication; steamships, cinema, radio and motor cars become as important as the railways and telegraphs that enabled the administrators of the British Empire in the earlier stories to stay in control of their territories. Familiar things, as Freud describes in his essay on 'The Uncanny', become shudderingly strange: a nameless misery can fill the satiny brightness of a rich Jew's Surrey mansion in 'The House Surgeon', despite its 'fortifying blaze of electric light', a petty naval officer is mesmerized by the cinematographic spectre of Mrs Bathurst leaving a train half the world away, and a tenant farmer sweats with terror while doggedly trying to get the better of his landlady in 'They'. Objects take on a life of their own – literally so in the fable 'The Ship That Found Herself' where the rivets, deck-beams, engine cylinders and other great and small parts of an iron ship learn, groaning and complaining like humans, to hold on and work together as a team through a violent Atlantic storm (the political allegory is transparent). More figuratively in 'Mary Postgate', the dead Wynn's existence as a beloved, indulged only child is implied by the exhaustive page-long inventory of his boyhood possessions including 'a dumb gramophone and cracked records', all carried down to be incinerated with his tin soldiers and jigsaws. Similarly, the uncanny communications from a dead poet in 'Wireless' are first mediated by objects: the hare's fur 'blown apart in ridges and streaks as the wind caught it' as it hangs outside an Italian shop on a freezing winter night (an image Hemingway was to borrow for the famous opening of 'In Another Country'), followed by the unforgettable interior of a chemist's shop:

> Across the street, blank shutters flung back the gaslight in cold smears; the dried pavement seemed to rough up in goose-flesh under the scouring of the savage wind ... Within, the flavours of cardamoms and chloric-ether disputed those of the pastilles and a score of drugs and perfume and soap scents. Our electric lights, set low down in the windows before the tun-bellied Rosamond jars, flung inward three monstrous daubs of red, blue, and green, that broke into kaleidoscopic lights on the faceted knobs of the drug-drawers, the cut-glass scent flagons, and the bulbs of the sparklet bottles. They flushed the white-tiled floor in gorgeous patches; splashed along the nickel-silver counter-rails, and turned the polished mahogany counter-panels to the likeness of intricate grained marbles – slabs of porphyry and malachite.

The garish opulence of these disturbingly vivid colours, objects and strange scents, so much livelier than the sick people who need them, parodies the sensuous romance of Keats's 'The Eve of St Agnes', while Shaynor, the consumptive shop assistant mesmerized by the blowsy 'Fanny Brand', is a debased, unconscious equivalent to Keats himself. As the wireless expert upstairs waits for the pinch of metallic dust in his glass tube to be cohered by the 'Hertzian waves' long enough to conduct an electric impulse to his Morse printer, so Shaynor's brown-fingered hand stained with chemicals writes the words of a dead poet, opening up infinite possibilities to the narrator – which prove to be a dead end, since the 'proof' of their authenticity is Shaynor's laborious invention of lines which the 'I' already knows.

A fascinated relish for the machinery of publicity – newspapers, music-halls, parliamentary question-time – powers the high-spirited revenge story 'The Village That Voted the Earth Was Flat', in which a group consisting of professional men – journalists, the wealthy music-hall impresario 'Bat' Masquerier and a Member of Parliament – irked by a speed trap and a rural magistrate's insolence, conspire to turn the unfortunate Huckley and its magistrate squire into an international joke. They manage this by publicizing a toxic combination of factual details and invented folklore about Huckley including its mythical 'Gubby Dance' and, in a brilliant stroke of Masquerier's ingenuity, by getting star actors dressed up as 'Geoplanarians' to persuade the villagers (with the help of much beer) into voting for a flat earth, and then commemorating the event with a hit song about the village. The story acquires an unnerving momentum that comes to alarm even its inventors – 'We couldn't stop it if we wanted to now' – until in a climactic scene of 'realistic' fantasy the whole House of Commons, 'without distinction of Party, fear of constituents, desire for office, or hope of emolument', bellows the song that has made the village into a global legend.

All the characters here, apart from the star singer 'Dal Benzaguen, come from a man's world. This is true of many late Kipling stories: servicemen recall destructive passions over their beer in 'Mrs Bathurst'; the Masons in 'The Janeites' and 'A Madonna of the Trenches' clean their paraphernalia and reminisce about the war; and ancient Roman sailors talk naval shop in 'The Manner of Men'. These tales communicate the charm of male companionship enhanced by the pleasure of craftsmanship beautifully executed: a Mason polishing the Emblems of Mortality to the exact shade 'betwixt the colour of ripe apricots an' a half-smoked meerschaum [pipe]' in 'The Janeites'; Mr Marsh in 'His Gift' expertly breaking an egg into hot fat; the Roman port inspector telling a young captain how not to over-ballast his ship in 'The Manner of Men'. Yet the other side of this all-male social world is an increasing fascination with women as sources of emotional or psychic power. The fact that there is nothing remotely feminist about Kipling's treatment of women (he was after all the man for whom, notoriously 'the female of the species is more deadly than the male') makes his representation of their powerful, often numinous 'otherness' the more interesting. One kind of powerful woman is the enigmatic Mrs Bathurst, not responsible for her self-destructive lover's death in the Bulawayo forest and yet somehow implicated in the lightning that charred all his body except the false teeth; or the shadowy Bella Armine in 'A Madonna of the Trenches', glimpsed only through her nephew's traumatic vision of her ghost gazing at a middle-aged sergeant, ''e was lookin' at 'er as though he could 'ave et 'er, an' she was lookin' at 'im the same way', before he calls her into the hut where he will suffocate himself to join her in death – or the even more elusive woman in 'Dayspring Mishandled' whose defiled memory Manallace sets himself to revenge through years of ingenious plotting.

While these femmes fatales are the focus of men's transcendent or destructive passions, another kind of woman disturbs the order of things by the power of her own desire. This happens most benignly in 'They', where the blind and childless clairvoyante's yearning calls the ghosts of children to her enchanted house, most spookily in 'The House Surgeon' where an old woman's concentrated brooding on what she believes to be her sister's damnable suicide in their old home feels to those living in it like a 'burning-glass' turned on them, most terribly in Mary Postgate's vengeful orgasmic 'rapture' over the dying German pilot (who may not even exist) as she burns the effects of the beloved bullying Wynn, and most powerfully of all perhaps in 'The Wish House' when Grace Ashcroft chooses pain and slow death in order to keep her ex-lover alive and single. Increasingly, these late stories foreground the subjectivities of women, with occasional exceptions like the viciously 'unappetising' Lady Castorley who is not directly shown until the very end of 'Dayspring Mishandled'. In 'Mary Postgate' and 'The Gardener' we see just what the repressed, matter-of-fact Mary and the disingenuously 'open' Helen, see – except perhaps when Mary tells herself, 'falling back on the teaching that had made her what she was', not to let herself 'dwell on these things', and when Helen encounters Christ's miraculous directness in the last resonant words of 'The Gardener'. As with most of Kipling's lower-class characters, Grace Ashcroft's point of view in 'The Wish House' is dramatized in dialect speech rather than being made the story's narrative focus; but the listener Liz confirms the truth of her words ('I lay you're further off lyin' now than in all your life') as Grace gradually unbandages first the story of her own love and loss, and finally the cancer by which she has taken on herself her lover's death – and, she believes or hopes, his capacity for loving anyone else: 'It *do* count, don't it – de pain?' The early Kipling with all his power could not have made a character ask that unanswered question.

Jan Montefiore 2011

NOTES

1.   Virginia Woolf, *A Room of One's Own* (Penguin, 1945), p. 101; John Willett, *The Theatre of Bertolt Brecht* (Eyre Methuen, 1959, rev. edn. 1977), p.91; Paul Theroux, *The Old Patagonian Express* (Hamish Hamilton, 1979); Martin Scofield, *T. S. Eliot: The Poems* (Cambridge University Press, 1988); Jan Montefiore, *Rudyard Kipling* (Northcote House, 2007).

2.   For criticism of Kipling's prose as mechanical, see Dixon Scott's 1912 essay in Roger Lancelyn Green (ed.), *Kipling: The Critical Heritage* (Routledge and Kegan Paul, 1971); for admiration of its delicate precision, see Randall Jarrell's 'On Preparing to read Kipling', repr. in his *Kipling, Auden & Co.: Essays and Reviews, 1935–1965* (Carcanet, 1982). Graham

Greene's 'Goats and Incense', in his *Collected Essays* (Bodley Head, 1969) finds both qualities.

3. Robert Buchanan's 1899 essay 'The Voice of the Hooligan', repr. in Lancelyn Green, *Critical Heritage*, attacks Kipling for vulgarity and jingoism; Benita Parry's 'The Content and Discontents of Kipling's Imperialism' (*New Formations*, 6, 1988) attacks him as a reactionary racist. J. M. S. Tompkins, *The Art of Rudyard Kipling* (Methuen, 1959, 2nd edn. 1965) praises Kipling's humanity. Danny Karlin admires the perceptiveness of 'On the City Wall' and 'The Man Who Would Be King' as allegories of the limitations of Empire, in *Rudyard Kipling: A Critical Edition of the Major Work* (Oxford University Press, 1999). Bart Moore-Gilbert's *Kipling and 'Orientalism'* (St Martin's Press and Croom Helm, 1986), Sara Suleri's *The Rhetoric of English India* (Chicago University Press, 1992), Zohreh T. Sullivan's *Narratives of Empire: The Fictions of Rudyard Kipling* (Routledge, 1993) and Thomas Richards, *The Imperial Archive: Knowledge and the Fantasy of Empire* (Verso, 1993) read Kipling's work as symptomatic of colonial fantasies and insecurities.

4. J. Lockwood Kipling, letter to Edith Plowden, quoted in Harry Ricketts, *The Unforgiving Minute: A Life of Rudyard Kipling* (Chatto and Windus, 1999), p. 164.

5. Edmund Wilson, 'The Kipling That Nobody Read', in his *The Wound and the Bow: Seven Studies in Literature* (Houghton Mifflin, 1941; repr. Methuen, 1961), p. 94.

6. K. Paustovsky, *Story of a Life IV: Years of Hope*, trans. Maya Harai and A. Thomson (Harvill Press, 1968), p. 119.

7. *Something of Myself and other Autobiographical Writings*, ed. Thomas Pinney (Cambridge University Press, 1985), p. 121.

8. R. G. Collingwood, *The Principles of Art* (Clarendon Press, 1938), p. 70.

9. W. H. Auden, 'In Memory of Sigmund Freud'.

10. Montefiore, *Rudyard Kipling*, p. 134.

11. Quoted in Paustovsky, *Years of Hope*, p. 165.

12. Letter to E. K. Robinson, 30 April 1886, *Letters of Rudyard Kipling*, ed. Thomas Pinney (Macmillan, 1990), vol. 1, p. 127.

13. Diary-letter to Margaret Burne-Jones, 1 June 1886, *Letters*, ed. Pinney, vol. 1, p. 131.

14. Sullivan, *Narratives of Empire*, p. 110.

15. Quoted in Lancelyn Green, *Critical Heritage*, p. 137.

Note on the Text

The earliest of these stories first appeared in Indian newspapers, the *Civil and Military Gazette* in Lahore and later *The Week's News* and the *Pioneer* in Allahabad; many were also reissued in the paper-cover 1888 Indian Railway Library series. Kipling later republished them in subsequent collections of stories which appeared in London. After Kipling's arrival in London in 1890 his stories usually appeared in British and American magazines before being published in permanent collections, where they remained in later collected editions including the Sussex Edition (1937–9), the last uniform edition to be supervised by Kipling, which is followed here.

Details of the date and place of each story's first appearance, and the collection in which it was eventually placed, are given in the notes at the end of the book.

Jan Montefiore 2011

Further Reading

BIBLIOGRAPHY

Richards, David A., *Rudyard Kipling: A Bibliography* (Yale University Press, 2009). Comprehensive, revised and updated.

Stewart J. M., *Rudyard Kipling: A Bibliographical Catologue* (Dalhousie University Press, 1959).

REFERENCE

Harbord, R. E., *A Reader's Guide to Rudyard Kipling*, 8 vols. (Canterbury: privately printed, 1955–65).

Radcliffe, John (gen. ed.), *New Reader's Guide to the Works of Rudyard Kipling*. An online Reader's Guide, updating Harbord; available through the Kipling Society's website.

Yule, Henry, and Burnell, A. C. (eds.), *Hobson-Jobson: A Glossary of Anglo-Indian Colloquial Words and Phrases and of Kindred Terms: Etymological Historical Geographical and Discursive* (John Murray, 1886); repr. as *Hobson-Jobson: The Anglo-Indian Dictionary* (Wordsworth, 1996).

BIOGRAPHY AND LETTERS

Allen, Charles, *Kipling Sahib: India and the Making of Rudyard Kipling* (Little, Brown, 2007).

Carrington, Charles, *The Life of Rudyard Kipling*, with epilogue (Macmillan, 1955). Memoir by Kipling's daughter Elsie Bambridge.

Cohen, Morton (ed.), *Rudyard Kipling to Rider Haggard: The Record of a Friendship* (Hutchinson, 1965).

Flanders, Judith, *A Circle of Sisters: Alice Kipling, Georgiana Burne-Jones, Agnes Poynter, Emily Baldwin* (Viking, 2001).

Gilbert, Elliott L. (ed.), 'O Beloved Kids': Rudyard Kipling's Letters to his Children (Weidenfeld and Nicolson, 1983).

Gilmour, David, The Long Recessional: The Imperial Life of Rudyard Kipling (John Murray, 2002).

Holt, Tone, and Holt Valmai, My Boy Jack? The Search for Kipling's Only Son (Pen & Sword, 1998).

Kemp, Sandra, and Lewis, Lisa (eds.), Rudyard Kipling: Writings on Writing (Cambridge University Press, 1996).

Kipling, Rudyard, Something of Myself and Other Autobiographical Writings, ed. Thomas Pinney (Cambridge University Press, 1985).

Letters of Rudyard Kipling, ed. Thomas Pinney, 6 vols. (Macmillan, 1990–2004).

Lycett, Andrew, Rudyard Kipling (Weidenfeld and Nicholson, 1999).

Nicolson, Adam, The Hated Wife: Carrie Kipling 1862–1939 (Faber and Faber, 2001).

Orel, H. (ed.), Kipling: Interviews and Recollections, 2 vols. (Macmillan, 1983).

Ricketts, Harry, The Unforgiving Minute: A Life of Rudyard Kipling (Chatto and Windus, 1999).

Wilson, Angus, The Strange Ride of Rudyard Kipling (Secker and Warburg, 1975).

CRITICISM

Bodelsen, C. A., Aspects of Kipling's Art (Manchester University Press, 1964).

Brantlinger, Patrick, Rule of Darkness: British Literature and Imperialism 1839–1940 (Cornell University Press, 1988).

——'Kipling's "The White Man's Burden" and its Afterlives', English Literature in Transition 50/2 (2007), repr. in Kipling Journal, 328 (September 2007).

Bristow, Joseph, Empire Boys: Adventures in a Man's World (HarperCollins, 1991).

Brogan, Hugh, Mowgli's Sons: Kipling and Baden-Powell's Scouts (Jonathan Cape, 1987).

——'The Great War and Rudyard Kipling', Kipling Journal, 286 (June 1998).

Cheyette, Bryan, 'Empire and Anarchy: John Buchan and Rudyard Kipling', in his Constructions of 'the Jew' in English Literature and Society (Routledge, 1993).

Crook, Nora, Kipling's Myths of Love and Death (Macmillan, 1990).

Gilbert, Elliott L. (ed.), Kipling and the Critics (Boston, Owen, 1966). Includes essays by Henry James, George Orwell, Edmund Wilson, T. S. Eliot, C. S. Lewis and Randall Jarrell.

—— *The Good Kipling: Studies in the Short Story* (1971; Ohio University Press, 1985).

Havholm, Peter, *Politics and Awe in Rudyard Kipling's Fiction* (Ashgate, 2008).

Hitchens, Christopher, 'The Bard of Empires', in his *Blood, Class and Empire: The Enduring Anglo-American Relationship* (Atlantic, 2004).

Hynes, Samuel, *War Imagined: The First World War in English Culture* (Bodley Head, 1990).

Islam, Shamsul, *Kipling's 'Law': A Study of his Philosophy of Life* (Unwin, 1975).

JanMohammed, Abdul, 'The Economy of Manichean Allegory: The Function of Radical Difference in Colonialist Literature', *Critical Inquiry*, 12/1 (1985).

Jarrell, Randall, 'On Preparing to Read Kipling', in his *A Sad Heart at the Supermarket* (Doubleday, 1962; repr. *Kipling, Auden & Co.: Essays and Reviews, 1935–1965* (Carcanet, 1982).

Kemp, Sandra, *Kipling's Hidden Narratives* (Blackwell, 1988).

Kinkead-Weekes, Mark, 'Vision in Kipling's novels', in Andrew Rutherford (ed.), *Kipling's Mind and Art* (Stanford University Press and Oliver & Boyd, 1964).

Kipling, John Lockwood, *Beast and Man in India: A Popular Sketch of Animals in their Relations with the People* (1892; repr. Kessinger, Montana, 2005).

Knoepflmacher, U. C., 'Female Power and Male Self-Assertion: Kipling and the Maternal', *Children's Literature*, 20 (1992).

—— 'Kipling's Just So Partner: The Dead Child as Collaborator and Muse', *Children's Literature*, 25 (1997).

Kutzer, Daphne, *Empire's Children: Empire and Imperialism in Classic British Children's Books* (Garland, 2000).

Lancelyn Green, Roger (ed.), *Kipling: The Critical Heritage* (Routledge and Kegan Paul, 1971).

—— *Kipling and the Children* (Elek, 1965).

Lewis, C. S. 'Kipling's World', in his *They Asked for a Paper* (Geoffrey Bles, 1961); repr. in Elliott L. Gilbert (ed.), *Kipling and the Critics* (Boston, Owen, 1966).

McBratney, John, *Imperial Subjects, Imperial Space: Kipling's Fiction of the Native-Born* (Ohio State University Press, 2002).

McClure, John, *Kipling and Conrad: The Colonial Fiction* (Harvard University Press, 1981).

Mallett, Philip (ed.), *Kipling Considered* (St Martin's Press, 1989).

Mason, Philip, *Kipling: The Glass, the Shadow and the Fire* (Macmillan, 1975).

Menand, Louis, 'Kipling in the History of Forms', in Maria DiBattista and Lucy McDiarmid (eds.), *High and Low Moderns: Literature and Culture 1889–1939* (Oxford University Press, 1996).

Montefiore, Jan, 'Latin, Arithmetic and Pedagogy: A Reading of Two Kipling

Fictions', in Howard Booth and Nigel Rigby (eds.), *Modernism and Empire* (Manchester University Press, 2000).

——*Rudyard Kipling* (Northcote House, 2007).

Moore-Gilbert, Bart, *Kipling and 'Orientalism'* (St Martin's Press and Croom Helm, 1986).

——(ed.), *Writing India 1757–1990* (Manchester University Press, 1996).

Nagai, Kaori, *Empire of Analogies: Kipling, India and Ireland* (Cork University Press, 2006).

Orel, Harold (ed.), *Critical Essays on Rudyard Kipling* (G. K. Hall & Co., 1989).

Park, Clara Claiborne, 'The River and the Road: Fashions in Forgiveness', *American Scholar*, 66/1 (1997), repr. *Kipling Journal*, 309 (June 2003).

Parry, Benita, 'The Content and Discontent of Kipling's Imperialism', *New Formations*, 6 (1988).

Randall, Don, *Kipling's Imperial Boy: Adolescence and Cultural Hybridity* (Palgrave, 2000).

Rao, K. Bhaskara, *Rudyard Kipling's India* (University of Oklahoma Press, 1967).

Richards, Thomas, *The Imperial Archive: Knowledge and the Fantasy of Empire* (Verso, 1993).

Rushdie, Salman, 'Kipling', in his *Imaginary Homelands: Essays and Criticism 1981–1991* (Granta, 1991).

Rutherford, Andrew (ed.), *Kipling's Mind and Art* (Stanford University Press and Oliver & Boyd, 1964). Includes essays by George Orwell, Edmund Wilson, Lionel Trilling, Noel Annan, W. W. Robson and Alan Sandison.

Said, Edward, *Orientalism* (Vintage, 1978).

——'The Pleasures of Imperialism', in his *Culture and Imperialism* (Viking, 1992).

Sandison, Alan, *The Wheel of Empire: A Study of the Imperial Idea* (Macmillan, 1967).

Stewart, J. I. M., *Rudyard Kipling* (Gollancz, 1966).

Suleri, Sara, *The Rhetoric of British India* (Chicago University Press, 1992).

Sullivan, Zohreh T., *Narratives of Empire: The Fictions of Rudyard Kipling* (Routledge, 1993).

Tate, Trudi, 'War Neurotics', in her *Modernism, History and the Great War* (Manchester University Press, 1998).

Tompkins, J. M. S., *The Art of Rudyard Kipling* (Methuen, 1959, 2nd edn., 1965).

Trotter, David, *The English Novel in History 1885–1920* (Routledge, 1993).

Williams, Patrick, '*Kim* and Orientalism', in Philip Mallett (ed.), *Kipling Considered* (St Martin's Press, 1989).

Winter, Jay, *Sites of Memory, Sites of Mourning: The Great War in European Cultural History* (Cambridge University Press, 1995).

Jan Montefiore 2011

The Man Who
Would Be King

THE GATE OF THE
HUNDRED SORROWS

If I can attain Heaven for a pice,[1] why should you be envious?
Opium-Smoker's Proverb

This is no work of mine. My friend, Gabral Misquitta, the half-caste,[2] spoke it all, between moonset and morning, six weeks before he died; and I took it down from his mouth as he answered my questions. So:

It lies between the Coppersmith's Gully and the pipe-stem-sellers' quarter, within a hundred yards, too, as the crow flies, of the Mosque of Wazir Khan.[3] I don't mind telling any one this much, but I defy him to find the Gate, however well he may think he knows the City. You might even go through the very gully it stands in a hundred times, and be none the wiser. We used to call the gully 'The Gully of the Black Smoke', but its native name is altogether different, of course. A loaded donkey couldn't pass between the walls; and, at one point, just before you reach the Gate, a bulged house-front makes people go along all sideways.

It isn't really a gate, though. It's a house. Old Fung-Tching had it first five years ago. He was a boot-maker in Calcutta. They say that he murdered his wife there when he was drunk. That was why he dropped bazar-rum and took to the Black Smoke instead. Later on, he came up North and opened the Gate as a house where you could get your smoke in peace and quiet. Mind you, it was a *pukka*,[4] respectable opium-house, and not one of those stifling, sweltering *chandoo-khanas*[5] that you can find all over the City. No; the old man knew his business thoroughly, and he was most clean for a Chinaman. He was a one-eyed little chap, not much more than five feet high, and both his middle fingers were gone. All the same, he was the handiest man at rolling black pills I have ever seen. Never seemed to be touched by the Smoke, either; and what he took day and night, night and day, was a caution. I've been at it five years, and I can do my fair share of the Smoke with any one; but I was a child to Fung-Tching that way. All the same, the old man was keen on his money: very keen; and that's what I can't understand. I heard he saved a good deal before he died, but his nephew has got all that now; and the old man's gone back to China to be buried.

He kept the big upper room, where his best customers gathered, as neat as a new pin. In one corner used to stand Fung-Tching's Joss[6] – almost as ugly as Fung-Tching – and there were always sticks burning under his nose; but you never smelt 'em when the pipes were going thick. Opposite the Joss was Fung-Tching's coffin. He had spent a good deal of his savings on that, and whenever a new man came to the Gate he was always introduced to it. It was lacquered black, with red-and-gold writings on it, and I've heard that Fung-Tching brought it out all the way from China. I don't know whether that's true or not, but I know that, if I came first in the evening, I used to spread my mat just at the foot of it. It was a quiet corner, you see, and a sort of breeze from the gully came in at the window now and then. Besides the mats, there was no other furniture in the room – only the coffin, and the old Joss all green and blue and purple with age and polish.

Fung-Tching never told us why he called the place 'The Gate of the Hundred Sorrows'. (He was the only Chinaman I know who used bad-sounding fancy names. Most of them are flowery. As you'll see in Calcutta.) We used to find that out for ourselves. Nothing grows on you so much, if you're white, as the Black Smoke. A yellow man is made different. Opium doesn't tell on him scarcely at all; but white and black suffer a good deal. Of course, there are some people that the Smoke doesn't touch any more than tobacco would at first. They just doze a bit, as one would fall asleep naturally, and next morning they are almost fit for work. Now, I was one of that sort when I began, but I've been at it for five years pretty steadily, and it's different now. There was an old aunt of mine, down Agra way, and she left me a little at her death. About sixty rupees a month secured. Sixty isn't much. I can recollect a time, seems hundreds and hundreds of years ago, that I was getting my three hundred a month, and pickings, when I was working on a big timber-contract in Calcutta.

I didn't stick to that work for long. The Black Smoke does not allow of much other business; and even though I am very little affected by it, as men go, I couldn't do a day's work now to save my life. After all, sixty rupees is what I want. When old Fung-Tching was alive he used to draw the money for me, give me about half of it to live on (I eat very little), and the rest he kept himself. I was free of the Gate at any time of the day and night, and could smoke and sleep there when I liked; so I didn't care. I know the old man made a good thing out of it; but that's no matter. Nothing matters much to me; and besides, the money always came fresh and fresh each month.

There was ten of us met at the Gate when the place was first opened. Me, and two Babus[7] from a Government Office somewhere in Anarkulli, but they got the sack and couldn't pay (no man who has to work in the daylight can do the Black Smoke for any length of time straight on); a Chinaman that was Fung-Tching's nephew; a bazar-woman[8] that had got a lot of money somehow; an English loafer – MacSomebody,[9] I think, but I have forgotten, – that smoked heaps, but never seemed to pay anything (they said he had saved Fung-Tching's life at some trial in Calcutta when he was a barrister); another Eurasian, like myself, from Madras; a half-caste woman, and a couple of men who said they had come from the North. I think they must have been Persians or Afghans or something. There are not more than five of us living now, but we come regular. I don't know what happened to the Babus; but the bazar-woman, she died after six months of the Gate, and I think Fung-Tching took her bangles and nose-ring for himself. But I'm not certain. The Englishman, he drank as well as smoked, and he dropped off. One of the Persians got killed in a row at night by the big well near the mosque a long time ago, and the Police shut up the well, because they said it was full of foul air. They found him dead at the bottom of it. So, you see, there is only me, the Chinaman, the half-caste woman that we call the Memsahib (she used to live with Fung-Tching), the other Eurasian, and one of the Persians. The Memsahib looks very old now. I think she was a young woman when the Gate was opened; but we are all old for the matter of that. Hundreds and hundreds of years old. It's very hard to keep count of time in the Gate, and, besides, time doesn't matter to me. I draw my sixty rupees fresh and fresh every month. A very, very long while ago, when I used to be getting three hundred and fifty rupees a month, and pickings, on a big timber-contract at Calcutta, I had a wife of sorts. But she's dead now. People said that I killed her by taking to the Black Smoke. Perhaps I did, but it's so long since that it doesn't matter. Sometimes, when I first came to the Gate, I used to feel sorry for it; but that's all over and done with long ago, and I draw my sixty rupees fresh and fresh every month, and am quite happy. Not *drunk* happy, you know, but always quiet and soothed and contented.

How did I take to it? It began at Calcutta. I used to try it in my own house, just to see what it was like. I never went very far, but I think my wife must have died then. Anyhow, I found myself here, and got to know Fung-Tching. I don't remember rightly how that came about; but he told me of the Gate and I used to go there, and, somehow, I have never got away from it since. Mind you, though, the Gate was a respectable place in Fung-Tching's time, where you could be comfortable, and not at all like the *chandoo-khanas* where the niggers go. No;

it was clean, and quiet, and not crowded. Of course, there were others besides us ten and the man; but we always had a mat apiece, with a wadded woollen headpiece, all covered with black and red dragons and things, just like the coffin in the corner.

At the end of one's third pipe the dragons used to move about and fight. I've watched 'em many and many a night through. I used to regulate my Smoke that way, and now it takes a dozen pipes to make 'em stir. Besides, they are all torn and dirty, like the mats, and old Fung-Tching is dead. He died a couple of years ago, and gave me the pipe I always use now – a silver one, with queer beasts crawling up and down the receiver-bottle below the cup. Before that, I think, I used a big bamboo stem with a copper cup, a very small one, and a green jade mouthpiece. It was a little thicker than a walking-stick stem, and smoked sweet, very sweet. The bamboo seemed to suck up the smoke. Silver doesn't, and I've got to clean it out now and then; that's a great deal of trouble, but I smoke it for the old man's sake. He must have made a good thing out of me, but he always gave me clean mats and pillows, and the best stuff you could get anywhere.

When he died, his nephew Tsin-ling took up the Gate, and he called it the 'Temple of the Three Possessions'; but we old ones speak of it as the 'Hundred Sorrows', all the same. The nephew does things very shabbily, and I think the Memsahib must help him. She lives with him; same as she used to do with the old man. The two let in all sorts of low people, niggers and all, and the Black Smoke isn't as good as it used to be. I've found burnt bran in my pipe over and over again. The old man would have died if that had happened in his time. Besides, the room is never cleaned, and all the mats are torn and cut at the edges. The coffin is gone – gone to China again – with the old man and two ounces of Smoke inside it, in case he should want 'em on the way.

The Joss doesn't get so many sticks burnt under his nose as he used to. That's a sign of ill-luck, as sure as death. He's all brown, too, and no one ever attends to him. That's the Memsahib's work, I know; because, when Tsin-ling tried to burn gilt paper before him, she said it was a waste of money, and, if he kept a stick burning very slowly, the Joss wouldn't know the difference. So now we've got the sticks mixed with a lot of glue, and they take half an hour longer to burn, and smell stinky. Let alone the smell of the room by itself. No business can get on if they try that sort of thing. The Joss doesn't like it. I can see that. Late at night, sometimes, he turns all sorts of queer colours – blue and green and red – just as he used to do when old Fung-Tching was alive; and he rolls his eyes and stamps his feet like a devil.

I don't know why I don't leave the place and smoke quietly in a little room of my own in the bazar. Most like, Tsin-ling would kill me if I went away – he draws my sixty rupees now – and besides, it's too much trouble, and I've grown to be very fond of the Gate. It's not much to look at. Not what it was in the old man's time, but I couldn't leave it. I've seen so many come in and out. And I've seen so many die here on the mats that I should be afraid of dying in the open now. I've seen some things that people would call strange enough; but nothing is strange when you're on the Black Smoke, except the Black Smoke. And if it was, it wouldn't matter.

Fung-Tching used to be very particular about his people, and never got in anyone who'd give trouble by dying messy and such. But the nephew isn't half so careful. He tells everywhere that he keeps a 'first-chop'[10] house. Never tries to get men in quietly, and make them comfortable like Fung-Tching did. That's why the Gate is getting a little bit more known than it used to be. Among the niggers, of course. The nephew daren't get a white, or, for matter of that, a mixed skin into the place. He has to keep us three; of course – me and the Memsahib and the other Eurasian. We're fixtures. But he wouldn't give us credit for a pipeful – not for anything.

One of these days, I hope, I shall die in the Gate. The Persian and the Madras man are terribly shaky now. They've got a boy to light their pipes for them. I always do that myself. Most like, I shall see them carried out before me. I don't think I shall ever outlive the Memsahib or Tsin-ling. Women last longer than men at the Black Smoke, and Tsin-ling has a deal of the old man's blood in him, though he does smoke cheap stuff. The bazar-woman knew when she was going two days before her time; and she died on a clean mat with a nicely-wadded pillow, and the old man hung up her pipe just above the Joss. He was always fond of her, I fancy. But he took her bangles just the same.

I should like to die like the bazar-woman – on a clean, cool mat with a pipe of good stuff between my lips. When I feel I'm going, I shall ask Tsin-ling for them, and he can draw my sixty rupees a month, fresh and fresh, as long as he pleases. Then I shall lie back, quiet and comfortable, and watch the black and red dragons have their last big fight together; and then . . .

Well, it doesn't matter. Nothing matters much to me – only I wish Tsin-ling wouldn't put bran into the Black Smoke.

IN THE HOUSE
OF SUDDHOO

A stone's throw out on either hand
From that well-ordered road we tread,
And all the world is wild and strange:
Churel[1] and ghoul[2] and *Djinn* and sprite
Shall bear us company to-night,
For we have reached the Oldest Land
Wherein the Powers of Darkness range.
From the Dusk to the Dawn

The House of Suddhoo, near the Taksali Gate,[3] is two-storeyed, with
four carved windows of old brown wood, and a flat roof. You may
recognise it by five red hand-prints arranged like the Five of Diamonds
on the whitewash between the upper windows. Bhagwan Dass the
grocer and a man who says he gets his living by seal-cutting[4] live in the
lower storey with a troop of wives, servants, friends, and retainers. The
two upper rooms used to be occupied by Janoo and Azizun, and a little
black-and-tan terrier that was stolen from an Englishman's house and
given to Janoo by a soldier. To-day, only Janoo lives in the upper rooms.
Suddhoo sleeps on the roof generally, except when he sleeps in the
street. He used to go to Peshawur in the cold weather to visit his son
who sells curiosities near the Edwardes Gate, and then he slept under
a real mud roof. Suddhoo is a great friend of mine, because his cousin
had a son who secured, thanks to my recommendation, the post of
head-messenger to a big firm in the station. Suddhoo says that God
will make me a Lieutenant-Governor one of these days. I daresay his
prophecy will come true. He is very, very old, with white hair and no
teeth worth showing, and he has outlived his wits – outlived nearly
everything except his fondness for his son at Peshawur. Janoo and
Azizun are Kashmiris, Ladies of the City, and theirs was an ancient and
more or less honourable profession; but Azizun has since married
a medical student from the North-West and has settled down to a
most respectable life somewhere near Bareilly.[5] Bhagwan Dass is an
extortioner and an adulterator.[6] He is very rich. The man who is

supposed to get his living by seal-cutting pretends to be very poor. This lets you know as much as is necessary of the four principal tenants in the House of Suddhoo. Then there is Me, of course; but I am only the chorus that comes in at the end to explain things. So I do not count.

Suddhoo was not clever. The man who pretended to cut seals was the cleverest of them all – Bhagwan Dass only knew how to lie – except Janoo. She was also beautiful, but that was her own affair.

Suddhoo's son at Peshawur was attacked by pleurisy, and old Suddhoo was troubled. The seal-cutter man heard of Suddhoo's anxiety and made capital out of it. He was abreast of the times. He got a friend in Peshawur to telegraph daily accounts of the son's health. And here the story begins.

Suddhoo's cousin's son told me, one evening, that Suddhoo wanted to see me; that he was too old and feeble to come personally, and that I should be conferring an everlasting honour on the House of Suddhoo if I went to him. I went; but I think, seeing how well off Suddhoo was then, that he might have sent something better than an *ekka*,[7] which jolted fearfully, to haul out a future Lieutenant-Governor to the City on a muggy April evening. The *ekka* did not run quickly. It was full dark when we pulled up opposite the door of Ranjit Singh's Tomb[8] near the main gate of the Fort. Here was Suddhoo, and he said that, by reason of my condescension, it was absolutely certain that I should become a Lieutenant-Governor while my hair was yet black. Then we talked about the weather and the state of my health, and the wheat crops, for fifteen minutes, in the Huzuri Bagh,[9] under the stars.

Suddhoo came to the point at last. He said that Janoo had told him that there was an order of the Sirkar[10] against magic, because it was feared that magic might one day kill the Empress of India.[11] I didn't know anything about the state of the law; but I fancied that something interesting was going to happen. I said that so far from magic being discouraged by the Government, it was highly commended. The greatest officials of the State practised it themselves. (If the Financial Statement isn't magic, I don't know what is.) Then, to encourage him further, I said that, if there was any *jadoo*[12] afoot, I had not the least objection to giving it my countenance and sanction, and to seeing that it was clean *jadoo* – white magic, as distinguished from the unclean *jadoo* which kills folk. It took a long time before Suddhoo admitted that this was just what he had asked me to come for. Then he told me, in jerks and quavers, that the man who said he cut seals was a sorcerer of the cleanest kind; that every day he gave Suddhoo news of the sick son in Peshawur more quickly than the lightning could fly, and that this news was always corroborated by the letters. Further, that he had told

Suddhoo how a great danger was threatening his son, which could be removed by clean *jadoo*; and, of course, heavy payment. I began to see exactly how the land lay, and told Suddhoo that I also understood a little *jadoo* in the Western line, and would go to his house to see that everything was done decently and in order. We set off together; and on the way Suddhoo told me that he had paid the seal-cutter between one hundred and two hundred rupees[13] already; and the *jadoo* of that night would cost two hundred more. Which was cheap, he said, considering the greatness of his son's danger; but I do not think he meant it.

The lights were all cloaked in the front of the house when we arrived. I could hear awful noises from behind the seal-cutter's shop-front, as if some one were groaning his soul out. Suddhoo shook all over, and while we groped our way upstairs told me that the *jadoo* had begun. Janoo and Azizun met us at the stair-head, and told us that the *jadoo*-work was coming off in their rooms, because there was more space there. Janoo is a lady of a free-thinking turn of mind. She whispered that the *jadoo* was an invention to get money out of Suddhoo, and that the seal-cutter would go to a hot place when he died. Suddhoo was nearly crying with fear and old age. He kept walking up and down the room in the half-light, repeating his son's name over and over again, and asking Azizun if the seal-cutter ought not to make a reduction in the case of his own landlord. Janoo pulled me over to the shadow in the recess of the carved bow-windows. The boards were up, and the rooms were only lit by one tiny oil-lamp. There was no chance of my being seen if I stayed still.

Presently, the groans below ceased, and we heard steps on the staircase. That was the seal-cutter. He stopped outside the door as the terrier barked and Azizun fumbled at the chain, and he told Suddhoo to blow out the lamp. This left the place in jet darkness, except for the red glow from the two hookahs[14] that belonged to Janoo and Azizun. The seal-cutter came in, and I heard Suddhoo throw himself down on the floor and groan. Azizun caught her breath, and Janoo backed on to one of the beds with a shudder. There was a clink of something metallic, and then shot up a pale blue-green flame near the ground. The light was just enough to show Azizun, pressed against one corner of the room with the terrier between her knees; Janoo, with her hands clasped, leaning forward as she sat on the bed; Suddhoo, face-down, quivering, and the seal-cutter.

I hope I may never see another man like that seal-cutter. He was stripped to the waist, with a wreath of white jasmine as thick as my wrist round his forehead, a salmon-coloured loin-cloth round his middle, and a steel bangle on each ankle. This was not awe-inspiring.

It was the face of the man that turned me cold. It was blue-grey in the
first place. In the second, the eyes were rolled back till you could only
see the whites of them; and, in the third, the face was the face of a
demon – a ghoul – anything you please except of the sleek, oily old
ruffian who sat in the daytime over his turning-lathe downstairs. He
was lying on his stomach with his arms turned and crossed behind him,
as if he had been thrown down pinioned. His head and neck were the
only parts of him off the floor. They were nearly at right angles to the
body, like the head of a cobra at spring. It was ghastly. In the centre of
the room, on the bare earth floor, stood a big, deep, brass basin, with
a pale blue-green light floating in the centre like a night-light. Round
that basin the man on the floor wriggled himself three times. How he
did it I do not know. I could see the muscles ripple along his spine and
fall smooth again; but I could not see any other motion. The head
seemed the only thing alive about him, except that slow curl and uncurl
of the labouring back-muscles. Janoo from the bed was breathing
seventy to the minute; Azizun held her hands before her eyes; and old
Suddhoo, fingering at the dirt that had got into his white beard, was
crying to himself. The horror of it was that the creeping, crawly thing
made no sound – only crawled! And, remember, this lasted for ten
minutes, while the terrier whined, and Azizun shuddered, and Janoo
gasped, and Suddhoo cried!

I felt the hair lift at the back of my head, and my heart thump like
a thermantidote-paddle.[15] Luckily, the seal-cutter betrayed himself by
his most impressive trick and made me calm again. After he had finished
that unspeakable triple crawl, he stretched his head away from the floor
as high as he could, and sent out a jet of fire from his nostrils. Now, I
knew how fire-spouting is done – I can do it myself – so I felt at ease.
The business was a fraud. If he had only kept to that crawl without
trying to raise the effect, goodness knows what I might not have
thought. Both the girls shrieked at the jet of fire, and the head dropped,
chin down on the floor, with a thud; the whole body lying there like a
corpse with its arms trussed. There was a pause of five full minutes
after this, and the blue-green flame died down. Janoo stooped to settle
one of her anklets, while Azizun turned her face to the wall and took
the terrier in her arms. Suddhoo put out an arm mechanically to Janoo's
hookah, and she slid it across the floor with her foot. Directly above
the body and on the wall were a couple of flaming portraits, in stamped-
paper frames, of the Queen and the Prince of Wales. They looked down
on the performance, and, to my thinking, seemed to heighten the
grotesqueness of it all.

Just when the silence was getting unendurable, the body turned over and rolled away from the basin to the side of the room, where it lay stomach-up. There was a faint 'plop' from the basin – exactly like the noise a fish makes when it takes a fly – and the green light in the centre revived.

I looked at the basin, and saw, bobbing in the water, the dried, shrivelled, black head of a native baby – open eyes, open mouth, and shaved scalp. It was worse, being so very sudden, than the crawling exhibition. We had no time to say anything before it began to speak.

Read Poe's account of the voice that came from the mesmerised dying man,[16] and you will realise less than one-half of the horror of that head's voice.

There was an interval of a second or two between each word, and a sort of 'ring, ring, ring', in the note of the voice, like the timbre of a bell. It pealed slowly, as if talking to itself, for several minutes before I got rid of my cold sweat. Then the blessed solution struck me. I looked at the body lying near the doorway, and saw, just where the hollow of the throat joins on the shoulders, a muscle that had nothing to do with any man's regular breathing twitching away steadily. The whole thing was a careful reproduction of the Egyptian teraphim[17] that one reads about sometimes; and the voice was as clever and as appalling a piece of ventriloquism as one could wish to hear. All this time the head was 'lip-lip-lapping' against the side of the basin, and speaking. It told Suddhoo, on his face again whining, of his son's illness and of the state of the illness up to the evening of that very night. I always shall respect the seal-cutter for keeping so faithfully to the time of the Peshawur telegrams. It went on to say that skilled doctors were night and day watching over the man's life; and that he would eventually recover if the fee to the potent sorcerer, whose servant was the head in the basin, were doubled.

Here the mistake from the artistic point of view came in. To ask for twice your stipulated fee in a voice that Lazarus[18] might have used when he rose from the dead, is absurd. Janoo, who is really a woman of masculine intellect, saw this as quickly as I did. I heard her say, 'Asli nahin! Fareib!'* scornfully under her breath; and just as she said so, the light in the basin died out, the head stopped talking, and we heard the room door creak on its hinges. Then Janoo struck a match, lit the lamp, and we saw that head, basin, and seal-cutter were gone. Suddhoo was wringing his hands, and explaining to any one who cared to listen that, if his chances of eternal salvation depended on it, he could not raise another two hundred rupees. Azizun was nearly in

* 'Not real. A trick.'

hysterics in the corner; while Janoo sat down composedly on one of the beds to discuss the probabilities of the whole thing being a *bunao*, or 'make-up'.

I explained as much as I knew of the seal-cutter's way of *jadoo*; but her argument was much more simple. 'The magic that is always demanding gifts is no true magic,' said she. 'My mother told me that the only potent love-spells are those which are told you for love. This seal-cutter man is a liar and a devil. I dare not tell, do anything, or get anything done, because I am in debt to Bhagwan Dass the *bunnia*[19] for two gold rings and a heavy anklet. I must get my food from his shop. The seal-cutter is the friend of Bhagwan Dass, and he would poison my food. A fool's *jadoo* has been going on for ten days, and has cost Suddhoo many rupees each night. The seal-cutter used black hens and lemons and charms before. He never showed us anything like this till to-night. Azizun is a fool, and will be *purdah-nashin** soon. Suddhoo has lost his strength and his wits. See now! I had hoped to get from Suddhoo many rupees while he lived, and many more after his death; and behold, he is spending everything on that offspring of a devil and a she-ass, the seal-cutter!'

Here I said, 'But what induced Suddhoo to drag *me* into the business? Of course I can speak to the seal-cutter, and he shall refund. The whole thing is child's talk – shame – and senseless.'

'Suddhoo *is* an old child,' said Janoo. 'He has lived on the roofs these seventy years and is as senseless as a milch-goat. He brought you here to assure himself that he was not breaking any law of the Sirkar, whose salt he ate many years ago. He worships the dust off the feet of the seal-cutter, and that cow-devourer has forbidden him to go and see his son. What does Suddhoo know of your laws or the lightning-post? *I* have to watch his money going day by day to that lying beast below.' Janoo stamped her foot on the floor and nearly cried with vexation; while Suddhoo was whimpering under a blanket in the corner, and Azizun was trying to guide the pipe-stem to his foolish old mouth.

Now, the case stands thus. Unthinkingly, I have laid myself open to the charge of aiding and abetting the seal-cutter in obtaining money under false pretences, which is forbidden by Section 420 of the Indian Penal Code. I am helpless in the matter for these reasons. I cannot inform the Police. What witnesses would support my statements? Janoo refuses flatly, and Azizun is a married woman somewhere near Bareilly – lost in this big India of ours. I dare not again take the law into my own

*Under coverture.

hands, and speak to the seal-cutter; for certain am I that, not only would Suddhoo disbelieve me, but this step would end in the poisoning of Janoo, who is bound hand and foot by her debt to the *bunnia*. Suddhoo is an old dotard; and whenever we meet mumbles my idiotic joke that the Sirkar rather patronises the Black Art than otherwise. His son is well now; but Suddhoo is completely under the influence of the seal-cutter, by whose advice he regulates the affairs of his life. Janoo watches daily the money that she hoped to wheedle out of Suddhoo taken by the seal-cutter, and becomes daily more furious and sullen.

She will never tell, because she dare not; but, unless something happens to prevent her, I am afraid that the seal-cutter will die of cholera – the white arsenic kind – about the middle of May. And thus I shall be privy to a murder in the House of Suddhoo!

THE STRANGE RIDE OF
MORROWBIE JUKES

Alive or dead – there is no other way.
Native Proverb

There is no invention about this tale. Jukes by accident stumbled upon a village that is well known to exist, though he is the only Englishman who has been there. A somewhat similar institution used to flourish on the outskirts of Calcutta, and there is a story that if you go into the heart of Bikanir,[1] which is in the heart of the Great Indian Desert, you shall come across, not a village, but a town where the Dead who did not die, but may not live, have established their headquarters. And, since it is perfectly true that in the same Desert is a wonderful city where all the rich money-lenders retreat after they have made their fortunes (fortunes so vast that the owners cannot trust even the strong hand of the Government to protect them, but take refuge in the water-less sands), and drive sumptuous C-spring barouches,[2] and buy beautiful girls, and decorate their palaces with gold and ivory and Minton tiles[3] and mother-o'-pearl, I do not see why Jukes's tale should not be true. He is a Civil Engineer, with a head for plans and distances and things of that kind, and he certainly would not take the trouble to invent imaginary traps. He could earn more by doing his legitimate work. He never varies the tale in the telling, and grows very hot and indignant when he thinks of the disrespectful treatment he received. He wrote this quite straightforwardly at first, but he has touched it up in places and introduced Moral Reflections: thus:

In the beginning it all arose from a slight attack of fever. My work necessitated my being in camp for some months between Pakpattan[4] and Mubarakpur[5] – a desolate sandy stretch of country as every one who has had the misfortune to go there may know. My coolies were neither more nor less exasperating than other gangs, and my work demanded sufficient attention to keep me from moping, had I been inclined to so unmanly a weakness.

On the 23rd December 1884 I felt a little feverish. There was a full moon at the time, and, in consequence, every dog near my tent was baying it. The brutes assembled in twos and threes and drove me frantic. A few days previously I had shot one loud-mouthed singer and suspended his carcass *in terrorem*[6] about fifty yards from my tent-door, but his friends fell upon, fought for, and ultimately devoured the body; and, as it seemed to me, sang their hymns of thanksgiving afterwards with renewed energy.

The light-headedness which accompanies fever acts differently on different men. My irritation gave way, after a short time, to a fixed determination to slaughter one huge black-and-white beast who had been foremost in song and first in flight throughout the evening. Thanks to a shaking hand and a giddy head I had already missed him twice with both barrels of my shot-gun, when it struck me that my best plan would be to ride him down in the open and finish him off with a hog-spear. This, of course, was merely the semi-delirious notion of a fever-patient; but I remember that it struck me at the time as being eminently practical and feasible.

I therefore ordered my groom to saddle Pornic and bring him round quietly to the rear of my tent. When the pony was ready, I stood at his head prepared to mount and dash out as soon as the dog should again lift up his voice. Pornic, by the way, had not been out of his pickets for a couple of days; the night air was crisp and chilly; and I was armed with a specially long and sharp pair of persuaders[7] with which I had been rousing a sluggish cob[8] that afternoon. You will easily believe, then, that when he was let go he went quickly. In one moment, for the brute bolted as straight as a die, the tent was left far behind, and we were flying over the smooth sandy soil at racing speed. In another we had passed the wretched dog, and I had almost forgotten why it was that I had taken horse and hog-spear.

The delirium of fever and the excitement of rapid motion through the air must have taken away the remnant of my senses. I have a faint recollection of standing upright in my stirrups, and of brandishing my hog-spear at the great white moon that looked down so calmly on my mad gallop; and of shouting challenges to the camelthorn bushes as they whizzed past. Once or twice, I believe, I swayed forward on Pornic's neck, and literally hung on by my spurs – as the marks next morning showed.

The wretched beast went forward like a thing possessed, over what seemed to be a limitless expanse of moonlit sand. Next, I remember, the ground rose suddenly in front of us, and as we topped the ascent I saw the waters of the Sutlej shining like a silver bar below. Then Pornic blundered heavily on his nose, and we rolled together down some unseen slope.

I must have lost consciousness, for when I recovered I was lying on my stomach in a heap of soft white sand, and the dawn was beginning to break dimly over the edge of the slope down which I had fallen. As the light grew stronger I saw I was at the bottom of a horseshoe-shaped crater of sand, opening on one side directly on to the shoals of the Sutlej. My fever had altogether left me, and, with the exception of a slight dizziness in the head, I felt no bad effects from the fall overnight.

Pornic, who was standing a few yards away, was naturally a good deal exhausted, but had not hurt himself in the least. His saddle, a favourite polo one, was much knocked about, and had been twisted under his belly. It took me some time to put him to rights, and in the meantime I had ample opportunities of observing the spot into which I had so foolishly dropped.

At the risk of being considered tedious, I must describe it at length; inasmuch as an accurate mental picture of its peculiarities will be of material assistance in enabling the reader to understand what follows.

Imagine then, as I have said before, a horseshoe-shaped crater of sand with steeply-graded sand walls about thirty-five feet high. (The slope, I fancy, must have been about 65°.) This crater enclosed a level piece of ground about fifty yards long by thirty at its broadest part, with a rude well in the centre. Round the bottom of the crater, about three feet from the level of the ground proper, ran a series of eighty-three semicircular, ovoid, square, and multilateral holes, all about three feet at the mouth. Each hole on inspection showed that it was carefully shored internally with drift-wood and bamboos, and over the mouth a wooden drip-board projected, like the peak of a jockey's cap, for two feet. No sign of life was visible in these tunnels, but a most sickening stench pervaded the entire amphitheatre – a stench fouler than any which my wanderings in Indian villages have introduced me to.

Having remounted Pornic, who was as anxious as I to get back to camp, I rode round the base of the horseshoe to find some place whence an exit would be practicable. The inhabitants, whoever they might be, had not thought fit to put in an appearance, so I was left to my own devices. My first attempt to 'rush' Pornic up the steep sand-banks showed me that I had fallen into a trap exactly on the same model as that which the ant-lion[9] sets for its prey. At each step the shifting sand poured down from above in tons, and rattled on the drip-boards of the holes like small shot. A couple of ineffectual charges sent us both rolling down to the bottom, half choked with the torrents of sand; and I was constrained to turn my attention to the river-bank.

Here everything seemed easy enough. The sand-hills ran down to the river edge, it is true, but there were plenty of shoals and shallows across which I could gallop Pornic, and find my way back to *terra firma*[10] by turning sharply to the right or the left. As I led Pornic over the sands I was startled by the faint pop of a rifle across the river; and at the same moment a bullet dropped with a sharp '*whit*' close to Pornic's head.

There was no mistaking the nature of the missile – a regulation Martini-Henry 'picket'.[11] About five hundred yards away a country-boat was anchored in mid-stream; and a jet of smoke drifting away from its bows in the still morning air showed me whence the delicate attention had come. Was ever a respectable gentleman in such an *impasse*? The treacherous sand-slope allowed no escape from a spot which I had visited most involuntarily, and a promenade on the river frontage was the signal for a bombardment from some insane native in a boat. I'm afraid that I lost my temper very much indeed.

Another bullet reminded me that I had better save my breath to cool my porridge; and I retreated hastily up the sands and back to the horseshoe, where I saw that the noise of the rifle had drawn sixty-five human beings from the badger-holes which I had up till that point supposed to be untenanted. I found myself in the midst of a crowd of spectators – about forty men, twenty women, and one child who could not have been more than five years old. They were all scantily clothed in that salmon-coloured cloth which one associates with Hindu mendicants, and, at first sight, gave me the impression of a band of loathsome *fakirs*.[12] The filth and repulsiveness of the assembly were beyond all description, and I shuddered to think what their life in the badger-holes must be.

Even in these days, when local self-government has destroyed the greater part of a native's respect for a Sahib,[13] I have been accustomed to a certain amount of civility from my inferiors, and on approaching the crowd naturally expected that there would be some recognition of my presence. As a matter of fact there was, but it was by no means what I had looked for.

The ragged crew actually laughed at me – such laughter I hope I may never hear again. They cackled, yelled, whistled, and howled as I walked into their midst; some of them literally throwing themselves down on the ground in convulsions of unholy mirth. In a moment I had let go Pornic's head, and, irritated beyond expression at the morning's adventure, commenced cuffing those nearest to me with all the force I could. The wretches dropped under my blows like ninepins, and the laughter gave place to wails for mercy; while those yet untouched clasped me round the knees, imploring me in all sorts of uncouth tongues to spare them.

In the tumult, and just when I was feeling very much ashamed of myself for having thus easily given way to my temper, a thin high voice murmured in English from behind my shoulder: 'Sahib! Sahib! Do you not know me? Sahib, it is Gunga Dass, the telegraph-master.'

I spun round quickly and faced the speaker.

Gunga Dass (I have, of course, no hesitation in mentioning the man's real name) I had known four years before as a Deccanee Brahmin[14] lent by the Punjab Government to one of the Khalsia States. He was in charge of a branch telegraph-office there, and when I had last met him was a jovial, full-stomached, portly Government servant with a marvellous capacity for making bad puns in English – a peculiarity which made me remember him long after I had forgotten his services to me in his official capacity. It is seldom that a Hindu makes English puns.

Now, however, the man was changed beyond all recognition. Caste-mark,[15] stomach, slate-coloured continuations,[16] and unctuous speech were all gone. I looked at a withered skeleton, turbanless and almost naked, with long matted hair and deep-set codfish-eyes. But for a crescent-shaped scar on the left cheek – the result of an accident for which I was responsible – I should never have known him. But it was indubitably Gunga Dass, and – for this I was thankful – an English-speaking native who might at least tell me the meaning of all that I had gone through that day.

The crowd retreated to some distance as I turned towards the miserable figure and ordered him to show me some method of escaping from the crater. He held a freshly-plucked crow in his hand, and in reply to my question climbed slowly to a platform of sand which ran in front of the holes, and commenced lighting a fire there in silence. Dried bents, sand-poppies, and drift-wood burn quickly; and I derived much consolation from the fact that he lit them with an ordinary sulphur match. When they were in a bright glow and the crow was neatly spitted in front thereof, Gunga Dass began without a word of preamble:

'There are only two kinds of men, sar – the alive and the dead. When you are dead you are dead, but when you are alive you live.' (Here the crow demanded his attention for an instant as it twirled before the fire in danger of being burnt to a cinder.) 'If you die at home and do not die when you come to the ghat[17] to be burnt you come here.'

The nature of the reeking village was made plain now, and all that I had known or read of the grotesque and the horrible paled before the fact just communicated by the ex-Brahmin. Sixteen years ago, when I first landed in Bombay, I had been told by a wandering Armenian of the existence, somewhere in India, of a place to which such Hindus as had the misfortune to recover from trance or catalepsy were conveyed and kept, and I recollect laughing heartily at what I was then pleased to consider a traveller's tale. Sitting at the bottom of the sand-trap, the memory of Watson's Hotel, with its swinging punkahs, white-robed servants, and the sallow-faced Armenian, rose up in my mind as vividly as a photograph, and I burst into a loud fit of laughter. The contrast was too absurd!

Gunga Dass, as he bent over the unclean bird, watched me curiously. Hindus seldom laugh, and his surroundings were not such as to move him that way. He removed the crow solemnly from the wooden spit and as solemnly devoured it. Then he continued his story, which I give in his own words: –

'In epidemics of the cholera you are carried to be burnt almost before you are dead. When you come to the riverside the cold air, perhaps, makes you alive, and then, if you are only a little alive, mud is put on your nose and mouth and you die conclusively. If you are rather more alive, more mud is put; but if you are too lively, they let you go and take you away. I was too lively, and made protestation with anger against the indignities that they endeavoured to press upon me. In those days I was Brahmin and proud man. Now I am dead man and eat' – here he eyed the well-gnawed breast-bone with the first sign of emotion that I had seen in him since we met – 'crows, and – other things. They took me from my sheets when they saw that I was too lively and gave me medicines for one week, and I survived successfully. Then they sent me by rail from my place to Okara Station,[18] with a man to take care of me; and at Okara Station we met two other men, and they conducted us three on camels, in the night, from Okara Station to this place, and they propelled me from the top to the bottom, and the other two succeeded, and I have been here ever since two and a half years. Once I was Brahmin and proud man, and now I eat crows.'

'There is no way of getting out?'

'None of what kind at all. When I first came I made experiments frequently, and all the others also, but we have always succumbed to the sand which is precipitated upon our heads.'

'But surely,' I broke in at this point, 'the river-front is open, and it is worth while dodging the bullets; while at night –'

I had already matured a rough plan of escape which a natural instinct of selfishness forbade me sharing with Gunga Dass. He, however, divined my unspoken thought almost as soon as it was formed; and, to my intense astonishment, gave vent to a long low chuckle of derision – the laughter, be it understood, of a superior or at least of an equal.

'You will not' – he had dropped the 'sir' after his first sentence – 'make any escape that way. But you can try. I have tried. Once only.'

The sensation of nameless terror which I had in vain attempted to strive against overmastered me completely. My long fast – it was now close upon ten o'clock, and I had eaten nothing since tiffin[19] on the previous day – combined with the violent agitation of the ride had exhausted me, and I verily believe that, for a few minutes, I acted as one mad. I hurled myself against the sand-slope. I ran round the base of the crater, blaspheming and praying by turns. I crawled out among the sedges of the river-front, only to be driven back each time in an agony of nervous dread by the rifle-bullets which cut up the sand round me – for I dared not face the death of a mad dog among that hideous crowd – and so fell, spent and raving, at the curb of the well. No one had taken the slightest notice of an exhibition which makes me blush hotly even when I think of it now.

Two or three men trod on my panting body as they drew water, but they were evidently used to this sort of thing, and had no time to waste upon me. Gunga Dass, indeed, when he had banked the embers of his fire with sand, was at some pains to throw half a cupful of fetid water over my head, an attention for which I could have fallen on my knees and thanked him, but he was laughing all the while in the same mirth-less, wheezy key that greeted me on my first attempt to force the shoals. And so, in a half-fainting state, I lay till noon. Then, being only a man after all, I felt hungry, and said as much to Gunga Dass, whom I had begun to regard as my natural protector. Following the impulse of the outer world when dealing with natives, I put my hand into my pocket and drew out four annas. The absurdity of the gift struck me at once, and I was about to replace the money.

Gunga Dass, however, cried: 'Give me the money, all you have, or I will get help, and we will kill you!'

A Briton's first impulse, I believe, is to guard the contents of his pockets; but a moment's thought showed me the folly of differing with the one man who had it in his power to make me comfortable; and with whose help it was possible that I might eventually escape from the crater. I gave him all the money in my possession, Rs. 9-8-5[20] – nine rupees, eight annas, and five pice – for I always keep small change as *bakshish*[21] when I am in camp. Gunga Dass clutched the coins, and hid them at once in his ragged loin-cloth, looking round to assure himself that no one had observed us.

'*Now* I will give you something to eat,' said he.

What pleasure my money could have given him I am unable to say; but inasmuch as it did please him I was not sorry that I had parted with it so readily, for I had no doubt that he would have had me killed if I had refused. One does not protest against the doings of a den of wild beasts; and my companions were lower than any beasts. While I ate what Gunga Dass had provided, a coarse *chapatti*[22] and a cupful of the foul well-water, the people showed not the faintest sign of curiosity – that curiosity which is so rampant, as a rule, in an Indian village.

I could even fancy that they despised me. At all events they treated me with the most chilling indifference, and Gunga Dass was nearly as bad. I plied him with questions about the terrible village, and received extremely unsatisfactory answers. So far as I could gather, it had been in existence from time immemorial – whence I concluded that it was at least a century old – and during that time no one had ever been known to escape from it. (I had to control myself here with both hands, lest the blind terror should lay hold of me a second time and drive me raving round the crater.) Gunga Dass took a malicious pleasure in emphasising this point and in watching me wince. Nothing that I could do would induce him to tell me who the mysterious 'They' were.

'It is so ordered,' he would reply, 'and I do not yet know any one who has disobeyed the orders.'

'Only wait till my servants find that I am missing,' I retorted, 'and I promise you that this place shall be cleared off the face of the earth, and I'll give you a lesson in civility, too, my friend.'

'Your servants would be torn in pieces before they came near this place; and, besides, you are dead, my dear friend. It is not your fault, of course, but none the less you are dead *and* buried.'

At irregular intervals supplies of food, I was told, were dropped down from the land side into the amphitheatre, and the inhabitants fought for them like wild beasts. When a man felt his death coming on he retreated to his lair and died there. The body was sometimes dragged out of the hole and thrown on to the sand, or allowed to rot where it lay.

The phrase 'thrown on to the sand' caught my attention, and I asked Gunga Dass whether this sort of thing was not likely to breed a pestilence.

'That,' said he, with another of his wheezy chuckles, 'you may see for yourself subsequently. You will have much time to make observations.'

Whereat, to his great delight, I winced once more and hastily continued the conversation: 'And how do you live here from day to day? What do you do?' The question elicited exactly the same answer as before – coupled with the information that 'this place is like your European Heaven; there is neither marrying nor giving in marriage.'

Gunga Dass had been educated at a Mission School, and, as he himself admitted, had he only changed his religion 'like a wise man', might have avoided the living grave which was now his portion. But as long as I was with him I fancy he was happy.

Here was a Sahib, a representative of the dominant race, helpless as a child and completely at the mercy of his native neighbours. In a deliberate lazy way he set himself to torture me as a schoolboy would devote a rapturous half-hour to watching the agonies of an impaled beetle, or as a ferret in a blind burrow might glue himself comfortably to the neck of a rabbit. The burden of his conversation was that there was no escape 'of no kind whatever', and that I should stay here till I died and was 'thrown on to the sand'. If it were possible to forejudge the conversation of the Damned on the advent of a new soul in their abode, I should say that they would speak as Gunga Dass did to me throughout that long afternoon. I was powerless to protest or answer; all my energies being devoted to a struggle against the inexplicable terror that threatened to overwhelm me again and again. I can compare the feeling to nothing except the struggles of a man against the overpowering nausea of the Channel passage[23] – only my agony was of the spirit and infinitely more terrible.

As the day wore on, the inhabitants began to appear in full strength to catch the rays of the afternoon sun, which were now sloping in at the mouth of the crater. They assembled by little knots, and talked among themselves without even throwing a glance in my direction. About four o'clock, so far as I could judge, Gunga Dass rose and dived into his lair for a moment, emerging with a live crow in his hands. The wretched bird was in a most draggled and deplorable condition, but seemed to be in no way afraid of its master. Advancing cautiously to the river-front, Gunga Dass stepped from tussock to tussock until he had reached a smooth patch of sand directly in the line of the boat's fire. The occupants of the boat took no notice. Here he stopped, and, with a couple of dexterous turns of the wrist, pegged the bird on its back with outstretched wings. As was only natural, the crow began to shriek at once and beat the air with its claws. In a few seconds the clamour had attracted the attention of a bevy of wild crows on a shoal a few hundred yards away, where they were discussing something that looked like a corpse. Half-a-dozen crows flew over at once to see what was going on, and also, as it proved, to attack the pinioned bird. Gunga Dass, who had lain down on a tussock, motioned to me to be quiet, though I fancy this was a needless precaution. In a moment, and before I could see how it happened, a wild crow, which had grappled with the shrieking and helpless bird, was entangled in the latter's claws, swiftly disengaged by Gunga Dass, and pegged down beside its companion in adversity. Curiosity, it seemed, overpowered the rest of the flock, and almost before Gunga Dass and I had time to withdraw to the tussock, two more captives were struggling in the upturned claws of the decoys. So the chase – if I can give it so dignified a name – continued until Gunga Dass had captured seven crows. Five of them he throttled at once, reserving two for further operations another day. I was a good deal impressed by this, to me, novel method of securing food, and complimented Gunga Dass on his skill.

'It is nothing to do,' said he. 'To-morrow you must do it for me. You are stronger than I am.'

This calm assumption of superiority upset me not a little, and I answered peremptorily: 'Indeed, you old ruffian? What do you think I have given you money for?'

'Very well,' was the unmoved reply. 'Perhaps not to-morrow, nor the day after, nor subsequently; but in the end, and for many years, you will catch crows and eat crows, and you will thank your European God that you have crows to catch and eat.'

I could have cheerfully strangled him for this, but judged it best under the circumstances to smother my resentment. An hour later I was eating one of the crows; and, as Gunga Dass had said, thanking my God that I had a crow to eat. Never as long as I live shall I forget that evening meal. The whole population were squatting on the hard sand platform opposite their dens, huddled over tiny fires of refuse and dried rushes. Death, having once laid his hand upon these men and forborne to strike, seemed to stand aloof from them now; for most of our company were old men, bent and worn and twisted with years, and women aged to all appearance as the Fates themselves.[24] They sat together in knots and talked – God only knows what they found to discuss – in low equable tones, curiously in contrast to the strident babble with which natives are accustomed to make day hideous. Now and then an access of that sudden fury which had possessed me in the morning would lay hold on a man or woman; and with yells and imprecations the sufferer would attack the steep slope until, baffled and bleeding, he fell back on the platform incapable of moving a limb. The others would never even raise their eyes when this happened, as men too well aware of the futility of their fellows' attempts and wearied with their useless repetition. I saw four such outbursts in the course of that evening.

Gunga Dass took an eminently businesslike view of my situation, and while we were dining – I can afford to laugh at the recollection now, but it was painful enough at the time – propounded the terms on which he would consent to 'do' for me. My nine rupees eight annas, he argued, at the rate of three annas a day, would provide me with food for fifty-one days, or about seven weeks; that is to say, he would be willing to cater for me for that length of time. At the end of it I was to look after myself. For a further consideration – *videlicet*[25] my boots – he would be willing to allow me to occupy the den next to his own, and would supply me with as much dried grass for bedding as he could spare.

'Very well, Gunga Dass,' I replied; 'to the first terms I cheerfully agree, but, as there is nothing on earth to prevent my killing you as you sit here and taking everything that you have' (I thought of the two invaluable crows at the time), 'I flatly refuse to give you my boots and shall take whichever den I please.'

The stroke was a bold one, and I was glad when I saw that it had succeeded. Gunga Dass changed his tone immediately, and disavowed all intention of asking for my boots. At the time it did not strike me as at all strange that I, a Civil Engineer, a man of thirteen years' standing in the Service, and, I trust, an average Englishman, should thus calmly threaten murder and violence against the man who had, for a consideration it is true, taken me under his wing. I had left the world, it seemed, for centuries. I was as certain then as I am now of my own existence, that in the accursed settlement there was no law save that of the strongest; that the living dead men had thrown behind them every canon[26] of the world which had cast them out; and that I had to depend for my own life on my strength and vigilance alone. The crew of the ill-fated *Mignonette*[27] are the only men who would understand my frame of mind. 'At present,' I argued to myself, 'I am strong and a match for six of these wretches. It is imperatively necessary that I should, for my own sake, keep both health and strength until the hour of my release comes – if it ever does.'

Fortified with these resolutions, I ate and drank as much as I could, and made Gunga Dass understand that I intended to be his master, and that the least sign of insubordination on his part would be visited with the only punishment I had it in my power to inflict – sudden and violent death. Shortly after this I went to bed. That is to say, Gunga Dass gave me a double armful of dried bents[28] which I thrust down the mouth of the lair to the right of his, and followed myself, feet foremost; the hole running about nine feet into the sand with a slight downward inclination, and being neatly shored with timbers. From my den, which faced the river-front, I was able to watch the waters of the Sutlej flowing past under the light of a young moon and compose myself to sleep as best I might.

The horrors of that night I shall never forget. My den was nearly as narrow as a coffin, and the sides had been worn smooth and greasy by the contact of innumerable naked bodies, added to which it smelt abominably. Sleep was altogether out of the question to one in my excited frame of mind. As the night wore on, it seemed that the entire amphitheatre was filled with legions of unclean devils that, trooping up from the shoals below, mocked the unfortunates in their lairs.

Personally I am not of an imaginative temperament – very few Engineers are – but on that occasion I was as completely prostrated with nervous terror as any woman. After half an hour or so, however, I was able once more to calmly review my chances of escape. Any exit by the steep sand walls was, of course, impracticable. I had been thoroughly convinced of this some time before. It was possible, just possible, that I might, in the uncertain moonlight, safely run the gauntlet of the rifle shots. The place was so full of terror for me that I was prepared to undergo any risk in leaving it. Imagine my delight, then, when after creeping stealthily to the river-front I found that the infernal boat was not there. My freedom lay before me in the next few steps!

By walking out to the first shallow pool that lay at the foot of the projecting left horn of the horseshoe, I could wade across, turn the flank of the crater, and make my way inland. Without a moment's hesitation I marched briskly past the tussocks where Gunga Dass had snared the crows, and out in the direction of the smooth white sand beyond. My first step from the tufts of dried grass showed me how utterly futile was any hope of escape; for, as I put my foot down, I felt an indescribable drawing, sucking motion of the sand below. Another moment and my leg was swallowed up nearly to the knee. In the moonlight the whole surface of the sand seemed to be shaken with devilish delight at my disappointment. I struggled clear, sweating with terror and exertion, back to the tussocks behind me and fell on my face.

My only means of escape from the semicircle was protected by a quicksand!

How long I lay I have not the faintest idea; but I was roused at last by the malevolent chuckle of Gunga Dass at my ear. 'I would advise you, Protector of the Poor,' (the ruffian was speaking English) 'to return to your house. It is unhealthy to lie down here. Moreover, when the boat returns you will most certainly be rifled at.' He stood over me in the dim light of the dawn, chuckling and laughing to himself. Suppressing my first impulse to catch the man by the neck and throw him on to the quicksand, I rose sullenly and followed him to the platform below the burrows.

Suddenly, and futilely, as I thought while I spoke, I asked: 'Gunga Dass, what is the good of the boat if I can't get out *anyhow*?' I recollect that even in my deepest trouble I had been speculating vaguely on the waste of ammunition in guarding an already well-protected foreshore.

Gunga Dass laughed again and made answer: 'They have the boat only in daytime. It is for the reason that *there is a way*. I hope we shall have the pleasure of your company for much longer time. It is a pleasant spot when you have been here some years and eaten roast crow long enough.'

I staggered, numbed and helpless, towards the fetid burrow allotted to me, and fell asleep. An hour or so later I was awakened by a piercing scream – the shrill, high-pitched scream of a horse in pain. Those who have once heard that will never forget the sound. I found some little difficulty in scrambling out of the burrow. When I was in the open, I saw Pornic, my poor old Pornic, lying dead on the sandy soil. How they had killed him I cannot guess. Gunga Dass explained that horse was better than crow, and 'greatest good of greatest number is political maxim.[29] We are now Republic, Mister Jukes, and you are entitled to a fair share of the beast. If you like, we will pass a vote of thanks. Shall I propose?'

Yes, we were a Republic indeed! A Republic of wild beasts penned at the bottom of a pit, to eat and fight and sleep till we died. I attempted no protest of any kind, but sat down and stared at the hideous sight in front of me. In less time almost than it takes me to write this, Pornic's body was divided, in some unclean way or other; the men and women had dragged the fragments on to the platform and were preparing their morning meal. Gunga Dass cooked mine. The almost irresistible impulse to fly at the sand walls until I was wearied laid hold of me afresh, and I had to struggle against it with all my might. Gunga Dass was offensively jocular till I told him that if he addressed another remark of any kind whatever to men I should strangle him where he sat. This silenced him till the silence became insupportable, and I bade him say something.

'You will live here till you die like the other Feringhi,'[30] he said coolly, watching me over the fragment of gristle that he was gnawing.

'What other Sahib, you swine? Speak at once, and don't stop to tell me a lie.'

'He is over there,' answered Gunga Dass, pointing to a burrow-mouth about four doors to the left of my own. 'You can see for yourself. He died in the burrow as you will die, and I will die, and as all these men and women and the one child will also die.'

'For pity's sake, tell me all you know about him. Who was he? When did he come, and when did he die?'

This appeal was a weak step on my part. Gunga Dass only leered and replied: 'I will not – unless you give me something first.'

Then I recollected where I was, and struck the man between the eyes, partially stunning him. He stepped down from the platform at once, and, cringing and fawning and weeping and attempting to embrace my feet, led me round to the burrow which he had indicated.

'I know nothing whatever about the gentleman. Your God be my witness that I do not. He was as anxious to escape as you were, and he was shot from the boat, though we all did all things to prevent him from attempting. He was shot here.' Gunga Dass laid his hand on his lean stomach and bowed to the earth.

'Well, and what then? Go on!'

'And then – and then, Your Honour, we carried him into his house and gave him water, and put wet cloths on the wound, and he laid down in his house and gave up the ghost.'

'In how long? In how long?'

'About half an hour after he received his wound. I call Vishnu[31] to witness,' yelled the wretched man, 'that I did everything for him. Everything which was possible, that I did!'

He threw himself down on the ground and clasped my ankles. But I had my doubts about Gunga Dass's benevolence, and kicked him off as he lay protesting.

'I believe you robbed him of everything he had. But I can find out in a minute or two. How long was the Sahib here?'

'Nearly a year and a half. I think he must have gone mad. But hear me swear, Protector of the Poor! Won't Your Honour hear me swear that I never touched an article that belonged to him? What is Your Worship going to do?'

I had taken Gunga Dass by the waist and had hauled him on to the platform opposite the deserted burrow. As I did so I thought of my wretched fellow-prisoner's unspeakable misery among all these horrors for eighteen months, and the final agony of dying like a rat in a hole, with a bullet-wound in the stomach. Gunga Dass fancied I was going to kill him and howled pitifully. The rest of the population, in the plethora that follows a full flesh meal, watched us without stirring.

'Go inside, Gunga Dass,' said I, 'and fetch it out.'

I was feeling sick and faint with horror now. Gunga Dass nearly rolled off the platform and howled aloud.

'But I am Brahmin, Sahib – a high-caste Brahmin. By your soul, by your father's soul, do not make me do this thing!'

'Brahmin or no Brahmin, by my soul and my father's soul, in you go!' I said, and, seizing him by the shoulders, I crammed his head into the mouth of the burrow, kicked the rest of him in, and, sitting down, covered my face with my hands.

At the end of a few minutes I heard a rustle and a creak; then Gunga Dass in a sobbing, choking whisper speaking to himself; then a soft thud – and I uncovered my eyes.

The dry sand had turned the corpse entrusted to its keeping into a yellow-brown mummy. I told Gunga Dass to stand off while I examined it. The body – clad in an olive-green hunting-suit much stained and worn, with leather pads on the shoulders – was that of a man between thirty and forty, above middle height, with light sandy hair, long moustache, and a rough unkempt beard. The left canine of the upper jaw was missing, and a portion of the lobe of the right ear was gone. On the second finger of the left hand was a ring – a shield-shaped bloodstone set in gold, with a monogram that might have been either 'B. K.' or 'B. L.' On the third finger of the right hand was a silver ring in the shape of a coiled cobra, much worn and tarnished. Gunga Dass deposited a handful of trifles he had picked out of the burrow at my feet, and, covering the face of the body with my handkerchief, I turned to examine these. I give the full list in the hope that it may lead to the identification of the unfortunate man:

1. Bowl of a briarwood pipe, serrated at the edge; much worn and blackened; bound with string at the screw.

2. Two patent-lever keys; wards of both broken.

3. Tortoise-shell-handled penknife, silver or nickel, name-plate marked with monogram 'B. K.'

4. Envelope, postmark undecipherable, bearing a Victorian stamp, addressed to 'Miss Mon – ' (rest illegible) – 'ham' – 'nt.'

5. Imitation crocodile-skin notebook with pencil. First forty-five pages blank; four and a half illegible; fifteen others filled with private memoranda relating chiefly to three persons – a Mrs L. Singleton, abbreviated several times to 'Lot Single', 'Mrs S. May', and 'Garmison', referred to in places as 'Jerry' or 'Jack'.

6. Handle of small-sized hunting-knife. Blade snapped short. Buck's horn, diamond-cut, with swivel and ring on the butt; fragment of cotton cord attached.

It must not be supposed that I inventoried all these things on the spot as fully as I have here written them down. The notebook first attracted my attention, and I put it in my pocket with a view to studying it later on. The rest of the articles I conveyed to my burrow for safety's sake, and there, being a methodical man, I inventoried them. I then returned to the corpse and ordered Gunga Dass to help me to carry it out to the river-front. While we were engaged in this, the exploded shell of an old brown cartridge dropped out of one of the pockets and rolled at my feet. Gunga Dass had not seen it; and I fell to thinking that a man does not carry exploded cartridge-cases, especially 'browns', which will not bear loading twice, about with him when shooting. In other words, that cartridge-case had been fired inside the crater. Consequently there must be a gun somewhere. I was on the verge of asking Gunga Dass, but checked myself, knowing that he would lie. We laid the body down on the edge of the quicksand by the tussocks. It was my intention to push it out and let it be swallowed up – the only possible mode of burial that I could think of. I ordered Gunga Dass to go away.

Then I gingerly put the corpse out on the quicksand. In doing so – it was lying face downward – I tore the frail and rotten khaki shooting-coat open, disclosing a hideous cavity in the back. I have already told you that the dry sand had, as it were, mummified the body. A moment's glance showed that the gaping hole had been caused by a gunshot wound; the gun must have been fired with the muzzle almost touching the back. The shooting-coat, being intact, had been drawn over the body after death, which must have been instantaneous. The secret of the poor wretch's death was plain to me in a flash. Some one of the crater, presumably Gunga Dass, must have shot him with his own gun – the gun that fitted the brown cartridges. He had never attempted to escape in the face of the rifle-fire from the boat.

I pushed the corpse out hastily, and saw it sink from sight literally in a few seconds. I shuddered as I watched. In a dazed, half-conscious way I turned to peruse the notebook. A stained and discoloured slip of paper had been inserted between the binding and the back, and dropped out as I opened the pages. This is what it contained: '*Four out from crow-clump; three left; nine out; two right; three back; two left; fourteen out; two left; seven out; one left; nine back; two right; six back; four right; seven back.*' The paper had been burnt and charred at the edges. What it meant I could not understand. I sat down on the dried bents turning it over and over between my fingers, until I was aware of Gunga Dass standing immediately behind me with glowing eyes and outstretched hands.

'Have you got it?' he panted. 'Will you not let me look at it also? I swear that I will return it.'

'Got what? Return what?' I asked.

'That which you have in your hands. It will help us both.' He stretched out his long bird-like talons, trembling with eagerness.

'I could never find it,' he continued. 'He had secreted it about his person. Therefore I shot him, but nevertheless I was unable to obtain it.'

Gunga Dass had quite forgotten his little fiction about the rifle-bullet. I heard him calmly. Morality is blunted by consorting with the Dead who are alive.

'What on earth are you raving about? What is it you want me to give you?'

'The piece of paper in the notebook. It will help us both. Oh, you fool! You fool! Can you not see what it will do for us? We shall escape!'

His voice rose almost to a scream, and he danced with excitement before me. I own I was moved at the chance of getting away.

'Do you mean to say that this slip of paper will help us? What does it mean?'

'Read it aloud! Read it aloud! I beg and I pray to you to read it aloud.'

I did so. Gunga Dass listened delightedly, and drew an irregular line in the sand with his fingers.

'See now! It was the length of his gun-barrels without the stock. I have those barrels. Four gun-barrels out from the place where I caught crows. Straight out; do you mind me? Then three left. Ah! Now well I remember how that man worked it out night after night. Then nine out, and so on. Out is always straight before you across the quicksand to the north. He told me so before I killed him.'

'But if you knew all this why didn't you get out before?'

'I did *not* know it. He told me that he was working it out a year and a half ago, and how he was working it out night after night when the boat had gone away, and he could get out near the quicksand safely. Then he said that we would get away together. But I was afraid that he would leave me behind one night when he had worked it all out, and so I shot him. Besides, it is not advisable that the men who once get in here should escape. Only I, and *I* am a Brahmin.'

The hope of escape had brought Gunga Dass's caste back to him. He stood up, walked about, and gesticulated violently. Eventually I managed to make him talk soberly, and he told me how this Englishman had spent six months night after night in exploring, inch by inch, the passage across the quicksand; how he had declared it to be simplicity itself up to within about twenty yards of the river-bank after turning the flank of the left horn of the horseshoe. This much he had evidently not completed when Gunga Dass shot him with his own gun.

In my frenzy of delight at the possibilities of escape I recollect shaking hands wildly with Gunga Dass, after we had decided that we were to make an attempt to get away that very night. It was weary work waiting throughout the afternoon.

About ten o'clock, as far as I could judge, when the moon had just risen above the lip of the crater, Gunga Dass made a move for his burrow to bring out the gun-barrels whereby to measure our path. All the other wretched inhabitants had retired to their lairs long ago. The guardian boat had drifted down-stream some hours before, and we were utterly alone by the crow-clump. Gunga Dass, while carrying the gun-barrels, let slip the piece of paper which was to be our guide. I stooped down hastily to recover it, and, as I did so, I was aware that the creature was aiming a violent blow at the back of my head with the gun-barrels. It was too late to turn round. I must have received the blow somewhere on the nape of the neck, for I fell senseless at the edge of the quicksand.

When I recovered consciousness the moon was going down, and I was sensible of intolerable pain in the back of my head. Gunga Dass had disappeared and my mouth was full of blood. I lay down again and prayed that I might die without more ado. Then the unreasoning fury which I have before mentioned laid hold upon me, and I staggered inland towards the walls of the crater. It seemed that some one was calling to me in a whisper – 'Sahib! Sahib! Sahib!' exactly as my bearer used to call me in the mornings. I fancied that I was delirious until a handful of sand fell at my feet. Then I looked up and saw a head peering down into the amphitheatre – the head of Dunnoo, my dog-boy, who attended to my collies. As soon as he had attracted my attention, he held up his hand and showed a rope. I motioned, staggering to and fro the while, that he should throw it down. It was a couple of leather punkah-ropes[32] knotted together, with a loop at one end. I slipped the loop over my head and under my arms; heard Dunnoo urge something forward; was conscious that I was being dragged, face downward, up the steep sand-slope, and the next instant found myself choked and half-fainting on the sand-hills overlooking the crater. Dunnoo, with his face ashy-grey in the moonlight, implored me not to stay, but to get back to my tent at once.

It seems that he had tracked Pornic's footprints fourteen miles across the sands to the crater; had returned and told my servants, who flatly refused to meddle with anyone, white or black, once fallen into the hideous Village of the Dead; whereupon Dunnoo had taken one of my ponies and a couple of punkah-ropes, returned to the crater, and hauled me out as I have described.

LISPETH

Look, you have cast out Love! What Gods are these
    You bid me please?
The Three in One, the One in Three? Not so!
    To my own Gods I go.
It may be they shall give me greater ease
Than your cold Christ and tangled Trinities.

The Convert

She was the daughter of Sonoo, a Hill-man of the Himalayas, and Jadéh his wife. One year their maize failed, and two bears spent the night in their only opium poppy-field just above the Sutlej Valley on the Kotgarh[1] side; so, next season, they turned Christian, and brought their baby to the Mission to be baptized. The Kotgarh Chaplain christened her Elizabeth, and 'Lispeth' is the Hill or *pahari*[2] pronunciation.

Later, cholera came into the Kotgarh Valley and carried off Sonoo and Jadéh, and Lispeth became half servant, half companion, to the wife of the then Chaplain of Kotgarh. This was after the reign of the Moravian missionaries[3] in that place, but before Kotgarh had quite forgotten her title of 'Mistress of the Northern Hills'.

Whether Christianity improved Lispeth, or whether the Gods of her own people would have done as much for her under any circumstances, I do not know; but she grew very lovely. When a Hill-girl grows lovely, she is worth travelling fifty miles over bad ground to look upon. Lispeth had a Greek face – one of those faces people paint so often, and see so seldom. She was of a pale, ivory colour, and, for her race, extremely tall. Also, she possessed eyes that were wonderful; and, had she not been dressed in the abominable print-cloths affected by Missions, you would, meeting her on the hillside unexpectedly, have thought her the original Diana of the Romans[4] going out to slay.

Lispeth took to Christianity readily, and did not abandon it when she reached womanhood, as do some Hill-girls. Her own people hated her because she had, they said, become a white woman and washed herself daily; and the Chaplain's wife did not know what to do with her. One cannot ask a stately goddess, five feet ten in her shoes, to clean plates and dishes. She played with the Chaplain's children and took

classes in the Sunday School, and read all the books in the house, and
grew more and more beautiful, like the Princesses in fairy tales. The
Chaplain's wife said that the girl ought to take service in Simla as a
nurse or something 'genteel'. But Lispeth did not want to take service.
She was very happy where she was.

When travellers – there were not many in those years – came in to
Kotgarh, Lispeth used to lock herself into her own room for fear they
might take her away to Simla, or out into the unknown world.

One day, a few months after she was seventeen years old, Lispeth
went out for a walk. She did not walk in the manner of English ladies
– a mile and a half out, with a carriage-ride back again. She covered
between twenty and thirty miles in her little constitutionals, all about
and about, between Kotgarh and Narkanda. This time she came back
at full dusk, stepping down the breakneck descent into Kotgarh with
something heavy in her arms. The Chaplain's wife was dozing in
the drawing-room when Lispeth came in breathing heavily and very
exhausted with her burden. Lispeth put it down on the sofa, and said
simply, 'This is my husband. I found him on the Bagi road. He has hurt
himself. We will nurse him, and when he is well your husband shall
marry him to me.'

This was the first mention Lispeth had ever made of her matrimonial
views, and the Chaplain's wife shrieked with horror. However, the man
on the sofa needed attention first. He was a young Englishman, and
his head had been cut to the bone by something jagged. Lispeth said
she had found him down the hillside, and had brought him in. He was
breathing queerly and was unconscious.

He was put to bed and tended by the Chaplain, who knew something
of medicine, and Lispeth waited outside the door in case she could be
useful. She explained to the Chaplain that this was the man she meant
to marry, and the Chaplain and his wife lectured her severely on the
impropriety of her conduct. Lispeth listened quietly, and repeated her
first proposition. It takes a great deal of Christianity to wipe out
uncivilised Eastern instincts, such as falling in love at first sight. Lispeth,
having found the man she worshipped, did not see why she should keep
silent as to her choice. She had no intention of being sent away, either.
She was going to nurse that Englishman until he was well enough to
marry her. That was her programme.

After a fortnight of slight fever and inflammation, the Englishman
recovered coherence and thanked the Chaplain and his wife, and Lispeth
– especially Lispeth – for their kindness. He was a traveller in the East,
he said – they never talked about 'globe-trotters'[5] in those days, when
the P. & O. fleet[6] was young and small – and had come from Dehra

Dun to hunt for plants and butterflies among the Simla[7] hills. No one at Simla, therefore, knew anything about him. He fancied that he must have fallen over the cliff while reaching out for a fern on a rotten tree-trunk, and that his coolies must have stolen his baggage and fled. He thought he would go back to Simla when he was a little stronger. He desired no more mountaineering.

He made small haste to go away, and recovered his strength slowly. Lispeth objected to being advised either by the Chaplain or his wife. Therefore the latter spoke to the Englishman, and told him how matters stood in Lispeth's heart. He laughed a good deal, and said it was very pretty and romantic, but, as he was engaged to a girl at Home, he fancied that nothing would happen. Certainly he would behave with discretion. He did that. Still, he found it very pleasant to talk to Lispeth, and walk with Lispeth, and say nice things to her, and call her pet names while he was getting strong enough to go away. It meant nothing at all to him, and everything in the world to Lispeth. She was very happy while the fortnight lasted, because she had found a man to love.

Being a savage by birth, she took no trouble to hide her feelings, and the Englishman was amused. When he went away, Lispeth walked with him up the Hill as far as Narkanda,[8] very troubled and very miserable. The Chaplain's wife, being a good Christian and disliking anything in the shape of fuss or scandal – Lispeth was beyond her management entirely – had told the Englishman to tell Lispeth that he was coming back to marry her. 'She is but a child, you know, and, I fear, at heart a heathen,' said the Chaplain's wife. So all the twelve miles up the Hill the Englishman, with his arm round Lispeth's waist, was assuring the girl that he would come back and marry her; and Lispeth made him promise over and over again. She wept on the Narkanda Ridge till he had passed out of sight along the Muttiani path.

Then she dried her tears and went in to Kotgarh again, and said to the Chaplain's wife, 'He will come back and marry me. He has gone to his own people to tell them so.' And the Chaplain's wife soothed Lispeth and said, 'He will come back.' At the end of two months Lispeth grew impatient, and was told that the Englishman had gone over the seas to England. She knew where England was, because she had read little geography primers; but, of course, she had no conception of the nature of the sea, being a Hill-girl. There was an old puzzle-map of the World in the house. Lispeth had played with it when she was a child. She unearthed it again, and put it together of evenings, and cried to herself, and tried to imagine where her Englishman was. As she had no ideas of distance or steamboats her notions were somewhat wild. It would not have made the least difference had she been perfectly correct, for the Englishman had no intention of coming back to marry a Hill-girl. He forgot all about her by the time he was butterfly-hunting in Assam. He wrote a book on the East afterwards. Lispeth's name did not appear there.

At the end of three months Lispeth made daily pilgrimage to Narkanda to see if her Englishman was coming along the road. It gave her comfort, and the Chaplain's wife finding her happier thought that she was getting over her 'barbarous and most indelicate folly'. A little later the walks ceased to help Lispeth, and her temper grew very bad. The Chaplain's wife thought this a profitable time to let her know the real state of affairs – that the Englishman had only promised his love to keep her quiet – that he had never meant anything, and that it was wrong and improper of Lispeth to think of marriage with an Englishman, who was of a superior clay, besides being promised in marriage to a girl of his own people. Lispeth said that all this was clearly impossible because he had said he loved her, and the Chaplain's wife had, with her own lips, asserted that the Englishman was coming back.

'How can what he and you said be untrue?' asked Lispeth.

'We said it as an excuse to keep you quiet, child,' said the Chaplain's wife.

'Then you have lied to me,' said Lispeth, 'you and he?'

The Chaplain's wife bowed her head, and said nothing. Lispeth was silent too for a little time; then she went out down the valley, and returned in the dress of a Hill-girl – infamously dirty, but without the nose-stud and ear-rings. She had her hair braided into the long pigtail, helped out with black thread, that Hill-women wear.

'I am going back to my own people,' said she. 'You have killed Lispeth. There is only left old Jadéh's daughter – the daughter of a *pahari* and the servant of Tarka Devi.[9] You are all liars, you English.'

By the time that the Chaplain's wife had recovered from the shock of the announcement that Lispeth had 'verted to her mother's Gods the girl had gone; and she never came back.

She took to her own unclean people savagely, as if to make up the arrears of the life she had stepped out of; and, in a little time, she married a wood-cutter who beat her after the manner of *paharis*, and her beauty faded soon.

'There is no law whereby you can account for the vagaries of the heathen,' said the Chaplain's wife, 'and I believe that Lispeth was always at heart an infidel.' Seeing she had been taken into the Church of England at the mature age of five weeks, this statement does not do credit to the Chaplain's wife.

Lispeth was a very old woman when she died. She had always a perfect command of English, and when she was sufficiently drunk could sometimes be induced to tell the story of her first love-affair.

It was hard then to realise that the bleared, wrinkled creature, exactly like a wisp of charred rag, could ever have been 'Lispeth of the Kotgarh Mission'.

BEYOND THE PALE

Love heeds not caste nor sleep a broken bed. I went in search of love and lost myself.

Hindu Proverb

A man should, whatever happens, keep to his own caste, race, and breed. Let the White go to the White and the Black to the Black. Then whatever trouble falls is in the ordinary course of things – neither sudden, alien, nor unexpected.

This is the story of a man who wilfully stepped beyond the safe limits of decent everyday society, and paid for it heavily.

He knew too much in the first instance; and he saw too much in the second. He took too deep an interest in native life; but he will never do so again.

Deep away in the heart of the City, behind Jitha Megji's *bustee*,[1] lies Amir Nath's Gully,[2] which ends in a dead-wall pierced by one grated window. At the head of the Gully is a big cow-byre,[3] and the walls on either side of the Gully are without windows. Neither Suchet Singh nor Gaur Chand approve of their women-folk looking into the world. If Durga Charan had been of their opinion he would have been a happier man to-day, and little Bisesa would have been able to knead her own bread. Her room looked out through the grated window into the narrow dark Gully where the sun never came and where the buffaloes wallowed in the blue slime. She was a widow, about fifteen years old, and she prayed the Gods, day and night, to send her a lover; for she did not approve of living alone.

One day, the man – Trejago his name was – came into Amir Nath's Gully on an aimless wandering; and, after he had passed the buffaloes, stumbled over a big heap of cattle-food.

Then he saw that the Gully ended in a trap, and heard a little laugh from behind the grated window. It was a pretty little laugh, and Trejago, knowing that, for all practical purposes, the old *Arabian Nights* are good guides, went forward to the window, and whispered that verse of 'The Love Song of Har Dyal' which begins:

Can a man stand upright in the face of the naked Sun; or a Lover in the Presence of his Beloved?

If my feet fail me, O Heart of my Heart, am I to blame, being blinded by the glimpse of your beauty?

There came the faint *tchink* of a woman's bracelets from behind the grating, and a little voice went on with the song at the fifth verse: –

Alas! alas! Can the Moon tell the Lotus of her love when the Gate of Heaven is shut and the clouds gather for the Rains?
They have taken my Beloved, and driven her with the pack-horses to the North.
There are iron chains on the feet that were set on my heart.
Call to the bowmen to make ready –

The voice stopped suddenly, and Trejago walked out of Amir Nath's Gully, wondering who in the world could have capped 'The Love Song of Har Dyal' so neatly.

Next morning, as he was driving to office, an old woman threw a packet into his dogcart. In the packet was the half of a broken glass bangle, one flower of the blood-red *dhak*,[4] a pinch of *bhusa* or cattle-food, and eleven cardamoms. That packet was a letter – not a clumsy compromising letter, but an innocent, unintelligible lover's epistle.

Trejago knew far too much about these things, as I have said. No Englishman should be able to translate object-letters. But Trejago spread all the trifles on the lid of his office-box and began to puzzle them out.

A broken glass bangle stands for a Hindu widow all India over; because, when her husband dies, a woman's bracelets are broken on her wrists. Trejago saw the meaning of the little bit of glass. The flower of the *dhak* means diversely 'desire', 'come', 'write', or 'danger', according to the other things with it. One cardamom means 'jealousy'; but when any article is duplicated in an object-letter, it loses its symbolic meaning and stands merely for one of a number indicating time, or, if incense, curds, or saffron be sent also, place. The message ran then: 'A widow – *dhak* flower and *bhusa*, – at eleven o'clock.' The pinch of *bhusa* enlightened Trejago. He saw – this kind of letter leaves much to instinctive knowledge – that the *bhusa* referred to the big heap of cattle-food over which he had fallen in Amir Nath's Gully, and that the message must come from the person behind the grating; she being a widow. So the message ran then: 'A widow, in the Gully in which is the heap of *bhusa*, desires you to come at eleven o'clock.'

Trejago threw all the rubbish into the fireplace and laughed. He knew that men in the East do not make love under windows at eleven in the forenoon, nor do women fix appointments a week in advance.

So he went, that very night at eleven, into Amir Nath's Gully, clad in a *boorka*,[5] which cloaks a man as well as a woman. Directly the gongs of the City made the hour, the little voice behind the grating took up 'The Love Song of Har Dyal' at the verse where the Panthan girl calls upon Har Dyal to return. The song is really pretty in the vernacular. In English you miss the wail of it. It runs something like this:

> Alone upon the housetops, to the North
>   I turn and watch the lightnings in the sky, –
> The glamour of thy footsteps in the North.
>   *Come back to me, Beloved, or I die!*
>
> Below my feet the still bazar is laid –
>   Far, far below the weary camels lie, –
> The camels and the captives of thy raid.
>   *Come back to me, Beloved, or I die!*
>
> My father's wife is old and harsh with years,
>   And drudge of all my father's house am I. –
> My bread is sorrow and my drink is tears.
>   *Come back to me, Beloved, or I die!*

As the song stopped, Trejago stepped up under the grating and whispered, 'I am here.'

Bisesa was good to look upon.

That night was the beginning of many strange things, and of a double life so wild that Trejago to-day sometimes wonders if it were not all a dream. Bisesa, or her old handmaiden who had thrown the object-letter, had detached the heavy grating from the brick-work of the wall; so that the window slid inside, leaving only a square of raw masonry into which an active man might climb.

In the daytime, Trejago drove through his routine of office work, or put on his calling-clothes and called on the ladies of the station, wondering how long they would know him if they knew of poor little Bisesa. At night, when all the City was still, came the walk under the evil-smelling *boorka*, the patrol through Jitha Megji's *bustee*, the quick turn into Amir Nath's Gully between the sleeping cattle and the dead walls, and then, last of all, Bisesa, and the deep, even breathing of the old woman who slept outside the door of the bare little room that Durga Charan allotted to his sister's daughter. Who or what Durga Charan was, Trejago never inquired; and why in the world he was not discovered and knifed never occurred to him till his madness was over, and Bisesa . . . But this comes later.

Bisesa was an endless delight to Trejago. She was as ignorant as a bird; and her distorted versions of the rumours from the outside world that had reached her in her room, amused Trejago almost as much as her lisping attempts to pronounce his name – 'Christopher'. The first syllable was always more than she could manage, and she made funny little gestures with her roseleaf hands, as one throwing the name away, and then, kneeling before Trejago, asked him, exactly as an English-woman would do, if he were sure he loved her. Trejago swore that he loved her more than anyone else in the world. Which was true.

After a month of this folly, the exigencies of his other life compelled Trejago to be especially attentive to a lady of his acquaintance. You may take it for a fact that anything of this kind is not only noticed and discussed by a man's own race, but by some hundred and fifty natives as well. Trejago had to walk with this lady and talk to her at the Bandstand, and once or twice to drive with her; never for an instant dreaming that this would affect his dearer, out-of-the-way life. But the news flew, in the usual mysterious fashion, from mouth to mouth, till Bisesa's duenna heard of it and told Bisesa. The child was so troubled that she did the household work evilly, and was beaten by Durga Charan's wife in consequence.

A week later, Bisesa taxed Trejago with the flirtation. She understood no gradations and spoke openly. Trejago laughed, and Bisesa stamped her little feet – little feet, light as marigold flowers, that could lie in the palm of a man's one hand.

Much that is written about Oriental passion and impulsiveness is exaggerated and compiled at second hand; but a little of it is true, and when an Englishman finds that little, it is quite as startling as any passion in his own proper life. Bisesa raged and stormed, and finally threatened to kill herself if Trejago did not at once drop the alien Memsahib who had come between them. Trejago tried to explain, and to show her that she did not understand these things from a Western standpoint. Bisesa drew herself up, and said simply: –

'I do not. I know only this – it is not good that I should have made you dearer than my own heart to me, Sahib. You are an Englishman. I am only a black girl' – she was fairer than bar-gold in the Mint, – 'and the widow of a black man.'

Then she sobbed and said: 'But on my soul and my Mother's soul, I love you. There shall no harm come to you, whatever happens to me.'

Trejago argued with the child, and tried to soothe her, but she seemed quite unreasonably disturbed. Nothing would satisfy her save that all relations between them should end. He was to go away at once. And he went. As he dropped out of the window, she kissed his forehead twice, and he walked home wondering.

A week, and then three weeks, passed without a sign from Bisesa. Trejago, thinking that the rupture had lasted quite long enough, went down to Amir Nath's Gully for the fifth time in the three weeks, hoping that his rap at the sill of the shifting grating would be answered. He was not disappointed.

There was a young moon, and one stream of light fell down into Amir Nath's Gully, and struck the grating, which was drawn away as he knocked. From the black dark, Bisesa held out her arms into the moonlight. Both hands had been cut off at the wrists, and the stumps were nearly healed.

Then, as Bisesa bowed her head between her arms and sobbed, some one in the room grunted like a wild beast, and something sharp – knife, sword, or spear, – thrust at Trejago in his *boorka*. The stroke missed his body, but cut into one of the muscles of the groin, find he limped slightly from the wound for the rest of his days.

The grating went into its place. There was no sign whatever from inside the house, – nothing but the moonlight strip on the high wall, and the blackness of Amir Nath's Gully behind.

The next thing Trejago remembers, after raging and shouting like a madman between those pitiless walls, is that he found himself near the river as the dawn was breaking, threw away his *boorka* and went home bareheaded.

What was the tragedy – whether Bisesa had, in a fit of causeless despair, told everything, or the intrigue had been discovered and she tortured to tell; whether Durga Charan knew his name, and what became of Bisesa – Trejago does not know to this day. Something horrible had happened, and the thought of what it must have been comes upon Trejago in the night now and again, and keeps him company till the morning. One special feature of the case is that he does not know where lies the front of Durga Charan's house. It may open on to a courtyard common to two or more houses, or it may lie behind any one of the gates of Jitha Megji's *bustee*. Trejago cannot tell. He cannot get Bisesa – poor little Bisesa – back again. He has lost her in the City where each man's house is as guarded and as unknowable as the grave; and the grating that opens into Amir Nath's Gully has been walled up.

But Trejago pays his calls regularly, and is reckoned a very decent sort of man.

There is nothing peculiar about him, except a slight stiffness, caused by a riding-strain, in the right leg.

DRAY WARA YOW DEE

For jealousy is the rage of a man: therefore he will not spare in the day of vengeance.

Proverbs vi. 34

Almonds and raisins, Sahib? Grapes from Kabul? Or a pony of the rarest if the Sahib will only come with me. He is thirteen-three, Sahib, plays polo, goes in a cart, carries a lady and – Holy Kurshed and the Blessed Imams, it is the Sahib himself! My heart is made fat and my eye glad. May you never be tired! As is cold water in the Tirah,[1] so is the sight of a friend in a far place. And what do *you* in this accursed land? South of Delhi, Sahib, you know the saying – 'Rats are the men and trulls[2] the women.' It was an order? Ahoo! An order is an order till one is strong enough to disobey. O my brother, O my friend, we have met in an auspicious hour! Is all well in the heart and the body and the house? In a lucky day have we two come together again.

I am to go with you? Your favour is great. Will there be picket-room in the compound? I have three horses and the bundles and the horse-boy. Moreover, remember that the police here hold me a horse-thief. What do these Lowland bastards know of horse-thieves? Do you remember that time in Peshawur when Kamal hammered on the gates of Jumrud – mountebank that he was – and lifted the Colonel's horses all in one night? Kamal is dead now, but his nephew has taken up the matter, and there will be more horses a-missing if the Khyber Levies do not look to it.

The Peace of God and the favour of His Prophet be upon this house and all that is in it! Shafiz Ullah, rope the mottled mare under the tree and draw water. The horses can stand in the sun, but double the felts over the loins. Nay, my friend, do not trouble to look them over. They are to sell to the Officer-fools who know so many things of the horse. The mare is heavy in foal; the grey is a devil unlicked; and the dun – but you know the trick of the peg. When they are sold I go back to Pubbi, or, it may be, the Valley of Peshawur.[3]

O friend of my heart, it is good to see you again. I have been bowing and lying all day to the Officer-Sahibs in respect to those horses; and my mouth is dry for straight talk. *Auggrh!* Before a meal tobacco is good. Do not join me, for we are not in our own country. Sit in the veranda and I will spread my cloth here. But first I will drink. *In the name of God returning thanks, thrice!* This is sweet water, indeed – sweet as the water of Sheoran when it comes from the snows.

They are all well and pleased in the North – Khoda Baksh and the others. Yar Khan has come down with the horses from Kurdistan – six-and-thirty head only, and a full half pack-ponies – and has said openly in the Kashmir Serai that you English should send guns and blow the Amir[4] into Hell. There are *fifteen* tolls now on the Kabul road; and at Dakka, when he thought he was clear, Yar Khan was stripped of all his Balkh stallions by the Governor! This is a great injustice, and Yar Khan is hot with rage. And of the others: Mahbub Ali is still at Pubbi,[5] writing God knows what. Tugluq Khan is in jail for the business of the Kohat Police Post. Faiz Beg came down from Ismail-ki-Dhera with a Bokhariot belt[6] for thee, my brother, at the closing of the year, but none knew whither thou hadst gone: there was no news left behind. The Cousins have taken a new run near Pakpattan to breed mules for the Government carts, and there is a story in the Bazar of a priest. Oho! Such a salt tale! Listen –

Sahib, why do you ask that? My clothes are fouled because of the dust on the road. My eyes are sad because of the glare of the sun. My feet are swollen because I have washed them in bitter water, and my cheeks are hollow because the food here is bad. Fire burn your money! What do I want with it? I am rich. I thought you were my friend. But you are like the others – a Sahib. Is a man sad? Give him money, say the Sahibs. Is he dishonoured? Give him money, say the Sahibs. Hath he a wrong upon his head? Give him money, say the Sahibs. Such are the Sahibs, and such art thou – even thou.

Nay, do not look at the feet of the dun. Pity it is that I ever taught you to know the legs of a horse. Footsore? Be it so. What of that? The roads are hard. And the mare footsore? She bears a double burden, Sahib.

And now, I pray you, give me permission to depart. Great favour and honour has the Sahib done me, and graciously has he shown his belief that the horses are stolen. Will it please him to send me to the Thana?[7] To call a sweeper and have me led away by one of these lizard-men?[8] I am the Sahib's friend. I have drunk water in the shadow of his house, and he has blackened my face. Remains there anything more to do? Will the Sahib give me eight annas[9] to make smooth the injury and – complete the insult – ?

Forgive me, my brother. I knew not – I know not now – what I say. Yes, I lied to you! I will put dust on my head – and I am an Afridi![10] The horses have been marched footsore from the Valley to this place, and my eyes are dim, and my body aches for the want of sleep, and my heart is dried up with sorrow and shame. But as it was my shame, so by God the Dispenser of Justice – by Allah-al-Mumit! – it shall be my own revenge!

We have spoken together with naked hearts before this, and our hands have dipped into the same dish, and thou hast been to me as a brother. Therefore I pay thee back with lies and ingratitude – as a Pathan. Listen now! When the grief of the soul is too heavy for endurance it may be a little eased by speech; and, moreover, the mind of a true man is as a well, and the pebble of confession dropped therein sinks and is no more seen. From the Valley have I come on foot, league by league, with a fire in my chest like the fire of the Pit. And why? Hast thou, then, so quickly forgotten our customs, among this folk who sell their wives and their daughters for silver? Come back with me to the North and be among men once more. Come back, when this matter is accomplished and I call for thee! The bloom of the peach-orchards is upon all the Valley, and *here* is only dust and a great stink. There is a pleasant wind among the mulberry trees, and the streams are bright with snow-water, and the caravans go up and the caravans go down, and a hundred fires sparkle in the gut of the Pass, and tent-peg answers hammer-nose, and pack-horse squeals to pack-horse across the drift-smoke of the evening. It is good in the North now. Come back with me. Let us return to our own people! Come!

Whence is my sorrow? Does a man tear out his heart and make fritters thereof over a slow fire for aught other than a woman? Do not laugh, friend of mine, for your time will also be. A woman of the Abazai[11] was she, and I took her to wife to staunch the feud between our village and the men of Ghor. I am no longer young? The lime has touched my beard? True. I had no need of the wedding? Nay, but I loved her. What saith Rahman?[12] 'Into whose heart Love enters, there is Folly *and naught else*. By a glance of the eye she hath blinded thee; and by the eyelids and the fringe of the eyelids taken thee into the captivity without ransom, *and naught else*.' Dost thou remember that song at the sheep-roasting in the Pindi camp among the Uzbegs[13] of the Amir?

The Abazai are dogs and their women the servants of sin. There was a lover of her own people, but of that her father told me naught. My friend, curse for me in your prayers, as I curse at each praying from the Fakr to the Isha,[14] the name of Daoud Shah, Abazai, whose head is still upon his neck, whose hands are still upon his wrists, who has done me dishonour, who has made my name a laughing-stock among the women of Little Malikand.

I went into Hindustan at the end of two months – to Cherat.[15] I was gone twelve days only; but I had said that I would be fifteen days absent. This I did to try her, for it is written: 'Trust not the incapable.' Coming up the gorge alone in the falling of the light, I heard the voice of a man singing at the door of my house; and it was the voice of Daoud Shah, and the song that he sang was '*Dray wara yow dee*' – 'All three are one.' It was as though a heel-rope had been slipped round my heart and all the Devils were drawing it tight past endurance. I crept silently up the hill-road, but the fuse of my matchlock[16] was wetted with the rain, and I could not slay Daoud Shah from afar. Moreover, it was in my mind to kill the woman also. Thus he sang, sitting outside my house, and, anon, the woman opened the door, and I came nearer, crawling on my belly among the rocks. I had only my knife to my hand. But a stone slipped under my foot, and the two looked down the hillside, and he, leaving his matchlock, fled from my anger, because he was afraid for the life that was in him. But the woman moved not till I stood in front of her, crying: 'O woman, what is this that thou hast done?' And she, void of fear, though she knew my thought, laughed, saying: 'It is a little thing. I loved him, and *thou* art a dog and cattle-thief coming by night. Strike!' And I, being still blinded by her beauty, for, O my friend, the women of the Abazai are very fair, said: 'Hast thou no fear?' And she answered: 'None – but only the fear that I do not die.' Then said I: 'Have no fear.' And she bowed her head, and I smote it off at the neck-bone so that it leaped between my feet. Thereafter the rage of our people came upon me, and I hacked off the breasts, that the men of Little Malikand might know the crime, and cast the body into the watercourse that flows to the Kabul river.[17] *Dray wara yow dee! Dray wara yow dee!* The body without the head, the soul without light, and my own darkling heart – all three are one – all three are one!

That night, making no halt, I went to Ghor and demanded news of Daoud Shah. Men said: 'He is gone to Pubbi for horses. What wouldst thou of him? There is peace between the villages.' I made answer: 'Ay! The peace of treachery and the love that the Devil Atala bore to Gurel.' So I fired thrice into the tower-gate and laughed and went my way.

In those hours, brother and friend of my heart's heart, the moon and the stars were as blood above me, and in my mouth was the taste of dry earth. Also, I broke no bread, and my drink was the rain of the valley of Ghor upon my face.

At Pubbi I found Mahbub Ali, the writer, sitting upon his charpoy,[18] and gave up my arms according to your Law. But I was not grieved, for it was in my heart that I should kill Daoud Shah with my bare hands thus – as a man strips a bunch of raisins. Mahbub Ali said: 'Daoud

Shah has even now gone hot-foot to Peshawur, and he will pick up his horses upon the road to Delhi, for it is said that the Bombay Tramway Company are buying horses there by the truck-load; eight horses to the truck.' And that was a true saying.

Then I saw that the hunting would be no little thing, for the man was gone into your borders to save himself against my wrath. And shall he save himself so? Am I not alive? Though he run northward to the Dora[19] and the snow, or southerly to the Black Water,[20] I will follow him, as a lover follows the footsteps of his mistress, and coming upon him I will take him tenderly – Aho! so tenderly! – in my arms, saying: 'Well hast thou done and well shalt thou be repaid.' And out of that embrace Daoud Shah shall not go forth with the breath in his nostrils. *Auggrh!* Where is the pitcher? I am as thirsty as a mother mare in the first month.

Your Law! What is your Law to me? When the horses fight on the runs do they regard the boundary pillars; or do the kites of Ali Musjid forbear because the carrion lies under the shadow of the Ghor Kuttri? The matter began across the Border. It shall finish where God pleases. Here; in my own country; or in Hell. All three are one.

Listen now, sharer of the sorrow of my heart, and I will tell of the hunting. I followed to Peshawur from Pubbi, and I went to and fro about the streets of Peshawur like a houseless dog, seeking for my enemy. Once I thought that I saw him washing his mouth in the conduit in the big square, but when I came up he was gone. It may be that it was he, and, seeing my face, he had fled.

A girl of the bazar said that he would go to Nowshera. I said: 'O heart's heart, does Daoud Shah visit thee?' And she said: 'Even so.' I said: 'I would fain see him, for we be friends parted for two years. Hide me, I pray, here in the shadow of the window-shutter, and I will wait for his coming.' And the girl said: 'O Pathan, look into my eyes!' And I turned, leaning upon her breast, and looked into her eyes, swearing that I spoke the very Truth of God. But she answered: 'Never friend waited friend with such eyes. Lie to God and the Prophet, but to a woman ye cannot lie. Get hence! There shall no harm befall Daoud Shah by cause of me.'

I would have strangled that girl but for the fear of your Police; and thus the hunting would have come to naught. Therefore I only laughed and departed, and she leaned over the window-bar in the night and mocked me down the street. Her name is Jamun.[21] When I have made my account with the man I will return to Peshawur and – her lovers shall desire her no more for her beauty's sake. She shall not be *Jamun*, but *Ak*,[22] the cripple among trees. Ho! ho! *Ak* shall she be!

At Peshawur I bought the horses and grapes, and the almonds and dried fruits, that the reason of my wanderings might be open to the Government, and that there might be no hindrance upon the road. But when I came to Nowshera he was gone; and I knew not where to go. I stayed one day at Nowshera, and in the night a Voice spoke in my ears as I slept among the horses. All night it flew round my head and would not cease from whispering. I was upon my belly, sleeping as the Devils sleep, and it may have been that the Voice was the voice of a Devil. It said: 'Go south, and thou shalt come upon Daoud Shah.' Listen, my brother and chiefest among friends – listen! Is the tale a long one? Think how it was long to me. I have trodden every league of the road from Pubbi to this place; and from Nowshera my guide was only the Voice and the lust of vengeance.

To the Uttock I went, but that was no hindrance to me. Ho! ho! A man may turn the word twice, even in his trouble. The Uttock was no *uttock* [obstacle] to me; and I heard the Voice above the noise of the waters beating on the big rock, saying: 'Go to the right.' So I went to Pindigheb, and in those days my sleep was taken from me utterly, and the head of the woman of the Abazai was before me night and day, even as it had fallen between my feet. *Dray wara yow dee! Dray wara yow dee!* Fire, ashes, and my couch, all three are one – all three are one!

Now I was far from the winter path of the dealers who had gone to Sialkot, and so south by the rail and the Big Road to the line of cantonments; but there was a Sahib in camp at Pindigheb who bought from me a white mare at a good price, and told me that one Daoud Shah had passed to Shahpur with horses. Then I saw that the warning of the Voice was true, and made swift to come to the Salt Hills. The Jhelum was in flood, but I could not wait, and, in the crossing, a bay stallion was washed down and drowned. Herein was God hard to me – not in respect of the beast, of that I had no care – but in this snatching. While I was upon the right bank urging the horses into the water, Daoud Shah was upon the left; for – *Alghias! Alghias!*[23] – the hoofs of my mare scattered the hot ashes of his fires when we came up the hither bank in the light of morning. But he had fled. His feet were made swift by the terror of Death. And I went south from Shahpur as the kite flies. I dared not turn aside lest I should miss my vengeance – which is my right. From Shahpur I skirted by the Jhelum, for I thought that he would avoid the Desert of the Rechna. But, presently, at Sahiwal, I turned away upon the road to Jhang, Samundri, and Gugera, till, upon a night, the mottled mare breasted the fence of the rail that runs to Montgomery. And that place was Okara, and the head of the woman of the Abazai lay upon the sand between my feet.

Thence I went to Fazilka, and they said that I was mad to bring starved horses there. The Voice was with me, and I was *not* mad, but only wearied, because I could not find Daoud Shah. It was written that I should not find him at Rania nor Bahadurgarh, and I came into Delhi from the west, and there also I found him not. My friend, I have seen many strange things in my wanderings. I have seen the Devils rioting across the Rechna as the stallions riot in spring. I have heard the *Djinns*[24] calling to each other from holes in the sand, and I have seen them pass before my face. There are no Devils, say the Sahibs? They are very wise, but they do not know all things about Devils or – horses. Ho! ho! I say to you who are laughing at my misery, that I have seen the Devils at high noon whooping and leaping on the shoals of the Chenab. And was I afraid? My brother, when the desire of a man is set upon one thing alone, he fears neither God nor Man nor Devil. If my vengeance failed, I would splinter the Gates of Paradise with the butt of my gun, or I would cut my way into Hell with my knife, and I would call upon Those who Govern there for the body of Daoud Shah. What love so deep as hate?

Do not speak. I know the thought in your heart. Is the white of this eye clouded? How does the blood beat at the wrist? There is no madness in my flesh, but only the vehemence of the desire that has eaten me up. Listen!

South of Delhi I knew not the country at all. Therefore I cannot say where I went, but I passed through many cities. I knew only that it was laid upon me to go south. When the horses could march no more, I threw myself upon the earth and waited till the day. There was no sleep with me in that journeying; and that was a heavy burden. Dost thou know, brother of mine, the evil of wakefulness that cannot break – when the bones are sore for lack of sleep, and the skin of the temples twitches with weariness, and yet – there is no sleep – there is no sleep? *Dray wara yow dee! Dray wara yow dee!* The eye of the Sun, the eye of the Moon, and my own unrestful eyes – all three are one – all three are one!

There was a city the name whereof I have forgotten, and there the Voice called all night. That was ten days ago. It has cheated me afresh.

I have come hither from a place called Hamirpur, and, behold, it is my Fate that I should meet with thee to my comfort, and the increase of friendship. This is a good omen. By the joy of looking upon thy face the weariness has gone from my feet, and the sorrow of my so long travel is forgotten. Also my heart is peaceful; for I know that the end is near.

It may be that I shall find Daoud Shah in this city going northward, since a Hillman will ever head back to his Hills when the spring warns.

And shall he see those hills of our country? Surely I shall overtake him! Surely my vengeance is safe! Surely God hath him in the hollow of His hand against my claiming! There shall no harm befall Daoud Shah till I come; for I would fain kill him quick and whole with the life sticking firm in his body. A pomegranate is sweetest when the cloves break away unwilling from the rind. Let it be in the daytime, that I may see his face, and my delight may be crowned.

And when I have accomplished the matter and my Honour is made clean, I shall return thanks unto God, the Holder of the Scales of the Law, and I shall sleep. From the night, through the day, and into the night again I shall sleep; and no dream shall trouble me.

And now, O my brother, the tale is all told. *Ahi! Ahi! Alghias! Ahi!*

AT THE PIT'S MOUTH

Men say it was a stolen tide –
    The Lord that sent it He knows all,
But in mine ear will aye abide
    The message that the bells let fall,
And awesome bells they were to me,
That in the dark rang 'Enderby.'[1]

JEAN INGELOW

Once upon a time there was a Man and his Wife and a Tertium Quid.[2]

All three were unwise, but the Wife was the unwisest. The Man should have looked after his Wife, who should have avoided the Tertium Quid, who, again, should have married a wife of his own, after clean and open flirtations, to which nobody can possibly object, round Jakko or Observatory Hill.[3] When you see a young man with his pony in a white lather and his hat on the back of his head, flying downhill at fifteen miles an hour to meet a girl who will be properly surprised to meet him, you naturally approve of that young man, and wish him Staff appointments, and take an interest in his welfare, and, as the proper time comes, give them sugar-tongs or side-saddles according to your means and generosity.

The Tertium Quid flew downhill on horseback, but it was to meet the Man's Wife; and when he flew uphill it was for the same end. The Man was in the Plains, earning money for his Wife to spend on dresses and four-hundred-rupee bracelets,[4] and inexpensive luxuries of that kind. He worked very hard, and sent her a letter or a postcard daily. She also wrote to him daily, and said that she was longing for him to come up to Simla. The Tertium Quid used to lean over her shoulder and laugh as she wrote the notes. Then the two would ride to the Post Office together.

Now, Simla is a strange place and its customs are peculiar; nor is any man who has not spent at least ten seasons there qualified to pass judgment on circumstantial evidence, which is the most untrustworthy in the Courts. For these reasons, and for others which need not appear, I decline to state positively whether there was anything irretrievably wrong in the relations between the Man's Wife and the Tertium Quid. If there was, and hereon you must form your own opinion, it was the

Man's Wife's fault. She was kittenish in her manners, wearing generally an air of soft and fluffy innocence. But she was deadlily learned and evil-instructed; and, now and again, when the mask dropped, men saw this, shuddered and – almost drew back. Men are occasionally particular, and the least particular men are always the most exacting.

Simla is eccentric in its fashion of treating friendships. Certain attachments which have set and crystallised through half-a-dozen seasons acquire almost the sanctity of the marriage bond, and are revered as such. Again, certain attachments equally old, and, to all appearance, equally venerable, never seem to win any recognised official status; while a chance-sprung acquaintance, not two months born, steps into the place which by right belongs to the senior. There is no law reducible to print which regulates these affairs.

Some people have a gift which secures them infinite toleration, and others have not. The Man's Wife had not. If she looked over the garden wall, for instance, women taxed her with stealing their husbands. She complained pathetically that she was not allowed to choose her own friends. When she put up her big white muff to her lips, and gazed over it and under her eyebrows at you as she said this thing, you felt that she had been infamously misjudged, and that all the other women's instincts were all wrong. Which was absurd. She was not allowed to own the Tertium Quid in peace; and was so strangely constructed that she would not have enjoyed peace had she been so permitted. She preferred some semblance of intrigue to cloak even her most commonplace actions.

After two months of riding, first round Jakko, then Elysium,[5] then Summer Hill, then Observatory Hill, then under Jutogh, and lastly up and down the Cart Road, as far as the Tara Devi gap[6] in the dusk, she said to the Tertium Quid, 'Frank, people say we are too much together, and people are so horrid.'

The Tertium Quid pulled his moustache, and replied that horrid people were unworthy of the consideration of nice people.

'But they have done more than talk – they have written – written to my hubby – I'm sure of it,' said the Man's Wife, and she pulled a letter from her husband out of her saddle-pocket and gave it to the Tertium Quid.

It was an honest letter, written by an honest man, then stewing in the Plains on two hundred rupees a month (for he allowed his wife eight hundred and fifty), and in a silk singlet and cotton trousers. It said that, perhaps, she had not thought of the unwisdom of allowing her name to be so generally coupled with the Tertium Quid's; that she was too much of a child to understand the dangers of that sort of thing; that he, her husband, was the last man in the world to interfere jealously with her little amusements and interests, but that it would be better were she to drop the Tertium Quid quietly and for her husband's sake. The letter was sweetened with many pretty little pet names, and it amused the Tertium Quid considerably. He and She laughed over it, so that you, fifty yards away, could see their shoulders shaking while the horses slouched along side by side.

Their conversation was not worth reporting. The upshot of it was that, next day, no one saw the Man's Wife and the Tertium Quid together. They had both gone down to the Cemetery, which, as a rule, is only visited officially by the inhabitants of Simla.

A Simla funeral with the clergyman riding, the mourners riding, and the coffin creaking as it swings between the bearers, is one of the most depressing things on this earth, particularly when the procession passes under the wet, dank dip beneath the Rockcliffe Hotel, where the sun is shut out, and all the hill streams are wailing and weeping together as they go down the valleys.

Occasionally folk tend the graves, but we in India shift and are transferred so often that, at the end of the second year, the Dead have no friends – only acquaintances who are far too busy amusing themselves up the hill to attend to old partners. The idea of using a Cemetery as a rendezvous is distinctly a feminine one. A man would have said simply, 'Let people talk. We'll go down the Mall.' A woman is made differently, especially if she be such a woman as the Man's Wife. She and the Tertium Quid enjoyed each other's society among the graves of men and women whom they had known and danced with aforetime.

They used to take a big horse-blanket and sit on the grass a little to the left of the lower end, where there is a dip in the ground, and where the occupied graves stop short and the ready-made ones are not ready. Each well-regulated Indian Cemetery keeps half-a-dozen graves perman-ently open for contingencies and incidental wear and tear. In the Hills these are more usually baby's size, because children who come up weakened and sick from the Plains often succumb to the effects of the Rains in the Hills or get pneumonia from their *ayahs*[7] taking them through damp pinewoods after the sun has set. In cantonments,[8] of course, the man's size is more in request; these arrangements varying with the climate and population.

One day when the Man's Wife and the Tertium Quid had just arrived in the Cemetery, they saw some coolies breaking ground. They had marked out a full-size grave, and the Tertium Quid asked them whether any Sahib was sick. They said that they did not know; but it was an order that they should dig a Sahib's grave.

'Work away,' said the Tertium Quid, 'and let's see how it's done.'

The coolies worked away, and the Man's Wife and the Tertium Quid watched and talked for a couple of hours while the grave was being deepened. Then a coolie, taking the earth in baskets as it was thrown up, jumped over the grave.

'That's queer,' said the Tertium Quid. 'Where's my ulster?'[9]

'What's queer?' said the Man's Wife.

'I have got a chill down my back – just as if a goose had walked over my grave.'

'Why do you look at the thing, then?' said the Man's Wife. 'Let us go.'

The Tertium Quid stood at the head of the grave, and stared without answering for a space. Then he said, dropping a pebble down, 'It is nasty – and cold: horribly cold. I don't think I shall come to the Cemetery any more. I don't think grave-digging is cheerful.'

The two talked and agreed that the Cemetery was depressing. They also arranged for a ride next day out from the Cemetery through the Mashobra Tunnel up to Fagoo[10] and back, because all the world was going to a garden-party at Viceregal Lodge, and all the people of Mashobra would go too.

Coming up the Cemetery road, the Tertium Quid's horse tried to bolt uphill, being tired with standing so long, and managed to strain a back sinew.

'I shall have to take the mare to-morrow,' said the Tertium Quid, 'and she will stand nothing heavier than a snaffle.'[11]

They made their arrangements to meet in the Cemetery, after allowing all the Mashobra people time to pass into Simla. That night it rained heavily, and, next day, when the Tertium Quid came to the trysting-place, he saw that the new grave had a foot of water in it, the ground being a tough and sour clay.

'Jove! That looks beastly,' said the Tertium Quid. 'Fancy being boarded up and dropped into that well!'

They then started off to Fagoo, the mare playing with the snaffle and picking her way as though she were shod with satin, and the sun shining divinely. The road below Mashobra to Fagoo is officially styled the Himalayan-Tibet Road; but in spite of its name it is not much more than six feet wide in most places, and the drop into the valley below may be anything between one and two thousand feet.

'Now we're going to Tibet,' said the Man's Wife merrily, as the horses drew near to Fagoo. She was riding on the cliff side.

'Into Tibet,' said the Tertium Quid, 'ever so far from people who say horrid things, and hubbies who write stupid letters. With you – to the end of the world!'

A coolie carrying a log of wood came round a corner, and the mare went wide to avoid him – forefeet in and haunches out, as a sensible mare should go.

'To the world's end,' said the Man's Wife, and looked unspeakable things over her near shoulder at the Tertium Quid.

He was smiling, but, while she looked, the smile froze stiff, as it were, on his face, and changed to a nervous grin – the sort of grin men wear when they are not quite easy in their saddles. The mare seemed to be sinking by the stern, and her nostrils cracked while she was trying to realise what was happening. The rain of the night before had rotted the drop-side of the Himalayan-Tibet Road, and it was giving way under her. 'What are you doing?' said the Man's Wife. The Tertium Quid gave no answer. He grinned nervously and set his spurs into the mare, who rapped with her forefeet on the road, and the struggle began. The Man's Wife screamed, 'Oh, Frank, get off!'

But the Tertium Quid was glued to the saddle – his face blue and white – and he looked into the Man's Wife's eyes. Then the Man's Wife clutched at the mare's head and caught her by the nose instead of the bridle. The brute threw up her head and went down with a scream, the Tertium Quid upon her, and the nervous grin still set on his face.

The Man's Wife heard the tinkle-tinkle of little stones and loose earth falling off the roadway, and the sliding roar of the man and horse going down. Then everything was quiet, and she called on Frank to leave his mare and walk up. But Frank did not answer. He was underneath the mare, nine hundred feet below, spoiling a patch of Indian corn.[12]

As the revellers came back from Viceregal Lodge in the mists of the evening, they met a temporarily insane woman, on a temporarily mad horse, swinging round the corners, with her eyes and her mouth open, and her head like the head of a Medusa.[13] She was stopped by a man at the risk of his life, and taken out of the saddle, a limp heap, and put on the bank to explain herself. This wasted twenty minutes, and then she was sent home in a lady's 'rickshaw, still with her mouth open and her hands picking at her riding-gloves.

She was in bed through the following three days, which were rainy; so she missed attending the funeral of the Tertium Quid, who was lowered into eighteen inches of water, instead of the twelve to which he had first objected.

A WAYSIDE COMEDY

Because to every purpose there is time and judgment, therefore the
misery of man is great upon him.

Ecclesiastes viii. 6

Fate and the Government of India have turned the Station of Kashima
into a prison; and, because there is no help for the poor souls who
are now lying there in torment, I write this story, praying that the
Government of India may be moved to scatter the European population
to the four winds.

Kashima is bounded on all sides by the rock-tipped circle of the
Dosehri hills. In spring, it is ablaze with roses. In summer, the roses die
and the hot winds blow from the hills. In autumn, the white mists from
the *jhils*[1] cover the place as with water, and in winter, the frosts nip
everything young and tender to earth-level. There is but one view in
Kashima – a stretch of perfectly flat pasture and plough-land, running
up to the grey-blue scrub of the Dosehri hills.

There are no amusements, except snipe and tiger shooting; but the
tigers have been long since hunted from their lairs in the rock-caves,
and the snipe only come once a year. Narkarra[2] – one hundred and
forty-three miles by road – is the nearest Station to Kashima. But
Kashima never goes to Narkarra, where there are at least twelve English
people. It stays within the circle of the Dosehri hills.

All Kashima acquits Mrs Vansuythen of any intention to do harm; but
all Kashima knows that she, and she alone, brought about their pain.

Boulte, the Engineer, Mrs Boulte, and Captain Kurrell know this.
They are the English population of Kashima, if we except Major
Vansuythen, who is of no importance whatever, and Mrs Vansuythen,
who is the most important of all.

You must remember, though you will not understand, that all laws
weaken in a small and hidden community where there is no public opinion.
When a man is absolutely alone in a Station he runs a certain risk of
falling into evil ways. This risk is multiplied by every addition to the
population up to twelve – the Jury-number. After that, fear and consequent
restraint begin, and human action becomes less grotesquely jerky.

There was deep peace in Kashima till Mrs Vansuythen arrived. She
was a charming woman, everyone said so everywhere; and she charmed

everyone. In spite of this, or, perhaps, because of this, since Fate is so perverse, she cared only for one man, and he was Major Vansuythen. Had she been plain or stupid, this matter would have been intelligible to Kashima. But she was a fair woman, with very still grey eyes, the colour of a lake just before the light of the sun touches it. No man who had seen those eyes could, later on, explain what fashion of woman she was to look upon. The eyes dazzled him. Her own sex said that she was 'not bad-looking, but spoilt by pretending to be so grave'. And yet her gravity was natural. It was not her habit to smile. She merely went through life, looking at those who passed; and the women objected while the men fell down and worshipped.

She knows and is deeply sorry for the evil she has done to Kashima; but Major Vansuythen cannot understand why Mrs Boulte does not drop in to afternoon tea at least three times a week. 'When there are only two women in one Station, they ought to see a great deal of each other,' says Major Vansuythen.

Long and long before ever Mrs Vansuythen came out of those far-away places where there is society and amusement, Kurrell had discovered that Mrs Boulte was the one woman in the world for him and – you dare not blame them. Kashima was as out of the world as Heaven or the Other Place, and the Dosehri hills kept their secret well. Boulte had no concern in the matter. He was in camp for a fortnight at a time. He was a hard, heavy man, and neither Mrs Boulte nor Kurrell pitied him. They had all Kashima and each other for their very, very own; and Kashima was the Garden of Eden in those days. When Boulte returned from his wanderings he would slap Kurrell between the shoulders and call him 'old fellow', and the three would dine together. Kashima was happy then when the Judgment of God seemed almost as distant as Narkarra or the railway that ran down to the sea. But the Government sent Major Vansuythen to Kashima, and with him came his wife.

The etiquette of Kashima is much the same as that of a desert island. When a stranger is cast away there, all hands go down to the shore to make him welcome. Kashima assembled at the masonry platform[3] close to the Narkarra Road, and spread tea for the Vansuythens. That ceremony was reckoned a formal call, and made them free of the Station, its rights and privileges. When the Vansuythens settled down they gave a tiny house-warming to all Kashima; and that made Kashima free of their house, according to the immemorial usage of the Station.

Then the Rains came, when no one could go into camp, and the Narkarra Road was washed away by the Kasun River, and in the cup-like pastures of Kashima the cattle waded knee-deep. The clouds dropped down from the Dosehri hills and covered everything.

At the end of the Rains Boulte's manner towards his wife changed and became demonstratively affectionate. They had been married twelve years, and the change startled Mrs Boulte, who hated her husband with the hate of a woman who has met with nothing but kindness from her mate, and, in the teeth of this kindness, has done him a great wrong. Moreover, she had her own trouble to fight with – her watch to keep over her own property, Kurrell. For two months the Rains had hidden the Dosehri hills and many other things besides; but, when they lifted, they showed Mrs Boulte that her man among men, her Ted – for she called him Ted in the old days when Boulte was out of earshot – was slipping the links of the allegiance.

'The Vansuythen Woman has taken him,' Mrs Boulte said to herself; and when Boulte was away, wept over her belief, in the face of the over-vehement blandishments of Ted. Sorrow in Kashima is as fortunate as Love because there is nothing to weaken it save the flight of Time. Mrs Boulte had never breathed her suspicion to Kurrell because she was not certain; and her nature led her to be very certain before she took steps in any direction. That is why she behaved as she did.

Boulte came into the house one evening, and leaned against the door-post of the drawing-room, chewing his moustache. Mrs Boulte was putting some flowers into a vase. There is a pretence of civilisation even in Kashima.

'Little woman,' said Boulte quietly, 'do you care for me?'

'Immensely,' said she, with a laugh. 'Can you ask it?'

'But I'm serious,' said Boulte. '*Do* you care for me?'

Mrs Boulte dropped the flowers, and turned round quickly. 'Do you want an honest answer?'

'Ye-es, I've asked for it.'

Mrs Boulte spoke in a low, even voice for five minutes, very distinctly, that there might be no misunderstanding her meaning. When Samson broke the pillars of Gaza,[4] he did a little thing, and one not to be compared with the deliberate pulling down of a woman's homestead about her own ears. There was no wise female friend to advise Mrs Boulte, the singularly cautious wife, to hold her hand. She struck at Boulte's heart, because her own was sick with suspicion of Kurrell, and worn out with the long strain of watching alone through the Rains. There was no plan or purpose in her speaking. The sentences made themselves; and Boulte listened, leaning against the doorpost with his hands in his pockets. When all was over, and Mrs Boulte began to breathe through her nose before breaking out into tears, he laughed and stared straight in front of him at the Dosehri hills.

'Is that all?' he said. 'Thanks, I only wanted to know, you know.'

'What are you going to do?' said the woman, between her sobs.

'Do! Nothing. What should I do? Kill Kurrell, or send you Home, or apply for leave to get a divorce? It's two days' *dâk*[5] into Narkarra.' He laughed again and went on: 'I'll tell you what *you* can do. You can ask Kurrell to dinner to-morrow – no, on Thursday, that will allow you time to pack – and you can bolt with him. I give you my word I won't follow.'

He took up his helmet and went out of the room, and Mrs Boulte sat till the moonlight streaked the floor, thinking and thinking and thinking. She had done her best upon the spur of the moment to pull the house down; but it would not fall. Moreover, she could not understand her husband, and she was afraid. Then the folly of her useless truthfulness struck her, and she was ashamed to write to Kurrell, saying, 'I have gone mad and told everything. My husband says that I am free to elope with you. Get a *dâk* for Thursday, and we will fly after dinner.' There was a cold-bloodedness about that procedure which did not appeal to her. So she sat still in her own house and thought.

At dinner-time Boulte came back from his walk, white and worn and haggard, and the woman was touched at his distress. As the evening wore on she muttered some expression of sorrow, something approaching to contrition. Boulte came out of a brown study and said, 'Oh, *that*! I wasn't thinking about that. By the way, what does Kurrell say to the elopement?'

'I haven't seen him,' said Mrs Boulte. 'Good God, is that all?'

But Boulte was not listening, and her sentence ended in a gulp.

The next day brought no comfort to Mrs Boulte, for Kurrell did not appear, and the new life that she, in the five minutes' madness of the previous evening, had hoped to build out of the ruins of the old, seemed to be no nearer.

Boulte ate his breakfast, advised her to see her Arab pony fed in the veranda, and went out. The morning wore through, and at mid-day the tension became unendurable. Mrs Boulte could not cry. She had finished her crying in the night, and now she did not want to be left alone. Perhaps the Vansuythen Woman would talk to her; and, since talking opens the heart, perhaps there might be some comfort to be found in her company. She was the only other woman in the Station.

In Kashima there are no regular calling-hours. Everyone can drop in upon every one else at pleasure. Mrs Boulte put on a big *terai* hat,[6] and walked across to the Vansuythens' house to borrow last week's *Queen*. The two compounds touched, and instead of going up the drive, she crossed through the gap in the cactus-hedge, entering the house from the back. As she passed through the dining-room, she heard, behind the *purdah* [7] that cloaked the drawing-room door, her husband's voice, saying:

'But on my Honour! On my Soul and Honour, I tell you she doesn't care for me. She told me so last night. I would have told you then if Vansuythen hadn't been with you. If it is for *her* sake that you'll have nothing to say to me, you can make your mind easy. It's Kurrell –'

'What?' said Mrs Vansuythen, with a hysterical little laugh. 'Kurrell! Oh, it can't be! You two must have made some horrible mistake. Perhaps you – you lost your temper, or misunderstood, or something. Things *can't* be as wrong as you say.'

Mrs Vansuythen had shifted her defence to avoid the man's pleading, and was desperately trying to keep him to a side-issue.

'There must be some mistake,' she insisted, 'and it can be all put right again.'

Boulte laughed grimly.

'It can't be Captain Kurrell! He told me that he had never taken the least – the least interest in your wife, Mr Boulte. Oh, *do* listen! He said he had not. He swore he had not,' said Mrs Vansuythen.

The *purdah* rustled, and the speech was cut short by the entry of a little thin woman, with big rings round her eyes. Mrs Vansuythen stood up with a gasp.

'What was that you said?' asked Mrs Boulte. 'Never mind that man. What did Ted say to you? What did he say to you? What did he say to you?'

Mrs Vansuythen sat down helplessly on the sofa, overborne by the trouble of her questioner.

'He said – I can't remember exactly what he said – but I understood him to say – that is – But, really, Mrs Boulte, isn't it rather a strange question?'

'*Will* you tell me what he said?' repeated Mrs Boulte. Even a tiger will fly before a bear robbed of her whelps, and Mrs Vansuythen was only an ordinarily good woman. She began in a sort of desperation: 'Well, he said that he never cared for you at all, and, of course, there was not the least reason why he should have, and – and – that was all.'

'You said he *swore* he had not cared for me. Was that true?'

'Yes,' said Mrs Vansuythen very softly.

Mrs Boulte wavered for an instant where she stood, and then fell forward fainting.

'What did I tell you?' said Boulte, as though the conversation had been unbroken. 'You can see for yourself. She cares for *him*.' The light began to break into his dull mind, and he went on: 'And he – what was *he* saying to you?'

But Mrs Vansuythen, with no heart for explanations or impassioned protestations, was kneeling over Mrs Boulte.

'Oh, you brute!' she cried. 'Are *all* men like this? Help me to get her into my room – and her face is cut against the table. Oh, *will* you be quiet, and help me to carry her? I hate you, and I hate Captain Kurrell. Lift her up carefully, and now – go! Go away!'

Boulte carried his wife into Mrs Vansuythen's bedroom, and departed before the storm of that lady's wrath and disgust, impenitent and burning with jealousy. Kurrell had been making love to Mrs Vansuythen – would do Vansuythen as great a wrong as he had done Boulte, who caught himself considering whether Mrs Vansuythen would faint if she discovered that the man she loved had forsworn her.

In the middle of these meditations, Kurrell came cantering along the road and pulled up with a cheery 'Good mornin'. Been mashing[8] Mrs Vansuythen as usual, eh? Bad thing for a sober, married man, that. What will Mrs Boulte say?'

Boulte raised his head and said slowly: 'Oh, you liar!' Kurrell's face changed. 'What's that?' he asked quickly.

'Nothing much,' said Boulte. 'Has my wife told you that you two are free to go off whenever you please? She has been good enough to explain the situation to me. You've been a true friend to me, Kurrell – old man – haven't you?'

Kurrell groaned, and tried to frame some sort of idiotic sentence about being willing to give 'satisfaction'.[9] But his interest in the woman was dead, had died out in the Rains, and, mentally, he was abusing her for her amazing indiscretion. It would have been so easy to have broken off the thing gently and by degrees, and now he was saddled with – Boulte's voice recalled him.

'I don't think I should get any satisfaction from killing you, and I'm pretty sure you'd get none from killing me.'

Then in a querulous tone, ludicrously disproportioned to his wrongs, Boulte added:–

'Seems rather a pity that you haven't the decency to keep to the woman, now you've got her. You've been a true friend to *her* too, haven't you?'

Kurrell stared long and gravely. The situation was getting beyond him.

'What do you mean?' he said.

Boulte answered, more to himself than the question: 'My wife came over to Mrs Vansuythen's just now; and it seems you'd been telling Mrs Vansuythen that you'd never cared for Emma. I suppose you lied, as usual. What had Mrs Vansuythen to do with you, or you with her? Try to speak the truth for once in a way.'

Kurrell took the double insult without wincing, and replied by another question: 'Go on. What happened?'

'Emma fainted,' said Boulte simply. 'But, look here, what had you been saying to Mrs Vansuythen?'

Kurrell laughed. Mrs Boulte had, with unbridled tongue, made havoc of his plans; and he could at least retaliate by hurting the man in whose eyes he was humiliated and shown dishonourable.

'Saying to her? What *does* a man tell a lie like that for? I suppose I said pretty much what you've said, unless I'm a good deal mistaken.'

'I spoke the truth,' said Boulte, again more to himself than Kurrell. 'Emma told me she hated me. She has no right in me.'

'No! I suppose not. You're only her husband, y'know. And what did Mrs Vansuythen say after you had laid your disengaged heart at her feet?'

Kurrell felt almost virtuous as he put the question.

'I don't think that matters,' Boulte replied; 'and it doesn't concern you.'

'But it does! I tell you it does' – began Kurrell shamelessly.

The sentence was cut by a roar of laughter from Boulte's lips. Kurrell was silent for an instant, and then he, too, laughed – laughed long and loudly, rocking in his saddle. It was an unpleasant sound – the mirthless mirth of these men on the long white line of the Narkarra Road. There were no strangers in Kashima, or they might have thought that captivity within the Dosehri hills had driven half the European population mad. The laughter ended abruptly, and Kurrell was the first to speak.

'Well, what are you going to do?'

Boulte looked up the road, and at the hills. 'Nothing,' said he quietly. 'What's the use? It's too ghastly for anything. We must let the old life go on. I can only call you a hound and a liar, and I can't go on calling you names for ever. Besides which, I don't feel that I'm much better. We can't get out of this place. What *is* there to do?'

Kurrell looked round the rat-pit of Kashima and made no reply. The injured husband took up the wondrous tale.

'Ride on, and speak to Emma if you want to. God knows *I* don't care what you do.'

He walked forward, and left Kurrell gazing blankly after him. Kurrell did not ride on either to see Mrs Boulte or Mrs Vansuythen. He sat in his saddle and thought, while his pony grazed by the roadside.

The whir of approaching wheels roused him. Mrs Vansuythen was driving home Mrs Boulte, white and wan, with a cut on her forehead.

'Stop, please,' said Mrs Boulte. 'I want to speak to Ted.'

Mrs Vansuythen obeyed, but as Mrs Boulte leaned forward, putting her hand upon the splash-board of the dog-cart, Kurrell spoke.

'I've seen your husband, Mrs Boulte.' There was no necessity for any further explanation.

The man's eyes were fixed, not upon Mrs Boulte, but her companion. Mrs Boulte saw the look.

'Speak to him!' she pleaded, turning to the woman at her side. 'Oh, speak to him! Tell him what you told me just now. Tell him you hate him! Tell him you hate him!'

She bent forward and wept bitterly, while the *sais,*[10] impassive, went forward to hold the horse. Mrs Vansuythen turned scarlet and dropped the reins. She wished to be no party to such unholy explanations.

'I've nothing to do with it,' she began coldly; but Mrs Boulte's sobs overcame her, and she addressed herself to the man. 'I don't know what I am to say, Captain Kurrell. I don't know what I can call you. I think you've – you've behaved abominably, and she has cut her forehead terribly against the table.'

'It doesn't hurt. It isn't anything,' said Mrs Boulte feebly. '*That* doesn't matter. Tell him what you told me. Say you don't care for him. Oh, Ted, *won't* you believe her?'

'Mrs Boulte has made me understand that you were – that you were fond of her once upon a time,' went on Mrs Vansuythen.

'Well!' said Kurrell brutally. 'It seems to me that Mrs Boulte had better be fond of her own husband first.'

'Stop!' said Mrs Vansuythen. 'Hear me first. I don't care – I don't want to know anything about you and Mrs Boulte; but I want *you* to know that I hate you, that I think you are a cur, and that I'll never, *never* speak to you again. Oh, I don't dare to say what I think of you, you – man!'

'I want to speak to Ted,' moaned Mrs Boulte, but the dog-cart rattled on, and Kurrell was left on the road, shamed, and boiling with wrath against Mrs Boulte.

He waited till Mrs Vansuythen was driving back to her own house, and, she being freed from the embarrassment of Mrs Boulte's presence, learned for the second time her opinion of himself and his actions.

In the evenings it was the wont of all Kashima to meet at the platform on the Narkarra Road, to drink tea and discuss the trivialities of the day. Major Vansuythen and his wife found themselves alone at the gathering-place for almost the first time in their remembrance; and the cheery Major, in the teeth of his wife's remarkably reasonable suggestion that the rest of the Station might be sick, insisted upon driving round to the two bungalows and unearthing the population.

'Sitting in the twilight!' said he, with great indignation, to the Boultes. 'That'll never do! Hang it all, we're one family here! You *must* come out, and so must Kurrell. I'll make him bring his banjo.'

So great is the power of honest simplicity and a good digestion over guilty consciences that all Kashima did turn out, even down to the banjo; and the Major embraced the company in one expansive grin. As he grinned, Mrs Vansuythen raised her eyes for an instant and looked at all Kashima. Her meaning was clear. Major Vansuythen would never know anything. He was to be the outsider in that happy family whose cage was the Dosehri hills.

'You're singing villainously out of tune, Kurrell,' said the Major truthfully. 'Pass me that banjo.'

And he sang in excruciating wise till the stars came out and all Kashima went to dinner.

That was the beginning of the New Life of Kashima – the life that Mrs Boulte made when her tongue was loosened in the twilight.

Mrs Vansuythen has never told the Major; and since he insists upon keeping up a burdensome geniality, she has been compelled to break her vow of not speaking to Kurrell. This speech, which must of necessity preserve the semblance of politeness and interest, serves admirably to keep alight the flame of jealousy and dull hatred in Boulte's bosom, as it awakens the same passions in his wife's heart. Mrs Boulte hates Mrs Vansuythen because she has taken Ted from her, and, in some curious fashion, hates her because Mrs Vansuythen – and here the wife's eyes see far more clearly than the husband's – detests Ted. And Ted – that gallant captain and honourable man – knows now that it is possible to hate a woman once loved, to the verge of wishing to silence her for ever with blows. Above all is he shocked that Mrs Boulte cannot see the error of her ways.

Boulte and he go out tiger-shooting together in all friendship. Boulte has put their relationship on a most satisfactory footing.

'You're a blackguard,' he says to Kurrell, 'and I've lost any self-respect I may ever have had; but when you're with me, I can feel certain that you are not with Mrs Vansuythen, or making Emma miserable.'

Kurrell endures anything that Boulte may say to him. Sometimes they are away for three days together, and then the Major insists upon his wife going over to sit with Mrs Boulte; although Mrs Vansuythen has repeatedly declared that she prefers her husband's company to any in the world. From the way in which she clings to him, she would certainly seem to be speaking the truth.

But of course, as the Major says, 'in a little Station we must all be friendly.'

THE STORY OF MUHAMMAD DIN

Who is the happy man? He that sees, in his own house at home,
little children crowned with dust, leaping and falling and crying.
Munichandra,[1] translated by Professor Peterson

The polo-ball was an old one, scarred, chipped, and dinted. It stood on
the mantelpiece among the pipe-stems which Imam Din, *khitmutgar*,[2]
was cleaning for me.

'Does the Heaven-born want this ball?' said Imam Din deferentially.

The Heaven-born set no particular store by it; but of what use was
a polo-ball to a *khitmutgar*?

'By your Honour's favour, I have a little son. He has seen this ball,
and desires it to play with. I do not want it for myself.'

No one would for an instant accuse portly old Imam Din of wanting
to play with polo-balls. He carried out the battered thing into the
veranda; and there followed a hurricane of joyful squeaks, a patter of
small feet, and the *thud-thud-thud* of the ball rolling along the ground.
Evidently the little son had been waiting outside the door to secure his
treasure. But how had he managed to see that polo-ball?

Next day, coming back from office half an hour earlier than usual,
I was aware of a small figure in the dining-room – a tiny, plump figure
in a ridiculously inadequate shirt which came, perhaps, half-way down
the tubby stomach. It wandered round the room, thumb in mouth,
crooning to itself as it took stock of the pictures. Undoubtedly this was
the 'little son'.

He had no business in my room, of course; but was so deeply absorbed
in his discoveries that he never noticed me in the doorway. I stepped into
the room and startled him nearly into a fit. He sat down on the ground
with a gasp. His eyes opened, and his mouth followed suit. I knew what
was coming, and fled, followed by a long, dry howl which reached the
servants' quarters far more quickly than any command of mine had ever
done. In ten seconds Imam Din was in the dining-room. Then despairing
sobs arose, and I returned to find Imam Din admonishing the small sinner,
who was using most of his shirt as a handkerchief.

'This boy,' said Imam Din judicially, 'is a *budmash*[3] – a big *budmash*. He will, without doubt, go to the *jail-khana*[4] for his behaviour.' Renewed yells from the penitent, and an elaborate apology to myself from Imam Din.

'Tell the baby,' said I, 'that the Sahib is not angry, and take him away.' Imam Din conveyed my forgiveness to the offender, who had now gathered all his shirt round his neck, stringwise, and the yell subsided into a sob. The two set off for the door. 'His name', said Imam Din, as though the name were part of the crime, 'is Muhammad Din, and he is a *budmash*.' Freed from present danger, Muhammad Din turned round in his father's arms, and said gravely, 'It is true that my name is Muhammad Din, Tahib, but I am not a *budmash*. I am a *man*!'

From that day dated my acquaintance with Muhammad Din. Never again did he come into my dining-room, but on the neutral ground of the garden we greeted each other with much state, though our conversation was confined to 'Talaam, Tahib' from his side, and 'Salaam,[5] Muhammad Din' from mine. Daily on my return from office, the little white shirt and the fat little body used to rise from the shade of the creeper-covered trellis where they had been hid; and daily I checked my horse here, that my salutation might not be slurred over or given unseemly.

Muhammad Din never had any companions. He used to trot about the compound, in and out of the castor-oil bushes, on mysterious errands of his own. One day I stumbled upon some of his handiwork far down the grounds. He had half buried the polo-ball in dust, and stuck six shrivelled old marigold flowers in a circle round it. Outside that circle again was a rude[6] square, traced out in bits of red brick alternating with fragments of broken china; the whole bounded by a little bank of dust. The water-man from the well-curb put in a plea for the small architect, saying that it was only the play of a baby and did not much disfigure my garden.

Heaven knows that I had no intention of touching the child's work then or later; but, that evening, a stroll through the garden brought me unawares full on it; so that I trampled, before I knew, marigold-heads, dust-bank, and fragments of broken soap-dish into confusion past all hope of mending. Next morning, I came upon Muhammad Din crying softly to himself over the ruin I had wrought. Some one had cruelly told him that the Sahib was very angry with him for spoiling the garden, and had scattered his rubbish, using bad language the while. Muhammad Din laboured for an hour at effacing every trace of the dust-bank and pottery fragments, and it was with a tearful and apologetic face that he said, 'Talaam, Tahib,' when I came home from office. A hasty inquiry resulted in Imam Din informing Muhammad Din that, by my singular favour, he was permitted to disport himself as he pleased. Whereat the child took heart and fell to tracing the ground-plan of an edifice which was to eclipse the marigold-polo-ball creation.

For some months the chubby little eccentricity revolved in his humble orbit among the castor-oil bushes and in the dust; always fashioning magnificent palaces from stale flowers thrown away by the bearer, smooth water-worn pebbles, bits of broken glass, and feathers pulled, I fancy, from my fowls – always alone, and always crooning to himself.

A gaily-spotted sea-shell was dropped one day close to the last of his little buildings; and I looked that Muhammad Din should build something more than ordinarily splendid on the strength of it. Nor was I disappointed. He meditated for the better part of an hour, and his crooning rose to a jubilant song. Then he began tracing in the dust. It would certainly be a wondrous palace, this one, for it was two yards long and a yard broad in ground-plan. But the palace was never completed.

Next day there was no Muhammad Din at the head of the carriage-drive, and no 'Talaam, Tahib' to welcome my return. I had grown accustomed to the greeting, and its omission troubled me. Next day Imam Din told me that the child was suffering slightly from fever and needed quinine. He got the medicine, and an English Doctor.

'They have no stamina, these brats,' said the Doctor, as he left Imam Din's quarters.

A week later, though I would have given much to have avoided it, I met on the road to the Mussulman burying-ground Imam Din, accompanied by one other friend, carrying in his arms, wrapped in a white cloth, all that was left of little Muhammad Din.

LITTLE TOBRAH

'Prisoner's head did not reach to the top of the dock,' as the English newspapers say. This case, however, was not reported because nobody cared by so much as a hempen rope for the life or death of Little Tobrah. The assessors in the red court-house sat upon him all through the long hot afternoon, and whenever they asked him a question he salaamed and whined. Their verdict was that the evidence was inconclusive, and the Judge concurred. It was true that the dead body of Little Tobrah's sister had been found at the bottom of the well, and Little Tobrah was the only human being within a half-mile radius at the time; but the child might have fallen in by accident. Therefore Little Tobrah was acquitted, and told to go where he pleased. This permission was not so generous as it sounds, for he had nowhere to go to, nothing in particular to eat, and nothing whatever to wear.

He trotted into the court-compound, and sat upon the well-kerb, wondering whether an unsuccessful dive into the black water below would end in a forced voyage across the other Black Water.[1] A groom put down an emptied nose-bag on the bricks, and Little Tobrah, being hungry, set himself to scrape out what wet grain the horse had overlooked.

'O Thief – and but newly set free from the terror of the Law! Come along!' said the groom, and Little Tobrah was led by the ear to a large and fat Englishman, who heard the tale of the theft. 'Hah!' said the Englishman three times (only he said a stronger word). 'Put him into the net[2] and take him home.' So Little Tobrah was thrown into the net of the cart, and, nothing doubting that he should be stuck like a pig, was driven to the Englishman's house. 'Hah!' said the Englishman as before. 'Wet grain, by Jove! Feed the little beggar, some of you, and we'll make a riding-boy of him! See? Wet grain, good Lord!'

'Give an account of yourself,' said the Head of the Grooms to Little Tobrah after the meal had been eaten, and the servants lay at ease in their quarters behind the house. 'You are not of the groom caste, unless it be for the stomach's sake. How came you into the court, and why? Answer, little devil's spawn!'

'There was not enough to eat,' said Little Tobrah calmly. 'This is a good place.'

'Talk straight talk,' said the Head Groom, 'or I will make you clean out the stable of that large red stallion who bites like a camel.'

'We be *Telis*,[3] oil-pressers,' said Little Tobrah, scratching his toes in the dust. 'We were *Telis* – my father, my mother, my brother, the elder by four years, myself, and the sister.'

'She who was found dead in the well?' said one who had heard something of the trial.

'Even so,' said Little Tobrah gravely. 'She who was found dead in the well. It befell upon a time, which is not in my memory, that the sickness came to the village where our oil-press stood, and first my sister was smitten as to her eyes, and went without sight, for it was *mata* – the smallpox. Thereafter, my father and my mother died of that same sickness, so we were alone – my brother who had twelve years, I who had eight, and the sister who could not see. Yet were there the bullock and the oil-press remaining, and we made shift to press the oil as before. But Surjun Dass, the grain-seller, cheated us in his dealings; and it was always a stubborn bullock to drive. We put marigold flowers for the Gods upon the neck of the bullock, and upon the great grinding-beam that rose through the roof; but we gained nothing thereby, and Surjun Dass was a hard man.'

'*Bapri-bap*,'[4] muttered the grooms' wives, 'to cheat a child so! But *we* know what the *bunnia*-folk[5] are, sisters.'

'The press was an old press, and we were not strong men – my brother and I; nor could we fix the neck of the beam firmly in the shackle.'

'Nay, indeed,' said the gorgeously-clad wife of the Head Groom, joining the circle. 'That is a strong man's work. When I was a maid in my father's house – '

'Peace, woman!' said the Head Groom. 'Go on, boy.'

'It is nothing,' said Little Tobrah. 'The big beam tore down the roof upon a day which is not in my memory, and with the roof fell much of the hinder wall, and both together upon our bullock, whose back was broken. Thus we had neither home, nor press, nor bullock – my brother, myself, and the sister who was blind. We went crying away from that place, hand-in-hand, across the fields; and our money was seven annas and six pies.[6] There was a famine in the land. I do not know the name of the land. So, on a night when we were sleeping, my brother took the five annas that remained to us and ran away. I do not know whither he went. The curse of my father be upon him! But I and the sister begged food in the villages, and there was none to give. Only all men said,

"Go to the Englishmen and they will give." I did not know what the Englishmen were; but they said that they were white, living in tents. I went forward; but I cannot say whither I went, and there was no more food for myself or the sister. And upon a hot night, she weeping and calling for food, we came to a well, and I bade her sit upon the kerb, and thrust her in, for, in truth, she could not see; and it is better to die than to starve.'

'*Ai! Ahi!*' wailed the grooms' wives in chorus; 'he thrust her in, for it is better to die than to starve!'

'I would have thrown myself in also, but that she was not dead and called to me from the bottom of the well, and I was afraid and ran. And one came out of the crops saying that I had killed her and defiled the well, and they took me before an Englishman, white and terrible, living in a tent, and me he sent here. But there were no witnesses, and it is better to die than to starve. She, furthermore, could not see with her eyes, and was but a little child.'

'Was but a little child,' echoed the Head Groom's wife. 'But who art thou, weak as a fowl and small as a day-old colt, what art *thou*?'

'I who was empty am now full,' said Little Tobrah, stretching himself upon the dust. 'And I would sleep.'

The groom's wife spread a cloth over him while Little Tobrah slept the sleep of the just.

THE FINANCES
OF THE GODS

The evening meal was ended in Dhunni Bhagat's *Chubara*,[1] and the old priests were smoking or counting their beads. A little naked child pattered in, with its mouth wide open, a handful of marigold flowers in one hand, and a lump of conserved tobacco in the other. It tried to kneel and make obeisance to Gobind,[2] but it was so fat that it fell forward on its shaven head, and rolled on its side, kicking and gasping, while the marigolds tumbled one way and the tobacco the other. Gobind laughed, set it up again, and blessed the marigold flowers as he received the tobacco.

'From my father,' said the child. 'He has the fever, and cannot come. Wilt thou pray for him, father?'

'Surely, littlest; but the smoke is on the ground, and the night-chill is in the air, and it is not good to go abroad naked in the autumn.'

'I have no clothes,' said the child, 'and all to-day I have been carrying cow-dung cakes[3] to the bazar. It was very hot, and I am very tired.' It shivered a little, for the twilight was cool.

Gobind lifted an arm under his vast tattered quilt of many colours, and made an inviting little nest by his side. The child crept in, and Gobind filled his brass-studded leather water-pipe with the new tobacco. When I came to the *Chubara* the shaven head with the tuft atop and the beady black eyes looked out of the folds of the quilt as a squirrel looks out from his nest, and Gobind was smiling while the child played with his beard.

I would have said something friendly, but remembered in time that if the child fell ill afterwards I should be credited with the Evil Eye, and that is a horrible possession.

'Sit thou still, Thumbling,' I said, as it made to get up and run away. 'Where is thy slate,[4] and why has the teacher let such an evil character loose on the streets when there are no police to protect us weaklings? In which ward dost thou try to break thy neck with flying kites from the house-tops?'

'Nay, Sahib, nay,' said the child, burrowing its face into Gobind's beard, and twisting uneasily. 'There was a holiday to-day among the schools, and I do not always fly kites. I play ker-li-kit like the rest.'

Cricket is the national game among the schoolboys of the Punjab, from the naked hedge-school children, who use an old kerosene-tin for wicket, to the BA's of the University, who compete for the Championship belt.

'Thou play kerlikit! Thou art half the height of the bat!' I said.

The child nodded resolutely. 'Yea, I *do* play. *Perlay-ball. Ow-at! Ran, ran, ran!*[5] I know it all.'

'But thou must not forget with all this to pray to the Gods according to custom,' said Gobind, who did not altogether approve of cricket and Western innovations.

'I do not forget,' said the child in a hushed voice.

'Also to give reverence to thy teacher, and' – Gobind's voice softened – 'to abstain from pulling holy men by the beard, little badling. Eh, eh, eh?'

The child's face was altogether hidden in the great white beard, and it began to whimper till Gobind soothed it as children are soothed all the world over, with the promise of a story.

'I did not think to frighten thee, senseless little one. Look up! Am I angry? *Arré, arré, arré!*[6] Shall I weep too, and of our tears make a great pond and drown us both, and then thy father will never get well, lacking thee to pull his beard? Peace, peace, and I will tell thee of the Gods. Thou hast heard many tales?'

'Very many, father.'

'Now, this is a new one which thou hast not heard. Long and long ago when the Gods walked with men as they do to-day, but that we have not faith to see, Shiv, the greatest of Gods, and Parbati his wife, were walking in the garden of a temple.'

'Which temple? That in the Nandgaon ward?' said the child.

'Nay, very far away. Maybe at Trimbak or Hurdwar, whither thou must make pilgrimage when thou art a man. Now, there was sitting in the garden under the jujube-trees[7] a mendicant that had worshipped Shiv for forty years, and he lived on the offerings of the pious, and meditated holiness night and day.'

'O father, was it thou?' said the child, looking up with large eyes.

'Nay, I have said it was long ago, and, moreover, this mendicant was married.'

'Did they put him on a horse with flowers on his head, and forbid him to go to sleep all night long? Thus they did to me when they made my wedding,' said the child, who had been married a few months before.

'And what didst thou do?' said I.

'I wept, and they called me evil names, and then I smote *her*, and we wept together.'

'Thus did not the mendicant,' said Gobind; 'for he was a holy man, and very poor. Parbati perceived him sitting naked by the temple steps where all went up and down, and she said to Shiv, "What shall men think of the Gods when the Gods thus scorn their worshippers? For forty years yonder man has prayed to us, and yet there be only a few grains of rice and some broken cowries before him after all. Men's hearts will be hardened by this thing." And Shiv said, "It shall be looked to," and so he called to the temple which was the temple of his son, Ganesh of the elephant head,[8] saying, "Son, there is a mendicant without who is very poor. What wilt thou do for him?" Then that great elephant-headed One awoke in the dark and answered, "In three days, if it be thy will, he shall have one lakh[9] of rupees." Then Shiv and Parbati went away.

'But there was a money-lender in the garden hidden among the marigolds' – the child looked at the ball of crumpled blossoms in its hands – 'ay, among the yellow marigolds, and he heard the Gods talking. He was a covetous man, and of a black heart, and he desired that lakh of rupees for himself. So he went to the mendicant and said, "O brother, how much do the pious give thee daily?" The mendicant said, "I cannot tell. Sometimes a little rice, sometimes a little pulse, and a few cowries and, it has been, pickled mangoes, and dried fish."'

'That is good,' said the child, smacking its lips.

'Then said the money-lender, "Because I have long watched thee, and learned to love thee and thy patience, I will give thee now five rupees for all thy earnings of the three days to come. There is only a bond to sign on the matter." But the mendicant said, "Thou art mad. In two months I do not receive the worth of five rupees," and he told the thing to his wife that evening. She, being a woman, said, "When did money-lender ever make a bad bargain? The wolf runs through the corn for the sake of the fat deer. Our fate is in the hands of the Gods. Pledge it not even for three days."

'So the mendicant returned to the money-lender, and would not sell. Then that wicked man sat all day before him offering more and more for those three days' earnings. First, ten, fifty, and a hundred rupees; and then, for he did not know when the Gods would pour down their gifts, rupees by the thousand, till he had offered half a lakh of rupees. Upon this sum the mendicant's wife shifted her counsel, and the mendicant signed the bond, and the money was paid in silver; great white bullocks bringing it by the cart-load. But saving only all that money, the mendicant received nothing from the Gods at all, and the heart of the money-lender was uneasy on account of expectation. Therefore at noon of the third day the money-lender went into the temple to spy upon the councils of the Gods, and to learn in what manner that gift might arrive. Even as he was making his prayers, a crack between the stones of the floor gaped, and, closing, caught him by the heel. Then he heard the Gods walking in the temple in the darkness of the columns, and Shiv called to his son Ganesh, saying, "Son, what hast thou done in regard to the lakh of rupees for the mendicant?" And Ganesh woke, for the money-lender heard the dry rustle of his trunk uncoiling, and he answered, "Father, one-half of the money has been paid, and the debtor for the other half I hold here fast by the heel."'

The child bubbled with laughter. 'And the money-lender paid the mendicant?' it said.

'Surely, for he whom the Gods hold by the heel must pay to the uttermost. The money was paid at evening, all silver, in great carts, and thus Ganesh did his work.'

'Nathu! Ohé, Nathu!'

A woman was calling in the dusk by the door of the courtyard.

The child began to wriggle. 'That is my mother,' it said.

'Go then, littlest,' answered Gobind; 'but stay a moment.'

He ripped a generous yard from his patchwork-quilt, put it over the child's shoulders, and the child ran away.

BAA BAA, BLACK SHEEP

Baa Baa, Black Sheep,
Have you any wool?
Yes, Sir, yes, Sir, three bags full.
One for the Master, one for the Dame –
None for the Little Boy that cries down the lane.

Nursery Rhyme

The First Bag

'When I was in my father's house, I was in a better place.'[1]

They were putting Punch to bed – the *ayah*[2] and the *hamal*[3] and Meeta, the big *Surti* boy,[4] with the red-and-gold turban. Judy, already tucked inside her mosquito-curtains, was nearly asleep. Punch had been allowed to stay up for dinner. Many privileges had been accorded to Punch within the last ten days, and a greater kindness from the people of his world had encompassed his ways and works, which were mostly obstreperous. He sat on the edge of his bed and swung his bare legs defiantly.

'Punch-*baba*[5] going to bye-lo?' said the *ayah* suggestively.

'No' said Punch. 'Punch-*baba* wants the story about the Ranee that was turned into a tiger. Meeta must tell it, and the *hamal* shall hide behind the door and make tiger-noises at the proper time.'

'But Judy-*baba* will wake up,' said the *ayah*.

'Judy-*baba* is waked,' piped a small voice from the mosquito-curtains. 'There was a Ranee that lived at Delhi. Go on, Meeta,' and she fell fast asleep again while Meeta began the story.

Never had Punch secured the telling of that tale with so little opposition. He reflected for a long time.

The *hamal* made the tiger-noises in twenty different keys.

'"Top!" said Punch authoritatively. 'Why doesn't Papa come in and say he is going to give me *put-put*?'[6]

'Punch-*baba* is going away,' said the *ayah*. 'In another week there will be no Punch-*baba* to pull my hair any more.' She sighed softly, for the boy of the household was very dear to her heart.

'Up the Ghauts[7] in a train?' said Punch, standing on his bed. 'All the way to Nassick where the Ranee-Tiger lives?'

'Not to Nassick this year, little Sahib,' said Meeta, lifting him on his shoulder. 'Down to the sea where the coconuts are thrown, and across the sea in a big ship. Will you take Meeta with you to *Belait?*'[8]

'You shall all come,' said Punch, from the height of Meeta's strong arms. 'Meeta and the *ayah* and the *hamal* and Bhini-in-the-Garden, and the salaam-Captain-Sahib-snake-man.'

There was no mockery in Meeta's voice when he replied: 'Great is the Sahib's favour,' and laid the little man down in the bed, while the *ayah*, sitting in the moonlight at the doorway, lulled him to sleep with an interminable canticle such as they sing in the Roman Catholic Church at Parel. Punch curled himself into a ball and slept.

Next morning Judy shouted that there was a rat in the nursery, and thus he forgot to tell her the wonderful news. It did not much matter, for Judy was only three and she would not have understood. But Punch was five; and he knew that going to England would be much nicer than a trip to Nassick.

Papa and Mamma sold the brougham[9] and the piano, and stripped the house, and curtailed the allowance of crockery for the daily meals, and took long counsel together over a bundle of letters bearing the Rocklington postmark.

'The worst of it is that one can't be certain of anything,' said Papa, pulling his moustache. 'The letters in themselves are excellent, and the terms are moderate enough.'

'The worst of it is that the children will grow up away from me,' thought Mamma; but she did not say it aloud.

'We are only one case among hundreds,' said Papa bitterly. 'You shall go Home again in five years, dear.'

'Punch will be ten then – and Judy eight. Oh, how long and long and long the time will be! And we have to leave them among strangers.'

'Punch is a cheery little chap. He's sure to make friends wherever he goes.'

'And who could help loving my Ju?'

They were standing over the cots in the nursery late at night, and I think that Mamma was crying softly. After Papa had gone away, she knelt down by the side of Judy's cot. The *ayah* saw her and put up a prayer that the Memsahib might never find the love of her children taken away from her and given to a stranger.

Mamma's own prayer was a slightly illogical one. Summarised it ran: 'Let strangers love my children and be as good to them as I should be, but let *me* preserve their love and their confidence for ever and ever. Amen.' Punch scratched himself in his sleep, and Judy moaned a little.

Next day they all went down to the sea, and there was a scene at the Apollo Bunder[10] when Punch discovered that Meeta could not come too, and Judy learned that the *ayah* must be left behind. But Punch found a thousand fascinating things in the rope, block, and steam-pipe line on the big P. & O. steamer long before Meeta and the *ayah* had dried their tears.

'Come back, Punch-*baba*,' said the *ayah*.

'Come back,' said Meeta, 'and be a *Burra Sahib* [a big man].'

'Yes,' said Punch, lifted up in his father's arms to wave good-bye. 'Yes, I will come back, and I will be a *Burra Sahib Bahadur* [a very big man indeed]!'

At the end of the first day Punch demanded to be set down in England, which he was certain must be close at hand. Next day there was a merry breeze, and Punch was very sick. 'When I come back to Bombay,' said Punch on his recovery, 'I will come by the road – in a broom-*gharri*.[11] This is a very naughty ship.'

The Swedish boatswain consoled him, and he modified his opinions as the voyage went on. There was so much to see and to handle and ask questions about that Punch nearly forgot the *ayah* and Meeta and the *hamal*, and with difficulty remembered a few words of the Hindustani once his second speech.

But Judy was much worse. The day before the steamer reached Southampton, Mamma asked her if she would not like to see the *ayah* again. Judy's blue eyes turned to the stretch of sea that had swallowed all her tiny past, and she said: '*Ayah*! What *ayah*?'

Mamma cried over her and Punch marvelled. It was then that he heard for the first time Mamma's passionate appeal to him never to let Judy forget Mamma. Seeing that Judy was young, ridiculously young, and that Mamma, every evening for four weeks past, had come into the cabin to sing her and Punch to sleep with a mysterious rune[12] that he called 'Sonny, my soul',[13] Punch could not understand what Mamma meant. But he strove to do his duty; for, the moment Mamma left the cabin, he said to Judy: 'Ju, you bemember Mamma?'

''Torse I do,' said Judy.

'Then *always* bemember Mamma, 'r else I won't give you the paper ducks that the red-haired Captain Sahib cut out for me.'

So Judy promised always to 'bemember Mamma'.

Many and many a time was Mamma's command laid upon Punch, and Papa would say the same thing with an insistence that awed the child.

'You must make haste and learn to write, Punch,' said Papa, 'and then you'll be able to write letters to us in Bombay.'

'I'll come into your room,' said Punch, and Papa choked.

Papa and Mamma were always choking in those days. If Punch took Judy to task for not 'bemembering', they choked. If Punch sprawled on the sofa in the Southampton lodging-house and sketched his future in purple and gold, they choked; and so they did if Judy put up her mouth for a kiss.

Through many days all four were vagabonds on the face of the earth – Punch with no one to give orders to, Judy too young for anything, and Papa and Mamma grave, distracted, and choking.

'Where,' demanded Punch, wearied of a loathsome contrivance on four wheels with a mound of luggage atop – '*where* is our broom-*gharri*? This thing talks so much that *I* can't talk. Where is our *own* broom-*gharri*? When I was at Bandstand before we comed away, I asked Inverarity Sahib why he was sitting in it, and he said it was his own. And I said, "I will *give* it you" – I like Inverarity Sahib – and I said, "Can you put your legs through the pully-wag loops by the windows?" And Inverarity Sahib said No, and laughed. *I* can put my legs through the pully-wag loops. I can put my legs through *these* pully-wag loops. Look! Oh, Mamma's crying again! I didn't know I wasn't not to do *so*.'

Punch drew his legs out of the loops of the four-wheeler: the door opened and he slid to the earth, in a cascade of parcels, at the door of an austere little villa whose gates bore the legend 'Downe Lodge'.[14] Punch gathered himself together and eyed the house with disfavour. It stood on a sandy road, and a cold wind tickled his knicker-bockered legs.

'Let us go away,' said Punch. 'This is not a pretty place.'

But Mamma and Papa and Judy had left the cab, and all the luggage was being taken into the house. At the doorstep stood a woman in black,[15] and she smiled largely, with dry chapped lips. Behind her was a man, big, bony, grey, and lame as to one leg[16] – behind him a boy of twelve,[17] black-haired and oily in appearance. Punch surveyed the trio, and advanced without fear, as he had been accustomed to do in Bombay when callers came and he happened to be playing in the veranda.

'How do you do?' said he. 'I am Punch.' But they were all looking at the luggage – all except the grey man, who shook hands with Punch, and said he was 'a smart little fellow'. There was much running about and banging of boxes, and Punch curled himself up on the sofa in the dining-room and considered things.

'I don't like these people,' said Punch. 'But never mind. We'll go away soon. We have always went away soon from everywhere. I wish we was gone back to Bombay *soon*.'

The wish bore no fruit. For six days Mamma wept at intervals, and showed the woman in black all Punch's clothes – a liberty which Punch resented: 'But p'raps she's a new white *ayah*,' he thought. 'I'm to call her Antirosa, but she doesn't call *me* Sahib. She says just Punch,' he confided to Judy. 'What is Antirosa?'

Judy didn't know. Neither she nor Punch had heard anything of an animal called an aunt. Their world had been Papa and Mamma, who knew everything, permitted everything, and loved everybody – even Punch when he used to go into the garden at Bombay and fill his nails with mould after the weekly nail-cutting, because, as he explained between two strokes of the slipper to his sorely-tried father, his fingers 'felt so new at the end'.

In an undefined way Punch judged it advisable to keep both parents between himself and the woman in black and the boy with black hair. He did not approve of them. He liked the grey man, who had expressed a wish to be called 'Uncleharri'. They nodded at each other when they met, and the grey man showed him a little ship with rigging that took up and down.

'She is a model of the *Brisk* – the little *Brisk* that was sore exposed that day at Navarino.'[18] The grey man hummed the last words and fell into a reverie. 'I'll tell you about Navarino, Punch, when we go for walks together; and you mustn't touch the ship, because she's the *Brisk*.'

Long before that walk, the first of many, was taken, they roused Punch and Judy in the chill dawn of a February morning to say Good-bye; and of all people in the wide earth to Papa and Mamma – both crying this time. Punch was very sleepy and Judy was cross.

'Don't forget us,' pleaded Mamma. 'Oh, my little son, don't forget us, and see that Judy remembers too.'

'I've told Judy to bemember,' said Punch, wriggling, for his father's beard tickled his neck, 'I've told Judy – ten – forty – 'leven thousand times. But Ju's so young – quite a baby – isn't she?'

'Yes,' said Papa, 'quite a baby, and you must be good to Judy, and make haste to learn to write and – and – and – '

Punch was back in his bed again. Judy was fast asleep, and there was the rattle of a cab below. Papa and Mamma had gone away. Not to Nassick; that was across the sea. To some place much nearer, of course, and equally of course they would return. They came back after dinner-parties, and Papa had come back after he had been to a place called 'The Snows', and Mamma with him, to Punch and Judy at Mrs Inverarity's house in Marine Lines. Assuredly they would come back again. So Punch fell asleep till the true morning, when the black-haired boy met him with the information that Papa and Mamma had gone to Bombay, and that he and Judy were to stay at Downe Lodge 'for ever'. Antirosa, tearfully appealed to for a contradiction, said that Harry had spoken the truth, and that it behoved Punch to fold up his clothes neatly on going to bed. Punch went out and wept bitterly with Judy, into whose fair head he had driven some ideas of the meaning of separation.

When a matured man discovers that he has been deserted by Providence, deprived of his God, and cast without help, comfort, or sympathy, upon a world which is new and strange to him, his despair, which may find expression in evil living, the writing of his experiences, or the more satisfactory diversion of suicide, is generally supposed to be impressive. A child, under exactly similar circumstances as far as its knowledge goes, cannot very well curse God and die.[19] It howls till its nose is red, its eyes are sore, and its head aches. Punch and Judy, through no fault of their own, had lost all their world. They sat in the hall and cried; the black-haired boy looking on from afar.

The model of the ship availed nothing, though the grey man assured Punch that he might pull the rigging up and down as much as he pleased; and Judy was promised free entry into the kitchen. They wanted Papa and Mamma, gone to Bombay beyond the seas, and their grief while it lasted was without remedy.

When the tears ceased the house was very still. Antirosa had decided that it was better to let the children 'have their cry out', and the boy had gone to school. Punch raised his head from the floor and sniffed mournfully. Judy was nearly asleep. Three short years had not taught her how to bear sorrow with full knowledge. There was a distant, dull boom in the air – a repeated heavy thud. Punch knew that sound in Bombay in the monsoon. It was the sea – the sea that must be traversed before anyone could get to Bombay.

'Quick, Ju!' he cried. 'We're close to the sea. I can hear it! Listen! That's where they've went. P'raps we can catch them if we was in time. They didn't mean to go without us. They've only forgot.'

'Iss,' said Judy. 'They've only forgotted. Less go to the sea.'

The hall-door was open and so was the garden-gate.

'It's very, very big, this place,' he said, looking cautiously down the road, 'and we will get lost. But *I* will find a man and order him to take me back to my house – like I did in Bombay.'

He took Judy by the hand, and the two ran hatless in the direction of the sound of the sea. Downe Lodge was almost the last of a range of newly-built houses running out, through a field of brick-mounds, to a heath where gipsies occasionally camped and where the Garrison Artillery of Rocklington[20] practised. There were few people to be seen, and the children might have been taken for those of the soldiery who ranged far. Half an hour the wearied little legs tramped across heath, potato-patch, and sand-dune.

'I'se so tired,' said Judy, 'and Mamma will be angry.'

'Mamma's *never* angry. I suppose she is waiting at the sea now while Papa gets tickets. We'll find them and go along with them. Ju, you mustn't sit down. Only a little more and we'll come to the sea. Ju, if you sit down I'll *thmack* you!' said Punch.

They climbed another dune, and came upon the great grey sea at low tide. Hundreds of crabs were scuttling about the beach, but there was no trace of Papa and Mamma, not even of a ship upon the waters – nothing but sand and mud for miles and miles.

And 'Uncleharri' found them by chance – very muddy and very forlorn – Punch dissolved in tears, but trying to divert Judy with an 'ickle trab', and Judy wailing to the pitiless horizon for 'Mamma, Mamma!' – and again 'Mamma!'

The Second Bag

> Ah, well-a-day, for we are souls bereaved!
> Of all the creatures under Heaven's wide scope
> We are most hopeless, who had once most hope,
> And most beliefless, who had most believed.
>   *The City of Dreadful Night.*[21]

All this time not a word about Black Sheep. He came later, and Harry, the black-haired boy, was mainly responsible for his coming.

Judy – who could help loving little Judy? – passed, by special permit, into the kitchen and thence straight to Aunty Rosa's heart. Harry was Aunty Rosa's one child, and Punch was the extra boy about the house. There was no special place for him or his little affairs, and he was forbidden to sprawl on sofas and explain his ideas about the manufacture of this world and his hopes for his future. Sprawling was lazy and wore out sofas, and little boys were not expected to talk. They were talked to, and the talking-to was intended for the benefit of their morals. As the unquestioned despot of the house at Bombay, Punch could not quite understand how he came to be of no account in this his new life.

Harry might reach across the table and take what he wanted; Judy might point and get what she wanted. Punch was forbidden to do either. The grey man was his great hope and stand-by for many months after

Mamma and Papa left, and he had forgotten to tell Judy to 'bemember Mamma'.

This lapse was excusable, because in the interval he had been introduced by Aunty Rosa to two very impressive things – an abstraction called God, the intimate friend and ally of Aunty Rosa, generally believed to live behind the kitchen-range because it was hot there – and a dirty brown book filled with unintelligible dots and marks. Punch was always anxious to oblige everybody. He therefore welded the story of the Creation on to what he could recollect of his Indian fairy tales, and scandalised Aunty Rosa by repeating the result to Judy. It was a sin, a grievous sin, and Punch was talked to for a quarter of an hour. He could not understand where the iniquity came in, but was careful not to repeat the offence, because Aunty Rosa told him that God had heard every word he had said and was very angry. If this were true why didn't God come and say so, thought Punch, and dismissed the matter from his mind. Afterwards he learned to know the Lord as the only thing in the world more awful than Aunty Rosa – as a Creature that stood in the background and counted the strokes of the cane.

But the reading was, just then, a much more serious matter than any creed. Aunty Rosa sat him upon a table and told him that A B meant ab.

'Why?' said Punch. 'A is a and B is bee. *Why* does A B mean ab?'

'Because I tell you it does,' said Aunty Rosa, 'and you've got to say it.'

Punch said it accordingly, and for a month, hugely against his will, stumbled through the brown book, not in the least comprehending what it meant. But Uncle Harry, who walked much and generally alone, was wont to come into the nursery and suggest to Aunty Rosa that Punch should walk with him. He seldom spoke, but he showed Punch all Rocklington, from the mud-banks and the sand of the back-bay to the great harbours where ships lay at anchor,[22] and the dockyards where the hammers were never still, and the marine-store shops, and the shiny brass counters in the Offices where Uncle Harry went once every three months with a slip of blue paper and received sovereigns[23] in exchange; for he held a wound-pension. Punch heard, too, from his lips the story of the battle of Navarino, where the sailors of the Fleet, for three days afterwards, were deaf as posts and could only sign to each other. 'That was because of the noise of the guns,' said Uncle Harry, 'and I have got the wadding of a bullet[24] somewhere inside me now.'

Punch regarded him with curiosity. He had not the least idea what wadding was, and his notion of a bullet was a dockyard cannon-ball bigger than his own head. How could Uncle Harry keep a

cannon-ball inside him? He was afraid to ask, for fear Uncle Harry
might be angry.

Punch had never known what anger – real anger – meant until one
terrible day when Harry had taken his paint-box to paint a boat with,
and Punch had protested. Then Uncle Harry had appeared on the scene
and, muttering something about 'strangers' children', had with a stick
smitten the black-haired boy across the shoulders till he wept and yelled,
and Aunty Rosa came in and abused Uncle Harry for cruelty to his
own flesh and blood, and Punch shuddered to the tips of his shoes. 'It
wasn't my fault,' he explained to the boy, but both Harry and Aunty
Rosa said that it was, and that Punch had told tales, and for a week
there were no more walks with Uncle Harry.

But that week brought a great joy to Punch.

He had repeated till he was thrice weary the statement that 'The Cat
lay on the Mat and the Rat came in.'

'Now I can truly read,' said Punch, 'and now I will never read
anything in the world.'

He put the brown book in the cupboard where his school-books
lived and accidentally tumbled out a venerable volume, without covers,
labelled *Sharpe's Magazine*. There was the most portentous picture of
a Griffin on the first page, with verses below. The Griffin carried off
one sheep a day from a German village, till a man came with a 'falchion'[25]
and split the Griffin open. Goodness only knew what a falchion was,
but there was the Griffin, and his history was an improvement upon
the eternal Cat.

'This', said Punch, 'means things, and now I will know all about
everything in all the world.' He read till the light failed, not understanding a tithe of the meaning, but tantalised by glimpses of new
worlds hereafter to be revealed.

'What is a "falchion"? What is a "e-wee lamb"? What is a "base
*uss*urper"? What is a "verdant me-ad"?' he demanded, with flushed
cheeks, at bedtime, of the astonished Aunty Rosa.

'Say your prayers and go to sleep,' she replied, and that was all the
help Punch then or afterwards found at her hands in the new and
delightful exercise of reading.

'Aunty Rosa only knows about God and things like that,' argued
Punch. 'Uncle Harry will tell me.'

The next walk proved that Uncle Harry could not help either; but
he allowed Punch to talk, and even sat down on a bench to hear about
the Griffin. Other walks brought other stories as Punch ranged farther
afield, for the house held large store of old books that no one ever
opened – from *Frank Fairlegh* in serial numbers, and the earlier poems

of Tennyson, contributed anonymously to *Sharpe's Magazine*, to '62 Exhibition Catalogues, gay with colours and delightfully incomprehensible, and odd leaves of *Gulliver's Travels*.

As soon as Punch could string a few pot-hooks[26] together he wrote to Bombay, demanding by return of post 'all the books in all the world'. Papa could not comply with this modest indent, but sent *Grimm's Fairy Tales* and a *Hans Andersen*. That was enough. If he were only left alone Punch could pass, at any hour he chose, into a land of his own, beyond reach of Aunty Rosa and her God, Harry and his teasements, and Judy's claims to be played with.

'Don't disturve me, I'm reading. Go and play in the kitchen,' grunted Punch. 'Aunty Rosa lets *you* go there.' Judy was cutting her second teeth and was fretful. She appealed to Aunty Rosa, who descended on Punch.

'I was reading,' he explained, 'reading a book. I *want* to read.'

'You're only doing that to show off,' said Aunty Rosa. 'But we'll see. Play with Judy now, and don't open a book for a week.'

Judy did not pass a very enjoyable playtime with Punch, who was consumed with indignation. There was a pettiness at the bottom of the prohibition which puzzled him.

'It's what I like to do,' he said, 'and she's found out that and stopped me. Don't cry, Ju – it wasn't your fault – *please* don't cry, or she'll say I made you.'

Ju loyally mopped up her tears, and the two played in their nursery, a room in the basement and half underground, to which they were regularly sent after the mid-day dinner while Aunty Rosa slept. She drank wine – that is to say, something from a bottle in the cellaret – for her stomach's sake, but if she did not fall asleep she would sometimes come into the nursery to see that the children were really playing. Now bricks, wooden hoops, ninepins, and chinaware cannot amuse for ever, especially when all Fairyland is to be won by the mere opening of a book, and, as often as not, Punch would be discovered reading to Judy or telling her interminable tales. That was an offence in the eyes of the law, and Judy would be whisked off by Aunty Rosa, while Punch was left to play alone, 'and be sure that I hear you doing it.'

It was not a cheering employ, for he had to make a playful noise. At last, with infinite craft, he devised an arrangement whereby the table could be supported as to three legs on toy bricks, leaving the fourth clear to bring down on the floor. He could work the table with one hand and hold a book with the other. This he did till an evil day when Aunty Rosa pounced upon him unawares and told him that he was 'acting a lie'.

'If you're old enough to do that,' she said – her temper was always worst after dinner – 'you're old enough to be beaten.'

'But – I'm – I'm not a animal!' said Punch aghast. He remembered Uncle Harry and the stick, and turned white. Aunty Rosa had hidden a light cane behind her, and Punch was beaten then and there over the shoulders. It was a revelation to him. The room-door was shut, and he was left to weep himself into repentance and work out his own gospel of life.

Aunty Rosa, he argued, had the power to beat him with many stripes. It was unjust and cruel, and Mamma and Papa would never have allowed it. Unless perhaps, as Aunty Rosa seemed to imply, they had sent secret orders. In which case he was abandoned indeed. It would be discreet in the future to propitiate Aunty Rosa, but then again, even in matters in which he was innocent, he had been accused of wishing to 'show off'. He had 'shown off' before visitors when he had attacked a strange gentleman – Harry's uncle, not his own – with requests for information about the Griffin and the falchion, and the precise nature of the Tilbury[27] in which Frank Fairlegh rode – all points of paramount interest which he was bursting to understand. Clearly it would not do to pretend to care for Aunty Rosa.

At this point Harry entered and stood afar off, eyeing Punch, a dishevelled heap in the corner of the room, with disgust.

'You're a liar – a young liar,' said Harry, with great unction, 'and you're to have tea down here because you're not fit to speak to us. And you're not to speak to Judy again till Mother gives you leave. You'll corrupt her. You're only fit to associate with the servant. Mother says so.'

Having reduced Punch to a second agony of tears, Harry departed upstairs with the news that Punch was still rebellious.

Uncle Harry sat uneasily in the dining-room. 'Damn it all, Rosa,' said he at last, 'can't you leave the child alone? He's a good enough little chap when I meet him.'

'He puts on his best manners with you, Henry,' said Aunty Rosa, 'but I'm afraid, I'm very much afraid, that he is the Black Sheep[28] of the family.'

Harry heard and stored up the name for future use. Judy cried till she was bidden to stop, her brother not being worth tears; and the evening concluded with the return of Punch to the upper regions and a private sitting at which all the blinding horrors of Hell were revealed to Punch with such store of imagery as Aunty Rosa's narrow mind possessed.

Most grievous of all was Judy's round-eyed reproach, and Punch went to bed in the depths of the Valley of Humiliation. He shared his room with Harry and knew the torture in store. For an hour and a half he had to answer that young gentleman's questions as to his motives for telling a lie, and a grievous lie, the precise quantity of punishment inflicted by Aunty Rosa, and had also to profess his deep gratitude for such religious instruction as Harry thought fit to impart.

From that day began the downfall of Punch, now Black Sheep.

'Untrustworthy in one thing, untrustworthy in all,' said Aunty Rosa, and Harry felt that Black Sheep was delivered into his hands. He would wake him up in the night to ask him why he was such a liar.

'I don't know,' Punch would reply.

'Then don't you think you ought to get up and pray to God for a new heart?'

'Y-yess.'

'Get out and pray, then!' And Punch would get out of bed with raging hate in his heart against all the world, seen and unseen. He was always tumbling into trouble. Harry had a knack of cross-examining him as to his day's doings, which seldom failed to lead him, sleepy and savage, into half-a-dozen contradictions – all duly reported to Aunty Rosa next morning.

'But it *wasn't* a lie,' Punch would begin, charging into a laboured explanation that landed him more hopelessly in the mire. 'I said that I didn't say my prayers *twice* over in the day, and *that* was on Tuesday. *Once* I did. I *know* I did, but Harry said I didn't,' and so forth, till the tension brought tears, and he was dismissed from the table in disgrace.

'You usen't to be as bad as this,' said Judy, awestricken at the catalogue of Black Sheep's crimes. 'Why are you so bad now?'

'I don't know,' Black Sheep would reply. 'I'm not, if I only wasn't bothered upside-down. I knew what I *did*, and I want to say so; but Harry always makes it out different somehow, and Aunty Rosa doesn't believe a word I say. Oh, Ju! Don't *you* say I'm bad too.'

'Aunty Rosa says you are,' said Judy. 'She told the Vicar so when he came yesterday.'

'Why does she tell all the people outside the house about me? It isn't fair,' said Black Sheep. 'When I was in Bombay, and was bad – *doing* bad, not made-up bad like this – Mamma told Papa, and Papa told me he knew, and that was all. *Outside* people didn't know too – even Meeta didn't know.'

'I don't remember,' said Judy wistfully. 'I was all little then. Mamma was just as fond of you as she was of me, wasn't she?'

''Course she was. So was Papa. So was everybody.'

'Aunty Rosa likes me more than she does you. She says that you are

a Trial and a Black Sheep, and I'm not to speak to you more than I
can help.'

'Always? Not outside of the times when you mustn't speak to me
at all?'

Judy nodded her head mournfully. Black Sheep turned away in
despair, but Judy's arms were round his neck.

'Never mind, Punch,' she whispered. 'I *will* speak to you just the
same as ever and ever. You're my own own brother though you are –
though Aunty Rosa says you're bad, and Harry says you are a little
coward. He says that if I pulled your hair hard, you'd cry.'

'Pull, then,' said Punch.

Judy pulled gingerly.

'Pull harder – as hard as you can! There! I don't mind how much
you pull it *now*. If you'll speak to me same as ever I'll let you pull it as
much as you like – pull it out if you like. But I know if Harry came and
stood by and made you do it I'd cry.'

So the two children sealed the compact with a kiss, and Black Sheep's
heart was cheered within him, and by extreme caution and careful
avoidance of Harry he acquired virtue, and was allowed to read
undisturbed for a week. Uncle Harry took him for walks, and consoled
him with rough tenderness, never calling him Black Sheep. 'It's good
for you, I suppose, Punch,' he used to say. 'Let us sit down. I'm getting
tired.' His steps led him now not to the beach, but to the Cemetery of
Rocklington, amid the potato-fields. For hours the grey man would sit
on a tombstone, while Black Sheep would read epitaphs, and then with
a sigh would stump home again.

'I shall lie there soon,' said he to Black Sheep, one winter evening,
when his face showed white as a worn silver coin under the light of the
lych-gate. 'You needn't tell Aunty Rosa.'

A month later he turned sharp round, ere half a morning walk was
completed, and stumped back to the house. 'Put me to bed, Rosa,' he
muttered. 'I've walked my last. The wadding has found me out.'

They put him to bed, and for a fortnight the shadow of his sickness
lay upon the house, and Black Sheep went to and fro unobserved. Papa
had sent him some new books, and he was told to keep quiet. He retired
into his own world, and was perfectly happy. Even at night his felicity
was unbroken. He could lie in bed and string himself tales of travel
and adventure while Harry was downstairs.

'Uncle Harry's going to die,' said Judy, who now lived almost entirely
with Aunty Rosa.

'I'm very sorry,' said Black Sheep soberly. 'He told me that a long
time ago.'

Aunty Rosa heard the conversation. 'Will nothing check your wicked tongue?' she said angrily. There were blue circles round her eyes.

Black Sheep retreated to the nursery and read *Cometh up as a Flower*[29] with deep and uncomprehending interest. He had been forbidden to open it on account of its 'sinfulness', but the bonds of the Universe were crumbling, and Aunty Rosa was in great grief.

'I'm glad,' said Black Sheep. 'She's unhappy now. It wasn't a lie, though. *I* knew. He told me not to tell.'

That night Black Sheep woke with a start. Harry was not in the room, and there was a sound of sobbing on the next floor. Then the voice of Uncle Harry, singing the song of the Battle of Navarino, came through the darkness:

> 'Our vanship was the *Asia* –
> The *Albion* and *Genoa*!'

'He's getting well,' thought Black Sheep, who knew the song through all its seventeen verses. But the blood froze at his little heart as he thought. The voice leapt an octave, and rang shrill as a boatswain's pipe:

> 'And next came on the lovely *Rose*,
> The *Philomel*, her fire-ship, closed,
> And the little *Brisk* was sore exposed
> That day at Navarino.'

'That day at Navarino, Uncle Harry!' shouted Black Sheep, half wild with excitement and fear of he knew not what.

A door opened, and Aunty Rosa screamed up the staircase: 'Hush! For God's sake hush, you little devil! Uncle Harry is *dead*!'

The Third Bag

> Journeys end in lovers' meeting,
> Every wise man's son doth know.[30]

'I wonder what will happen to me now,' thought Black Sheep, when semi-pagan rites peculiar to the burial of the Dead in middle-class houses had been accomplished, and Aunty Rosa, awful in black crape, had returned to this life. 'I don't think I've done anything bad that she knows of I suppose I will soon. She will be very cross after Uncle

Harry's dying, and Harry will be cross too. I'll keep in the nursery.'

Unfortunately for Punch's plans, it was decided that he should be sent to a day-school which Harry attended. This meant a morning walk with Harry, and perhaps an evening one; but the prospect of freedom in the interval was refreshing. 'Harry'll tell everything I do, but I won't do anything,' said Black Sheep. Fortified with this virtuous resolution, he went to school only to find that Harry's version of his character had preceded him, and that life was a burden in consequence. He took stock of his associates. Some of them were unclean, some of them talked in dialect, many dropped their h's, and there were two Jews and a negro, or someone quite as dark, in the assembly. 'That's a *hubshi*,'[31] said Black Sheep to himself. 'Even Meeta used to laugh at a *hubshi*. I don't think this is a proper place.' He was indignant for at least an hour, till he reflected that any expostulation on his part would be by Aunty Rosa construed into 'showing off', and that Harry would tell the boys.

'How do you like school?' said Aunty Rosa at the end of the day.

'I think it is a very nice place,' said Punch quietly.

'I suppose you warned the boys of Black Sheep's character?' said Aunty Rosa to Harry.

'Oh yes,' said the censor of Black Sheep's morals. 'They know all about him.'

'If I was with my father,' said Black Sheep, stung to the quick, 'I shouldn't *speak* to those boys. He wouldn't let me. They live in shops. I saw them go into shops – where their fathers live and sell things.'

'You're too good for that school, are you?' said Aunty Rosa, with a bitter smile. 'You ought to be grateful, Black Sheep, that those boys speak to you at all. It isn't every school that takes little liars.'

Harry did not fail to make much capital out of Black Sheep's ill-considered remark; with the result that several boys, including the *hubshi*, demonstrated to Black Sheep the eternal equality of the human race by smacking his head, and his consolation from Aunty Rosa was that it 'served him right for being vain'. He learned, however, to keep his opinions to himself, and by propitiating Harry in carrying books and the like to get a little peace. His existence was not too joyful. From nine till twelve he was at school, and from two to four, except on Saturdays. In the evenings he was sent down into the nursery to prepare his lessons for the next day, and every night came the dreaded cross-questionings at Harry's hand. Of Judy he saw but little. She was deeply religious – at six years of age Religion is easy to come by – and sorely divided between her natural love for Black Sheep and her love for Aunty Rosa, who could do no wrong.

The lean woman returned that love with interest, and Judy, when she dared, took advantage of this for the remission of Black Sheep's penalties. Failures in lessons at school were punished at home by a week without reading other than school-books, and Harry brought the news of such a failure with glee. Further, Black Sheep was then bound to repeat his lessons at bedtime to Harry, who generally succeeded in making him break down, and consoled him by gloomiest forebodings for the morrow. Harry was at once spy, practical joker, inquisitor, and Aunty Rosa's deputy executioner. He filled his many posts to admiration. From his actions, now that Uncle Harry was dead, there was no appeal. Black Sheep had not been permitted to keep any self-respect at school: at home he was, of course, utterly discredited, and grateful for any pity that the servant-girls – they changed frequently at Downe Lodge because they, too, were liars – might show. 'You're just fit to row in the same boat with Black Sheep,' was a sentiment that each new Jane or Eliza might expect to hear, before a month was over, from Aunty Rosa's lips; and Black Sheep was used to ask new girls whether they had yet been compared to him. Harry was 'Master Harry' in their mouths; Judy was officially 'Miss Judy'; but Black Sheep was never anything more than Black Sheep *tout court*.[32]

As time went on and the memory of Papa and Mamma became wholly overlaid by the unpleasant task of writing them letters, under Aunty Rosa's eye, each Sunday, Black Sheep forgot what manner of life he had led in the beginning of things. Even Judy's appeals to 'try and remember about Bombay' failed to quicken him.

'I can't remember,' he said. 'I know I used to give orders and Mamma kissed me.'

'Aunty Rosa will kiss you if you are good,' pleaded Judy.

'Ugh! I don't want to be kissed by Aunty Rosa. She'd say I was doing it to get something more to eat.'

The weeks lengthened into months, and the holidays came; but just before the holidays Black Sheep fell into deadly sin.

Among the many boys whom Harry had incited to 'punch Black Sheep's head because he daren't hit back', was one more aggravating than the rest, who, in an unlucky moment, fell upon Black Sheep when Harry was not near. The blows stung, and Black Sheep struck back at random with all the power at his command. The boy dropped and whimpered. Black Sheep was astounded at his own act, but, feeling the unresisting body under him, shook it with both his hands in blind fury and then began to throttle his enemy; meaning honestly to slay him. There was a scuffle, and Black Sheep was torn off the body by Harry and some colleagues, and cuffed home tingling but exultant. Aunty Rosa was out. Pending her arrival, Harry set himself to lecture Black

Sheep on the sin of murder – which he described as the offence of Cain.[33]

'Why didn't you fight him fair? What did you hit him when he was down for, you little cur?'

Black Sheep looked up at Harry's throat and then at a knife on the dinner-table.

'I don't understand,' he said wearily. 'You always set him on me and told me I was a coward when I blubbed. Will you leave me alone until Aunty Rosa comes in? She'll beat me if you tell her I ought to be beaten; so it's all right.'

'It's all wrong,' said Harry magisterially. 'You nearly killed him, and I shouldn't wonder if he dies.'

'Will he die?' said Black Sheep.

'I daresay,' said Harry, 'and then you'll be hanged, and go to Hell.'

'All right,' said Black Sheep, picking up the table-knife. 'Then I'll kill *you* now. You say things and do things and – and *I* don't know how things happen, and you never leave me alone – and I don't care *what* happens!'

He ran at the boy with the knife, and Harry fled upstairs to his room, promising Black Sheep the finest thrashing in the world when Aunty Rosa returned. Black Sheep sat at the bottom of the stairs, the table-knife in his hand, and wept for that he had not killed Harry. The servant-girl came up from the kitchen, took the knife away, and consoled him. But Black Sheep was beyond consolation. He would be badly beaten by Aunty Rosa; then there would be another beating at Harry's hands; then Judy would not be allowed to speak to him; then the tale would be told at school, and then –

There was no one to help and no one to care, and the best way out of the business was by death. A knife would hurt, but Aunty Rosa had told him, a year ago, that if he sucked paint he would die. He went into the nursery, unearthed the now disused Noah's Ark, and sucked the paint off as many animals as remained. It tasted abominably, but he had licked Noah's Dove clean by the time Aunty Rosa and Judy returned. He went upstairs and greeted them with: 'Please, Aunty Rosa, I believe I've nearly killed a boy at school, and I've tried to kill Harry, and when you've done all about God and Hell, will you beat me and get it over?'

The tale of the assault as told by Harry could only be explained on the ground of possession by the Devil. Wherefore Black Sheep was not only most excellently beaten, once by Aunty Rosa, and once, when thoroughly cowed down, by Harry, but he was further prayed for at family prayers, together with Jane, who had stolen a cold rissole from the pantry, and snuffled audibly as her sin was brought before the Throne of Grace. Black Sheep was sore and stiff but triumphant. He would die that very night and be rid of them all. No, he would ask for no forgiveness from Harry, and at bed-time would stand no questioning at Harry's hands, even though addressed as 'Young Cain'.

'I've been beaten,' said he, 'and I've done other things. I don't care what I do. If you speak to me to-night, Harry, I'll get out and try to kill you. Now you can kill me if you like.'

Harry took his bed into the spare room, and Black Sheep lay down to die.

It may be that the makers of Noah's Arks know that their animals are likely to find their way into young mouths, and paint them accordingly. Certain it is that the common, weary next morning broke through the windows and found Black Sheep quite well and a good deal ashamed of himself, but richer by the knowledge that he could, in extremity, secure himself against Harry for the future.

When he descended to breakfast on the first day of the holidays, he was greeted with the news that Harry, Aunty Rosa, and Judy were going away to Brighton, while Black Sheep was to stay in the house with the servant. His latest outbreak suited Aunty Rosa's plans admirably. It gave her good excuse for leaving the extra boy behind. Papa in Bombay, who really seemed to know a young sinner's wants to the hour, sent, that week, a package of new books. And with these, and the society of Jane on board-wages,[34] Black Sheep was left alone for a month.

The books lasted for ten days. They were eaten too quickly in long gulps of twelve hours at a time. Then came days of doing absolutely nothing, of dreaming dreams and marching imaginary armies up and down stairs, of counting the number of banisters, and of measuring the length and breadth of every room in handspans – fifty down the side, thirty across, and fifty back again. Jane made many friends, and, after receiving Black Sheep's assurance that he would not tell of her absences, went out daily for long hours. Black Sheep would follow the rays of the sinking sun from the kitchen to the dining-room and thence upward to his own bedroom until all was grey dark, and he ran down to the kitchen fire and read by its light. He was happy in that he was left alone and could read as much as he pleased. But, later, he grew afraid of the shadows of window-curtains and the flapping of doors and the creaking of shutters. He went out into the garden, and the rustling of the laurel-bushes frightened him.

He was glad when they all returned – Aunty Rosa, Harry, and Judy – full of news, and Judy laden with gifts. Who could help loving loyal little Judy? In return for all her merry babblement, Black Sheep confided

to her that the distance from the hall-door to the top of the first landing
was exactly one hundred and eighty-four handspans. He had found it
out himself!

Then the old life recommenced; but with a difference, and a new
sin. To his other iniquities Black Sheep had now added a phenomenal
clumsiness – was as unfit to trust in action as he was in word. He himself
could not account for spilling everything he touched, upsetting glasses
as he put his hand out, and bumping his head against doors that were
manifestly shut. There was a grey haze upon all his world, and it
narrowed month by month, until at last it left Black Sheep almost alone
with the flapping curtains that were so like ghosts, and the nameless
terrors of broad daylight that were only coats on pegs after all.

Holidays came and holidays went, and Black Sheep was taken to
see many people whose faces were all exactly alike; was beaten when
occasion demanded, and tortured by Harry on all possible occasions;
but defended by Judy through good and evil report, though she hereby
drew upon herself the wrath of Aunty Rosa.

The weeks were interminable and Papa and Mamma were clean
forgotten. Harry had left school and was a clerk in a Banking-Office.
Freed from his presence, Black Sheep resolved that he should no longer
be deprived of his allowance of pleasure-reading. Consequently when
he failed at school he reported that all was well, and conceived a large
contempt for Aunty Rosa as he saw how easy it was to deceive her. 'She
says I'm a little liar when I don't tell lies, and now I do, she doesn't
know,' thought Black Sheep. Aunty Rosa had credited him in the past
with petty cunning and stratagem that had never entered into his head.
By the light of the sordid knowledge that she had revealed to him he
paid her back full tale. In a household where the most innocent of his
motives, his natural yearning for a little affection, had been interpreted
into a desire for more bread and jam, or to ingratiate himself with
strangers and so put Harry into the background, his work was easy.
Aunty Rosa could penetrate certain kinds of hypocrisy, but not all. He
set his child's wits against hers and was no more beaten. It grew monthly
more and more of a trouble to read the school-books, and even the
pages of the open-print story-books danced and were dim. So Black
Sheep brooded in the shadows that fell about him and cut him off from
the world, inventing horrible punishments for 'dear Harry', or plotting
another line of the tangled web of deception that he wrapped round
Aunty Rosa.

Then the crash came and the cobwebs were broken. It was impossible
to foresee everything. Aunty Rosa made personal inquiries as to Black
Sheep's progress and received information that startled her. Step by

step, with a delight as keen as when she convicted an underfed house-maid of the theft of cold meats, she followed the trail of Black Sheep's delinquencies. For weeks and weeks, in order to escape banishment from the book-shelves, he had made a fool of Aunty Rosa, of Harry, of God, of all the world! Horrible, most horrible, and evidence of an utterly depraved mind.

Black Sheep counted the cost. 'It will only be one big beating and then she'll put a card with "Liar" on my back, same as she did before. Harry will whack me and pray for me, and she will pray for me at prayers and tell me I'm a Child of the Devil and give me hymns to learn. But I've done all my reading and she never knew. She'll say she knew all along. She's an old liar too,' said he.

For three days Black Sheep was shut in his own bedroom – to prepare his heart. 'That means two beatings. One at school and one here. *That* one will hurt most.' And it fell even as he thought. He was thrashed at school before the Jews and the *hubshi* for the heinous crime of carrying home false reports of progress. He was thrashed at home by Aunty Rosa on the same count, and then the placard was produced. Aunty Rosa stitched it between his shoulders and bade him go for a walk with it upon him.

'If you make me do that,' said Black Sheep very quietly, 'I shall burn this house down, and perhaps I'll kill you. I don't know whether I *can* kill you – you're so bony – but I'll try.'

No punishment followed this blasphemy, though Black Sheep held himself ready to work his way to Aunty Rosa's withered throat, and grip there till he was beaten off. Perhaps Aunty Rosa was afraid, for Black Sheep, having reached the Nadir of Sin, bore himself with a new recklessness.

In the midst of all the trouble there came a visitor from over the seas to Downe Lodge, who knew Papa and Mamma, and was commissioned to see Punch and Judy. Black Sheep was sent to the drawing-room and charged into a solid tea-table laden with china.

'Gently, gently, little man,' said the visitor, turning Black Sheep's face to the light slowly. 'What's that big bird on the palings?'

'What bird?' asked Black Sheep.

The visitor looked deep down into Black Sheep's eyes for half a minute, and then said suddenly: 'Good God, the little chap's nearly blind!'

It was a most businesslike visitor. He gave orders, on his own responsibility, that Black Sheep was not to go to school or open a book until Mamma came home. 'She'll be here in three weeks, as you know, of course,' said he, 'and I'm Inverarity Sahib. I ushered you into this wicked world, young man, and a nice use you seem to have made of your time. You must do nothing whatever. Can you do that?'

'Yes,' said Punch in a dazed way. He had known that Mamma was coming. There was a chance, then, of another beating. Thank Heaven, Papa wasn't coming too. Aunty Rosa had said of late that he ought to be beaten by a man.

For the next three weeks Black Sheep was strictly allowed to do nothing. He spent his time in the old nursery looking at the broken toys, for all of which account must be rendered to Mamma. Aunty Rosa hit him over the hands if even a wooden boat were broken. But that sin was of small importance compared to the other revelations, so darkly hinted at by Aunty Rosa. 'When your Mother comes, and hears what I have to tell her, she may appreciate you properly,' she said grimly, and mounted guard over Judy lest that small maiden should attempt to comfort her brother, to the peril of her soul.

And Mamma came – in a four-wheeler – fluttered with tender excitement. Such a Mamma! She was young, frivolously young, and beautiful, with delicately flushed cheeks, eyes that shone like stars, and a voice that needed no appeal of outstretched arms to draw little ones to her heart. Judy ran straight to her, but Black Sheep hesitated. Could this wonder be 'showing off'? She would not put out her arms when she knew of his crimes. Meantime was it possible that by fondling she wanted to get anything out of Black Sheep? Only all his love and all his confidence; but that Black Sheep did not know. Aunty Rosa withdrew and left Mamma, kneeling between her children, half laughing, half crying, in the very hall where Punch and Judy had wept five years before.

'Well, chicks, do you remember me?'

'No,' said Judy frankly, 'but I said, "God bless Papa and Mamma" ev'vy night.'

'A little,' said Black Sheep. 'Remember I wrote to you every week, anyhow. That isn't to show off, but 'cause of what comes afterwards.'

'What comes after? What should come after, my darling boy?' And she drew him to her again. He came awkwardly, with many angles. 'Not used to petting,' said the quick Mother-soul. 'The girl is.'

'She's too little to hurt anyone,' thought Black Sheep, 'and if I said I'd kill her, she'd be afraid. I wonder what Aunty Rosa will tell.'

There was a constrained late dinner, at the end of which Mamma picked up Judy and put her to bed with endearments manifold. Faithless little Judy had shown her defection from Aunty Rosa already. And that lady resented it bitterly. Black Sheep rose to leave the room.

'Come and say good-night,' said Aunty Rosa, offering a withered cheek.

'Huh!' said Black Sheep. 'I never kiss you, and I'm not going to show off. Tell that woman what I've done, and see what she says.'

Black Sheep climbed into bed feeling that he had lost Heaven after a glimpse through the gates. In half an hour 'that woman' was bending over him. Black Sheep flung up his right arm. It wasn't fair to come and hit him in the dark. Even Aunty Rosa never tried that. But no blow followed.

'Are you showing off? I won't tell you anything more than Aunty Rosa has, and *she* doesn't know everything,' said Black Sheep as clearly as he could for the arms round his neck.

'Oh, my son – my little, little son! It was my fault – *my* fault, darling – and yet how could we help it? Forgive me, Punch.' The voice died out in a broken whisper, and two hot tears fell on Black Sheep's forehead.

'Has she been making you cry too?' he asked. 'You should see Jane cry. But you're nice, and Jane is a Born Liar – Aunty Rosa says so.'

'Hush, Punch, hush! My boy, don't talk like that. Try to love me a little bit – a little bit. You don't know how I want it. Punch-*baba*, come back to me! I am your Mother – your own Mother – and never mind the rest. I know – yes, I know, dear. It doesn't matter now. Punch, won't you care for me a little?'

It is astonishing how much petting a big boy of ten can endure when he is quite sure that there is no one to laugh at him. Black Sheep had never been made much of before, and here was this beautiful woman treating him – Black Sheep, the Child of the Devil and the inheritor of undying flame – as though he were a small God.

'I care for you a great deal, Mother dear,' he whispered at last, 'and I'm glad you've come back; but are you sure Aunty Rosa told you everything?'

'Everything. What *does* it matter? But – ' the voice broke with a sob that was also laughter – 'Punch, my poor, dear, half-blind darling, don't you think it was a little foolish of you?'

'*No*. It saved a lickin'.'

Mamma shuddered and slipped away in the darkness to write a long letter to Papa. Here is an extract:

'. . . Judy is a dear, plump little prig who adores the woman, and wears with as much gravity as her religious opinions – only eight, Jack! – a venerable horse-hair atrocity which she calls her Bustle! I have just burnt it, and the child is asleep in my bed as I write. She will come to me at once. Punch I cannot quite understand. He is well nourished, but seems to have been worried into a system of small deceptions which the woman magnifies into deadly sins. Don't you recollect our own upbringing, dear, when the Fear of the Lord was so often the beginning of falsehood?[35] I shall win Punch to me before long. I am taking the children away into the country to get them to know me, and, on the whole, I am content, or shall be when you come home, dear boy, and then, thank God, we shall be all under one roof again at last!'

Three months later, Punch, no longer Black Sheep, has discovered that he is the veritable owner of a real, live, lovely Mamma, who is also a sister, comforter, and friend, and that he must protect her till the Father comes home. Deception does not suit the part of a protector, and, when one can do anything without question, where is the use of deception?

'Mother would be awfully cross if you walked through that ditch,' says Judy, continuing a conversation.

'Mother's never angry,' says Punch. 'She'd just say, "You're a little *pagal* [idiot]"; and that's not nice, but I'll show.'

Punch walks through the ditch and mires himself to the knees. 'Mother dear,' he shouts, 'I'm just as dirty as I can pos-*sib*-ly be!'

'Then change your clothes as quickly as you pos-*sib*-ly can!' Mother's clear voice rings out from the house. 'And don't be a little *pagal*!'

'There! Told you so,' says Punch. 'It's all different now, and we are just as much Mother's as if she had never gone.'

Not altogether, O Punch, for when young lips have drunk deep of the bitter waters of Hate, Suspicion, and Despair, all the Love in the world will not wholly take away that knowledge; though it may turn darkened eyes for a while to the light, and teach Faith where no Faith was.

THE MAN WHO
WOULD BE KING

'Brother to a Prince and fellow to a beggar if he be found worthy.'[1]

The Law,[2] as quoted, lays down a fair conduct of life, and one not easy to follow. I have been fellow to a beggar again and again under circumstances which prevented either of us finding out whether the other was worthy. I have still to be brother to a Prince, though I once came near to kinship with what might have been a veritable King, and was promised the reversion of a Kingdom – army, law-courts, revenue, and policy all complete. But, to-day, I greatly fear that my King is dead, and if I want a crown I must go hunt it for myself.

The beginning of everything was in a railway train upon the road to Mhow from Ajmir.[3] There had been a Deficit in the Budget, which necessitated travelling, not Second-class, which is only half as dear as First-class, but by Intermediate, which is very awful indeed. There are no cushions in the Intermediate class, and the population are either Intermediate, which is Eurasian,[4] or Native, which for a long night journey is nasty, or Loafer, which is amusing though intoxicated. Intermediates do not buy from refreshment-rooms. They carry their food in bundles and pots, and buy sweets from the native sweetmeat-sellers, and drink the roadside water. That is why in the hot weather Intermediates are taken out of the carriages dead, and in all weathers are most properly looked down upon.

My particular Intermediate happened to be empty till I reached Nasirabad, when a big black-browed gentleman in shirt-sleeves entered, and, following the custom of Intermediates, passed the time of day. He was a wanderer and a vagabond like myself, but with an educated taste for whisky. He told tales of things he had seen and done, of out-of-the-way corners of the Empire into which he had penetrated, and of adventures in which he risked his life for a few days' food.

'If India was filled with men like you and me, not knowing more than the crows where they'd get their next day's rations, it isn't seventy millions of revenue the land would be paying – it's seven hundred millions,' said he; and as I looked at his mouth and chin I was disposed to agree with him.

We talked politics – the politics of Loaferdom, that sees things from the underside where the lath and plaster is not smoothed off – and we talked postal arrangements because my friend wanted to send a telegram back from the next station to Ajmir, the turning-off place from the Bombay to the Mhow line as you travel westward. My friend had no money beyond eight annas, which he wanted for dinner, and I had no money at all, owing to the hitch in the Budget before mentioned. Further, I was going into a wilderness where, though I should resume touch with the Treasury, there were no telegraph offices. I was, therefore, unable to help him in any way.

'We might threaten a Station-master, and make him send a wire on tick,' said my friend, 'but that'd mean inquiries for you and for me, and I've got my hands full these days. Did you say you are travelling back along this line within any days?'

'Within ten,' I said.

'Can't you make it eight?' said he. 'Mine is rather urgent business.'

'I can send your telegram within ten days if that will serve you,' I said.

'I couldn't trust the wire to fetch him, now I think of it. It's this way. He leaves Delhi on the 23rd for Bombay. That means he'll be running through Ajmir about the night of the 23rd.'

'But I'm going into the Indian Desert,' I explained.

'Well *and* good,' said he. 'You'll be changing at Marwar Junction to get into Jodhpore territory – you must do that – and he'll be coming through Marwar Junction in the early morning of the 24th by the Bombay Mail. Can you be at Marwar Junction on that time? 'Twon't be inconveniencing you because I know that there's precious few pickings to be got out of these Central India States – even though you pretend to be correspondent of the *Backwoodsman*.'[5]

'Have you ever tried that trick?' I asked.

'Again and again, but the Residents find you out, and then you get escorted to the border before you've time to get your knife into them. But about my friend here. I *must* give him a word o' mouth to tell him what's come to me or else he won't know where to go. I would take it more than kind of you if you was to come out of Central India in time to catch him at Marwar Junction, and say to him: "He has gone South for the week." He'll know what that means. He's a big man with a red beard, and a great swell he is. You'll find him sleeping like a gentleman with all his luggage round him in a second-class compartment. But don't you be afraid. Slip down the window, and say: "He has gone South for the week," and he'll tumble. It's only cutting your time of stay in those parts by two days. I ask you as a stranger – going to the West,' he said with emphasis.

'Where have *you* come from?' said I.

'From the East,' said he, 'and I am hoping that you will give him the message on the Square – for the sake of my Mother[6] as well as your own.'

Englishmen are not usually softened by appeals to the memory of their mothers, but for certain reasons, which will be fully apparent, I saw fit to agree.

'It's more than a little matter,' said he, 'and that's why I asked you to do it – and now I know that I can depend on you doing it. A second-class carriage at Marwar Junction, and a red-haired man asleep in it. You'll be sure to remember. I get out at the next station, and I must hold on there till he comes or sends me what I want.'

'I'll give the message if I catch him,' I said, 'and for the sake of your Mother as well as mine I'll give you a word of advice. Don't try to run the Central India States just now as the correspondent of the *Backwoodsman*. There's a real one knocking about there, and it might lead to trouble.'

'Thank you,' said he simply, 'and when will the swine be gone? I can't starve because he's ruining my work. I wanted to get hold of the Degumber Rajah down here about his father's widow, and give him a jump.'

'What did he do to his father's widow, then?'

'Filled her up with red pepper and slippered her to death as she hung from a beam. I found that out myself, and I'm the only man that would dare going into the State to get hush-money for it. They'll try to poison me, same as they did in Chortumna when I went on the loot there. But you'll give the man at Marwar Junction my message?'

He got out at a little roadside station, and I reflected. I had heard, more than once, of men personating correspondents of newspapers and bleeding small Native States with threats of exposure, but I had never met any of the caste before. They lead a hard life, and generally die with great suddenness. The Native States have a wholesome horror of English newspapers which may throw light on their peculiar methods of government, and do their best to choke correspondents with champagne, or drive them out of their mind with four-in-hand barouches. They do not understand that nobody cares a straw for the internal administration of Native States so long as oppression and crime are kept within decent limits, and the ruler is not drugged, drunk, or diseased from one end of the year to the other. They are the dark places of the earth, full of unimaginable cruelty, touching the Railway and the Telegraph on one side, and, on the other, the days of Harun-al-Raschid.[7] When I left the train I did business with divers Kings,[8] and in eight days passed through many changes of life. Sometimes I wore dress-clothes and consorted with Princes and Politicals,[9] drinking from crystal and eating from silver. Sometimes I lay out upon the ground and devoured what I could get, from a plate made of leaves, and drank the running water, and slept under the same rug as my servant. It was all in the day's work.

Then I headed for the Great Indian Desert upon the proper date, as I had promised, and the night mail set me down at Marwar Junction, where a funny, little, happy-go-lucky, native-managed railway runs to Jodhpore. The Bombay Mail from Delhi makes a short halt at Marwar. She arrived as I got in, and I had just time to hurry to her platform and go down the carriages. There was only one second-class on the train. I slipped the window and looked down upon a flaming red beard, half covered by a railway rug. That was my man, fast asleep, and I dug him gently in the ribs. He woke with a grunt, and I saw his face in the light of the lamps. It was a great and shining face.

'Tickets again?' said he.

'No,' said I. 'I am to tell you that he has gone South for the week. He has gone South for the week!'

The train had begun to move out. The red man rubbed his eyes. 'He has gone South for the week,' he repeated. 'Now that's just like his impidence. Did he say that I was to give you anything? Cause I won't.'

'He didn't,' I said, and dropped away, and watched the red lights die out in the dark. It was horribly cold because the wind was blowing off the sands. I climbed into my own train – not an Intermediate carriage this time – and went to sleep.

If the man with the beard had given me a rupee I should have kept it as a memento of a rather curious affair. But the consciousness of having done my duty was my only reward.

Later on I reflected that two gentlemen like my friends could not do any good if they forgathered and personated correspondents of newspapers, and might, if they blackmailed one of the little rat-trap states of Central India or Southern Rajputana, get themselves into serious difficulties. I therefore took some trouble to describe them as accurately as I could remember to people who would be interested in deporting them; and succeeded, so I was later informed, in having them headed back from the Degumber borders.

Then I became respectable, and returned to an office where there were no Kings and no incidents outside the daily manufacture of a newspaper. A newspaper office seems to attract every conceivable sort of person, to the prejudice of discipline. Zenana-mission ladies[10] arrive, and beg that the Editor will instantly abandon all his duties to describe

a Christian prize-giving in a back-slum of a perfectly inaccessible village;
Colonels who have been overpassed for command sit down and sketch
the outline of a series of ten, twelve, or twenty-four leading articles on
Seniority *versus* Selection; Missionaries wish to know why they have
not been permitted to escape from their regular vehicles of abuse and
swear at a brother-missionary under special patronage of the editorial
We; stranded theatrical companies troop up to explain that they cannot
pay for their advertisements, but on their return from New Zealand or
Tahiti will do so with interest; inventors of patent punkah-pulling
machines, carriage couplings, and unbreakable swords and axle-trees,
call with specifications in their pockets and hours at their disposal;
tea-companies enter and elaborate their prospectuses with the office
pens; secretaries of ball-committees clamour to have the glories of their
last dance more fully described; strange ladies rustle in and say, 'I want
a hundred lady's cards printed *at once*, please,' which is manifestly part
of an Editor's duty; and every dissolute ruffian that ever tramped the
Grand Trunk Road makes it his business to ask for employment as a
proof-reader. And, all the time, the telephone-bell is ringing madly, and
Kings are being killed on the Continent, and Empires are saying, 'You're
another,' and Mister Gladstone[11] is calling down brimstone upon the
British Dominions, and the little black copy-boys are whining, '*kaa-pi
chay-ha-yeh*' [copy wanted] like tired bees, and most of the paper is as
blank as Modred's shield.[12]

But that is the amusing part of the year. There are six other months
when none ever comes to call, and the thermometer walks inch by inch
up to the top of the glass, and the office is darkened to just above reading-
light, and the press-machines are red-hot of touch, and nobody writes
anything but accounts of amusements in the Hill-stations or obituary
notices. Then the telephone becomes a tinkling terror, because it tells you
of the sudden deaths of men and women that you knew intimately, and
the prickly-heat covers you with a garment, and you sit down and write:
'A slight increase of sickness is reported from the Khuda Janta Khan
District. The outbreak is purely sporadic in its nature, and, thanks to the
energetic efforts of the District authorities, is now almost at an end. It
is, however, with deep regret we record the death, etc.'

Then the sickness really breaks out, and the less recording and
reporting the better for the peace of the subscribers. But the Empires
and the Kings continue to divert themselves as selfishly as before, and
the Foreman thinks that a daily paper really ought to come out once
in twenty-four hours, and all the people at the Hill-stations in the middle
of their amusements say: 'Good gracious! Why can't the paper be
sparkling? I'm sure there's plenty going on up here.'

That is the dark half of the moon, and, as the advertisements say, 'must be experienced to be appreciated.'

It was in that season, and a remarkably evil season, that the paper began running the last issue of the week on Saturday night, which is to say Sunday morning, after the custom of a London paper. This was a great convenience, for immediately after the paper was put to bed, the dawn would lower the thermometer from 96° to almost 84° for half an hour, and in that chill – you have no idea how cold is 84° on the grass until you begin to pray for it – a very tired man could get off to sleep ere the heat roused him.

One Saturday night it was my pleasant duty to put the paper to bed alone. A King or a courtier or courtesan or a Community was going to die or get a new Constitution, or do something that was important on the other side of the world, and the paper was to be held open till the latest possible minute in order to catch the telegram.

It was a pitchy black night, as stifling as a June night can be, and the *loo*, the red-hot wind from the westward, was booming among the tinder-dry trees and pretending that the rain was on its heels. Now and again a spot of almost boiling water would fall on the dust with the flop of a frog, but all our weary world knew that was only pretence. It was a shade cooler in the press-room than the office, so I sat there, while the type ticked and clicked, and the night-jars hooted at the windows, and the all but naked compositors wiped the sweat from their foreheads, and called for water. The thing that was keeping us back, whatever it was, would not come off, though the *loo* dropped and the last type was set, and the whole round earth stood still in the choking heat, with its finger on its lip, to wait the event. I drowsed, and wondered whether the telegraph was a blessing, and whether this dying man, or struggling people, might be aware of the inconvenience the delay was causing. There was no special reason beyond the heat and worry to make tension, but, as the clock-hands crept up to three o'clock, and the machines spun their fly-wheels two or three times to see that all was in order before I said the word that would set them off, I could have shrieked aloud.

Then the roar and rattle of the wheels shivered the quiet into little bits. I rose to go away, but two men in white clothes stood in front of me. The first one said: 'It's him!' The second said: 'So it is!' And they both laughed almost as loudly as the machinery roared, and mopped their foreheads. 'We seed there was a light burning across the road, and we were sleeping in that ditch there for coolness, and I said to my friend here, "The office is open. Let's come along and speak to him as turned us back from the Degumber State,"' said the smaller of the two. He was the man I had met in the Mhow train, and his fellow was the red-haired man of

Marwar Junction. There was no mistaking the eyebrows of the one or the beard of the other.

I was not pleased, because I wished to go to sleep, not to squabble with loafers. 'What do you want?' I asked.

'Half an hour's talk with you, cool and comfortable, in the office,' said the red-bearded man. 'We'd *like* some drink – the Contrack doesn't begin yet, Peachey, so you needn't look – but what we really want is advice. We don't want money. We ask you as a favour, because we found out you did us a bad turn about Degumber State.'

I led from the press-room to the stifling office with the maps on the walls, and the red-haired man rubbed his hands. 'That's something like,' said he. 'This was the proper shop to come to. Now, sir, let me introduce to you Brother Peachey Carnehan, that's him, and Brother Daniel Dravot, that is *me*, and the less said about our professions the better, for we have been most things in our time. Soldier, sailor, compositor, photographer, proof-reader, street-preacher, *and* correspondent of the *Backwoodsman* when we thought the paper wanted one. Carnehan is sober, and so am I. Look at us first, and see that's sure. It will save you cutting into my talk. We'll take one of your cigars apiece, and you shall see us light up.'

I watched the test. The men were absolutely sober, so I gave them each a tepid whisky and soda.

'Well *and* good,' said Carnehan of the eyebrows, wiping the froth from his moustache. 'Let *me* talk now, Dan. We have been all over India, mostly on foot. We have been boiler-fitters, engine-drivers, petty contractors, and all that, and we have decided that India isn't big enough for such as us.'

They certainly were too big for the office. Dravot's beard seemed to fill half the room and Carnehan's shoulders the other half, as they sat on the big table. Carnehan continued: 'The country isn't half worked out because they that governs it won't let you touch it. They spend all their blessed time in governing it, and you can't lift a spade, nor chip a rock, nor look for oil, nor anything like that, without all the Government saying, "Leave it alone, and let us govern." Therefore, such *as* it is, we will let it alone, and go away to some other place where a man isn't crowded and can come to his own. We are not little men, and there is nothing that we are afraid of except Drink, and we have signed a Contrack on that. *Therefore*, we are going away to be Kings.'

'Kings in our own right,' muttered Dravot.

'Yes, of course,' I said. 'You've been tramping in the sun, and it's a very warm night, and hadn't you better sleep over the notion? Come to-morrow.'

'Neither drunk nor sunstruck,' said Dravot. 'We have slept over the notion half a year, and require to see Books and Atlases, and we have decided that there is only one place now in the world that two strong men can Sar-a-*whack*.[13] They call it Kafiristan.[14]. By my reckoning it's the top right-hand corner of Afghanistan, not more than three hundred miles from Peshawur.

They have two-and-thirty heathen idols there, and we'll be the thirty-third and fourth. It's a mountaineous country, and the women of those parts are very beautiful.'

'But that is provided against in the Contrack,' said Carnehan. 'Neither Woman nor Liqu-or, Daniel.'

'And that's all we know, except that no one has gone there, and they fight; and in any place where they fight, a man who knows how to drill men can always be a King. We shall go to those parts and say to any King we find – "D'you want to vanquish your foes?" and we will show him how to drill men; for that we know better than anything else. Then we will subvert that King and seize his Throne and establish a Dy-nasty.'

'You'll be cut to pieces before you're fifty miles across the Border,' I said. 'You have to travel through Afghanistan to get to that country. It's one mass of mountains and peaks and glaciers, and no Englishman has been through it. The people are utter brutes, and even if you reached them you couldn't do anything.'

'That's more like,' said Carnehan. 'If you could think us a little more mad we would be more pleased. We have come to you to know about this country, to read a book about it, and to be shown maps. We want you to tell us that we are fools and to show us your books.' He turned to the bookcases.

'Are you at all in earnest?' I said.

'A little,' said Dravot sweetly. 'As big a map as you have got, even if it's all blank where Kafiristan is, and any books you've got. We can read, though we aren't very educated.'

I uncased the big thirty-two-miles-to-the-inch map of India, and two smaller Frontier maps, hauled down volume INF-KAN of the *Encyclopedia Britannica*, and the men consulted them.

'See here!' said Dravot, his thumb on the map. 'Up to Jagdallak, Peachey and me know the road. We was there with Roberts' Army.[15] We'll have to turn off to the right at Jagdallak through Laghman territory. Then we get among the hills – fourteen thousand feet – fifteen thousand – it will be cold work there, but it don't look very far on the map.'

I handed him Wood on the *Sources of the Oxus*.[16] Carnehan was deep in the *Encyclopedia*.

'They're a mixed lot,' said Dravot reflectively; 'and it won't help us to know the names of their tribes. The more tribes the more they'll fight, and the better for us. From Jagdallak to Ashang – H'mm!'

'But all the information about the country is as sketchy and inaccurate as can be,' I protested. 'No one knows anything about it really. Here's the file of the *United Services' Institute*.[17] Read what Bellew[18] says.'

'Blow Bellew!' said Carnehan. 'Dan, they're a stinkin' lot of heathens, but this book here says they think they're related to us English.'

I smoked while the men pored over Raverty,[19] Wood, the maps, and the *Encyclopedia*.

'There is no use your waiting,' said Dravot politely. 'It's about four o'clock now. We'll go before six o'clock if you want to sleep, and we won't steal any of the papers. Don't you sit up. We're two harmless lunatics, and if you come to-morrow evening down to the Serai we'll say good-bye to you.'

'You *are* two fools,' I answered. 'You'll be turned back at the Frontier or cut up the minute you set foot in Afghanistan. Do you want any money or a recommendation down-country? I can help you to the chance of work next week.'

'Next week we shall be hard at work ourselves, thank you,' said Dravot. 'It isn't so easy being a King as it looks. When we've got our Kingdom in going order we'll let you know, and you can come up and help us to govern it.'

'Would two lunatics make a Contrack like that?' said Carnehan, with subdued pride, showing me a greasy half-sheet of notepaper on which was written the following. I copied it, then and there, as a curiosity:

This Contract between me and you persuing witnesseth in the name of God – Amen and so forth.

(One)   That me and you will settle this matter together; i.e. to be Kings of Kafiristan.

(Two)   That you and me will not, while this matter is being settled, look at any Liquor, nor any Woman black, white, or brown, so as to get mixed up with one or the other harmful.

(Three) That we conduct ourselves with Dignity and Discretion, and if one of us gets into trouble the other will stay by him.

    Signed by you and me this day.

      Peachey Taliaferro Carnehan.

      Daniel Dravot.

      Both Gentlemen at Large.

'There was no need for the last article,' said Carnehan, blushing modestly; 'but it looks regular. Now you know the sort of men that loafers are – we *are* loafers, Dan, until we get out of India – and *do* you think that we would sign a Contrack like that unless we was in earnest? We have kept away from the two things that make life worth having.'

'You won't enjoy your lives much longer if you are going to try this idiotic adventure. Don't set the office on fire,' I said, 'and go away before nine o'clock.'

I left them still poring over the maps and making notes on the back of the 'Contrack'. 'Be sure to come down to the Serai to-morrow,' were their parting words.

The Kumharsen Serai is the great four-square sink of humanity where the strings of camels and horses from the North load and unload. All the nationalities of Central Asia may be found there, and most of the folk of India proper. Balkh and Bokhara there meet Bengal and Bombay, and try to draw eye-teeth. You can buy ponies, turquoises, Persian pussy-cats, saddle-bags, fat-tailed sheep and musk in the Kumharsen Serai, and get many strange things for nothing. In the afternoon I went down to see whether my friends intended to keep their word or were lying there drunk.

A priest attired in fragments of ribbons and rags stalked up to me, gravely twisting a child's paper whirligig. Behind him was his servant bending under the load of a crate of mud toys. The two were loading up two camels, and the inhabitants of the Serai watched them with shrieks of laughter.

'The priest is mad,' said a horse-dealer to me. 'He is going up to Kabul to sell toys to the Amir. He will either be raised to honour or have his head cut off. He came in here this morning and has been behaving madly ever since.'

'The witless are under the protection of God,' stammered a flat-cheeked Uzbeg in broken Hindi. 'They foretell future events.'

'Would they could have foretold that my caravan would have been cut up by the Shinwaris almost within shadow of the Pass!' grunted the Yusufzai agent of a Rajputana trading-house whose goods had been diverted into the hands of other robbers just across the Border, and whose misfortunes were the laughing-stock of the bazar. 'Ohé, priest, whence come you and whither do you go?'

'From Roum[20] have I come,' shouted the priest, waving his whirligig; 'from Roum, blown by the breath of a hundred devils across the sea! O thieves, robbers, liars, the blessing of Pir Khan on pigs, dogs, and perjurers! Who will take the Protected of God[21] to the North to sell

charms that are never still to the Amir? The camels shall not gall, the
sons shall not fall sick, and the wives shall remain faithful while they
are away, of the men who give me place in their caravan. Who will
assist me to slipper the King of the Roos[22] with a golden slipper with
a silver heel? The protection of Pir Khan[23] be upon his labours!' He
spread out the skirts of his gaberdine and pirouetted between the lines
of tethered horses.

'There starts a caravan from Peshawur to Kabul in twenty days,
Huzrut,'[24] said the Yusufzai trader. 'My camels go therewith. Do thou
also go and bring us good luck.'

'I will go even now!' shouted the priest. 'I will depart upon my
winged camels, and be at Peshawur in a day! Ho! Hazar[25] Mir Khan,'
he yelled to his servant, 'drive out the camels, but let me first mount
my own.'

He leaped on the back of his beast as it knelt, and, turning round to
me, cried: 'Come thou also, Sahib, a little along the road, and I will sell
thee a charm – an amulet that shall make thee King of Kafiristan.'

Then the light broke upon me, and I followed the two camels out
of the Serai till we reached open road and the priest halted.

'What d'you think o' that?' said he in English. 'Carnehan can't talk
their patter, so I've made him my servant. He makes a handsome servant.
'Tisn't for nothing that I've been knocking about the country for
fourteen years. Didn't I do that talk neat? We'll hitch on to a caravan
at Peshawur till we get to Jagdallak, and then we'll see if we can get
donkeys for our camels, and strike into Kafiristan. Whirligigs for the
Amir, oh, Lor! Put your hand under the camel-bags and tell me what
you feel.'

I felt the butt of a Martini,[26] and another and another.

'Twenty of 'em,' said Dravot placidly. 'Twenty of 'em and ammunition
to correspond, under the whirligigs and the mud dolls.'

'Heaven help you if you are caught with those things!' I said. 'A
Martini is worth her weight in silver among the Pathans.'

'Fifteen hundred rupees of capital – every rupee we could beg,
borrow, or steal – are invested on these two camels,' said Dravot. 'We
won't get caught. We're going through the Khyber[27] with a regular
caravan. Who'd touch a poor mad priest?'

'Have you got everything you want?' I asked, overcome with
astonishment.

'Not yet, but we shall soon. Give us a memento of your kindness,
Brother. You did me a service, yesterday, and that time in Marwar. Half
my Kingdom shall you have, as the saying is.' I slipped a small charm
compass[28] from my watch-chain and handed it up to the priest.

'Good-bye,' said Dravot, giving me hand cautiously. 'It's the last time we'll shake hands with an Englishman these many days. Shake hands with him, Carnehan,' he cried, as the second camel passed me.

Carnehan leaned down and shook hands. Then the camels passed away along the dusty road, and I was left alone to wonder. My eye could detect no failure in the disguises. The scene in the Serai proved that they were complete to the native mind. There was just the chance, therefore, that Carnehan and Dravot would be able to wander through Afghanistan without detection. But, beyond, they would find death – certain and awful death.

Ten days later a native correspondent, giving me the news of the day from Peshawur, wound up his letter with: 'There has been much laughter here on account of a certain mad priest who is going in his estimation to sell petty gauds and insignificant trinkets which he ascribes as great charms to HH the Amir of Bokhara. He passed through Peshawur and associated himself to the Second Summer caravan that goes to Kabul. The merchants are pleased because through superstition they imagine that such mad fellows bring good fortune.'

The two, then, were beyond the Border. I would have prayed for them, but, that night, a real King died in Europe, and demanded an obituary notice.

The wheel of the world swings through the same phases again and again. Summer passed and winter thereafter, and came and passed again. The daily paper continued and I with it, and upon the third summer there fell a hot night, a night-issue, and a strained waiting for something to be telegraphed from the other side of the world, exactly as had happened before. A few great men had died in the past two years, the machines worked with more clatter, and some of the trees in the office garden were a few feet taller. But that was all the difference.

I passed over to the press-room, and went through just such a scene as I have already described. The nervous tension was stronger than it had been two years before, and I felt the heat more acutely. At three o'clock I cried, 'Print off,' and turned to go, when there crept to my chair what was left of a man. He was bent into a circle, his head was sunk between his shoulders, and he moved his feet one over the other like a bear. I could hardly see whether he walked or crawled – this rag-wrapped, whining cripple who addressed me by name, crying that he was come back. 'Can you give me a drink?' he whimpered. 'For the Lord's sake, give me a drink!'

I went back to the office, the man following with groans of pain, and I turned up the lamp.

'Don't you know me?' he gasped, dropping into a chair, and he turned his drawn face, surmounted by a shock of grey hair, to the light.

I looked at him intently. Once before had I seen eyebrows that met over the nose in an inch-broad black band, but for the life of me I could not recall where.

'I don't know you,' I said, handing him the whisky. 'What can I do for you?'

He took a gulp of the spirit raw, and shivered in spite of the suffocating heat.

'I've come back,' he repeated; 'and I was the King of Kafiristan – me and Dravot – crowned Kings we was! In this office we settled it – you setting there and giving us the books. I am Peachey – Peachey Taliaferro Carnehan, and you've been setting here ever since – oh, Lord!'

I was more than a little astonished, and expressed my feelings accordingly.

'It's true,' said Carnehan, with a dry cackle, nursing his feet, which were wrapped in rags. 'True as gospel. Kings we were, with crowns upon our heads – me and Dravot – poor Dan – oh, poor, poor Dan, that would never take advice, not though I begged of him!'

'Take the whisky,' I said, 'and take your own time. Tell me all you can recollect of everything from beginning to end. You got across the Border on your camels, Dravot dressed as a mad priest and you his servant. Do you remember that?'

'I ain't mad – yet, but I shall be that way soon. Of course I remember. Keep looking at me, or maybe my words will go all to pieces. Keep looking at me in my eyes and don't say anything.'

I leaned forward and looked into his face as steadily as I could. He dropped one hand upon the table and I grasped it by the wrist. It was twisted like a bird's claw, and upon the back was a ragged red diamond-shaped scar.

'No, don't look there. Look at *me*,' said Carnehan. 'That comes afterwards, but for the Lord's sake don't distrack me. We left with that caravan, me and Dravot playing all sorts of antics to amuse the people we were with. Dravot used to make us laugh in the evenings when all the people was cooking their dinners – cooking their dinners, and . . . what did they do then? They lit little fires with sparks that went into Dravot's beard, and we all laughed – fit to die. Little red fires they was, going into Dravot's big red beard – so funny.' His eyes left mine and he smiled foolishly.

'You went as far as Jagdallak with that caravan,' I said at a venture, 'after you had lit those fires. To Jagdallak where you turned off to try to get into Kafiristan.'

'No, we didn't neither. What are you talking about? We turned off before Jagdallak, because we heard the roads was good. But they wasn't good enough for our two camels – mine and Dravot's. When we left the caravan, Dravot took off all his clothes and mine too, and said we would be heathen, because the Kafirs didn't allow Mohammedans to talk to them. So we dressed betwixt and between, and such a sight as Daniel Dravot I never saw yet nor expect to see again. He burned half his beard, and slung a sheep-skin over his shoulder, and shaved his head into patterns. He shaved mine, too, and made me wear outrageous things to look like a heathen. That was in a most mountaineous country, and our camels couldn't go along any more because of the mountains. They were tall and black, and coming home I saw them fight like wild goats – there are lots of goats in Kafiristan. And these mountains, they never keep still, no more than the goats. Always fighting they are, and don't let you sleep at night.'

'Take some more whisky,' I said very slowly. 'What did you and Daniel Dravot do when the camels could go no farther because of the rough roads that led into Kafiristan?'

'What did which do? There was a party called Peachey Taliaferro Carnehan that was with Dravot. Shall I tell you about him? He died out there in the cold. Slap from the bridge fell old Peachey, turning and twisting in the air like a penny whirligig that you can sell to the Amir. – No; they was two for three-ha'pence, those whirligigs, or I am much mistaken and woeful sore . . . And then these camels were no use, and Peachey said to Dravot – "For the Lord's sake let's get out of this before our heads are chopped off," and with that they killed the camels all among the mountains, not having anything in particular to eat, but first they took off the boxes with the guns and the ammunition, till two men came along driving four mules. Dravot up and dances in front of them, singing: "Sell me four mules." Says the first man: "If you are rich enough to buy, you are rich enough to rob"; but before ever he could put his hand to his knife, Dravot breaks his neck over his knee, and the other party runs away. So Carnehan loaded the mules with the rifles that was taken off the camels, and together we starts forward into those bitter cold mountaineous parts, and never a road broader than the back of your hand.'

He paused for a moment, while I asked him if he could remember the nature of the country through which he had journeyed.

'I am telling you as straight as I can, but my head isn't as good as it might be. They drove nails through it to make me hear better how Dravot died. The country was mountaineous, and the mules were most contrary, and the inhabitants was dispersed and solitary. They went up and up, and down and down, and that other party, Carnehan, was imploring of Dravot not to sing and whistle so loud, for fear of bringing down the tremenjus avalanches. But Dravot says that if a King couldn't sing it wasn't worth being King, and whacked the mules over the rump, and never took no heed for ten cold days. We came to a big level valley all among the mountains, and the mules were near dead, so we killed them, not having anything in special for them or us to eat. We sat upon the boxes, and played odd and even with the cartridges that was jolted out.

'Then ten men with bows and arrows ran down that valley, chasing twenty men with bows and arrows, and the row was tremenjus. They was fair men – fairer than you or me – with yellow hair and remarkable well built. Says Dravot, unpacking the guns: "This is the beginning of the business. We'll fight for the ten men," and with that he fires two rifles at the twenty men, and drops one of them at two hundred yards from the rock where he was sitting. The other men began to run, but Carnehan and Dravot sits on the boxes picking them off at all ranges, up and down the valley. Then we goes up to the ten men that had run across the snow too, and they fires a footy little arrow at us. Dravot he shoots above their heads and they all falls down flat. Then he walks over them and kicks them, and then he lifts them up and shakes hands all round to make them friendly like. He calls them and gives them the boxes to carry, and waves his hand for all the world as though he was King already. They takes the boxes and him across the valley and up the hill into a pine-wood on the top, where there was half-a-dozen big stone idols. Dravot he goes to the biggest – a fellow they call Imbra[29] – and lays a rifle and a cartridge at his feet, rubbing his nose respectful with his own nose, patting him on the head, and saluting in front of it. He turns round to the men and nods his head, and says: "That's all right. I'm in the know too, and all these old jim-jams[30] are my friends." Then he opens his mouth and points down it, and when the first man brings him food, he says: "No"; and when the second man brings him food, he says: "No"; but when one of the old priests and the boss of the village brings him food, he says: "Yes," very haughty, and eats it slow. That was how we came to our first village, without any trouble, just as though we had tumbled from the skies. But we tumbled from one of those damned rope-bridges, you see, and – you couldn't expect a man to laugh much after that?'

'Take some more whisky and go on,' I said. 'That was the first village you came into. How did you get to be King?'

'I wasn't King,' said Carnehan. 'Dravot he was the King, and a handsome man he looked with the gold crown on his head and all.

Him and the other party stayed in that village, and every morning
Dravot sat by the side of old Imbra, and the people came and worshipped. That was Dravot's order. Then a lot of men came into the valley,
and Carnehan and Dravot picks them off with the rifles before they
knew where they was, and runs down into the valley and up again the
other side and finds another village, same as the first one, and the people
all falls down flat on their faces, and Dravot says: "Now what is the
trouble between you two villages?" and the people points to a woman,
as fair as you or me, that was carried off, and Dravot takes her back
to the first village and counts up the dead – eight there was. For each
dead man Dravot pours a little milk on the ground and waves his arms
like a whirligig, and "That's all right," says he. Then he and Carnehan
takes the big boss of each village by the arm and walks them down
into the valley, and shows them how to scratch a line with a spear right
down the valley, and gives each a sod of turf from both sides of the
line. Then all the people comes down and shouts like the devil and all,
and Dravot says: "Go and dig the land, and be fruitful and multiply,"[31]
which they did, though they didn't understand. Then we asks the names
of things in their lingo – bread and water and fire and idols and such,
and Dravot leads the priest of each village up to the idol, and says he
must sit there and judge the people, and if anything goes wrong he is
to be shot.

'Next week they was all turning up the land in the valley as quiet
as bees and much prettier, and the priests heard all the complaints and
told Dravot in dumb show what it was about. "That's just the beginning," says Dravot. "They think we're Gods." He and Carnehan picks
out twenty good men and shows them how to click off a rifle, and form
fours, and advance in line, and they was very pleased to do so, and
clever to see the hang of it. Then he takes out his pipe and his baccy-
pouch and leaves one at one village, and one at the other, and off we
two goes to see what was to be done in the next valley. That was all
rock, and there was a little village there, and Carnehan says: "Send 'em
to the old valley to plant," and takes 'em there, and gives 'em some
land that wasn't took before. They were a poor lot, and we blooded
'em with a kid before letting 'em into the new Kingdom. That was to
impress the people, and then they settled down quiet, and Carnehan
went back to Dravot, who had got into another valley, all snow and
ice and most mountaineous. There was no people there and the Army
got afraid, so Dravot shoots one of them, and goes on till he finds some
people in a village, and the Army explains that unless the people wants
to be killed they had better not shoot their little matchlocks;[32] for they
had matchlocks. We makes friends with the priest, and I stays there

alone with two of the Army, teaching the men how to drill, and a thundering big Chief comes across the snow with kettle-drums and horns twanging, because he heard there was a new God kicking about. Carnehan sights for the brown of the men half a mile across the snow and wings one of them. Then he sends a message to the Chief that, unless he wished to be killed, he must come and shake hands with me and leave his arms behind. The Chief comes alone first, and Carnehan shakes hands with him and whirls his arms about, same as Dravot used, and very much surprised that Chief was, and strokes my eyebrows. Then Carnehan goes alone to the Chief, and asks him in dumb show if he had an enemy he hated. "I have," says the Chief. So Carnehan weeds out the pick of his men, and sets the two of the Army to show them drill, and at the end of two weeks the men can manoeuvre about as well as Volunteers. So he marches with the Chief to a great big plain on the top of a mountain, and the Chief's men rushes into a village and takes it; we three Martinis firing into the brown of the enemy. So we took that village too, and I gives the Chief a rag from my coat and says, "Occupy till I come";[33] which was scriptural. By way of a reminder, when me and the Army was eighteen hundred yards away, I drops a bullet near him standing on the snow, and all the people falls flat on their faces. Then I sends a letter to Dravot wherever he be by land or by sea.'

At the risk of throwing the creature out of train I interrupted: 'How could you write a letter up yonder?'

'The letter? – Oh! – The letter! Keep looking at me between the eyes, please. It was a string-talk letter, that we'd learned the way of it from a blind beggar in the Punjab.'

I remembered that there had once come to the office a blind man with a knotted twig and a piece of string which he wound round the twig according to some cipher of his own. He could, after the lapse of days or weeks, repeat the sentence which he had reeled up. He had reduced the alphabet to eleven primitive sounds, and tried to teach me his method, but I could not understand.

'I sent that letter to Dravot,' said Carnehan; 'and told him to come back because this Kingdom was growing too big for me to handle, and then I struck for the first valley, to see how the priests were working. They called the village we took along with the Chief, Bashkai, and the first village we took, Er-Heb. The priests at Er-Heb was doing all right, but they had a lot of pending cases about land to show me, and some men from another village had been firing arrows at night. I went out and looked for that village, and fired four rounds at it from a thousand yards. That used all the cartridges I cared to spend, and I waited for Dravot, who had been away two or three months, and I kept my people quiet.

'One morning I heard the devil's own noise of drums and horns, and Dan Dravot marches down the hill with his Army and a tail of hundreds of men, and, which was the most amazing, a great gold crown on his head. "My Gord, Carnehan," says Daniel, "this is a tremenjus business, and we've got the whole country as far as it's worth having. I am the son of Alexander by Queen Semiramis,[34] and you're my younger brother and a God too! It's the biggest thing we've ever seen. I've been marching and fighting for six weeks with the Army, and every footy little village for fifty miles has come in rejoiceful; and more than that, I've got the key of the whole show, as you'll see, and I've got a crown for you! I told 'em to make two of 'em at a place called Shu, where the gold lies in the rock like suet in mutton. Gold I've seen, and turquoise I've kicked out of the cliffs, and there's garnets in the sands of the river, and here's a chunk of amber that a man brought me. Call up all the priests and, here, take your crown."

'One of the men opens a black hair bag, and I slips the crown on. It was too small and too heavy, but I wore it for the glory. Hammered gold it was – five pound weight, like a hoop of a barrel.

'"Peachey," says Dravot, "we don't want to fight no more. The Craft's the trick,[35] so help me!" and he brings forward that same Chief that I left at Bashkai – Billy Fish we called him afterwards, because he was so like Billy Fish that drove the big tank-engine at Mach on the Bolan[36] in the old days. "Shake hands with him," says Dravot, and I shook hands and nearly dropped, for Billy Fish gave me the Grip. I said nothing, but tried him with the Fellow Craft Grip.[37] He answers all right, and I tried the Master's Grip, but that was a slip. "A Fellow Craft he is!" I says to Dan. "Does he know the Word?" – "He does," says Dan, "and all the priests know. It's a miracle! The Chiefs and the priests can work a Fellow Craft Lodge in a way that's very like ours, and they've cut the marks on the rocks,[38] but they don't know the Third Degree, and they've come to find out. It's Gord's Truth! I've known these long years that the Afghans knew up to the Fellow Craft Degree, but this is a miracle. A God and a Grand-Master of the Craft am I, and a Lodge in the Third Degree I will open, and we'll raise the head priests and the Chiefs of the villages."

'"It's against all the law,"[39] I says, "holding a Lodge without warrant from any one; and you know we never held office in any Lodge."

'"It's a master-stroke o' policy," says Dravot. "It means running the country as easy as a four-wheeled bogie on a down grade. We can't stop to inquire now, or they'll turn against us. I've forty Chiefs at my heel, and passed and raised according to their merit they shall be. Billet these men on the villages, and see that we run up a Lodge of some kind. The temple of Imbra will do for the Lodge-room. The women must make aprons as you show them. I'll hold a levee of Chiefs to-night and Lodge to-morrow."

'I was fair run off my legs, but I wasn't such a fool as not to see what a pull this Craft business gave us. I showed the priests' families how to make aprons of the degrees, but for Dravot's apron[40] the blue border and marks was made of turquoise lumps on white hide, not cloth. We took a great square stone in the temple for the Master's chair, and little stones for the officers' chairs, and painted the black pavement with white squares, and did what we could to make things regular.

'At the levee which was held that night on the hillside with big bonfires, Dravot gives out that him and me were Gods and sons of Alexander,[41] and Past Grand-Masters in the Craft, and was come to make Kafiristan a country where every man should eat in peace and drink in quiet, and 'specially obey us. Then the Chiefs come round to shake hands, and they were so hairy and white and fair it was just shaking hands with old friends. We gave them names according as they was like men we had known in India – Billy Fish, Holly Dilworth, Pikky Kergan, that was Bazar-master when I was at Mhow, and so on, and so on.

'The most amazing miracles was at Lodge next night. One of the old priests was watching us continuous, and I felt uneasy, for I knew we'd have to fudge the Ritual, and I didn't know what the men knew. The old priest was a stranger come in from beyond the village of Bashkai. The minute Dravot puts on the Master's apron that the girls had made for him, the priest fetches a whoop and a howl, and tries to overturn the stone that Dravot was sitting on. "It's all up now," I says. "That comes of meddling with the Craft without warrant!" Dravot never winked an eye, not when ten priests took and tilted over the Grand-Master's chair – which was to say the stone of Imbra. The priest begins rubbing the bottom end of it to clear away the black dirt, and presently he shows all the other priests the Master's Mark,[42] same as was on Dravot's apron, cut into the stone. Not even the priests of the temple of Imbra knew it was there. The old chap falls flat on his face at Dravot's feet and kisses 'em. "Luck again," says Dravot, across the Lodge to me; "they say it's the missing Mark that no one could understand the why of. We're more than safe now." Then he bangs the butt of his gun for a gavel and says: "By virtue of the authority vested in me by my own right hand[43] and the help of Peachey, I declare myself Grand-Master of all Freemasonry in Kafiristan in this the Mother Lodge o' the country, and King of Kafiristan equally with Peachey!" At that he puts on his crown and I puts on mine – I was doing Senior Warden – and we opens the Lodge in most ample form. It was a amazing miracle! The priests moved in Lodge through the first two degrees almost without telling, as if the memory was coming back to them. After that, Peachey and Dravot raised such as was worthy – high priests and Chiefs of far-off villages. Billy Fish was the first, and I can tell you we scared the soul out of him. It was not in any way according to Ritual, but it served our turn. We didn't raise more than ten of the biggest men, because we didn't want to make the Degree common. And they was clamouring to be raised.

'"In another six months," says Dravot, "we'll hold another Communication,[44] and see how you are working." Then he asks them about their villages, and learns that they was fighting one against the other, and was sick and tired of it. And when they wasn't doing that they was fighting with the Mohammedans. "You can fight those when they come into our country," says Dravot. "Tell off every tenth man of your tribes for a Frontier guard, and send two hundred at a time to this valley to be drilled. Nobody is going to be shot or speared any more so long as he does well, and I know that you won't cheat me, because you're white people – sons of Alexander – and not like common, black Mohammedans. You are *my* people, and by God," says he, running off into English at the end, "I'll make a damned fine Nation of you, or I'll die in the making!"

'I can't tell all we did for the next six months, because Dravot did a lot I couldn't see the hang of, and he learned their lingo in a way I never could. My work was to help the people plough, and now and again go out with some of the Army and see what the other villages were doing, and make 'em throw rope-bridges across the ravines which cut up the country horrid. Dravot was very kind to me, but when he walked up and down in the pine-wood pulling that bloody red beard of his with both fists I knew he was thinking plans I could not advise about, and I just waited for orders.

'But Dravot never showed me disrespect before the people. They were afraid of me and the Army, but they loved Dan. He was the best of friends with the priests and the Chiefs; but any one could come across the hills with a complaint, and Dravot would hear him out fair, and call four priests together and say what was to be done. He used to call in Billy Fish from Bashkai, and Pikky Kergan from Shu, and an old Chief we called Kafoozelum – it was like enough to his real name – and hold councils with 'em when there was any fighting to be done in small villages. That was his Council of War, and the four priests of Bashkai, Shu, Khawak, and Madora was his Privy Council. Between the lot of 'em they sent me, with forty men and twenty rifles and sixty men carrying turquoises, into the Ghorband country to buy those hand-made Martini rifles, that come out of the Amir's workshops at Kabul, from one of the Amir's Herati regiments that would have sold the very teeth out of their mouths for turquoises.

'I stayed in Ghorband a month, and gave the Governor there the pick of my baskets for hush-money, and bribed the Colonel of the regiment some more, and, between the two and the tribespeople, we got more than a hundred hand-made Martinis, a hundred good Kohat *jezails*[45] that'll throw to six hundred yards, and forty man-loads of very bad ammunition for the rifles. I came back with what I had, and distributed 'em among the men that the Chiefs sent in to me to drill. Dravot was too busy to attend to those things, but the old Army that we first made helped me, and we turned out five hundred men that could drill, and two hundred that knew how to hold arms pretty straight. Even those corkscrewed, hand-made guns was a miracle to them. Dravot talked big about powder-shops and factories, walking up and down in the pine-wood when the winter was coming on.

'"I won't make a Nation," says he. "I'll make an Empire! These men aren't niggers; they're English! Look at their eyes – look at their mouths. Look at the way they stand up. They sit on chairs in their own houses. They're the Lost Tribes, or something like it, and they've grown to be English. I'll take a census in the spring if the priests don't get frightened. There must be a fair two million of 'em in these hills. The villages are full o' little children. Two million people – two hundred and fifty thousand fighting men – and all English! They only want the rifles and a little drilling. Two hundred and fifty thousand men, ready to cut in on Russia's right flank when she tries for India! Peachey, man," he says, chewing his beard in great hunks, "we shall be Emperors – Emperors of the Earth! Rajah Brooke[46] will be a suckling to us. I'll treat with the Viceroy on equal terms. I'll ask him to send me twelve picked English – twelve that I know of – to help us govern a bit. There's Mackray, Sergeant-pensioner at Segowli – many's the good dinner he's given me, and his wife a pair of trousers. There's Donkin, the Warder of Tounghoo Jail. There's hundreds that I could lay my hand on if I was in India. The Viceroy shall do it for me. I'll send a man through in the spring for those men, and I'll write for a Dispensation from the Grand Lodge for what I've done as Grand-Master. That – and all the Sniders[47] that'll be thrown out when the native troops in India take up the Martini. They'll be worn smooth, but they'll do for fighting in these hills. Twelve English, a hundred thousand Sniders run through the Amir's country in driblets – I'd be content with twenty thousand in one year – and we'd be an

Empire. When everything was shipshape, I'd hand over the crown – this crown I'm wearing now – to Queen Victoria on my knees, and she'd say: 'Rise up, Sir Daniel Dravot.' Oh, it's big! It's big, I tell you! But there's so much to be done in every place – Bashkai, Khawak, Shu, and everywhere else."

"'What is it?' I says. "There are no more men coming in to be drilled this autumn. Look at those fat, black clouds. They're bringing the snow."

"'It isn't that," says Daniel, putting his hand very hard on my shoulder; "and I don't wish to say anything that's against you, for no other living man would have followed me and made me what I am as you have done. You're a first-class Commander-in-Chief, and the people know you; but – it's a big country, and somehow you can't help me, Peachey, in the way I want to be helped."

"'Go to your blasted priests, then!' I said, and I was sorry when I made that remark, but it did hurt me sore to find Daniel talking so superior when I'd drilled all the men, and done all he told me.

"'Don't let's quarrel, Peachey," says Daniel without cursing. "You're a King too, and the half of this Kingdom is yours; but can't you see, Peachey, we want cleverer men than us now – three or four of 'em, that we can scatter about for our Deputies. It's a hugeous great State, and I can't always tell the right thing to do, and I haven't time for all I want to do, and here's winter coming on and all." He stuffed half his beard into his mouth, all red like the gold of his crown.

"'I'm sorry, Daniel," says I. "I've done all I could. I've drilled the men and shown the people how to stack their oats better; and I've brought in those tinware rifles from Ghorband – but I know what you're driving at. I take it Kings always feel oppressed that way."

"'There's another thing too," says Dravot, walking up and down. "The winter's coming and these people won't be giving much trouble, and if they do we can't move about. I want a wife."

"'For Gord's sake, leave the women alone!' I says. "We've both got all the work we can, though I *am* a fool. Remember the Contrack, and keep clear o' women."

"'The Contrack only lasted till such time as we was Kings; and Kings we have been these months past," says Dravot, weighing his crown in his hand. "You go get a wife too, Peachey – a nice, strappin', plump girl that'll keep you warm in the winter. They're prettier than English girls, and we can take the pick of 'em. Boil 'em once or twice in hot water and they'll come out like chicken and ham."

"'Don't tempt me!' I says. "I will not have any dealings with a woman not till we are a dam' sight more settled than we are now. I've been doing the work o' two men, and you've been doing the work o' three. Let's lie off a bit, and see if we can get some better tobacco from Afghan country and run in some good liquor; but no women."

'"Who's talking o' *women*?" says Dravot. "I said *wife* – a Queen to breed a King's son for the King. A Queen out of the strongest tribe, that'll make them your blood-brothers, and that'll lie by your side and tell you all the people thinks about you and their own affairs. That's what I want."

'"Do you remember that Bengali woman I kept at Mogul Serai when I was a platelayer?" says I. "A fat lot o' good she was to me. She taught me the lingo and one or two other things; but what happened? She ran away with the Station-master's servant and half my month's pay. Then she turned up at Dadur Junction in tow of a half-caste, and had the impidence to say I was her husband – all among the drivers in the running-shed too!"

'"We've done with that," says Dravot; "these women are whiter than you or me, and a Queen I will have for the winter months."

'"For the last time o' asking, Dan, do *not*," I says. "It'll only bring us harm. The Bible says that Kings ain't to waste their strength on women,[48] 'specially when they've got a raw new Kingdom to work over."

'"For the last time of answering, I will," said Dravot, and he went away through the pine-trees looking like a big red devil, the sun being on his crown and beard and all.

'But getting a wife was not as easy as Dan thought. He put it before the Council, and there was no answer till Billy Fish said that he'd better ask the girls. Dravot damned them all round. "What's wrong with me?" he shouts, standing by the idol Imbra. "Am I a dog or am I not enough of a man for your wenches? Haven't I put the shadow of my hand over this country? Who stopped the last Afghan raid?" It was me really, but Dravot was too angry to remember. "Who bought your guns? Who repaired the bridges? Who's the Grand-Master of the Sign cut in the stone?" says he, and he thumped his hand on the block that he used to sit on in Lodge, and at Council, which opened like Lodge always. Billy Fish said nothing and no more did the others. "Keep your hair on, Dan," said I; "and ask the girls. That's how it's done at Home, and these people are quite English."

'"The marriage of the King is a matter of State," says Dan, in a red-hot rage, for he could feel, I hope, that he was going against his better mind. He walked out of the Council-room, and the others sat still, looking at the ground.

'"Billy Fish," says I to the Chief of Bashkai, "what's the difficulty here? A straight answer to a true friend."

'"You know," says Billy Fish. "How should a man tell you who knows everything? How can daughters of men marry Gods or Devils? It's not proper."

'I remembered something like that in the Bible; but if, after seeing us as long as they had, they still believed we were Gods, 'twasn't for me to undeceive them.

'"A God can do anything," says I. "If the King is fond of a girl he'll not let her die." – "She'll have to," said Billy Fish. "There are all sorts of Gods and Devils in these mountains, and now and again a girl marries one of them and isn't seen any more. Besides, you two know the Mark cut in the stone. Only the Gods know that. We thought you were men till you showed the Sign of the Master."

'I wished then that we had explained about the loss of the genuine secrets of a Master-Mason at the first go-off; but I said nothing. All that night there was a blowing of horns in a little dark temple half-way down the hill, and I heard a girl crying fit to die. One of the priests told us that she was being prepared to marry the King.

'"I'll have no nonsense of that kind," says Dan. "I don't want to interfere with your customs, but I'll take my own wife." – "The girl's a little bit afraid," says the priest. "She thinks she's going to die, and they are a-heartening of her up down in the temple."

'"Hearten her very tender, then," says Dravot, "or I'll hearten you with the butt of a gun so you'll never want to be heartened again." He licked his lips, did Dan, and stayed up walking about more than half the night, thinking of the wife that he was going to get in the morning. I wasn't any means comfortable, for I knew that dealings with a woman in foreign parts, though you was a crowned King twenty times over, could not but be risky. I got up very early in the morning while Dravot was asleep, and I saw the priests talking together in whispers, and the Chiefs talking together too, and they looked at me out of the corners of their eyes.

'"What is up, Fish?" I says to the Bashkai man, who was wrapped up in his furs and looking splendid to behold.

'"I can't rightly say," says he; "but if you can make the King drop all this nonsense about marriage, you'll be doing him and me and yourself a great service."

'"That I do believe," says I. "But sure, you know, Billy, as well as me, having fought against and for us, that the King and me are nothing more than two of the finest men that God Almighty ever made. Nothing more, I do assure you."

'"That may be," says Billy Fish, "and yet I should be sorry if it was." He sinks his head upon his great fur cloak for a minute and thinks.

"King," says he, "be you man or God or Devil, I'll stick by you to-day. I have twenty of my men with me, and they will follow me. We'll go to Bashkai until the storm blows over."

'A little snow had fallen in the night, and everything was white except them greasy fat clouds that blew down and down from the north. Dravot came out with his crown on his head, swinging his arms and stamping his feet, and looking more pleased than Punch.

'"For the last time, drop it, Dan," says I in a whisper. "Billy Fish here says that there will be a row."

'"A row among my people!" says Dravot. "Not much. Peachey, you're a fool not to get a wife too. Where's the girl?" says he with a voice as loud as the braying of a jackass. "Call up all the Chiefs and priests, and let the Emperor see if his wife suits him."

'There was no need to call any one. They were all there leaning on their guns and spears round the clearing in the centre of the pine-wood. A lot of priests went down to the little temple to bring up the girl, and the horns blew fit to wake the dead. Billy Fish saunters round and gets as close to Daniel as he could, and behind him stood his twenty men with matchlocks. Not a man of them under six feet. I was next to Dravot, and behind me was twenty men of the regular Army. Up comes the girl, and a strapping wench she was, covered with silver and turquoises, but white as death, and looking back every minute at the priests.

'"She'll do," said Dan, looking her over. "What's to be afraid of, lass? Come and kiss me." He puts his arm round her. She shuts her eyes, gives a bit of a squeak, and down goes her face in the side of Dan's flaming red beard.

'"The slut's bitten me!" says he, clapping his hand to his neck, and, sure enough, his hand was red with blood. Billy Fish and two of his matchlock-men catches hold of Dan by the shoulders and drags him into the Bashkai lot, while the priests howls in their lingo: "Neither God nor Devil but a man!" I was all taken aback, for a priest cut at me in front, and the Army behind began firing into the Bashkai men.

'"God A'mighty!" says Dan. "What is the meaning o' this?"

'"Come back! Come away!" says Billy Fish. "Ruin and Mutiny's the matter. We'll break for Bashkai if we can."

'I tried to give some sort of orders to my men – the men o' the regular Army – but it was no use, so I fired into the brown of 'em with an English Martini and drilled three beggars in a line. The valley was full of shouting, howling people, and every soul was shrieking, "Not a God nor a Devil but only a man!" The Bashkai troops stuck to Billy Fish all they were worth, but their matchlocks wasn't half as good as the Kabul breech-loaders, and four of them dropped. Dan was bellowing like a bull, for he was very wrathy; and Billy Fish had a hard job to prevent him running out at the crowd.

'"We can't stand," says Billy Fish. "Make a run for it down the valley! The whole place is against us." The matchlock-men ran, and we went down the valley in spite of Dravot. He was swearing horrible and crying out he was a King. The priests rolled great stones on us, and the regular Army fired hard, and there wasn't more than six men, not counting Dan; Billy Fish, and me, that came down to the bottom of the valley alive.

'Then they stopped firing and the horns in the temple blew again. "Come away – for God's sake come away!" says Billy Fish. "They'll send runners out to all the villages before ever we get to Bashkai. I can protect you there, but I can't do anything now."

'My own notion is that Dan began to go mad in his head from that hour. He stared up and down like a stuck pig. Then he was all for walking back alone and killing the priests with his bare hands; which he could have done. "An Emperor am I," says Daniel, "and next year I shall be a Knight of the Queen."

'"All right, Dan," says I; "but come along now while there's time."

'"It's your fault," says he, "for not looking after your Army better. There was mutiny in the midst, and you didn't know – you damned engine-driving, plate-laying, missionary's-pass-hunting hound!" He sat upon a rock and called me every name he could lay tongue to. I was too heart-sick to care, though it was all his foolishness that brought the smash.

'"I'm sorry, Dan," says I, "but there's no accounting for natives. This business is our 'Fifty-Seven.[49] Maybe we'll make something out of it yet, when we've got to Bashkai."

'"Let's get to Bashkai, then," says Dan, "and, by God, when I come back here again I'll sweep the valley so there isn't a bug in a blanket left!"

'We walked all that day, and all that night Dan was stumping up and down on the snow, chewing his beard and muttering to himself.

'"There's no hope o' getting clear," said Billy Fish. "The priests will have sent runners to the villages to say that you are only men. Why didn't you stick on as Gods till things was more settled? I'm a dead man," says Billy Fish, and he throws himself down on the snow and begins to pray to his Gods.

'Next morning we was in a cruel bad country – all up and down, no level ground at all, and no food either. The six Bashkai men looked at Billy Fish hungry-ways as if they wanted to ask something, but they said never a word. At noon we came to the top of a flat mountain all covered with snow, and when we climbed up into it, behold, there was an Army in position waiting in the middle!

'"The runners have been very quick," says Billy Fish, with a little bit of a laugh. "They are waiting for us."

'Three or four men began to fire from the enemy's side, and a chance shot took Daniel in the calf of the leg. That brought him to his senses. He looks across the snow at the Army, and sees the rifles that we had brought into the country.

'"We're done for," says he. "They are Englishmen, these people, – and it's my blasted nonsense that has brought you to this. Get back, Billy Fish, and take your men away. You've done what you could, and now cut for it. Carnehan," says he, "shake hands with me and go along with Billy. Maybe they won't kill you. I'll go and meet 'em alone. It's me that did it. Me, the King!"

'"Go!" says I. "Go to Hell, Dan! I'm with you here. Billy Fish, you clear out, and we two will meet those folk."

'"I'm a Chief," says Billy Fish, quite quiet. "I stay with you. My men can go."

'The Bashkai fellows didn't wait for a second word, but ran off, and Dan and me and Billy Fish walked across to where the drums were drumming and the horns were horning. It was cold – awful cold. I've got that cold in the back of my head now. There's a lump of it there.'

The punkah-coolies had gone to sleep. Two kerosene lamps were blazing in the office, and the perspiration poured down my face and splashed on the blotter as I leaned forward. Carnehan was shivering, and I feared that his mind might go. I wiped my face, took a fresh grip of the piteously mangled hands, and said: 'What happened after that?'

The momentary shift of my eyes had broken the clear current.

'What was you pleased to say?' whined Carnehan. 'They took them without any sound. Not a little whisper all along the snow, not though the King knocked down the first man that set hand on him – not though old Peachey fired his last cartridge into the brown of 'em. Not a single solitary sound did those swines make. They just closed up tight, and I tell you their furs stunk. There was a man called Billy Fish, a good friend of us all, and they cut his throat, sir, then and there, like a pig; and the King kicks up the bloody snow and says: "We've had a dashed fine run for our money. What's coming next?" But Peachey, Peachey Taliaferro, I tell you, sir, in confidence as betwixt two friends, he lost his head, sir. No, he didn't neither. The King lost his head, so he did, all along o' one of those cunning rope-bridges. Kindly let me have the paper-cutter, sir. It tilted this way. They marched him a mile across that snow to a rope-bridge over a ravine with a river at the bottom. You may have seen such. They prodded him behind like an ox. "Damn your eyes!" says the King. "D'you suppose I can't die like a gentleman?" He turns to Peachey – Peachey that was crying like a child. "I've brought you to this, Peachey," says he. "Brought you out of your happy life to be killed in Kafiristan, where you was late Commander-in-Chief of the Emperor's forces. Say you forgive me, Peachey." – "I do," says Peachey. "Fully and freely do I forgive you, Dan." – "Shake hands, Peachey," says he. "I'm going now." Out he goes, looking neither right nor left, and when he was plumb in the middle of those dizzy dancing ropes – "Cut, you beggars," he shouts; and they cut, and old Dan fell, turning round and round and round, twenty thousand miles, for he took half an hour to fall till he struck the water, and I could see his body caught on a rock with the gold crown close beside.

'But do you know what they did to Peachey between two pine-trees? They crucified him, sir, as Peachey's hands will show. They used wooden pegs for his hands and his feet; and he didn't die. He hung there and screamed, and they took him down next day, and said it was a miracle that he wasn't dead. They took him down – poor old Peachey that hadn't done them any harm – that hadn't done them any –'

He rocked to and fro and wept bitterly, wiping his eyes with the back of his scarred hands and moaning like a child for some ten minutes.

'They was cruel enough to feed him up in the temple, because they said he was more of a God than old Daniel that was a man. Then they turned him out on the snow, and told him to go home, and Peachey came home in about a year, begging along the roads quite safe; for Daniel Dravot he walked before and said: "Come along, Peachey. It's a big thing we're doing." The mountains they danced at night, and the mountains they tried to fall on Peachey's head, but Dan he held up his hand, and Peachey came along bent double. He never let go of Dan's hand, and he never let go of Dan's head. They gave it to him as a present in the temple, to remind him not to come again, and though the crown was pure gold, and Peachey was starving, never would Peachey sell the same. You knew Dravot, sir! You knew Right Worshipful Brother Dravot! Look at him now!'

He fumbled in the mass of rags round his bent waist; brought out a black horsehair bag embroidered with silver thread, and shook therefrom on to my table – the dried, withered head of Daniel Dravot! The morning sun that had long been paling the lamps struck the red beard and blind sunken eyes; struck, too, a heavy circlet of gold studded with raw turquoises, that Carnehan placed tenderly on the battered temples.

'You behold now,' said Carnehan, 'the Emperor in his habit as he lived – the King of Kafiristan with his crown upon his head. Poor old Daniel that was a monarch once!'

I shuddered, for, in spite of defacements manifold, I recognised the head of the man of Marwar Junction. Carnehan rose to go. I attempted to stop him. He was not fit to walk abroad. 'Let me take away the whisky, and give me a little money,' he gasped. 'I was a King once. I'll go to the Deputy-Commissioner and ask to set in the Poorhouse till I get my health. No, thank you, I can't wait till you get a carriage for me. I've urgent private affairs – in the South – at Marwar.'

He shambled out of the office and departed in the direction of the Deputy-Commissioner's house. That day at noon I had occasion to go down the blinding hot Mall, and I saw a crooked man crawling along the white dust of the roadside, his hat in his hand, quavering dolorously after the fashion of street-singers at Home. There was not a soul in sight, and he was out of all possible earshot of the houses. And he sang through his nose, turning his head from right to left:

> 'The Son of God goes forth to war,
>   A kingly crown to gain;
> His blood-red banner streams afar!
>   Who follows in his train?'[50]

I waited to hear no more, but put the poor wretch into my carriage and drove him off to the nearest missionary for eventual transfer to the Asylum. He repeated the hymn twice while he was with me, whom he did not in the least recognise, and I left him singing it to the missionary.

Two days later I inquired after his welfare of the Superintendent of the Asylum.

'He was admitted suffering from sunstroke. He died early yesterday morning,' said the Superintendent. 'Is it true that he was half an hour bare-headed in the sun at mid-day?'

'Yes,' said I, 'but do you happen to know if he had anything upon him by any chance when he died?'

'Not to my knowledge,' said the Superintendent.

And there the matter rests.

NABOTH

This was how it happened; and the truth is also an allegory of Empire.[1] I met him at the corner of my garden, an empty basket on his head, and an unclean cloth round his loins. That was all the property to which Naboth had the shadow of a claim when I first saw him. He opened our acquaintance by begging. He was very thin and showed nearly as many ribs as his basket; and he told me a long story about fever and a lawsuit, and an iron cauldron that had been seized by the court in execution of a decree. I put my hand into my pocket to help Naboth, as kings of the East have helped alien adventurers to the loss of their kingdoms. A rupee had hidden in my waistcoat lining. I never knew it was there, and gave the trove to Naboth as a direct gift from Heaven. He replied that I was the only legitimate Protector of the Poor he had ever known.

Next morning he reappeared, a little fatter in the round, and curled himself into knots in the front veranda. He said I was his father and his mother, and the direct descendant of all the Gods in his Pantheon, besides controlling the destinies of the universe. He himself was but a sweetmeat-seller, and much less important than the dirt under my feet. I had heard this sort of thing before, so I asked him what he wanted. My rupee, quoth Naboth, had raised him to the everlasting heavens, and he wished to prefer a request. He wished to establish a sweet-meatpitch near the house of his benefactor, to gaze on my revered countenance as I went to and fro illumining the world. I was graciously pleased to give permission, and he went away with his head between his knees.

Now at the far end of my garden the ground slopes toward the public road, and the slope is crowned with a thick shrubbery. There is a short carriage-road from the house to the Mall, which passes close to the shrubbery. Next afternoon I saw that Naboth had seated himself at the bottom of the slope, down in the dust of the public road, and in the full glare of the sun, with a starved basket of greasy sweets in front of him. He had gone into trade once more on the strength of my munificent donation, and the ground was as Paradise by my honoured favour. Remember, there was only Naboth, his basket, the sunshine, and the grey dust when the sap[2] of my Empire first began.

Next day he had moved himself up the slope nearer to my shrubbery, and waved a palm-leaf fan to keep the flies off the sweets. So I judged that he must have done a fair trade.

Four days later I noticed that he had backed himself and his basket under the shadow of the shrubbery, and had tied an Isabella-coloured[3] rag between two branches in order to make more shade. There were plenty of sweets in his basket. I thought that trade must certainly be looking up.

Seven weeks later the Government took up a plot of ground for a Chief Court close to the end of my compound, and employed nearly four hundred coolies on the foundations. Naboth bought a blue-and-white striped blanket, a brass lamp-stand, and a small boy, to cope with the rush of trade, which was tremendous.

Five days later he bought a huge, fat, red-backed account-book, and a glass ink-stand. Thus I saw that the coolies had been getting into his debt, and that commerce was increasing on legitimate lines of credit. Also I saw that the one basket had grown into three, and that Naboth had backed and hacked into the shrubbery, and made himself a nice little clearing for the proper display of the basket, the blanket, the books, and the boy.

One week and five days later he had built a mud fireplace in the clearing, and the fat account-book was overflowing. He said that God created few Englishmen of my kind, and that I was the incarnation of all human virtues. He offered me some of his sweets as tribute, and by accepting these I acknowledged him as my feudatory[4] under the skirt of my protection.

Three weeks later I noticed that the boy was in the habit of cooking Naboth's mid-day meal for him, and Naboth was beginning to grow a stomach. He had hacked away more of my shrubbery, and owned another and a fatter account-book.

Eleven weeks later Naboth had eaten his way nearly through that shrubbery, and there was a reed hut with a bedstead outside it, standing in the little glade that he had eroded. Two dogs and a baby slept on the bedstead. So I fancied Naboth had taken a wife. He said that he had, by my favour, done this thing, and that I was several times finer than Krishna.

Six weeks and two days later a mud wall had grown up at the back of the hut. There were fowls in front and it smelt a little. The Municipal Secretary said that a cesspool was forming in the public road from the drainage of my compound, and that I must take steps to clear it away. I spoke to Naboth. He said I was Lord Paramount of his earthly concerns, and the garden was all my own property, and sent me some more sweets in a second-hand duster.

Two months later a coolie bricklayer was killed in a scuffle that took place opposite Naboth's Vineyard. The Inspector of Police said it was a serious case, went into my servants' quarters, insulted my butler's wife, and wanted to arrest my butler. The curious thing about the murder was that most of the coolies were drunk at the time. Naboth pointed out that my name was a strong shield between him and his enemies, and he expected that another baby would be born to him shortly.

Four months later the hut was *all* mud walls, very solidly built, and Naboth had used most of my shrubbery for his five goats. A silver watch and an aluminium chain shone upon his very round stomach. My servants were alarmingly drunk several times, and used to waste the day with Naboth when they got the chance. I spoke to Naboth. He said, by my favour and the glory of my countenance, he would make all his womenfolk ladies, and that if any one hinted that he was running an illicit still[5] under the shadow of the tamarisks, why, I, his Suzerain,[6] was to prosecute.

A week later he hired a man to make several dozen square yards of trellis-work to put round the back of his hut, that his women-folk might be screened from the public gaze. The man went away in the evening, and left his day's work to pave the short cut from the public road to my house. I was driving home in the dusk, and turned the corner by Naboth's Vineyard quickly. The next thing I knew was that the horses of the phaeton[7] were stamping and plunging in the strongest sort of bamboo net-work. Both beasts came down. One rose with nothing more than chipped knees. The other was so badly kicked that I was forced to shoot him.

Naboth is gone now, and his hut is ploughed into its native mud with sweetmeats instead of salt[8] for a sign that the place is accursed. I have built a summer-house to overlook the end of the garden, and it is as a fort on my frontier whence I guard my Empire.

I know exactly how Ahab felt.[9] He has been shamefully misrepresented in the Scriptures.

ON THE CITY WALL

Then she[1] let them down by a cord through the window; for her house was upon the town wall, and she dwelt upon the wall.

Joshua ii. 15

Lalun is a member of the most ancient profession in the world. Lilith[2] was her very-great-grand-mamma, and that was before the days of Eve, as every one knows. In the West, people say rude things about Lalun's profession, and write lectures about it, and distribute the lectures to young persons in order that Morality may be preserved. In the East, where the profession is hereditary, descending from mother to daughter, nobody writes lectures or takes any notice; and that is a distinct proof of the inability of the East to manage its own affairs.

Lalun's real husband, for even ladies of Lalun's profession in the East must have husbands, was a big jujube-tree.[3] Her Mamma, who had married a fig-tree, spent ten thousand rupees on Lalun's wedding, which was blessed by forty-seven clergymen of Mamma's Church, and distributed five thousand rupees in charity to the poor. And that was the custom of the land. The advantages of having a jujube-tree for a husband are obvious. You cannot hurt his feelings, and he looks imposing.

Lalun's husband stood on the plain outside the City walls, and Lalun's house was upon the east wall facing the river. If you fell from the broad window-seat you dropped thirty feet sheer into the City Ditch. But if you stayed where you should and looked forth, you saw all the cattle of the City being driven down to water, the students of the Government College playing cricket, the high grass and trees that fringed the river-bank, the great sand-bars that ribbed the river, the red tombs of dead Emperors beyond the river, and very far away through the blue heat-haze a glint of the snows of the Himalayas.

Wali Dad used to lie in the window-seat for hours at a time watching this view. He was a young Mohammedan who was suffering acutely from education of the English variety and knew it. His father had sent him to a Mission-school to get wisdom, and Wali Dad had absorbed more than ever his father or the Missionaries intended he should. When his father died, Wali Dad was independent and spent two years experimenting with the creeds of the Earth and reading books that are of no use to anybody.

After he had made an unsuccessful attempt to enter the Roman Catholic Church and the Presbyterian fold at the same time (the Missionaries found him out and called him names; but they did not understand his trouble), he discovered Lalun on the City wall and became the most constant of her few admirers. He possessed a head that English artists at home would rave over and paint amid impossible surroundings – a face that female novelists would use with delight through nine hundred pages. In reality he was only a clean-bred young Mohammedan, with pencilled eyebrows, small-cut nostrils, little feet and hands, and a very tired look in his eyes. By virtue of his twenty-two years he had grown a neat black beard which he stroked with pride and kept delicately scented. His life seemed to be divided between borrowing books from me and making love to Lalun in the window-seat. He composed songs about her, and some of the songs are sung to this day in the City from the Street of the Mutton-Butchers to the Copper-Smiths' ward.

One song, the prettiest of all, says that the beauty of Lalun was so great that it troubled the hearts of the British Government and caused them to lose their peace of mind. That is the way the song is sung in the streets; but, if you examine it carefully and know the key to the explanation, you will find that there are three puns in it – on 'beauty', 'heart', and 'peace of mind', – so that it runs: 'By the subtlety of Lalun the administration of the Government was troubled and it lost such-and-such a man.' When Wali Dad sings that song his eyes glow like hot coals, and Lalun leans back among the cushions and throws bunches of jasmine-buds at Wali Dad.

But first it is necessary to explain something about the Supreme Government which is above all and below all and behind all. Gentlemen come from England, spend a few weeks in India, walk round this great Sphinx of the Plains, and write books upon its ways and its works, denouncing or praising it as their own ignorance prompts. Consequently all the world knows how the Supreme Government conducts itself. But no one, not even the Supreme Government, knows everything about the administration of the Empire. Year by year England sends out fresh drafts for the first fighting-line, which is officially called the Indian Civil Service. These die, or kill themselves by overwork, or are worried to death, or broken in health and hope in order that the land may be protected from death and sickness, famine and war, and may eventually become capable of standing alone. It will never stand alone, but the idea is a pretty one, and men are willing to die for it, and yearly the work of pushing and coaxing and scolding and petting the country into good living goes forward. If an advance be made all credit is given to the native, while the Englishmen stand back and wipe their foreheads. If a failure occurs the Englishmen step forward and take the blame. Overmuch tenderness of this kind has bred a strong belief among many natives that the native is capable of administering the country, and many devout Englishmen believe this also, because the theory is stated in beautiful English with all the latest political colours.

There are other men who, though uneducated, see visions and dream dreams, and they, too, hope to administer the country in their own way – that is to say, with a garnish of Red Sauce. Such men must exist among two hundred million people, and, if they are not attended to, may cause trouble and even break the great idol called *Pax Britannica*,[4] which, as the newspapers say, lives between Peshawur and Cape Comorin.[5] Were the Day of Doom to dawn tomorrow, you would find the Supreme Government 'taking measures to allay popular excitement', and putting guards upon the graveyards that the Dead might troop forth orderly. The youngest Civilian would arrest Gabriel on his own responsibility if the Archangel could not produce a Deputy-Commissioner's permission to 'make music or other noises' as the licence says.

Whence it is easy to see that mere men of the flesh who would create a tumult must fare badly at the hands of the Supreme Government. And they do. There is no outward sign of excitement; there is no confusion; there is no knowledge. When due and sufficient reasons have been given, weighed and approved, the machinery moves forward, and the dreamer of dreams and the seer of visions is gone from his friends and following. He enjoys the hospitality of Government; there is no restriction upon his movements within certain limits; but he must not confer any more with his brother dreamers. Once in every six months the Supreme Government assures itself that he is well and takes formal acknowledgment of his existence. No one protests against his detention, because the few people who know about it are in deadly fear of seeming to know him; and never a single newspaper 'takes up his case' or organises demonstrations on his behalf, because the newspapers of India have got behind that lying proverb which says the Pen is mightier than the Sword, and can walk delicately.

So now you know as much as you ought about Wali Dad, the educational mixture, and the Supreme Government.

Lalun has not yet been described. She would need, so Wali Dad says, a thousand pens of gold, and ink scented with musk. She has been variously compared to the Moon, the Dil Sagar Lake, a spotted quail, a gazelle, the Sun on the Desert of Kutch, the Dawn, the Stars, and the young bamboo. These comparisons imply that she is beautiful exceedingly according to the native standards, which are practically the same as those of the West. Her eyes are black and her hair is black, and her eyebrows are black as leeches; her mouth is tiny and says witty things; her hands are tiny and have saved much money; her feet are tiny and have trodden on the naked hearts of many men. But, as Wali Dad sings: 'Lalun *is* Lalun, and when you have said that, you have only come to the Beginnings of Knowledge.'

The little house on the City wall was just big enough to hold Lalun, and her maid, and a pussy-cat with a silver collar. A big pink-and-blue cut-glass chandelier hung from the ceiling of the reception room. A petty Nawab had given Lalun the horror, and she kept it for politeness' sake. The floor of the room was of polished chunam,[6] white as curds. A latticed window of carved wood was set in one wall; there was a profusion of squabby pluffy cushions and fat carpets everywhere, and Lalun's silver hookah, studded with turquoises, had a special little carpet all to its shining self. Wali Dad was nearly as permanent a fixture as the chandelier. As I have said, he lay in the window-seat and meditated on Life and Death and Lalun – 'specially Lalun. The feet of the young men of the City tended to her doorways and then – retired, for Lalun was a particular maiden, slow of speech, reserved of mind, and not in the least inclined to orgies which were nearly certain to end in strife. 'If I am of no value, I am unworthy of this honour,' said Lalun. 'If I am of value, they are unworthy of Me.' And that was a crooked sentence.

In the long hot nights of latter April and May all the City seemed to assemble in Lalun's little white room to smoke and to talk. Shiahs[7] of the grimmest and most uncompromising persuasion; Sufis[8] who had lost all belief in the Prophet and retained but little in God; wandering Hindu priests passing southward on their way to the Central India fairs and other affairs; Pundits in black gowns, with spectacles on their noses and undigested wisdom in their insides; bearded headmen of the wards; Sikhs with all the details of the latest ecclesiastical scandal in the Golden Temple;[9] red-eyed priests from beyond the Border, looking like trapped wolves and talking like ravens; MA's of the University, very superior and very voluble – all these people and more also you might find in the white room. Wali Dad lay in the window-seat and listened to the talk.

'It is Lalun's *salon*,' said Wali Dad to me, 'and it is electic[10] – is not that the word? Outside of a Freemasons' Lodge I have never seen such gatherings. *There* I dined once with a Jew – a Yahoudi!' He spat into the City Ditch with apologies for allowing national feelings to overcome him. 'Though I have lost every belief in the world,' said he, 'and try to be proud of my losing, I cannot help hating a Jew. Lalun admits no Jews here.'

'But what in the world do all these men do?' I asked.

'The curse of our country,' said Wali Dad. 'They talk. It is like the Athenians – always hearing and telling some new thing.[11] Ask the Pearl and she will show you how much she knows of the news of the City and the Province. Lalun knows everything.'

'Lalun,' I said at random – she was talking to a gentleman of the Kurd persuasion who had come in from God-knows-where – 'when does the 175th Regiment go to Agra?'

'It does not go at all,' said Lalun, without turning her head. 'They have ordered the 118th to go in its stead. That Regiment goes to Lucknow in three months, unless they give a fresh order.'

'That is so,' said Wali Dad, without a shade of doubt. 'Can you, with your telegrams and your newspapers, do better? Always hearing and telling some new thing,' he went on. 'My friend, has your God ever smitten a European nation for gossiping in the bazars? India has gossiped for centuries – always standing in the bazars until the soldiers go by. Therefore – you are here to-day instead of starving in your own country, and I am not a Mohammedan – I am a Product – a Demnition Product.[12] *That* also I owe to you and yours: that I cannot make an end to my sentence without quoting from your authors.' He pulled at the hookah and mourned, half feelingly, half in earnest, for the shattered hopes of his youth. Wali Dad was always mourning over something or other – the country of which he despaired, or the creed in which he had lost faith, or the life of the English which he could by no means understand.

Lalun never mourned. She played little songs on the *sitar*,[13] and to hear her sing, 'O Peacock, cry again,' was always a fresh pleasure. She knew all the songs that have ever been sung, from the war-songs of the South, that make the old men angry with the young men and the young men angry with the State, to the love-songs of the North, where the swords whinny-whicker like angry kites[14] in the pauses between the kisses, and the Passes fill with armed men, and the Lover is torn from his Beloved and cries Ai! Ai! Ai! evermore. She knew how to make up tobacco for the pipe so that it smelt like the Gates of Paradise and wafted you gently through them. She could embroider strange things in gold and silver, and dance softly with the moonlight when it came in at the window. Also she knew the hearts of men, and the heart of the City, and whose wives were faithful and whose untrue, and more of the secrets of the Government Offices than are good to be set down in this place. Nasiban, her maid, said that her jewelry was worth ten thousand pounds, and that, some night, a thief would enter and murder her for its possession; but Lalun said that all the

City would tear that thief limb from limb, and that he, whoever he was, knew it.

So she took her *sitar* and sat in the window-seat, and sang a song of old days that had been sung by a girl of her profession in an armed camp on the eve of a great battle – the day before the Fords of the Jumna ran red and Sivaji[15] fled fifty miles to Delhi with a Toorkh stallion at his horse's tail and another Lalun on his saddle-bow. It was what men call a Mahratta *laonee*,[16] and it said:

> 'Their warrior forces Chimnajee
>   Before the Peishwa led,
> The Children of the Sun and Fire
>   Behind him turned and fled.'

And the chorus said:

> 'With them there fought who rides so free
>   With sword and turban red,
> The warrior-youth who earns his fee
>   At peril of his head.'

'At peril of his head,' said Wali Dad in English to me. 'Thanks to your Government, all our heads are protected, and with the educational facilities at my command' – his eyes twinkled wickedly – 'I might be a distinguished member of the local administration. Perhaps, in time, I might even be a member of a Legislative Council.'

'Don't speak English,' said Lalun, bending over her *sitar* afresh. The chorus went out from the City wall to the blackened wall of Fort Amara which dominates the City. No man knows the precise extent of Fort Amara. Three kings built it hundreds of years ago, and they say that there are miles of underground rooms beneath its walls. It is peopled with many ghosts, a detachment of Garrison Artillery, and a Company of Infantry. In its prime it held ten thousand men and filled its ditches with corpses.

'At peril of his head,' sang Lalun again and again.

A head moved on one of the ramparts – the grey head of an old man – and a voice, rough as shark-skin on a sword-hilt, sent back the last line of the chorus and broke into a song that I could not understand, though Lalun and Wali Dad listened intently.

'What is it?' I asked. 'Who is it?'

'A consistent man,' said Wali Dad. 'He fought you in '46, when he was a warrior-youth; refought you in '57, and he tried to fight you in '71,[17] but you had learned the trick of blowing men from guns too well. Now he is old; but he would still fight if he could.'

'Is he a Wahabi,[18] then? Why should he answer to a Mahratta *laonee* if he be Wahabi – or Sikh?' said I.

'I do not know,' said Wali Dad. 'He has lost, perhaps, his religion. Perhaps he wishes to be a King. Perhaps he *is* a King. I do not know his name.'

'That is a lie, Wali Dad. If you know his career you must know his name.'

'That is quite true. I belong to a nation of liars. I would rather not tell you his name. Think for yourself.'

Lalun finished her song, pointed to the Fort, and said simply: 'Khem Singh.'

'Hm,' said Wali Dad. 'If the Pearl chooses to tell you, the Pearl is a fool.'

I translated to Lalun, who laughed. 'I choose to tell what I choose to tell. They kept Khem Singh in Burma,' said she. 'They kept him there for many years until his mind was changed in him. So great was the kindness of the Government. Finding this, they sent him back to his own country that he might look upon it before he died. He is an old man, but when he looks upon this his country his memory will come. Moreover, there be many who remember him.'

'He is an Interesting Survival,' said Wali Dad, pulling at the pipe. 'He returns to a country now full of educational and political reform, but, as the Pearl says, there are many who remember him. He was once a great man. There will never be any more great men in India. They will all, when they are boys, go whoring after strange gods,[19] and they will become citizens – "fellow-citizens" – "illustrious fellow-citizens". What is it that the native papers call them?'

Wali Dad seemed to be in a very bad temper. Lalun looked out of the window and smiled into the dust-haze. I went away thinking about Khem Singh, who had once made history with a thousand followers, and would have been a princeling but for the power of the Supreme Government aforesaid.

The Senior Captain Commanding Fort Amara was away on leave, but the Subaltern, his Deputy, had drifted down to the Club, where I found him and inquired of him whether it was really true that a political prisoner had been added to the attractions of the Fort. The Subaltern explained at great length, for this was the first time that he had held command of the Fort, and his glory lay heavy upon him.

'Yes,' said he, 'a man was sent in to me about a week ago from down the line – a thorough gentleman, whoever he is. Of course I did all I could for him. He had his two servants and some silver cooking-pots, and he looked for all the world like a native officer. I called him Subadar Sahib.[20] Just as well to be on the safe side, y'know. "Look here, Subadar Sahib," I said, "you're handed over to my authority, and I'm supposed to guard you. Now I don't want to make your life hard, but you must make things easy for me. All the Fort is at your disposal, from the flagstaff to the dry Ditch, and I shall be happy to entertain you in any way I can, but you mustn't take advantage of it. Give me your word that you won't try to escape, Subadar Sahib, and I'll give you my word that you shall have no heavy guard put over you." I thought the best way of getting at him was by going at him straight, y'know; and it was, by Jove! The old man gave me his word, and moved about the Fort as contented as a sick crow. He's a rummy chap – always asking to be told where he is and what the buildings about him are. I had to sign a slip of blue paper when he turned up, acknowledging receipt of his body and all that, and I'm responsible, y'know, that he doesn't get away. Queer thing, though, looking after a Johnnie old enough to be your grandfather, isn't it? Come to the Fort one of these days and see him.'

For reasons which will appear, I never went to the Fort while Khem Singh was then within its walls. I knew him only as a grey head seen from Lalun's window – a grey head and a harsh voice. But natives told me that, day by day, as he looked upon the fair lands round Amara, his memory came back to him and, with it, the old hatred against the Government that had been nearly effaced in far-off Burma. So he raged up and down the West face of the Fort from morning till noon and from evening till the night, devising vain things in his heart, and croaking war-songs when Lalun sang on the City wall. As he grew more acquainted with the Subaltern he unburdened his old heart of some of the passions that had withered it. 'Sahib,' he used to say, tapping his stick against the parapet, 'when I was a young man I was one of twenty thousand horsemen who came out of the City and rode round the plain here. Sahib, I was the leader of a hundred, then of a thousand, then of five thousand, and now!' – he pointed to his two servants. 'But from the beginning to-day I would cut the throats of all the Sahibs in the land if I could. Hold me fast, Sahib, lest I get away and return to those who would follow me. I forgot them when I was in Burma, but now that I am in my own country again, I remember everything.'

'Do you remember that you have given me your Honour not to make your tendance a hard matter?' said the Subaltern.

'Yes, to you, only to you, Sahib,' said Khem Singh. 'To you because you are of a pleasant countenance. If my turn comes again, Sahib, I will not hang you nor cut your throat.'

'Thank you,' said the Subaltern gravely, as he looked along the line of guns that could pound the City to powder in half an hour. 'Let us go into our own quarters, Khem Singh. Come and talk with me after dinner.'

Khem Singh would sit on his own cushion at the Subaltern's feet, drinking heavy, scented aniseed brandy in great gulps, and telling strange stories of Fort Amara, which had been a palace in the old days, of Begums and Ranees tortured to death – in the very vaulted chamber that now served as a messroom; would tell stories of Sobraon[21] that made the Subaltern's cheeks flush and tingle with pride of race, and of the Kuka rising from which so much was expected and the fore-knowledge of which was shared by a hundred thousand souls. But he never told tales of '57 because, as he said, he was the Subaltern's guest, and '57 is a year that no man, Black or White, cares to speak of. Once only, when the aniseed brandy had slightly affected his head, he said: 'Sahib, speaking now of a matter which lay between Sobraon and the affair of the Kukas, it was ever a wonder to us that you stayed your hand at all, and that, having stayed it, you did not make the land one prison. Now I hear from without that you do great honour to all men of our country and by your own hands are destroying the Terror of your Name which is your strong rock and defence. This is a foolish thing. Will oil and water mix? Now in '57 –'

'I was not born then, Subadar Sahib,' said the Subaltern, and Khem Singh reeled to his quarters.

The Subaltern would tell me of these conversations at the Club, and my desire to see Khem Singh increased. But Wali Dad, sitting in the window-seat of the house on the City wall, said that it would be a cruel thing to do, and Lalun pretended that I preferred the society of a grizzled old Sikh to hers.

'Here is tobacco, here is talk, here are many friends and all the news of the City, and, above all, here is myself. I will tell you stories and sing you songs, and Wali Dad will talk his English nonsense in your ears. Is that worse than watching the caged animal yonder? Go to-morrow then, if you must, but to-day such-and-such an one will be here, and he will speak of wonderful things.'

It happened that To-morrow never came, and the warm heat of the latter Rains gave place to the chill of early October almost before I was aware of the flight of the year. The Captain Commanding the Fort returned from leave and took over charge of Khem Singh according to the laws of seniority. The Captain was not a nice man. He called all natives 'niggers', which, besides being extreme bad form, shows gross ignorance.[22]

'What's the use of telling off two Tommies to watch that old nigger?' said he.

'I fancy it soothes his vanity,' said the Subaltern. 'The men are ordered to keep well out of his way, but he takes them as a tribute to his importance, poor old chap.'

'I won't have Line men taken off regular guards in this way. Put on a couple of Native Infantry.'

'Sikhs?'[23] said the Subaltern, lifting his eyebrows.

'Sikhs, Pathans, Dogras[24] – they're all alike, these black people,' and the Captain talked to Khem Singh in a manner which hurt that old gentleman's feelings. Fifteen years before, when he had been caught for the second time, every one looked upon him as a sort of tiger. He liked being regarded in this light. But he forgot that the world goes forward in fifteen years, and many Subalterns are promoted to Captaincies.

'The Captain-pig is in charge of the Fort?' said Khem Singh to his native guard every morning. And the native guard said: 'Yes, Subadar Sahib,' in deference to his age and his air of distinction; but they did not know who he was.

In those days the gathering in Lalun's little white room was always large and talked more than before.

'The Greeks,' said Wali Dad, who had been borrowing my books, 'the inhabitants of the city of Athens, where they were always hearing and telling some new thing, rigorously secluded their women – who were fools. Hence the glorious institution of the heterodox women[25] – is it not? – who were amusing and *not* fools. All the Greek philosophers delighted in their company. Tell me, my friend, how it goes now in Greece and the other places upon the Continent of Europe. Are your women-folk also fools?'

'Wali Dad,' I said, 'you never speak to us about your women-folk and we never speak about ours to you. That is the bar between us.'

'Yes,' said Wali Dad, 'it is curious to think that our common meeting-place should be here, in the house of a common – how do you call *her*?' He pointed with the pipe-mouth to Lalun.

'Lalun is nothing but Lalun,' I said, and that was perfectly true. 'But if you took your place in the world, Wali Dad, and gave up dreaming dreams –'

'I might wear an English coat and trousers. I might be a leading Mohammedan pleader. I might be received even at the Commissioner's tennis-parties where the English stand on one side and the natives on the other, in order to promote social intercourse throughout the Empire.'

Heart's Heart,' said he to Lalun quickly, 'the Sahib says that I ought to quit you.'

'The Sahib is always talking stupid talk,' returned Lalun with a laugh. 'In this house I am a Queen and thou art a King. The Sahib' – she put her arms above her head and thought for a moment – 'the Sahib shall be our Vizier[26] – thine and mine, Wali Dad – because he has said that thou shouldst leave me.'

Wali Dad laughed immoderately, and I laughed too. 'Be it so,' said he. 'My friend, are you willing to take this lucrative Government appointment? Lalun, what shall his pay be?'

But Lalun began to sing, and for the rest of the time there was no hope of getting a sensible answer from her or Wali Dad. When the one stopped, the other began to quote Persian poetry with a triple pun in every other line. Some of it was not strictly proper, but it was all very funny, and it only came to an end when a fat person in black, with gold pince-nez, sent up his name to Lalun, and Wali Dad dragged me into the twinkling night to walk in a big rose-garden and talk heresies about Religion and Governments and a man's career in life.

The Mohurrum, the great mourning-festival[27] of the Mohammedans, was close at hand, and the things that Wali Dad said about religious fanaticism would have secured his expulsion from the loosest-thinking Muslim sect. There were the rose-bushes round us, the stars above us, and from every quarter of the City came the boom of the big Mohurrum drums. You must know that the City is divided in fairly equal proportions between the Hindus and the Mussulmans, and where both creeds belong to the fighting races, a big religious festival gives ample chance for trouble. When they can – that is to say, when the authorities are weak enough to allow it – the Hindus do their best to arrange some minor feast-day of their own in time to clash with the period of general mourning for the martyrs Hasan and Hussain, the heroes of the Mohurrum. Gilt and painted paper representations of their tombs are borne with shouting and wailing, music, torches, and yells, through the principal thoroughfares of the City; which fakements are called *tazias*.[28] Their passage is rigorously laid down beforehand by the Police, and detachments of Police accompany each *tazia*, lest the Hindus should throw bricks at it and the peace of the Queen and the heads of Her loyal subjects should thereby be broken. Mohurrum time in a 'fighting' town means anxiety to all the officials, because, if a riot breaks out, the officials and not the rioters are held responsible. The former must foresee everything, and while not making their precautions ridiculously elaborate, must see that they are at least adequate.

'Listen to the drums!' said Wali Dad. 'That is the heart of the people

– empty and making much noise. How, think you, will the Mohurrum go this year? *I* think that there will be trouble.'

He turned down a side-street and left me alone with the stars and a sleepy Police patrol. Then I went to bed and dreamed that Wali Dad had sacked the City and I was made Vizier, with Lalun's silver pipe for mark of office.

All day the Mohurrum drums beat in the City, and all day deputations of tearful Hindu gentlemen besieged the Deputy-Commissioner with assurances that they would be murdered are next dawning by the Mohammedans. 'Which,' said the Deputy-Commissioner, in confidence to the Head of Police, 'is a pretty fair indication that the Hindus are going to make 'emselves unpleasant. I think we can arrange a little surprise for them. I have given the heads of both Creeds fair warning. If they choose to disregard it, so much the worse for them.'

There was a large gathering in Lalun's house that night, but of men that I had never seen before, if I except the fat gentleman in black with the gold pince-nez. Wali Dad lay in the window-seat, more bitterly scornful of his Faith and its manifestations than I had ever known him. Lalun's maid was very busy cutting up and mixing tobacco for the guests. We could hear the thunder of the drums as the processions accompanying each *tazia* marched to the central gathering-place in the plain outside the City, preparatory to their triumphant re-entry and circuit within the walls. All the streets seemed ablaze with torches, and only Fort Amara was black and silent.

When the noise of the drums ceased, no one in the white room spoke for a time. 'The first *tazia* has moved off,' said Wali Dad, looking to the plain.

'That is very early,' said the man with the pince-nez. 'It is only half-past eight.' The company rose and departed.

'Some of them were men from Ladakh,'[29] said Lalun, when the last had gone. 'They brought me brick-tea such as the Russians sell, and a tea-urn from Peshawur. Show me, now, how the English Memsahibs make tea.'

The brick-tea was abominable. When it was finished Wali Dad suggested going into the streets. 'I am nearly sure that there will be trouble to-night,' he said. 'All the City thinks so, and *Vox Populi* is *Vox Dei*,[30] as the Babus say. Now I tell you that at the corner of the Padshahi Gate you will find my horse all this night if you want to go about and to see things. It is a most disgraceful exhibition. Where is the pleasure of saying "*Ya Hasan! Ya Hussain!*"[31] twenty thousand times in a night?'

All the processions – there were two-and-twenty of them – were now well within the City walls. The drums were beating afresh, the crowd were howling 'Ya Hasan! Ya Hussain!' and beating their breasts, the brass bands were playing their loudest, and at every corner where space allowed, Mohammedan preachers were telling the lamentable story of the death of the Martyrs. It was impossible to move except with the crowd, for the streets were not more than twenty feet wide. In the Hindu quarters the shutters of all the shops were up and cross-barred. As the first *tazia*, a gorgeous erection, ten feet high, was borne aloft on the shoulders of a score of stout men into the semi-darkness of the Gully of the Horsemen, a brickbat crashed through its talc and tinsel sides.

'Into thy hands, O Lord!'[32] murmured Wali Dad profanely, as a yell went up from behind, and a native officer of Police jammed his horse through the crowd. Another brickbat followed, and the *tazia* staggered and swayed where it had stopped.

'Go on! In the name of the Sirkar,[33] go forward!' shouted the Police-man, but there was an ugly cracking and splintering of shutters, and the crowd halted, with oaths and growlings, before the house whence the brickbat had been thrown.

Then, without any warning, broke the storm – not only in the Gully of the Horsemen, but in half-a-dozen other places. The *tazias* rocked like ships at sea, the long pole-torches dipped and rose round them while the men shouted: 'The Hindus are dishonouring the *tazias*! Strike! strike! Into their temples for the Faith!' The six or eight Policemen with each *tazia* drew their batons, and struck as long as they could in the hope of forcing the mob forward, but they were overpowered, and as contingents of Hindus poured into the streets, the fight became general. Half a mile away where the *tazias* were yet untouched the drums and the shrieks of 'Ya Hasan! Ya Hussain!' continued, but not for long. The priests at the corners of the streets knocked the legs from the bedsteads that supported their pulpits and smote for the Faith, while stones fell from the silent houses upon friend and foe, and the packed streets bellowed: '*Din! Din! Din!*' A *tazia* caught fire, and was dropped for a flaming barrier between Hindu and Mussulman at the corner of the Gully. Then the crowd surged forward, and Wali Dad drew me close to the stone pillar of a well.

'It was intended from the beginning!' he shouted in my ear, with more heat than blank unbelief should be guilty of. 'The bricks were carried up to the houses beforehand. These swine of Hindus! We shall be killing kine in their temples[34] to-night!'

Tazia after *tazia*, some burning, others torn to pieces, hurried past us and the mob with them, howling, shrieking, and striking at the house doors in their flight. At last we saw the reason of the rush. Hugonin, the Assistant District Superintendent of Police, a boy of twenty, had got together thirty constables and was forcing the crowd through the streets. His old grey Police-horse showed no sign of uneasiness as it was spurred breast-on into the crowd, and the long dog-whip with which he had armed himself was never still.

'They know we haven't enough Police to hold 'em,' he cried as he passed me, mopping a cut on his face. 'They *know* we haven't! Aren't any of the men from the Club coming down to help? Get on, you sons of burnt fathers!' The dog-whip cracked across the writhing backs, and the constables smote afresh with baton and gun-butt. With these passed the lights and the shouting, and Wali Dad began to swear under his breath. From Fort Amara shot up a single rocket; then two side by side. It was the signal for troops.

Petitt, the Deputy-Commissioner, covered with dust and sweat, but calm and gently smiling, cantered up the clean-swept street in rear of the main body of the rioters. 'No one killed yet,' he shouted. 'I'll keep 'em on the run till dawn! Don't let 'em halt, Hugonin! Trot 'em about till the troops come.'

The science of the defence lay solely in keeping the mob on the move. If they had breathing-space they would halt and fire a house, and then the work of restoring order would be more difficult, to say the least of it. Flames have the same effect on a crowd as blood has on a wild beast.

Word had reached the Club, and men in evening-dress were beginning to show themselves and lend a hand in heading off and breaking up the shouting masses with stirrup-leathers, whips, or chance-found staves. They were not very often attacked, for the rioters had sense enough to know that the death of a European would not mean one hanging but many, and possibly the appearance of the thrice-dreaded Artillery. The clamour in the City redoubled. The Hindus had descended into the streets in real earnest and ere long the mob returned. It was a strange sight. There were no *tazias* – only their riven platforms – and there were no Police. Here and there a City dignitary, Hindu or Mohammedan, was vainly imploring his co-religionists to keep quiet and behave themselves – advice for which his white beard was pulled. Then a native officer of Police, unhorsed but still using his spurs with effect, would be borne along, warning all the crowd of the danger of insulting the Government. Everywhere men struck aimlessly with sticks, grasping each other by the throat, howling and foaming with rage, or beat with their bare hands on the doors of the houses.

'It is a lucky thing that they are fighting with natural weapons,' I said to Wali Dad, 'else we should have half the City killed.'

I turned as I spoke and looked at his face. His nostrils were distended, his eyes were fixed, and he was smiting himself softly on the breast. The crowd poured by with renewed riot – a gang of Mussulmans hard pressed by some hundred Hindu fanatics. Wali Dad left my side with an oath, and shouting: '*Ya Hasan! Ya Hussain!*' plunged into the thick of the fight, where I lost sight of him.

I fled by a side alley to the Padshahi Gate, where I found Wali Dad's horse, and thence rode to the Fort. Once outside the City wall, the tumult sank to a dull roar, very impressive under the stars and reflecting great credit on the fifty thousand angry able-bodied men who were making it. The troops who, at the Deputy-Commissioner's instance, had been ordered to rendezvous quietly near the Fort, showed no signs of being impressed. Two companies of Native Infantry, a squadron of Native Cavalry, and a company of British Infantry were kicking their heels in the shadow of the East face, waiting for orders to march in. I am sorry to say that they were all pleased, unholily pleased, at the chance of what they called 'a little fun'. The senior officers, to be sure, grumbled at having been kept out of bed, and the English troops pretended to be sulky, but there was joy in the hearts of all the sub-alterns, and whispers ran up and down the line: 'No ball-cartridge – what a beastly shame!' 'D'you think the beggars will really stand up to us?' 'Hope I shall meet my money-lender there. I owe him more than I can afford.' 'Oh, they won't let us even unsheath swords.' 'Hurrah! Up goes the fourth rocket. Fall in, there!'

The Garrison Artillery, who to the last cherished a wild hope that they might be allowed to bombard the City at a hundred yards' range, lined the parapet above the East gateway and cheered themselves hoarse as the British Infantry doubled along the road to the Main Gate of the City. The Cavalry cantered on to the Padshahi Gate, and the Native Infantry marched slowly to the Gate of the Butchers. The surprise was intended to be of a distinctly unpleasant nature, and to come on top of the defeat of the Police, who had been just able to keep the Mohammedans from firing the houses of a few leading Hindus. The bulk of the riot lay in the north and north-west wards. The east and south-east were by this time dark and silent, and I rode hastily to Lalun's house, for I wished to tell her to send someone in search of Wali Dad. The house was unlighted, but the door was open, and I climbed upstairs in the darkness. One small lamp in the white room showed Lalun and her maid leaning half out of the window, breathing heavily and evidently pulling at something that refused to come.

'Thou art late – very late,' gasped Lalun without turning her head. 'Help us now, O Fool, if thou hast not spent thy strength howling among the *tazias*. Pull! Nasiban and I can do no more! O Sahib, is it you? The Hindus have been hunting an old Mohammedan round the Ditch with clubs. If they find him again they will kill him. Help us to pull him up.'

I put my hands to the long red silk waist-cloth that was hanging out of the window, and we three pulled and pulled with all the strength at our command. There was something very heavy at the end, and it swore in an unknown tongue as it kicked against the City wall.

'Pull, oh, pull!' said Lalun at the last. A pair of brown hands grasped the window-sill and a venerable Mohammedan tumbled upon the floor, very much out of breath. His jaws were tied up, his turban had fallen over one eye, and he was dusty and angry.

Lalun hid her face in her hands for an instant and said something about Wali Dad that I could not catch.

Then, to my extreme gratification, she threw her arms round my neck and murmured pretty things. I was in no haste to stop her; and Nasiban, being a handmaiden of tact, turned to the big jewel-chest that stands in the corner of the white room and rummaged among the contents. The Mohammedan sat on the floor and glared.

'One service more, Sahib, since thou hast come so opportunely,' said Lalun. 'Wilt thou' – it is very nice to be thou-ed by Lalun – 'take this old man across the City – the troops are everywhere, and they might hurt him, for he is old – to the Kumharsen Gate? There I think he may find a carriage to take him to his house. He is a friend of mine, and thou art – more than a friend – therefore I ask this.'

Nasiban bent over the old man, tucked something into his belt, and I raised him up and led him into the streets. In crossing from the east to the west of the City there was no chance of avoiding the troops and the crowd. Long before I reached the Gully of the Horsemen I heard the shouts of the British Infantry crying cheerily: '*Hutt*, ye beggars! *Hutt*, ye devils! Get along! Go forward, there!' Then followed the ringing of rifle-butts and shrieks of pain. The troops were banging the bare toes of the mob with their gun-butts – for not a bayonet had been fixed. My companion mumbled and jabbered as we walked on until we were carried back by the crowd and had to force our way to the troops. I caught him by the wrist and felt a bangle there – the iron bangle of the Sikhs[35] – but I had no suspicions, for Lalun had only ten minutes before put her arms round me. Thrice we were carried back by the crowd, and when we made our way past the British Infantry it was to meet the Sikh Cavalry driving another mob before them with the butts of their lances.

'What are these dogs?' said the old man.

'Sikhs of the Cavalry, Father,' I said, and we edged our way up the line of horses two abreast and found the Deputy-Commissioner, his helmet smashed on his head, surrounded by a knot of men who had come down from the Club as amateur constables and had helped the Police mightily.

'We'll keep 'em on the run till dawn,' said Petitt. 'Who's your villainous friend?'

I had only time to say: 'The Protection of the Sirkar!' when a fresh crowd flying before the Native Infantry carried us a hundred yards nearer to the Kumharsen Gate, and Petitt was swept away like a shadow.

'I do not know – I cannot see – this is all new to me!' moaned my companion. 'How many troops are there in the City?'

'Perhaps five hundred,' I said.

'A lakh[36] of men beaten by five hundred – and Sikhs among them! Surely, surely, I am an old man, but – the Kumharsen Gate is new. Who pulled down the stone lions? Where is the conduit? Sahib, I am a very old man, and, alas, I – I cannot stand.' He dropped in the shadow of the Kumharsen Gate where there was no disturbance. A fat gentleman wearing gold pince-nez came out of the darkness.

'You are most kind to bring my old friend,' he said suavely. 'He is a landholder of Akala. He should not be in a big City when there is religious excitement. But I have a carriage here. You are quite truly kind. Will you help me to put him into the carriage? It is very late.'

We bundled the old man into a hired victoria that stood close to the gate, and I turned back to the house on the City wall. The troops were driving the people to and fro, while the Police shouted, 'To your houses! Get to your houses!' and the dog-whip of the Assistant District Superintendent cracked remorselessly. Terror-stricken *bunnias*[37] clung to the stirrups of the Cavalry, crying that their houses had been robbed (which was a lie), and the burly Sikh horsemen patted them on the shoulder and bade them return to those houses lest a worse thing should happen. Parties of five or six British soldiers, joining arms, swept down the side-gullies, their rifles on their backs, stamping, with shouting and song, upon the toes of Hindu and Mussulman. Never was religious enthusiasm more systematically squashed; and never were poor breakers of the peace more utterly weary and footsore. They were routed out of holes and corners, from behind well-pillars and byres, and bidden to go to their houses. If they had no houses to go to, so much the worse for their toes.

On returning to Lalun's door I stumbled over a man at the threshold. He was sobbing hysterically and his arms flapped like the wings of a goose. It was Wali Dad, Agnostic and Unbeliever, shoeless, turbanless, and frothing at the mouth, the flesh on his chest bruised and bleeding from the vehemence with which he had smitten himself. A broken torch-handle lay by his side, and his quivering lips murmured, '*Ya Hasan! Ya Hussain!*' as I stooped over him. I pushed him a few steps up the staircase, threw a pebble at Lalun's City window and hurried home.

Most of the streets were very still, and the cold wind that comes before the dawn whistled down them. In the centre of the Square of the Mosque a man was bending over a corpse. The skull had been smashed in by gun-butt or bamboo-stave.

'It is expedient that one man should die for the people,'[38] said Petitt grimly, raising the shapeless head. 'These brutes were beginning to show their teeth too much.'

And from afar we could hear the soldiers singing 'Two Lovely Black Eyes'[39] as they drove the remnant of the rioters within doors.

Of course you can guess what happened? I was not so clever. When the news went abroad that Khem Singh had escaped from the Fort, I did not, since I was then living this story, not writing it, connect myself, or Lalun, or the fat gentleman of the gold pince-nez, with his disappearance. Nor did it strike me that Wali Dad was the man who should have convoyed him across the City, or that Lalun's arms round my neck were put there to hide the money that Nasiban gave to Khem Singh, and that Lalun had used me and my white face as even a better safeguard than Wali Dad who proved himself so untrustworthy. All that I knew at the time was that, when Fort Amara was taken up with the riots, Khem Singh profited by the confusion to get away, and that his two Sikh guards also escaped.

But later on I received full enlightenment; and so did Khem Singh. He fled to those who knew him in the old days, but many of them were dead and more were changed, and all knew something of the Wrath of the Government. He went to the young men, but the glamour of his name had passed away, and they were entering native regiments or Government offices, and Khem Singh could give them neither pension, decorations, nor influence – nothing but a glorious death with their back to the mouth of a gun. He wrote letters and made promises, and the letters fell into bad hands, and a wholly insignificant subordinate officer of Police tracked them down and gained promotion thereby. Moreover, Khem Singh was old, and aniseed brandy was scarce, and he had left his silver cooking-pots in Fort Amara with his nice warm bedding, and the gentleman with the gold pince-nez was told by Those who had employed him that Khem Singh as a popular leader was not worth the money paid.

'Great is the mercy of these fools of English!' said Khem Singh when the situation was put before him. 'I will go back to Fort Amara of my own free will and gain honour. Give me good clothes to return in.'

So, at his own time, Khem Singh knocked at the wicket-gate of the Fort and walked to the Captain and the Subaltern, who were nearly grey-headed on account of correspondence that daily arrived from Simla marked 'Private'.

'I have come back, Captain Sahib,' said Khem Singh. 'Put no more guards over me. It is no good out yonder.'

A week later I saw him for the first time to my knowledge, and he made as though there were an understanding between us.

'It was well done, Sahib,' said he, 'and greatly I admired your astuteness in thus boldly facing the troops when I, whom they would have doubtless torn to pieces, was with you. Now there is a man in Fort Ooltagarh whom a bold man could with ease help to escape. This is the position of the Fort as I draw it on the sand – '

But I was thinking how I had become Lalun's Vizier after all.

'THE CITY OF DREADFUL NIGHT'

The dense wet heat that hung over the face of the land, like a blanket, prevented all hope of sleep in the first instance. The cicalas helped the heat, and the yelling jackals the cicalas. It was impossible to sit still in the dark, empty, echoing house and watch the punkah beat the dead air. So, at ten o'clock of the night, I set my walking-stick on end in the middle of the garden, and waited to see how it would fall. It pointed directly down the moonlit road that leads to the City of Dreadful Night. The sound of its fall disturbed a hare. She limped from her form and ran across to a disused Mohammedan burial-ground, where the jawless skulls and rough-butted shank-bones, heartlessly exposed by the July rains, glimmered like mother o' pearl on the rain-channelled soil. The heated air and the heavy earth had driven the very dead upward for coolness' sake. The hare limped on, snuffed curiously at a fragment of a smoke-stained lamp-shard, and died out, in the shadow of a clump of tamarisk trees.

The mat-weaver's hut under the lee of the Hindu temple was full of sleeping men who lay like sheeted corpses. Overhead blazed the unwinking eye of the Moon. Darkness gives at least a false impression of coolness. It was hard not to believe that the flood of light from above was warm. Not so hot as the Sun, but still sickly warm, and heating the heavy air beyond what was our due. Straight as a bar of polished steel ran the road to the City of Dreadful Night; and on either side of the road lay corpses disposed on beds in fantastic attitudes – one hundred and seventy bodies of men. Some shrouded all in white with bound-up mouths; some naked and black as ebony in the strong light; and one – that lay face upwards with dropped jaw, far away from the others – silvery white and ashen grey.

'A leper asleep; and the remainder wearied coolies, servants, small shopkeepers, and drivers from the hack-stand hard by. The scene – a main approach to Lahore city, and the night a warm one in August.' This was all that there was to be seen; but by no means all that one could see. The witchery of the moonlight was everywhere; and the world was horribly changed. The long line of the naked dead, flanked by the rigid silver statue, was not pleasant to look upon. It was made up of men alone. Were the womenkind, then, forced to sleep in the shelter of the stifling mud huts as best they might? The fretful wail of a child from a low mud roof answered the question. Where the children are the mothers must be also to look after them. They need care on these sweltering nights. A black little bullet-head peeped over the coping, and a thin – a painfully thin – brown leg was slid over on to the gutter-pipe. There was a sharp clink of glass bracelets; a woman's arm showed for an instant above the parapet, twined itself round the lean little neck, and the child was dragged back, protesting, to the shelter of the bedstead. His thin, high-pitched shriek died out in the thick air almost as soon as it was raised; for even the children of the soil found it too hot to weep.

More corpses; more stretches of moonlit, white road; a string of sleeping camels at rest by the wayside; a vision of scudding jackals; *ekka*-ponies[1] asleep – the harness still on their backs, and the brass-studded country carts, winking in the moonlight – and again more corpses. Wherever a grain-cart atilt, a tree-trunk, a sawn log, a couple of bamboos and a few handfuls of thatch cast a shadow, the ground is covered with them. They lie – some face downwards, arms folded, in the dust; some with clasped hands flung up above their heads; some curled up dog-wise; some thrown like limp gunny-bags[2] over the side of the grain-carts; and some bowed with their brows on their knees in the full glare of the Moon. It would be a comfort if they were only given to snoring; but they are not, and the likeness to corpses is unbroken in all respects save one. The lean dogs snuff at them and turn away. Here and there a tiny child lies on his father's bedstead, and a protecting arm is thrown round it in every instance. But, for the most part, the children sleep with their mothers on the house-tops. Yellow-skinned, white-toothed pariahs[3] are not to be trusted within reach of brown bodies.

A stifling hot blast from the mouth of the Delhi Gate nearly ends my resolution of entering the City of Dreadful Night at this hour. It is a compound of all evil savours, animal and vegetable, that a walled city can brew in a day and a night. The temperature within the motionless groves of plantain and orange-trees outside the city walls seems chilly by comparison. Heaven help all sick persons and young children within the city to-night! The high house-walls are still radiating heat savagely, and from obscure side gullies fetid breezes eddy that ought to poison a buffalo. But the buffaloes do not heed. A drove of them are parading the vacant main street, stopping now and then to lay their ponderous muzzles against the closed shutters of a grain-dealer's shop, and to blow thereon like grampuses.[4]

Then silence follows – the silence that is full of the night noises of a great city. A stringed instrument of some kind is just, and only just, audible. High overhead someone throws open a window, and the rattle of the woodwork echoes down in the empty street. On one of the roofs a hookah is in full blast, and the men are talking softly as the pipe gutters. A little farther on the noise of conversation is more distinct. A slit of light shows itself between the sliding shutters of a shop. Inside, a stubble-bearded, weary-eyed trader is balancing his account-books among the bales of cotton prints that surround him. Three sheeted figures bear him company, and throw in a remark from time to time. First he makes an entry, then a remark; then passes the back of his hand across his streaming forehead. The heat in the built-in street is fearful. Inside the shops it must be almost unendurable. But the work goes on steadily; entry, guttural growl, and uplifted hand-stroke succeeding each other with the precision of clockwork.

A policeman – turbanless and fast asleep – lies across the road on the way to the Mosque of Wazir Khan.[5] A bar of moonlight falls across the forehead and eyes of the sleeper, but he never stirs. It is close upon midnight, and the heat seems to be increasing. The open square in front of the Mosque is crowded with corpses; and a man must pick his way carefully for fear of treading on them. The moonlight stripes the Mosque's high front of coloured enamel-work in broad diagonal bands; and each separate dreaming pigeon in the niches and corners of the masonry throws a squab little shadow. Sheeted ghosts rise up wearily from their pallets, and flit into the dark depths of the building. Is it possible to climb to the top of the great Minars,[6] and thence to look down on the city? At all events the attempt is worth making, and the chances are that the door of the staircase will be unlocked. Unlocked it is, but a deeply sleeping janitor lies across the threshold, face turned to the Moon. A rat dashes out of his turban at the sound of approaching footsteps. The man grunts, opens his eyes for a minute, turns round, and goes to sleep again. All the heat of a decade of fierce Indian summers is stored in the pitch-black, polished walls of the corkscrew staircase. Half-way up there is something alive, warm, and feathery; and it snores. Driven from step to step as it catches the sound of my advance, it flutters to the top and reveals itself as a yellow-eyed, angry kite.[7] Dozens of kites are asleep on this and the other Minars, and on the domes below. There is the shadow of a cool, or at least a less sultry breeze at this height; and, refreshed thereby, I turn to look on the City of Dreadful Night.

Doré might have drawn it! Zola[8] could describe it – this spectacle of sleeping thousands in the moonlight and in the shadow of the Moon. The roof-tops are crammed with men, women, and children, and the air is full of undistinguishable noises. They are restless in the City of Dreadful Night; and small wonder. The marvel is that they can even breathe. If you gaze intently at the multitude you can see that they are almost as uneasy as a daylight crowd, but the tumult is subdued. Everywhere, in the strong light, you can watch the sleepers turning to and fro, shifting their beds and again resettling them. In the pit-like courtyards of the houses there is the same movement.

The pitiless Moon shows it all. Shows, too, the plains outside the city, and here and there a hand's-breadth of the Ravee[9] without the walls. Shows lastly, a splash of glittering silver on a house-top almost directly below the mosque Minar. Some poor soul has risen to throw a jar of water over his fevered body; the tinkle of the falling water strikes faintly on the ear. Two or three other men, in far-off corners of the City of Dreadful Night, follow his example, and the water flashes like heliographic signals.[10] A small cloud passes over the face of the Moon, and the city and its inhabitants – clear drawn in black and white before – fade into masses of black and deeper black. Still the unrestful noise continues, the sigh of a great city overwhelmed with the heat, and of a people seeking in vain for rest. It is only the lower-class women who sleep on the house-tops. What must the torment be in the latticed zenanas, where a few lamps are still twinkling? There are footfalls in the court below. It is the *Muezzin*[11] – faithful minister; but he ought to have been here an hour ago to tell the Faithful that prayer is better than sleep – the sleep that will not come to the city.

The *Muezzin* fumbles for a moment with the door of one of the Minars, disappears awhile, and a bull-like roar – a magnificent bass thunder – tells that he has reached the top of the Minar. They must hear the cry to the banks of the shrunken Ravee itself! Even across the courtyard it is almost overpowering. The cloud drifts by and shows him outlined in black against the sky, hands laid upon his ears, and broad chest heaving with the play of his lungs – '*Allah ho Akbar!*';[12] then a pause while another *Muezzin* somewhere in the direction of the Golden Temple takes up the call – '*Allah ho Akbar!*' Again and again, four times in all, and from the bedsteads a dozen men have risen up already. – 'I bear witness that there is no God but God.' What a splendid cry it is, the proclamation of the creed that brings men out of their beds by scores at midnight! Once again he thunders through the same phrase, shaking with the vehemence of his own voice; and then, far and near, the night air rings with 'Mohammed is the Prophet of God.' It is as though he were flinging his defiance to the far-off horizon, where the summer lightning plays and leaps like a bared sword. Every *Muezzin* in the city is in full cry, and some men on the roof-tops are beginning to kneel. A long pause precedes the last cry, '*La ilaha Illallah*!'[13] and the silence closes up on it, as the ram[14] on the head of a cotton-bale.

The *Muezzin* stumbles down the dark stairway grumbling in his beard. He passes the arch of the entrance and disappears. Then the stifling silence settles down over the City of Dreadful Night. The kites on the Minar sleep again, snoring more loudly, the hot breeze comes up in puffs and lazy eddies, and the Moon slides down towards the horizon. Seated with both elbows on the parapet of the tower, one can watch and wonder over that heat-tortured hive till the dawn. 'How do they live down there? What do they think of? When will they awake?' More tinkling of sluiced water-pots; faint jarring of wooden bedsteads moved into or out of the shadows; uncouth music of stringed instruments softened by distance into a plaintive wail, and one low grumble of far-off thunder. In the courtyard of the mosque the janitor, who lay across the threshold of the Minar when I came up, starts wildly in his sleep, throws his hands above his head, mutters something, and falls back again. Lulled by the snoring of the kites – they snore like over-gorged humans – I drop off into an uneasy doze, conscious that three o'clock has struck, and that there is a slight – a very slight – coolness in the atmosphere. The city is absolutely quiet now, but for some vagrant dog's love-song. Nothing save dead heavy sleep.

Several weeks of darkness pass after this. For the Moon has gone out. The very dogs are still, and I watch for the first light of the dawn before making my way homeward. Again the noise of shuffling feet. The morning call is about to begin, and my night watch is over. '*Allah ho Akbar! Allah ho Akbar!*' The east grows grey, and presently saffron; the dawn wind comes up as though the *Muezzin* had summoned it; and, as one man, the City of Dreadful Night rises from its bed and turns its face towards the dawning day. With return of life comes return of sound. First a low whisper, then a deep bass hum; for it must be remembered that the entire city is on the house-tops. My eyelids weighed down with the arrears of long-deferred sleep, I escape from the Minar through the courtyard and out into the square beyond, where the sleepers have risen, stowed away the bedsteads, and are discussing the morning hookah. The minute's freshness of the air has gone, and it is as hot as at first.

'Will the Sahib, out of his kindness, make room?' What is it? Something borne on men's shoulders comes by in the half-light, and I stand back. A woman's corpse going down to the burning-ghat, and a bystander says, 'She died at midnight from the heat.' So the City was of Death as well as Night after all.

AT THE END OF
THE PASSAGE

The sky is lead, and our faces are red,
   And the Gates of Hell are opened and riven,
   And the winds of Hell are loosened and driven,
   And the dust flies up in the face of Heaven,
And the clouds come down in a fiery sheet,
   Heavy to raise and hard to be borne.
And the soul of man is turned from his meat,
   Turned from the trifles for which he has striven,
   Sick in his body, and heavy-hearted,
And his soul flies up like the dust in the street,
   Breaks from his flesh and is gone and departed
Like the blasts that they blow on the cholera-horn.
                     Himalayan[1]

Four men, each entitled to 'life, liberty, and the pursuit of happiness',[2] sat at a table playing whist. The thermometer marked – for them – one hundred and one degrees of heat. The room was darkened[3] till it was only just possible to distinguish the pips of the cards and the very white faces of the players. A tattered, rotten punkah[4] of whitewashed calico was puddling the hot air and whining dolefully at each stroke. Outside lay gloom of a November day in London. There was neither sky, sun, nor horizon, – nothing but a brown-purple haze of heat. It was as though the earth were dying of apoplexy.[5]

From time to time clouds of tawny dust rose from the ground without wind or warning, flung themselves tablecloth-wise among the tops of the parched trees, and came down again. Then a whirling dust-devil would scutter across the plain for a couple of miles, break, and fall outward, though there was nothing to check its flight save a long low line of piled railway-sleepers white with the dust, a cluster of huts made of mud, condemned rails, and canvas, and the one squat four-roomed bungalow that belonged to the assistant engineer in charge of a section of the Gaudhari State line then under construction.

The four, stripped to the thinnest of sleeping-suits, played whist crossly, with wranglings as to leads and returns. It was not the best kind of whist, but they had taken some trouble to arrive at it. Mottram of the Indian Survey[6] had ridden thirty and railed one hundred miles from his lonely post in the desert since the night before; Lowndes of the Civil Service, on special duty in the Political Department,[7] had come as far to escape for an instant the miserable intrigues of an impoverished Native State whose king alternately fawned and blustered for more money from the pitiful revenues contributed by hard-wrung peasants and despairing camel-breeders; Spurstow, the doctor of the line, had left a cholera-stricken camp of coolies to look after itself for forty-eight hours while he associated with white men once more. Hummil, the assistant engineer, was the host. He stood fast and received his friends thus every Sunday if they could come in. When one of them failed to appear, he would send a telegram to his last address, in order that he might know whether the defaulter were dead or alive. There are very many places in the East where it is not good or kind to let your acquaintances drop out of sight even for one short week.

The players were not conscious of any special regard for each other. They squabbled whenever they met; but they ardently desired to meet, as men without water desire to drink. They were lonely folk who understood the dread meaning of loneliness. They were all under thirty years of age, – which is too soon for any man to possess that knowledge.

'Pilsener?' said Spurstow, after the second rubber, mopping his forehead.

'Beer's out, I'm sorry to say, and there's hardly enough soda-water for to-night,' said Hummil.

'What filthy bad management!' Spurstow snarled.

'Can't help it. I've written and wired; but the trains don't come through regularly yet. Last week the ice ran out, – as Lowndes knows.'

'Glad I didn't come. I could ha' sent you some if I had known, though. Phew! it's too hot to go on playing bumble-puppy.'[8] This with a savage scowl at Lowndes, who only laughed. He was a hardened offender.

Mottram rose from the table and looked out of a chink in the shutters.

'What a sweet day!' said he.

The company yawned all together and betook themselves to an aimless investigation of all Hummil's possessions, – guns, tattered novels, saddlery, spurs, and the like. They had fingered them a score of times before, but there was really nothing else to do.

'Got anything fresh?' said Lowndes.

'Last week's *Gazette of India*, and a cutting from a Home paper. My father sent it out. It's rather amusing.'

'One of those vestrymen[9] that call 'emselves MP's again, is it?' said Spurstow, who read his newspapers when he could get them.

'Yes. Listen to this. It's to your address, Lowndes. The man was making a speech to his constituents, and he piled it on. Here's a sample: "And I assert unhesitatingly that the Civil Service in India is the preserve – the pet preserve – of the aristocracy of England. What does the democracy – what do the masses – get from that country, which we have step by step fraudulently annexed? I answer, nothing whatever. It is farmed with a single eye to their own interests by the scions of the aristocracy. They take good care to maintain their lavish scale of incomes, to avoid or stifle any inquiries into the nature and conduct of their administration, while they themselves force the unhappy peasant to pay with the sweat of his brow for all the luxuries in which they are lapped."' Hummil waved the cutting above his head. "'Ear! 'ear!' said his audience.

Then Lowndes, meditatively: 'I'd give – I'd give three months' pay to have that gentleman spend one month with me and see how the free and independent native prince works things. Old Timbersides' – this was his flippant title for an honoured and decorated feudatory prince – 'has been wearing my life out this week past for money. By Jove, his latest performance was to send me one of his women as a bribe!'

'Good for you! Did you accept it?' said Mottram.

'No. I rather wish I had, now. She was a pretty little person, and she yarned away to me about the horrible destitution among the king's women-folk. The darlings haven't had any new clothes for nearly a month, and the old man wants to buy a new drag[10] from Calcutta, – solid silver railings and silver lamps, and trifles of that kind. I've tried to make him understand that he has played the deuce with the revenues for the last twenty years and must go slow. He can't see it.'

'But he has the ancestral treasure-vaults to draw on. There must be three millions at least in jewels and coin under his palace,' said Hummil.

'Catch a native king disturbing the family treasure! The priests forbid it except as the last resort. Old Timbersides has added something like a quarter of a million to the deposit in his reign.'

'Where the mischief does it all come from?' said Mottram.

'The country. The state of the people is enough to make you sick. I've known the tax-men wait by a milch-camel till the foal was born and then hurry off the mother for arrears. And what can I do? I can't get the Court clerks to give me any accounts; I can't raise anything more than a fat smile from the commander-in-chief when I find out the troops are three months in arrears; and old Timbersides begins to weep when I speak to him. He has taken to the King's Peg heavily, – liqueur brandy for whisky, and Heidsieck[11] for soda-water.'

'That's what the Rao of Jubela took to. Even a native can't last long at that,' said Spurstow. 'He'll go out.'

'And a good thing, too. Then I suppose we'll have a council of regency, and a tutor for the young prince, and hand him back his kingdom with ten years' accumulations.'

'Whereupon that young prince, having been taught all the vices of the English, will play ducks and drakes with the money and undo ten years' work in eighteen months. I've seen that business before,' said Spurstow. 'I should tackle the king with a light hand if I were you, Lowndes. They'll hate you quite enough under any circumstances.'

'That's all very well. The man who looks on can talk about the light hand; but you can't clean a pig-sty with a pen dipped in rose-water. I know my risks; but nothing has happened yet. My servant's an old Pathan, and he cooks for me. They are hardly likely to bribe him, and I don't accept food from my true friends, as they call themselves. Oh, but it's weary work! I'd sooner be with you, Spurstow. There's shooting near your camp.'

'Would you? I don't think it. About fifteen deaths a day don't incite a man to shoot anything but himself. And the worst of it is that the poor devils look at you as though you ought to save them. Lord knows, I've tried everything. My last attempt was empirical, but it pulled an old man through. He was brought to me apparently past hope, and I gave him gin and Worcester sauce with cayenne. It cured him; but I don't recommend it.'

'How do the cases run generally?' said Hummil.

'Very simply indeed. Chlorodyne,[12] opium pill, chlorodyne, collapse, nitre,[13] bricks to the feet, and then – the burning-ghat. The last seems to be the only thing that stops the trouble. It's black cholera,[14] you know. Poor devils! But, I will say, little Bunsee Lal, my apothecary, works like a demon. I've recommended him for promotion if he comes through it all alive.'

'And what are your chances, old man?' said Mottram.

'Don't know; don't care much; but I've sent the letter in. What are you doing with yourself generally?'

'Sitting under a table in the tent and spitting on the sextant[15] to keep it cool,' said the man of the Survey. 'Washing my eyes to avoid ophthalmia,[16] which I shall certainly get, and trying to make a sub-surveyor understand that an error of five degrees in an angle isn't quite so small as it looks. I'm altogether alone, y' know, and shall be till the end of the hot weather.'

'Hummil's the lucky man,' said Lowndes, flinging himself into a long chair. 'He has an actual roof – torn as to the ceiling-cloth, but still a roof – over his head. He sees one train daily. He can get beer and soda-water and ice 'em when God is good. He has books, pictures,' – they were torn from the *Graphic*,[17] – 'and the society of the excellent sub-contractor Jevins, besides the pleasure of receiving us weekly.'

Hummil smiled grimly. 'Yes, I'm the lucky man, I suppose. Jevins is luckier.'

'How? Not –'

'Yes. Went out. Last Monday.'

'By his own hand?' said Spurstow quickly, hinting the suspicion that was in everybody's mind. There was no cholera near Hummil's section. Even fever gives a man at least a week's grace, and sudden death generally implied self-slaughter.

'I judge no man this weather,' said Hummil. 'He had a touch of the sun, I fancy; for last week, after you fellows had left, he came into the veranda and told me that he was going home to see his wife, in Market Street, Liverpool, that evening.

'I got the apothecary in to look at him, and we tried to make him lie down. After an hour or two he rubbed his eyes and said he believed he had had a fit, – hoped he hadn't said anything rude. Jevins had a great idea of bettering himself socially. He was very like Chucks[18] in his language.'

'Well?'

'Then he went to his own bungalow and began cleaning a rifle. He told the servant that he was going to shoot buck in the morning. Naturally he fumbled with the trigger, and shot himself through the head – accidentally. The apothecary sent in a report to my chief, and Jevins is buried somewhere out there. I'd have wired to you, Spurstow, if you could have done anything.'

'You're a queer chap,' said Mottram. 'If you'd killed the man yourself you couldn't have been more quiet about the business.'

'Good Lord! what does it matter?' said Hummil calmly. 'I've got to do a lot of his overseeing work in addition to my own. I'm the only person that suffers. Jevins is out of it, – by pure accident, of course, but out of it. The apothecary was going to write a long screed on suicide. Trust a Babu[19] to drivel when he gets the chance.'

'Why didn't you let it go in as suicide?' said Lowndes.

'No direct proof. A man hasn't many privileges in this country, but he might at least be allowed to mishandle his own rifle. Besides, some day I may need a man to smother up an accident to myself. Live and let live. Die and let die.'

'You take a pill,' said Spurstow, who had been watching Hummil's white face narrowly. 'Take a pill, and don't be an ass. That sort of talk is skittles. Anyhow, suicide is shirking your work. If I were Job[20] ten times over, I should be so interested in what was going to happen next that I'd stay on and watch.'

'Ah! I've lost that curiosity,' said Hummil.

'Liver out of order?' said Lowndes feelingly.

'No. Can't sleep. That's worse.'

'By Jove, it is!' said Mottram. 'I'm that way every now and then, and the fit has to wear itself out. What do you take for it?'

'Nothing. What's the use? I haven't had ten minutes' sleep since Friday morning.'

'Poor chap! Spurstow, you ought to attend to this,' said Mottram. 'Now you mention it, your eyes *are* rather gummy and swollen.'

Spurstow, still watching Hummil, laughed lightly. 'I'll patch him up, later on. Is it too hot, do you think, to go for a ride?'

'Where to?' said Lowndes wearily. 'We shall have to go away at eight, and there'll be riding enough for us then. I hate a horse when I have to use him as a necessity. Oh, heavens! what is there to do?'

'Begin whist again, at chick points ['a chick' is supposed to be eight shillings] and a gold mohur on the rub,'[21] said Spurstow promptly.

'Poker. A month's pay all round for the pool, – no limit, – and fifty-rupee raises. Somebody would be broken before we got up,' said Lowndes.

'Can't say that it would give me any pleasure to break any man in this company,' said Mottram. 'There isn't enough excitement in it, and it's foolish.' He crossed over to the worn and battered little camp-piano, – wreckage of a married household that had once held the bungalow, – and opened the case.

'It's used up long ago,' said Hummil. 'The servants have picked it to pieces.'

The piano was indeed hopelessly out of order, but Mottram managed to bring the rebellious notes into a sort of agreement, and there rose from the ragged keyboard something that might once have been the ghost of a popular music-hall song. The men in the long chairs turned with evident interest as Mottram banged the more lustily.

'That's good!' said Lowndes. 'By Jove! the last time I heard that song was in '79, or thereabouts, just before I came out.'

'Ah!' said Spurstow with pride, 'I was Home in '80.' And he mentioned a song of the streets popular at that date.

Mottram executed it roughly. Lowndes criticised and volunteered emendations. Mottram dashed into another ditty, not of the music-hall character, and made as if to rise.

'Sit down,' said Hummil. 'I didn't know that you had any music in your composition. Go on playing until you can't think of anything more. I'll have that piano tuned up before you come again. Play something festive.'

Very simple indeed were the tunes to which Mottram's art and the limitations of the piano could give effect, but the men listened with pleasure, and in the pauses talked all together of what they had seen or heard when they were last at Home. A dense dust-storm sprung up outside, and swept roaring over the house, enveloping it in the choking darkness of midnight, but Mottram continued unheeding, and the crazy tinkle reached the ears of the listeners above the flapping of the tattered ceiling-cloth.

In the silence after the storm he glided from the more directly personal songs of Scotland, half humming them as he played, into the Evening Hymn.

'Sunday,' said he, nodding his head.

'Go on. Don't apologise for it,' said Spurstow.

Hummil laughed long and riotously. 'Play it, by all means. You're full of surprises to-day. I didn't know you had such a gift of finished sarcasm. How does that thing go?'

Mottram took up the tune.

'Too slow by half. You miss the note of gratitude,' said Hummil. 'It ought to go to the "Grasshopper's Polka", – this way.' And he chanted, *prestissimo*,[22]

> 'Glory to thee, my God, this night,
> For all the blessings of the light.[23]

'That shows we really feel our blessings. How does it go on? –

> 'If in the night I sleepless lie,
> My soul with sacred thoughts supply;
> May no ill dreams disturb my rest, –

'Quicker, Mottram! –

> 'Or powers of darkness me molest!

'Bah! what an old hypocrite you are!'

'Don't be an ass,' said Lowndes. 'You are at full liberty to make fun of anything else you like, but leave that hymn alone. It's associated in my mind with the most sacred recollections – '

'Summer evenings in the country, – stained-glass window, – light going out, and you and she jamming your heads together over one hymn-book,' said Mottram.

'Yes, and a fat old cockchafer[24] hitting you in the eye when you walked home. Smell of hay, and a moon as big as a bandbox[25] sitting on the top of a haycock; bats, – roses, – milk and midges,' said Lowndes.

'Also mothers. I can just recollect my mother singing me to sleep with that when I was a little chap,' said Spurstow.

The darkness had fallen on the room. They could hear Hummil squirming in his chair.

'Consequently,' said he testily, 'you sing it when you are seven fathom[26] deep in Hell! It's an insult to the intelligence of the Deity to pretend we're anything but tortured rebels.'

'Take *two* pills,' said Spurstow; 'that's tortured liver.'

'The usually placid Hummil is in a vile bad temper. I'm sorry for his coolies to-morrow,' said Lowndes, as the servants brought in the lights and prepared the table for dinner.

As they were settling into their places about the miserable goat-chops and the smoked tapioca pudding, Spurstow took occasion to whisper to Mottram, 'Well done, David!'

'Look after Saul,[27] then,' was the reply.

'What are you two whispering about?' said Hummil suspiciously.

'Only saying that you are a damned poor host. This fowl can't be cut,' returned Spurstow with a sweet smile. 'Call this a dinner?'

'I can't help it. You don't expect a banquet, do you?'

Throughout that meal Hummil contrived laboriously to insult directly and pointedly all his guests in succession, and at each insult Spurstow kicked the aggrieved persons under the table; but he dared not exchange a glance of intelligence with either of them. Hummil's face was white and pinched, while his eyes were unnaturally large. No man dreamed for a moment of resenting his savage personalities, but as soon as the meal was over they made haste to get away.

'Don't go. You're just getting amusing, you fellows. I hope I haven't said anything that annoyed you. You're such touchy devils.' Then, changing the note into one of almost abject entreaty, Hummil added, 'I say, you surely aren't going?'

'In the language of the blessed Jorrocks, where I dines I sleeps,'[28] said Spurstow. 'I want to have a look at your coolies to-morrow, if you don't mind. You can give me a place to lie down in, I suppose?'

The others pleaded the urgency of their several duties next day, and, saddling up, departed together, Hummil begging them to come next Sunday. As they jogged off, Lowndes unbosomed himself to Mottram: –

'. . . And I never felt so like kicking a man at his own table in my life. He said I cheated at whist, and reminded me I was in debt! Told you you were as good as a liar to your face! You aren't half indignant enough over it.'

'Not I,' said Mottram. 'Poor devil! Did you ever know old Hummy behave like that before or within a hundred miles of it?'

'That's no excuse. Spurstow was hacking my shin all the time, so I kept a hand on myself. Else I should have – '

'No, you wouldn't. You'd have done as Hummy did about Jevins; judge no man this weather. By Jove! the buckle of my bridle is hot in my hand! Trot out a bit, and 'ware rat-holes.'

Ten minutes' trotting jerked out of Lowndes one very sage remark when he pulled up, sweating from every pore: –

'Good thing Spurstow's with him to-night.'

'Ye-es. Good man, Spurstow. Our roads turn here. See you again next Sunday, if the sun doesn't bowl me over.'

'S'pose so, unless old Timbersides' Finance Minister manages to dress some of my food. Good-night, and – God bless you!'

'What's wrong now?'

'Oh, nothing.' Lowndes gathered up his whip, and, as he flicked Mottram's mare on the flank, added, 'You're not a bad little chap, – that's all.' And the mare bolted half a mile across the sand, on the word.

In the assistant engineer's bungalow Spurstow and Hummil smoked the pipe of silence together, each narrowly watching the other. The capacity of a bachelor's establishment is as elastic as its arrangements are simple. A servant cleared away the dining-room table, brought in a couple of rude native bedsteads made of tape strung on a light wood frame, flung a square of cool Calcutta matting over each, set them side by side, pinned two towels to the punkah so that their fringes should just sweep clear of the sleeper's nose and mouth, and announced that the couches were ready.

The men flung themselves down, ordering the punkah-coolies by all the powers of Hell to pull. Every door and window was shut, for the outside air was that of an oven. The atmosphere within was only 104°, as the thermometer bore witness, and heavy with the foul smell of badly trimmed kerosene lamps; and this stench, combined with that of native tobacco, baked brick, and dried earth, sends the heart of many a strong man down to his boots, for it is the smell of the Great Indian Empire when she turns herself for six months into a house of torment. Spurstow packed his pillows craftily so that he reclined rather than lay, his head at a safe elevation above his feet. It is not good to sleep on a low pillow in the hot weather if you happen to be of thick-necked build, for you may pass with lively snores and gugglings from natural sleep into the deep slumber of heat-apoplexy.

'Pack your pillows,' said the doctor sharply, as he saw Hummil preparing to lie down at full length.

The night-light was trimmed; the shadow of the punkah wavered across the room, and the '*flick*' of the punkah-towel and the soft whine of the rope through the wall-hole followed it. Then the punkah flagged, almost ceased. The sweat poured from Spurstow's brow. Should he go out and harangue the coolie? It started forward again with a savage jerk, and a pin came out of the towels. When this was replaced, a tomtom in the coolie-lines began to beat with the steady throb of a swollen artery inside some brain-fevered skull. Spurstow turned on his side and swore gently. There was no movement on Hummil's part. The man had composed himself as rigidly as a corpse, his hands clinched at his sides. The respiration was too hurried for any suspicion of sleep. Spurstow looked at the set face. The jaws were clinched, and there was a pucker round the quivering eyelids.

'He's holding himself as tightly as ever he can,' thought Spurstow. 'What in the world is the matter with him? – Hummil!'

'Yes,' in a thick constrained voice.

'Can't you get to sleep?'

'No.'

'Head hot? Throat feeling bulgy? or how?'

'Neither, thanks. I don't sleep much, you know.'

'Feel pretty bad?'

'Pretty bad, thanks. There is a tomtom outside, isn't there? I thought it was my head at first . . . Oh, Spurstow, for pity's sake give me something that will put me asleep, – sound asleep, – if it's only for six hours!' He sprang up, trembling from head to foot. 'I haven't been able to sleep naturally for days, and I can't stand it! – I can't stand it!'

'Poor old chap!'

'That's no use. Give me something to make me sleep. I tell you I'm nearly mad. I don't know what I say half my time. For three weeks I've had to think and spell out every word that has come through my lips before I dared say it. Isn't that enough to drive a man mad? I can't see things correctly now, and I've lost my sense of touch. My skin aches – my skin aches! Make me sleep. Oh, Spurstow, for the love of God make me sleep sound. It isn't enough merely to let me dream. Let me sleep!'

'All right, old man, all right. Go slow; you aren't half as bad as you think.'

The flood-gates of reserve once broken, Hummil was clinging to him like a frightened child. 'You're pinching my arm to pieces.'

'I'll break your neck if you don't do something for me. No, I didn't mean that. Don't be angry, old fellow.' He wiped the sweat off himself as he fought to regain composure. 'I'm a bit restless and off my oats, and perhaps you could recommend some sort of sleeping mixture, – bromide of potassium.'

'Bromide of skittles! Why didn't you tell me this before? Let go of my arm, and I'll see if there's anything in my cigarette-case to suit your complaint.' Spurstow hunted among his day-clothes, turned up the lamp, opened a little silver cigarette-case, and advanced on the expectant Hummil with the daintiest of fairy squirts.

'The last appeal of civilisation,' said he, 'and a thing I hate to use. Hold out your arm. Well, your sleeplessness hasn't ruined your muscle; and what a thick hide it is! Might as well inject a buffalo subcutaneously. Now in a few minutes the morphia will begin working. Lie down and wait.'

A smile of unalloyed and idiotic delight began to creep over Hummil's face. 'I think,' he whispered, – 'I think I'm going off now. Gad! it's positively heavenly! Spurstow, you must give me that case to keep; you – ' The voice ceased as the head fell back.

'Not for a good deal,' said Spurstow to the unconscious form. 'And now, my friend, sleeplessness of your kind being very apt to relax the moral fibre in little matters of life and death, I'll just take the liberty of spiking your guns.'

He paddled into Hummil's saddle-room in his bare feet and uncased a twelve-bore rifle, an express, and a revolver. Of the first he unscrewed the nipples and hid them in the bottom of a saddlery-case; of the second he abstracted the lever, kicking it behind a big wardrobe. The third he merely opened, and knocked the doll-head bolt of the grip up with the heel of a riding-boot.

'That's settled,' he said, as he shook the sweat off his hands. 'These little precautions will at least give you time to turn. You have too much sympathy with gun-room accidents.'

And as he rose from his knees, the thick muffled voice of Hummil cried in the doorway, 'You fool!'

Such tones they use who speak in the lucid intervals of delirium to their friends a little before they die.

Spurstow started, dropping the pistol. Hummil stood in the doorway, rocking with helpless laughter.

'That was awf'ly good of you, I'm sure,' he said, very slowly, feeling for his words. 'I don't intend to go out by my own hand at present. I say, Spurstow, that stuff won't work. What shall I do? What shall I do?' And panic terror stood in his eyes.

'Lie down and give it a chance. Lie down at once.'

'I daren't. It will only take me half-way again, and I shan't be able to get away this time. Do you know, it was all I could do to come out just now? Generally I am as quick as lightning; but you had clogged my feet. I was nearly caught.'

'Oh yes, I understand. Go and lie down.'

'No, it isn't delirium; but it was an awfully mean trick to play on me. Do you know I might have died?'

As a sponge rubs a slate clean, so some power unknown to Spurstow had wiped out of Hummil's face all that stamped it for the face of a man, and he stood at the doorway in the expression of his lost innocence. He had slept back into terrified childhood.

'Is he going to die on the spot?' thought Spurstow. Then, aloud, 'All right, my son. Come back to bed, and tell me all about it. You couldn't sleep; but what was all the rest of the nonsense?'

'A place, – a place down there,' said Hummil, with simple sincerity. The drug was acting on him by waves, and he was flung from the fear of a strong man to the fright of a child as his nerves gathered sense or were dulled.

'Good God! I've been afraid of it for months past, Spurstow. It has made every night hell to me; and yet I'm not conscious of having done anything wrong.'

'Be still, and I'll give you another dose. We'll stop your nightmares, you unutterable idiot!'

'Yes, but you must give me so much that I can't get away. You must make me quite sleepy, – not just a little sleepy. It's so hard to run then.'

'I know it; I know it. I've felt it myself. The symptoms are exactly as you describe.'

'Oh, don't laugh at me, confound you! Before this awful sleeplessness came to me I've tried to rest on my elbow and put a spur in the bed to sting me when I fell back. Look!'

'By Jove! the man has been rowelled like a horse! Ridden by the nightmare with a vengeance! And we all thought him sensible enough. Heaven send us understanding! You like to talk, don't you?'

'Yes, sometimes. Not when I'm frightened. *Then* I want to run. Don't you?'

'Always. Before I give you your second dose try to tell me exactly what your trouble is.'

Hummil spoke in broken whispers for nearly ten minutes, whilst Spurstow looked into the pupils of his eyes and passed his hand before them once or twice.

At the end of the narrative the silver cigarette-case was produced, and the last words that Hummil said as he fell back for the second time were, 'Put me quite to sleep; for if I'm caught I die, – I die!'

'Yes, yes; we all do that sooner or later, – thank Heaven who has set a term to our miseries,' said Spurstow, settling the cushions under the head. 'It occurs to me that unless I drink something I shall go out before my time. I've stopped sweating, and – I wear a seventeen-inch collar.' He brewed himself scalding hot tea, which is an excellent remedy against heat-apoplexy if you take three or four cups of it in time. Then he watched the sleeper.

'A blind face that cries and can't wipe its eyes, a blind face that chases him down corridors! H'm! Decidedly, Hummil ought to go on leave as soon as possible; and, sane or otherwise, he undoubtedly did rowel himself most cruelly. Well, Heaven send us understanding!'

At mid-day Hummil rose, with an evil taste in his mouth, but an unclouded eye and a joyful heart.

'I was pretty bad last night, wasn't I?' said he.

'I have seen healthier men. You must have had a touch of the sun. Look here: if I write you a swingeing medical certificate, will you apply for leave on the spot?'

'No.'

'Why not? You want it.'

'Yes, but I can hold on till the weather's a little cooler.'

'Why should you, if you can get relieved on the spot?'

'Burkett is the only man who could be sent; and he's a born fool.'

'Oh, never mind about the line. You aren't so important as all that. Wire for leave, if necessary.'

Hummil looked very uncomfortable.

'I can hold on till the Rains,' he said evasively.

'You can't. Wire to headquarters for Burkett.'

'I won't. If you want to know why, particularly, Burkett is married, and his wife's just had a kid, and she's up at Simla, in the cool, and Burkett has a very nice billet that takes him into Simla from Saturday to Monday. That little woman isn't at all well. If Burkett was transferred she'd try to follow him. If she left the baby behind she'd fret herself to death. If she came, – and Burkett's one of those selfish little beasts who are always talking about a wife's place being with her husband, – she'd die. It's murder to bring a woman here just now. Burkett hasn't the physique of a rat. If he came here he'd go out; and I know she hasn't any money, and I'm pretty sure she'd go out too. I'm salted in a sort of way, and I'm not married. Wait till the Rains, and then Burkett can get thin down here. It'll do him heaps of good.'

'Do you mean to say that you intend to face – what you have faced, till the Rains break?'

'Oh, it won't be so bad, now you've shown me a way out of it. I can always wire to you. Besides, now I've once got into the way of sleeping, it'll be all right. Anyhow, I shan't put in for leave. That's the long and the short of it.'

'My great Scott! I thought all that sort of thing was dead and done with.'

'Bosh! You'd do the same yourself. I feel a new man, thanks to that cigarette-case. You're going over to camp now, aren't you?'

'Yes; but I'll try to look you up every other day, if I can.'

'I'm not bad enough for that. I don't want you to bother. Give the coolies gin and ketchup.'

'Then you feel all right?'

'Fit to fight for my life, but not to stand out in the sun talking to you. Go along, old man, and bless you!'

Hummil turned on his heel to face the echoing desolation of his bungalow, and the first thing he saw standing in the veranda was the figure of himself. He had met a similar apparition once before, when he was suffering from overwork and the strain of the hot weather.

'This is bad, – already,' he said, rubbing his eyes. 'If the thing slides away from me all in one piece, like a ghost, I shall know it is only my eyes and stomach that are out of order. If it walks – my head is going.'

He approached the figure, which naturally kept at an unvarying distance from him, as is the use of all spectres that are born of overwork. It slid through the house and dissolved into swimming specks within the eyeball as soon as it reached the burning light of the garden. Hummil went about his business till even. When he came in to dinner he found himself sitting at the table. The vision rose and walked out hastily. Except that it cast no shadow it was in all respects real.

No living man knows what that week held for Hummil. An increase of the epidemic kept Spurstow in camp among the coolies, and all he could do was to telegraph to Mottram, bidding him go to the bungalow and sleep there. But Mottram was forty miles away from the nearest telegraph, and knew nothing of anything save the needs of the Survey till he met, early on Sunday morning, Lowndes and Spurstow heading towards Hummil's for the weekly gathering.

'Hope the poor chap's in a better temper,' said the former, swinging himself off his horse at the door. 'I suppose he isn't up yet.'

'I'll just have a look at him,' said the doctor. 'If he's asleep there's no need to wake him.'

And an instant later, by the tone of Spurstow's voice calling upon them to enter, the men knew what had happened. There was no need to wake him.

The punkah was still being pulled over the bed, but Hummil had departed this life at least three hours.

The body lay on its back, hands clinched by the side, as Spurstow had seen it lying seven nights previously. In the staring eyes was written terror beyond the expression of any pen.

Mottram, who had entered behind Lowndes, bent over the dead and touched the forehead lightly with his lips. 'Oh, you lucky, lucky devil!' he whispered.

But Lowndes had seen the eyes, and withdrew shuddering to the other side of the room.

'Poor chap! poor old chap! And the last time I met him I was angry. Spurstow, we should have watched him. Has he – ?'

Deftly Spurstow continued his investigations, ending by a search round the room.

'No, he hasn't,' he snapped. 'There's no trace of anything. Call the servants.'

They came, eight or ten of them, whispering and peering over each other's shoulders.

'When did your Sahib go to bed?' said Spurstow.

'At eleven or ten, we think,' said Hummil's personal servant.

'He was well then? But how should you know?'

'He was not ill, as far as our comprehension extended. But he had slept very little for three nights. This I know, because I saw him walking much, and specially in the heart of the night.'

As Spurstow was arranging the sheet, a big straight-necked hunting-spur tumbled on the ground. The doctor groaned. The personal servant peeped at the body.

'What do you think, Chuma?' said Spurstow, catching the look on the dark face.

'Heaven-born,[29] in my poor opinion, this that was my master has descended into the Dark Places, and there has been caught because he was not able to escape with sufficient speed. We have the spur for evidence that he fought with Fear. Thus have I seen men of my race do with thorns when a spell was laid upon them to overtake them in their sleeping hours and they dared not sleep.'

'Chuma, you're a mud-head. Go out and prepare seals to be set on the Sahib's property.'

'God has made the Heaven-born. God has made me. Who are we, to inquire into the dispensations of God? I will bid the other servants hold aloof while you are reckoning the tale of the Sahib's property. They are all thieves, and would steal.'

'As far as I can make out, he died from – oh, anything; stoppage of the heart's action, heat-apoplexy, or some other visitation,' said Spurstow to his companions. 'We must make an inventory of his effects, and so on.'

'He was scared to death,' insisted Lowndes. 'Look at those eyes! For pity's sake don't let him be buried with them open!'

'Whatever it was, he's clear of all the trouble now,' said Mottram softly.

Spurstow was peering into the open eyes.

'Come here,' said he. 'Can you see anything there?'

'I can't face it!' whimpered Lowndes. 'Cover up the face! Is there any fear on earth that can turn a man into that likeness? It's ghastly. Oh, Spurstow, cover it up!'

'No fear – on earth,' said Spurstow. Mottram leaned over his shoulder and looked intently.

'I see nothing except some grey blurs in the pupil. There can be nothing there, you know.'

'Even so. Well, let's think. It'll take half a day to knock up any sort of coffin; and he must have died at midnight. Lowndes, old man, go out and tell the coolies to break ground next to Jevins's grave. Mottram, go round the house with Chuma and see that the seals are put on things. Send a couple of men to me here, and I'll arrange.'

The strong-armed servants when they returned to their own kind told a strange story of the Doctor Sahib vainly trying to call their master back to life by magic arts, – to wit, the holding of a little green box that clicked to each of the dead man's eyes, and of a bewildered muttering on the part of the Doctor Sahib, who took the little green box away with him.

The resonant hammering of a coffin-lid is no pleasant thing to hear, but those who have experience maintain that much more terrible is the soft swish of the bed-linen, the reeving and unreeving of the bed-tapes,[30] when he who has fallen by the roadside is apparelled for burial, sinking gradually as the tapes are tied over, till the swaddled shape touches the floor and there is no protest against the indignity of hasty disposal.

At the last moment Lowndes was seized with scruples of conscience. 'Ought you to read the service, – from beginning to end?' said he to Spurstow.

'I intend to. You're my senior as a Civilian. You can take it if you like.'

'I didn't mean that for a moment. I only thought if we could get a chaplain from somewhere, – I'm willing to ride anywhere, – and give poor Hummil a better chance. That's all.'

'Bosh!' said Spurstow, as he framed his lips to the tremendous words[31] that stand at the head of the burial service.

After breakfast they smoked a pipe in silence to the memory of the dead. Then Spurstow said absently: –

''Tisn't in medical science.'

'What?'

'Things in a dead man's eye.'

'For goodness' sake leave that horror alone!' said Lowndes. 'I've seen a native die of pure fright when a tiger chivied him. I know what killed Hummil.'

'The deuce you do! I'm going to try to see.' And the doctor retreated into the bath-room with a Kodak camera. After a few minutes there was the sound of something being hammered to pieces, and he emerged, very white indeed.

'Have you got a picture?' said Mottram. 'What does the thing look like?'

'It was impossible, of course. You needn't look, Mottram. I've torn up the films. There was nothing there. It was impossible.'

'That,' said Lowndes, very distinctly, watching the shaking hand striving to relight the pipe, 'is a damned lie.'

Mottram laughed uneasily. 'Spurstow's right,' he said. 'We're all in such a state now that we'd believe anything. For pity's sake let's try to be rational.'

There was no further speech for a long time. The hot wind whistled without, and the dry trees sobbed. Presently the daily train, winking brass, burnished steel, and spouting steam, pulled up panting in the intense glare. 'We'd better go on on that,' said Spurstow. 'Go back to work. I've written my certificate. We can't do any more good here, and work 'll keep our wits together. Come on.'

No one moved. It is not pleasant to face railway journeys at mid-day in June. Spurstow gathered up his hat and whip, and, turning in the doorway, said:

'There may be Heaven, – there must be Hell.
Meantime, there is our life here. We-ell?'[32]

Neither Mottram nor Lowndes had any answer to the question.

THE DRUMS OF THE
FORE AND AFT

In the Army List they still stand as 'The Fore and Fit Princess Hohen-zollern-Sigmaringen-Anspach's Merthyr-Tydfilshire Own Royal Loyal Light Infantry, Regimental District 329A', but the Army through all its barracks and canteens knows them now as the 'Fore and Aft'. They may in time do something that shall make their new title honourable, but at present they are bitterly ashamed, and the man who calls them 'Fore and Aft' does so at the risk of the head which is on his shoulders.

Two words breathed into the stables of a certain Cavalry Regiment will bring the men out into the streets with belts and mops and bad language; but a whisper of 'Fore and Aft' will bring out this Regiment with rifles.

Their one excuse is that they came again and did their best to finish the job in style. But for a time all their world knows that they were openly beaten, whipped, dumb-cowed, shaking, and afraid. The men know it; their officers know it; the Horse Guards know it, and when the next war comes the enemy will know it also. There are two or three Regiments of the Line that have a black mark against their names which they will then wipe out; and it will be excessively inconvenient for the troops upon whom they do their wiping.

The courage of the British soldier is officially supposed to be above proof,[1] and, as a general rule, it is so. The exceptions are decently shovelled out of sight, only to be referred to in the freshet of unguarded talk that occasionally swamps a Mess-table at midnight. Then one hears strange and horrible stories of men not following their officers, of orders being given by those who had no right to give them, and of disgrace that, but for the standing luck of the British Army, might have ended in brilliant disaster. These are unpleasant stories to listen to, and the Messes tell them under their breath, sitting by the big wood fires, and the young officer bows his head and thinks to himself, please God, his men shall never behave unhandily.

The British soldier is not altogether to be blamed for occasional lapses; but this verdict he should not know. A moderately intelligent

General will waste six months in mastering the craft of the particular war that he may be waging; a Colonel may utterly misunderstand the capacity of his Regiment for three months after it has taken the field; and even a Company Commander may err and be deceived as to the temper and temperament of his own handful: wherefore the soldier, and the soldier of to-day more particularly, should not be blamed for falling back. He should be shot or hanged afterwards – to encourage the others;[2] but he should not be vilified in newspapers, for that is want of tact and waste of space.

He has, let us say, been in the service of the Empress for, perhaps, four years. He will leave in another two years. He has no inherited morals, and four years are not sufficient to drive toughness into his fibre, or to teach him how holy a thing is his Regiment. He wants to drink, he wants to enjoy himself – in India he wants to save money – and he does not in the least like getting hurt. He has received just sufficient education to make him understand half the purport of the orders he receives, and to speculate on the nature of clean, incised, and shattering wounds. Thus, if he is told to deploy under fire preparatory to an attack, he knows that he runs a very great risk of being killed while he is deploying, and suspects that he is being thrown away to gain ten minutes' time. He may either deploy with desperate swiftness, or he may shuffle, or bunch, or break, according to the discipline under which he has lain for four years.

Armed with imperfect knowledge, cursed with the rudiments of an imagination, hampered by the intense selfishness of the lower classes, and unsupported by any regimental associations, this young man is suddenly introduced to an enemy who in Eastern lands is always ugly, generally tall and hairy, and frequently noisy. If he looks to the right and the left and sees old soldiers – men of twelve years' service, who, he knows, know what they are about – taking a charge, rush, or demonstration without embarrassment, he is consoled and applies his shoulder to the butt of his rifle with a stout heart. His peace is the greater if he hears a senior, who has taught him his soldiering and broken his head on occasion, whispering: 'They'll shout and carry on like this for five minutes. Then they'll rush in, and then we've got 'em by the short hairs!'

But, on the other hand, if he sees only men of his own term of service turning white and playing with their triggers, and saying: 'What the Hell's up now?' while the Company Commanders are sweating into their sword-hilts and shouting: 'Front rank, fix bayonets! Steady there – steady! Sight for three hundred – no, for five! Lie down, all! Steady! Front rank, kneel!' and so forth, he becomes unhappy; and grows acutely miserable when he hears a comrade turn over with the rattle of fire-irons falling into the fender, and the grunt of a pole-axed ox. If he can be moved about a little and allowed to watch the effect of his own fire on the enemy he feels merrier, and may be then worked up to the blind passion of fighting, which is, contrary to general belief, controlled by a chilly Devil and shakes men like ague. If he is not moved about, and begins to feel cold at the pit of the stomach, and in that crisis is badly mauled, and hears orders that were never given, he will break, and he will break badly; and of all things under the light of the sun there is nothing more terrible than a broken British regiment. When the worst comes to the worst and the panic is really epidemic, the men must be e'en let go, and the Company Commanders had better escape to the enemy and stay there for safety's sake. If they can be made to come again they are not pleasant men to meet; because they will not break twice.

About thirty years from this date, when we have succeeded in half-educating everything that wears trousers, our Army will be a beautifully unreliable machine. It will know too much and it will do too little. Later still, when all men are at the mental level of the officer of to-day, it will sweep the earth. Speaking roughly, you must employ either blackguards or gentlemen, or, best of all, blackguards commanded by gentlemen, to do butcher's work with efficiency and dispatch. The ideal soldier should, of course, think for himself – the *Pocket-book*[3] says so. Unfortunately, to attain this virtue he has to pass through the phase of thinking *of* himself, and that is misdirected genius. A blackguard may be slow to think for himself, but he is genuinely anxious to kill, and a little punishment teaches him how to guard his own skin and perforate another's. A powerfully prayerful Highland Regiment, officered by rank Presbyterians, is, perhaps, one degree more terrible in action than a hard-bitten thousand of irresponsible Irish ruffians led by most improper young unbelievers. But these things prove the rule – which is that the midway men are not to be trusted alone. They have ideas about the value of life and an upbringing that has not taught them to go on and take the chances. They are carefully unprovided with a backing of comrades who have been shot over, and until that backing is re-introduced, as a great many Regimental Commanders intend it shall be, they are more liable to disgrace themselves than the size of the Empire or the dignity of the Army allows. Their officers are as good as good can be, because their training begins early, and God has arranged that a clean-run youth of the British middle classes shall, in the matter of backbone, brains, and bowels, surpass all other youths. For this reason a child of eighteen will stand up, doing nothing, with a tin sword in his hand and joy in his heart until he is dropped. If he dies, he dies like a gentleman. If he lives, he writes Home that he has been 'potted', 'sniped', 'chipped', or 'cut over', and sits down to besiege Government for a wound-gratuity until the next little war breaks out, when he perjures himself before a Medical Board, blarneys his Colonel, burns incense round his Adjutant, and is allowed to go to the Front once more.

Which homily brings me directly to a brace of the most finished little fiends that ever banged drum or tootled fife in the Band of a British regiment. They ended their sinful career by open and flagrant mutiny and were shot for it. Their names were Jakin and Lew – Piggy Lew – and they were bold, bad drummer-boys,[4] both of them frequently birched by the Drum-Major of the Fore and Fit.

Jakin was a stunted child of fourteen, and Lew was about the same age. When not looked after, they smoked and drank. They swore habitually after the manner of the barrack-room, which is cold swearing and comes from between clinched teeth; and they fought religiously once a week. Jakin had sprung from some London gutter and may or may not have passed through Dr Barnardo's hands[5] ere he arrived at the dignity of drummer-boy. Lew could remember nothing except the Regiment and the delight of listening to the Band from his earliest years. He hid somewhere in his grimy little soul a genuine love for music, and was most mistakenly furnished with the head of a cherub: insomuch that beautiful ladies who watched the Regiment in church were wont to speak of him as a 'darling'. They never heard his vitriolic comments on their manners and morals, as he walked back to barracks with the Band and matured fresh causes of offence against Jakin.

The other drummer-boys hated both lads on account of their illogical conduct. Jakin might be pounding Lew, or Lew might be rubbing Jakin's head in the dirt, but any attempt at aggression on the part of an outsider was met by the combined forces of Lew and Jakin; and the consequences were painful. The boys were the Ishmaels[6] of the corps, but wealthy Ishmaels, for they sold battles in alternate weeks for the sport of the barracks when they were not pitted against other boys; and thus they amassed money.

On this particular day there was dissension in the camp. They had just been convicted afresh of smoking, which is bad for little boys who use plug tobacco,[7] and Lew's contention was that Jakin had 'stunk so 'orrid bad from keepin' the pipe in 'is pocket', that he and he alone was responsible for the birching they were both tingling under.

'I tell you I 'id the pipe back o' barracks,' said Jakin pacifically.

'You're a bloomin' liar,' said Lew without heat.

'You're a bloomin' little barstard,' said Jakin, strong in the knowledge that his own ancestry was unknown.

Now there is one word in the extended vocabulary of barrack-room abuse that cannot pass without comment. You may call a man a thief and risk nothing. You may even call him a coward without finding more than a boot whiz past your ear, but you must not call a man a bastard unless you are prepared to prove it on his front teeth.

'You might ha' kep' that till I wasn't so sore,' said Lew sorrowfully, dodging round Jakin's guard.

'I'll make you sorer,' said Jakin genially, and got home on Lew's alabaster forehead. All would have gone well and this story, as the books say, would never have been written, had not his evil fate prompted the Bazar-Sergeant's son,[8] a long, employless man of five-and-twenty, to put in an appearance after the first round. He was eternally in need of money, and knew that the boys had silver.

'Fighting again,' said he. 'I'll report you to my father, and he'll report you to the Colour-Sergeant.'

'What's that to you?' said Jakin with an unpleasant dilation of the nostrils.

'Oh! nothing to *me*. You'll get into trouble, and you've been up too often to afford that.'

'What the Hell do you know about what we've done?' asked Lew the Seraph. '*You* aren't in the Army, you lousy, cadging civilian.'

He closed in on the man's left flank.

'Jes' 'cause you find two gentlemen settlin' their diff'rences with their fistes you stick in your ugly nose where you aren't wanted. Run 'ome to your 'arf-caste slut of a Ma – or we'll give you what-for,' said Jakin.

The man attempted reprisals by knocking the boys' heads together. The scheme would have succeeded had not Jakin punched him vehemently in the stomach, or had Lew refrained from kicking his shins. They fought together, bleeding and breathless, for half an hour, and, after heavy punishment, triumphantly pulled down their opponent as terriers pull down a jackal.

'Now,' gasped Jakin, 'I'll give you what-for.' He proceeded to pound the man's features while Lew stamped on the outlying portions of his anatomy. Chivalry is not a strong point in the composition of the average drummer-boy. He fights, as do his betters, to make his mark.

Ghastly was the ruin that escaped, and awful was the wrath of the Bazar-Sergeant. Awful, too, was the scene in Orderly-Room when the two reprobates appeared to answer the charge of half-murdering a 'civilian', The Bazar-Sergeant thirsted for a criminal action, and his son lied. The boys stood to attention while the black clouds of evidence accumulated.

'You little devils are more trouble than the rest of the Regiment put together,' said the Colonel angrily. 'One might as well admonish thistle-down, and I can't well put you in cells or under stoppages. You must be birched again.'

'Beg y' pardon, sir. Can't we say nothin' in our own defence, sir?' shrilled Jakin.

'Hey! What? Are you going to argue with *me*?' said the Colonel.

'No, sir,' said Lew. 'But if a man come to you, sir, and said he was going to report you, sir, for 'avin' a bit of a turn-up with a friend, sir, an' wanted to get money out o' *you*, sir –'

The Orderly-Room exploded in a roar of laughter. 'Well?' said the Colonel.

'That was what that measly *jarnwar*⁹ there did, sir, and 'e'd'a' *done* it, sir, if we 'adn't prevented 'im. We didn't 'it 'im much, sir. 'E'adn't no manner o' right to interfere with us, sir. I don't mind bein' birched by the Drum-Major, sir, nor yet reported by *any* Corp'ral, but I'm – but I don't think it's fair, sir, for a civilian to come an' talk over a man in the Army.'

A second shout of laughter shook the Orderly-Room, but the Colonel was grave.

'What sort of characters have these boys?' he asked of the Regimental Sergeant-Major.

'Accordin' to the Bandmaster, sir,' returned that revered official – the only soul in the Regiment whom the boys feared – 'they do everything *but* lie, sir.'

'Is it like we'd go for that man for fun, sir?' said Lew, pointing to the plaintiff.

'Oh, admonished – admonished!' said the Colonel testily, and when the boys had gone he read the Bazar-Sergeant's son a lecture on the sin of unprofitable meddling, and gave orders that the Bandmaster should keep the Drums in better discipline.

'If either of you comes to practice again with so much as a scratch on your two ugly little faces,' thundered the Bandmaster, 'I'll tell the Drum-Major to take the skin off your backs. Understand that, you young devils.'

Then he repented of his speech for just the length of time that Lew, looking like a seraph in red worsted embellishments, took the place of one of the trumpets – in hospital – and rendered the echo of a battle-piece. Lew certainly was a musician, and had often in his more exalted moments expressed a yearning to master every instrument of the Band.

'There's nothing to prevent your becoming a Bandmaster, Lew,' said the Bandmaster, who had composed waltzes of his own, and worked day and night in the interests of the Band.

'What did he say?' demanded Jakin after practice.

'Said I might be a bloomin' Bandmaster, an' be asked in to 'ave a glass o' sherry-wine on Mess-nights.'

'Ho! Said you might be a bloomin' non-combatant, did 'e! That's just about wot 'e would say. When I've put in my boy's service – it's a bloomin' shame that doesn't count for pension – I'll take on as a privit. Then I'll be a Lance[10] in a year – knowin' what I know about the ins an' outs o' things. In three years I'll be a bloomin' Sergeant. I won't marry then, not me! I'll 'old on and learn the orf'cers' ways an' apply for exchange into a reg'ment that doesn't know all about me. Then I'll be a bloomin' orf'cer. Then I'll ask you to 'ave a glass o' sherry-wine, *Mister* Lew, an' you'll bloomin' well 'ave to stay in the ante-room while the Mess-Sergeant brings it to your dirty 'ands.'

''S'pose I'm going to be a Bandmaster? Not me, quite. I'll be a orf'cer too. There's nothin' like takin' to a thing an' stickin' to it, the Schoolmaster says. The Reg'ment don't go 'ome for another seven years. I'll be a Lance then or near to.'

Thus the boys discussed their futures, and conducted themselves piously for a week. That is to say, Lew started a flirtation with the Colour-Sergeant's daughter, aged thirteen – 'not,' as he explained to Jakin, 'with any intention o' matrimony, but by way o' keepin' my 'and in.' And the black-haired Cris Delighan enjoyed that flirtation more than previous ones, and the other drummer-boys raged furiously together, and Jakin preached sermons on the dangers of 'bein' tangled along o' petticoats'.

But neither love nor virtue would have held Lew long in the paths of propriety had not the rumour gone abroad that the Regiment was to be sent on active service, to take part in a war which, for the sake of brevity, we will call 'The War of the Lost Tribes'.[11]

The barracks had the rumour almost before the Mess-room, and of all the nine hundred men in barracks not ten had seen a shot fired in anger. The Colonel had, twenty years ago, assisted at a Frontier expedition; one of the Majors had seen service at the Cape;[12] a confirmed deserter in E Company had helped to clear streets in Ireland; but that was all. The Regiment had been put by for many years. The overwhelming mass of its rank and file had from three to four years' service; the non-commissioned officers were under thirty years old; and men and sergeants alike had forgotten to speak of the stories written in brief upon the Colours[13] – the New Colours that had been formally blessed by an Archbishop in England ere the Regiment came away.

They wanted to go to the Front – they were enthusiastically anxious to go – but they had no knowledge of what war meant, and there was none to tell them. They were an educated Regiment, the percentage of school-certificates in their ranks was high, and most of the men could do more than read and write. They had been recruited in loyal observance of the territorial idea; but they themselves had no notion of that idea. They were made up of drafts from an over-populated manufacturing district. The system had put flesh and muscle upon their small bones, but it could not put heart into the sons of those who for generations had done over-much work for over-scanty pay, had sweated in drying-rooms, stooped over looms, coughed among white lead, and shivered on lime-barges. The men had found food and rest in the Army, and now they were going to fight 'niggers' – people who ran away if you shook a stick at them. Wherefore they cheered lustily when the rumour ran, and the shrewd, clerkly non-commissioned officers speculated on the chances of *batta*[14] and of saving their pay. At Headquarters men said: 'The Fore and Fit have never been under fire within the last generation. Let us, therefore, break them in easily by setting them to guard lines of communication.' And this would have been done but for the fact that British Regiments were wanted – badly wanted – at the Front, and there were doubtful Native Regiments that could fill the minor duties. 'Brigade 'em with two strong Regiments,' said Headquarters. 'They may be knocked about a bit, but they'll learn their business before they come through. Nothing like a night-alarm and a little cutting-up of stragglers to make a Regiment smart in the field. Wait till they've had half-a-dozen sentries' throats cut.'

The Colonel wrote with delight that the temper of his men was excellent, that the Regiment was all that could be wished, and as sound as a bell. The Majors smiled with a sober joy, and the subalterns waltzed in pairs down the Mess-room after dinner, and nearly shot themselves at revolver-practice. But there was consternation in the hearts of Jakin and Lew. What was to be done with the Drums? Would the Band go to the Front? How many of the Drums would accompany the Regiment?

They took counsel together, sitting in a tree and smoking.

'It's more than a bloomin' toss-up they'll leave us be'ind at the Depôt with the women. You'll like that,' said Jakin sarcastically.

''Cause o' Cris, y' mean? Wot's a woman, or a 'ole bloomin' Depôt o' women, 'longside o' the chanst of field-service? You know I'm as keen on goin' as you,' said Lew.

'Wish I was a bloomin' bugler,' said Jakin sadly. 'They'll take Tom Kidd along, that I can plaster a wall with, an' like as not they won't take us.'

'Then let's go an' make Tom Kidd so bloomin' sick 'e can't bugle no more. You 'old 'is 'ands an' I'll kick him,' said Lew, wriggling on the branch.

'That ain't no good neither. We ain't the sort o' characters to presoom on our rep'tations – they're bad. If they leave the Band at the Depôt we don't go, and no error *there*. If they take the Band we may get cast for medical unfitness. Are you medical fit, Piggy?' said Jakin, digging Lew in the ribs with force.

'Yus,' said Lew with an oath. 'The Doctor says your 'eart's weak through smokin' on an empty stummick. Throw a chest an' I'll try yer.'

Jakin threw out his chest, which Lew smote with all his might. Jakin turned very pale, gasped, crowed, screwed up his eyes, and said: 'That's all right.'

'You'll do,' said Lew. 'I've 'eard o' men dyin' when you 'it 'em fair on the breastbone.'

'Don't bring us no nearer goin', though,' said Jakin. 'Do you know where we're ordered?'

'Gawd knows, an' 'E won't split on a pal. Somewheres up to the Front to kill Paythans – hairy big beggars that turn you inside out if they get 'old o' you. They say their women are good-lookin', too.'

'Any loot?' asked the abandoned Jakin.

'Not a bloomin' anna, they say, unless you dig up the ground an' see what the niggers 'ave 'id. They're a poor lot.' Jakin stood upright on the branch and gazed across the plain.

'Lew,' said he, 'there's the Colonel comin'. Colonel's a good old beggar. Let's go an' talk to 'im.'

Lew nearly fell out of the tree at the audacity of the suggestion. Like Jakin he feared not God, neither regarded he Man, but there are limits even to the audacity of drummer-boy, and to speak to a Colonel was –

But Jakin had slid down the trunk and doubled in the direction of the Colonel. That officer was walking wrapped in thought and visions of a CB – yes, even a KCB,[15] for had he not at command one of the best Regiments of the Line – the Fore and Fit? And he was aware of two small boys charging down upon him. Once before it had been solemnly reported to him that 'the Drums were in a state of mutiny', Jakin and Lew being the ringleaders. This looked like an organised conspiracy.

The boys halted at twenty yards, walked to the regulation four paces, and saluted together, each as well-set-up as a ramrod and little taller.

The Colonel was in a genial mood; the boys appeared very forlorn and unprotected on the desolate plain, and one of them was handsome.

'Well?' said the Colonel, recognising them. 'Are you going to pull me down in the open? I'm sure I never interfere with you, even though' – he sniffed suspiciously – 'you have been smoking.'

It was time to strike while the iron was hot. Their hearts beat tumultuously.

'Beg y' pardon, sir,' began Jakin. 'The Reg'ment's ordered on active service, sir?'

'So I believe,' said the Colonel courteously.

'Is the Band goin', sir?' said both together. Then, without pause, 'We're goin', sir, ain't we?'

'You!' said the Colonel, stepping back the more fully to take in the two small figures. 'You! You'd die in the first march.'

'No, we wouldn't, sir. We can march with the Reg'ment anywheres – p'rade an' anywhere else,' said Jakin.

'If Tom Kidd goes 'e'll shut up like a clasp-knife,' said Lew. 'Tom 'as very-close veins in both 'is legs, sir.'

'Very how much?'

'Very-close veins, sir. That's why they swells after long p'rade, sir. If 'e can go, we can go, sir.'

Again the Colonel looked at them long and intently.

'Yes, the Band is going,' he said as gravely as though he had been addressing a brother officer. 'Have you any parents, either of you two?'

'No, sir,' rejoicingly from Lew and Jakin. 'We're both orphans, sir. There's no one to be considered of on our account, sir.'

'You poor little sprats, and you want to go up to the Front with the Regiment, do you? Why?'

'I've wore the Queen's uniform for two years,' said Jakin. 'It's very 'ard, sir, that a man don't get no recompense for doin' of 'is dooty, sir.'

'An' – an' if I don't go, sir,' interrupted Lew, 'the Bandmaster 'e says 'e'll catch an' make a bloo – a blessed musician o' me, sir. Before I've seen any service, sir.'

The Colonel made no answer for a long time. Then he said quietly: 'If you're passed by the Doctor I daresay you can go. I shouldn't smoke if I were you.'

The boys saluted and disappeared. The Colonel walked home and told the story to his wife, who nearly cried over it. The Colonel was well pleased. If that was the temper of the children, what would not the men do?

Jakin and Lew entered the boys' barrack-room with great stateliness, and refused to hold any conversation with their comrades for at least ten minutes. Then, bursting with pride, Jakin drawled: 'I've bin inter-vooin' the Colonel. Good old beggar is the Colonel. Says I to 'im, "Colonel," says I, "let me go to the Front, along o' the Reg'ment." – "To the Front you shall go," says 'e, "an' I only wish there was more like you among the dirty little devils that bang the bloomin' drums." Kidd, if you throw your 'coutrements[16] at me for tellin' you the truth to your own advantage, your legs 'll swell.'

None the less there was a battle-royal in the barrack-room, for the boys were consumed with envy and hate, and neither Jakin nor Lew behaved in conciliatory wise.

'I'm goin' out to say adoo to my girl,' said Lew, to cap the climax. 'Don't none o' you touch my kit, because it's wanted for active service; me bein' specially invited to go by the Colonel.'

He strolled forth and whistled in the clump of trees at the back of the Married Quarters till Cris came to him, and, the preliminary kisses being given and taken, Lew began to explain the situation.

'I'm goin' to the Front with the Reg'ment,' he said valiantly.

'Piggy, you're a little liar,' said Cris, but her heart misgave her, for Lew was not in the habit of lying.

'Liar yourself, Cris,' said Lew, slipping an arm round her. 'I'm goin'. When the Reg'ment marches out you'll see me with 'em, all galliant and gay. Give us another kiss, Cris, on the strength of it.'

'If you'd on'y 'a' stayed at the Depôt – where you *ought* to ha' bin – you could get as many of 'em as – as you dam' please,' whimpered Cris, putting up her mouth.

'It's 'ard, Cris. I grant you it's 'ard. But what's a man to do? If I'd 'a' stayed at the Depôt, you wouldn't think anything of me.'

'Like as not, but I'd 'ave you with me, Piggy. An' all the thinkin' in the world isn't like kissin'.'

'An' all the kissin' in the world isn't like 'avin' a medal to wear on the front o' your coat.'

'*You* won't get no medal.'

'Oh yus, I shall though. Me an' Jakin are the only actin'-drummers that'll be took along. All the rest is full men, an' we'll get our medals with them.'

'They might ha' taken anybody but you, Piggy. You'll get killed – you're so venturesome. Stay with me, Piggy, darlin', down at the Depôt, an' I'll love you true, for ever.'

'Ain't you goin' to do that *now*, Cris? You said you was.'

'O' course I am, but t' other's more comfortable. Wait till you've growed a bit, Piggy. You aren't no taller than me now.'

'I've bin in the Army for two years an' I'm not goin' to get out of a chanst o' seein' service, an' don't you try to make me do so. I'll come back, Cris, an' when I take on as a man I'll marry you – marry you when I'm a Lance.'

'Promise, Piggy?'

Lew reflected on the future as arranged by Jakin a short time previously, but Cris's mouth was very near to his own.

'I promise, s'elp me Gawd!' said he.

Cris slid an arm round his neck.

'I won't 'old you back no more, Piggy. Go away an' get your medal, an' I'll make you a new button-bag as nice as I know how,' she whispered.

'Put some o' your 'air into it, Cris, an' I'll keep it in my pocket so long's I'm alive.'

Then Cris wept anew, and the interview ended. Public feeling among the drummer-boys rose to fever pitch and the lives of Jakin and Lew became unenviable. Not only had they been permitted to enlist two years before the regulation boy's age – fourteen – but, by virtue, it seemed, of their extreme youth, they were now allowed to go to the Front – which thing had not happened to acting-drummers within the knowledge of boy. The Band which was to accompany the Regiment had been cut down to the regulation twenty men, the surplus returning to the ranks. Jakin and Lew were attached to the Band as supernumeraries, though they would much have preferred being Company buglers.

'Don't matter much,' said Jakin, after the medical inspection. 'Be thankful that we're 'lowed to go at all. The Doctor 'e said that if we could stand what we took from the Bazar-Sergeant's son we'd stand pretty nigh anything.'

'Which we will,' said Lew, looking tenderly at the ragged and ill-made housewife[17] that Cris had given him, with a lock of her hair worked into a sprawling 'L' upon the cover.

'It was the best I could,' she sobbed. 'I wouldn't let mother nor the Sergeants' tailor 'elp me. Keep it always, Piggy, an' remember I love you true.'

They marched to the railway station, nine hundred and sixty strong, and every soul in cantonments turned out to see them go. The drummers gnashed their teeth at Jakin and Lew marching with the Band, the married women wept upon the platform, and the Regiment cheered its noble self black in the face.

'A nice level lot,' said the Colonel to the Second-in-Command as they watched the first four companies entraining.

'Fit to do anything,' said the Second-in-Command enthusiastically.

'But it seems to me they're a thought too young and tender for the work in hand. It's bitter cold up at the Front now.'

'They're sound enough,' said the Colonel. 'We must take our chance of sick casualties.'

So they went northward, ever northward, past droves and droves of camels, armies of camp-followers, and legions of laden mules, the throng thickening day by day, till with a shriek the train pulled up at a hopelessly congested junction where six lines of temporary track accommodated six forty-wagon trains; where whistles blew, Babus sweated, and Commissariat[18] officers swore from dawn till far into the night amid the wind-driven chaff of the fodder-bales and the lowing of a thousand steers.[19]

'Hurry up – you're badly wanted at the Front,' was the message that greeted the Fore and Fit, and the occupants of the Red Cross carriages told the same tale.

''Tisn't so much the bloomin' fightin',' gasped a head-bound trooper of Hussars[20] to a knot of admiring Fore and Fits. ''Tisn't so much the bloomin' fightin', though there's enough o' that. It's the bloomin' food an' the bloomin' climate. Frost all night 'cept when it hails, an' bilin' sun all day, an' the water stinks fit to knock you down. I got my 'ead chipped like a' egg; I've got pneumonia too, an' my guts is all out o' order. 'Tain't no bloomin' picnic in those parts, I can tell you.'

'Wot are the niggers like?' demanded a private.

'There's some prisoners in that train yonder. Go an' look at 'em. They're the aristocracy o' the country. The common folk are a dashed sight uglier. If you want to know what they fight with, reach under my seat an' pull out the long knife that's there.'

They dragged out and beheld for the first time the grim, bone-handled, triangular Afghan knife. It was almost as long as Lew.

'That's the thing to jint ye,' said the trooper feebly. 'It can take off a man's arm at the shoulder as easy as slicin' butter. I halved the beggar that used that 'un, but there's more of his likes up above. They don't understand thrustin', but they're devils to slice.'

The men strolled across the tracks to inspect the Afghan prisoners. They were unlike any 'niggers' that the Fore and Fit had ever met – these huge, black-haired, scowling sons of the Beni-Israel.[21] As the men stared the Afghans spat freely and muttered one to another with lowered eyes.

'My eyes! Wot awful swine!' said Jakin, who was in the rear of the procession. 'Say, old man, how you got *puckrowed*,[22] eh? *Kiswasti*[23] you wasn't hanged for your ugly face, hey?'

The tallest of the company turned, his leg-irons clanking at the movement, and stared at the boy. 'See!' he cried to his fellows in Pushtu. 'They send children against us. What a people, and what fools!'

'*Hya!*' said Jakin, nodding his head cheerily. 'You go down-country. *Khana* get, *peenikapanee* get – live like a bloomin' Rajah *ke marfik*. That's a better *bundobust*[24] than baynit get it in your innards. Good-bye, ole man. Take care o' your beautiful figure-'ed, an' try to look *kushy*.'[25]

The men laughed and fell in for their first march, when they began to realise that a soldier's life was not all beer and skittles. They were much impressed with the size and bestial ferocity of the 'niggers' whom they had now learned to call 'Paythans', and more with the exceeding discomfort of their own surroundings. Twenty old soldiers in the corps would have taught them how to make themselves moderately snug at night, but they had no old soldiers, and, as the troops on the line of march said, 'they lived like pigs'. They learned the heart-breaking cursedness of camp-kitchens and camels and the depravity of an EP tent[26] and a wither-wrung[27] mule. They studied animalculae in water, and developed a few cases of dysentery in that study.

At the end of their third march they were disagreeably surprised by the arrival in their camp of a hammered iron slug[28] which, fired from a steady rest at seven hundred yards, flicked out the brains of a private seated by the fire. This robbed them of their peace for a night, and was the beginning of a long-range fire carefully calculated to that end. In the daytime they saw nothing except an unpleasant puff of smoke from a crag above the line of march. At night there were distant spurts of flame and occasional casualties, which set the whole camp blazing into the gloom and, occasionally, into opposite tents. Then they swore vehemently, and vowed that this was magnificent but not war.

Indeed it was not. The Regiment could not halt for reprisals against the sharpshooters of the countryside. Its duty was to go forward and make connection with the Scotch and Gurkha troops with which it was brigaded. The Afghans knew this, and knew too, after their first tentative shots, that they were dealing with a raw regiment. Thereafter they devoted themselves to the task of keeping the Fore and Fit on the strain. Not for anything would they have taken equal liberties with a seasoned corps – with the wicked little Gurkhas, whose delight it was to lie out in the open on a dark night and stalk their stalkers – with the terrible, big men dressed in women's clothes,[29] who could be heard praying to their God in the nightwatches, and whose peace of mind no amount of sniping could shake – or with those vile Sikhs, who marched so ostentatiously unprepared, and who dealt out such grim reward to those who tried to profit by that unpreparedness. This white regiment was different – quite different. It slept like a hog, and, like a hog, charged in every direction when it was roused. Its sentries walked with a footfall that could be heard for a quarter of a mile; would fire at anything that moved – even a driven donkey[30] – and when they had once fired, could be scientifically 'rushed' and laid out, a horror and an offence against the morning sun. Then there were camp-followers who straggled and could be cut up without fear. Their shrieks would disturb the white boys, and the loss of their services would inconvenience them sorely.

Thus, at every march, the hidden enemy became bolder and the Regiment writhed and twisted under attacks it could not avenge. The crowning triumph was a sudden night-rush ending in the cutting of many tent-ropes, the collapse of the sodden canvas, and a glorious knifing of the men who struggled and kicked below. It was a great deed, neatly carried out, and it shook the already shaken nerves of the Fore and Fit. All the courage that they had been required to exercise up to this point was the 'two o'clock in the morning courage';[31] and, so far, they had only succeeded in shooting their own comrades and losing their sleep.

Sullen, discontented, cold, savage, sick, with their uniforms dulled and unclean, the Fore and Fit joined their Brigade.

'I hear you had a tough time of it coming up,' said the Brigadier. But when he saw the hospital-sheets his face fell.

'This is bad,' said he to himself. 'They're as rotten as sheep.' And aloud to the Colonel: 'I'm afraid we can't spare you just yet. We want all we have, else I should have given you ten days to recover in.'

The Colonel winced. 'On my honour, sir,' he returned, 'there is not the least necessity to think of sparing us. My men have been rather mauled and upset without a fair return. They only want to go in somewhere where they can see what's before them.'

'Can't say I think much of the Fore and Fit,' said the Brigadier in confidence to his Brigade-Major. 'They've lost all their soldiering, and, by the trim of them, might have marched through the country from the other side. A more fagged-out set of men I never put eyes on.'

'Oh, they'll improve as the work goes on. The parade gloss has been rubbed off a little, but they'll put on field polish before long,' said the Brigade-Major. 'They've been mauled, and they don't quite understand it.'

They did not. All the hitting was on one side, and it was cruelly hard hitting, with accessories that made them sick. There was also the real sickness that laid hold of a strong man and dragged him howling to the grave. Worst of all, their officers knew just as little of the country as the men themselves, and looked as if they did. The Fore and Fit were

in a thoroughly unsatisfactory condition, but they believed that all
would be well if they could once get a fair go-in at the enemy. Pot-shots
up and down the valleys were unsatisfactory, and the bayonet never
seemed to get a chance. Perhaps it was as well, for a long-limbed Afghan
with a knife had a reach of eight feet, and could carry away lead that
would disable three Englishmen.

The Fore and Fit would like some rifle-practice at the enemy – all
seven hundred rifles blazing together. That wish showed the mood of
the men.

The Gurkhas walked into their camp, and in broken barrack-room
English strove to fraternise with them; offered them pipes of tobacco
and stood them treat at the canteen. But the Fore and Fit, not knowing
much of the nature of the Gurkhas, treated them as they would treat
any other 'niggers', and the little men in green trotted back to their firm
friends the Highlanders, and with many grins confided to them: 'That
dam' white regiment no dam' use. Sulky – ugh! Dirty – ugh! *Hya*, any
tot for Johnny?' Whereat the Highlanders smote the Gurkhas as to the
head, and told them not to vilify a British regiment, and the Gurkhas
grinned cavernously, for the Highlanders were their elder brothers and
entitled to the privileges of kinship. The common soldier who touches
a Gurkha is more than likely to have his head sliced open.

Three days later the Brigadier arranged a battle according to the
rules of war and the peculiarity of the Afghan temperament. The enemy
were massing in inconvenient strength among the hills, and the moving
of many green standards warned him that the tribes were 'up' in aid
of the Afghan regular troops. A squadron and a half of Bengal Lancers
represented the available Cavalry, and two screw-guns[32] borrowed from
a column thirty miles away, the Artillery at the General's disposal.

'If they stand, as I've a very strong notion they will, I fancy we shall
see an infantry fight that will be worth watching,' said the Brigadier.
'We'll do it in style. Each regiment shall be played into action by its
Band, and we'll hold the Cavalry in reserve.'

'For *all* the reserve?' somebody asked.

'For all the reserve; because we're going to crumple them up,' said
the Brigadier, who was an extraordinary Brigadier, and did not believe
in the value of a reserve when dealing with Asiatics. Indeed, when you
come to think of it, had the British Army consistently waited for reserves
in all its little affairs, the boundaries of Our Empire would have stopped
at Brighton beach.

That battle was to be a glorious battle.

The three regiments debouching from three separate gorges, after
duly crowning the heights above, were to converge from the centre,

left, and right upon what we will call the Afghan army, then stationed towards the lower extremity of a flat-bottomed valley. Thus it will be seen that three sides of the valley practically belonged to the English, while the fourth was strictly Afghan property. In the event of defeat the Afghans had the rocky hills to fly to, where the fire from the guerilla tribes in aid would cover their retreat. In the event of victory these same tribes would rush down and lend their weight to the rout of the British.

The screw-guns were to shell the head of each Afghan rush that was made in close formation, and the Cavalry, held in reserve in the right valley, were to gently stimulate the break-up which would follow on the combined attack. The Brigadier, sitting upon a rock overlooking the valley, would watch the battle unrolled at his feet. The Fore and Fit would debouch from the central gorge, the Gurkhas from the left, and the Highlanders from the right, for the reason that the left flank of the enemy seemed as though it required the most hammering. It was not every day that an Afghan force would take ground in the open, and the Brigadier was resolved to make the most of it.

'If we only had a few more men,' he said plaintively, 'we could surround the creatures and crumple 'em up thoroughly. As it is, I'm afraid we can only cut them up as they run. It's a great pity.'

The Fore and Fit had enjoyed unbroken peace for five days, and were beginning, in spite of dysentery, to recover their nerve. But they were not happy, for they did not know the work in hand, and had they known, would not have known how to do it. Throughout those five days in which old soldiers might have taught them the craft of the game, they discussed together their misadventures in the past – how such an one was alive at dawn and dead ere the dusk, and with what shrieks and struggles such another had given up his soul under the Afghan knife. Death was a new and horrible thing to the sons of mechanics who were used to die decently of zymotic[33] disease; and their careful conservation in barracks had done nothing to make them look upon it with less dread.

Very early in the dawn the bugles began to blow, and the Fore and Fit, filled with a misguided enthusiasm, turned out without waiting for a cup of coffee and a biscuit; and were rewarded by being kept under arms in the cold while the other regiments leisurely prepared for the fray. All the world knows that it is ill taking the breeks off a Highlander.[34] It is much iller to try to make him stir unless he is convinced of the necessity for haste.

The Fore and Fit waited, leaning upon their rifles and listening to the protests of their empty stomachs. The Colonel did his best to remedy the default of lining as soon as it was borne in upon him that the affair would not begin at once, and so well did he succeed that the coffee was just ready when – the men moved off, their Band leading. Even then there had been a mistake in time, and the Fore and Fit came out into the valley ten minutes before the proper hour. Their Band wheeled to the right after reaching the open, and retired behind a little rocky knoll still playing while the Regiment went past.

It was not a pleasant sight that opened on the uninstructed view, for the lower end of the valley appeared to be filled by an army in position – real and actual regiments attired in red coats,[35] and – of this there was no doubt – firing Martini-Henry[36] bullets which cut up the ground a hundred yards in front of the leading company. Over that pock-marked ground the Regiment had to pass, and it opened the ball with a general and profound courtesy to the piping pickets; ducking in perfect time, as though it had been brazed[37] on a rod. Being half capable of thinking for itself, it fired a volley by the simple process of pitching its rifle into its shoulder and pulling the trigger. The bullets may have accounted for some of the watchers on the hillside, but they certainly did not affect the mass of enemy in front, while the noise of the rifles drowned any orders that might have been given.

'Good God!' said the Brigadier, sitting on the rock high above all. 'That battalion has spoilt the whole show. Hurry up the others, and let the screw-guns get off.'

But the screw-guns, in working round the heights, had stumbled upon a wasps' nest of a small mud fort which they incontinently shelled at eight hundred yards, to the huge discomfort of the occupants, who were unaccustomed to weapons of such devilish precision.

The Fore and Fit continued to go forward, but with shortened stride. Where were the other regiments, and why did these niggers use Martinis? They took open order instinctively, lying down and firing at random, rushing a few paces forward and lying down again, according to the regulations. Once in this formation, each man felt himself desperately alone, and edged in towards his fellow for comfort's sake.

Then the crack of his neighbour's rifle at his ear led him to fire as rapidly as he could – again for the sake of the comfort of the noise. The reward was not long delayed. Five volleys plunged the files in banked smoke impenetrable to the eye, and the bullets began to take ground twenty or thirty yards in front of the firers, as the weight of the bayonet dragged down and to the right arms wearied with holding the kick of the jolting Martini. The Company Commanders peered helplessly through the smoke, the more nervous mechanically trying to fan it away with their helmets.

'High and to the left!' bawled a Captain till he was hoarse. 'No good! Cease firing, and let it drift away a bit.'

Three and four times the bugles shrieked the order, and when it was obeyed the Fore and Fit looked that their foe should be lying before them in mown swaths of men. A light wind drove the smoke to leeward, and showed the enemy still in position and apparently unaffected. A quarter of a ton of lead had been buried a furlong in front of them, as the ragged earth attested,

That was not demoralising to the Afghans, who have not European nerves. They were waiting for the mad riot to die down, and were firing quietly into the heart of the smoke. A private of the Fore and Fit spun up his company shrieking with agony, another was kicking the earth and gasping, and a third, ripped through the lower intestines by a jagged bullet, was calling aloud on his comrades to put him out of his pain. These were the casualties, and they were not soothing to hear or see. The smoke cleared to a dull haze.

Then the foe began to shout with a great shouting, and a mass – a black mass – detached itself from the main body, and rolled over the ground at horrid speed. It was composed of, perhaps, three hundred men, who would shout and fire and slash if the rush of their fifty comrades who were determined to die carried home. The fifty were Ghazis,[38] half maddened with drugs and wholly mad with religious fanaticism.

When they rushed the British fire ceased, and in the lull the order was given to close ranks and meet them with the bayonet.

Any one who knew the business could have told the Fore and Fit that the only way of dealing with a Ghazi rush is by volleys at long ranges; because a man who means to die, who desires to die, who will gain Heaven by dying, must, in nine cases out of ten, kill a man who has a lingering prejudice in favour of life. Where they should have closed and gone forward, the Fore and Fit opened out and skirmished, and where they should have opened out and fired, they closed and waited.

A man dragged from his blankets half awake and unfed is never in a pleasant frame of mind. Nor does his happiness increase when he watches the whites of the eyes of three hundred six-foot fiends upon whose beards the foam is lying, upon whose tongues is a roar of wrath, and in whose hands are yard-long knives.

The Fore and Fit heard the Gurkha bugles bringing that regiment forward at the double, while the neighing of the Highland pipes came from the left. They strove to stay where they were, though the bayonets wavered down the line like the oars of a ragged boat. Then they felt body to body the amazing physical strength of their foes; a shriek of pain ended the rush, and the knives fell amid scenes not to be told. The men clubbed together and smote blindly – as often as not at their own fellows. Their front crumpled like paper, and the fifty Ghazis passed on; their backers, now drunk with success, fighting as madly as they.

Then the rear ranks were bidden to close up, and the subalterns dashed into the stew – alone. For the rear ranks had heard the clamour in front, the yells and the howls of pain, and had seen the dark stale blood that makes afraid. They were not going to stay. It was the rushing of the camps over again. Let their officers go to Hell, if they chose; they would get away from the knives.

'Come on!' shrieked the subalterns, and their men, cursing them, drew back, each closing into his neighbour and wheeling round.

Charteris and Devlin, subalterns of the last company, faced their death alone in the belief that their men would follow.

'You've killed me, you cowards,' sobbed Devlin and dropped, cut from the shoulder-strap to the centre of the chest, and a fresh detachment of his men retreating, always retreating, trampled him under foot as they made for the pass whence they had emerged . . .

> 'I kissed her in the kitchen and I kissed her in the hall.
> Child'un, child'un, follow me!
> "Oh, Golly," said the cook, "is he gwine to kiss us all?"
> Halla – Halla – Halla – Hallelujah!'

The Gurkhas were pouring through the left gorge and over the heights at the double to the invitation of their Regimental Quick-step. The black rocks were crowned with dark green spiders as the bugles gave tongue jubilantly:

> 'In the morning! In the morning *by* the bright light!
> When Gabriel blows his trumpet in the morning!'

The Gurkha rear companies tripped and blundered over loose stones. The front files halted for a moment to take stock of the valley and to settle stray bootlaces. Then a happy little sigh of contentment soughed down the ranks, and it was as though the land smiled, for behold there below were the enemy, and it was to meet them that the Gurkhas had doubled so hastily. There was much enemy. There would be amusement. The little men hitched their *kukris*[39] well to hand, and gaped expectantly at their officers as terriers grin ere the stone is cast for them to fetch. The Gurkhas' ground sloped downward to the valley, and they enjoyed a fair view of the proceedings. They sat upon the boulders to watch, for their officers were not going to waste their wind in assisting to repulse a Ghazi rush more than half a mile away. Let the white men look to their own front.

'Hi! yi!' said the Subadar-Major,[40] who was sweating profusely. 'Dam' fools yonder, stand close-order! This is no time for close order, it is the time for volleys. Ugh!'

Horrified, amused, and indignant, the Gurkhas beheld the retirement of the Fore and Fit with a running chorus of oaths and commentaries.

'They run! The white men run! Colonel Sahib, may *we* also do a little running?' murmured Runbir Thappa, the Senior Jemadar.[41]

But the Colonel would have none of it. 'Let the beggars be cut up a little,' said he wrathfully. 'Serves 'em right. They'll be prodded into facing round in a minute.' He looked through his field-glasses, and caught the glint of an officer's sword.

'Beating 'em with the flat – damned conscripts! How the Ghazis are walking into them!' said he.

The Fore and Fit, heading back, bore with them their officers. The narrowness of the pass forced the mob into solid formation, and the rear rank delivered some sort of a wavering volley. The Ghazis drew off, for they did not know what reserves the gorge might hide. Moreover, it was never wise to chase white men too far. They returned as wolves return to cover, satisfied with the slaughter that they had done, and only stopping to slash at the wounded on the ground. A quarter of a mile had the Fore and Fit retreated, and now, jammed in the pass, were quivering with pain, shaken and demoralised with fear, while the officers, maddened beyond control, smote the men with the hilts and the flats of their swords.

'Get back! Get back, you cowards – you women! Right about face – column of companies, form – you hounds!' shouted the Colonel, and the subalterns swore aloud. But the Regiment wanted to go – to get anywhere out of the range of those merciless knives. It swayed to and fro irresolutely with shouts and outcries, while from the right the Gurkhas dropped volley after volley of cripple-stopper Snider bullets[42] at long range into the mob of the Ghazis returning to their own troops.

The Fore and Fit Band, though protected from direct fire by the rocky knoll under which it had sat down, fled at the first rush. Jakin and Lew would have fled also, but their short legs left them fifty yards in the rear, and by the time the Band had mixed with the Regiment, they were painfully aware that they would have to close in alone and unsupported.

'Get back to that rock,' gasped Jakin. 'They won't see us there.'

And they returned to the scattered instruments of the Band, their hearts nearly bursting their ribs.

'Here's a nice show for *us*,' said Jakin, throwing himself full length on the ground. 'A bloomin' fine show for British Infantry! Oh, the devils! They've gone an' left us alone here! Wot'll we do?'

Lew took possession of a cast-off water-bottle, which naturally was full of canteen rum, and drank till he coughed again.

'Drink,' said he shortly. 'They'll come back in a minute or two – you see.'

Jakin drank, but there was no sign of the Regiment's return. They could hear a dull clamour from the head of the valley of retreat, and saw the Ghazis slink back, quickening their pace as the Gurkhas fired at them.

'We're all that's left of the Band, an' we'll be cut up as sure as death,' said Jakin.

'I'll die game, then,' said Lew thickly, fumbling with his tiny drummer's sword. The drink was working on his brain as it was on Jakin's.

''Old on! I know somethin' better than fightin',' said Jakin, 'stung by the splendour of a sudden thought'[43] due chiefly to rum. 'Tip our bloomin' cowards yonder the word to come back. The Paythan beggars are well away. Come on, Lew! We won't get 'urt. Take the fife[44] an' give me the drum. The Old Step for all your bloomin' guts are worth! There's a few of our men comin' back now. Stand up, ye drunken little defaulter. By your right – quick march!'

He slipped the drum-sling over his shoulder, thrust the fife into Lew's hand, and the two boys marched out of the cover of the rock into the open, making a hideous hash of the first bars of the 'British Grenadiers'.[45]

As Lew had said, a few of the Fore and Fit were coming back sullenly and shamefacedly under the stimulus of blows and abuse. Their red coats shone at the head of the valley, and behind them were wavering bayonets. But between this shattered line and the enemy, who with Afghan suspicion feared that the hasty retreat meant an ambush, and had not moved therefore, lay half a mile of level ground dotted only with the wounded.

The tune settled into full swing and the boys kept shoulder to shoulder, Jakin banging the drum as one possessed. The one fife made a thin and pitiful squeaking, but the tune carried far, even to the Gurkhas.

'Come on, you dorgs!' muttered Jakin to himself. 'Are we to play for hever?' Lew was staring straight in front of him and marching more stiffly than ever he had done on parade.

And in bitter mockery of the distant mob, the old tune of the Old Line shrilled and rattled:

> 'Some talk of Alexander,
>   And some of Hercules;
> Of Hector and Lysander,
>   And such great names as these!'

There was a far-off clapping of hands from the Gurkhas, and a roar from the Highlanders in the distance, but never a shot was fired by British or Afghan. The two little red dots moved forward in the open parallel to the enemy's front.

> 'But of all the world's great heroes
>   There's none that can compare,
> With a tow-row-row-row-row-row,
>   To the British Grenadier!'

The men of the Fore and Fit were gathering thick at the entrance to the plain. The Brigadier on the heights far above was speechless with rage. Still no movement from the enemy. The day stayed to watch the children.

Jakin halted and beat the long roll of the Assembly, while the fife squealed despairingly.

'Right about face! Hold up, Lew, you're drunk,' said Jakin. They wheeled and marched back:

> 'Those heroes of antiquity
>   Ne'er saw a cannon-ball,
> Nor knew the force o' powder'

'Here they come!' said Jakin. 'Go on, Lew':

> 'To scare their foes withal!'

The Fore and Fit were pouring out of the valley. What officers had said to men in that time of shame and humiliation will never be known; for neither officers nor men speak of it now.

'They are coming anew!' shouted a priest among the Afghans. 'Do not kill the boys! Take them alive, and they shall be of our faith.'

But the first volley had been fired, and Lew dropped on his face. Jakin stood for a minute, spun round and collapsed, as the Fore and

Fit came forward, the curses of their officers in their ears, and in their hearts the shame of open shame.

Half the men had seen the drummers die, and they made no sign. They did not even shout. They doubled out straight across the plain in open order, and they did not fire.

'This,' said the Colonel of Gurkhas softly, 'is the real attack, as it should have been delivered. Come on, my children.'

'Ulu-lu-lu-lu!' squealed the Gurkhas, and came down with a joyful clicking of *kukris* – the vicious Gurkha knives.

On the right there was no rush. The Highlanders, cannily commending their souls to God (for it matters as much to a dead man whether he has been shot in a Border scuffle or at Waterloo), opened out and fired according to their custom, that is to say, without heat and without intervals, while the screw-guns, having disposed of the impertinent mud fort aforementioned, dropped shell after shell into the clusters round the flickering green standards on the heights.

'Charrging is an unfortunate necessity,' murmured the Colour-Sergeant of the right company of the Highlanders. 'It makes the men sweer so – but I am thinkin' that it will come to a charrge if these black devils stand much longer. Stewarrt, man, you're firing into the eye of the sun, and he'll not take any harm for Government ammuneetion. A foot lower and a great deal slower! What are the English doing? They're very quiet there in the centre. Running again?'

The English were not running. They were hacking and hewing and stabbing, for though one white man is seldom physically a match for an Afghan in a sheepskin or wadded coat, yet, through the pressure of many white men behind, and a certain thirst for revenge in his heart, he becomes capable of doing much with both ends of his rifle. The Fore and Fit held their fire till one bullet could drive through five or six men, and the front of the Afghan force gave on the volley. They then selected their men, and slew them with deep gasps, and short hacking coughs, and groanings of leather belts against strained bodies, and realised for the first time that an Afghan attacked is far less formidable than an Afghan attacking: which fact old soldiers might have told them.

But they had no old soldiers in their ranks.

The Gurkhas' stall at the bazar was the noisiest, for the men were engaged – to a nasty noise as of beef being cut on the block – with the *kukri*, which they preferred to the bayonet; well knowing how the Afghan hates the half-moon blade.

As the Afghans wavered, the green standards on the mountain moved down to assist them in a last rally. This was unwise. The Lancers chafing in the right gorge had thrice despatched their only subaltern as galloper to report on the progress of affairs. On the third occasion he returned, with a bullet-graze on his knee, swearing strange oaths in Hindustani, and saying that all things were ready. So that squadron swung round the right of the Highlanders with a wicked whistling of wind in the pennons of its lances, and fell upon the remnant just when, according to all the rules of war, it should have waited for the foe to show more signs of wavering.

But it was a dainty charge, deftly delivered, and it ended by the Cavalry finding itself at the head of the pass by which the Afghans intended to retreat; and down the track that the lances had made streamed two companies of the Highlanders, which was never intended by the Brigadier. The new development was successful. It detached the enemy from his base as a sponge is torn from a rock, and left him ringed about with fire in that pitiless plain. And as a sponge is chased round the bath-tub by the hand of the bather, so were the Afghans chased till they broke into little detachments much more difficult to dispose of than large masses.

'See!' quoth the Brigadier. 'Everything has come as I arranged. We've cut their base, and now we'll bucket 'em to pieces.'

A direct hammering was all that the Brigadier had dared to hope for, considering the size of the force at his disposal; but men who stand or fall by the errors of their opponents may be forgiven for turning Chance into Design. The bucketing went forward merrily. The Afghan forces were upon the run – the run of wearied wolves who snarl and bite over their shoulders. The red lances dipped by twos and threes, and, with a shriek, up rose the lance-butt, like a spar on a stormy sea, as the trooper cantering forward cleared his point. The Lancers kept between their prey and the steep hills, for all who could were trying to escape from the valley of death. The Highlanders gave the fugitives two hundred yards' law, and then brought them down, gasping and choking, ere they could reach the protection of the boulders above. The Gurkhas followed suit; but the Fore and Fit were killing on their own account, for they had penned a mass of men between their bayonets and a wall of rock, and the flash of the rifles was lighting the wadded coats.

'We cannot hold them, Captain Sahib!' panted a Rissaldar[46] of Lancers. 'Let us try the carbine.[47] The lance is good, but it wastes time.'

They tried the carbine, and still the enemy melted away – fled up the hills by hundreds when there were only twenty bullets to stop them. On the heights the screw-guns ceased firing – they had run out of ammunition – and the Brigadier groaned, for the musketry fire could not sufficiently smash the retreat. Long before the last volleys were fired the doolies[48] were out in force looking for the wounded. The battle was over, and, but for want of fresh troops, the Afghans would have been wiped off the earth. As it was they counted their dead by hundreds, and nowhere were the dead thicker than in the track of the Fore and Fit.

But the Regiment did not cheer with the Highlanders, nor did they dance uncouth dances with the Gurkhas among the dead. They looked under their brows at the Colonel as they leaned upon their rifles and panted.

'Get back to camp, you! Haven't you disgraced yourselves enough for one day? Go and look to the wounded. It's all you're fit for,' said the Colonel. Yet for the past hour the Fore and Fit had been doing all that mortal commander could expect. They had lost heavily because they did not know how to set about their business with proper skill, but they had borne themselves gallantly, and this was their reward.

A young and sprightly Colour-Sergeant, who had begun to imagine himself a hero, offered his water-bottle to a Highlander, whose tongue was black with thirst. 'I drink with no cowards,' answered the youngster huskily, and, turning to a Gurkha, said, '*Hya*, Johnny! Drink water got it?' The Gurkha grinned and passed his bottle. The Fore and Fit said no word.

They went back to camp when the field of strife had been a little mopped up and made presentable, and the Brigadier, who saw himself a Knight in three months, was the only soul who was complimentary to them. The Colonel was heartbroken, and the officers were savage and sullen.

'Well,' said the Brigadier, 'they are young troops, of course, and it was not unnatural that they should retire in disorder for a bit.'

'Oh, my only Aunt Maria!' murmured a junior Staff Officer. 'Retire in disorder! It was a bally run!'

'But they came again, as we all know,' cooed the Brigadier, the Colonel's ashy-white face before him, 'and they behaved as well as could possibly be expected. Behaved beautifully, indeed. I was watching them. It isn't a matter to take to heart, Colonel. As some German General said of his men, they wanted to be shooted over a little, that was all.' To himself he said – 'Now they're blooded[49] I can give 'em responsible work. It's as well that they got what they did. Teach 'em more than any amount of rifle flirtations, that will – later – run alone and bite. Poor old Colonel, though!'

All that afternoon the heliograph winked and flickered on the hills, striving to tell the good news to a mountain forty miles away. And in the evening there arrived, dusty, sweating, and sore, a misguided Correspondent who had gone out to assist at a trumpery village-burning, and who had read off the message from afar, cursing his luck the while.

'Let's have the details somehow – as full as ever you can, please. It's the first time I've ever been left this campaign,' said the Correspondent to the Brigadier, and the Brigadier, nothing loath, told him how an Army of Communication had been crumpled up, destroyed, and all but annihilated by the craft, strategy, wisdom, and foresight of the Brigadier.

But some say, and among these be the Gurkhas who watched on the hillside, that that battle was won by Jakin and Lew, whose little bodies were borne up just in time to fit two gaps at the head of the big ditch-grave for the dead under the heights of Jagai.

WITH THE MAIN GUARD

Der jungere Uhlanen
Sit round mit open mouth
While Breitmann tell dem sdories
Of fightin' in the South;
Und gif dem moral lessons,
How before der battle pops,
Take a little prayer to Himmel
Und a goot long drink of Schnapps.

C. G. LELAND[1]

'Mary Mother av Mercy, fwhat the divil possist us to take an' kape this melancolious counthry? Answer me that, sorr.'

It was Mulvaney who was speaking. The time was one o'clock of a stifling June night, and the place was the main gate of Fort Amara, most desolate and least desirable of all fortresses in India. What I was doing there at that hour is a question which only concerns M'Grath the Sergeant of the Guard, and the men on the gate.

'Slape,' said Mulvaney, 'is a shuparfluous necessity. This Gyard'll shtay lively till relieved.' He himself was stripped to the waist; Learoyd on the next bedstead was dripping from the skinful of water[2] which Ortheris, clad only in white trousers, had just sluiced over his shoulders; and a fourth private was muttering uneasily as he dozed open-mouthed in the glare of the great guard-lantern. The heat under the bricked archway was terrifying.

'The worrst night that iver I remimber. Eyah! Is all Hell loose this tide?' said Mulvaney. A puff of burning wind lashed through the wicket-gate like a wave of the sea, and Ortheris swore.

'Are ye more heasy, Jock?' he said to Learoyd. 'Put yer 'ead between your legs. It'll go orf in a minute.'

'Ah doan't care. Ah would not care, but ma heart is plaayin' tivvy-tivvy on ma ribs. Let ma die! Oh, leave ma die!' groaned the huge Yorkshireman, who was feeling the heat acutely, being of fleshy build.

The sleeper under the lantern roused for a moment and raised himself on his elbow. 'Die and be damned then!' he said. '*I'm* damned and I can't die!'

'Who's that?' I whispered, for the voice was new to me.

'Gentleman born,' said Mulvaney; 'Corp'ril wan year, Sargint nex'. Red-hot on his C'mission, but dhrinks like a fish. He'll be gone before the cowld weather's here. So!'

He slipped his boot, and with the naked toe just touched the trigger of his Martini. Ortheris misunderstood the movement, and the next instant the Irishman's rifle was dashed aside, while Ortheris stood before him, his eyes blazing with reproof.

'You!' said Ortheris. 'My Gawd, *you*! If it was you, wot would *we* do?'

'Kape quiet, little man,' said Mulvaney, putting him aside, but very gently; ''tis not me, nor will ut be me whoile Dinah Shadd's here. I was but showin' somethin'.'

Learoyd, bowed on his bedstead, groaned, and the gentleman-ranker sighed in his sleep. Ortheris took Mulvaney's tendered pouch, and we three smoked gravely for a space while the dust-devils danced on the glacis[3] and scoured the red-hot plain.

'Pop?' said Ortheris, wiping his forehead.

'Don't tantalise wid talkin' av dhrink, or I'll shtuff you into your own breech-block an' – fire you off!' grunted Mulvaney.

Ortheris chuckled, and from a niche in the veranda produced six bottles of gingerade.

'Where did ye get ut, ye Machiavel?' said Mulvaney. ''Tis no bazar pop.'

''Ow do *I* know wot the orf'cers drink?' answered Ortheris. 'Arst the mess-man.'

'Ye'll have a Disthrict Coort-Martial settin' on ye yet, me son,' said Mulvaney, 'but' – he opened a bottle – 'I will not report ye this time. Fwhat's in the mess-kid[4] is mint for the belly, as they say, 'specially whin that mate is dhrink. Here's luck! A bloody war or a – no, we've got the sickly season. War, thin!' – he waved the innocent 'pop' to the four quarters of heaven. 'Bloody war! North, East, South, an' West! Jock, ye quakin' hayrick, come an' dhrink.'

But Learoyd, half mad with the fear of death presaged in the swelling veins of his neck, was begging his Maker to strike him dead, and fighting for more air between his prayers. A second time Ortheris drenched the quivering body with water, and the giant revived.

'An' Ah divn't see thot a mon is i' fettle for gooin' on to live; an' Ah divn't see thot there is owt for t' livin' for. Hear now, lads! Ah'm tired – tired. There's nobbut watter i' ma bones. Leave ma die!'

The hollow of the arch gave back Learoyd's broken whisper in a bass boom. Mulvaney looked at me hopelessly, but I remembered how the madness of despair had once fallen upon Ortheris, that weary, weary afternoon on the banks of the Khemi River, and how it had been exorcised by the skilful magician Mulvaney.

'Talk, Terence!' I said, 'or we shall have Learoyd slinging loose, and he'll be worse than Ortheris was. Talk! He'll answer to your voice.'

Almost before Ortheris had deftly thrown all the rifles of the guard on Mulvaney's bedstead, the Irishman's voice was uplifted as that of one in the middle of a story, and, turning to me, he said: –

'In barricks or out av it, as *you* say, sorr, an Irish rig'mint is the divil an' more. 'Tis only fit for a young man wid eddicated fisteses. Oh, the crame av disrupshin is an Irish rig'mint, an' rippin', tearin', ragin' scattherers in the field av war! My first rig'mint was Irish – Faynians[5] an' rebils to the heart av their marrow was they, an' *so* they fought for the Widdy[6] betther than most, bein' contrairy – Irish. They was the Black Tyrone. You've heard av thim, sorr?'

Heard of them! I knew the Black Tyrone for the choicest collection of unmitigated blackguards, dogstealers, robbers of hen-roosts, assault-ers of innocent citizens, and recklessly daring heroes in the Army List. Half Europe and half Asia has had cause to know the Black Tyrone – good luck be with their tattered Colours[7] as Glory has ever been!

'They *was* hot pickils an' ginger! I cut a man's head tu deep wid me belt in the days av me youth, an', afther some circumstances which I will obliterate, I came to the Ould Rig'mint, bearin' the character av a man wid hands an' feet. But, as I was goin' to tell you, I fell acrost[8] the Black Tyrone agin wan day whin we wanted thim powerful bad. Orth'ris, me son, fwhat was the name av that place where they sint wan comp'ny av us an' wan av the Tyrone roun' a hill an' down agin, all for to tache the Paythans something they'd niver learned before? Afther Ghuzni 'twas.'

'Don't know what the bloomin' Paythans called it. We called it Silver's Theayter. You know that, sure!'

'Silver's Theatre – so 'twas. A gut betwix' two hills, as black as a bucket, an' as thin as a gurl's waist. There was over-many Paythans for our convaynience in the gut, an' begad they called thimsilves a Reserve – bein' impident by natur'! Our Scotchies an' lashin's av Gurkys was poundin' into some Paythan rig'mints, I think 'twas. Scotchies an' Gurkys are twins bekaze they're so onlike, an' they get dhrunk together whin God plazes. As I was sayin', they sint wan comp'ny av the Ould an' wan av the Tyrone to double up the hill an' clane out the Paythan Reserve. Orf'cers was scarce in thim days, fwhat wid dysint'ry an' not takin' care av thimsilves, an' we was sint out wid only wan orf'cer for the comp'ny; but he was a Man that had his feet beneath him an' all his teeth in their sockuts.'

'Who was he?' I asked.

'Captain O'Neil – Old Crook – Cruik-na-bulleen – him that I tould ye that tale av whin he was in Burma.* Hah! He was a Man. The Tyrone tuk a little orf'cer bhoy, but divil a bit was he in command, as I'll dimonsthrate prisintly. We an' they came over the brow av the hill, wan on each side av the gut, an' there was that ondacint Reserve waitin' down below like rats in a pit.

'"Howld on, men," sez Crook, who tuk a mother's care av us always. "Rowl some rocks on thim by way av visitin'-kyards." We hadn't rowled more than twinty bowlders, an' the Paythans was beginnin' to swear tremenjus, whin the little orf'cer bhoy av the Tyrone shqueaks out acrost the valley: "Fwhat the divil an' all are you doin', shpoilin' the fun for my men? Do ye not see they'll stand?"

'"Faith, that's a rare pluckt wan!" sez Crook. "Niver mind the rocks, men. Come along down an' take tay wid thim!"

'"There's damned little sugar in ut!" sez my rear-rank man; but Crook heard.

'"Have ye not all got spoons?" he sez, laughin', an' down we wint as fast as we cud. Learoyd bein' sick at the Base, he, av coorse, was not there.'

'Thot's a lie!' said Learoyd, dragging his bedstead nearer. 'Ah gotten *thot* theer, an' you knaw it, Mulvaaney.' He threw up his arms, and from the right armpit ran, diagonally through the fell of his chest, a thin white line terminating near the fourth left rib.

'My mind's goin',' said Mulvaney, the unabashed. 'Ye were there. Fwhat was I thinkin' av? 'Twas another man, av coorse. Well, you'll remimber thin, Jock, how we an' the Tyrone met wid a bang at the bottom an' got jammed past all movin' among the Paythans?'

'Ow! It *was* a tight 'ole. I was squeezed till I thought I'd bloomin' well bust,' said Ortheris, rubbing his stomach meditatively.

''Twas no place for a little man, but *wan* little man' – Mulvaney put his hand on Ortheris's shoulder – 'saved the life av me. There we shtuck, for divil a bit did the Paythans flinch, an' divil a bit dare we; our business bein' to clear 'em out. An' the most exthryordinar' thing av all was that we an' they just rushed into each other's arrums, an' there was no firin' for a long time. Nothin' but knife an' bay'nit when we cud get our

*Now first of the foemen of Boh Da Thone
Was Captain O'Neil of the Black Tyrone.
The Ballad of Boh Da Thone

hands free: an' that was not often. We was breast-on to thim, an' the Tyrone was yelpin' behind av us in a way I didn't see the lean av at first. But I knew later, an' so did the Paythans.

'"Knee to knee!" sings out Crook, wid a laugh whin the rush av our comin' into the gut shtopped, an' he was huggin' a hairy great Paythan, neither bein' able to do anything to the other, tho' both was wishful.

'"Breast to breast!" he sez, as the Tyrone was pushin' us forward closer an' closer.

'"An' hand over back!"⁹ sez a Sargint that was behin'. I saw a sword lick out past Crook's ear, an' the Paythan was tuk in the apple av his throat like a pig at Dromeen Fair.

'"Thank ye, Brother Inner Guard," sez Crook, cool as a cucumber widout salt. "I wanted that room." An' he wint forward by the thickness av a man's body, havin' turned the Paythan undher him. The man bit the heel off Crook's boot in his death-bite.

'"Push, men!" sez Crook. "Push, ye paper-backed beggars!" he sez. "Am *I* to pull ye through?" So we pushed, an' we kicked, an' we swung, an' we swore, an' the grass bein' slippery, our heels wudn't bite, an' God help the front-rank man that wint down that day!'

''Ave you ever bin in the Pit hentrance o' the Vic. on a thick night?' interrupted Ortheris. 'It was worse nor that, for they was goin' one way, an' we wouldn't 'ave it. Leastaways, I 'adn't much to say.'

'Faith, me son, ye said ut, thin. I kep' this little man betune my knees as long as I cud, but he was pokin' roun' wid his bay'nit, blindin' an' stiffin' feroshus. The divil of a man is Orth'ris in a ruction – aren't ye?' said Mulvaney.

'Don't make game!' said the Cockney. 'I knowed I wasn't no good then, but I guv 'em compot from the lef' flank when we opened out. No!' he said, bringing down his hand with a thump on the bedstead, 'a bay'nit ain't no good to a little man – might as well 'ave a bloomin' fishin'-rod! I 'ate a clawin', maulin' mess, but gimme a breech that's wore out a bit an' hamminition one year in store, to let the powder kiss the bullet, an' put me somewheres where I ain't trod on by 'ulking swine like you, an' s'elp me Gawd, I could bowl you over five times outer seven at height 'undred. Would yer try, you lumberin' Hirishman?'

'No, ye wasp. I've seen ye do ut. I say there's nothin' better than the bay'nit, wid a long reach, a double twist av ye can, an' a slow recover.'

'Dom the bay'nit,' said Learoyd, who had been listening intently. 'Look a-here!' He picked up a rifle an inch below the foresight with an underhanded action, and used it exactly as a man would use a dagger.

'Sitha,' said he softly, 'thot's better than owt, for a mon can bash t'

faace wi' thot, an', if he divn't, he can breeak t' forearm o' t' guaard.
'Tis nut i' t' books, though. Gie me t' butt.'

'Each does ut his own way, like makin' love,' said Mulvaney quietly;
'the butt or the bay'nit or the bullet accordin' to the natur' av the man.
Well, as I was sayin', we shtuck there breathin' in each other's faces an'
swearin' powerful; Orth'ris cursin' the mother that bore him bekaze
he was not three inches taller.

'Prisintly he sez: "Duck, ye lump, an' I can get at a man over your
shoulther!"

'"You'll blow me head off," I sez, throwin' my arrum clear; "go
through under my arrumpit, ye bloodthirsty little scutt," sez I, "but
don't shtick me or I'll wring your ears round."

'Fwhat was ut ye gave the Paythan man forninst me, him that cut
at me whin I cudn't move hand or foot? Hot or cowld was ut?'

'Cold,' said Ortheris, 'up an' under the rib-jints. 'E come down flat.
Best for you 'e did.'

'Thrue, me son! This jam thing that I'm talkin' about lasted for five
minut's good, an' thin we got our arrums clear an' wint in. I mis-
remimber exactly fwhat I did, but I didn't want Dinah to be a widdy
at the depôt. Thin, afther some promishcuous hackin' we shtuck again,
an' the Tyrone behin' was callin' us dogs an' cowards an' all manner
av names; we barrin' their way.

'"Fwhat ails the Tyrone?" thinks I. "They've the makin's av a most
convanient fight here."

'"A man behind me sez beseechful an' in a whisper: "Let me get at
thim! For the love av Mary, give me room beside ye, ye tall man!"

'"An' who are you that's so anxious to be kilt?" sez I, widout turnin'
my head, for the long knives was dancin' in front like the sun on
Donegal Bay whin ut's rough.

'"We've seen our dead,"[10] he sez, squeezin' into me; "our dead that
was men two days gone! An' me that was his cousin by blood cud not
bring Tim Coulan off! Let me get on," he sez, "let me get to thim or I'll
run ye through the back!"

'"My troth," thinks I, "if the Tyrone have seen their dead, God help
the Paythans this day!" An' thin I knew why the Tyrone was ragin'
behind us as they was.

'I gave room to the man, an' he ran forward wid the Haymakers'
Lift on his bay'nit an' swung a Paythan clear off his feet by the belly-
band av the brute, an' the iron bruk at the lockin'-ring.[11]

'"Tim Coulan 'll slape aisy to-night," sez he wid a grin; an' the next
minut' his head was in two halves and he wint down grinnin' by
sections.

'The Tyrone was pushin' an' pushin' in, an' our men was swearin' at thim, an' Crook was workin' away in front av us all, his sword-arrum swingin' like a pump-handle an' his revolver spittin' like a cat. But the strange thing av ut was the quiet that lay upon. 'Twas like a fight in a drame – excipt for thim that was dead.

'Whin I gave room to the Irishman I was expinded an' forlorn in my inside. 'Tis a way I have, savin' your presince, sorr, in action. "Let me out, bhoys," sez I, backin' in among thim. "I'm goin' to be onwell!" Faith, they gave me room at the wurrud, though they wud not ha' given room for all Hell wid the chill off. When I got clear, I was, savin' your presince, sorr, outrajis sick bekaze I had dhrunk heavy that day.

'Well an' far out av harm was a Sargint av the Tyrone sittin' on the little orf'cer bhoy who had stopped Crook from rowlin' the rocks. Oh, he was a beautiful bhoy, an' the long black curses was slidin' out av his innocint mouth like mornin'-jew from a rose!

'"Fwhat have you got there?" sez I to the Sargint.

'"Wan av Her Majesty's bantams wid his spurs up," sez he. "He's goin' to Coort-Martial me."

'"Let me go!" sez the little orf'cer bhoy. "Let me go and command me men!" manin' thereby the Black Tyrone which was beyond any command – even av they had made the Divil Field-Orf'cer.

'"His father howlds my mother's cow-feed in Clonmel," sez the man that was sittin' on him. "Will I go back to *his* mother an' tell her that I've let him throw himsilf away? Lie still, ye little pinch of dynamite, an' Coort-Martial me afterwards."

'"Good," sez I; "'tis the likes av him makes the likes av the Commander-in-Chief, but we must presarve thim. Fwhat d'you want to do, sorr?" sez I, very politeful.

'"Kill the beggars – kill the beggars!" he shqueaks, his big blue eyes brimmin' wid tears.

'"An' how'll ye do that?" sez I. "You've shquibbed off your revolver like a child wid a cracker; you can make no play wid that fine large sword av yours; an' your hand's shakin' like an asp on a leaf.[12] Lie still and grow," sez I.

'"Get back to your comp'ny," sez he; "you're insolint!"

'"All in good time," sez I, "but I'll have a dhrink first."

'Just thin Crook comes up, blue an' white all over where he wasn't red.

'"Wather!" sez he; "I'm dead wid drouth! Oh, but it's a gran' day!"

'He dhrank half a skinful, and the rest he tilts into his chest, an' it fair hissed on the hairy hide av him. He sees the little orf'cer bhoy undher the Sargint.

'"Fwhat's yonder?" sez he.

'"Mutiny, sorr," sez the Sargint, an' the orf'cer bhoy begins pleadin' pitiful to Crook to be let go; but divil a bit wud Crook budge.

'"Kape him there," he sez; "'tis no child's work this day. By the same token," sez he, "I'll confishcate that iligant nickel-plated scent-sprinkler av yours, for my own has been vomitin' dishgraceful!"

'The fork av his hand was black wid the back-spit av the machine. So he tuk the orf'cer bhoy's revolver. Ye may look, sorr, but, by my faith, *there's a dale more done in the field than iver gets into Field Ordhers!*

'"Come on, Mulvaney," sez Crook; "is this a Coort-Martial?" The two av us wint back together into the mess an' the Paythans was still standin' up. They was not *too* impart'nint though, for the Tyrone was callin' wan to another to remimber Tim Coulan.

'Crook holted[13] outside av the strife an' looked anxious, his eyes rowlin' roun'.

'"Fwhat is ut, sorr?" sez I; "can I get ye anything?"

'"Where's a bugler?" sez he.

'I wint into the crowd – our men was dhrawin' breath behin' the Tyrone, who was fightin' like sowls in tormint – an' prisintly I came acrost little Frehan, our bugler bhoy, pokin' roun' among the best wid a rifle an' bay'nit.

'"Is amusin' yoursilf fwhat you're paid for, ye limb?" sez I, catchin' him by the scruff. "Come out av that an' attind to your jooty," I sez; but the bhoy was not plazed.

'"I've got wan," sez he, grinnin', "big as you, Mulvaney, an' fair half as ugly. Let me go get another."

'I was dishplazed at the personability av that remark, so I tucks him under my arrum an' carries him to Crook, who was watchin' how the fight wint. Crook cuffs him till the bhoy cries, an' thin sez nothin' for a whoile.

'The Paythans began to flicker onaisy, an' our men roared. "Opin ordher! Double!" sez Crook. "Blow, child, blow for the honour av the British Arrmy!"

'That bhoy blew like a typhoon, an' the Tyrone an' we opind out as the Paythans bruk, an' I saw that fwhat had gone before wud be kissin' an' huggin' to fwhat was to come. We'd dhruv thim into a broad part av the gut whin they gave, an' thin we opind out an' fair danced down the valley, dhrivin' thim before us. Oh, 'twas lovely, an' stiddy, too! There was the Sargints on the flanks av what was left av us, kapin' touch, an' the fire was runnin' from flank to flank, an' the Paythans was dhroppin'. We opind out wid the widenin' av the valley, an' whin the valley narrowed we closed agin like the shticks on a lady's fan, an' at the far ind av the gut where they thried to stand, we fair blew them off their feet, for we had expinded very little ammunition by reason av the knife-work.'

'*I* used thirty rounds goin' down that valley,' said Ortheris, 'an' it was gentleman's work. Might 'a' done it in a white 'andkerchief an' pink silk stockin's, that part. *Hi* was on in that piece.'

'You cud ha' heard the Tyrone yellin' a mile away,' said Mulvaney, 'an' 'twas all their Sargints cud do to get thim off. They was mad – mad – mad! Crook sits down in the quiet that fell whin we had gone down the valley, an' covers his face wid his hands. Prisintly we all came back agin accordin' to our natur's and disposishins, for they, mark you, show through the hide av a man in that hour.

'"Bhoys! bhoys!" sez Crook to himsilf. "I misdoubt we cud ha' engaged at long range an' saved betther men than me." He looked at our dead an' said no more.

'"Captain dear," sez a man av the Tyrone, comin' up wid his mouth bigger than iver his mother kissed ut, spittin' blood like a whale; "Captain dear," sez he, "if wan or two in the shtalls have been dishcommoded, the gallery have enjoyed the performinces av a Roshus."[14]

'Thin I knew that man for the Dublin dock-rat he was – wan av the bhoys that made the lessee av Silver's Theatre grey before his time wid tearin' out the bowils av the benches an' throwin' thim into the pit. So I passed the wurrud that I knew whin I was in the Tyrone an' we lay in Dublin. "I don't know who 'twas," I whishpers, "an' I don't care, but anyways I'll knock the face av you, Tim Kelly."

'"Eyah!" sez the man, "was you there too? We'll call ut Silver's Theatre." Half the Tyrone, knowin' the ould place, tuk ut up: so we called ut Silver's Theatre.

'The little orf'cer bhoy av the Tyrone was thremblin' an' cryin'. He had no heart for the Coort-Martials that he talked so big upon. "Ye'll do well later," sez Crook, very quiet, "for not bein' allowed to kill yoursilf for amusemint."

'"I'm a dishgraced man!" sez the little orf'cer bhoy.

'"Put me undher arrest, sorr, if you will, but, by my sowl, I'd do ut agin sooner than face your mother wid you dead," sez the Sargint that had sat on his head, standin' to attenshin an' salutin'. But the young wan only cried as tho' his little heart was breakin'.

'Thin another man av the Tyrone came up, wid the fog av fightin' on him.'

'The what, Mulvaney?'

'Fog av fightin'. You know, sorr, that, like makin' love, ut takes each man diff'rint. Now, I can't help bein' powerful sick whin I'm in action.

Orth'ris, here, niver stops swearin' from ind to ind, an' the only time that Learoyd opins his mouth to sing is whin he is messin' wid other people's heads; for he's a dhirty fighter is Jock. Recruities sometime cry, an' sometime they don't know fwhat they do, an' sometime they are all for cuttin' throats an' such-like dhirtiness; but some men get heavy-dead-dhrunk on the fightin'. This man was. He was staggerin', an' his eyes were half shut, an' we cud hear him dhraw breath twinty yards away. He sees the little orf'cer bhoy, an' comes up, talkin' thick an' drowsy to himsilf. "Blood the young whelp!"[15] he sez; "Blood the young whelp"; an' wid that he threw up his arrums, shpun roun', an' dropped at our feet, dead as a Paythan, an' there was niver sign or scratch on him. They said 'twas his heart was rotten, but oh, 'twas a quare thing to see!

'Thin we wint to bury our dead, for we wud not lave thim to the Paythans, an' in movin' among the haythen we nearly lost that little orf'cer bhoy. He was for givin' wan divil wather and layin' him aisy against a rock. "Be careful, sorr," sez I; "a wounded Paythan's worse than a live wan." My troth, before the words was out av me mouth, the man on the ground fires at the orf'cer bhoy lanin' over him, an' I saw the helmit fly. I dropped the butt on the face av the man an' tuk his pistol. The little orf'cer bhoy turned very white, for the hair av half his head was singed away.

'"I tould you so, sorr!" sez I; an', afther that, whin he wanted to help a Paythan I stud wid the muzzle contagious to the ear. They dared not do anythin' but curse. The Tyrone was growlin' like dogs over a bone that has been taken away too soon, for they had seen their dead an' they wanted to kill ivry sowl on the ground. Crook tould thim that he'd blow the hide off any man that misconducted himsilf; but, seeing that ut was the first time the Tyrone had iver seen their dead, I do not wondher they was on the sharp. 'Tis a shameful sight! Whin I first saw ut I wud niver ha' given quarter to any man north of the Khyber – no, nor woman either, for the wimmen used to come out afther dhark – Auggrh!

'Well, evenshually we buried our dead an' tuk away our wounded, an' come over the brow av the hills to see the Scotchies an' the Gurkys takin' tay with the Paythans in bucketsfuls. We were a gang av dissolute ruffians, for the blood had caked the dust, an' the sweat had cut the cake, an' our bay'nits was hangin' like butchers' steels betune our legs, an' most av us was marked one way or another.

'A Staff Orf'cer man, clane as a new rifle, rides up an' sez: "What damned scarecrows are you?"

'"A comp'ny av Her Majesty's Black Tyrone an' wan av the Ould

Rig'mint," sez Crook very quiet, givin' our visitors the flure as 'twas.

'"Oh!" sez the Staff Orf'cer. "Did you dislodge that Reserve?"

'"No!" sez Crook, an' the Tyrone laughed.

'"Thin fwhat the divil have ye done?"

'"Disthroyed ut," sez Crook, an' he took us on, but not before Toomey that was in the Tyrone sez aloud, his voice somewhere in his stummick: "Fwhat in the name av misfortune does this parrit widout a tail mane by shtoppin' the road av his betthers?"

'The Staff Orf'cer wint blue, an' Toomey makes him pink by changin' to the voice av a minowdherin' woman an' sayin': "Come an' kiss me, Major dear, for me husband's at the wars an' I'm all alone at the depôt."

'The Staff Orf'cer wint away, an' I cud see Crook's shoulthers shakin'.

'His Corp'ril checks Toomey. "Lave me alone," sez Toomey, widout a wink. "I was his batman[16] before he was married an' he knows fwhat I mane, av you don't. There's nothin' like livin' in the hoight av society." D'you remimber that, Orth'ris?'

'Yuss. Toomey, 'e died in 'orspital, next week it was, 'cause I bought 'arf his kit; an' I remember after that – '

'GUARRD, TURN OUT!'

The Relief had come; it was four o'clock. 'I'll catch a kyart for you, sorr,' said Mulvaney, diving hastily into his accoutrements. 'Come up to the top av the Fort an' we'll pershue our invistigations into M'Grath's shtable.' The relieved guard strolled round the main bastion on its way to the swimming-bath, and Learoyd grew almost talkative. Ortheris looked into the Fort Ditch and across the plain. 'Ho! it's weary waitin' for Ma-ary!' he hummed; 'but I'd like to kill some more bloomin' Paythans before my time's up. War! Bloody war! North, East, South, and West.'

'Amen,' said Learoyd slowly.

'Fwhat's here?' said Mulvaney, checking at a blur of white by the foot of the old sentry-box. He stooped and touched it. 'It's Norah – Norah M'Taggart! Why, Nonie darlin', fwhat are ye doin' out av your mother's bed at this time?'

The two-year-old child of Sergeant M'Taggart must have wandered for a breath of cool air to the very verge of the parapet of the Fort Ditch. Her tiny night-shift was gathered into a wisp round her neck and she moaned in her sleep. 'See there!' said Mulvaney; 'poor lamb! Look at the heat-rash on the innocint shkin av her. 'Tis hard – crool hard even for us. Fwhat must it be for these? Wake up, Nonie, your mother will be woild about you. Begad, the child might ha' fallen into the Ditch!'

He picked her up in the growing light, and set her on his shoulder, and her fair curls touched the grizzled stubble of his temples. Ortheris and Learoyd followed snapping their fingers, while Norah smiled at them a sleepy smile. Then carolled Mulvaney, clear as a lark, dancing the baby on his arm:

> "'If any young man should marry you,
>   Say nothin' about the joke;
>   That iver ye slep' in a sinthry-box,
>   Wrapped up in a soldier's cloak.'"

'Though, on my sowl, Nonie,' he said gravely, 'there was not much cloak about you. Niver mind, you won't dhress like this ten years to come. Kiss your frinds an' run along to your mother.'

Nonie, set down close to the Married Quarters, nodded with the quiet obedience of the soldier's child, but, ere she pattered off over the flagged path, held up her lips to be kissed by the Three Musketeers. Ortheris wiped his mouth with the back of his hand and swore sentimentally; Learoyd turned pink; and the two walked away together. The Yorkshireman lifted up his voice and gave in thunder the chorus of *The Sentry-Box*, while Ortheris piped at his side.

'Bin to a bloomin' sing-song, you two?' said the Artilleryman, who was taking his cartridge down to the Morning Gun. 'You're over merry for these dashed days.'

> "'I bid ye take care o' the brat," said he,
>   "For it comes of a noble race,"'

Learoyd bellowed. The voices died out in the swimming-bath.

'Oh, Terence!' I said, dropping into Mulvaney's speech, when we were alone, 'it's you that have the Tongue!'

He looked at me wearily; his eyes were sunk in his head, and his face was drawn and white. 'Eyah!' said he; 'I've blandandhered thim through the night somehow, but can thim that helps others help thimsilves? Answer me that, sorr!'

And over the bastions of Fort Amara broke the pitiless day.

ON GREENHOW HILL

To Love's low voice she lent a careless ear;
Her hand within his rosy fingers lay,
A chilling weight. She would not turn or hear;
But with averted face went on her way.
But when pale Death, all featureless and grim,
Lifted his bony hand, and beckoning
Held out his cypress-wreath, she followed him,
And Love was left forlorn and wondering,
That she who for his bidding would not stay,
At Death's first whisper rose and went away.

Rivals[1]

'Ohe, Ahmed Din! Shafiz Ullah, *ahoo!* Bahadur Khan, where are you?
Come out of the tents, as I have done, and fight against the English.
Don't kill your own kin! Come out to me!'

The deserter from a native corps was crawling round the outskirts
of the camp, firing at intervals, and shouting invitations to his old
comrades. Misled by the rain and the darkness, he came to the English
wing of the camp, and with his yelping and rifle-practice disturbed the
men. They had been making roads all day, and were tired.

Ortheris was sleeping at Learoyd's feet. 'Wot's all that?' he said
thickly. Learoyd snored, and a Snider[2] bullet ripped its way through
the tent wall. The men swore. 'It's that bloomin' deserter from the
Aurangabadis,' said Ortheris. 'Git up, some one, an' tell 'im 'e's come
to the wrong shop.'

'Go to sleep, little man,' said Mulvaney, who was steaming nearest
the door. 'I can't arise an' expaytiate wid him. 'Tis rainin' entrenchin'
tools outside.'

''Tain't because you bloomin' can't. It's 'cause you bloomin' won't,
ye long, limp, lousy, lazy beggar, you. 'Ark to 'im 'owlin'!'

'Wot's the good of argifying? Put a bullet into the swine! 'E's keepin'
us awake!' said another voice.

A subaltern shouted angrily, and a dripping sentry whined from the
darkness: –

''Tain't no good, sir. I can't see 'im. 'E's 'idin' somewhere down 'ill.'

Ortheris tumbled out of his blanket. 'Shall I try to get 'im, sir?' said he.

'No,' was the answer. 'Lie down. I won't have the whole camp shooting all round the clock. Tell him to go and pot his friends.'

Ortheris considered for a moment. Then, putting his head under the tent wall, he called, as a 'bus-conductor calls in a block, ''Igher up, there! 'Igher up!'

The men laughed, and the laughter was carried down wind to the deserter, who, hearing that he had made a mistake, went off to worry his own regiment half a mile away. He was received with shots; the Aurangabadis were very angry with him for disgracing their colours.

'An' that's all right,' said Ortheris, withdrawing his head as he heard the hiccough of the Sniders in the distance. 'S'elp me Gawd, tho', that man's not fit to live – messin' with my beauty-sleep this way.'

'Go out and shoot him in the morning, then,' said the subaltern incautiously. 'Silence in the tents now. Get your rest, men.'

Ortheris lay down with a happy little sigh, and in two minutes there was no sound except the rain on the canvas and the all-embracing and elemental snoring of Learoyd.

The camp lay on a bare ridge of the Himalayas, and for a week had been waiting for a flying column to make connection. The nightly rounds of the deserter and his friends had become a nuisance.

In the morning the men dried themselves in hot sunshine and cleaned their grimy accoutrements. The native regiment was to take its turn of road-making that day while the Old Regiment loafed.

'I'm goin' to lay for a shot at that man,' said Ortheris, when he had finished washing out his rifle. ''E comes up the watercourse every evenin' about five o'clock. If we go and lie out on the north 'ill a bit this afternoon we'll get 'im.'

'You're a bloodthirsty little mosquito,' said Mulvaney, blowing blue clouds into the air. 'But I suppose I will have to come wid you. Fwhere's Jock?'

'Gone out with the Mixed Pickles, 'cause 'e thinks 'isself a bloomin' marksman,' said Ortheris with scorn.

The 'Mixed Pickles' were a detachment of picked shots, generally employed in clearing spurs of hills when the enemy were too impertinent. This taught the young officers how to handle men, and did not do the enemy much harm. Mulvaney and Ortheris strolled out of camp, and passed the Aurangabadis going to their road-making.

'You've got to sweat to-day,' said Ortheris genially. 'We're going to get your man. You didn't knock 'im out last night by any chanst, any of you?'

'No. The pig went away mocking us. I had one shot at him,' said a private. 'He's my cousin, and *I* ought to have cleared our dishonour. But good luck to you.'

They went cautiously to the north hill, Ortheris leading, because, as he explained, 'this is a long-range show, an' I've got to do it.' His was an almost passionate devotion to his rifle, which, by barrack-room report, he was supposed to kiss every night before turning in. Charges and scuffles he held in contempt, and, when they were inevitable, slipped between Mulvaney and Learoyd, bidding them to fight for his skin as well as their own. They never failed him. He trotted along, questing like a hound on a broken trail,[3] through the wood of the north hill. At last he was satisfied, and threw himself down on the soft pine-needled slope that commanded a clear view of the watercourse and a brown, bare hillside beyond it. The trees made a scented darkness in which an army corps could have hidden from the sun-glare without.

''Ere's the tail o' the wood,' said Ortheris. ''E's got to come up the watercourse, 'cause it gives 'im cover. We'll lay 'ere. 'Tain't not 'arf so bloomin' dusty neither.'

He buried his nose in a clump of scentless white violets. No one had come to tell the flowers that the season of their strength was long past, and they had bloomed merrily in the twilight of the pines.

'This is something like,' he said luxuriously. 'Wot a 'evinly clear drop for a bullet acrost. How much d'you make it, Mulvaney?'

'Sivin hundher'. Maybe a trifle less, bekaze the air's so thin.'

Wop! wop! wop! went a volley of musketry on the rear face of the north hill.

'Curse them Mixed Pickles firin' at nothin'! They'll scare 'arf the country.'

'Thry a sightin' shot in the middle of the row,' said Mulvaney, the man of many wiles. 'There's a red rock yonder he'll be sure to pass. Quick!'

Ortheris ran his sight up to six hundred yards and fired. The bullet threw up a feather of dust by a clump of gentians at the base of the rock.

'Good enough!' said Ortheris, snapping the scale down. 'You snick your sights to mine or a little lower. You're always firin' high. But remember, first shot to me. O Lordy! but it's a lovely afternoon.'

The noise of the firing grew louder, and there was a tramping of men in the wood. The two lay very quiet, for they knew that the British soldier is desperately prone to fire at anything that moves or calls. Then Learoyd appeared, his tunic ripped across the breast by a bullet, looking ashamed of himself. He flung down on the pine-needles, breathing in snorts.

'One o' them dommed gardeners o' th' Pickles,' said he, fingering the rent. 'Firin' to th' right flank, when he knowed I was there. If I knew who he was I'd 'a' rippen the hide offan him. Look at ma tunic!'

'That's the spishil trustability av a marksman. Train him to hit a fly wid a stiddy rest at sivin hundher, an' he'll loose on anythin' he sees or hears up to th' mile. You're well out av that fancy-firin' gang, Jock. Stay here.'

'Bin firin' at the bloomin' wind in the bloomin' tree-tops,' said Ortheris with a chuckle. 'I'll show you some firin' later on.'

They wallowed in the pine-needles, and the sun warmed them where they lay. The Mixed Pickles ceased firing, and returned to camp, and left the wood to a few scared apes. The watercourse lifted up its voice in the silence, and talked foolishly to the rocks. Now and again the dull thump of a blasting charge three miles away told that the Aurangabadis were in difficulties with their road-making. The men smiled as they listened and lay still, soaking in the warm leisure. Presently, Learoyd, between the whiffs of his pipe: –

'Seems queer – about 'im yonder – desertin' at all.'

''E'll be a bloomin' side queerer when I've done with 'im,' said Ortheris. They were talking in whispers, for the stillness of the wood and the desire of slaughter lay heavy upon them.

'I make no doubt he had his reasons for desertin'; but, my faith! I make less doubt ivry man has good reason for killin' him,' said Mulvaney.

'Happen there was a lass tewed up wi' it. Men do more than more for t' saake of a lass.'

'They make most av us 'list.[4] They've no manner av right to make us desert.'

'Ah; they make us 'list, or their fathers do,' said Learoyd softly, his helmet over his eyes.

Ortheris's brows contracted savagely. He was watching the valley. 'If it's a girl I'll shoot the beggar twice over, an' second time for bein' a fool. You're blasted sentimental all of a sudden. Thinkin' o' your last near shave?'

'Nay, lad. Ah was but thinkin' o' what has happened.'

'An' fwhat has happened, ye lumberin' child av calamity, that you're lowing like a cow-calf at the back av the pasture, an' suggestin' invijus excuses for the man Stanley's goin' to kill? Ye'll have to wait another hour yet, little man. Spit it out, Jock, an' bellow melojus to the moon. It takes an earthquake or a bullet-graze to fetch aught out av you.

Discourse, Don Juan! The a-moors av Lotharius[5] Learoyd! Stanley, kape a rowlin' rig'mintal eye on the valley.'

'It's along o' yon hill there,' said Learoyd, watching the bare sub-Himalayan spur that reminded him of his Yorkshire moors. He was speaking more to himself than his fellows. 'Ay,' said he, 'Rumbolds Moor stands up ovver Skipton town, an' Greenhow Hill stands up ovver Pately Brig. I reckon yo've never heeard tell o' Greenhow Hill, but yon bit o' bare stuff if there was nobbut a white road windin' is like it; strangely like. Moors an' moors an' moors, wi' never a tree for shelter, an' grey houses wi' flagstone rooves, and peewits cryin', an' a windhover goin' to and fro just like these kites. And cold! A wind that cuts you like a knife. You could tell Greenhow Hill folk by the red-apple colour o' their cheeks an' nose-tips, and their blue eyes, driven into pin-points by the wind. Miners mostly, burrowin' for lead i' th' hillsides, followin' the trail of th' ore vein same as a field-rat. It was the roughest minin' I ever seen. Yo'd come on a bit o' creakin' wood windlass like a well-head an' you was let down i' th' bight[6] of a rope, fendin' yoursen off the side wi' one hand, carryin' a candle stuck in a lump o' clay wi' t' other, an' clickin' hold of a rope wi' t' other hand.'

'An' that's three av thim,' said Mulvaney. 'Must be a good climate in those parts.'

Learoyd took no heed.

'An' then yo' came to a level, where you crept on your hands and knees through a mile o' windin' drift,[7] an' you come out into a cave-place as big as Leeds Town Hall, wi' a engine pumpin' water from workin's 'at went deeper still. It's a queer country, let alone minin', for the hill is full of those natural caves, an' the rivers an' the becks drops into what they call potholes, an' come out again miles away.'

'Wot was you doin' there?' said Ortheris.

'I was a young chap then, an' mostly went wi' 'osses, leadin' coal and lead ore; but at the time I'm tellin' on I was drivin' the wagon-team i' th' big sumph.[8] I didn't belong to that countryside by rights. I went there because of a little difference at home, an' at fost I took up wi' a rough lot. One night we'd been drinkin', an' I must ha' hed more than I could stand, or happen th' ale was none so good. Though i' them days, By for God, I niver seed bad ale.' He flung his arms over his head, and gripped a vast handful of white violets. 'Nah,' said he, 'I niver seed th' ale I could not drink, the bacca I could not smoke, nor the lass I could not kiss. Well, we mun have a race home, the lot on us. I lost all t' others, an' when I was climbin' ovver one of them walls built o' loose stones, I comes down into the ditch, stones and all, an' broke my arm. Not as I knawed much about it, for I fell on t' back of my head, an' was knocked stupid like. An' when I come to mysen it were mornin', an' I were lyin' on the settle i' Jesse Roantree's house-place, an' 'Liza Roantree was settin' sewin'. I ached all ovver, and my mouth were like a lime-kiln. She gave me a drink out of a china mug wi' gold letters – "A Present from Leeds" – as I looked at many and many a time at after. "Yo're to lie still while Dr Warbottom comes, because your arm's broken, and father has sent a lad to fetch him. He found yo' when he was goin' to work, an' carried yo' here on his back," sez she. "Oa!" sez I; an' I shet my eyes, for I felt ashamed o' mysen. "Father's gone to his work these three hours, an' he said he'd tell 'em to get somebody to drive the tram." The clock ticked, an' a bee comed in the house, an' they rung i' my head like mill-wheels. An' she give me another drink an' settled the pillow. "Eh, but yo're young to be getten drunk an' such-like, but yo' won't do it again, will yo'?" – Noa, sez I, I wouldn't if she'd nobbut stop they mill-wheels clatterin'.'

'Faith, ut's a good thing to be nursed by a woman whin you're sick!' said Mulvaney. 'Dir' chape at the price av twenty broken heads.'

Ortheris turned to frown across the valley. He had not been nursed by many women in his life.

'An' then Dr Warbottom comes ridin' up, an' Jesse Roantree along wi' 'im. He was a high-larned doctor, but he talked wi' poor folk same as theirsens. "What's ta bin agaate[9] on naa?" he sings out. "Brekkin' tha thick head?" An' he felt me all ovver. "That's none broken. Tha's nobbut knocked a bit sillier than ordinary, an' that's daaft eneaf." An' soa he went on, callin' me all the naames he could think on, but settin' my arm, wi' Jesse's help, as careful as could be. "Yo' mun let the big oaf bide here a bit, Jesse," he says, when he hed strapped me up an' given me a dose o' physic; "an' you an' 'Liza will tend him, though he's scarcelins worth the trouble. An' tha'll lose tha work," sez he, "an' tha'll be upon th' Sick Club for a couple o' months an' more. Doesn't tha think tha's a fool?"'

'But whin was a young man, high or low, the other av a fool, I'd like to know?' said Mulvaney. 'Sure, folly's the only safe way to wisdom, for I've thried ut.'

'Wisdom!' grinned Ortheris, scanning his comrades with uplifted chin. 'You're bloomin' Solomons, you two, ain't you?'

Learoyd went calmly on, with a steady eye like an ox chewing the cud.

'And that was how I comed to know 'Liza Roantree. There's some tunes as she used to sing – aw, she were always singin' – that fetches Greenhow Hill before my eyes as fair as yon brow across there. And she would learn me to sing bass, an' I was to go to the chapel wi' 'em, where Jesse and she led the singin', th' owd man playin' the fiddle. He was a strange chap, old Jesse, fair mad wi' music, an' he med me promise to learn the big fiddle when my arm was better. It belonged to him, and it stood up in a big case alongside o' th' eight-day clock, but Willie Satterthwaite, as played it in the chapel, had getten deaf as a door-post, and it vexed Jesse, as he had to rap him ovver his head wi' th' fiddle-stick to make him give ovver sawin' at th' right time.

'But there was a black drop in it all, an' it was a man in a black coat that brought it. When th' Primitive Methodist preacher came to Green-how, he would always stop wi' Jesse Roantree, an' he laid hold of me from th' beginning. It seemed I wor a soul to be saved, and he meaned to do it. At th' same time I jealoused[10] 'at he were keen o' savin' 'Liza Roantree's soul as well, and I could ha' killed him many a time. An' this went on till one day I broke out, an' borrowed th' brass for a drink from 'Liza. After fower days I come back, wi' my tail between my legs, just to see 'Liza again. But Jesse were at home an' th' preacher – th' Reverend Amos Barraclough. 'Liza said naught, but a bit o' red come into her face as were white of a regular thing. Says Jesse, tryin' his best to be civil, "Nay, lad, it's like this. Yo've getten to choose which way it's goin' to be. I'll ha' nobody across ma doorstep as goes a-drinkin', an' borrows my lass's money to spend i' their drink. Ho'd tha tongue, 'Liza," sez he, when she wanted to put in a word 'at I were welcome to th' brass, and she were none afraid that I wouldn't pay it back. Then the Reverend cuts in, seein' as Jesse were losin' his temper, an' they fair beat me among them. But it were 'Liza, as looked an' said nowt, as did more than either o' their tongues, an' soa I concluded to get converted.'

'Fwhat!' shouted Mulvaney. Then, checking himself, he said softly, 'Let be! Let be! Sure the Blessed Virgin is the mother av all religion an' most women; an' there's a dale av piety in a girl if the men wud only let ut stay there. I'd ha' been convarted mesilf undher the circumstances.'

'Nay, but,' pursued Learoyd with a blush, 'I meaned it.'

Ortheris laughed as loudly as he dared, having regard to his business at the time.

'Ay, Ortheris, you may laugh, but you didn't know yon preacher Barraclough – a little white-faced chap, wi' a voice as 'ud wile a bird offan a bush, and a way o' layin' hold of folks as med them think they'd never had a live man for a friend before. You never saw him, an' – an' – you never seed 'Liza Roantree – never seed 'Liza Roantree . . . Happen it was as much 'Liza as th' preacher and her father, but anyways they all meaned it, an' I was fair shamed o' mysen, an' soa I become what they called a changed character. And when I think on, it's hard to believe as yon chap going to prayer-meetin's, chapel, and class-meetin's[11] were me. But I niver had nowt to say for mysen, though there was a deal o' shoutin', and old Sammy Strother, as were almost clemmed to death and doubled up with the rheumatics, would sing out, "Joyful! Joyful!" and 'at it were better to go up to heaven in a coal-basket than down to hell i' a coach an' six. And he would put his poor old claw on my shoulder, sayin', "Doesn't tha feel it, tha great lump? Doesn't tha feel it?" An' sometimes I thought I did, and then again I thought I didn't, an' how was that?'

'The iverlastin' natur' av mankind,' said Mulvaney. 'An', further-more, I misdoubt you were built for the Primitive Methodians. They're a new corps anyways. I hold by the Ould Church, for she's the mother av them all – ay, an' the father, too. I like her bekaze she's most remarkable rig'mintal in her fittings. I may die in Honolulu, Nova Zambra, or Cape Cayenne, but wherever I die, me bein' fwhat I am, an' a priest handy, I go under the same ordhers an' the same wurruds an' the same unction as tho' the Pope himsilf come down from the roof av St Peter's to see me off. There's neither high nor low, nor broad nor deep, nor betwixt nor between wid her, an' that's fwhat I like. But mark you, she's no manner av Church for a wake man, bekaze she takes the body and the sowl av him, unless he has his proper work to do. I rimimber when my father died that was three months comin' to his grave; begad, he'd ha' sold the shebeen[12] above our heads for ten minut's' quittance av purgathory. An' he did all he cud. That's why I say ut takes a strong man to dale with the Ould Church, an' for that reason you'll find so many women go there. An' that same's a conundrum.'

'Wot's the use o' worrittin' 'bout these things?' said Ortheris. 'You're bound to find all out quicker nor you want to, any'ow.' He jerked the cartridge out of the breech-block into the palm of his hand. ''Ere's my chaplain,' he said, and made the venomous black-headed bullet bow like a marionette. ''E's goin' to teach a man all about which is which, an' wot's true, after all, before sundown. But wot 'appened after that, Jock?'

'There was one thing they boggled at, and almost shut th' gate i' my face for, and that were my dog Blast, th' only one saved out o' a litter o' pups as was blowed up when a keg o' minin' powder loosed off in th' store-keeper's hut. They liked his name no better than his business, which were fightin' every dog he comed across; a rare good dog, wi' spots o' black and pink on his face, one ear gone, and lame o' one side wi' being driven in a basket through an iron roof, a matter of half a mile.

'They said I mun give him up 'cause he were worldly and low; and would I let mysen be shut out of heaven for the sake on a dog? "Nay," says I, "if th' door isn't wide enough for th' pair on us, we'll stop outside, for we'll none be parted." And th' preacher spoke up for Blast, as had a likin' for him from the fost – I reckon that was why I come to like th' preacher – and wouldn't hear o' changin' his naame to Bless, as some o' them wanted. Soa th' pair on us became reg'lar chapel-members. But it's hard for a young chap o' my build to cut traces from the world, th' flesh, an' the devil all iv a heap. Yet I stuck to it for a long time, while th' lads as used to stand about th' town-end an' lean ovver th' bridge, spittin' into th' beck o' a Sunday, would call after me, "Sitha,[13] Learoyd, when's ta beean to preach, 'cause we're comin' to hear tha?" – "Ho'd tha jaw. He hasn't getten th' white choaker[14] on ta morn," another lad would say, and I had to double my fists hard i' th' bottom of my Sunday coat, and say to mysen, "If 'twere Monday and I warn't a member o' the Primitive Methodists, I'd leather all th' lot of yond'." That was th' hardest of all – to know that I could fight and I mustn't fight.'

Sympathetic grunts from Mulvaney.

'Soa what wi' singin', practisin', and class-meetin's, and th' big fiddle, as he med me take between my knees, I spent a deal o' time i' Jesse Roantree's house-place. But often as I was there, th' preacher fared to me to go oftener, and both th' old man an' th' young woman were pleased to have him. He lived i' Pately Brig, as were a goodish step off, but he come. He come all the same. I liked him as well or better as any man I'd ever seen i' one way, and yet I hated him wi' all my heart i' t' other, and we watched each other like cat and mouse, but civil as you please, for I was on my best behaviour, and he was that fair and oppen that I was bound to be fair wi' him. Rare good company he was, if I hadn't wanted to wring his cliver little neck half of the time. Often and often when he was goin' from Jesse's I'd set him a bit on the road.'

'See 'im 'ome, you mean?' said Ortheris.

'Ay. It's a way we have i' Yorkshire o' seein' friends off. Yon was a friend as I didn't want to come back, and he didn't want me to come back neither, and so we'd walk together towards Pately, and then he'd set me back again, and there we'd be wal two o'clock i' the mornin' settin' each other to an' fro like a blasted pair o' pendulums 'twixt hill and valley, long after th' light had gone out i' 'Liza's window, as both on us had been looking at, pretending to watch the moon.'

'Ah!' broke in Mulvaney, 'ye'd no chanst against the maraudhin' psalm-singer. They'll take the airs an' the graces instid av the man nine times out av tin, an' they only find the blunder later – the women.'

'That's just where yo're wrong,' said Learoyd, reddening under the

freckled tan of his cheeks. 'I was th' fost wi 'Liza, an' yo'd think that
were enough. But th' parson were a steady-gaited sort o' chap, and
Jesse were strong o' his side, and all th' women i' the congregation
dinned it to 'Liza 'at she were fair fond to take up wi' a wastrel ne'er-
do-weel like me, as was scarcelins respectable an' a fighting dog at his
heels. It was all very well for her to be doing me good and saving my
soul, but she must mind as she didn't do hersen harm. They talk o' rich
folk bein' stuck-up an' genteel, but for cast-iron pride o' respectability
there's nowt like poor chapel folk. It's as cold as th' wind o' Greenhow
Hill – ay, and colder, for 'twill never change. And now I come to think
on't, one o't' strangest things I know is 'at they couldn't abide th'
thought o' soldiering. There's a vast o' fightin' i' th' Bible, and there's
a deal of Methodists i' th' Army; but to hear chapel folk talk yo'd think
that soldierin' were next door, an' t'other side, to hangin'. I' their
meetin's all their talk is o' fightin'. When Sammy Strother were stuck
for summat to say in his prayers, he'd sing out, "Th' sword o' th' Lord
and o' Gideon."[15] They were allus at it about puttin' on th' whole
armour o' righteousness,[16] an' fightin' the good fight[17] o' faith. And
then, atop o' 't all, they held a prayer-meetin' ovver a young chap as
wanted to 'list, and nearly deafened him, till he picked up his hat and
fair ran away. And they'd tell tales in th' Sunday-school o' bad lads as
had been thumped and brayed for bird-nestin' o' Sundays and playin'
truant o' week-days, and how they took to wrestlin', dog-fightin',
rabbit-runnin', an' drinkin', till at last, as if 'twere a hepitaph on a
gravestone, they dommed him across th' moors wi', "an' then he went
and 'listed for a soldier," an' they'd all fetch a deep breath, and throw
up their eyes like a hen drinkin'.'

'Fwhy is ut?' said Mulvaney, bringing down his hand on his thigh
with a crack. 'In the name av God, fwhy is ut? I've seen ut, tu. They
chate an' they swindle an' they lie an' they slander, an' fifty things
fifty times worse; but the last an' the worst by their reckonin' is to
serve the Widdy honust. Ut's like the talk av childher – seein' things
all round.'

'Plucky lot of fightin' good fights of whatsername they'd do if we
didn't see they had a quiet place to fight in. And such fightin' as theirs
is! Cats on the tiles. T'other callin' to which to come on. I'd give a
month's pay to get some o' them broad-backed beggars in London
sweatin' through a day's road-makin' an' a night's rain. They'd carry
on a deal afterwards – same as we're supposed to carry on. I've bin
turned out of a measly 'arf-licence pub down Lambeth way, full o'
greasy kebmen, 'fore now,' said Ortheris with an oath.

'Maybe you were dhrunk,' said Mulvaney soothingly.

'Worse nor that. The Forders[18] were drunk. *I* was wearin' the Queen's uniform.'

'I'd no particular thought to be a soldier i' them days,' said Learoyd, still keeping his eye on the bare hill opposite, 'but this sort o' talk put it i' my head. They was so good, th' chapel folk, that they tumbled ovver t'other side. But I stuck to it for 'Liza's sake, 'specially as she was learning me to sing the bass part in a horotorio as Jesse were gettin' up. She sung like a throstle hersen, and we had practisin's night after night for a matter of three months.'

'I know what a horotorio is,' said Ortheris pertly. 'It's a sort of chaplain's sing-song – words all out of the Bible, and hullabaloojah choruses.'

'Most Greenhow Hill folks played some instrument or t'other, an' they all sung so you might have heard them miles away, and they were so pleased wi' the noise they made they didn't fare to want anybody to listen. The preacher sung high seconds when he wasn't playin' the flute, an' they set me, as hadn't got far wi't' big fiddle, again' Willie Satterthwaite, to jog his elbow when he had to get agate playin'. Old Jesse was happy if ever a man was, for he were th' conductor an' th' fost fiddle an' th' leadin' singer, beatin' time wi' his fiddle-stick, till at times he'd rap wi' it on the table, and cry out, "Now, you mun all stop; it's my turn." And he'd face round to his front, fair sweatin' wi' pride, to sing th' tenor solos. But he were grandest i' th' choruses, waggin' his head, flinging his arms round like a windmill, and singin' hissen black in the face. A rare singer were Jesse.

'Yo' see, I was not o' much account wi' 'em all exceptin' to 'Liza Roantree, and I had a deal o' time settin' quiet at meetin's and horotorio practices to hearken their talk, and if it were strange to me at beginnin', it got stranger still at after, when I was shut on it, and could study what it meaned.

'Just after th' horotorios came off, 'Liza, as had allus been weakly like, was took very bad. I walked Dr Warbottom's horse up and down a deal of times while he were inside, where they wouldn't let me go, though I fair ached to see her.

'"She'll be better i' noo, lad – better i' noo," he used to say. "Tha mun ha' patience." Then they said if I was quiet I might go in, and th' Reverend Amos Barraclough used to read to her lyin' propped up among th' pillows. Then she began to mend a bit, and they let me carry her on to th' settle, and when it got warm again she went about same as afore. Th' preacher and me and Blast was a deal together i' them days, and i' one way we was rare good comrades. But I could ha' stretched him time and again wi' a good will. I mind one day he said he would like to go down into th' bowels o' th' earth, and see how th' Lord had builded th' framework o' th' everlastin' hills. He were one of them chaps as had a gift o' sayin' things. They rolled off the tip of his cliver tongue, same as Mulvaney here, as would ha' made a rare good preacher if he had nobbut given his mind to it. I lent him a suit o' miner's kit as almost buried th' little man, and his white face down i' th' coat-collar and hat-flap looked like the face of a boggart,[19] and he cowered down i' th' bottom o' the wagon. I was drivin' a tram as led up a bit of an incline, up to th' cave where the engine was pumpin', and where th' ore was brought up and put into th' wagons as went down o' theirsen, me puttin' th' brake on and th' horses a-trottin' after. Long as it was daylight we were good friends, but when we got fair into th' dark, and could nobbut see th' day shinin' at the hole like a lamp at a street-end, I feeled downright wicked. Ma religion dropped all away from me when I looked back at him as were always comin' between me and 'Liza. The talk was 'at they were to be wed when she got better, an' I couldn't get her to say yes or nay to it. He began to sing a hymn in his thin voice, and I came out wi' a chorus that was all cussin' an' swearin' at my horses, an' I began to know how I hated him. He were such a little chap, too. I could drop him wi' one hand down Garstang's Copper-hole – a place where th' beck slithered ovver th' edge on a rock, and fell wi' a bit of a whisper into a pit as no rope i' Greenhow could plumb.'

Again Learoyd rooted up the innocent violets. 'Ay, he should see th' bowels o' th' earth an' never nowt else. I could take him a mile or two along th' drift, and leave him wi' his candle doused to cry hallelujah, wi' none to hear him and say amen. I was to lead him down th' ladder-way to th' drift where Jesse Roantree was workin', and why shouldn't he slip on th' ladder, wi' my feet on his fingers till they loosed grip, and put him down wi' my heel? If I went fost down th' ladder I could click hold on him and chuck him ovver my head, so as he should go squushin' down the shaft breakin' his bones at ev'ry timberin' as Bill Appleton did when he was fresh, and hadn't a bone left when he wrought to th' bottom. Niver a blasted leg to walk from Pately. Niver an arm to put round 'Liza Roantree's waist. Niver no more – niver no more.'

The thick lips curled back over the yellow teeth, and that flushed face was not pretty to look upon. Mulvaney nodded sympathy, and Ortheris, moved by his comrade's passion, brought up the rifle to his shoulder, and searched the hillside for his quarry, muttering ribaldry about a sparrow, a spout, and a thunderstorm. The voice of the watercourse supplied the necessary small-talk till Learoyd picked up his story.

'But it's none so easy to kill a man like yon. When I'd given up my horses to th' lad as took my place and I was showin' th' preacher th' workin's, shoutin' into his ear across th' clang o' th' pumpin' engines, I saw he were afraid o' nowt; and when the lamplight showed his black eyes, I could feel as he was masterin' me again. I were no better nor Blast chained up short and growlin' i' the depths of him while a strange dog went safe past.

'"Th'art a coward and a fool," I said to mysen; an' I wrestled i' my mind again' him till, when we come to Garstang's Copper-hole, I laid hold o' the preacher and lifted him up ovver my head and held him into the darkest on it. "Now, lad," I says, "it's to be one or t'other on us – thee or me – for 'Liza Roantree. Why, isn't thee afraid for thysen?" I says, for he were still i' my arms as a sack. "Nay; I'm but afraid for thee, my poor lad, as knows nowt," says he. I set him down on th' edge, an' th' beck run stiller, an' there was no more buzzin' in my head like when th' bee comed through th' window o' Jesse's house. "What dost tha mean?" says I.

'"I've often thought as thou ought to know," says he, "but 'twas hard to tell thee. 'Liza Roantree's for neither on us, nor for nobody o' this earth. Dr Warbottom says – and he knows her, and her mother before her – that she is in a decline, and she cannot live six months longer. He's known it for many a day. Steady, John! Steady!" says he. And that weak little man pulled me further back and set me again' him, and talked it all ovver quiet and still, me turnin' a bunch o' candles in my hand, and countin' them ovver and ovver again as I listened. A deal on it were th' regular preachin' talk, but there were a vast lot as med me begin to think as he were more of a man than I'd ever given him credit for, till I were cut as deep for him as I were for mysen.

'Six candles we had, and we crawled and climbed all that day while they lasted, and I said to mysen, "'Liza Roantree hasn't six months to live." And when we came into th' daylight again we were like dead men to look at, an' Blast come behind us without so much as waggin' his tail. When I saw 'Liza again she looked at me a minute and says, "Who's telled tha? For I see tha knows." And she tried to smile as she kissed me, and I fair broke down.

'Yo' see, I was a young chap i' them days, and had seen nowt o' life, let alone death, as is allus a-waitin'. She told me as Dr Warbottom said as Greenhow air was too keen, an' they were goin' to Bradford, to Jesse's brother David, as worked i' a mill, and I mun hold up like a man and a Christian, an' she'd pray for me. Well, an' they went away, and the preacher that same back end o' th' year were appointed to another circuit, as they call it, and I were left alone on Greenhow Hill.

'I tried, and I tried hard, to stick to th' chapel, but 'tweren't th' same thing at after. I hadn't 'Liza's voice to follow i' th' singin', nor her eyes a-shinin' acrost their heads. And i' th' class-meetings they said as I mun have some experiences to tell, and I hadn't a word to say for mysen.

'Blast an' me moped a good deal, an' happen we didn't behave ourselves ovver well, for they dropped us an' wondered however they'd come to take us up. I can't tell how we got through th' time, while i' th' winter I gave up my job and went to Bradford. Old Jesse were at th' door o' th' house, in a long street o' little houses. He'd been sendin' th' children 'way as were clatterin' their clogs in th' causeway, for she were asleep.

'"Is it thee?" he says; "but yo're not to see her. I'll none have her wakened for a nowt like thee. She's goin' fast, and she mun go in peace. Tha'lt never be good for nowt i' th' world, and as long as thou lives thou'll never play the big fiddle. Get away, lad, get away!" So he shut the door softly i' my face.

'Nobody never made Jesse my master, but it seemed to me he was about right, and I went away into the town an' knocked up against a recruitin'-sergeant. The old tales o' th' chapel folk came buzzin' into my head. I was to get away, and this were th' regular road for the likes o' me. I 'listed there an' then, took th' Widow's shillin', an' had a bunch o' ribbons pinned i' my hat.

'But next day I found my way to David Roantree's door, and Jesse came to open it. Says he, "Tha's come back again wi' th' Devil's colours flyin' – thy true colours, as I always telled thee."

'But I begged an' prayed of him to let me see her nobbut to say good-bye, till a woman calls down th' stairway, "She says John Learoyd's to come up." Th' old man shifts aside in a flash, and lays his hand on my arm, quite gentle-like. "But tha'lt be quiet, John," says he, "for she's rare and weak. Tha was allus a good lad."

'Her eyes were all alive wi' light, and her hair was thick on the pillow round her, but her cheeks were thin – thin to frighten a man that's strong. "Nay, father, yo' mayn't say th' Devil's colours. Them ribbons is pretty." An' she held out her hands for th' hat, an' she put all straight as a woman will wi' ribbons. "Nay, but what they're pretty," she says. "Eh, but I'd ha' liked to see thee i' thy red coat, John, for thou was allus my own lad – my very own lad, and none else."

'She lifted up her arms, an' they come round my neck i' a gentle grip, an' they slacked away, an' she seemed fainting. "Now yo' mun get away, lad," says Jesse, and I picked up my hat and I came downstairs.

'Th' recruitin'-sergeant were waitin' for me at th' corner public-house. "Yo've seen your sweetheart?" says he. "Yes, I've seen her," says

I. "Well, we'll have a quart now, an' yo'll do your best to forget her," says he, bein' one o' them smart, bustlin' chaps. "Ay, Sergeant," says I. "Forget her." And I've been forgettin' her ever since.'

He threw away the wilted clump of white violets as he spoke. Ortheris suddenly rose to his knees, his rifle at his shoulder, and peered across the valley in the clear afternoon light. His chin cuddled the stock, and there was a twitching of the muscles of the right cheek as he sighted; Private Stanley Ortheris was engaged on his business. A speck of white crawled up the watercourse.

'See that beggar? . . . Got 'im.'

Seven hundred yards away, and a full two hundred down the hillside, the deserter of the Aurangabadis pitched forward, rolled down a red rock, and lay very still, with his face in a clump of blue gentians, while a big raven flapped out of the pine-wood to make investigation.

'That's a clane shot, little man,' said Mulvaney.

Learoyd thoughtfully watched the smoke clear away. 'Happen there was a lass tewed up wi' him, too,' said he.

Ortheris did not reply. He was staring across the valley, with the smile of the artist who looks on the completed work.

WITHOUT BENEFIT OF CLERGY

Before my Spring I garnered Autumn's gain,
Out of her time my field was white with grain,
  The year gave up her secrets to my woe.
Forced and deflowered each sick season lay,
In mystery of increase and decay;
I saw the sunset ere men saw the day,
  Who am too wise in that I should not know.

                                        Bitter Waters[1]

I

'But if it be a girl?'

'Lord of my life, it cannot be. I have prayed for so many nights, and sent gifts to Sheikh Badl's shrine so often, that I know God will give us a son – a man-child that shall grow into a man. Think of this and be glad. My mother shall be his mother till I can take him again, and the mullah of the Pattan mosque shall cast his nativity – God send he be born in an auspicious hour! – and then, and then thou wilt never weary of me, thy slave.'

'Since when hast thou been a slave, my queen?'

'Since the beginning – till this mercy came to me. How could I be sure of thy love when I knew that I had been bought with silver?'

'Nay, that was the dowry. I paid it to thy mother.'

'And she has buried it, and sits upon it all day long like a hen. What talk is yours of dower! I was bought as though I had been a Lucknow dancing-girl instead of a child.'

'Art thou sorry for the sale?'

'I have sorrowed; but to-day I am glad. Thou wilt never cease to love me now? – answer, my king.'

'Never – never. No.'

'Not even though the *mem-log* – the white women of thine own blood – love thee? And remember, I have watched them driving in the evening; they are very fair.'

'I have seen fire-balloons by the hundred. I have seen the moon, and – then I saw no more fire-balloons.'

Ameera clapped her hands and laughed. 'Very good talk,' she said. Then with an assumption of great stateliness, 'It is enough. Thou hast my permission to depart, – if thou wilt.'

The man did not move. He was sitting on a low red-lacquered couch in a room furnished only with a blue-and-white floor-cloth, some rugs, and a very complete collection of native cushions. At his feet sat a woman of sixteen, and she was all but all the world in his eyes. By every rule and law she should have been otherwise, for he was an Englishman, and she a Mussulman's daughter bought two years before from her mother, who, being left without money, would have sold Ameera shrieking to the Prince of Darkness if the price had been sufficient.

It was a contract entered into with a light heart; but even before the girl had reached her bloom she came to fill the greater portion of John Holden's life. For her, and the withered hag her mother, he had taken a little house overlooking the great red-walled city, and found, – when the marigolds had sprung up by the well in the courtyard, and Ameera had established herself according to her own ideas of comfort, and her mother had ceased grumbling at the inadequacy of the cooking-places, the distance from the daily market, and at matters of house-keeping in general, – that the house was to him his home. Anyone could enter his bachelor's bungalow by day or night, and the life that he led there was an unlovely one. In the house in the city his feet only could pass beyond the outer courtyard to the women's rooms; and when the big wooden gate was bolted behind him he was king in his own territory, with Ameera for queen. And there was going to be added to this kingdom a third person whose arrival Holden felt inclined to resent. It interfered with his perfect happiness. It disarranged the orderly peace of the house that was his own. But Ameera was wild with delight at the thought of it, and her mother not less so. The love of a man, and particularly a white man, was at the best an inconstant affair, but it might, both women argued, be held fast by a baby's hands. 'And then,' Ameera would always say, 'then he will never care for the white *mem-log*. I hate them all – I hate them all.'

'He will go back to his own people in time,' said the mother; 'but by the blessing of God that time is yet afar off.'

Holden sat silent on the couch thinking of the future, and his thoughts were not pleasant. The drawbacks of a double life are manifold. The Government, with singular care, had ordered him out of the station for a fortnight on special duty in the place of a man who was watching by the bedside of a sick wife. The verbal notification of the transfer had been edged by a cheerful remark that Holden ought to think himself lucky in being a bachelor and a free man. He came to break the news to Ameera.

'It is not good,' she said slowly, 'but it is not all bad. There is my mother here, and no harm will come to me – unless indeed I die of pure joy. Go thou to thy work and think no troublesome thoughts. When the days are done I believe . . . nay, I am sure. And – and then I shall lay *him* in thy arms, and thou wilt love me for ever. The train goes to-night, at midnight, is it not? Go now, and do not let thy heart be heavy by cause of me. But thou wilt not delay in returning? Thou wilt not stay on the road to talk to the bold white *mem-log*? Come back to me swiftly, my life.'

As he left the courtyard to reach his horse that was tethered to the gate-post, Holden spoke to the white-haired old watchman who guarded the house, and bade him under certain contingencies despatch the filled-up telegraph-form that Holden gave him. It was all that could be done, and with the sensations of a man who has attended his own funeral Holden went away by the night mail to his exile. Every hour of the day he dreaded the arrival of the telegram, and every hour of the night he pictured to himself the death of Ameera. In consequence his work for the State was not of first-rate quality, nor was his temper towards his colleagues of the most amiable. The fortnight ended without a sign from his home, and, torn to pieces by his anxieties, Holden returned to be swallowed up for two precious hours by a dinner at the Club, wherein he heard, as a man hears in a swoon, voices telling him how execrably he had performed the other man's duties, and how he had endeared himself to all his associates. Then he fled on horseback through the night with his heart in his mouth. There was no answer at first to his blows on the gate, and he had just wheeled his horse round to kick it in when Pir Khan appeared with a lantern and held his stirrup.

'Has aught occurred?' said Holden.

'The news does not come from my mouth, Protector of the Poor, but – ' He held out his shaking hand as befitted the bearer of good news who is entitled to a reward.

Holden hurried through the courtyard. A light burned in the upper room. His horse neighed in the gateway, and he heard a shrill little wail that sent all the blood into the apple of his throat. It was a new voice, but it did not prove that Ameera was alive.

'Who is there?' he called up the narrow brick stair-case.

There was a cry of delight from Ameera, and then the voice of the mother, tremulous with old age and pride: 'We be two women and – the – man – thy – son.'

On the threshold of the room Holden stepped on a naked dagger, that was laid there to avert ill-luck, and it broke at the hilt under his impatient heel.

'God is great!' cooed Ameera in the half-light. 'Thou hast taken his misfortunes on thy head.'

'Ay, but how is it with thee, life of my life? Old woman, how is it with her?'

'She has forgotten her sufferings for joy that the child is born. There is no harm; but speak softly,' said the mother.

'It only needed thy presence to make me all well' said Ameera. 'My king, thou hast been very long away. What gifts hast thou for me? Ah, ah! It is that bring gifts this time. Look, my life, look. Was there ever such a babe? Nay, I am too weak even to clear my arm from him.'

'Rest then, and do not talk. I am here, *bachari* [little woman].'

'Well said, for there is a bond and a heel-rope [*peecharee*] between us now that nothing can break. Look – canst thou see in this light? He is without spot or blemish. Never was such a man-child. *Ya illah!* he shall be a pundit – no, a trooper of the Queen. And, my life, dost thou love me as well as ever, though am faint and sick and worn? Answer truly.'

'Yea. I love as I have loved, with all my soul. Lie still, pearl, and rest.'

'Then do not go. Sit by my side here – so. Mother the lord of this house needs a cushion. Bring it.' There was an almost imperceptible movement on the part of the new life that lay in the hollow of Ameera's arm. 'Aho!' she said, her voice breaking with love. 'The babe is a champion from his birth. He is kicking me in the side with mighty kicks. Was there ever such a babe! And he is ours to us – thine and mine. Put thy hand on his head, but carefully, for he is very young, and men are unskilled in such matters.'

Very cautiously Holden touched with the tips of his fingers the downy head.

'He is of the Faith,' said Ameera; 'for lying here in the night-watches I whispered the call to prayer and the profession of faith into his ears. And it is most marvellous that he was born upon a Friday,[2] as I was born. Be careful of him, my life; but he can almost grip with his hands.'

Holden found one helpless little hand that closed feebly on his finger. And the clutch ran through his body till it settled about his heart. Till then his sole thought had been for Ameera. He began to realise that there was someone else in the world, but he could not feel that it was a veritable son with a soul. He sat down to think, and Ameera dozed lightly.

'Get hence, Sahib,' said her mother under her breath. 'It is not good that she should find you here on waking. She must be still.'

'I go,' said Holden submissively. 'Here be rupees. See that my *baba* gets fat and finds all that he needs.'

The chink of the silver roused Ameera. 'I am his mother, and no hireling,' she said weakly. 'Shall I look to him more or less for the sake of money? Mother, give it back. I have borne my lord a son.'

The deep sleep of weakness came upon her almost before the sentence was completed. Holden went down to the courtyard very softly with his heart at ease. Pir Khan, the old watchman, was chuckling with delight. 'This house is now complete,' he said, and without further comment thrust into Holden's hands the hilt of a sabre worn many years ago when he, Pir Khan, served the Queen in the Police. The bleat of a tethered goat came from the well-kerb.

'There be two,' said Pir Khan, 'two goats of the best. I bought them, and they cost much money; and since there is no birth-party assembled their flesh will be all mine. Strike craftily, Sahib! 'Tis an ill-balanced sabre at the best. Wait till they raise their heads from cropping the marigolds.'

'And why?' said Holden, bewildered.

'For the birth-sacrifice. What else? Otherwise the child being unguarded from fate may die. The Protector of the Poor knows the fitting words to be said.'

Holden had learned them once with little thought that he would ever speak them in earnest. The touch of the cold sabre-hilt in his palm turned suddenly to the clinging grip of the child upstairs – the child that was his own son – and a dread of loss filled him.

'Strike!' said Pir Khan. 'Never life came into the world but life was paid for it. See, the goats have raised their heads. Now! With a drawing cut!'

Hardly knowing what he did, Holden cut twice as he muttered the Mohammedan prayer that runs: 'Almighty! In place of this my son I offer life for life, blood for blood, head for head, bone for bone, hair for hair, skin for skin.' The waiting horse snorted and bounded in his pickets at the smell of the raw blood that spirted over Holden's riding-boots.

'Well smitten!' said Pir Khan, wiping the sabre. 'A swordsman was lost in thee. Go with a light heart, Heaven-born. I am thy servant, and the servant of thy son. May the Presence live a thousand years and . . . the flesh of the goats is all mine?' Pir Khan drew back richer by a month's pay. Holden swung himself into the saddle and rode off through the low-hanging wood-smoke of the evening. He was full of riotous exultation, alternating with a vast vague tenderness directed towards no particular object, that made him choke as he bent over the neck of his uneasy horse. 'I never felt like this in my life,' he thought. 'I'll go to the Club and pull myself together.'

A game of pool was beginning, and the room was full of men. Holden entered, eager to get to the light and the company of his fellows, singing at the top of his voice:

> 'In Baltimore a-woalking, a lady I did meet!'

'Did you?' said the Club Secretary from his corner. 'Did she happen to tell you that your boots were wringing wet? Great goodness, man, it's blood!'

'Bosh!' said Holden, picking his cue from the rack. 'May I cut in? It's dew. I've been riding through high crops. My faith! my boots are in a mess though!

> 'And if it be a girl she shall wear a wedding-ring,
> And if it be a boy he shall fight for his King,
> With his dirk, and his cap, and his little jacket blue,
> He shall walk the quarter-deck – '

'Yellow on blue – green next player,' said the marker monotonously.

'*He shall walk the quarter-deck*, – Am I green, marker? *He shall walk the quarter-deck*, – eh! that's a bad shot, – *as his daddy used to do!*'

'I don't see that you have anything to crow about,' said a zealous junior Civilian acidly. 'The Government is not exactly pleased with your work when you relieved Sanders.'

'Does that mean a wigging from headquarters?' said Holden with an abstracted smile. 'I think I can stand it.'

The talk beat up round the ever-fresh subject of each man's work, and steadied Holden till it was time to go to his dark empty bungalow, where his butler received him as one who knew all his affairs. Holden remained awake for the greater part of the night, and his dreams were pleasant ones.

II

'How old is he now?'

'*Ya illah!* What a man's question! He is all but six weeks old; and on this night I go up to the house-top with thee; my life, to count the stars. For that is auspicious. And he was born on a Friday under the sign of the Sun, and it has been told to me that he will outlive us both and get wealth. Can we wish for aught better, beloved?'

'There is nothing better. Let us go up to the roof, and thou shalt count the stars – but a few only, for the sky is heavy with cloud.'

'The winter rains are late, and maybe they come out of season. Come, before all the stars are hid. I have put on my richest jewels.'

'Thou hast forgotten the best of all.'

'*Ai!* Ours. He comes also. He has never yet seen the skies.'

Ameera climbed the narrow staircase that led to the flat roof. The child, placid and unwinking, lay in the hollow of her right arm, gorgeous in silver-fringed muslin with a small skull-cap on his head. Ameera wore all that she valued most. The diamond nose-stud that takes the place of the Western patch in drawing attention to the curve of the nostril, the gold ornament in the centre of the forehead studded with tallow-drop emeralds and flawed rubies, the heavy circlet of beaten gold that was fastened round her neck by the softness of the pure metal, and the chinking curb-patterned silver anklets hanging low over the rosy ankle-bone. She was dressed in jade-green muslin as befitted a daughter of the Faith, and from shoulder to elbow and elbow to wrist ran bracelets of silver tied with floss silk, frail glass bangles slipped over the wrist in proof of the slenderness of the hand, and certain heavy gold bracelets that had no part in her country's ornaments, but, since they were Holden's gift and fastened with a cunning European snap, delighted her immensely.

They sat down by the low white parapet of the roof, overlooking the city and its lights.

'They are happy down there,' said Ameera. 'But I do not think that they are as happy as we. Nor do I think the white *mem-log* are as happy. And thou?'

'I know they are not.'

'How dost thou know?'

'They give their children over to the nurses.'

'I have never seen that,' said Ameera with a sigh, 'nor do I wish to see. *Ahi!*' – she dropped her head on Holden's shoulder – 'I have counted forty stars, and I am tired. Look at the child, love of my life, he is counting too.'

The baby was staring with round eyes at the dark of the heavens. Ameera placed him in Holden's arms, and he lay there without a cry.

'What shall we call him among ourselves?' she said. 'Look! Art thou ever tired of looking? He carries thy very eyes. But the mouth –'

'Is thine, most dear. Who should know better than I?'

''Tis such a feeble mouth. Oh, so small! And yet it holds my heart between its lips. Give him to me now. He has been too long away.'

'Nay, let him lie; he has not yet begun to cry.'

'When he cries thou wilt give him back – eh? What a man of mankind thou art! If he cried he were only the dearer to me. But, my life, what little name shall we give him?'

The small body lay close to Holden's heart. It was utterly helpless and very soft. He scarcely dared to breathe for fear of crushing it. The caged green parrot that is regarded as a sort of guardian-spirit in most native households moved on its perch and fluttered a drowsy wing.

'There is the answer,' said Holden. 'Mian Mittu has spoken. He shall be The Parrot. When he is ready he will talk mightily and run about. Mian Mittu is The Parrot in thy – in the Mussulman tongue, is it not?'

'Why put me so far off?' said Ameera fretfully. 'Let it be like unto some English name – but not wholly. For he is mine.'

'Then call him Tota, for that is likest English.'

'Ay, Tota, and that is still The Parrot. Forgive me, my lord, for a minute ago, but in truth he is too little to wear all the weight of Mian Mittu for name. He shall be Tota – our Tota to us. Hearest thou, O small one? Littlest, thou art Tota.' She touched the child's cheek, and he waking wailed, and it was necessary to return him to his mother, who soothed him with the wonderful rhyme of *Aré koko, Jaré koko!*[3] which says:

> 'Oh, crow! Go, crow! Baby's sleeping sound,
> And the wild plums grow in the jungle, only a penny a pound.
> Only a penny a pound, *baba*, only a penny a pound.'

Reassured many times as to the price of those plums, Tota cuddled himself down to sleep. The two sleek, white well-bullocks in the court-yard were steadily chewing the cud of their evening meal; old Pir Khan squatted at the head of Holden's horse, his Police sabre across his knees, pulling drowsily at a big water-pipe that croaked like a bull-frog in a pond. Ameera's mother sat spinning in the lower veranda, and the wooden gate was shut and barred. The music of a marriage-procession came to the roof above the gentle hum of the city, and a string of flying-foxes crossed the face of the low moon.

'I have prayed,' said Ameera after a long pause, 'I have prayed for two things. First, that I may die in thy stead if thy death is demanded, and in the second, that I may die in the place of the child. I have prayed to the Prophet and to Bibi Miriam [the Virgin Mary]. Thinkest thou either will hear?'

'From thy lips who would not hear the lightest word?'

'I asked for straight talk, and thou hast given me sweet talk. Will my prayers be heard?'

'How can I say? God is very good.'

'Of that I am not sure. Listen now. When I die, or the child dies, what is thy fate? Living, thou wilt return to the bold white *mem-log*, for kind calls to kind.'

'Not always.'

'With a woman, no; with a man it is otherwise. Thou wilt in this life, later on, go back to thine own folk. That I could almost endure, for I should be dead. But in thy very death thou wilt be taken away to a strange place and a Paradise that I do not know.'

'Will it be Paradise?'

'Surely, for who would harm thee? But we two – I and the child – shall be elsewhere, and we cannot come to thee, nor canst thou come to us. In the old days, before the child was born, I did not think of these things; but now I think of them always. It is very hard talk.'

'It will fall as it will fall. To-morrow we do not know, but to-day and love we know well. Surely we are happy now.'

'So happy that it were well to make our happiness assured. And thy Bibi Miriam should listen to me; for she is also a woman. But then she would envy me! It is not seemly for men to worship a woman.'

Holden laughed aloud at Ameera's little spasm of jealousy.

'Is it not seemly? Why didst thou not turn me from worship of thee, then?'

'Thou a worshipper! And of me? My king, for all thy sweet words, well I know that I am thy servant and thy slave, and the dust under thy feet. And I would not have it otherwise. See!'

Before Holden could prevent her she stooped forward and touched his feet; recovering herself with a little laugh she hugged Tota closer to her bosom. Then, almost savagely: –

'Is it true that the bold white *mem-log* live for three times the length of my life? Is it true that they make their marriages not before they are old women?'

'They marry as do others – when they are women.'

'That I know, but they wed when they are twenty-five. Is that true?'

'That is true.'

'*Ya illah!*[4] At twenty-five! Who would of his own will take a wife even of eighteen? She is a woman – ageing every hour. Twenty-five! I shall be an old woman at that age, and – Those *mem-log* remain young forever. How I hate them!'

'What have they to do with us?'

'I cannot tell. I know only that there may now be alive on this earth a woman ten years older than I who may come to thee and take thy love ten years after I am an old woman, grey-headed, and the nurse of Tota's son. That is unjust and evil. They should die too.'

'Now, for all thy years thou art a child, and shalt be picked up and carried down the staircase.'

'Tota! Have a care for Tota, my lord! Thou at least art as foolish as any babe!' Ameera tucked Tota out of harm's way in the hollow of her neck, and was carried downstairs laughing in Holden's arms, while Tota opened his eyes and smiled after the manner of the lesser angels.

He was a silent infant, and, almost before Holden could realise that he was in the world, developed into a small gold-coloured little god and unquestioned despot of the house overlooking the city. Those were months of absolute happiness to Holden and Ameera – happiness withdrawn from the world, shut in behind the wooden gate that Pir Khan guarded. By day Holden did his work with an immense pity for such as were not so fortunate as himself and a sympathy for small children that amazed and amused many mothers at the little station-gatherings. At nightfall he returned to Ameera, – Ameera, full of the wondrous doings of Tota; how he had been seen to clap his hands together and move his fingers with intention and purpose – which was manifestly a miracle – how, later, he had of his own initiative crawled out of his low bedstead on to the floor and swayed on both feet for the space of three breaths.

'And they were long breaths, for my heart stood still with delight,' said Ameera.

Then Tota took the beasts into his councils – the well-bullocks, the little grey squirrels, the mongoose that lived in a hole near the well, and especially Mian Mittu, the parrot, whose tail he grievously pulled, and Mian Mittu screamed till Ameera and Holden arrived.

'Oh, villain! Child of strength! This to thy brother on the house-top! *Tobah, tobah!*[5] Fie! Fie! But I know a charm to make him wise as Suleiman and Aflatoun [Solomon and Plato]. Now look,' said Ameera. She drew from an embroidered bag a handful of almonds. 'See! we count seven. In the name of God!'

She placed Mian Mittu, very angry and rumpled, on the top of his cage, and seating herself between the babe and the bird she cracked and peeled an almond less white than her teeth. 'This is a true charm, my life, and do not laugh. See! I give the parrot one-half and Tota the other.' Mian Mittu with careful beak took his share from between Ameera's lips, and she kissed the other half into the mouth of the child, who ate it slowly with wondering eyes. 'This I will do each day of seven, and without doubt he who is ours will be a bold speaker and wise. Eh, Tota, what wilt thou be when thou art a man and I am grey-headed?' Tota tucked his fat legs into adorable creases. He could crawl, but he was not going to waste the spring of his youth in idle speech. He wanted Mian Mittu's tail to tweak.

When he was advanced to the dignity of a silver belt – which, with a magic square engraved on silver and hung round his neck, made up the greater part of his clothing – he staggered on a perilous journey down the garden to Pir Khan, and proffered him all his jewels in exchange for one little ride on Holden's horse, having seen his mother's mother chaffering with pedlars in the veranda. Pir Khan wept and set the untried feet on his own grey head in sign of fealty, and brought the bold adventurer to his mother's arms, vowing that Tota would be a leader of men ere his beard was grown.

One hot evening, while he sat on the roof between his father and mother watching the never-ending warfare of the kites that the city boys flew, he demanded a kite of his own with Pir Khan to fly it, because he had a fear of dealing with anything larger than himself, and when Holden called him a 'spark', he rose to his feet and answered slowly in defence of his new found individuality, '*Hum 'park nahin hai. Hum adm hai* [I am no spark, but a man.]'

The protest made Holden choke and devote himself very seriously to a consideration of Tota's future. He need hardly have taken the trouble. The delight of that life was too perfect to endure. Therefore it was taken away as many things are taken away in India – suddenly and without warning. The little lord of the house, as Pir Khan called him, grew sorrowful and complained of pains who had never known the meaning of pain. Ameera, wild with terror, watched him through the night, and in the dawning of the second day the life was shaken out of him by fever – the seasonal autumn fever. It seemed altogether impossible that he could die, and neither Ameera nor Holden at first believed the evidence of the little body on the bedstead. Then Ameera beat her head against the wall and would have flung herself down the well in the garden had Holden not restrained her by main force.

One mercy only was granted to Holden. He rode to his office in broad daylight and found waiting him an unusually heavy mail that demanded concentrated attention and hard work. He was not, however, alive to this kindness of the Gods.

III

The first shock of a bullet is no more than a brisk pinch. The wrecked body does not send in its protest to the soul till ten or fifteen seconds

later. Holden realised his pain slowly, exactly as he had realised his
happiness, and with the same imperious necessity for hiding all trace
of it. In the beginning he only felt that there had been a loss, and that
Ameera needed comforting, where she sat with her head on her knees
shivering as Mian Mittu from the house-top called, *Tota! Tota! Tota!*
Later all his world and the daily life of it rose up to hurt him. It was
an outrage that any one of the children at the band-stand in the evening
should be alive and clamorous, when his own child lay dead. It was
more than mere pain when one of them touched him, and stories told
by over-fond fathers of their children's latest performances cut him to
the quick. He could not declare his pain. He had neither help, comfort,
nor sympathy; and Ameera at the end of each weary day would lead
him through the hell of self-questioning reproach which is reserved for
those who have lost a child, and believe that with a little – just a little
more care – it might have been saved.

'Perhaps,' Ameera would say, 'I did not take sufficient heed. Did I, or
did I not? The sun on the roof that day when he played so long alone
and I was – *ahi!* braiding my hair – it may be that the sun then bred the
fever. If I had warned him from the sun he might have lived. But, oh, my
life, say that I am guiltless! Thou knowest that I loved him as I love thee.
Say that there is no blame on me, or I shall die – I shall die!'

'There is no blame, – before God, none. It was written, and how could
we do aught to save? What has been, has been. Let it go, beloved.'

'He was all my heart to me. How can I let the thought go when my
arm tells me every night that he is not here? *Ahi! Ahi!* Oh, Tota, come
back to me – come back again, and let us be all together as it was
before!'

'Peace, peace! For thine own sake, and for mine also, if thou lovest
me – rest.'

'By this I know thou dost not care; and how shouldst thou? The
white men have hearts of stone and souls of iron. Oh, that I had married
a man of mine own people – though he beat me – and had never eaten
the bread of an alien!'

'Am I an alien – mother of my son?'

'What else – Sahib? . . . Oh, forgive me – forgive! The death has driven
me mad. Thou art the life of my heart, and the light of my eyes, and the
breath of my life, and – and I have put thee from me, though it was but
for a moment. If thou goest away, to whom shall I look for help? Do not
be angry. Indeed, it was the pain that spoke and not thy slave.'

'I know, I know. We be two who were three. The greater need
therefore that we should be one.'

They were sitting on the roof as of custom. The night was a warm one in early spring, and sheet-lightning was dancing on the horizon to a broken tune played by far-off thunder. Ameera settled herself in Holden's arms.

'The dry earth is lowing like a cow for the rain, and I – I am afraid. It was not like this when we counted the stars. But thou lovest me as much as before, though a bond is taken away? Answer!'

'I love more because a new bond has come out of the sorrow that we have eaten together, and that thou knowest.'

'Yea, I knew,' said Ameera in a very small whisper. 'But it is good to hear thee say so, my life, who art so strong to help. I will be a child no more, but a woman and an aid to thee. Listen! Give me my *sitar*[6] and I will sing bravely.'

She took the light silver-studded *sitar* and began a song of the great hero Rajah Rasalu.[7] The hand failed on the strings, the tune halted, checked, and at a low note turned off to the poor little nursery-rhyme about the wicked crow:

> 'And the wild plums grow in the jungle, only a penny a pound.
> Only a penny a pound, *baba* – only . . .'

Then came the tears, and the piteous rebellion against fate till she slept, moaning a little in her sleep, with the right arm thrown clear of the body as though it protected something that was not there. It was after this night that life became a little easier for Holden. The ever-present pain of loss drove him into his work, and the work repaid him by filling up his mind for nine or ten hours a day. Ameera sat alone in the house and brooded, but grew happier when she understood that Holden was more at ease, according to the custom of women. They touched happiness again, but this time with caution.

'It was because we loved Tota that he died. The jealousy of God was upon us,' said Ameera. 'I have hung up a large black jar before our window to turn the evil eye from us, and we must make no protestations of delight, but go softly underneath the stars, lest God find us out. Is that not good talk, worthless one?'

She had shifted the accent on the word that means 'beloved', in proof of the sincerity of her purpose. But the kiss that followed the new christening was a thing that any deity might have envied. They went about henceforward saying, 'It is naught, it is naught'; and hoping that all the Powers heard.

The Powers were busy on other things. They had allowed thirty million people four years of plenty, wherein men fed well and the crops were certain, and the birth-rate rose year by year; the Districts reported a purely agricultural population varying from nine hundred to two thousand to the square mile of the overburdened earth; and the Member for Lower Tooting, wandering about India in top-hat and frock-coat, talked largely of the benefits of British rule, and suggested as the one thing needful the establishment of a duly qualified electoral system and a general bestowal of the franchise. His long-suffering hosts smiled and made him welcome, and when he paused to admire, with pretty picked words, the blossom of the blood-red *dhak*-tree[8] that had flowered untimely for a sign of what was coming, they smiled more than ever.

It was the Deputy-Commissioner of Kot-Kumharsen, staying at the Club for a day, who lightly told a tale that made Holden's blood run cold as he overheard the end.

'He won't bother any one any more. Never saw a man so astonished in my life. By Jove, I thought he meant to ask a question in the House about it. Fellow-passenger in his ship – dined next him – bowled over by cholera and died in eighteen hours. You needn't laugh, you fellows. The Member for Lower Tooting is awfully angry about it; but he's more scared. I think he's going to take his enlightened self out of India.'

'I'd give a good deal if he were knocked over. It might keep a few vestrymen[9] of his kidney to their own parish. But what's this about cholera? It's full early for anything of that kind,' said the warden of an unprofitable salt-lick.

'Don't know,' said the Deputy-Commissioner reflectively. 'We've got locusts with us. There's sporadic cholera all along the north – at least we're calling it sporadic for decency's sake. The spring crops are short in five Districts, and nobody seems to know where the Rains are. It's nearly March now. I don't want to scare anybody, but it seems to me that Nature's going to audit her accounts with a big red pencil this summer.'

'Just when I wanted to take leave, too!' said a voice across the room.

'There won't be much leave this year, but there ought to be a great deal of promotion. I've come in to persuade the Government to put my pet canal on the list of famine-relief works. It's an ill wind that blows no good. I shall get that canal finished at last.'

'Is it the old programme then,' said Holden; 'famine, fever, and cholera?'

'Oh no. Only local scarcity and an unusual prevalence of seasonal sickness. You'll find it all in the reports if you live till next year. You're a lucky chap. *You* haven't got a wife to send out of harm's way. The hill-stations ought to be full of women this year.'

'I think you're inclined to exaggerate the talk in the bazars,' said a young Civilian in the Secretariat. 'Now I have observed – '

'I daresay you have,' said the Deputy-Commissioner, 'but you've a great deal more to observe, my son. In the meantime, I wish to observe to you – ' and he drew him aside to discuss the construction of the canal that was so dear to his heart. Holden went to his bungalow and began to understand that he was not alone in the world, and also that he was afraid for the sake of another, – which is the most soul-satisfying fear known to man.

Two months later, as the Deputy had foretold, Nature began to audit her accounts with a red pencil. On the heels of the spring reapings came a cry for bread, and the Government, which had decreed that no man should die of want, sent wheat. Then came the cholera from all four quarters of the compass. It struck a pilgrim-gathering of half a million at a sacred shrine. Many died at the feet of their god; the others broke and ran over the face of the land carrying the pestilence with them. It smote a walled city and killed two hundred a day. The people crowded the trains, hanging on to the footboards and squatting on the roofs of the carriages, and the cholera followed them, for at each station they dragged out the dead and the dying. They died by the roadside, and the horses of the Englishmen shied at the corpses in the grass. The Rains did not come, and the earth turned to iron lest man should escape death by hiding in her. The English sent their wives away to the Hills and went about their work, coming forward as they were bidden to fill the gaps in the fighting-line. Holden, sick with fear of losing his chiefest treasure on earth, had done his best to persuade Ameera to go away with her mother to the Himalayas.

'Why should I go?' said she, one evening on the roof.

'There is sickness, and people are dying, and all the white *mem-log* have gone.'

'All of them?'

'All – unless perhaps there remain some old scald-head[10] who vexes her husband's heart by running risk of death.'

'Nay; who stays is my sister, and thou must not abuse her, for I will be a scald-head too. I am glad all the bold *mem-log* are gone.'

'Do I speak to a woman or a babe? Go to the Hills, and I will see to it that thou goest like a queen's daughter. Think, child. In a red-lacquered bullock-cart, veiled and curtained, with brass peacocks upon the pole and red cloth hangings. I will send two orderlies for guard and – '

'Peace! Thou art the babe in speaking thus. What use are those toys to me? *He* would have patted the bullocks and played with the housings.

For his sake, perhaps, – thou hast made me very English – I might have gone. Now, I will not. Let the *mem-log* run.'

'Their husbands are sending them, beloved.'

'Very good talk. Since when hast thou been my husband to tell me what to do? I have but borne thee a son. Thou art only all the desire of my soul to me. How shall I depart when I know that if evil befall thee by the breadth of so much as my littlest finger-nail – is that not small? – I should be aware of it though I were in Paradise. And here, this summer, thou mayest die – *ai, janee*,[11] die! and in dying they might call to tend thee a white woman, and she would rob me in the last of thy love!'

'But love is not born in a moment or on a death-bed!'

'What dost thou know of love, stoneheart? She would take thy thanks at least and, by God and the Prophet and Bibi Miriam the mother of thy Prophet, that I will never endure. My lord and my love, let there be no more foolish talk of going away. Where thou art, I am. It is enough.' She put an arm round his neck and a hand on his mouth.

There are not many happinesses so complete as those that are snatched under the shadow of the sword. They sat together and laughed, calling each other openly by every pet name that could move the wrath of the Gods. The city below them was locked up in its own torments. Sulphur fires blazed in the streets; the conches in the Hindu temples screamed and bellowed, for the Gods were inattentive in those days. There was a service in the great Mohammedan shrine, and the call to prayer from the minarets was almost unceasing. They heard the wailing in the houses of the dead, and once the shriek of a mother who had lost a child and was calling for its return. In the grey dawn they saw the dead borne out through the city gates, each litter with its own little knot of mourners. Wherefore they kissed each other and shivered.

It was a red and heavy audit, for the land was very sick and needed a little breathing-space ere the torrent of cheap life should flood it anew. The children of immature fathers and undeveloped mothers made no resistance. They were cowed and sat still, waiting till the sword should be sheathed in November if it were so willed. There were gaps among the English, but the gaps were filled. The work of superintending famine-relief, cholera-sheds, medicine-distribution, and what little sanitation was possible, went forward because it was so ordered.

Holden had been told to keep himself in readiness to move to replace the next man who should fall. There were twelve hours in each day when he could not see Ameera, and she might die in three. He was considering what his pain would be if he could not see her for three months, or if she died out of his sight. He was absolutely certain that her death would be demanded – so certain, that when he looked up from the telegram and saw Pir Khan breathless in the doorway, he laughed aloud. 'And?' said he, –

'When there is a cry in the night and the spirit flutters into the throat, who has a charm that will restore? Come swiftly, Heaven-born! It is the black cholera.'[12]

Holden galloped to his home. The sky was heavy with clouds, for the long-deferred Rains were near and the heat was stifling. Ameera's mother met him in the courtyard, whimpering, 'She is dying. She is nursing herself into death. She is all but dead. What shall I do, Sahib?'

Ameera was lying in the room in which Tota had been born. She made no sign when Holden entered, because the human soul is a very lonely thing and, when it is getting ready to go away, hides itself in a misty borderland where the living may not follow. The black cholera does its work quietly and without explanation. Ameera was being thrust out of life as though the Angel of Death had himself put his hand upon her. The quick breathing seemed to show that she was either afraid or in pain, but neither eyes nor mouth gave any answer to Holden's kisses. There was nothing to be said or done. Holden could only wait and suffer. The first drops of the rain began to fall on the roof and he could hear shouts of joy in the parched city.

The soul came back a little and the lips moved. Holden bent down to listen. 'Keep nothing of mine,' said Ameera. 'Take no hair from my head. *She* would make thee burn it later on. That flame I should feel. Lower! Stoop lower! Remember only that I was thine and bore thee a son. Though thou wed a white woman to-morrow, the pleasure of receiving in thine arms thy first son is taken from thee for ever. Remember me when thy son is born – the one that shall carry thy name before all men. His misfortunes be on my head. I bear witness – I bear witness' – the lips were forming the words on his ear – 'that there is no God but – thee, beloved!'[13]

Then she died. Holden sat still, and all thought was taken from him, – till he heard Ameera's mother lift the curtain.

'Is she dead, Sahib?'

'She is dead.'

'Then I will mourn, and afterwards take an inventory of the furniture in this house. For that will be mine. The Sahib does not mean to resume it? It is so little, so very little, Sahib, and I am an old woman. I would like to lie softly.'

'For the mercy of God be silent a while. Go out and mourn where I cannot hear.'

'Sahib, she will be buried in four hours.'

'I know the custom. I shall go ere she is taken away. That matter is in thy hands. Look to it that the bed on which – on which she lies – '

'Aha! That beautiful red-lacquered bed. I have long desired – '

'That the bed is left here untouched for my disposal. All else in the house is thine. Hire a cart, take everything, go hence, and before sunrise let there be nothing in this house but that which I have ordered thee to respect.'

'I am an old woman. I would stay at least for the days of mourning, and the Rains have just broken. Whither shall I go?'

'What is that to me? My order is that there is a going. The house-gear is worth a thousand rupees and my orderly shall bring thee a hundred rupees tonight.'

'That is very little. Think of the cart-hire.'

'It shall be nothing unless thou goest, and with speed. O woman, get hence and leave me with my dead!'

The mother shuffled down the staircase, and in her anxiety to take stock of the house-fittings forgot to mourn. Holden stayed by Ameera's side, and the rain roared on the roof. He could not think connectedly by reason of the noise, though he made many attempts to do so. Then four sheeted ghosts glided dripping into the room and stared at him through their veils. They were the washers of the dead. Holden left the room and went out to his horse. He had come in a dead, stifling calm through ankle-deep dust. He found the courtyard a rain-lashed pond alive with frogs; a torrent of yellow water ran under the gate, and a roaring wind drove the bolts of the rain like buckshot against the mud walls. Pir Khan was shivering in his little hut by the gate, and the horse was stamping uneasily in the water.

'I have been told the Sahib's order,' said Pir Khan. 'It is well. This house is now desolate. I go also, for my monkey-face would be a reminder of that which has been. Concerning the bed, I will bring that to thy house yonder in the morning; but remember, Sahib, it will be to thee a knife turning in a green wound. I go upon a pilgrimage, and I will take no money. I have grown fat in the protection of the Presence whose sorrow is my sorrow. For the last time I hold his stirrup.'

He touched Holden's foot with both hands and the horse sprang out into the road, where the creaking bamboos were whipping the sky and all the frogs were chuckling. Holden could not see for the rain in his face. He put his hands before his eyes and muttered:–

'Oh, you brute! You utter brute!'

The news of his trouble was already in his bungalow. He read the knowledge in his butler's eyes when Ahmed Khan brought in food, and for the first and last time in his life laid a hand upon his master's shoulder, saying, 'Eat, Sahib, eat. Meat is good against sorrow. I also have known. Moreover the shadows come and go, Sahib; the shadows come and go. These be curried eggs.'

Holden could neither eat nor sleep. The heavens sent down eight inches of rain in that night and washed the earth clean. The waters tore down walls, broke roads, and scoured open the shallow graves on the Mohammedan burying-ground. All next day it rained, and Holden sat still in his house considering his sorrow. On the morning of the third day he received a telegram which said only, 'Ricketts, Myndonie. Dying. Holden relieve. Immediate.' Then he thought that before he departed he would look at the house wherein he had been master and lord. There was a break in the weather, and the rank earth steamed with vapour.

He found that the rains had torn down the mud pillars of the gateway, and the heavy wooden gate that had guarded his life hung lazily from one hinge. There was grass three inches high in the courtyard; Pir Khan's lodge was empty, and the sodden thatch sagged between the beams. A grey squirrel was in possession of the veranda as if the house had been untenanted for thirty years instead of three days. Ameera's mother had removed everything except some mildewed matting. The *tick-tick* of the little scorpions as they hurried across the floor was the only sound in the house. Ameera's room and the other one where Tota had lived were heavy with mildew; and the narrow staircase leading to the roof was streaked and stained with rain-borne mud. Holden saw all these things, and came out again to meet in the road Durga Dass, his landlord, – portly, affable, clothed in white muslin, and driving a Cee-spring buggy. He was overlooking his property to see how the roofs stood the stress of the first rains.

'I have heard,' said he, 'you will not take this place any more, Sahib?'

'What are you going to do with it?'

'Perhaps I shall let it again.'

'Then I will keep it on while I am away.'

Durga Dass was silent for some time. 'You shall not take it on, Sahib,' he said: 'When I was a young man I also – but to-day I am a member of the Municipality. Ho! Ho! No. When the birds have gone what need to keep the nest? I will have it pulled down – the timber will sell for something always. It shall be pulled down, and the Municipality shall make a road across, as they desire, from the burning-ghat[14] to the city wall, so that no man may say where this house stood.'

THE BRIDGE-BUILDERS

The least that Findlayson, of the Public Works Department, expected was a CIE: he dreamed of a CSI:[1] indeed, his friends told him that he deserved more. For three years he had endured heat and cold, disappointment, discomfort, danger, and disease, with responsibility almost too heavy for one pair of shoulders; and day by day, through that time, the great Kashi[2] Bridge over the Ganges had grown under his charge. Now, in less than three months, if all went well, His Excellency the Viceroy would open the bridge in state, an Archbishop would bless it, the first train-load of soldiers would come over it, and there would be speeches.

Findlayson, CE,[3] sat in his trolley on a construction-line that ran along one of the main revetments – the huge stone-faced banks that flared away north and south for three miles on either side of the river – and permitted himself to think of the end. With its approaches, his work was one mile and three-quarters in length; a lattice-girder bridge, trussed with the Findlayson truss, standing on seven-and-twenty brick piers. Each one of those piers was twenty-four feet in diameter, capped with red Agra stone and sunk eighty feet below the shifting sand of the Ganges' bed. Above them ran the railway-line fifteen feet broad; above that, again, a cart-road of eighteen feet, flanked with footpaths. At either end rose towers of red brick, loopholed for musketry and pierced for big guns, and the ramp of the road was being pushed forward to their haunches. The raw earth-ends were crawling and alive with hundreds upon hundreds of tiny asses climbing out of the yawning borrow-pit below with sackfuls of stuff; and the hot afternoon air was filled with the noise of hooves, the rattle of the drivers' sticks, and the swish and roll-down of the dirt. The river was very low, and on the dazzling white sand between the three centre piers stood squat cribs of railway-sleepers, filled within and daubed without with mud, to support the last of the girders as those were riveted up. In the little deep water left by the drought, an overhead crane travelled to and fro along its spile-pier,[4] jerking sections of iron into place, snorting and backing and grunting as an elephant grunts in the timber-yard. Riveters by the hundred swarmed about the lattice side-work and the iron roof of the railway-line, hung from invisible staging under the bellies of the girders, clustered round the throats of the piers, and rode on the overhang of the footpath-stanchions; their fire-pots and the spurts of flame that answered each hammer-stroke showing no more than pale yellow in the sun's glare. East and west and north and south the construction-trains rattled and shrieked up and down the embankments, the piled trucks of brown and white stone banging behind them till the side-boards were unpinned, and with a roar and a grumble a few thousand tons more material were thrown out to hold the river in place.

Findlayson, CE, turned on his trolley and looked over the face of the country that he had changed for seven miles around. Looked back on the humming village of five thousand workmen; up-stream and down, along the vista of spurs and sand; across the river to the far piers, lessening in the haze; overhead to the guard-towers – and only he knew how strong those were – and with a sigh of contentment saw that his work was good. There stood his bridge before him in the sunlight, lacking only a few weeks' work on the girders of the three middle piers – his bridge, raw and ugly as original sin, but *pukka*[5] – permanent – to endure when all memory of the builder – even of the splendid Findlayson truss – had perished. Practically, the thing was done.

Hitchcock, his assistant, cantered along the line on a little switch-tailed Kabuli pony, who, through long practice, could have trotted securely over a trestle, and nodded to his chief.

'All but,' said he, with a smile.

'I've been thinking about it,' the senior answered. 'Not half a bad job for two men, is it?'

'One – and a half. 'Gad, what a Cooper's Hill[6] cub I was when I came on the works!' Hitchcock felt very old in the crowded experiences of the past three years, that had taught him power and responsibility.

'You *were* rather a colt,' said Findlayson. 'I wonder how you'll like going back to office work when this job's over.'

'I shall hate it!' said the young man, and, as he went on, his eye followed Findlayson's, and he muttered, 'Isn't it damned good?'

'I think we'll go up the Service together,' Findlayson said to himself. 'You're too good a youngster to waste on another man. Cub thou wast; assistant thou art. Personal assistant, and at Simla, thou shalt be, if any credit comes to me out of the business!'

Indeed, the burden of the work had fallen altogether on Findlayson and his assistant, the young man whom he had chosen because of his rawness to break to his own needs. There were labour-contractors by

the half-hundred – fitters and riveters, European, borrowed from the
railway workshops, with perhaps twenty white and half-caste subordinates to direct, under direction, the bevies of workmen – but none
knew better than these two, who trusted each other, how the underlings
were not to be trusted. They had been tried many times in sudden crises
– by slipping of booms, by breaking of tackle, failure of cranes, and
the wrath of the river – but no stress had brought to light any man
among them whom Findlayson and Hitchcock would have honoured
by working as remorselessly as they worked themselves. Findlayson
thought it over from the beginning: the months of office work destroyed
at a blow when the Government of India, at the last moment, added
two feet to the width of the bridge, under the impression that bridges
were cut out of paper, and so brought to ruin at least half an acre of
calculations – and Hitchcock, new to disappointment, buried his head
in his arms and wept; the heart-breaking delays over the filling of the
contracts in England; the futile correspondences hinting at great wealth
of commission if one, only one, rather doubtful consignment were
passed; the war that followed the refusal; the careful, polite obstruction
at the other end that followed the war, till young Hitchcock, putting
one month's leave to another month, and borrowing ten days from
Findlayson, spent his poor little savings of a year in a wild dash to
London, and there, as his own tongue asserted and the later consign-
ments proved, put the fear of God into a man so great that he feared
only Parliament, and said so till Hitchcock wrought with him across
his own dinner-table, and – he feared the Kashi Bridge and all who
spoke in its name. Then there was the cholera that came in the night
to the village by the bridge-works; and after the cholera the smallpox.
The fever they had always with them. Hitchcock had been appointed
a magistrate of the third class with whipping powers, for the better
government of the community, and Findlayson watched him wield his
powers temperately, learning what to overlook and what to look after.
It was a long, long reverie, and it covered storm, sudden freshets,[7] death
in every manner and shape, violent and awful rage against red tape half
frenzying a mind that knows it should be busy on other things; drought,
sanitation, finance; birth, wedding, burial, and riot in the village of
twenty warring castes; argument, expostulation, persuasion, and the
blank despair that a man goes to bed upon, thankful that his rifle is all
in pieces in the gun-case. Behind everything rose the black frame of the
Kashi Bridge – plate by plate, girder by girder, span by span – and each
pier of it recalled Hitchcock, the all-round man, who had stood by his
chief without failing from the very first to this last.

So the bridge was two men's work – unless one counted Peroo, as

Peroo certainly counted himself. He was a Lascar,[8] a Kharva from Bulsar,[9] familiar with every port between Rockhampton[10] and London, who had risen to the rank of serang[11] on the British India boats, but wearying of routine musters and clean clothes had thrown up the Service and gone inland, where men of his calibre were sure of employment. For his knowledge of tackle and the handling of heavy weights, Peroo was worth almost any price he might have chosen to put upon his services; but custom decreed the wage of the overhead-men, and Peroo was not within many silver pieces of his proper value. Neither running water nor extreme heights made him afraid; and, as an ex-serang, he knew how to hold authority. No piece of iron was so big or so badly placed that Peroo could not devise a tackle to lift it – a loose-ended, sagging arrangement, rigged with a scandalous amount of talking, but perfectly equal to the work in hand. It was Peroo who had saved the girder of Number Seven Pier from destruction when the new wire rope jammed in the eye of the crane, and the huge plate tilted in its slings, threatening to slide out sideways. Then the native workmen lost their heads with great shoutings, and Hitchcock's right arm was broken by a falling T-plate, and he buttoned it up in his coat and swooned, and came to and directed for four hours till Peroo, from the top of the crane, reported, 'All's well,' and the plate swung home. There was no one like Peroo, serang, to lash and guy and hold, to control the donkey-engines,[12] to hoist a fallen locomotive craftily out of the borrow-pit into which it had tumbled; to strip and dive, if need be, to see how the concrete blocks round the piers stood the scouring of Mother Gunga,[13] or to adventure up-stream on a monsoon night and report on the state of the embankment-facings. He would interrupt the field-councils of Findlayson and Hitchcock without fear, till his wonderful English, or his still more wonderful *lingua-franca*, half Portuguese and half Malay, ran out and he was forced to take string and show the knots that he would recommend. He controlled his own gang of tacklemen – mysterious relatives from Kutch Mandvi[14] gathered month by month and tried to the uttermost. No consideration of family or kin allowed Peroo to keep weak hands or a giddy head on the pay-roll. 'My honour is the honour of this bridge,' he would say to the about-to-be-dismissed. 'What do I care for *your* honour? Go and work on a steamer. That is all you are fit for.'

The little cluster of huts where he and his gang lived centred round the tattered dwelling of a sea-priest – one who had never set foot on Black Water,[15] but had been chosen as ghostly counsellor by two generations of sea-rovers, all unaffected by port missions or those creeds which are thrust upon sailors by agencies along Thames' bank. The priest of the Lascars had nothing to do with their caste, or indeed with anything at all. He ate the offerings of his church, and slept and smoked, and slept again, 'for,' said Peroo, who had haled him a thousand miles inland, 'he is a very holy man. He never cares what you eat so long as you do not eat beef, and that is good, because on land we worship Shiva, we Kharvas; but at sea on the Kumpani's boats we attend strictly to the orders of the Burra Malum [the first mate], and on this bridge we observe what Finlinson Sahib says.'

Findlayson Sahib had that day given orders to clear the scaffolding from the guard-tower on the right bank, and Peroo with his mates was casting loose and lowering down the bamboo poles and planks as swiftly as ever they had whipped the cargo out of a coaster.

From his trolley he could hear the whistle of the serang's silver pipe and the creak and clatter of the pulleys. Peroo was standing on the topmost coping of the tower, clad in the blue dungaree[16] of his abandoned Service, and as Findlayson motioned to him to be careful, for his was no life to throw away, he gripped the last pole, and, shading his eyes ship-fashion, answered with the long-drawn wail of the foc'sle look-out: '*Ham dekhta hai*' ['I am looking out']. Findlayson laughed, and then sighed. It was years since he had seen a steamer, and he was sick for Home. As his trolley passed under the tower, Peroo descended by a rope, ape-fashion, and cried: 'It looks well now, Sahib. Our bridge is all but done. What think you Mother Gunga will say when the rail runs over?'

'She has said little so far. It was never Mother Gunga that delayed us.'

'There is always time for her; and none the less there has been delay. Has the Sahib forgotten last autumn's flood, when the stone-boats were sunk without warning – or only a half-day's warning?'

'Yes, but nothing save a big flood could hurt us now. The spurs are holding well on the west bank.'

'Mother Gunga eats great allowances. There is always room for more stone on the revetments. I tell this to the Chota Sahib'[17] – he meant Hitchcock – 'and he laughs.'

'No matter, Peroo. Another year thou wilt be able to build a bridge in thine own fashion.'

The Lascar grinned. 'Then it will not be in this way – with stonework sunk under water, as the *Quetta*[18] was sunk. I like sus-sus-pen-sheen bridges that fly from bank to bank, with one big step, like a gangplank. Then no water can hurt. When does the Lord Sahib come to open the bridge?'

'In three months, when the weather is cooler.'

'Ho! ho! He is like the Burra Malum. He sleeps below while the work is being done. Then he comes upon the quarter-deck and touches with his finger, and says: "This is not clean! Dam' jiboonwallah!"[19]

'But the Lord Sahib does not call me a dam' jiboonwallah, Peroo.'

'No, Sahib; but he does not come on deck till the work is all finished. Even the Burra Malum of the *Nerbudda* said once at Tuticorin – '

'Bah! Go! I am busy.'

'I, also!' said Peroo, with an unshaken countenance. 'May I take the light dinghy now and row along the spurs?'

'To hold them up with thy hands? They are, I think, sufficiently heavy.'

'Nay, Sahib. It is thus. At sea, on the Black Water, we have room to be blown up and down without care. Here we have no room at all. Look you, we have put the river into a dock, and run her between stone sills.'

Findlayson smiled at the 'we'.

'We have bitted and bridled her. She is not like the sea, that can beat against a soft beach. She is Mother Gunga – in irons.' His voice fell a little.

'Peroo, thou hast been up and down the world more even than I. Speak true talk, now. How much dost thou in thy heart believe of Mother Gunga?'

'All that our priest says. London is London, Sahib. Sydney is Sydney, and Port Darwin is Port Darwin. Also Mother Gunga is Mother Gunga, and when I come back to her banks I know this and worship. In London I did *pujah*[20] to the big Temple by the river for the sake of the God within . . . Yes, I will not take the cushions in the dinghy.'

Findlayson mounted his horse and trotted to the shed of a bungalow that he shared with his assistant. The place had become home to him in the last three years. He had grilled in the heat, sweated in the Rains, and shivered with fever under the rude thatch roof; the limewash beside the door was covered with rough drawings and formulae, and the sentry-path trodden in the matting of the veranda showed where he had walked alone. There is no eight-hour limit to an engineer's work, and the evening meal with Hitchcock was eaten booted and spurred. Over their cigars they listened to the hum of the village as the gangs came up from the river-bed and the lights began to twinkle.

'Peroo has gone up the spurs in your dinghy. He's taken a couple of nephews with him, and he's lolling in the stern like a commodore,' said Hitchcock.

'That's all right. He's got something on his mind. You'd think that ten years in the British India boats would have knocked most of his religion out of him.'

'So it has,' said Hitchcock, chuckling. 'I overheard him the other day in the middle of a most atheistical talk with that fat old *guru* of theirs. Peroo denied the efficacy of prayer, and wanted the *guru* to go to sea and watch a gale out with him, and see if he could stop a monsoon.'

'All the same, if you carried off his *guru* he'd leave us like a shot. He was yarning away to me about praying to the dome of St Paul's when he was in London.'

'He told me that the first time he went into the engine-room of a steamer, when he was a boy, he prayed to the low-press cylinder.'

'Not half a bad thing to pray to, either. He's propitiating his own Gods now, and he wants to know what Mother Gunga will think of a bridge being run across her. Who's there?' A shadow darkened the doorway, and a telegram was put into Hitchcock's hand.

'She ought to be pretty well used to it by this time. Only a *tar*.[21] It ought to be Ralli's answer about the new rivets . . . Great Heavens!' Hitchcock jumped to his feet.

'What is it?' said the senior, and took the form. '*That's* what Mother Gunga thinks, is it?' he said, reading. 'Keep cool, young 'un. We've got all our work cut out for us. Let's see. Muir wires, half an hour ago: "*Floods on the Ramgunga. Look out.*" Well, that gives us – one, two – nine and a half for the flood to reach Melipur Ghat and seven's sixteen and a half to Latodi – say fifteen hours before it comes down to us.'

'Curse that hill-fed sewer of a Ramgunga! Findlayson, this is two months before anything could have been expected, and the left bank is littered up with stuff still. Two full months before time!'

'That's why it happens. I've only known Indian rivers for five-and-twenty years, and I don't pretend to understand 'em. Here comes another *tar*.' Findlayson opened the telegram. 'Cockran, this time, from the Ganges Canal: "*Heavy rains here. Bad.*" He might have saved the last word. Well, we don't want to know any more. We've got to work the gangs all night and clean up the river-bed. You'll take the east bank and work out to meet me in the middle. Get everything that floats below the bridge. We shall have quite enough river-craft coming down adrift anyhow, without letting the stone-boats ram the piers. What have you got on the east bank that needs looking after?'

'Pontoon, one big pontoon with the overhead crane on it. T'other overhead crane on the mended pontoon, with the cart-road rivets from Twenty to Twenty-three piers – two construction lines, and a turning-spur. The pilework must take its chance,' said Hitchcock.

'All right. Roll up everything you can lay hands on. We'll give the gang fifteen minutes more to eat their grub.'

Close to the veranda stood a big night-gong, never used except for flood, or fire in the village. Hitchcock had called for a fresh horse, and was off to his side of the bridge when Findlayson took the cloth-bound stick and smote with the rubbing stroke that brings out the full thunder of the metal.

Long before the last rumble ceased every night-gong in the village had taken up the warning. To these were added the hoarse screaming of conches in the little temples; the throbbing of drums and tom-toms; and from the European quarters, where the riveters lived, M'Cartney's bugle, a weapon of offence on Sundays and festivals, brayed desperately, calling to 'Stables'. Engine after engine toiling home along the spurs after her day's work whistled in reply till the whistles were answered from the far bank. Then the big gong thundered thrice for a sign that it was flood and not fire; conch, drum, and whistle echoed the call, and the village quivered to the sound of bare feet running upon soft earth. The order in all cases was to stand by the day's work and wait instructions. The gangs poured by in the dusk; men stopping to knot a loin-cloth or fasten a sandal; gang-foremen shouting to their subordinates as they ran or paused by the tool-issue sheds for bars and mattocks; locomotives creeping down their tracks wheel-deep in the crowd, till the brown torrent disappeared into the dusk of the river-bed, raced over the pilework, swarmed along the lattices, clustered by the cranes, and stood still, each man in his place.

Then the troubled beating of the gong carried the order to take up everything and bear it beyond highwater mark, and the flare-lamps broke out by the hundred between the webs of dull iron as the riveters began a night's work racing against the flood that was to come. The girders of the three centre piers – those that stood on the cribs[22] – were all but in position. They needed just as many rivets as could be driven into them, for the flood would assuredly wash out the supports, and the ironwork would settle down on the caps of stone if they were not blocked at the ends. A hundred crowbars strained at the sleepers of the temporary line that fed the unfinished piers. It was heaved up in lengths, loaded into trucks, and backed up the bank beyond flood-level by the groaning locomotives. The tool-sheds on the sands melted away before the attack of shouting armies, and with them went the stacked ranks of Government stores, iron-bound boxes of rivets, pliers, cutters, duplicate parts of the riveting-machines, spare pumps and chains. The big crane would be the last to be shifted, for she was hoisting all the heavy stuff up to the main structure of the bridge. The concrete blocks on the fleet of stone-boats were dropped overside, where there was any depth of water, to guard the piers, and the empty boats themselves were poled under the bridge down-stream. It was here that Peroo's pipe shrilled loudest, for the first stroke of the big gong had brought back the dinghy at racing speed, and Peroo and his people were stripped to the waist, working for the honour and credit which are better than life.

'I knew she would speak,' he cried. '*I* knew, but the telegraph gave us good warning. O sons of unthinkable begetting – children of unspeakable shame – are we here for the look of the thing?' It was two feet of wire rope frayed at the ends, and it did wonders as Peroo leaped from gunnel to gunnel, shouting the language of the sea.

Findlayson was more troubled for the stone-boats than anything else. M'Cartney, with his gangs, was blocking up the ends of the three doubtful spans, but boats adrift, if the flood chanced to be a high one, might endanger the girders; and there was a very fleet in the shrunken channels.

'Get them behind the swell of the guard-tower,' he shouted to Peroo. 'It will be dead-water there; get them below the bridge.'

'Very good. *I* know. We are mooring them with wire rope,' was the answer. 'Heh! Listen to the Chota Sahib. He is working hard.'

From across the river came an almost continuous whistling of locomotives, backed by the rumble of stone. Hitchcock at the last minute was spending a few hundred more trucks of Tarakee stone in reinforcing his spurs and embankments.

'The bridge challenges Mother Gunga,' said Peroo, with a laugh. 'But when *she* talks I know whose voice will be the loudest.'

For hours the naked men worked, screaming and shouting under the lights. It was a hot, moonless night; the end of it was darkened by clouds and a sudden squall that made Findlayson very grave.

'She moves!' said Peroo, just before the dawn. 'Mother Gunga is awake! Hear!' He dipped his hand over the side of a boat and the current mumbled on it. A little wave hit the side of a pier with a crisp slap.

'Six hours before her time,' said Findlayson, mopping his forehead savagely. 'Now we can't depend on anything. We'd better clear all hands out of the river-bed.'

Again the big gong beat, and a second time there was the rushing of naked feet on earth and ringing iron; the clatter of tools ceased. In the silence, men heard the dry yawn of water crawling over thirsty sand.

Foreman after foreman shouted to Findlayson, who had posted himself by the guard-tower, that his section of the river-bed had been cleaned out, and when the last voice dropped, Findlayson hurried over the bridge till the iron plating of the permanent way gave place to the temporary plank-walk over the three centre piers, and there he met Hitchcock.

'All clear your side?' said Findlayson. The whisper rang in the box of latticework.

'Yes, and the east channel's filling now. We're utterly out of our reckoning. When is this thing down on us?'

'There's no saying. She's filling as fast as she can. Look!' Findlayson pointed to the planks below his feet, where the burned sand, defiled by months of work, was beginning to whisper and fizz.

'What orders?' said Hitchcock.

'Call the roll – count stores – sit on your hunkers – and pray for the bridge. That's all I can think of. Good-night. Don't risk your life trying to fish out anything that may go down-stream.'

'Oh, I'll be as prudent as you are! 'Night! Heavens, how she's filling! Here's the rain in earnest!' Findlayson picked his way back to his bank, sweeping the last of M'Cartney's riveters before him. The gangs had spread themselves along the embankments, regardless of the cold rain of the dawn, and there they waited for the flood. Only Peroo kept his men together behind the swell of the guard-tower, where the stone-boats lay tied fore and aft with hawsers, wire rope, and chains.

A shrill wail ran along the line, growing to a yell, half fear and half wonder: the face of the river whitened from bank to bank between the stone facings, and the far-away spurs went out in spouts of foam. Mother Gunga had come bank-high in haste, and a wall of chocolate-coloured water was her messenger. There was a shriek above the roar of the water, the complaint of the spans coming down on their blocks as the cribs were whirled out from under their bellies. The stone-boats groaned and ground each other in the eddy that swung round the abutments and their clumsy masts rose higher and higher against the dim skyline.

'Before she was shut between these walls we knew what she would do. Now she is thus cramped God only knows what she will do!' said Peroo, watching the furious turmoil round the guard-tower. 'Ohé! Fight, then! Fight hard! It is thus that a woman wears herself out.'

But Mother Gunga would not fight as Peroo desired. After the first down-stream plunge there came no more walls of water, but the river lifted herself bodily, as a snake when she drinks in midsummer, plucking and fingering along the revetments, and banking up behind the piers till even Findlayson began to recalculate the strength of his work.

When day came the village gasped. 'Only last night,' men said, turning to each other, 'it was as a town in the river-bed. Look now!'

And they looked and wondered afresh at the deep water, the racing water that licked the throat of the piers. The farther bank was veiled by rain, into which the bridge ran out and vanished; the spurs up-stream were marked by no more than eddies and spoutings, and down-stream the pent river, once freed of her guide-lines, had spread like a sea to the horizon. Then hurried by, rolling in the water, dead men and oxen together, with here and there a patch of thatched roof that melted when it touched a pier.

'Big flood,' said Peroo, and Findlayson nodded. It was as big a flood as he had any wish to watch. His bridge would stand what was upon her now, but not very much more; and if by any of a thousand chances there happened to be a weakness in the embankments, Mother Gunga would carry his honour to the sea with the other raffle. Worst of all, there was nothing to do except to sit still; and Findlayson sat still under his mackintosh till his helmet became pulp on his head, and his boots were over-ankle in mire. He took no count of time, for the river was marking the hours, inch by inch and foot by foot, along the embankment, and he listened, numb and hungry, to the straining of the stone-boats, the hollow thunder under the piers, and the hundred noises that make the full note of a flood. Once a dripping servant brought him food, but he could not eat; and once he thought that he heard a faint toot from a locomotive across the river, and then he smiled. The bridge's failure would hurt his assistant not a little, but Hitchcock was a young man with his big work yet to do. For himself the crash meant everything – everything that made a hard life worth the living. They would say, the men of his own profession – he remembered the half-pitying things that he himself had said when Lockhart's big water-works burst and broke down in brick-heaps and sludge, and Lockhart's spirit broke in him and he died. He remembered what he himself had said when the Sumao Bridge went out in the big cyclone by the sea; and most he remembered poor Hartopp's face three weeks later, when the shame had marked it. His bridge was twice the size of Hartopp's, and it carried the Findlayson truss as well as the new pier-shoe – the Findlayson bolted shoe. There were no excuses in his Service. Government might listen, perhaps, but his own kind would judge him by his bridge, as that stood or fell. He went over it in his head, plate by plate, span by span, brick by brick, pier by pier, remembering, comparing, estimating, and recalculating, lest there should be any mistake; and through the long hours and through the flights of formulae that danced and wheeled before him a cold fear would come to pinch his heart. His side of the sum was beyond question; but what man knew Mother Gunga's arthimetic? Even as he was making all sure by the multiplication-table, the river might be scooping pot-holes to the very bottom of any one of those eighty-foot piers that carried his reputation. Again a servant came to him with food, but his mouth was dry, and he could only drink and return to the decimals in his brain. And the river was still rising. Peroo, in a mat shelter-coat, crouched at his feet, watching now his face and now the face of the river, but saying nothing.

At last the Lascar rose and floundered through the mud towards the village, but he was careful to leave an ally to watch the boats.

Presently he returned, most irreverently driving before him the priest of his creed – a fat old man, with a grey beard that whipped the wind with the wet cloth that blew over his shoulder. Never was seen so lamentable a *guru*.

'What good are offerings and little kerosene lamps and dry grain,' shouted Peroo, 'if squatting in the mud is all that thou canst do? Thou hast dealt long with the Gods when they were contented and well-wishing. Now they are angry. Speak to them!'

'What is a man against the Wrath of Gods?' whined the priest, cowering as the wind took him. 'Let me go to the temple, and I will pray there.'

'Son of a pig, pray *here*! Is there no return for salt fish and curry powder and dried onions? Call aloud! Tell Mother Gunga we have had enough. Bid her be still for the night. I cannot pray, but I have served in the Kumpani's boats, and when men did not obey my orders I – ' A flourish of the wire-rope colt[23] rounded the sentence, and the priest, breaking from his disciple, fled to the village.

'Fat pig!' said Peroo. 'After all that we have done for him! When the flood is down I will see to it that we get a new *guru*. Finlinson Sahib, it darkens for night now, and since yesterday nothing has been eaten. Be wise, Sahib. No man can endure watching and great thinking on an empty belly. Lie down, Sahib. The river will do what the river will do.'

'The bridge is mine; I cannot leave it.'

'Wilt thou hold it up with thy hands, then?' said Peroo, laughing. 'I was troubled for my boats and sheers *before* the flood came. Now we are in the hands of the Gods. The Sahib will not eat and lie down? Take these, then. They are meat and good toddy together, and they kill all weariness, besides the fever that follows the rain. I have eaten nothing else to-day at all.'

He took a small tin tobacco-box from his sodden waist-belt and thrust it into Findlayson's hand, saying, 'Nay, do not be afraid. It is no more than opium – clean Malwa opium!'

Findlayson shook two or three of the dark-brown pellets into his hand, and, hardly knowing what he did, swallowed them. The stuff was at least a good guard against fever – the fever that was creeping upon him out of the wet mud – and he had seen what Peroo could do in the stewing mists of autumn on the strength of a dose from the tin box.

Peroo nodded with bright eyes. 'In a little – in a little the Sahib will find that he thinks well again. I too will – ' He dived into his treasure-box, resettled the rain-coat over his head, and squatted down to watch the boats. It was too dark now to see beyond the first pier, and the night seemed to have given the river new strength. Findlayson stood with his chin on his chest, thinking. There was one point about one of the piers – the Seventh – that he had not fully settled in his mind. The figures would not shape themselves to the eye except one by one and at enormous intervals of time. There was a sound, rich and mellow in his ears, like the deepest note of a double-bass – an entrancing sound upon which he pondered for several hours, as it seemed. Then Peroo was at his elbow, shouting that a wire hawser had snapped and the stone-boats were loose. Findlayson saw the fleet open and swing out fanwise to a long-drawn shriek of wire straining across gunnels.

'A tree hit them. They will all go,' cried Peroo. 'The main hawser has parted. What does the Sahib do?'

An immensely complex plan had suddenly flashed into Findlayson's mind. He saw the ropes running from boat to boat in straight lines and angles – each rope a line of white fire. But there was one rope which was the master-rope. He could see that rope. If he could pull it once, it was absolutely and mathematically certain that the disordered fleet would reassemble itself in the backwater behind the guard-tower. But why, he wondered, was Peroo clinging so desperately to his waist as he hastened down the bank? It was necessary to put the Lascar aside, gently and slowly, because it was necessary to save the boats, and, further, to demonstrate the extreme ease of the problem that looked so difficult. And then – but it was of no conceivable importance – a wire rope raced through his hand, burning it, the high bank disappeared, and with it all the slowly dispersing factors of the problem. He was sitting in the rainy darkness – sitting in a boat that spun like a top, and Peroo was standing over him.

'I had forgotten,' said the Lascar slowly, 'that to those fasting and unused the opium is worse than any wine. Those who die in Gunga go to the Gods. Still, I have no desire to present myself before such great ones. Can the Sahib swim?'

'What need? He can fly – fly as swiftly as the wind,' was the thick answer.

'He is mad!' muttered Peroo under his breath. 'And he threw me aside like a bundle of dung-cakes. Well, he will not know his death. The boat cannot live an hour here even if she strike nothing. It is not good to look at death with a clear eye.'

He refreshed himself again from the tin box, squatted down in the bows of the reeling, pegged, and stitched craft,[24] staring through the mist at the nothing that was there. A warm drowsiness crept over Findlayson, the Chief Engineer, whose duty was with his bridge. The heavy raindrops struck him with a thousand tingling little thrills, and the weight of all time since time was made hung heavy on his eyelids. He thought and perceived that he was perfectly secure, for the water was so solid that a man could surely step out upon it, and, standing still with his legs apart to keep his balance – this was the most important point – would be borne with great and easy speed to the shore. But yet a better plan came to him. It needed only an exertion of will for the soul to hurl the body ashore as wind drives paper; to waft it kite-fashion to the bank. Thereafter – the boat spun dizzily – suppose the high wind got under the freed body? Would it tower up like a kite and pitch headlong on the far-away sands, or would it duck about beyond control through all eternity? Findlayson gripped the gunnel to anchor himself, for it seemed that he was on the edge of taking the flight before he had settled all his plans. Opium has more effect on the white man than the black. Peroo was only comfortably indifferent to accidents. 'She cannot live,' he grunted. 'Her seams open already. If she were even a dinghy with oars we could have ridden it out; but a box with holes is no good. Finlinson Sahib, she fills.'

'*Achcha!* I am going away. Come thou also.'

In his mind Findlayson had already escaped from the boat, and was circling high in air to find a rest for the sole of his foot. His body – he was really sorry for its gross helplessness – lay in the stern, the water rushing about its knees.

'How very ridiculous!' he said to himself, from his eyrie. 'That – is Findlayson – chief of the Kashi Bridge. The poor beast is going to be drowned, too. Drowned when it's close to shore. I'm – I'm on shore already. Why doesn't it come along?'

To his intense disgust, he found his soul back in his body again, and that body spluttering and choking in deep water. The pain of the reunion was atrocious, but it was necessary, also, to fight for the body. He was conscious of grasping wildly at wet sand, and striding prodigiously, as one strides in a dream, to keep foothold in the swirling water, till at last he hauled himself clear of the hold of the river, and dropped, panting, on wet earth.

'Not this night,' said Peroo in his ear. 'The Gods have protected us.' The Lascar moved his feet cautiously, and they rustled among dried stumps. 'This is some island of last year's indigo crop,' he went on. 'We shall find no men here; but have great care, Sahib; all the snakes of a hundred miles have been flooded out. Here comes the lightning, on the heels of the wind. Now we shall be able to look; but walk carefully.'

Findlayson was far and far beyond any fear of snakes, or indeed any merely human emotion. He saw, after he had rubbed the water from his eyes, with an immense clearness, and trod, so it seemed to himself, with world-encompassing strides. Somewhere in the night of time he had built a bridge – a bridge that spanned illimitable levels of shining seas; but the Deluge had swept it away, leaving this one island under heaven for Findlayson and his companion, sole survivors of the breed of man.

An incessant lightning, forked and blue, showed all that there was to be seen on the little patch in the flood – a clump of thorn, a clump of swaying, creaking bamboos, and a grey gnarled peepul[25] overshadowing a Hindu shrine, from whose dome floated a tattered red flag. The holy man whose summer resting-place it was had long since abandoned it, and the weather had broken the red-daubed image of his God. The two men stumbled, heavy-limbed and heavy-eyed, over the ashes of a brick-set cooking-place, and dropped down under the shelter of the branches, while the rain and river roared together.

The stumps of the indigo crackled, and there was a smell of cattle, as a huge and dripping Brahmini Bull[26] shouldered his way under the tree. The flashes revealed the trident mark of Shiva on his flank, the insolence of head and hump, the luminous stag-like eyes, the brow crowned with a wreath of sodden marigold blooms, and the silky dewlap that nigh swept the ground. There was a noise behind him of other beasts coming up from the flood-line through the thicket, a sound of heavy feet and deep breathing.

'Here be more besides ourselves,' said Findlayson, his head against the tree-bole, looking through half-shut eyes, wholly at ease.

'Truly,' said Peroo thickly, 'and no small ones.'

'What are they, then? I do not see clearly.'

'The Gods. Who else? Look!'

'Ah, true! The Gods surely – the Gods.' Findlayson smiled as his head fell forward on his chest. Peroo was eminently right. After the Flood, who should be alive in the land except the Gods that made it – the Gods to whom his village prayed nightly – the Gods who were in all men's mouths and about all men's ways? He could not raise his head or stir a finger for the trance that held him, and Peroo was smiling vacantly at the lightning.

The Bull paused by the shrine, his head lowered to the damp earth. A green Parrot[27] in the branches preened his wet wings and screamed against the thunder as the circle under the tree filled with the shifting shadows of beasts. There was a Blackbuck at the Bull's heels – such a buck as Findlayson in his far-away life upon earth might have seen in dreams – a buck with a royal head, ebon back, silver belly, and gleaming straight horns. Beside him, her head bowed to the ground, the green eyes burning under the heavy brows, with restless tail switching the dead grass, paced a Tigress, full-bellied and deep-jowled.

The Bull crouched beside the shrine, and there leaped from the darkness a monstrous grey Ape, who seated himself man-wise in the place of the fallen image, and the rain spilled like jewels from the hair of his neck and shoulders.

Other shadows came and went behind the circle, among them a drunken Man flourishing staff and drinking-bottle. Then a hoarse bellow broke out from near the ground. 'The flood lessens even now,' it cried. 'Hour by hour the water falls, and their bridge still stands!'

'My bridge,' said Findlayson to himself. 'That must be very old work now. What have the Gods to do with my bridge?'

His eyes rolled in the darkness following the roar. A Crocodile – the blunt-nosed, ford-haunting Mugger[28] of the Ganges – draggled herself before the beasts, lashing furiously to right and left with her tail.

'They have made it too strong for me. In all this night I have only torn away a handful of planks. The walls stand! The towers stand! They have chained my flood, and my river is not free any more. Heavenly Ones, take this yoke away! Give me clear water between bank and bank! It is I, Mother Gunga, that speak. The Justice of the Gods! Deal me the Justice of the Gods!'

'What said I?' whispered Peroo. 'This is in truth a *Punchayet*[29] of the Gods. Now we know that all the world is dead, save you and I, Sahib.'

The Parrot screamed and fluttered again, and the Tigress, her ears flat to her head, snarled wickedly.

Somewhere in the shadow a great trunk and gleaming tusks swayed to and fro, and a low gurgle broke the silence that followed on the snarl.

'We be here,' said a deep voice, 'the Great Ones. One only and very many. Shiv, my father, is here, with Indra. Kali[30] has spoken already. Hanuman listens also.'

'Kashi is without her Kotwal[31] to-night,' shouted the Man with the drinking-bottle, flinging his staff to the ground, while the island rang to the baying of hounds. 'Give her the Justice of the Gods!'

'Ye were still when they polluted my waters,' the great Crocodile bellowed. 'Ye made no sign when my river was trapped between the walls. I had no help save my own strength, and that failed – the strength

of Mother Gunga failed – before their guard-towers. What could I do?
I have done everything. Finish now, Heavenly Ones!'

'I brought the death; I rode the spotted sickness from hut to hut of
their workmen, and yet they would not cease.' A nose-slitten, hide-worn
Ass,[32] lame, scissor-legged, and galled, limped forward. 'I cast the death
at them out of my nostrils, but they would not cease.'

Peroo would have moved, but the opium lay heavy upon him.

'Bah!' he said, spitting. 'Here is Sitala herself; Mata – the smallpox.
Has the Sahib a handkerchief to put over his face?'

'Small help!' said the Crocodile. 'They fed me the corpses for a
month, and I flung them out on my sand-bars, but their work went
forward. Demons they are, and sons of demons! And ye left Mother
Gunga alone for their fire-carriage to make a mock of. The Justice of
the Gods on the bridge-builders!'

The Bull turned the cud in his mouth and answered slowly, 'If the
Justice of the Gods caught all who made a mock of holy things, there
would be many dark altars in the land, Mother.'

'But this goes beyond a mock,' said the Tigress, darting forward a
griping paw. 'Thou knowest, Shiv, and ye too, Heavenly Ones; ye know
that they have defiled Gunga. Surely they must come to the Destroyer.
Let Indra judge.'

The Buck made no movement as he answered, 'How long has this
evil been?'

'Three years, as men count years,' said the Mugger, close pressed to
the earth.

'Does Mother Gunga die, then, in a year, that she is so anxious to
see vengeance now? The deep sea was where she runs but yesterday,
and to-morrow the sea shall cover her again as the Gods count that
which men call time. Can any say that this their bridge endures till
to-morrow?' said the Buck.

There was a long hush, and in the clearing of the storm the full moon
stood up above the dripping trees.

'Judge ye, then,' said the Mugger sullenly. 'I have spoken my shame.
The flood falls still. I can do no more.'

'For my own part' – it was the voice of the great Ape seated within
the shrine – 'it pleases me well to watch these men, remembering that
I also builded no small bridge[33] in the world's youth.'

'They say, too,' snarled the Tiger, 'that these men came of the wreck
of thy armies, Hanuman,[34] and therefore thou hast aided – '

'They toil as my armies toiled in Lanka, and they believe that their
toil endures. Indra is too high, but, Shiv, thou knowest how the land is
threaded with their fire-carriages.'

'Yea, I know,' said the Bull. 'Their Gods instructed them in the matter.'

A laugh ran round the circle.

'Their Gods! What should their Gods know? They were born yesterday, and those that made them are scarcely yet cold,' said the Mugger. 'To-morrow their Gods will die.'

'Ho!' said Peroo. 'Mother Gunga talks good talk. I told that to the Padre-Sahib who preached on the *Mombasa*, and he asked the Burra Malum to put me in irons for a great rudeness.'

'Surely they make these things to please their Gods,' said the Bull again.

'Not altogether,' the Elephant rolled forth. 'It is for the profit of my *mahajuns*[35] – my fat money-lenders that worship me at each new year, when they draw my image at the head of the account-books. I, looking over their shoulders by lamplight, see that the names in the books are those of men in far places – for all the towns are drawn together by the fire-carriage, and the money comes and goes swiftly, and the account-books grow as fat as – myself. And I, who am Ganesh of Good Luck, I bless my peoples.'

'They have changed the face of the land – which is *my* land. They have killed and made new towns on my banks,' said the Mugger.

'It is but the shifting of a little dirt. Let the dirt dig in the dirt if it pleases the dirt,' answered the Elephant.

'But afterwards?' said the Tiger. 'Afterwards they will see that Mother Gunga can avenge no insult, and they fall away from her first, and later from us all, one by one. In the end, Ganesh, we are left with naked altars.'

The drunken Man staggered to his feet, and hiccupped vehemently in the face of the assembled Gods.

'Kali lies. My sister lies. Also this my stick is the Kotwal of Kashi, and he keeps tally of my pilgrims. When the time comes to worship Bhairon – and it is always time – the fire-carriages move one by one, and each bears a thousand pilgrims. They do not come afoot any more, but rolling upon wheels, and my honour is increased.'

'Gunga, I have seen thy bed at Prayag[36] black with the pilgrims,' said the Ape, leaning forward, 'and but for the fire-carriage they would have come slowly and in fewer numbers. Remember.'

'They come to me always,' Bhairon went on thickly. 'By day and night they pray to me, all the Common People in the fields and the roads. Who is like Bhairon to-day? What talk is this of changing faiths? Is my staff Kotwal of Kashi for nothing? He keeps the tally, and he says that never were so many altars as to-day, and the fire-carriage serves them well. Bhairon am I – Bhairon of the Common People, and the chiefest of the Heavenly Ones to-day. Also my staff says – '

'Peace, thou!' lowed the Bull. 'The worship of the schools is mine, and they talk very wisely, asking whether I be one or many, as is the delight of my people, and ye know what I am. Kali, my wife, thou knowest also.'

'Yea, I know,' said the Tigress, with lowered head.

'Greater am I than Gunga also. For ye know who moved the minds of men that they should count Gunga holy among the rivers. Who die in that water – ye know how men say – come to Us without punishment, and Gunga knows that the fire-carriage has borne to her scores upon scores of such anxious ones; and Kali knows that she has held her chiefest festivals among the pilgrimages that are fed by the fire-carriage. Who smote at Puri, under the Image there,[37] her thousands in a day and a night, and bound the sickness to the wheels of the fire-carriages, so that it ran from one end of the land to the other? Who but Kali? Before the fire-carriage came it was a heavy toil. The fire-carriages have served thee well, Mother of Death. But I speak for mine own altars, who am not Bhairon of the Common Folk, but Shiv. Men go to and fro, making words and telling talk of strange Gods, and I listen. Faith follows faith among my people in the schools, and I have no anger; for when the words are said, and the new talk is ended, to Shiv men return at the last.'

'True. It is true,' murmured Hanuman. 'To Shiv and to the others, Mother, they return. I creep from temple to temple in the North, where they worship one God and His Prophet; and presently my image is alone within their shrines.'

'Small thanks,' said the Buck, turning his head slowly. 'I am that One and His Prophet also.'

'Even so, Father,' said Hanuman. 'And to the South I go who am the oldest of the Gods as men know the Gods, and presently I touch the shrines of the new faiths and the Woman whom we know is hewn twelve-armed, and still they call her Mary.'

'Small thanks, brother,' said the Tigress. 'I am that Woman.'

'Even so, sister; and I go West among the fire-carriages, and stand before the bridge-builders in many shapes, and because of me they change their faiths and are very wise. Ho! ho! I am the builder of bridges indeed – bridges between this and that, and each bridge leads surely to Us in the end. Be content, Gunga. Neither these men nor those that follow them mock thee at all.'

'Am I alone, then, Heavenly Ones? Shall I smooth out my flood lest unhappily I bear away their walls? Will Indra dry my springs in the hills and make me crawl humbly between their wharfs? Shall I bury me in the sand ere I offend?'

'And all for the sake of a little iron bar with the fire-carriage atop. Truly, Mother Gunga is always young!' said Ganesh the Elephant. 'A child had not spoken more foolishly. Let the dirt dig in the dirt ere it return to the dirt. I know only that my people grow rich and praise me. Shiv has said that the men of the schools do not forget; Bhairon is content for his crowd of the Common People: and Hanuman laughs.'

'Surely I laugh,' said the Ape. 'My altars are few beside those of Ganesh or Bhairon, but the fire-carriages bring me new worshippers from beyond the Black Water – the men who believe that their God is toil. I run before them beckoning, and they follow Hanuman.'

'Give them the toil that they desire, then,' said the Mugger. 'Make a bar across my flood and throw the water back upon the bridge. Once thou wast strong in Lanka, Hanuman. Stoop and lift my bed.'

'Who gives life can take life.' The Ape scratched in the mud with a long forefinger. 'And yet, who would profit by the killing? Very many would die.'

There came up from the water a snatch of a love-song such as the boys sing when they watch their cattle in the noon heats of late spring. The Parrot screamed joyously, sidling along his branch with lowered head as the song grew louder, and in a patch of clear moonlight stood revealed the young herd, the darling of the Gopis,[38] the idol of dreaming maids and of mothers ere their children are born – Krishna the Well-beloved.[39] He stooped to knot up his long wet hair, and the Parrot fluttered to his shoulder.

'Fleeting and singing, and singing and fleeting,' hiccupped Bhairon. 'Those make thee late for the council, brother.'

'And then?' said Krishna, with a laugh, throwing back his head. 'Ye can do little without me or Karma[40] here.' He fondled the Parrot's plumage and laughed again. 'What is this sitting and talking together? I heard Mother Gunga roaring in the dark, and so came quickly from a hut where I lay warm. And what have ye done to Karma, that he is so wet and silent? And what does Mother Gunga here? Are the heavens full that ye must come paddling in the mud beast-wise? Karma, what do they do?'

'Gunga has prayed for a vengeance on the bridge-builders, and Kali is with her. Now she bids Hanuman whelm the bridge, that her honour may be made great,' cried the Parrot. 'I waited here, knowing that thou wouldst come, O my master!'

'And the Heavenly Ones said nothing? Did Gunga and the Mother of Sorrows out-talk them? Did none speak for my people?'

'Nay,' said Ganesh, moving uneasily from foot to foot; 'I said it was but dirt at play, and why should we stamp it flat?'

'I was content to let them toil – well content,' said Hanuman.

'What had I to do with Gunga's anger?' said the Bull.

'I am Bhairon of the Common Folk, and this my staff is Kotwal of all Kashi. I spoke for the Common People.'

'Thou?' The young God's eyes sparkled.

'Am I not the first of the Gods in their mouths today?' returned Bhairon, unabashed. 'For the sake of the Common People I said – very many wise things which I have now forgotten – but this my staff – '

Krishna turned impatiently, saw the Mugger at his feet, and kneeling, slipped an arm round the cold neck. 'Mother,' he said gently, 'get thee to thy flood again. The matter is not for thee. What harm shall thy honour take of this live dirt? Thou hast given them their fields new year after year, and by thy flood they are made strong. They come all to thee at the last. What need to slay them now? Have pity, Mother, for a little – and it is only for a little.'

'If it be only for a little – ' the slow beast began.

'Are they Gods, then?' Krishna returned with a laugh, his eyes looking into the dull eyes of the Mugger. 'Be certain that it is only for a little. The Heavenly Ones have heard thee, and presently justice will be done. Go now, Mother, to the flood again. Men and cattle are thick on the waters – the banks fall – the villages melt because of thee.'

'But the bridge – the bridge stands.' The Mugger turned grunting into the undergrowth as Krishna rose.

'It is ended,' said the Tigress viciously. 'There is no more justice from the Heavenly Ones. Ye have made shame and sport of Gunga, who asked no more than a few score lives.'

'Of *my* people – who lie under the leaf-roofs of the village yonder – of the young girls, and the young men who sing to them in the dark – of the child that will be born next morn – of that which was begotten to-night,' said Krishna. 'And when all is done, what profit? To-morrow sees them at work. Ay, if ye swept the bridge out from end to end they would begin anew. Hear me! Bhairon is drunk always. Hanuman mocks his people with new riddles.'

'Nay, but they are very old ones,' the Ape said, laughing.

'Shiv bears the talk of the schools and the dreams of the holy men; Ganesh thinks only of his fat traders; but I – I live with these my people, asking for no gifts, and so receiving them hourly.'

'And very tender art thou of thy people,' said the Tigress.

'They are my own. The old women dream of me, turning in their sleep; the maids look and listen for me when they go to fill their *lotahs*[41] by the river. I walk by the young men waiting without the gates at dusk, and I call over my shoulder to the white-beards. Ye know, Heavenly Ones, that I alone of us all walk upon the earth continually, and have no pleasure in our heavens so long as a green blade springs here, or there are two voices at twilight in the standing crops. Wise are ye, but ye live far off, forgetting whence ye came. So do I not forget. And the fire-carriage feeds your shrines, ye say? And the fire-carriages bring a thousand pilgrimages where but ten came in the old years? True. That is true to-day.'

'But to-morrow they are dead, brother,' said Ganesh.

'Peace!' said the Bull, as Hanuman leaned forward again. 'And to-morrow, beloved – what of tomorrow?'

'This only. A new word creeping from mouth to mouth among the Common Folk – a word that neither man nor God can lay hold of – an evil word – a little lazy word among the Common Folk, saying (and none know who set that word afoot) that they weary of ye, Heavenly Ones.'

The Gods laughed together softly. 'And then, beloved?' they said.

'And to cover that weariness they, my people, will bring to thee, Shiv, and to thee, Ganesh, at first greater offerings and a louder noise of worship. But the word has gone abroad, and, after, they will pay fewer dues to your fat Brahmins. Next they will forget your altars, but so slowly that no man can say how his forgetfulness began.'

'I knew – I knew! I spoke this also, but they would not hear,' said the Tigress. 'We should have slain – we should have slain!'

'It is too late now. Ye should have slain at the beginning, when the men from across the water had taught our folk nothing. Now my people see their work, and go away thinking. They do not think of the Heavenly Ones altogether. They think of the fire-carriage and the other things that the bridge-builders have done, and when your priests thrust forward hands asking alms, they give unwillingly a little. That is the beginning, among one or two, or five or ten – for I, moving among my people, know what is in their hearts.'

'And the end, Jester of the Gods? What shall the end be?' said Ganesh.

'The end shall be as it was in the beginning, O slothful son of Shiv! The flame shall die upon the altars and the prayer upon the tongue till ye become little Gods again – Gods of the jungle – names that the hunters of rats and noosers of dogs whisper in the thicket and among the caves – rag-Gods, pot Godlings of the tree, and the village-mark, as ye were at the beginning. That is the end, Ganesh, for thee, and for Bhairon – Bhairon of the Common People.'

'It is very far away,' grunted Bhairon. 'Also, it is a lie.'

'Many women have kissed Krishna. They told him this to cheer their own hearts when the grey hairs came, and he has told us the tale,' said the Bull, below his breath.

'Their Gods came, and we changed them. I took the Woman and made her twelve-armed. So shall we twist all their Gods,' said Hanuman.

'Their Gods! This is no question of their Gods – one or three – man or woman. The matter is with the people. *They* move, and not the Gods of the bridge-builders,' said Krishna.

'So be it. I have made a man worship the fire-carriage as it stood still breathing smoke, and he knew not that he worshipped me,' said Hanuman the Ape. 'They will only change a little the names of their Gods. I shall lead the builders of the bridges as of old; Shiv shall be worshipped in the schools by such as doubt and despise their fellows; Ganesh shall have his *mahajuns*, and Bhairon the donkey-drivers, the pilgrims, and the sellers of toys. Beloved, they will do no more than change the names, and that we have seen a thousand times.'

'Surely they will do no more than change the names,' echoed Ganesh: but there was an uneasy movement among the Gods.

'They will change more than the names. Me alone they cannot kill, so long as maiden and man meet together or the spring follows the winter rains. Heavenly Ones, not for nothing have I walked upon the earth. My people know not now what they know; but I, who live with them, I read their hearts. Great Kings, the beginning of the end is born already. The fire-carriages shout the names of new Gods that are *not* the old under new names. Drink now and eat greatly! Bathe your faces in the smoke of the altars before they grow cold! Take dues and listen to the cymbals and the drums, Heavenly Ones, while yet there are flowers and songs. As men count time the end is far off; but as we who know reckon it is to-day. I have spoken.'

The young God ceased, and his brethren looked at each other long in silence.

'This I have not heard before,' Peroo whispered in his companion's ear. 'And yet sometimes, when I oiled the brasses in the engine-room of the *Goorkha*,[42] I have wondered if our priests were so wise – so wise. The day is coming, Sahib. They will be gone by the morning.'

A yellow light broadened in the sky, and the tone of the river changed as the darkness withdrew.

Suddenly the Elephant trumpeted aloud as though a man had goaded him.

'Let Indra judge! Father of all, speak thou! What of the things we have heard? Has Krishna lied indeed? Or – '

'Ye know,' said the Buck, rising to his feet. 'Ye know the Riddle of the Gods. When Brahm[43] ceases to dream, the Heavens and the Hells and Earth disappear. Be content. Brahm dreams still. The dreams come and go, and the nature of the dreams changes, but still Brahm dreams. Krishna has walked too long upon earth, and yet I love him the more for the tale he has told. The Gods change, beloved – all save One!'

'Ay, all save one that makes love in the hearts of men,' said Krishna, knotting his girdle. 'It is but a little time to wait, and ye shall know if I lie.'

'Truly it is but a little time, as thou sayest, and we shall know. Get thee to thy huts again, beloved, and make sport for the young things, for still Brahm dreams. Go, my children! Brahm dreams – and till He wakes, the Gods die not.'

'Whither went they?' said the Lascar, awe-struck, shivering a little with the cold.

'God knows!' said Findlayson. The river and the island lay in full daylight now, and there was never mark of hoof or pug[44] on the wet earth under the peepul. Only a parrot screamed in the branches, bringing down showers of water-drops as he fluttered his wings.

'Up! We are cramped with cold! Has the opium died out? Canst thou move, Sahib?'

Findlayson staggered to his feet and shook himself. His head swam and ached, but the work of the opium was over, and, as he sluiced his forehead in a pool, the Chief Engineer of the Kashi Bridge was wondering how he had managed to fall upon the island, what chances the day offered of return, and, above all, how his work stood.

'Peroo, I have forgotten much. I was under the guard-tower watching the river; and then – Did the flood sweep us away?'

'No. The boats broke loose, Sahib, and' (if the Sahib had forgotten about the opium, decidedly Peroo would not remind him) 'in striving to retie them, so it seemed to me – but it was dark – a rope caught the Sahib and threw him upon a boat. Considering that we two, with Hitchcock Sahib, built, as it were, that bridge, I came also upon the boat, which came riding on horseback, as it were, on the nose of this island, and so, splitting, cast us ashore. I made a great cry when the boat left the wharf, and without doubt Hitchcock Sahib will come for us. As for the bridge, so many have died in the building that it cannot fall.'

A fierce sun, that drew out all the smell of the sodden land, had followed the storm, and in that clear light there was no room for a man to think of dreams of the dark. Findlayson stared up-stream, across the blaze of moving water, till his eyes ached. There was no sign of any bank to the Ganges, much less of a bridge-line.

'We came down far,' he said. 'It was wonderful that we were not drowned a hundred times.'

'That was the least of the wonder, for no man dies before his time. I have seen Sydney, I have seen London, and twenty great ports, but' – Peroo looked at the damp, discoloured shrine under the peepul – 'never man has seen that we saw here.'

'What?'

'Has the Sahib forgotten; or do we black men only see the Gods?'

'There was a fever upon me.' Findlayson was still looking uneasily across the water. 'It seemed that the island was full of beasts and men talking, but I do not remember. A boat could live in this water now, I think.'

'Oho! Then it *is* true. "When Brahm ceases to dream, the Gods die." Now I know, indeed, what he meant. Once, too, the *guru* said as much to me; but then I did not understand. Now I am wise.'

'What?' said Findlayson over his shoulder.

Peroo went on as if he were talking to himself. 'Six – seven – ten monsoons since, I was watch on the foc'sle of the *Rewah* – the Kumpani's big boat – and there was a big *tufan*,[45] green and black water beating; and I held fast to the life-lines, choking under the waters. Then I thought of the Gods – of Those whom we saw to-night' – he stared curiously at Findlayson's back, but the white man was looking across the flood. 'Yes, I say of Those whom we saw this night past, and I called upon Them to protect me. And while I prayed, still keeping my look-out, a big wave came and threw me forward upon the ring of the great black bow-anchor, and the *Rewah* rose high and high, leaning towards the left-hand side, and the water drew away from beneath her nose, and I lay upon my belly, holding the ring, and looking down into those great deeps. Then I thought, even in the face of death, if I lose hold I die, and for me neither the *Rewah* nor my place by the galley where the rice is cooked, nor Bombay, nor Calcutta, nor even London, will be any more for me. "How shall I be sure," I said, "that the Gods to whom I pray will abide at all?" This I thought, and the *Rewah* dropped her nose as a hammer falls, and all the sea came in and slid me backwards along the foc'sle and over the break of the foc'sle, and I very badly bruised my shin against the donkey-engine; but I did not die, and I have seen the Gods. They are good for live men, but for the dead – They have spoken Themselves. Therefore, when I come to the village I will beat the *guru* for talking riddles which are no riddles. When Brahm ceases to dream, the Gods go.'

'Look up-stream. The light blinds. Is there smoke yonder?'

Peroo shaded his eyes with his hands. 'He is a wise man and quick. Hitchcock Sahib would not trust a rowboat. He has borrowed the Rao Sahib's steam-launch, and comes to look for us. I have always said that there should have been a steam-launch on the bridge-works for us.'

The territory of the Rao of Baraon lay within ten miles of the bridge; and Findlayson and Hitchcock had spent a fair portion of their scanty leisure in playing billiards and shooting blackbuck with the young man. He had been bear-led[46] by an English tutor of sporting tastes for some five or six years, and was now royally wasting the revenues accumulated during his minority by the Indian Government. His steam-launch, with its silver-plated rails, striped silk awning, and mahogany decks, was a new toy which Findlayson had found horribly in the way when the Rao came to look at the bridge-works.

'It's great luck,' murmured Findlayson, but he was none the less afraid, wondering what news might be of the bridge.

The gaudy blue-and-white funnel came down-stream swiftly. They could see Hitchcock in the bows, with a pair of opera-glasses, and his face was unusually white. Then Peroo hailed, and the launch made for the tail of the island. The Rao Sahib, in tweed shooting-suit and a seven-hued turban, waved his royal hand, and Hitchcock shouted. But he need have asked no questions, for Findlayson's first demand was for his bridge.

'All serene! 'Gad, I never expected to see you again, Findlayson. You're seven *koss*[47] down-stream. Yes, there's not a stone shifted anywhere; but how are you? I borrowed the Rao Sahib's launch, and he was good enough to come along. Jump in.'

'Ah, Finlinson, you are very well, eh? That was most unprecedented calamity last night, eh? My royal palace, too, it leaks like the devil, and the crops will also be short all about my country. Now you shall back her out, Hitchcock. I – I do not understand steam-engines. You are wet? You are cold, Finlinson? I have some things to eat here, and you will take a good drink.'

'I'm immensely grateful, Rao Sahib. I believe you've saved my life. How did Hitchcock – '

'Oho! His hair was upon end. He rode to me in the middle of the night and woke me up in the arms of Morphus.[48] I was most truly concerned, Finlinson, so I came too. My head-priest he is very angry just now. We will go quick, Mister Hitchcock. I am due to attend at twelve forty-five in the state temple, where we sanctify some new idol. If not so I would have asked you to spend the day with me. They are dam'-bore, these religious ceremonies, Finlinson, eh?'

Peroo, well known to the crew, had possessed himself of the wheel, and was taking the launch craftily up-stream. But while he steered he was, in his mind, handling two feet of partially untwisted wire rope; and the back upon which he beat was the back of his *guru*.

THE MALTESE CAT

They had good reason to be proud, and better reason to be afraid, all twelve of them; for, though they had fought their way, game by game, up the teams entered for the polo tournament, they were meeting the Archangels that afternoon in the final match; and the Archangels' men were playing with half-a-dozen ponies apiece. As the game was divided into six quarters of eight minutes each, that meant a fresh pony after every halt. The Skidars' team, even supposing there were no accidents, could only supply one pony for every other change; and two to one is heavy odds. Again, as Shiraz, the grey Syrian, pointed out, they were meeting the pink and pick of the polo-ponies of Upper India; ponies that had cost from a thousand rupees each, while they themselves were a cheap lot gathered, often from country carts, by their masters who belonged to a poor but honest native infantry regiment.

'Money means pace and weight,' said Shiraz, rubbing his black silk nose dolefully along his neat-fitting boot,[1] 'and by the maxims of the game as I know it – '

'Ah, but we aren't playing the maxims,' said the Maltese Cat. 'We're playing the game, and we've the great advantage of knowing the game. Just think a stride, Shiraz. We've pulled up from bottom to second place in two weeks against all those fellows on the ground here; and that's because we play with our heads as well as with our feet.'

'It makes me feel undersized and unhappy all the same,' said Kittiwynk, a mouse-coloured mare with a red browband and the cleanest pair of legs that ever an aged pony owned. 'They've twice our size, these others.'

Kittiwynk looked at the gathering and sighed. The hard, dusty Umballa polo-ground was lined with thousands of soldiers, black and white, not counting hundreds and hundreds of carriages, and drags, and dog-carts,[2] and ladies with brilliant-coloured parasols, and officers in uniform and out of it, and crowds of natives behind them; and orderlies on camels who had halted to watch the game, instead of carrying letters up and down the Station, and native horse-dealers running about on thin-eared Baluchi mares, looking for a chance to sell a few first-class polo-ponies. Then there were the ponies of thirty teams that had entered for the Upper India Free-for-All Cup – nearly every pony of worth and dignity from Mhow to Peshawur, from Allahabad to Multan; prize ponies, Arabs, Syrian, Barb, countrybred, Deccanee, Waziri, and Kabul ponies of every colour and shape and temper that you could imagine. Some of them were in mat-roofed stables close to the polo-ground, but most were under saddle while their masters, who had been defeated in the earlier games, trotted in and out and told each other exactly how the game should have been played.

It was a glorious sight, and the come-and-go of the little quick hoofs, and the incessant salutations of ponies that had met before on other polo-grounds or racecourses, were enough to drive a four-footed thing wild.

But the Skidars' team were careful not to know their neighbours, though half the ponies on the ground were anxious to scrape acquaintance with the little fellows that had come from the North, and, so far, had swept the board.

'Let's see,' said a soft, golden-coloured Arab, who had been playing very badly the day before, to the Maltese Cat, 'didn't we meet in Abdul Rahman's stable in Bombay four seasons ago? I won the Paikpattan Cup next season, you may remember.'

'Not me,' said the Maltese Cat politely. 'I was at Malta then, pulling a vegetable cart. I don't race. I play the game.'

'O-oh!' said the Arab, cocking his tail and swaggering off.

'Keep yourselves to yourselves,' said the Maltese Cat to his companions. 'We don't want to rub noses with all those goose-rumped half-breeds of Upper India. When we've won this Cup they'll give their shoes to know us.'

'We shan't win the Cup,' said Shiraz. 'How do you feel?'

'Stale as last night's feed after a musk-rat has run over it,' said Polaris, a rather heavy-shouldered grey, and the rest of the team agreed with him.

'The sooner you forget that the better,' said the Maltese Cat cheerfully. 'They've finished tiffin[3] in the big tent. We shall be wanted now. If your saddles are not comfy, kick. If your bits aren't easy, rear, and let the *saises* know whether your boots are tight.'

Each pony had his *sais*, his groom, who lived and ate and slept with the pony, and had betted a great deal more than he could afford on the result of the game. There was no chance of anything going wrong, and, to make sure, each *sais* was shampooing the legs of his pony to the last minute. Behind the *saises* sat as many of the Skidars' regiment as had leave to attend the match – about half the native officers, and a hundred or two dark, black-bearded men with the regimental pipers nervously fingering the big be-ribboned bagpipes. The Skidars were what they call a Pioneer regiment; and the bagpipes made the national music of half the men. The native officers held bundles of polo-sticks, long cane-handled mallets, and as the grand-stand filled after lunch they arranged themselves by ones and twos at different points round the ground, so that if a stick were broken the player would not have far to ride for a new one. An impatient British cavalry band struck up 'If you want to know the time, ask a p'leeceman!' and the two umpires in light dust-coats danced out on two little excited ponies. The four players of the Archangels' team followed, and the sight of their beautiful mounts made Shiraz groan again.

'Wait till we know,' said the Maltese Cat. 'Two of 'em are playing in blinkers,[4] and that means they can't see to get out of the way of their own side, or they *may* shy at the umpires' ponies. They've *all* got white web reins that are sure to stretch or slip!'

'And,' said Kittiwynk, dancing to take the stiffness out of her, 'they carry their whips in their hands instead of on their wrists. Hah!'

'True enough. No man can manage his stick and his reins and his whip that way,' said the Maltese Cat. 'I've fallen over every square yard of the Malta ground, and *I* ought to know.' He quivered his little flea-bitten[5] withers just to show how satisfied he felt; but his heart was not so light. Ever since he had drifted into India on a troopship, taken, with an old rifle, as part payment for a racing debt, the Maltese Cat had played and preached polo to the Skidars' team on the Skidars' stony polo-ground. Now a polo-pony is like a poet. If he is born with a love for the game he can be made. The Maltese Cat knew that bamboos grew solely in order that polo-balls might be turned from their roots, that grain was given to ponies to keep them in hard condition, and that ponies were shod to prevent them slipping on a turn. But, besides all these things, he knew every trick and device of the finest game of the world, and for two seasons he had been teaching the others all he knew or guessed.

'Remember,' he said for the hundredth time as the riders came up, 'we *must* play together, and you *must* play with your heads. Whatever happens, follow the ball. Who goes out first?'

Kittiwynk, Shiraz, Polaris, and a short high little bay fellow with tremendous hocks and no withers worth speaking of (he was called Corks) were being girthed up, and the soldiers in the background stared with all their eyes.

'I want you men to keep quiet,' said Lutyens, the captain of the team, 'and especially *not* to blow your pipes.'

'Not if we win, Captain Sahib?' asked a piper.

'If we win, you can do what you please,' said Lutyens with a smile, as he slipped the loop of his stick over his wrist, and wheeled to canter to his place. The Archangels' ponies were a little bit above themselves on account of the many-coloured crowd so close to the ground. Their riders were excellent players, but they were a team of crack players instead of a crack team; and that made all the difference in the world. They honestly meant to play together, but it is very hard for four men, each the best of the team he is picked from, to remember that in polo no brilliancy of hitting or riding makes up for playing alone. Their captain shouted his orders to them by name, and it is a curious thing that if you call his name aloud in public after an Englishman you make him hot and fretty. Lutyens said nothing to his men because it had all been said before. He pulled up Shiraz, for he was playing 'back', to guard the goal. Powell on Polaris was half-back, and Macnamara and Hughes on Corks and Kittiwynk were forwards. The tough bamboo-root ball was put into the middle of the ground one hundred and fifty yards from the ends, and Hughes crossed sticks, heads-up, with the captain of the Archangels, who saw fit to play forward, and that is a place from which you cannot easily control the team. The little click as the cane-shafts met was heard all over the ground, and then Hughes made some sort of quick wrist-stroke that just dribbled the ball a few yards. Kittiwynk knew that stroke of old, and followed as a cat follows a mouse. While the captain of the Archangels was wrenching his pony round Hughes struck with all his strength, and next instant Kittiwynk was away, Corks following close behind her, their little feet pattering like rain-drops on glass.

'Pull out to the left,' said Kittiwynk between her teeth, 'it's coming our way, Corks!'

The back and half-back of the Archangels were tearing down on her just as she was within reach of the ball. Hughes leaned forward with a loose rein, and cut it away to the left almost under Kittiwynk's feet, and it hopped and skipped off to Corks, who saw that, if he were not quick, it would run beyond the boundaries. That long bouncing drive gave the Archangels time to wheel and send three men across the ground to head off Corks. Kittiwynk stayed where she was, for she knew the game. Corks was on the ball half a fraction of a second before the others came up, and Macnamara, with a back-handed stroke, sent it back across the ground to Hughes, who saw the way clear to the Archangels' goal, and smacked the ball in before anyone quite knew what had happened.

'That's luck,' said Corks, as they changed ends. 'A goal in three minutes for three hits and no riding to speak of.'

'Don't know,' said Polaris. 'We've made 'em angry too soon. Shouldn't wonder if they try to rush us off our feet next time.'

'Keep the ball hanging then,' said Shiraz. 'That wears out every pony that isn't used to it.'

Next time there was no easy galloping across the ground. All the Archangels closed up as one man, but there they stayed, for Corks, Kittiwynk, and Polaris were somewhere on the top of the ball, marking time among the rattling sticks, while Shiraz circled about outside, waiting for a chance.

'*We* can do this all day,' said Polaris, ramming his quarters into the side of another pony. 'Where do you think you're shoving to?'

'I'll – I'll be driven in an *ekka*[6] if I know,' was the gasping reply, 'and I'd give a week's feed to get my blinkers off. I can't see anything.'

'The dust *is* rather bad. Whew! That was one for my off hock. Where's the ball, Corks?'

'Under my tail. Anyhow a man's looking for it there. This is beautiful. They can't use their sticks, and it's driving 'em wild. Give old Blinkers a push and he'll go over!'

'Here, don't touch me! I can't see. I'll – I'll back out, I think,' said the pony in blinkers, who knew that if you can't see all round your head you cannot prop yourself against a shock.

Corks was watching the ball where it lay in the dust close to his near fore, with Macnamara's shortened stick tap-tapping it from time to time. Kittiwynk was edging her way out of the scrimmage, whisking her stump of a tail with nervous excitement.

'Ho! They've got it,' she snorted. 'Let me out!' and she galloped like a rifle-bullet just behind a tall lanky pony of the Archangels, whose rider was swinging up his stick for a stroke.

'Not to-day, thank you,' said Hughes, as the blow slid off his raised stick, and Kittiwynk laid her shoulder to the tall pony's quarters, and shoved him aside just as Lutyens on Shiraz sent the ball where it had come from, and the tall pony went skating and slipping away to the left. Kittiwynk, seeing that Polaris had joined Corks in the chase for the ball up the ground, dropped into Polaris's place, and then time was called.

The Skidars' ponies wasted no time in kicking or fuming. They knew each minute's rest meant so much gain, and trotted off to the rails and their *saises*, who began to scrape and blanket and rub them at once.

'Whew!' said Corks, stiffening up to get all the tickle out of the big vulcanite[7] scraper. 'If we were playing pony for pony we'd bend those

Archangels double in half an hour. But they'll bring out fresh ones and fresh ones, and fresh ones after that – you see.'

'Who cares?' said Polaris. 'We've drawn first blood. Is my hock swelling?'

'Looks puffy,' said Corks. 'You must have got rather a wipe. Don't let it stiffen. You'll be wanted again in half an hour.'

'What's the game like?' said the Maltese Cat.

'Ground's like your shoe, except where they've put too much water on it,' said Kittiwynk. 'Then it's slippery. Don't play in the centre. There's a bog there. I don't know how their next four are going to behave, but we kept the ball hanging and made 'em lather for nothing. Who goes next? Two Arabs and a couple of countrybreds! That's bad. What a comfort it is to wash your mouth out!'

Kitty was talking with the neck of a leather-covered soda-water bottle between her teeth and trying to look over her withers at the same time. This gave her a very coquettish air.

'What's bad?' said Grey Dawn, giving to the girth and admiring his well-set shoulders.

'You Arabs can't gallop fast enough to keep yourselves warm – that's what Kitty means,' said Polaris, limping to show that his hock needed attention. 'Are you playing "back", Grey Dawn?'

'Looks like it,' said Grey Dawn, as Lutyens swung himself up. Powell mounted the Rabbit, a plain bay countrybred much like Corks, but with mulish ears. Macnamara took Faiz Ullah, a handy short-backed little red Arab with a long tail, and Hughes mounted Benami, an old and sullen brown beast, who stood over in front more than a polo-pony should.

'Benami looks like business,' said Shiraz. 'How's your temper, Ben?' The old campaigner hobbled off without answering, and the Maltese Cat looked at the new Archangel ponies prancing about on the ground. They were four beautiful blacks, and they saddled big enough and strong enough to eat the Skidars' team and gallop away with the meal inside them.

'Blinkers again,' said the Maltese Cat. 'Good enough!'

'They're chargers – cavalry chargers!' said Kittiwynk indignantly. '*They*'ll never see thirteen-three again.'

'They've all been fairly measured and they've all got their certificates,' said the Maltese Cat, 'or they wouldn't be here. We must take things as they come along, and keep our eyes on the ball.'

The game began, but this time the Skidars were penned to their own end of the ground, and the watching ponies did not approve of that.

'Faiz Ullah is shirking, as usual,' said Polaris, with a scornful grunt.

'Faiz Ullah is eating whip,' said Corks. They could hear the leather-thonged polo-quirt lacing the little fellow's well-rounded barrel. Then the Rabbit's shrill neigh came across the ground. 'I can't do all the work,' he cried.

'Play the game, don't talk,' the Maltese Cat whickered; and all the ponies wriggled with excitement, and the soldiers and the grooms gripped the railings and shouted. A black pony with blinkers had singled out old Benami, and was interfering with him in every possible way. They could see Benami shaking his head up and down and flapping his underlip.

'There'll be a fall in a minute,' said Polaris. 'Benami is getting stuffy.'

The game flickered up and down between goal-post and goal-post, and the black ponies were getting more confident as they felt they had the legs of the others. The ball was hit out of a little scrimmage, and Benami and the Rabbit followed it; Faiz Ullah only too glad to be quiet for an instant.

The blinkered black pony came up like a hawk, with two of his own side behind him, and Benami's eye glittered as he raced. The question was which pony should make way for the other; each rider was perfectly willing to risk a fall in a good cause. The black who had been driven nearly crazy by his blinkers trusted to his weight and his temper; but Benami knew how to apply his weight and how to keep his temper. They met, and there was a cloud of dust. The black was lying on his side with all the breath knocked out of his body. The Rabbit was a hundred yards up the ground with the ball, and Benami was sitting down. He had slid nearly ten yards, but he had had his revenge, and sat cracking his nostrils till the black pony rose.

'That's what you get for interfering. Do you want any more?' said Benami, and he plunged into the game. Nothing was done, because Faiz Ullah would not gallop, though Macnamara beat him whenever he could spare a second. The fall of the black pony had impressed his companions tremendously, and so the Archangels could not profit by Faiz Ullah's bad behaviour.

But as the Maltese Cat said, when time was called and the four came back blowing and dripping, Faiz Ullah ought to have been kicked all round Umballa. If he did not behave better next time, the Maltese Cat promised to pull out his Arab tail by the root and eat it.

There was no time to talk, for the third four were ordered out.

The third quarter of a game is generally the hottest, for each side thinks that the others must be pumped; and most of the winning play in a game is made about that time.

Lutyens took over the Maltese Cat with a pat and a hug, for Lutyens valued him more than anything else in the world. Powell had Shikast, a little grey rat with no pedigree and no manners outside polo; Macnamara mounted Bamboo, the largest of the team, and Hughes took Who's Who, *alias* The Animal. He was supposed to have Australian blood in his veins, but he looked like a clothes-horse, and you could whack him on the legs with an iron crowbar without hurting him.

They went out to meet the very flower of the Archangels' team, and when Who's Who saw their elegantly booted legs and their beautiful satiny skins he grinned a grin through his light, well-worn bridle.

'My word!' said Who's Who. 'We must give 'em a little football. Those gentlemen need a rubbing-down.'

'No biting,' said the Maltese Cat warningly, for once or twice in his career Who's Who had been known to forget himself in that way.

'Who said anything about biting? I'm not playing tiddlywinks. I'm playing the game.'

The Archangels came down like a wolf on the fold, for they were tired of football and they wanted polo. They got it and much more. Just after the game began, Lutyens hit a ball that was coming towards him rapidly, and it rose in the air, as a ball sometimes will, with the whirr of a frightened partridge. Shikast heard, but could not see it for the minute, though he looked everywhere and up into the air as the Maltese Cat had taught him. When he saw it ahead and overhead, he went forward with Powell as fast as he could put foot to ground. It was then that Powell, a quiet and level-headed man as a rule, became inspired and played a stroke which sometimes comes off successfully on a quiet afternoon of long practice. He took his stick in both hands, and standing up in his stirrups, swiped at the ball in the air, Manipur fashion. There was one second of paralysed astonishment, and then all four sides of the ground went up in a yell of applause and delight as the ball flew true (you could see the amazed Archangels ducking in their saddles to get out of the line of flight, and looking at it with open mouths), and the regimental pipes of the Skidars squealed from the railings as long as the pipers had breath.

Shikast heard the stroke; but he heard the head of the stick fly off at the same time. Nine hundred and ninety-nine ponies out of a thousand would have gone tearing on after the ball with a useless player pulling at their heads, but Powell knew him, and he knew Powell; and the instant he felt Powell's right leg shift a trifle on the saddle-flap he headed for the boundary, where a native officer was frantically waving a new stick. Before the shouts had ended Powell was armed again.

Once before in his life the Maltese Cat had heard that very same stroke played off his own back, and had profited by the confusion it made. This time he acted on experience, and leaving Bamboo to guard the goal in case of accidents, came through the others like a flash, head and tail low, Lutyens standing up to ease him – swept on and on before the other side knew what was the matter, and nearly pitched on his head between the Archangels' goal-posts as Lutyens tipped the ball in after a straight scurry of a hundred and fifty yards. If there was one thing more than another upon which the Maltese Cat prided himself it was on this quick, streaking kind of run half across the ground. He did not believe in taking balls round the field unless you were clearly over-matched. After this they gave the Archangels five minutes' football, and an expensive fast pony hates football because it rumples his temper.

Who's Who showed himself even better than Polaris in this game. He did not permit any wriggling away, but bored joyfully into the scrimmage as if he had his nose in a feed-box, and were looking for something nice. Little Shikast jumped on the ball the minute it got clear, and every time an Archangel pony followed it he found Shikast standing over it asking what was the matter.

'If we can live through this quarter,' said the Maltese Cat, 'I shan't care. Don't take it out of yourselves. Let *them* do the lathering.'

So the ponies, as their riders explained afterwards, 'shut up'. The Archangels kept them tied fast in front of their goal, but it cost the Archangels' ponies all that was left of their tempers; and ponies began to kick, and men began to repeat compliments, and they chopped at the legs of Who's Who, and he set his teeth and stayed where he was, and the dust stood up like a tree over the scrimmage till that hot quarter ended.

They found the ponies very excited and confident when they went to their *saises*; and the Maltese Cat had to warn them that the worst of the game was coming.

'Now *we* are all going in for the second time,' said he, 'and *they* are trotting out fresh ponies. You'll think you can gallop, but you'll find you can't; and then you'll be sorry.'

'But two goals to nothing is a halter-long lead,' said Kittiwynk, prancing.

'How long does it take to get a goal?' the Maltese Cat answered. 'For pity's sake, don't run away with the notion that the game is half-won just because we happen to be in luck now. They'll ride you into the grand-stand if they can. You mustn't give 'em a chance. Follow the ball.'

'Football, as usual?' said Polaris. 'My hock's half as big as a nose-bag.'

'Don't let them have a look at the ball if you can help it. Now leave me alone. I must get all the rest I can before the last quarter.'

He hung down his head and let all his muscles go slack; Shikast, Bamboo, and Who's Who copying his example.

'Better not watch the game,' he said. 'We aren't playing, and we shall only take it out of ourselves if we grow anxious. Look at the ground and pretend it's fly-time.'

They did their best, but it was hard advice to follow. The hoofs were drumming and the sticks were rattling all up and down the ground, and yells of applause from the English troops told that the Archangels were pressing the Skidars hard. The native soldiers behind the ponies groaned and grunted, and said things in undertones, and presently they heard a long-drawn shout and a clatter of hurrahs!

'One to the Archangels,' said Shikast, without raising his head. 'Time's nearly up. Oh, my sire and – dam!'

'Faiz Ullah,' said the Maltese Cat, 'if you don't play to the last nail in your shoes this time, I'll kick you on the ground before all the other ponies.'

'I'll do my best when my time comes,' said the little Arab sturdily.

The *saises* looked at each other gravely as they rubbed their ponies' legs. This was the first time when long purses began to tell, and everybody knew it. Kittiwynk and the others came back with the sweat dripping over their hoofs and their tails telling sad stories.

'They're better than we are,' said Shiraz. 'I knew how it would be.'

'Shut your big head,' said the Maltese Cat; 'we've one goal to the good yet.'

'Yes, but it's two Arabs and two countrybreds to play now,' said Corks. 'Faiz Ullah, remember!' He spoke in a biting voice.

As Lutyens mounted Grey Dawn he looked at his men, and they did not look pretty. They were covered with dust and sweat in streaks. Their yellow boots were almost black, their wrists were red and lumpy, and their eyes seemed two inches deep in their heads, but the expression in their eyes was satisfactory.

'Did you take anything at tiffin?' said Lutyens, and the team shook their heads. They were too dry to talk.

'All right. The Archangels did. They are worse pumped than we are.'

'They've got the better ponies,' said Powell. 'I shan't be sorry when this business is over.'

That fifth quarter was a sad one in every way. Faiz Ullah played like a little red demon; and the Rabbit seemed to be everywhere at once, and Benami rode straight at anything and everything that came in his way,

while the umpires on their ponies wheeled like gulls outside the shifting
game. But the Archangels had the better mounts – they had kept their
racers till late in the game – and never allowed the Skidars to play football.
They hit the ball up and down the width of the ground till Benami and
the rest were outpaced. Then they went forward, and time and again
Lutyens and Grey Dawn were just, and only just, able to send the ball
away with a long splitting backhander. Grey Dawn forgot that he was
an Arab; and turned from grey to blue as he galloped. Indeed, he forgot
too well, for he did not keep his eyes on the ground as an Arab should,
but stuck out his nose and scuttled for the dear honour of the game. They
had watered the ground once or twice between the quarters, and a careless
waterman had emptied the last of his skinful all in one place near the
Skidars' goal. It was close to the end of play, and for the tenth time Grey
Dawn was bolting after a ball when his near hind foot slipped on the
greasy mud and he rolled over and over, pitching Lutyens just clear of
the goal-post; and the triumphant Archangels made their goal. Then time
was called – two goals all; but Lutyens had to be helped up, and Grey
Dawn rose with his near hind leg strained somewhere.

'What's the damage?' said Powell, his arm round Lutyens.

'Collar-bone, of course,' said Lutyens between his teeth. It was the
third time he had broken it in two years, and it hurt him.

Powell and the others whistled. 'Game's up,' said Hughes.

'Hold on. We've five good minutes yet, and it isn't my right hand,'
said Lutyens. 'We'll stick it out.'

'I say,' said the captain of the Archangels, trotting up. 'Are you hurt,
Lutyens? We'll wait if you care to put in a substitute. I wish – I mean
– the fact is, you fellows deserve this game if any team does. Wish we
could give you a man or some of our ponies – or something.'

'You're awfully good, but we'll play it to a finish, I think.'

The captain of the Archangels stared for a little. 'That's not half
bad,' he said, and went back to his own side, while Lutyens borrowed
a scarf from one of his native officers and made a sling of it. Then an
Archangel galloped up with a big bath-sponge and advised Lutyens to
put it under his arm-pit to ease his shoulder, and between them they
tied up his left arm scientifically, and one of the native officers leaped
forward with four long glasses that fizzed and bubbled.

The team looked at Lutyens piteously, and he nodded. It was the
last quarter, and nothing would matter after that. They drank out the
dark golden drink, and wiped their moustaches, and things looked
more hopeful.

The Maltese Cat had pushed his nose into the front of Lutyens' shirt,
and was trying to say how sorry he was.

'He knows,' said Lutyens proudly. 'The little beggar knows. I've played him without a bridle before now – for fun.'

'It's no fun now,' said Powell. 'But we haven't a decent substitute.'

'No,' said Lutyens. 'It's the last quarter, and we've got to make our goal and win. I'll trust the Cat.'

'If you fall this time you'll suffer a little,' said Macnamara.

'I'll trust the Cat,' said Lutyens.

'You hear that?' said the Maltese Cat proudly to the others. 'It's worth while playing polo for ten years to have that said of you. Now then, my sons, come along. We'll kick up a little bit, just to show the Archangels *this* team haven't suffered.'

And, sure enough, as they went on to the ground the Maltese Cat, after satisfying himself that Lutyens was home in the saddle, kicked out three or four times, and Lutyens laughed. The reins were caught up anyhow in the tips of his strapped fingers, and he never pretended to rely on them. He knew the Cat would answer to the least pressure of the leg, and by way of showing off – for his shoulder hurt him very much – he bent the little fellow in a close figure-of-eight in and out between the goal-posts. There was a roar from the native officers and men, who dearly loved a piece of *dugabashi* [horse-trick work], as they called it, and the pipes very quietly and scornfully droned out the first bars of a common bazar-tune called 'Freshly Fresh and Newly New', just as a warning to the other regiments that the Skidars were fit. All the natives laughed.

'And now,' said the Cat, as they took their place, 'remember that this is the last quarter, and follow the ball!'

'Don't need to be told,' said Who's Who.

'Let me go on. All those people on all four sides will begin to crowd in – just as they did at Malta. You'll hear people calling out, and moving forward and being pushed back, and that is going to make the Archangel ponies very unhappy. But if a ball is struck to the boundary, you go after it, and let the people get out of your way. I hopped over the pole of a four-in-hand once, and picked a game out of the dust by it. Back me up when I run, and follow the ball.'

There was a sort of an all-round sound of sympathy and wonder as the last quarter opened, and then there began exactly what the Maltese Cat had foreseen. People crowded in close to the boundaries, and the Archangels' ponies kept looking sideways at the narrowing space. If you know how a man feels to be cramped at tennis – not because he wants to run out of the court, but because he likes to know that he can at a pinch – you will guess how ponies must feel when they are playing in a box of human beings.

'I'll bend some of those men if I can get away,' said Who's Who, as he rocketed behind the ball; and Bamboo nodded without speaking. They were playing the last ounce in them, and the Maltese Cat had left the goal undefended to join them. Lutyens gave him every order that he could to bring him back, but this was the first time in his career that the little wise grey had ever played polo on his own responsibility, and he was going to make the most of it.

'What are you doing here?' said Hughes, as the Cat crossed in front of him and rode off an Archangel.

'The Cat's in charge – mind the goal!' shouted Lutyens, and bowing forward hit the ball full, and followed on, forcing the Archangels towards their own goal.

'No football,' said the Cat. 'Keep the ball by the boundaries and cramp 'em. Play open order and drive 'em to the boundaries.'

Across and across the ground in big diagonals flew the ball, and whenever it came to a flying rush and a stroke close to the boundaries the Archangel ponies moved stiffly. They did not care to go headlong at a wall of men and carriages, though if the ground had been open they could have turned on a sixpence.

'Wriggle her up the sides,' said the Cat. 'Keep her close to the crowd. They hate the carriages. Shikast, keep her up this side.'

Shikast with Powell lay left and right behind the uneasy scuffle of an open scrimmage, and every time the ball was hit away Shikast galloped on it at such an angle that Powell was forced to hit it towards the boundary; and when the crowd had been driven away from that side, Lutyens would send the ball over to the other, and Shikast would slide desperately after it till his friends came down to help. It was billiards, and no football, this time – billiards in a corner pocket; and the cues were not well chalked.

'If they get us out in the middle of the ground they'll walk away from us. Dribble her along the sides,' cried the Cat.

So they dribbled all along the boundary, where a pony could not come on their right-hand side; and the Archangels were furious, and the umpires had to neglect the game to shout at the people to get back, and several blundering mounted policemen tried to restore order, all close to the scrimmage, and the nerves of the Archangels' ponies stretched and broke like cobwebs.

Five or six times an Archangel hit the ball up into the middle of the ground, and each time the watchful Shikast gave Powell his chance to send it back, and after each return, when the dust had settled, men could see that the Skidars had gained a few yards.

Every now and again there were shouts of ''Side! Off side!' from the spectators; but the teams were too busy to care, and the umpires had all they could do to keep their maddened ponies clear of the scuffle.

At last Lutyens missed a short easy stroke, and the Skidars had to fly back helter-skelter to protect their own goal, Shikast leading. Powell stopped the ball with a backhander when it was not fifty yards from the goal-posts, and Shikast spun round with a wrench that nearly hoisted Powell out of his saddle.

'Now's our last chance,' said the Cat, wheeling like a cockchafer on a pin. 'We've got to ride it out. Come along.'

Lutyens felt the little chap take a deep breath, and, as it were, crouch under his rider. The ball was hopping towards the right-hand boundary, an Archangel riding for it with both spurs and a whip; but neither spur nor whip would make his pony stretch himself as he neared the crowd. The Maltese Cat glided under his very nose, picking up his hind legs sharp, for there was not a foot to spare between his quarters and the other pony's bit. It was as neat an exhibition as fancy figure-skating. Lutyens hit with all the strength he had left, but the stick slipped a little in his hand, and the ball flew off to the left instead of keeping close to the boundary. Who's Who was far across the ground, thinking hard as he galloped. He repeated, stride for stride, the Cat's manoeuvres with another Archangel pony, nipping the ball away from under his bridle, and clearing his opponent by half a fraction of an inch, for Who's Who was clumsy behind. Then he drove away towards the right as the Maltese Cat came up from the left; and Bamboo held a middle course exactly between them. The three were making a sort of Government-broad-arrow-shaped attack; and there was only the Archangels' back to guard the goal; but immediately behind them were three Archangels racing all they knew, and mixed up with them was Powell, sending Shikast along on what he felt was their last hope. It takes a very good man to stand up to the rush of seven crazy ponies in the last quarter of a Cup game, when men are riding with their necks for sale, and the ponies are delirious. The Archangels' back missed his stroke, and pulled aside just in time to let the rush go by. Bamboo and Who's Who shortened stride to give the Maltese Cat room, and Lutyens got the goal with a clean, smooth, smacking stroke that was heard all over the field. But there was no stopping the ponies. They poured through the goal-posts in one mixed mob, winners and losers together, for the pace had been terrific. The Maltese Cat knew by experience what would happen, and, to save Lutyens, turned to the right with one last effort that strained a back-sinew beyond hope of repair. As he did so he heard the right-hand goal-post crack as a pony cannoned into it – crack, splinter, and fall like a mast. It had been sawed three parts through in case of accidents, but it upset the pony nevertheless, and he blundered into another, who blundered into the left-hand post, and then there was confusion and dust and wood. Bamboo was lying on the ground, seeing stars; an Archangel pony rolled beside him, breathless and angry; Shikast had sat down dog-fashion to avoid falling over the others, and was sliding along on his little bob-tail in a cloud of dust; and Powell was sitting on the ground, hammering with his stick and trying to cheer. All the others were shouting at the top of what was left of their voices, and the men who had been spilt were shouting too. As soon as the people saw no one was hurt, ten thousand native and English shouted and clapped and yelled, and before any one could stop them the pipers of the Skidars broke on to the ground, with all the native officers and men behind them, and marched up and down, playing a wild northern tune called 'Zakhme Bagān', and through the insolent blaring of the pipes and the high-pitched native yells you could hear the Archangels' band hammering 'For they are all jolly good fellows', and then reproachfully to the losing team, 'Ooh, Kafoozalum! Kafoozalum! Kafoozalum!'

Besides all these things and many more, there was a Commander-in-Chief, and an Inspector-General of Cavalry, and the principal Veterinary Officer in all India, standing on the top of a regimental coach, yelling like schoolboys; and Brigadiers and Colonels and Commissioners, and hundreds of pretty ladies joined the chorus. But the Maltese Cat stood with his head down, wondering how many legs were left to him; and Lutyens watched the men and ponies pick themselves out of the wreck of the two goal-posts, and he patted the Cat very tenderly.

'I say,' said the captain of the Archangels, spitting a pebble out of his mouth, 'will you take three thousand for that pony – as he stands?'

'No, thank you. I've an idea he's saved my life,' said Lutyens, getting off and lying down at full length. Both teams were on the ground too, waving their boots in the air, and coughing and drawing deep breaths, as the *saises* ran up to take away the ponies, and an officious water-carrier sprinkled the players with dirty water till they sat up.

'My Aunt!' said Powell, rubbing his back and looking at the stumps of the goal-posts. 'That was a game!'

They played it over again, every stroke of it, that night at the big dinner, when the Free-for-All Cup was filled and passed down the table, and emptied and filled again, and everybody made most eloquent speeches. About two in the morning, when there might have been some singing, a wise little, plain little, grey little head looked in through the open door.

'Hurrah! Bring him in,' said the Archangels; and his *sais*, who was very happy indeed, patted the Maltese Cat on the flank, and he limped in to the blaze of light and the glittering uniforms, looking for Lutyens. He was used to Messes, and officers' bedrooms, and places where ponies are not usually encouraged, and in his youth had jumped on and off a Mess-table for a bet. So he behaved himself very politely, and ate bread dipped in salt, and was petted all round the table, moving gingerly; and they drank his health, because he had done more to win the Cup than any man or horse on the ground.

That was glory and honour enough for the rest of his days, and the Maltese Cat did not complain much when his veterinary surgeon said that he would be no good for polo any more. When Lutyens married, his wife did not allow him to play, so he was forced to be an umpire; and his pony on these occasions was a flea-bitten grey with a neat polo-tail, lame all round, but desperately quick on his feet, and, as everybody knew, Past Pluperfect Prestissimo Player of the Game.

'THE FINEST STORY
IN THE WORLD'

'Or ever the knightly years were gone
With the old world to the grave,
I was King in Babylon
And you were a Christian Slave.'
W. E. HENLEY

His name was Charlie Mears. He was the only son of his mother, who was a widow, and he lived in the north of London, coming into the City every day to work in a bank. He was twenty years old and was full of aspirations. I met him in a public billiard-saloon where the marker called him by his first name, and he called the marker 'Bullseye'. Charlie explained, a little nervously, that he had only come to the place to look on; and since looking on at games of skill is not a cheap amusement for the young, I suggested that Charlie should go back to his mother.

That was our first step towards better acquaintance. He would call on me sometimes in the evenings instead of running about London with his fellow-clerks; and before long, speaking of himself as a young man must, he told me of his aspirations, which were all literary. He desired to make himself an undying name chiefly through verse, though he was not above sending stories of love and death to the penny-in-the-slot journals. It was my fate to sit still while Charlie read me poems of many hundred lines, and bulky fragments of plays that would surely shake the world. My reward was his unreserved confidence, and the self-revelations and troubles of a young man are almost as holy as those of a maiden. Charlie had never fallen in love, but was anxious to do so on the first opportunity. He believed in all things good and all things honourable, but at the same time was curiously careful to let me see that he knew his way about the world as befitted a bank-clerk on twenty-five shillings[1] a week. He rhymed 'dove' with 'love' and 'moon' with 'June', and devoutly believed that they had never so been rhymed before. The long lame gaps in his plays he filled up with hasty words of apology and description, and swept on, seeing all that he intended to do so clearly that he esteemed it already done, and turned to me for applause.

I fancy that his mother did not encourage his aspirations; and I know that his writing-table at home was the edge of his washstand.[2] This he told me almost at the outset of our acquaintance – when he was ravaging my bookshelves, and a little before I was implored to speak the truth as to his chances of 'writing something really great, you know'. Maybe I encouraged him too much, for, one night, he called on me, his eyes flaming with excitement, and said breathlessly: –

'Do you mind – can you let me stay here and write all this evening? I won't interrupt you, I won't really. There's no place for me to write in at my mother's.'

'What's the trouble?' I said, knowing well what that trouble was.

'I've a notion in my head that would make the most splendid story that was ever written. Do let me write it out here. It's *such* a notion!'

There was no resisting the appeal. I set him a table; he hardly thanked me, but plunged into his work at once. For half an hour the pen scratched without stopping. Then Charlie sighed and tugged his hair. The scratching grew slower, there were more erasures, and at last ceased. The finest story in the world would not come forth.

'It looks such awful rot now,' he said mournfully. 'And yet it seemed so good when I was thinking about it. What's wrong?'

I could not dishearten him by saying the truth. So I answered: 'Perhaps you don't feel in the mood for writing.'

'Yes, I do – except when I look at this stuff. Ugh!'

'Read me what you've done,' I said.

He read, and it was wondrous bad, and he paused at all the specially turgid sentences, expecting a little approval; for he was proud of those sentences, as I knew he would be.

'It needs compression,' I suggested cautiously.

'I hate cutting my things down. I don't think you could alter a word here without spoiling the sense. It reads better aloud than when I was writing it.'

'Charlie, you're suffering from an alarming disease afflicting a numerous class. Put the thing by, and tackle it again in a week.'

'I want to do it at once. What do you think of it?'

'How can I judge from a half-written tale? Tell me the story as it lies in your head.'

Charlie told, and in the telling there was everything that his ignorance had so carefully prevented from escaping into the written word. I looked at him, wondering whether it were possible that he did not know the originality, the power of the notion that had come in his way? It was distinctly a Notion among notions. Men had been puffed up with pride by ideas not a title as excellent and practicable. But Charlie babbled on serenely, interrupting the current of pure fancy with samples of horrible sentences which he purposed to use. I heard him out to the end. It would be folly to allow his thought to remain in his own inept hands; when I could do so much with it. Not all that could be done indeed; but oh, so much!

'What do you think?' he said at last. 'I fancy I shall call it "The Story of a Ship".'

'I think the idea's pretty good; but you won't be able to handle it for ever so long. Now I – '

'Would it be of any use to you? Would you care to take it? I should be proud,' said Charlie promptly.

There are few things sweeter in this world than the guileless, hot-headed, intemperate, open admiration of a junior. Even a woman in her blindest devotion does not fall into the gait of the man she adores, tilt her bonnet to the angle at which he wears his hat, or interlard her speech with his pet oaths. And Charlie did all these things. Still it was necessary to salve my conscience before I possessed myself of Charlie's thoughts.

'Let's make a bargain. I'll give you a fiver for the notion,' I said.

Charlie became a bank-clerk at once.

'Oh, that's impossible. Between two pals, you know, if I may call you so, and speaking as a man of the world, I couldn't. Take the notion if it's any use to you. I've heaps more.'

He had – none knew this better than I – but they were the notions of other men.

'Look at it as a matter of business – between men of the world,' I returned. 'Five pounds will buy you any number of poetry-books. Business is business, and you may be sure I shouldn't give that price unless – '

'Oh, if you put it *that* way,' said Charlie, visibly moved by the thought of the books. The bargain was clinched with an agreement that he should at unstated intervals come to me with all the notions that he possessed, should have a table of his own to write at, and unquestioned right to inflict upon me all his poems and fragments of poems. Then I said, 'Now tell me how you came by this idea.'

'It came by itself.' Charlie's eyes opened a little.

'Yes, but you told me a great deal about the hero that you must have read before somewhere.'

'I haven't any time for reading, except when you let me sit here, and on Sundays I'm on my bicycle or down the River all day. There's nothing wrong about the hero, is there?'

'Tell me again and I shall understand clearly. You say that your hero went pirating. How did he live?'

'He was on the lower deck of this ship-thing that I was telling you about.'

'What sort of ship?'

'It was the kind rowed with oars, and the sea spurts through the oar-holes, and the men row sitting up to their knees in water. Then there's a bench running down between the two lines of oars, and an overseer with a whip walks up and down the bench to make the men work.'

'How do you know that?'

'It's in my tale. There's a rope running overhead, looped to the upper deck, for the overseer to catch hold of when the ship rolls. When the overseer misses the rope once and falls among the rowers, remember the hero laughs at him and gets licked for it. He's chained to his oar, of course – the hero.'

'How is he chained?'

'With an iron band round his waist fixed to the bench he sits on, and a sort of handcuff on his left wrist chaining him to the oar. He's on the lower deck where the worst men are sent, and the only light comes from the hatchways and through the oar-holes. Can't you imagine the sunlight just squeezing through between the handle and the hole and wobbling about as the ship moves?'

'I can, but I can't imagine your imagining it.'

'How could it be any other way? Now you listen to me. The long oars on the upper deck are managed by four men to each bench, the lower ones by three, and the lowest of all by two. Remember it's quite dark on the lowest deck and all the men there go mad. When a man dies at his oar on that deck he isn't thrown overboard, but cut up in his chains and stuffed through the oar-hole in little pieces.'

'Why?' I demanded amazed, not so much at the information as the tone of command in which it was flung out.

'To save trouble and to frighten the others. It needs two overseers to drag a man's body up to the top deck; and if the men at the lower-deck oars were left alone, of course they'd stop rowing and try to pull up the benches by all standing up together in their chains.'

'You've a most provident imagination. Where have you been reading about galleys and galley-slaves?'

'Nowhere that I remember. I row a little when I get the chance. But, perhaps, if you say so, I may have read something.'

He went away shortly afterwards to deal with booksellers, and I wondered how a bank-clerk aged twenty could put into my hands with

a profligate abundance of detail, all given with absolute assurance, the
story of extravagant and bloodthirsty adventure, riot, piracy, and death
in unnamed seas. He had led his hero a desperate dance through revolt
against the overseers, to command of a ship of his own, and at last to
the establishment of a kingdom on an island 'somewhere in the sea,
you know'; and, delighted with my paltry five pounds, had gone out
to buy the notions of other men, that these might teach him how to
write. I had the consolation of knowing that this notion was mine by
right of purchase, and I thought that I could make something of it.

When next he came to me he was drunk – royally drunk on many
poets for the first time revealed to him. His pupils were dilated, his
words tumbled over each other, and he wrapped himself in quotations
– as a beggar would enfold himself in the purple of emperors. Most of
all was he drunk on Longfellow.[3]

'Isn't it splendid? Isn't it superb?' he cried, after hasty greetings.
'Listen to this:

> '"Wouldst thou," – so the helmsman answered,
> "Learn the secret of the sea?
> Only those who brave its dangers
> Comprehend its mystery!"

By Gum!

> '"Only those who brave its dangers
> Comprehend its mystery,"'

he repeated twenty times, walking up and down the room and forgetting
me. 'But *I* can understand it too,' he said to himself. 'I don't know how
to thank you for that fiver. And this; listen:

> "I remember the black wharves and the slips,
> And the sea-tides tossing free;
> And Spanish sailors with bearded lips,
> And the beauty and mystery of the ships,
> And the magic of the sea."

I haven't braved any dangers, but I feel as if I knew all about it.'

'You certainly seem to have a grip of the sea. Have you ever seen
it?'

'When I was a little chap I went to Brighton once. We used to live
in Coventry, though, before we came to London. I never saw it,

> '"When descends on the Atlantic
>   The gigantic
>   Storm-wind of the Equinox."'

He shook me by the shoulder to make me understand the passion that was shaking himself.

'When that storm comes,' he continued, 'I think that all the oars in the ship that I was talking about get broken, and the rowers have their chests smashed in by the oar-heads bucking. By the way, have you done anything with that notion of mine yet?'

'No. I was waiting to hear more of it from you. Tell me how in the world you're so certain about the fittings of the ship. You know nothing of ships?'

'I don't know. It's as real as anything to me until I try to write it down. I was thinking about it only last night in bed, after you had lent me *Treasure Island*; and I made up a whole lot of new things to go into the story.'

'What sort of things?'

'About the food the men ate; rotten figs and black beans and wine in a skin bag, passed from bench to bench.'

'Was the ship built so long ago as *that*?'

'As what? I don't know whether it was long ago or not. It's only a notion, but sometimes it seems just as real as if it was true. Do I bother you with talking about it?'

'Not in the least. Did you make up anything else?'

'Yes, but it's nonsense.' Charlie flushed a little.

'Never mind; let's hear about it.'

'Well, I was thinking over the story, and after a while I got out of bed and wrote down on a piece of paper the sort of stuff the men might be supposed to scratch on their oars with the edges of their handcuffs. It seemed to make the thing more lifelike. It *is* so real to me, y' know.'

'Have you the paper on you?'

'Ye–es, but what's the use of showing it? It's only a lot of scratches. All the same, we might have 'em reproduced in the book on the front page.'

'I'll attend to those details. Show me what your men wrote.'

He pulled out of his pocket a sheet of notepaper, with a single line of scratches upon it, and I put this carefully away.

'What is it supposed to mean in English?' I said.

'Oh, I don't know. I mean it to mean "I'm beastly tired." It's great nonsense,' he repeated, 'but all those men in the ship seem as real as real people to me. *Do* do something to the notion soon. I should like to see it written and printed.'

'But all you've told me would make a long book.'

'Make it then. You've only to sit down and write it out.'

'Give me a little time. Have you any more notions?'

'Not just now. I'm reading all the books I've bought. They're splendid.'

When he had left I looked at the sheet of notepaper with the inscription upon it. Then I took my head tenderly between both hands, to make certain that it was not coming off or turning round. Then ... but there seemed to be no interval between quitting my rooms and finding myself arguing with a policeman outside a door marked *Private* in a corridor of the British Museum. All I demanded, as politely as possible, was 'the Greek antiquities man'. The policeman knew nothing except the rules of the Museum, and it became necessary to forage through all the houses and offices inside the gates. An elderly gentleman called away from his lunch put an end to my search by holding the notepaper between finger and thumb and sniffing at it scornfully.

'What does this mean? H'mm,' said he. 'So far as I can ascertain it is an attempt to write extremely corrupt Greek on the part' – here he glared at me with intention – 'of an extremely illiterate – ah – person.' He read slowly from the paper, '*Pollock, Erckmann, Tauchnitz, Henniker*'[4] – four names familiar to me.

'Can you tell me what the corruption is supposed to mean – the gist of the thing?' I asked.

'"I have been – many times – overcome with weariness in this particular employment." That is the meaning.' He returned me the paper, and I fled without a word of thanks, explanation, or apology.

I might have been excused for forgetting much. To me of all men had been given the chance to write the most marvellous tale in the world, nothing less than the story of a Greek galley-slave, as told by himself. Small wonder that his dreaming had seemed real to Charlie! The Fates that are so careful to shut the doors of each successive life behind us had, in this case, been neglectful, and Charlie was looking, though that he did not know, where never man had been permitted to look with full knowledge since Time began. Above all, he was absolutely ignorant of the knowledge sold to me for five pounds; and he would retain that ignorance, for bank-clerks do not understand metempsychosis,[5] and a sound commercial education does not include Greek. He would supply me – here I capered among the dumb gods of Egypt and laughed in their battered faces – with material to make my tale sure – so sure that the world would hail it as an impudent and vamped fiction. And I – I alone would know that it was absolutely and literally true. I – I alone held this jewel to my hand for the cutting and polishing!

Therefore I danced again among the gods of the Egyptian Court till a policeman saw me and took steps in my direction.

It remained now only to encourage Charlie to talk, and here there was no difficulty. But I had forgotten those accursed books of poetry. He came to me time after time, as useless as a surcharged phonograph – drunk on Byron, Shelley, or Keats. Knowing now what the boy had been in his past lives, and desperately anxious not to lose one word of his babble, I could not hide from him my respect and interest. He misconstrued both into respect for the present soul of Charlie Mears, to whom life was as new as it was to Adam, and interest in his readings; and stretched my patience to breaking-point by reciting poetry – not his own now, but that of others. I wished every English poet blotted out of the memory of mankind. I blasphemed the mightiest names of song because they had drawn Charlie from the path of direct narrative, and would, later, spur him to imitate them; but I choked down my impatience until the first flood of enthusiasm should have spent itself and the boy returned to his dreams.

'What's the use of my telling you what *I* think, when these chaps wrote things for the angels to read?' he growled, one evening. 'Why don't *you* write something like theirs?'

'I don't think you're treating me quite fairly,' I said, speaking under strong restraint.

'I've given you the story,' he said shortly, replunging into 'Lara'.[6]

'But I want the details.'

'The things I make up about that damned ship that you call a galley? They're quite easy. You can just make 'em up for yourself. Turn up the gas a little; I want to go on reading.'

I could have broken the gas-globe over his head for his amazing stupidity. I could indeed make up things for myself did I only know what Charlie did not know that he knew. But since the doors were shut behind me I could only wait his youthful pleasure and strive to keep him in good temper. One minute's want of guard might spoil a priceless revelation: now and again he would toss his books aside – he kept them in my rooms, for his mother would have been shocked at the waste of good money had she seen them – and launched into his sea-dreams. Again I cursed all the poets of England. The plastic mind of the bank-clerk had been overlaid, coloured, and distorted by that which he had read, and the result as delivered was a confused tangle of other voices most like the mutter and hum through a City telephone in the busiest part of the day.

He talked of the galley – his own galley had he but known it – with illustrations borrowed from 'The Bride of Abydos'. He pointed the experiences of his hero with quotations from 'The Corsair', and threw in deep and desperate moral reflections from 'Cain' and 'Manfred', expecting me to use them all. Only when the talk turned on Longfellow were the jarring cross-currents dumb, and I knew that Charlie was speaking the truth as he remembered it.

'What do you think of this?' I said one evening, as soon as I understood the medium in which his memory worked best, and, before he could expostulate, read him nearly the whole of 'The Saga of King Olaf'![7]

He listened open-mouthed, flushed, his hands drumming on the back of the sofa where he lay, till I came to the Song of Einar Tamberskelver and the verse:

> 'Einar then, the arrow taking
>   From the loosened string,
> Answered, "That was Norway breaking
>   From thy hand, O King!"'

He gasped with pure delight of sound.

'That's better than Byron, a little?' I ventured.

'Better! Why, it's *true*! How could he have known?' I went back and repeated:

> '"What was that?" said Olaf, standing
>   On the quarter-deck.
> "Something heard I like the stranding
>   Of a shattered wreck."'

'How could he have known how the ships crash and the oars rip out and go *z-zzp* all along the line? Why, only the other night . . . But go back, please, and read "The Skerry of Shrieks" again.'

'No, I'm tired. Let's talk. What happened the other night?'

'I had an awful dream about that galley of ours. I dreamed I was drowned in a fight. You see, we ran alongside another ship in harbour. The water was dead still except where our oars whipped it up. You know where I always sit in the galley?' He spoke haltingly at first, under a fine English fear of being laughed at.

'No. That's news to me,' I answered meekly, my heart beginning to beat.

'On the fourth oar from the bow on the right side on the upper deck. There were four of us at that oar, all chained. I remember watching the water and trying to get my handcuffs off before the row began. Then we closed up on the other ship, and all their fighting-men jumped over our bulwarks, and my bench broke and I was pinned down with the three other fellows on top of me, and the big oar jammed across our backs.'

'Well?' Charlie's eyes were alive and alight. He was looking at the wall behind my chair.

'I don't know how we fought. The men were trampling all over my back, and I lay low. Then our rowers on the left side – tied to their oars, you know – began to yell and back water. I could hear the water sizzle, and we spun round like a cockchafer,[8] and I knew, lying where I was, that there was a galley coming up bow-on to ram us on the left side. I could just lift up my head and see her sail over the bulwarks. We wanted to meet her bow to bow, but it was too late. We could only turn a little bit because the galley on our right had hooked herself on to us and stopped our moving. Then, by Gum! there was a crash! Our left oars began to break as the other galley, the moving one, y'know, stuck her nose into them. Then the lower-deck oars shot up through the deck planking, butt first, and one of them jumped clear up into the air and came down again close at my head.'

'How was that managed?'

'The moving galley's bow was plunking them back through their own oar-holes, and I could hear no end of a shindy on the decks below. Then her nose caught us nearly in the middle, and we tilted sideways, and the fellows in the right-hand galley unhitched their hooks and ropes, and threw things on to our upper deck – arrows, and hot pitch or something that stung, and we went up and up and up on the left side, and the right side dipped, and I twisted my head round and saw the water stand still as it topped the right bulwarks. Then it curled over and crashed down on the whole lot of us on the right side, and I felt it hit my back, and I woke.'

'One minute, Charlie. When the sea topped the bulwarks, what did it look like?' I had my reasons for asking. A man of my acquaintance had once gone down with a leaking ship in a still sea, and had seen the water-level pause for an instant ere it fell on the deck.

'It looked just like a banjo-string drawn tight, and it seemed to stay there for years,' said Charlie.

Exactly! The other man had said: 'It looked like a silver wire laid down along the bulwarks, and I thought it was never going to break.' He had paid everything except the bare life for this little valueless piece of knowledge, and I had travelled ten thousand weary miles to meet him and take his knowledge at second hand. But Charlie, the bank-clerk on twenty-five shillings a week, who had never been out of sight of a made road, knew it all. It was no consolation to me that once in his lives he had been forced to die for his gains. I also must have died scores of times, but behind me, because I could have used my knowledge, the doors were shut.

'And then?' I said, trying to put away the devil of envy.

'The funny thing was, though, in all the row I didn't feel a bit astonished or frightened. It seemed as if I'd been in a good many fights, because I told my next man so when the row began. But that cad of an overseer on my deck wouldn't unloose our chains and give us a chance. He always said that we'd all be set free after a battle, but we never were – we never were.' Charlie shook his head mournfully.

'What a scoundrel!'

'I should say he was. He never gave us enough to eat, and sometimes we were so thirsty that we used to drink salt water. I can taste that salt water still.'

'Now tell me something about the harbour where the fight was fought.'

'I didn't dream about that. I know it was a harbour, though; because we were tied up to a ring on a white wall and all the face of the stone under water was covered with wood to prevent our ram getting chipped when the tide made us rock.'

'That's curious. Our hero commanded the galley, didn't he?'

'Didn't he just! He stood by the bows and shouted like a good 'un. He was the man who killed the overseer.'

'But you were all drowned together, Charlie, weren't you?'

'I can't make that fit quite,' he said, with a puzzled look. 'The galley must have gone down with all hands, and yet I fancy that the hero went on living afterwards. Perhaps he climbed into the attacking ship. I wouldn't see that, of course. I was dead, you know.'

He shivered slightly and protested that he could remember no more.

I did not press him further, but to satisfy myself that he lay in ignorance of the workings of his own mind, deliberately introduced him to Mortimer Collins's *Transmigration*,[9] and gave him a sketch of the plot before he opened the pages.

'What rot it all is!' he said frankly, at the end of an hour. 'I don't understand his nonsense about the Red Planet Mars and the King, and the rest of it. Chuck me the Longfellow again.'

I handed him the book and wrote out as much as I could remember of his description of the sea-fight, appealing to him from time to time for confirmation of fact or detail. He would answer without raising his eyes from the book, as assuredly as though all his knowledge lay before him on the printed page. I spoke under the normal key of my voice that the current might not be broken, and I knew that he was not aware of what he was saying, for his thoughts were out on the sea with Longfellow.

'Charlie,' I asked, 'when the rowers on the galleys mutinied how did they kill their overseers?'

'Tore up the benches and brained 'em. That happened when a heavy sea was running. An overseer on the lower deck slipped from the centre plank and fell among the rowers. They choked him to death against the side of the ship with their chained hands quite quietly, and it was too dark for the other overseer to see what had happened. When he asked, he was pulled down too and choked, and the lower deck fought their way up deck by deck, with the pieces of the broken benches banging behind 'em. How they howled!'

'And what happened after that?'

'I don't know. The hero went away – red hair and red beard and all. That was after he had captured our galley, I think.'

The sound of my voice irritated him, and he motioned slightly with his left hand as a man does when interruption jars.

'You never told me he was red-headed before, or that he captured your galley,' I said, after a discreet interval.

Charlie did not raise his eyes.

'He was as red as a red bear,' said he abstractedly. 'He came from the North; they said so in the galley when he asked for rowers – not slaves, but free men. Afterwards – years and years afterwards – news came from another ship, or else he came back – '

His lips moved in silence. He was rapturously retasting some poem before him.

'Where had he been, then?' I was almost whispering that the sentence might come gently to whichever section of Charlie's brain was working on my behalf.

'To the Beaches – the Long and Wonderful Beaches!' was the reply after a minute of silence.

'To Furdurstrandi?'[10] I asked, tingling from head to foot.

'Yes, to Furdurstrandi.' He pronounced the word in a new fashion. 'And I too saw – ' The voice failed.

'Do you know what you have said?' I shouted incautiously.

He lifted his eyes, fully roused now. 'No!' he snapped. 'I wish you'd let a chap go on reading. Hark to this:

> '"But Othere, the old sea-captain,
>   He neither paused nor stirred
> Till the King listened, and then
>   Once more took up his pen
>   And wrote down every word.

> '"And to the King of the Saxons,
>   In witness of the truth,
>   Raising his noble head,
>   He stretched his brown hand and said,
>   'Behold this walrus-tooth!' "[11]

By Jove, what chaps those must have been, to go sailing all over the shop never knowing where they'd fetch the land! Hah!'

'Charlie,' I pleaded, 'if you'll only be sensible for a minute or two I'll make our hero in our tale every inch as good as Othere.'

'Umph! Longfellow wrote that poem. I don't care about writing things any more. I want to read.' He was thoroughly out of tune now, and raging over my own ill-luck, I left him.

Conceive yourself at the door of the world's treasure-house guarded by a child – an idle, irresponsible child playing knuckle-bones[12] – on whose favour depends the gift of the key, and you will imagine onehalf my torment. Till that evening Charlie had spoken nothing that might not lie within the experiences of a Greek galley-slave. But now, or there was no virtue in books, he had talked of some desperate adventure of the Vikings, of Thorfinn Karlsefne's sailing to Wineland,[13] which is America, in the ninth or tenth century. The battle in the harbour he had seen; and his own death he had described. But this was a much more startling plunge into the past. Was it possible that he had skipped half-a-dozen lives, and was then dimly remembering some episode of a thousand years later? It was a maddening jumble, and the worst of it was that Charlie Mears in his normal condition was the last person in the world to clear it up. I could only wait and watch, but I went to bed that night full of the wildest imaginings. There was nothing that was not possible if Charlie's detestable memory only held good.

I might rewrite the Saga of Thorfinn Karlsefne as it had never been written before; might tell the story of the first discovery of America, myself the discoverer. But I was entirely at Charlie's mercy, and so long as there was a three-and-sixpenny Bohn volume[14] within his reach Charlie would not tell. I dared not curse him openly. I hardly dared jog his memory, for I was dealing with the experiences of a thousand years ago, told through the mouth of a boy of to-day; and a boy is affected by every change of tone and gust of opinion, so that he must lie even when he most desires to speak the truth.

I saw no more of Charlie for nearly a week. When next I met him it was in Gracechurch Street with a bill-book[15] chained to his waist. Business took him over London Bridge, and I accompanied him. He was very full of the importance of that book and magnified it. As we passed over the Thames we paused to look at a steamer unloading great slabs of white and brown marble. A barge drifted under the steamer's stern and a lonely ship's cow in that barge bellowed. Charlie's face changed from the face of the bank-clerk to that of an unknown and – though he would not have believed this – a much shrewder man. He flung out his arm across the parapet of the bridge and, laughing very loudly, said: –

'When they heard *our* bulls bellow the Skroelings ran away!'

I waited only for an instant, but the barge and the cow had disappeared under the bows of the steamer before I answered.

'Charlie, what do you suppose are Skroelings?'

'Never heard of 'em before. They sound like a new kind of sea-gull. What a chap you are for asking questions!' he replied. 'I have to go to the cashier of the Omnibus Company yonder. Will you wait for me and we can lunch somewhere together? I've a notion for a poem.'

'No, thanks. I'm off. You're sure you know nothing about Skroelings?'

'Not unless he's been entered for the Liverpool Handicap.' He nodded and disappeared in the crowd.

Now it is written in the Saga of Eric the Red or that of Thorfinn Karlsefne, that nine hundred years ago, when Karlsefne's galleys came to Leif's booths, which Leif had erected in the unknown land called Markland, which may or may not have been Rhode Island, the Skroelings – and the Lord He knows who these may or may not have been! – came to trade with the Vikings, and ran away because they were frightened at the bellowing of the cattle which Thorfinn had brought with him in the ships. But what in the world could a Greek slave know of that affair? I wandered up and down among the streets trying to unravel the mystery, and the more I considered it the more baffling it grew. One thing only seemed certain, and that certainty took away my breath for the moment. If I came to full knowledge of anything at all, it would not be one life of the soul in Charlie Mears's body, but half-a-dozen – half-a-dozen several and separate existences spent on blue water in the morning of the world!

Then I reviewed the situation.

Obviously if I used my knowledge I should stand alone and unapproachable until all men were as wise as myself. That would be something, but, manlike, I was ungrateful. It seemed bitterly unfair that Charlie's memory should fail me when I needed it most. Great Powers Above! – I looked up at them through the fog-smoke – did the Lords of Life and Death know what this meant to me? Nothing less than eternal fame of the best kind, that comes from One, and is shared by one alone. I would be content – remembering Clive,[16] I stood astounded at my own moderation – with the mere right to tell one story, to work out one little contribution to the light literature of the day. If Charlie were permitted full recollection for one hour – for sixty short minutes – of existences that had extended over a thousand years – I would forgo all profit and honour from all that I should make of his speech. I would take no share in the commotion that would follow throughout the particular corner of the earth that calls itself 'the world'. The thing should be put forth anonymously. Nay, I would make other men believe that they had written it. They would hire bull-hided, self-advertising Englishmen to bellow it abroad. Preachers would found a fresh conduct of life upon it, swearing that it was new and that they had lifted the fear of death from all mankind. Every Orientalist in Europe would patronise it discursively with Sanskrit and Pali texts. Terrible women would invent unclean variants of the men's belief for the elevation of their sisters. Churches and religions would war over it. Between the hailing and restarting of an omnibus I foresaw the scuffles that would arise among half-a-dozen denominations all professing 'the doctrine of the True Metempsychosis as applied to the world and the New Era'; and saw, too, the respectable English newspapers shying, like frightened kine, over the beautiful simplicity of the tale. The mind leaped forward a hundred – two hundred – a thousand years. I saw with sorrow that men would mutilate and garble the story; that rival creeds would turn it up-side-down till, at last, the Western world, which clings to the dread of Death more closely than the hope of Life, would set it aside as an interesting superstition and stampede after some faith so long forgotten that it seemed altogether new. Upon this I changed the terms of the bargain that I would make with the Lords of Life and Death. Only let me know, let me write, the story with sure knowledge that I wrote the truth, and I would burn the manuscript as a solemn sacrifice. Five minutes after the last line was written I would destroy it all. But I must be allowed to write it with absolute certainty.

There was no answer. The flaming colours of an Aquarium poster[17] caught my eye, and I wondered whether it would be wise or prudent to lure Charlie into the hands of the professional mesmerist there, and whether, if he were under his power, he would speak of his past lives. If he did, and if people believed him . . . but Charlie would be frightened and flustered, or made conceited by the interviews. In either case he would begin to lie through fear or vanity. He was safest in my own hands.

'They are very funny fools, your English,' said a voice at my elbow, and turning round I recognised a casual acquaintance, a young Bengali law student, called Grish Chunder, whose father had sent him to England to become civilised. The old man was a retired native official, and on an income of five pounds a month contrived to allow his son two hundred pounds a year, and the run of his teeth in a city where he could pretend to be the cadet of a royal house, and tell stories of the brutal Indian bureaucrats who ground the faces of the poor.

Grish Chunder was a young, fat, full-bodied Bengali, dressed with scrupulous care in frock-coat, tall hat, light trousers, and tan gloves. But I had known him in the days when the brutal Indian Government paid for his university education, and he contributed cheap sedition to the *Sachi Durpan*, and intrigued with the wives of his fourteen-year-old schoolmates.

'That is very funny and very foolish,' he said, nodding at the poster. 'I am going down to the Northbrook Club.[18] Will you come too?'

I walked with him for some time. 'You are not well,' he said. 'What is there on your mind? You do not talk.'

'Grish Chunder, you've been too well educated to believe in a God, haven't you?'

'Oah, yes, *here*! But when I go home I must conciliate popular superstition, and make ceremonies of purification, and my women will anoint idols.'

'And hang up *tulsi*[19] and feast the *purohit*,[20] and take you back into caste again, and make a good *khuttri*[21] of you again, you advanced Freethinker. And you'll eat *desi*[22] food, and like it all, from the smell in the courtyard to the mustard oil over you.'

'I shall very much like it,' said Grish Chunder unguardedly. 'Once a Hindu – always a Hindu. But I like to know what the English think they know.'

'I'll tell you something that one Englishman knows. It's an old tale to you.'

I began to tell the story of Charlie in English, but Grish Chunder put a question in the vernacular, and the history went forward naturally in the tongue best suited for its telling. After all, it could never have been told in English. Grish Chunder heard me, nodding from time to time, and then came up to my rooms, where I finished the tale.

'*Beshak*,' he said philosophically. '*Lekin darwaza band hai*. [Without doubt. But the door is shut.] I have heard of this remembering of previous existences among my people. It is, of course, an old tale with us, but to happen to an Englishman – a cow-fed *Mlech*[23] – an outcaste. By Jove, that is *most* peculiar!'

'Outcaste yourself, Grish Chunder! You eat cow-beef every day. Let's think the thing over. The boy remembers his incarnations.'

'Does he know that?' said Grish Chunder quietly, swinging his legs as he sat on my table. He was speaking in his English now.

'He does not know anything. Would I speak to you if he did? Go on!'

'There is no going on at all. If you tell *that* to your friends they will say you are mad and put it in the papers. Suppose, now, you prosecute for libel.'

'Let's leave that out of the question entirely. Is there any chance of his being made to speak?'

'There is a chance. Oah, yess! But *if* he spoke it would mean that all this world would end now – *instanto* – fall down on your head. These things are not allowed, you know. As I said, the door is shut.'

'Not a ghost of a chance?'

'How can there be? You are a Christi-án, and it is forbidden to eat, in your books, of the Tree of Life, or else you would never die. How shall you all fear death if you all know what your friend does not know that he knows? I am afraid to be kicked, but I am not afraid to die, because I know what I know. You are not afraid to be kicked, but you are afraid to die. If you were not, by God! you English would be all over the shop in an hour, upsetting the balances of power, and making commotions. It would not be good. But no fear. He will remember a little and a little less, and he will call it dreams. Then he will forget altogether. When I passed my First Arts Examination in Calcutta that was all in the cram-book on Wordsworth.[24] "Trailing clouds of glory", you know.'

'This seems to be an exception to the rule.'

'There are no exceptions to rules. Some are not so hard-looking as others, but they are all the same when you touch. If this friend of yours said so-and-so and so-and-so, indicating that he remembered all his lost lives, or one piece of a lost life, he would not be in the bank another hour. He would be what you call sacked because he was mad, and they would send him to an asylum for lunatics. You can see that, my friend.'

'Of course I can, but I wasn't thinking of him. His name need never appear in the story.'

'Ah! I see. That story will never be written. You can try.'

'I am going to.'

'For your own credit and for the sake of money, *of* course?'

'No. For the sake of writing the story. On my honour, that will be all.'

'Even then there is no chance. You cannot play with the Gods. It is a very pretty story now. As they say, Let it go on that – I mean, at that. Be quick; he will not last long.'

'How do you mean?'

'What I say. He has never, so far, thought about a woman.'

'Hasn't he, though!' I remembered some of Charlie's confidences.

'I mean, no woman has thought about him. When that comes – *bus* – *hogya*[25] – all up! I know. There are millions of women here. House-maids, for instance. They kiss you behind doors.'

I winced at the thought of my story being ruined by a housemaid. And yet nothing was more probable.

Grish Chunder grinned.

'Yes – also pretty girls – cousins of his house, and perhaps *not* of his house. One kiss that he gives back again and remembers will cure all this nonsense, or else –'

'Or else what? Remember he does not know that he knows.'

'I know that. Or else, if nothing happens he will become immersed in the trade and the financial speculation like the rest. It must be so. You can see that it must be so. But the woman will come first, *I* think.'

There was a rap at the door, and Charlie charged in impetuously. He had been released from the office, and by the look in his eyes I could see that he had come over for a long talk; most probably with poems in his pockets. Charlie's poems were very wearying, but sometimes they led him to speak about the galley.

Grish Chunder looked at him keenly for a minute.

'I beg your pardon,' Charlie said uneasily; 'I didn't know you had anyone with you.'

'I am going,' said Grish Chunder.

He drew me into the lobby as he departed.

'That is your man,' he said quickly. 'I tell you he will never speak all you wish. That is rot – bosh. But he would be most good to make to see things. Suppose now we pretend that it was only play' – I had never seen Grish Chunder so excited – 'and pour the ink-pool into his hand. Eh, what do you think? I tell you that he could see *anything* that a man could see. Let me get the ink and the camphor. He is a seer and he will tell us very many things.'

'He may be all you say, but I'm not going to trust him to your gods and devils.'

'It will not hurt him. He will only feel a little stupid and dull when he wakes up. You have seen boys look into the ink-pool before.'

'That is the reason why I am not going to see it any more. You'd better go, Grish Chunder.'

He went, insisting far down the staircase that it was throwing away my only chance of looking into the future.

This left me unmoved, for I was concerned for the past, and no peering of hypnotised boys into mirrors and ink-pools would help me to that. But I recognised Grish Chunder's point of view and sympathised with it.

'What a big black brute that was!' said Charlie, when I returned to him. 'Well, look here, I've just done a poem. Did it instead of playing dominoes after lunch. May I read it?'

'Let me read it to myself.'

'Then you miss the proper expression. Besides, you always make my things sound as if the rhymes were all wrong.'

'Read it aloud, then. You're like the rest of 'em.'

Charlie mouthed me his poem, and it was not much worse than the average of his verses. He had been reading his books faithfully, but he was not pleased when I told him that I preferred my Longfellow undiluted with Charlie.

Then we began to go through the MS line by line, Charlie parrying every objection and correction with:

'Yes, that may be better, but you don't catch what I'm driving at.'

Charlie was, in one way at least, very like one kind of poet.

There was a pencil scrawl at the back of the paper, and 'What's that?' I said.

'Oh, that's not poetry at all. It's some rot I wrote last night before I went to bed, and it was too much bother to hunt for rhymes; so I made it a sort of blank verse instead.'

Here is Charlie's 'blank verse':

'We pulled for you when the wind was against us and the sails were low.
    Will you never let us go?
We ate bread and onions when you took towns, or ran aboard quickly when you were beaten back by the foe.
The captains walked up and down the deck in fair weather singing songs, but we were below.
We fainted with our chins on the oars and you did not see that we were idle, for we still swung to and fro.
    Will you never let us go?
The salt made the oar-handles like shark-skin; our knees were cut to the bone with salt-cracks; our hair was stuck to our foreheads; and our lips were cut to our gums, and you whipped us because we could not row.
    Will you never let us go?
But in a little time we shall run out of the portholes as the water runs along the oar-blade, and though you tell the others to row after

us you will never catch us till you catch the oar-thresh and tie up the
winds in the belly of the sail. Aho!

    Will you never let us go?'

'H'm. What's oar-thresh, Charlie?'

'The water washed up by the oars. That's the sort of song they might
sing in the galley, y' know. Aren't you ever going to finish that story
and give me some of the profits?'

'It depends on yourself. If you'd only told me more about your hero
in the first instance it might have been finished by now. You're so hazy
in your notions.'

'I only want to give you the general notion of it – the knocking about
from place to place and the fighting and all that. Can't you fill in the
rest yourself? Make the hero save a girl on a pirate-galley and marry
her or do something.'

'You're a really helpful collaborator. I suppose the hero went through
some few adventures before he married.'

'Well, then, make him a very artful card – a low sort of man – a sort
of political man who went about making treaties and breaking them
– a black-haired chap who hid behind the mast when the fighting
began.'

'But you said the other day that he was red-haired.'

'I couldn't have. Make him black-haired, of course. You've no
imagination.'

Seeing that I had just discovered the entire principles upon which
the half-memory falsely called imagination is based, I felt entitled to
laugh, but forbore for the sake of the tale.

'You're right. *You*'re the man with imagination. A black-haired chap
in a decked ship,' I said.

'No, an open ship – like a big boat.'

This was maddening.

'Your ship has been built and designed, closed and decked in; you
said so yourself,' I protested.

'No, no, not that ship. That was open or half-decked because – By
Jove, you're right. You made me think of the hero as a red-haired chap.
Of course, if he were red, the ship would be an open one with painted
sails.'

Surely, I thought, he would remember now that he had served in
two galleys at least – in a three-decked Greek one under the black-haired
'political man', and again in a Viking's open sea-serpent under the man
'red as a red bear' who went to Markland. The Devil prompted me to
speak.

'Why "of course", Charlie?' said I.

'I don't know. Are you making fun of me?'

The current was broken for the time being. I took up a note-book and pretended to make many entries in it.

'It's a pleasure to work with an imaginative chap like yourself,' I said, after a pause. 'The way that you've brought out the character of the hero is simply wonderful.'

'Do you think so?' he answered, with a pleased flush. 'I often tell myself that there's more in me than my mo – than people think.'

'There's an enormous amount in you.'

'Then, won't you let me send an essay on "The Ways of Bank-Clerks" to *Tit-Bits*,[26] and get the guinea prize?'

'That wasn't exactly what I meant, old fellow: perhaps it would be better to wait a little and go ahead with the galley-story.'

'Ah, but I shan't get the credit of that. *Tit-Bits* would publish my name and address if I win. What are you grinning at? They would.'

'I know it. Suppose you go for a walk. I want to look through my notes about our story.'

Now this reprehensible youth who left me, a little hurt and put aback, might for aught he or I knew have been one of the crew of the *Argo*[27] – had been certainly slave or comrade to Thorfinn Karlsefne. Therefore he was deeply interested in guinea competitions. Remembering what Grish Chunder had said I laughed aloud. The Lords of Life and Death would never allow Charlie Mears to speak with full knowledge of his pasts, and I must even piece out what he had told me with my own poor inventions while Charlie wrote of the ways of bank-clerks.

I got together and placed on one file all my notes; and the net result was not cheering. I read them a second time. There was nothing that might not have been compiled at second hand from other people's books – except, perhaps, the story of the fight in the harbour. The adventures of a Viking had been written many times before; the history of a Greek galley-slave was no new thing, and though I wrote both, who could challenge or confirm the accuracy of my details? I might as well tell a tale of two thousand years hence. The Lords of Life and Death were as cunning as Grish Chunder had hinted. They would allow nothing to escape that might trouble or make easy the minds of men. Though I was convinced of this, yet I could not leave the tale alone. Exaltation followed reaction, not once, but twenty times in the next few weeks. My moods varied with the March sunlight and flying clouds. By night or in the beauty of a spring morning I perceived that I could write that tale and shift continents thereby. In the wet windy afternoons I saw that the tale might indeed be written, but would be nothing more than a faked, false-varnished, sham-rusted piece of Wardour Street work[28] in the end. Then I blessed Charlie in many ways – though it was no fault of his. He seemed to be busy with prize competitions, and I saw less and less of him as the weeks went by and the earth cracked and grew ripe to spring, and the buds swelled in their sheaths. He did not care to read or talk of what he had read, and there was a new ring of self-assertion in his voice. I hardly cared to remind him of the galley when we met; but Charlie alluded to it on every occasion, always as a story from which money was to be made.

'I think I deserve twenty-five per cent, don't I, at least?' he said, with beautiful frankness. 'I supplied all the ideas, didn't I?'

This greediness for silver was a new side in his nature. I assumed that it had been developed in the City, where Charlie was picking up the curious nasal drawl of the underbred City man.

'When the thing's done we'll talk about it. I can't make anything of it at present. Red-haired or black-haired heroes are equally difficult.'

He was sitting by the fire staring at the red coals. 'I can't understand what you find so difficult. It's all as clear as mud to me,' he replied. A jet of gas puffed out between the bars, took light, and whistled softly. 'Suppose we take the red-haired hero's adventures first, from the time that he came south to my galley and captured it and sailed to the Beaches.'

I knew better now than to interrupt Charlie. I was out of reach of pen and paper, and dared not move to get them lest I should break the current. The gas-jet puffed and whinnied, Charlie's voice dropped almost to a whisper, and he told a tale of the sailing of an open galley to Furdurstrandi, of sunsets on the open sea, seen under the curve of the one sail evening after evening when the galley's beak was notched into the centre of the sinking disc, and 'we sailed by that, for we had no other guide,' quoth Charlie. He spoke of a landing on an island and explorations in its woods, where the crew killed three men whom they found asleep under the pines. Their ghosts, Charlie said, followed the galley, swimming and choking in the water, and the crew cast lots and threw one of their number overboard as a sacrifice to the strange gods whom they had offended. Then they ate seaweed when their provisions failed, and their legs swelled, and their leader, the red-haired man, killed two rowers who mutinied, and after a year spent among the woods they set sail for their own country, and a wind that never failed carried them back so safely that they all slept at night. This and much more Charlie told. Sometimes the voice fell so low that I could not catch the words, though every nerve was on the strain. He spoke of their leader, the red-haired man, as a pagan speaks of his God; for it was he who cheered them and slew them impartially as he thought best for their needs; and it was he who steered them for three days among floating ice, each floe crowded with strange beasts that 'tried to sail with us', said Charlie, 'and we beat them back with the handles of the oars.'

The gas-jet went out, a burnt coal gave way, and the fire settled with a tiny crash to the bottom of the grate. Charlie ceased speaking, and I said no word.

'By Jove!' he said at last, shaking his head. 'I've been staring at the fire till I'm dizzy. What was I going to say?'

'Something about the galley book.'

'I remember now. It's twenty-five per cent of the profits, isn't it?'

'It's anything you like when I've done the tale.'

'I wanted to be sure of that. I must go now. I've – I've an appointment.' And he left me.

Had not my eyes been held I might have known that that broken muttering over the fire was the swan-song of Charlie Mears. But I thought it the prelude to fuller revelation. At last and at last I should cheat the Lords of Life and Death!

When next Charlie came to me I received him with rapture. He was nervous and embarrassed, but his eyes were very full of light, and his lips a little parted.

'I've done a poem,' he said; and then, quickly: 'It's the best I've ever done. Read it.' He thrust it into my hand and retreated to the window.

I groaned inwardly. It would be the work of half an hour to criticise – that is to say, praise – the poem sufficiently to please Charlie. Then I had good reason to groan, for Charlie, discarding his favourite centipede metres,[29] had launched into shorter and choppier verse, and verse with a motive at the back of it. This is what I read:

> 'The day is most fair, the cheery wind
>   Halloos behind the hill,
> Where he bends the wood as seemeth good,
>   And the sapling to his will!
> Riot, O wind; there is that in my blood
>   That would not have thee still!
>
> 'She gave me herself, O Earth, O Sky;
>   Grey sea, she is mine alone!
> Let the sullen boulders hear my cry,
>   And rejoice tho' they be but stone!

'Mine! I have won her, O good brown Earth,
   Make merry! 'Tis hard on Spring;
Make merry – my love is doubly worth
   All worship your fields can bring!
Let the hind that tills you feel my mirth
   At the early harrowing!'

'Yes, it's the early harrowing, past a doubt,' I said, with a dread at my heart. Charlie smiled, but did not answer.

'Red cloud of the sunset, tell it abroad;
   I am victor. Greet me, O Sun,
Dominant master and absolute lord
   Over the soul of one!'

'Well?' said Charlie, looking over my shoulder.

I thought it far from well, and very evil indeed when he silently laid a photograph on the paper – the photograph of a girl with a curly head and a foolish slack mouth.

'Isn't it – isn't it wonderful?' he whispered, pink to the tips of his ears, wrapped in the rosy mystery of first love. 'I didn't know. I didn't think. It came like a thunderclap.'

'Yes. It comes like a thunderclap. Are you very happy, Charlie?'

'My God, – she – she loves me!' He sat down repeating the last words to himself. I looked at the hairless face, the narrow shoulders already bowed by desk-work, and wondered when, where, and how he had loved in his past lives.

'What will your mother say?' I asked cheerfully.

'I don't care a damn what she says!'

At twenty the things for which one does not care a damn should, properly, be many, but one must not include mothers in the list. I told him this gently; and he described Her, even as Adam must have described to the newly-named beasts the glory and tenderness and beauty of Eve. Incidentally I learned that She was a tobacconist's assistant with a weakness for pretty dress, and had told him four or five times already that She had never been kissed by a man before.

Charlie spoke on and on, and on; while I, separated from him by thousands of years, was considering the beginnings of things. Now I understood why the Lords of Life and Death shut the doors so carefully behind us. It is that we may not remember our first and most beautiful wooings. Were this not so, our world would be without inhabitants in a hundred years.

'Now, about that galley-story,' I said still more cheerfully, in a pause in the rush of the speech.

Charlie looked up as though he had been hit. 'The galley – what galley? Good heavens, don't joke, man! This is serious! You don't know how serious it is!'

Grish Chunder was right. Charlie had tasted the love of woman that kills remembrance, and the finest story in the world would never be written.

THE SHIP THAT FOUND HERSELF

We now, held in captivity,
  Spring to our labour nor grieve!
See now, how it is blesseder,
  Brothers, to give than receive!
Keep trust, wherefore ye were made,
  Paying the duty ye owe;
For a clean thrust and the sheer of the blade
  Shall carry us where we should go.
                    Song of the Engines.

It was her first voyage, and though she was but a cargo-steamer of twelve hundred tons, she was the very best of her kind, the outcome of forty years of experiments and improvements in framework and machinery; and her designers and owner thought as much of her as though she had been the *Lucania*.[1] Any one can make a floating hotel that will pay expenses if he puts enough money into the saloons, and charges for private baths, suites of rooms, and such-like; but in these days of competition and low freights every square inch of a cargo-boat must be built for cheapness, great hold-capacity, and a certain steady speed. This boat was, perhaps, two hundred and forty feet long and thirty-two feet wide, with arrangements that enabled her to carry cattle on her main and sheep on her upper deck if she wanted to; but her great glory was the amount of cargo that she could store away in her holds. Her owners – they were a very well-known Scotch firm – came round with her from the North, where she had been launched and christened and fitted, to Liverpool, where she was to take cargo for New York; and the owner's daughter, Miss Frazier, went to and fro on the clean decks, admiring the new paint and the brass-work, and the patent winches, and particularly the strong, straight bow, over which she had cracked a bottle of champagne when she named the steamer the *Dimbula*. It was a beautiful September afternoon, and the boat in all her newness – she was painted lead-colour with a red funnel – looked very fine indeed. Her house-flag was flying, and her whistle from time to time acknowledged the salutes of friendly boats, who saw that she was new to the High and Narrow Seas and wished to make her welcome.

'And now,' said Miss Frazier delightedly, to the captain, 'she's a real ship, isn't she? It seems only the other day Father gave the order for her, and now – and now – isn't she a beauty!' The girl was proud of the firm, and talked as though she were the controlling partner.

'Oh, she's no so bad,' the skipper replied cautiously. 'But I'm sayin' that it takes more than christenin' to mak' a ship. In the nature o' things, Miss Frazier, if ye follow me, she's just irons and rivets and plates put into the form of a ship. She has to find herself yet.'

'I thought Father said she was exceptionally well found.'[2]

'So she is,' said the skipper, with a laugh. 'But it's this way wi' ships, Miss Frazier. She's all here, but the parrts of her have not learned to work together yet. They've had no chance.'

'The engines are working beautifully. I can hear them.'

'Yes, indeed. But there's more than engines to a ship. Every inch of her, ye'll understand, has to be livened up and made to work wi' its neighbour – sweetenin' her, we call it, technically.'

'And how will you do it?' the girl asked.

'We can no more than drive and steer her, and so forth; but if we have rough weather this trip – it's likely – she'll learn the rest by heart! For a ship, ye'll obsairve, Miss Frazier, is in no sense a reegid body closed at both ends. She's a highly complex structure o' various an' conflictin' strains, wi' tissues that must give an' tak', accordin' to her perrsonal modulus of elasteecity.' Mr Buchanan, the chief engineer, was coming towards them. 'I'm sayin' to Miss Frazier here that our little *Dimbula* has to be sweetened yet, and nothin' but a gale will do it. How's all wi' your engines, Buck?'

'Well enough – true by plumb an' rule, o' course; but there's no spontaneeity yet.' He turned to the girl. 'Take my word, Miss Frazier, and maybe ye'll comprehend later; even after a pretty girl's christened a ship it does not follow that there's such a thing as a ship under the men that work her.'

'I was sayin' the very same, Mr Buchanan,' the skipper interrupted.

'That's more metaphysical than I can follow,' said Miss Frazier, laughing.

'Why so? Ye're good Scotch, an' – I knew your mother's father, he was fra' Dumfries – ye've a vested right in metapheesics, Miss Frazier, just as ye have in the *Dimbula*,' the engineer said.

'Eh, well, we must go down to the deep watters, an' earn Miss Frazier her deevidends. Will you not come to my cabin for tea?' said the skipper.

'We'll be in dock the night, and when you're goin' back to Glasgie ye can think of us loadin' her down an' drivin' her forth – all for your sake.'

In the next few days they stowed some two thousand tons' dead weight into the *Dimbula*, and took her out from Liverpool. As soon as she met the lift of the open water, she naturally began to talk. If you lay your ear to the side of the cabin the next time you are in a steamer, you will hear hundreds of little voices in every direction, thrilling and buzzing, and whispering and popping, and gurgling and sobbing and squeaking exactly like a telephone in a thunderstorm. Wooden ships shriek and growl and grunt, but iron vessels throb and quiver through all their hundreds of ribs and thousands of rivets. The *Dimbula* was very strongly built, and every piece of her had a letter or number, or both, to describe it; and every piece had been hammered, or forged, or rolled, or punched by man, and had lived in the roar and rattle of the shipyard for months. Therefore, every piece had its own separate voice in exact proportion to the amount of trouble spent upon it. Cast-iron, as a rule, says very little; but mild steel plates and wrought-iron, and ribs and beams that have been much bent and welded and riveted, talk continuously. Their conversation, of course, is not half as wise as our human talk, because they are all, though they do not know it, bound down one to the other in a black darkness, where they cannot tell what is happening near them, nor what will overtake them next.

As soon as she had cleared the Irish coast a sullen, grey-headed old wave of the Atlantic climbed leisurely over her straight bows, and sat down on the steam-capstan used for hauling up the anchor. Now the capstan and the engine that drove it had been newly painted red and green; besides which, nobody likes being ducked.

'Don't you do that again,' the capstan sputtered through the teeth of his cogs. 'Hi! Where's the fellow gone?'

The wave had slouched overside with a plop and a chuckle; but 'Plenty more where he came from,' said a brother-wave, and went through and over the capstan, who was bolted firmly to an iron plate on the iron deck-beams below.

'Can't you keep still up there?' said the deck-beams. 'What's the matter with you? One minute you weigh twice as much as you ought to, and the next you don't!'

'It isn't my fault,' said the capstan. 'There's a green brute outside that comes and hits me on the head.'

'Tell that to the shipwrights! You've been in position for months and you've never wriggled like this before. If you aren't careful you'll strain *us*.'

'Talking of strain,' said a low, rasping, unpleasant voice, 'are any of you fellows – you deck-beams, we mean – aware that those exceedingly ugly knees[3] of yours happen to be riveted into our structure – *ours*?'

'Who might you be?' the deck-beams inquired.

'Oh, nobody in particular,' was the answer. 'We're only the port and starboard upper-deck stringers; and if you persist in heaving and hiking like this, we shall be reluctantly compelled to take steps.'

Now the stringers of the ship are long iron girders, so to speak, that run lengthways from stern to bow. They keep the iron frames (what are called ribs in a wooden ship) in place, and also help to hold the ends of the deck-beams, which go from side to side of the ship. Stringers always consider themselves most important, because they are so long.

'You will take steps – will you?' This was a long echoing rumble. It came from the frames – scores and scores of them, each one about eighteen inches distant from the next, and each riveted to the stringers in four places. 'We think you will have a certain amount of trouble in *that*'; and thousands and thousands of the little rivets that held everything together whispered: 'You will. You will! Stop quivering and be quiet. Hold on, brethren! Hold on! Hot Punches! What's that?'

Rivets have no teeth, so they cannot chatter with fright; but they did their best as a fluttering jar swept along the ship from stern to bow, and she shook like a rat in a terrier's mouth.

An unusually severe pitch, for the sea was rising, had lifted the big throbbing screw nearly to the surface, and it was spinning round in a kind of soda-water – half sea and half air – going much faster than was proper, because there was no true water for it to work in. As it sank again, the engines – and they were triple expansion, three cylinders in a row – snorted through all their three pistons. 'Was that a joke, you fellow outside? It's an uncommonly poor one. How are we to do our work if you fly off the handle that way?'

'I didn't fly off the handle,' said the screw, twirling huskily at the end of the screw-shaft. 'If I had, you'd have been scrap-iron by this time. The sea dropped away from under me, and I had nothing to catch hold of. That's all.'

'That's all, d'you call it?' said the thrust-block, whose business it is to take the push of the screw; for if a screw had nothing to hold it back it would crawl right into the engine-room. (It is the holding back of the screwing action that gives the drive to a ship.) 'I know I do my work deep down and out of sight, but I warn you I expect justice. All I ask for is bare justice. Why can't you push steadily and evenly, instead of whizzing like a whirligig, and making me hot under all my collars.' The thrust-block had six collars, each faced with brass, and he did not wish to get them heated.

All the bearings that supported the fifty feet of screw-shaft as it ran to the stern whispered: 'Justice – give us justice.'

'I can only give you what I can get,' the screw answered. 'Look out! It's coming again!'

He rose with a roar as the *Dimbula* plunged, and 'whack – flack – whack – whack' went the engines furiously, for they had little to check them.

'I'm the noblest outcome of human ingenuity – Mr Buchanan says so,' squealed the high-pressure cylinder. 'This is simply ridiculous!' The piston went up savagely, and choked, for half the steam behind it was mixed with dirty water. 'Help! Oiler! Fitter! Stoker! Help! I'm choking,' it gasped. 'Never in the history of maritime invention has such a calamity overtaken one so young and strong. And if I go, who's to drive the ship?'

'Hush! Oh, hush!' whispered the Steam, who, of course, had been to sea many times before. He used to spend his leisure ashore in a cloud, or a gutter, or a flower-pot, or a thunderstorm, or anywhere else where water was needed. 'That's only a little priming, a little carrying-over, as they call it. It'll happen all night, on and off. I don't say it's nice, but it's the best we can do under the circumstances.'

'What difference can circumstances make? I'm here to do my work – on clean, dry steam. Blow circumstances!' the cylinder roared.

'The circumstances will attend to the blowing. I've worked on the North Atlantic run a good many times – it's going to be rough before morning.'

'It isn't distressingly calm now,' said the extra-strong frames – they were called web-frames – in the engine-room. 'There's an upward thrust that we don't understand, and there's a twist that is very bad for our brackets and diamond-plates, and there's a sort of west-north-westerly pull that follows the twist, which seriously annoys us. We mention this because we happened to cost a good deal of money, and we feel sure that the owner would not approve of our being treated in this frivolous way.'

'I'm afraid the matter is out of the owner's hands for the present,' said the Steam, slipping into the condenser. 'You're left to your own devices till the weather betters.'

'I wouldn't mind the weather,' said a flat bass voice below; 'it's this confounded cargo that's breaking my heart. I'm the garboard-strake, and I'm twice as thick as most of the others, and I ought to know something.'

The garboard-strake is the lowest plate in the bottom of a ship, and the *Dimbula's* garboard-strake was nearly three-quarters of an inch mild steel.

'The sea pushes me up in a way I should never have expected,' the strake went on, 'and the cargo pushes me down, and, between the two, I don't know what I'm supposed to do.'

'When in doubt, hold on,' rumbled the Steam, making head in the boilers.

'Yes; but there's only dark, and cold, and hurry, down here; and how do I know whether the other plates are doing their duty? Those bulwark-plates up above, I've heard, ain't more than five-sixteenths of an inch thick – scandalous, I call it.'

'I agree with you,' said a huge web-frame by the main cargo-hatch. He was deeper and thicker than all the others, and curved half-way across the ship in the shape of half an arch, to support the deck where deck-beams would have been in the way of cargo coming up and down. 'I work entirely unsupported, and I observe that I am the sole strength of this vessel, so far as my vision extends. The responsibility, I assure you, is enormous. I believe the money-value of the cargo is over one hundred and fifty thousand pounds. Think of that!'

'And every pound of it is dependent on my personal exertions.' Here spoke a sea-valve that communicated directly with the water outside, and was seated not very far from the garboard-strake. 'I rejoice to think that I am a Prince-Hyde Valve, with best Para rubber facings. Five patents cover me – I mention this without pride – five separate and several patents, each one finer than the other. At present I am screwed fast. Should I open, you would immediately be swamped. This is incontrovertible!'

Patent things always use the longest words they can. It is a trick that they pick up from their inventors.

'That's news,' said a big centrifugal bilge-pump. 'I had an idea that you were employed to clean decks and things with. At least, I've used you for that more than once. I forget the precise number, in thousands, of gallons which I am guaranteed to throw per hour; but I assure you, my complaining friends, that there is not the least danger. I alone am capable of clearing any water that may find its way here. By my Biggest Deliveries, we pitched then!'

The sea was getting up in a workmanlike style. It was a dead westerly gale, blown from under a ragged opening of green sky, narrowed on all sides by fat, grey clouds; and the wind bit like pincers as it fretted the spray into lacework on the flanks of the waves.

'I tell you what it is,' the foremast telephoned down its wire-stays.

'I'm up here, and I can take a dispassionate view of things. There's an organised conspiracy against us. I'm sure of it, because every single one of these waves is heading directly for our bows. The whole sea is concerned in it – and so's the wind. It's awful!'

'What's awful?' said a wave, drowning the capstan for the hundredth time.

'This organised conspiracy on your part,' the capstan gurgled, taking his cue from the mast.

'Organised bubbles and spindrift! There has been a depression in the Gulf of Mexico. Excuse me!' He leaped overside; but his friends took up the tale one after another.

'Which has advanced –' That wave hove green water over the funnel.

'As far as Cape Hatteras[4] –' He drenched the bridge.

'And is now going out to sea – to sea – to sea!' The third wave went free in three surges, making a clean sweep of a boat, which turned bottom-up and sank in the darkening troughs alongside, while the broken falls whipped the davits.[5]

'That's all there is to it,' seethed the white water roaring through the scuppers. 'There's no animus in our proceedings. We're only meteorological corollaries.'

'Is it going to get any worse?' said the bow-anchor chained down to the deck, where he could only breathe once in five minutes.

'Not knowing, can't say. Wind may blow a bit by midnight. Thanks awfully. Good-bye.'

The wave that spoke so politely had travelled some distance aft, and found itself all mixed up on the deck amidships, which was a well-deck sunk between high bulwarks. One of the bulwark-plates, which was hung on hinges to open outward, had swung out, and passed the bulk of the water back to the sea again with a clean smack.

'Evidently that's what I'm made for,' said the plate, closing again with a sputter of pride. 'Oh no, you don't, my friend!'

The top of a wave was trying to get in from the outside, but as the plate did not open in that direction, the defeated water spurted back.

'Not bad for five-sixteenths of an inch,' said the bulwark-plate. 'My work, I see, is laid down for the night'; and it began opening and shutting with the motion of the ship as it was designed to do.

'We are not what you might call idle,' groaned all the frames together, as the *Dimbula* climbed a big wave, lay on her side at the top, and shot into the next hollow, twisting in the descent. A huge swell pushed up exactly under her middle, and her bow and stern hung free with nothing to support them. Then one joking wave caught her up at the bow, and another at the stern, while the rest of the water slunk away from under her just to see how she would like it; so she was held up at her two ends only, and the weight of the cargo and the machinery fell on the groaning iron keels and bilge-stringers.

'Ease off! Ease off, there!' roared the garboard-strake. 'I want one-eighth of an inch fair play. D'you hear me, you rivets!'

'Ease off! Ease off!' cried the bilge-stringers. 'Don't hold us so tight to the frames!'

'Ease off!' grunted the deck-beams, as the *Dimbula* rolled fearfully. 'You've cramped our knees into the stringers, and we can't move. Ease off, you flat-headed little nuisances.'

Then two converging seas hit the bows, one on each side, and fell away in torrents of streaming thunder.

'Ease off!' shouted the forward collision-bulkhead. 'I want to crumple up, but I'm stiffened in every direction. Ease off, you dirty little forge-filings. Let me breathe!'

All the hundreds of plates that are riveted to the frames, and make the outside skin of every steamer, echoed the call, for each plate wanted to shift and creep a little, and each plate, according to its position, complained against the rivets.

'We can't help it! *We* can't help it!' they murmured in reply. 'We're put here to hold you, and we're going to do it. You never pull us twice in the same direction. If you'd say what you were going to do next, we'd try to meet your views.'

'As far as I could feel,' said the upper-deck planking, and that was four inches thick, 'every single iron near me was pushing or pulling in opposite directions. Now, what's the sense of that? My friends, let us all pull together.'

'Pull any way you please,' roared the funnel, 'so long as you don't try your experiments on *me*. I need seven wire ropes, all pulling in different directions, to hold me steady. Isn't that so?'

'We believe you, my boy!' whistled the funnel-stays through their clenched teeth, as they twanged in the wind from the top of the funnel to the deck.

'Nonsense! We must all pull together,' the decks repeated. 'Pull lengthways.'

'Very good,' said the stringers; 'then stop pushing sideways when you get wet. Be content to run gracefully fore and aft, and curve in at the ends as we do.'

'No! – No curves at the ends! A very slight workmanlike curve from side to side, with a good grip at each knee, and little pieces welded on,' said the deck-beams.

'Fiddle!' cried the iron pillars of the deep, dark hold. 'Who ever heard of curves? Stand up straight; be a perfectly round column, and carry tons of good solid weight – like that! There!' A big sea smashed on the deck above, and the pillars stiffened themselves to the load.

'Straight up and down is not bad,' said the frames, who ran that way in the sides of the ship, 'but you must also expand yourselves sideways. Expansion is the law of life, children. Open out! open out!'

'Come back!' said the deck-beams savagely, as the upward heave of the sea made the frames try to open. 'Come back to your bearings, you slack-jawed irons!'

'Rigidity! Rigidity! Rigidity!' thumped the engines. 'Absolute, unvarying rigidity – rigidity!'

'You see!' whined the rivets in chorus. 'No two of you will ever pull alike, and – and you blame it all on us. We only know how to go through a plate and bite down on both sides so that it can't, and mustn't, and shan't move.'

'I've got one fraction of an inch play, at any rate,' said the garboardstrake, triumphantly. So he had, and all the bottom of the ship felt the easier for it.

'Then we're no good,' sobbed the bottom rivets. 'We were ordered – we were ordered – never to give; and we've given, and the sea will come in, and we'll all go to the bottom together! First we're blamed for everything unpleasant, and now we haven't the consolation of having done our work.'

'Don't say I told you,' whispered the Steam consolingly; 'but, between you and me and the last cloud I came from, it was bound to happen sooner or later. You *had* to give a fraction, and you've given without knowing it. Now, hold on, as before.'

'What's the use?' a few hundred rivets chattered. 'We've given – we've given; and the sooner we confess that we can't keep the ship together, and go off our little heads, the easier it will be. No rivet forged can stand this strain.'

'No one rivet was ever meant to. Share it among you,' the Steam answered.

'The others can have my share. I'm going to pull out,' said a rivet in one of the forward plates.

'If you go, others will follow,' hissed the Steam. 'There's nothing so contagious in a boat as rivets going. Why, I knew a little chap like you – he was an eighth of an inch fatter, though – on a steamer – to be sure, she was only nine hundred tons, now I come to think of it – in exactly the same place as you are. He pulled out in a bit of a bobble of a sea, not half as bad as this, and he started all his friends on the same butt-strap, and the plates opened like a furnace door, and I had to climb into the nearest fog-bank, while the boat went down.'

'Now that's peculiarly disgraceful,' said the rivet. 'Fatter than me, was he, and in a steamer half our tonnage? Reedy little peg! I blush for the family, sir.' He settled himself more firmly than ever in his place, and the Steam chuckled.

'You see,' he went on, quite gravely, 'a rivet, and especially a rivet in your position, is really the one indispensable part of the ship.'

The Steam did not say that he had whispered the very same thing to every single piece of iron aboard. There is no sense in telling too much truth.

And all that while the little *Dimbula* pitched and chopped, and swung and slewed, and lay down as though she were going to die, and got up as though she had been stung, and threw her nose round and round in circles half-a-dozen times as she dipped; for the gale was at its worst. It was inky black, in spite of the tearing white froth on the waves, and, to top everything, the rain began to fall in sheets, so that you could not see your hand before your face. This did not make much difference to the ironwork below, but it troubled the foremast a good deal.

'Now it's all finished,' he said dismally. 'The conspiracy is too strong for us. There is nothing left but to –'

'*Hurraar! Brrrraaah! Brrrrrrp!*' roared the Steam through the fog-horn, till the decks quivered. 'Don't be frightened, below. It's only me, just throwing out a few words, in case any one happens to be rolling round to-night.'

'You don't mean to say there's anyone except *us* on the sea in such weather?' said the funnel in a husky snuffle.

'Scores of 'em,' said the Steam, clearing its throat. '*Rrrrrraaa! Brraaaaa! Prrrrp!* It's a trifle windy up here; and, Great Boilers! how it rains!'

'We're drowning,' said the scuppers. They had been doing nothing else all night, but this steady thrash of rain above them seemed to be the end of the world.

'That's all right. We'll be easier in an hour or two. First the wind and then the rain: Soon you may make sail again! *Grrraaaaaah! Drrrraaaa! Drrrp!* I have a notion that the sea is going down already. If it does you'll learn something about rolling. We've only pitched till now. By the way, aren't you chaps in the hold a little easier than you were?'

There was just as much groaning and straining as ever, but it was not so loud or squeaky in tone; and when the ship quivered she did not jar stiffly, like a poker hit on the floor, but gave with a supple little waggle, like a perfectly balanced golf-club.

'We have made a most amazing discovery,' said the stringers, one after another. 'A discovery that entirely changes the situation. We have found, for the first time in the history of shipbuilding, that the inward pull of the deck-beams and the outward thrust of the frames lock us, as it were, more closely in our places, and enable us to endure a strain which is entirely without parallel in the records of marine architecture.'

The Steam turned a laugh quickly into a roar up the fog-horn. 'What massive intellects you great stringers have!' he said softly, when he had finished.

'We also,' began the deck-beams, 'are discoverers and geniuses. We are of opinion that the support of the hold-pillars materially helps us. We find that we lock up on them when we are subjected to a heavy and singular weight of sea above.'

Here the *Dimbula* shot down a hollow, lying almost on her side, – righting at the bottom with a wrench and a spasm.

'In these cases – are you aware of this, Steam? – the plating at the bows, and particularly at the stern – we would also mention the floors beneath us – help *us* to resist any tendency to spring.' The frames spoke in the solemn, awed voice which people use when they have just come across something entirely new for the very first time.

'I'm only a poor puffy little flutterer,' said the Steam, 'but I have to stand a good deal of pressure in my business. It's all tremendously interesting. Tell us some more. You fellows are so strong.'

'Watch us and you'll see,' said the bow-plates proudly. 'Ready, behind there! Here's the Father and Mother of Waves coming! Sit tight, rivets all!' A great sluicing comber thundered by, but through the scuffle and confusion the Steam could hear the low, quick cries of the ironwork as the various strains took them – cries like these: 'Easy, now – easy! *Now* push for all your strength! Hold out! Give a fraction! Hold up! Pull in! Shove crossways! Mind the strain at the ends! Grip, now! Bite tight! Let the water get away from under – and there she goes!'

The wave raced off into the darkness, shouting, 'Not bad, that, if it's your first run!' and the drenched and ducked ship throbbed to the beat of the engines inside her. All three cylinders were white with the salt spray that had come down through the engine-room hatch; there was white fur on the canvas-bound steam-pipes, and even the bright-work deep below was speckled and soiled; but the cylinders had learned to make the most of steam that was half water, and were pounding along cheerfully.

'How's the noblest outcome of human ingenuity hitting it?' said the Steam, as he whirled through the engine-room.

'Nothing for nothing in this world of woe,' the cylinders answered, as though they had been working for centuries, 'and precious little for seventy-five pounds' head. We've made two knots this last hour and a quarter! Rather humiliating for eight hundred horse-power, isn't it?'

'Well, it's better than drifting astern, at any rate. You seem rather less – how shall I put it? – stiff in the back than you were.'

'If you'd been hammered as we've been this night, you wouldn't be stiff–iff–iff, either. Theoreti–retti–retti–cally, of course, rigidity is the thing. Purrr – purr – practically, there has to be a little give and take. We found that out by working on our sides for five minutes at a stretch – chch – chh. How's the weather?'

'Sea's going down fast,' said the Steam.

'Good business,' said the high-pressure cylinder. 'Whack her up, boys. They've given us five pounds more steam'; and he began humming the first bars of 'Said the young Obadiah to the old Obadiah', which, as you may have noticed, is a pet tune among engines not built for high speed. Racing-liners with twin-screws sing 'The Turkish Patrol' and the overture to 'The Bronze Horse', and 'Madame Angot', till something goes wrong, and then they render Gounod's 'Funeral March of a Marionette', with variations.

'You'll learn a song of your own some fine day,' said the Steam, as he flew up the fog-horn for one last bellow.

Next day the sky cleared and the sea dropped a little, and the *Dimbula* began to roll from side to side till every inch of iron in her was sick and giddy. But luckily they did not all feel ill at the same time: otherwise she would have opened out like a wet paper box.

The Steam whistled warnings as he went about his business. It is in this short, quick roll and tumble that follows a heavy sea that most of the accidents happen, for then everything thinks that the worst is over and goes off guard. So he orated and chattered till the beams and frames and floors and stringers and the rest had learned how to lock down and lock up on one another, and endure this new kind of strain.

They found ample time to practise, for they were sixteen days at sea, and it was foul weather till within a hundred miles of New York. The *Dimbula* picked up her pilot, and came in covered with salt and red rust. Her funnel was dirty grey from top to bottom; two boats had been carried away; three copper ventilators looked like hats after a fight with the police; the bridge had a dimple in the middle of it; the house that covered the steam steering-gear was split as with hatchets; there was a bill for small repairs in the engine-room almost as long as the screw-shaft; the forward cargo-hatch fell into bucket-staves when they raised the iron cross-bars; and the steam-capstan had been badly wrenched on its bed. Altogether, as the skipper said, it was 'a pretty general average'.

'But she's soupled,' he said to Mr Buchanan. 'For all her dead weight she rode like a yacht. Ye mind that last blow off the Banks? I am proud of her, Buck.'

'It's vara good,' said the chief engineer, looking along the dishevelled decks. 'Now a man judgin' superfeecially would say we were a wreck, but we know otherwise – by experience.'

Naturally everything in the *Dimbula* fairly stiffened with pride, and the foremast and the forward collision-bulkhead, who are pushing creatures, begged the Steam to warn the Port of New York of their arrival. 'Tell those big boats all about us,' they said. 'They seem to take us quite as a matter of course.'

It was a glorious, clear, dead calm morning, and in single file, with less than half a mile between each, their bands playing and their tug-boats shouting and waving handkerchiefs, were the *Majestic,* the *Paris,* the *Touraine,* the *Servia,* the *Kaiser Wilhelm II,* and the *Werkendam,* all statelily going out to sea. As the *Dimbula* shifted her helm to give the great boats clear way, the Steam (who knows far too much to mind making an exhibition of himself now and then) shouted: –

'Oyez! Oyez! Oyez! Princes, Dukes, and Barons of the High Seas! Know ye by these presents, we are the *Dimbula,* fifteen days nine hours from Liverpool, having crossed the Atlantic with three thousand ton of cargo for the first time in our career! We have not foundered. We are here. *'Eer! 'Eer!* We are not disabled. But we have had a time wholly unparalleled in the annals of shipbuilding! Our decks were swept! We pitched; we rolled! We thought we were going to die! *Hi! Hi!* But we didn't. We wish to give notice that we have come to New York all the way across the Atlantic, through the worst weather in the world; and we are the *Dimbula!* We are–arr–ha–ha–ha-r-r-r!'

The beautiful line of boats swept by as steadily as the procession of the Seasons. The *Dimbula* heard the *Majestic* say, 'Hmph!' and the *Paris* grunted, 'How!' and the *Touraine* said, 'Oui!' with a little coquettish flicker of steam; and the *Servia* said, 'Haw!' and the *Kaiser* and the *Werkendam* said, 'Hoch!' Dutch-fashion – and that was absolutely all.

'I did my best,' said the Steam gravely, 'but I don't think they were much impressed with us, somehow. Do you?'

'It's simply disgusting,' said the bow-plates. 'They might have seen what we've been through. There isn't a ship on the sea that has suffered as we have – is there, now?'

'Well, I wouldn't go so far as that,' said the Steam, 'because I've worked on some of those boats, and sent them through weather quite as bad as the fortnight that we've had, in six days; and some of them are a little over ten thousand tons, I believe. Now I've seen the *Majestic,* for instance, ducked from her bows to her funnel; and I've helped the *Arizona,*[6] I think she was, to back off an iceberg she met with one dark night; and I had to run out of the *Paris*'s engine-room,[7] one day, because there was thirty foot of water in it. Of course, I don't deny –' The Steam shut off suddenly, as a tug-boat, loaded with a political club and a brass band, that had been to see a New York Senator off to Europe, crossed their bows, going to Hoboken. There was a long silence that reached, without a break, from the cut-water to the propeller-blades of the *Dimbula.*

Then a new, big voice said slowly and thickly, as though the owner had just waked up: 'It's my conviction that I have made a fool of myself.'

The Steam knew what had happened at once; for when a ship finds herself all the talking of the separate pieces ceases and melts into one voice, which is the Soul of the Ship.

'Who are you?' he said, with a laugh.

'I am the *Dimbula,* of course. I've never been anything else except that – and a fool!'

The tug-boat, which was doing its very best to be run down, got away just in time, its band playing clashily and brassily a popular but impolite air:

> 'In the days of old Rameses – are you on?
> In the days of old Rameses – are you on?
> In the days of old Rameses,
> That story had paresis,
> Are you on – are you on – are you on?'

'Well, I'm glad you've found yourself,' said the Steam. 'To tell the truth, I was a little tired of talking to all those ribs and stringers. Here's Quarantine. After that we'll go to our wharf and clean up a little, and – next month we'll do it all over again.'

MRS BATHURST

The day that I chose to visit HMS *Peridot* in Simon's Bay[1] was the day that the Admiral had chosen to send her up the coast. She was just steaming out to sea as my train came in, and since the rest of the Fleet were either coaling[2] or busy at the rifle-ranges a thousand feet up the hill, I found myself stranded, lunchless, on the sea-front with no hope of return to Cape Town before 5 p.m. At this crisis I had the luck to come across my friend Inspector Hooper,[3] Cape Government Railways, in command of an engine and a brake-van chalked for repair.

'If you get something to eat,' he said, 'I'll run you down to Glengariff siding till the goods comes along. It's cooler there than here, you see.'

I got food and drink from the Greeks who sell all things at a price, and the engine trotted us a couple of miles up the line to a bay of drifted sand and a plank-platform half buried in sand not a hundred yards from the edge of the surf. Moulded dunes, whiter than any snow, rolled far inland up a brown-and-purple valley of splintered rocks and dry scrub. A crowd of Malays hauled at a net beside two blue-and-green boats on the beach; a picnic party danced and shouted barefoot where a tiny river trickled across the flat, and a circle of dry hills, whose feet were set in sands of silver, locked us in against a seven-coloured sea. At either horn of the bay the railway line, cut just above high-water mark, ran round a shoulder of piled rocks, and disappeared.

'You see, there's always a breeze here,' said Hooper, opening the door as the engine left us in the siding on the sand, and the strong south-easter buffeting under Elsie's Peak dusted sand into our tickey beer.[4] Presently he sat down to a file full of spiked documents. He had returned from a long trip up-country, where he had been reporting on damaged rolling-stock, as far away as Rhodesia. The weight of the bland wind on my eyelids; the song of it under the car-roof, and high up among the rocks; the drift of fine grains chasing each other musically ashore; the tramp of the surf; the voices of the picnickers; the rustle of Hooper's file, and the presence of the assured sun, joined with the beer to cast me into magical slumber. The hills of False Bay[5] were just dissolving into those of fairyland when I heard footsteps on the sand outside, and the clink of our couplings.

'Stop that!' snapped Hooper, without raising his head from his work. 'It's those dirty little Malay boys, you see: they're always playing with the trucks . . .'

'Don't be hard on 'em. The railway's a general refuge in Africa,' I replied.

''Tis – up-country at any rate. That reminds me,' – he felt in his waistcoat-pocket – 'I've got a curiosity for you from Wankies[6] – beyond Bulawayo. It's more of a souvenir perhaps than – '

'The old hotel's inhabited,' cried a voice. 'White men, from the language. Marines to the front! Come on, Pritch. Here's your Belmont.[7] Wha – i – i!'

The last word dragged like a rope as Mr Pyecroft ran round to the open door, and stood looking up into my face. Behind him an enormous Sergeant of Marines trailed a stalk of dried seaweed, and dusted the sand nervously from his fingers.

'What are you doing here?' I asked. 'I thought the *Hierophant* was down the coast?'

'We came in last Tuesday – from Tristan d'Acunha – for overhaul, and we shall be in dockyard 'ands for two months, with boiler-seatings.'

'Come and sit down.' Hooper put away the file.

'This is Mr Hooper of the Railway,' I explained, as Pyecroft turned to haul up the black-moustached sergeant.

'This is Sergeant Pritchard, of the *Agaric*, an old shipmate,' said he. 'We were strollin' on the beach.' The monster blushed and nodded. He filled up one side of the van when he sat down.

'And this is my friend, Mr Pyecroft,' I added to Hooper, already busy with the extra beer which my prophetic soul had bought from the Greeks.

'*Moi aussi*,' quoth Pyecroft, and drew out beneath his coat a labelled quart bottle.[8]

'Why, it's Bass!' cried Hooper.

'It was Pritchard,' said Pyecroft. 'They can't resist him.'

'That's not so,' said Pritchard mildly.

'Not *verbatim*[9] per'aps, but the look in the eye came to the same thing.'

'Where was it?' I demanded.

'Just on beyond here – at Kalk Bay. She was slappin' a rug in a back veranda. Pritch 'adn't more than brought his batteries to bear, before she stepped indoors an' sent it flyin' over the wall.'

Pyecroft patted the warm bottle.

'It was all a mistake,' said Pritchard. 'I shouldn't wonder if she mistook me for Maclean. We're about of a size.'

I had heard householders of Muizenberg, St James, and Kalk Bay complain of the difficulty of keeping beer or good servants at the seaside, and I began to see the reason. None the less, it was excellent Bass, and I too drank to the health of that large-minded maid.

'It's the uniform that fetches 'em, an' they fetch it,' said Pyecroft. 'My simple navy blue is respectable, but not fascinatin'. Now Pritch in 'is Number One rig[10] is always "purr Mary, on the terrace"[11] – *ex officio* as you might say.'

'She took me for Maclean, I tell you,' Pritchard insisted. 'Why – why, – to listen to him you wouldn't think that only yesterday – '

'Pritch,' said Pyecroft, 'be warned in time. If we begin tellin' what we know about each other we'll be turned out of the pub. Not to mention aggravated desertion on several occasions – '

'Never anything more than absence without leaf – I defy you to prove it,' said the Sergeant hotly. 'An', if it comes to that, how about Vancouver[12] in '87?'

'How about it? Who pulled bow in the gig going ashore? Who told Boy Niven . . . ?'

'Surely you were court-martialled for that?' I said. The story of Boy Niven who lured seven or eight able-bodied seamen and marines into the woods of British Columbia used to be a legend of the Fleet.

'Yes, we were court-martialled to rights,' said Pritchard, 'but we should have been tried for murder if Boy Niven 'adn't been unusually tough. 'E told us e 'ad an uncle 'oo'd give us land to farm. 'E said he was born at the back o' Vancouver Island, and *all* the time the beggar was a balmy Barnado Orphan!'

'*But* we believed him,' said Pyecroft. 'I did – you did – Paterson did – an' 'oo was the Marine that married the coconut-woman after-wards – him with the mouth?'

'Oh, Jones, Spit-Kid Jones. I 'aven't thought of 'im in years,' said Pritchard. 'Yes, Spit-Kid believed it, an' George Anstey and Moon. We were very young an' very curious.'

'*But* lovin' an' trustful to a degree,' said Pyecroft.

'Remember when 'e told us to walk in single file for fear o' bears? Remember, Pye, when 'e 'opped about in that bog full o' ferns an' sniffed an' said 'e could smell the smoke of 'is uncle's farm? An' *all* the time it was a dirty little outlyin' uninhabited island. We walked round it in a day, an' come back to our boat lyin' on the beach. A whole day Boy Niven kept us walkin' in circles lookin' for 'is uncle's farm! He said 'is uncle was compelled by the law of the land to give us a farm!'

'Don't get hot, Pritch. We believed,' said Pyecroft.

"'E'd been readin' books. 'E only did it to get a run ashore an' 'ave 'imself talked of. A day an' a night – eight of us – followin' Boy Niven round an uninhabited island in the Vancouver archipelago! Then the picket came for us an' a nice pack o' idiots we looked!'

'What did you get for it?' Hooper asked.

'Heavy thunder with continuous lightning for two hours. Thereafter sleet-squalls, a confused sea, and cold, unfriendly weather till conclusion o' cruise,' said Pyecroft. 'It was only what we expected, but what we felt – an' I assure you, Mr Hooper, even a sailor-man has a heart to break – was bein' told that we able seamen an' promisin' marines 'ad misled Boy Niven. Yes, we poor back-to-the-landers was supposed to 'ave misled him! He rounded on us, o' course, an' got off easy.'

'Excep' for what we gave 'im in the steerin'-flat[13] when we came out o' cells. 'Eard anything of 'im lately, Pye?'

'Signal Boatswain in the Channel Fleet, I believe – Mr L. L. Niven is.'

'An' Anstey died o' fever in Benin,' Pritchard mused. 'What come to Moon? Spit-Kid we know about.'

'Moon – Moon! Now where did I last . . . ? Oh yes, when I was in the *Palladium*. I met Quigley at Buncrana Station. He told me Moon 'ad run when the *Astrild* sloop was cruising among the South Seas three years back. He always showed signs o' bein' a Mormonastic beggar. Yes, he slipped off quietly an' they 'adn't time to chase 'im round the islands even if the navigatin' officer 'ad been equal to the job.'

'Wasn't he?' said Hooper.

'Not so. Accordin' to Quigley the *Astrild* spent half 'er commission rompin' up the beach like a she turtle, an' the other half 'atching turtles' eggs on the top o' numerous reefs. When she was docked at Sydney 'er copper looked like Aunt Maria's washing on the line – an' her 'midship frames was sprung. The commander swore the dockyard 'ad done it haulin' the pore thing on to the slips. They *do* do strange things at sea, Mr Hooper.'

'Ah! I'm not a taxpayer,' said Hooper, and opened a fresh bottle. The Sergeant seemed to be one who had a difficulty in dropping subjects.

'How it all comes back, don't it?' he said. 'Why, Moon must 'ave 'ad sixteen years' service before he ran.'

'It takes 'em at all ages. Look at – you know,' said Pyecroft.

'Who?' I asked.

'A Service man within eighteen months of his pension[14] is the party you're thinkin' of,' said Pritchard. 'A warrant 'oo's name begins with a V., isn't it?'

'But, in a way o' puttin' it, we can't say that he actually did desert,' Pyecroft suggested.

'Oh no,' said Pritchard. 'It was only permanent absence up-country without leaf. That was all.'

'Up-country?' said Hooper. 'Did they circulate his description?'

'What for?' said Pritchard, most impolitely.

'Because deserters are like columns in the war. They don't move away from the line, you see. I've known a chap caught at Salisbury[15] that way tryin' to get to Nyassa. They tell me, but o'course I don't know, that they don't ask questions on the Nyassa Lake Flotilla up there. I've heard of a P. & O. quartermaster in full command of an armed launch there.'

'Do you think Click 'ud ha' gone up that way?' Pritchard asked.

'There's no saying. He was sent up to Bloemfontein to take over some Navy ammunition left in the fort. We know he took it over and saw it into the trucks. Then there was no more Click – then or thereafter. Four months ago it transpired, and thus the *casus belli*[16] stands at present,' said Pyecroft.

'What were his marks?' said Hooper again.

'Does the Railway get a reward for returnin' 'em, then?' said Pritchard.

'If I did d'you suppose I'd talk about it?' Hooper retorted angrily.

'You seemed so very interested,' said Pritchard with equal crispness.

'Why was he called Click?' I asked, to tide over an uneasy little break in the conversation. The two men were staring at each other very fixedly.

'Because of an ammunition hoist carryin' away,' said Pyecroft. 'And it carried away four of 'is teeth – on the lower port side, wasn't it, Pritch? The substitutes which 'e bought weren't screwed home, in a manner o' sayin'. When he talked fast they used to lift a little on the bed-plate. 'Ence, "Click." They called 'im a superior man, which is what we'd call a long, black-'aired, genteelly-speakin', 'alf-bred beggar on the lower deck.'

'Four false teeth in the lower left jaw,' said Hooper, his hand in his waistcoat-pocket. 'What tattoo-marks?'

'Look here,' began Pritchard, half rising. 'I'm sure we're very grateful to you as a gentleman for your 'orspitality, but per'aps we may 'ave made an error in – '

I looked at Pyecroft for aid – Hooper was crimsoning rapidly.

'If the fat marine now occupying the foc'sle will kindly bring 'is *status quo*[17] to an anchor yet once more, we may be able to talk like gentlemen – not to say friends,' said Pyecroft. 'He regards you, Mr Hooper, as a emissary of the Law.'

'I only wish to observe that when a gentleman exhibits such a peculiar, or I should rather say, such a *bloomin'* curiosity in identification-marks as our friend 'ere – '

'Mr Pritchard,' I interposed, 'I'll take all the responsibility for Mr Hooper.'

'An' *you'll* apologise all round,' said Pyecroft. 'You're a rude little man, Pritch.'

'But how was I – ' he began, wavering.

'I don't know an' I don't care. Apologise!'

The giant looked round bewildered and took our little hands into his vast grip, one by one.

'I was wrong,' he said, meekly as a sheep. 'My suspicions was unfounded. Mr Hooper, I apologise.'

'You did quite right to look out for your own end o' the line,' said Hooper. 'I'd ha' done the same with a gentleman I didn't know, you see. If you don't mind I'd like to hear a little more o' your Mr Vickery. It's safe with me, you see.'

'Why did Vickery run – ?' I began, but Pyecroft's smile made me turn my question to 'Who was she?'

'She kep' a little hotel at Hauraki – near Auckland,' said Pyecroft.

'By Gawd!' roared Pritchard, slapping his hand on his leg. 'Not Mrs Bathurst!'

Pyecroft nodded slowly, and the Sergeant called all the powers of darkness to witness his bewilderment.

'So far as I could get at it, Mrs B. was the lady in question.'

'But Click was married,' cried Pritchard.

'An' 'ad a fifteen-year-old daughter. 'E's shown me her photograph. Settin' that aside, so to say, 'ave you ever found these little things make much difference? Because *I* haven't.'

'Good Lord Alive an' Watchin'! . . . Mrs Bathurst. . . .' Then with another roar: 'You can say what you please, Pye, but you don't make me believe it was any of 'er fault. She wasn't *that*!'

'If I was going to say what I please, I'd begin by callin' you a silly ox an' work up to the 'igher pressures at leisure. I'm trying to say solely what transpired. M'reover, for once you're right. It wasn't her fault.'

'You couldn't 'aven't made me believe it if it 'ad been,' was the answer.

Such faith in a Sergeant of Marines interested me greatly. 'Never mind about that,' I cried. 'Tell me what she was like.'

'She was a widow,' said Pyecroft. 'Left so very young and never re-spliced. She kep' a little hotel for warrants and non-coms[18] close to Auckland, an' she always wore black silk, and 'er neck – '

'You ask what she was like,' Pritchard broke in. 'Let me give you an instance. I was at Auckland first in '97, at the end o' the *Marroquin*'s commission, an' as I'd been promoted I went up with the others. She used to look after us all, an' she never lost by it – not a penny! "Pay me now," she'd say, "or settle later. I know you won't let me suffer. Send the money from home if you like." Why, gentlemen all, I tell you I've seen that lady take 'er own gold watch an' chain off 'er neck in the bar an' pass it to a bo'sun 'oo'd come ashore without 'is ticker an' 'ad to catch the last boat. "I don't know your name," she said, "but when you've done with it, you'll find plenty that know me on the front. Send it back by one o' them." And it was worth thirty pounds if it was worth 'arf-a-crown. The little gold watch, Pye, with the blue monogram at the back. But, as I was sayin', in those days she kep' a beer that agreed with me – Slits it was called. One way an' another I must 'ave punished a good few bottles of it while we was in the bay – comin' ashore every night or so. Chaffin' across the bar, like, once when we were alone, "Mrs B.," I said, "when next I call I want you to remember that this is my particular – just as you're my particular." (She'd let you go *that* far!) "Just as you're my particular," I said. "Oh, thank you, Sergeant Pritchard," she says, an' put 'er hand up to the curl be'ind 'er ear. Remember that way she had, Pye?'

'I think so,' said the sailor.

'Yes, "Thank you, Sergeant Pritchard," she says. "The least I can do is to mark it for you in case you change your mind. There's no great demand for it in the Fleet," she says, "but to make sure I'll put it at the back o' the shelf," an' she snipped off a piece of her hair-ribbon with that old dolphin cigar-cutter on the bar – remember it, Pye? – an' she tied a bow round what was left – just four bottles. That was '97 – no, '96. In '98 I was in the *Resilient* – China station – full commission. In Nineteen One, mark you, I was in the *Carthusian*, back in Auckland Bay again. Of course I went up to Mrs B.'s with the rest of us to see how things were goin'. They were the same as ever. (Remember the big tree on the pavement by the side-bar, Pye?) I never said anythin' in special (there was too many of us talkin' to her), but she saw me at once.'

'That wasn't difficult?' I ventured.

'Ah, but wait. I was comin' up to the bar, when, "Ada," she says to her niece, "get me Sergeant Pritchard's particular," and, gentlemen all, I tell you before I could shake 'ands with the lady, there were those four bottles o' Slits, with 'er 'air-ribbon in a bow round each o' their necks, set down in front o' me, an' as she drew the cork she looked at me under her eyebrows in that blindish way she had o' lookin', an',

"Sergeant Pritchard," she says, "I do 'ope you 'aven't changed your mind about your particulars." That's the kind o' woman she was – after five years!'

'I don't *see* her yet somehow,' said Hooper, but with sympathy.

'She – she never scrupled to feed a lame duck or set 'er foot on a scorpion at any time of 'er life,' Pritchard added valiantly.

'That don't help me either. My mother's like that for one.'

The giant heaved inside his uniform and rolled his eyes at the car-roof. Said Pyecroft suddenly:

'How many women have you been intimate with all over the world, Pritch?'

Pritchard blushed plum-colour to the short hairs of his seventeen-inch neck.

''Undreds,' said Pyecroft. 'So've I. How many of 'em can you remember in your own mind, settin' aside the first – an' per'aps the last – *and one more*?'

'Few, wonderful few, now I tax myself,' said Sergeant Pritchard relievedly.

'An' how many times might you 'ave been at Auckland?'

'One – two,' he began – 'why, I can't make it more than three times in ten years. But I can remember every time that I ever saw Mrs B.'

'So can I – an' I've only been to Auckland twice – how she stood an' what she was sayin' an' what she looked like. That's the secret. 'Tisn't beauty, so to speak, nor good talk necessarily. It's just It. Some women 'll stay in a man's memory if they once walk down a street, but most of 'em you can live with a month on end, an' next commission you'd be put to it to certify whether they talked in their sleep or not, as one might say.'

'Ah!' said Hooper. 'That's more the idea. I've known just two women of that nature.'

'An' it was no fault o' theirs?' asked Pritchard.

'None whatever. I know *that*!'

'An' if a man gets struck with that kind o' woman, Mr Hooper?' Pritchard went on.

'He goes crazy – or just saves himself,' was the slow answer.

'You've hit it,' said the Sergeant. 'You've seen an' known somethin' in the course o' your life, Mr Hooper. I'm lookin' at you!' He set down his bottle.

'And how often had Vickery seen her?' I asked.

'That's the dark an' bloody mystery,' Pyecroft answered. 'I'd never come across 'im till I come out in the *Hierophant* just now, an' there wasn't anyone in the ship who knew much about 'im. You see, he was what you call a superior man. 'E spoke to me once or twice about Auckland and Mrs B. on the voyage out. I called that to mind subsequently. There must 'ave been a good deal between 'em, to my way o' thinkin'. Mind you, I'm only giving you my *résumé* of it all, because all I know is second-'and, so to speak, or rather I should say more than second-'and.'

'How?' said Hooper peremptorily. 'You must have seen it or heard it.'

'Ye-es,' said Pyecroft. 'I used to think seein' and hearin' was the only regulation aids to ascertainin' facts, but as we get older we get more accommodatin'. The cylinders work easier, I suppose. . . . Were you in Cape Town last December when Phyllis's Circus came?'

'No – up-country,' said Hooper, a little nettled at the change of venue.

'I ask because they 'ad a new turn of a scientific nature called "Home and Friends for a Tickey".'

'Oh, you mean the cinematograph – the pictures of prize-fights and steamers. I've seen 'em up-country.'

'Biograph or cinematograph was what I was alludin' to. London Bridge with the omnibuses – a troopship goin' to the war – marines on parade at Portsmouth, an' the Plymouth Express arrivin' at Paddin'ton.'

'Seen 'em all. Seen 'em all,' said Hooper impatiently.

'We *Hierophants* came in just before Christmas week an' leaf was easy.'

'I think a man gets fed up with Cape Town quicker than anywhere else on the station. Why, even Durban's more like Nature. We was there for Christmas,' Pritchard put in.

'Not bein' a devotee of Indian *peeris*,[19] as our Doctor said to the Pusser,[20] I can't exactly say. Phyllis's was good enough after musketry practice at Mozambique. I couldn't get off the first two or three nights on account of what you might call an imbroglio with our Torpedo Lieutenant in the submerged flat, where some pride of the West Country had sugared up a gyroscope; but I remember Vickery went ashore with our Carpenter Rigdon – old Crocus we called him. As a general rule Crocus never left 'is ship unless an' until he was 'oisted out with a winch, but *when* 'e went 'e would return noddin' like a lily gemmed with dew. We smothered 'im down below that night, but the things 'e said about Vickery as a fittin' playmate for a warrant-officer of 'is cubic capacity, before we got 'im quiet, was what I should call pointed.'

'I've been with Crocus – in the *Redoubtable*,' said the Sergeant. ''E's a character if there is one.'

'Next night I went into Cape Town with Dawson and Pratt; but just

at the door of the Circus I came across Vickery. "Oh!" 'e says, "you're
the man I'm looking for. Come and sit next me. This way to the shillin'
places!" I went astern at once, protestin', because tickey seats better suited
my so-called finances. "Come on," says Vickery, "I'm payin'." Naturally
I abandoned Pratt and Dawson in anticipation o' drinks to match the
seats. "No," 'e says, when this was 'inted – "not now. Not now. As many
as you please afterwards, but I want you sober for the occasion." I caught
'is face under a lamp just then, an' the appearance of it quite cured me
of my thirst. Don't mistake. It didn't frighten me. It made me anxious. I
can't tell you what it was like, but that was the effect which it 'ad on me.
If you want to know, it reminded me of those things in bottles in those
herbalistic shops at Plymouth – preserved in spirits of wine. White an'
crumply things – previous to birth, as you might say.'

'You 'ave a beastial mind, Pye,' said the Sergeant, relighting his
pipe.

'Per'aps. We were in the front row, an' "Home an' Friends" came
on early. Vickery touched me on the knee when the number went up.
"If you see anything that strikes you," 'e says, "drop me a hint"; then
'e went on clicking. We saw London Bridge an' so forth an' so on, an'
it was most interestin'. I'd never seen it before. You 'eard a little dynamo
like buzzin', but the pictures were the real thing – alive an' movin'.'

'I've seen 'em,' said Hooper. 'Of course they are taken from the very
thing itself – you see.'

'Then the Western Mail came in to Paddin'ton on the big magic-
lantern sheet. First we saw the platform empty an' the porters standin'
by. Then the engine come in, head-on, an' the women in the front row
jumped, she headed so straight. Then the doors opened an' the passengers
came out an' the porters got the luggage – just like life. Only – only
when anyone came down too far towards us that was watchin', they
walked right out o' the picture, so to speak. I was 'ighly interested, I
can tell you. So were all of us. I watched an old man with a rug 'oo'd
dropped a book an' was tryin' to pick it up, when quite slowly, from
be'ind two porters – carryin' a little reticule an' lookin' from side to
side – comes out Mrs Bathurst. There was no mistakin' the walk in a
hundred thousand. She come forward – right forward – she looked out
straight at us with that blindish look which Pritch alluded to. She
walked on and on till she melted out of the picture – like – like a shadow
jumpin' over a candle, an' as she went I 'eard Dawson in the tickey
seats be'ind sing out: "Christ! there's Mrs B.!"'

Hooper swallowed his spittle and leaned forward intently.

'Vickery touched me on the knee again. He was clickin' his four
false teeth, with his jaw down like an enteric at the last kick.[21] "Are

you sure?" says he. "Sure," I says. "Didn't you 'ear Dawson give tongue? Why, it's the woman herself." "I was sure before," 'e says, "but I brought you to make sure. Will you come again with me to-morrow?"

"'Willingly," I says. "It's like meetin' old friends."

"'Yes," 'e says, openin' his watch, "very like. It will be four-and-twenty hours less four minutes before I see her again. Come and have a drink," 'e says. "It may amuse *you*, but it's no sort of earthly use to me." He went out shaking his head an' stumblin' over people's feet as if he was drunk already. I anticipated a swift drink an' a speedy return, because I wanted to see the performin' elephants. Instead o' which Vickery began to navigate the town at the rate o' knots, lookin' in at a bar every three minutes approximate Greenwich time. I'm not a drinkin' man, though there are those present' – he cocked his unforgettable eye at me – 'who may have seen me more or less imbued with the fragrant spirit. None the less when I drink I like to do it at anchor an' not at an average speed of eighteen knots on the measured mile. There's a tank as you might say at the back o' that big hotel up the hill – what do they call it?'

'The Molteno Reservoir,' I suggested, and Hooper nodded.

'That was his limit o' drift. We walked there an' we come down through the Gardens – there was a South-Easter blowin' – an' we finished up by the Docks. Then we bore up the road to Salt River, and wherever there was a pub Vickery put in sweatin'. He didn't look at what 'e drunk – he didn't look at the change. He walked an' he drunk an' he perspired in rivers. I understood why old Crocus 'ad come back in the condition 'e did, because Vickery an' I 'ad two an' a half hours o' this gipsy manoeuvres, an' when we got back to the station there wasn't a dry atom on or in me.'

'Did he say anything?' Pritchard asked.

'The sum total of' is conversation from 7.45 p.m. till 11.15 p.m. was "Let's have another." Thus the mornin' an' the evenin' were the first day,[22] as Scripture says ... To abbreviate a lengthy narrative, I went into Cape Town for five consecutive nights with Master Vickery, and in that time I must 'ave logged about fifty knots over the ground an' taken in two gallon o' all the worst spirits south the Equator. The evolution never varied. Two shilling seats for us two; five minutes o' the pictures, an' perhaps forty-five seconds o' Mrs B. walking down towards us with that blindish look in 'er eyes an' the reticule in 'er hand. Then out – walk – drink till train-time.'

'What did you think?' said Hooper, his hand fingering his waistcoat-pocket.

'Several things,' said Pyecroft. 'To tell you the truth, I aren't quite

done thinkin' about it yet. Mad? The man was a dumb lunatic – must
'ave been for months – years p'r'aps. I know somethin' o' maniacs, as
every man in the Service must. I've been shipmates with a mad skipper
– an' a lunatic Number One, but never both together, I thank 'Eavin.
I could give you the names o' three captains now 'oo ought to be in
an asylum, but you don't find me interferin' with the mentally afflicted
till they begin to lay about 'em with rammers an' winch-handles. Only
once I crept up a little into the wind towards Master Vickery. "I wonder
what she's doin' in England," I says. "Don't it seem to you she's lookin'
for somebody?" That was in the Gardens again, with the South-Easter
blowin' as we were makin' our desperate round. "She's lookin' for
me," 'e says, stoppin' dead under a lamp an' clickin'. When he wasn't
drinkin', in which case all 'is teeth clicked on the glass, 'e was clickin'
'is four false teeth like a Marconi ticker.[23] "Yes! lookin' for me," 'e
said, an' he went on very softly an' as you might say affectionately.
"*But*," he went on, "in future, Mr Pyecroft, I should take it kindly
of you if you'd confine your remarks to the drinks set before you.
Otherwise," 'e says, "with the best will in the world towards you, I
may find myself guilty of murder! Do you understand?" 'e says.
"Perfectly," I says, "but would it at all soothe you to know that in such
a case the chances o' your being killed are precisely equivalent to the
chances o' me being outed?" "Why, no," 'e says. "I'm almost afraid
that 'ud be a temptation." Then I said – we was right under the lamp
by that arch at the end o' the Gardens where the trams come round
– "Assumin' murder was done – or attempted murder – I put it to you
that you would still be left so badly crippled, as one might say, that
your subsequent capture by the police – to 'oom you would 'ave to
explain – would be largely inevitable." "That's better," 'e says, passin'
'is hands over 'is forehead. "That's much better, because," 'e says, "do
you know, as I am now, Pye, I'm not so sure if I could explain anything
much." Those were the only particular words I had with 'im in our
walks as I remember.'

'What walks!' said Hooper. 'Oh, my soul, what walks!'

'They were chronic,' said Pyecroft gravely, 'but I didn't anticipate
any danger till the Circus left. Then I anticipated that, bein' deprived
of 'is stimulant, he might react on me, so to say, with a hatchet.
Consequently, after the final performance an' the ensuin' wet walk, I
kep' myself aloof from my superior officer on board in the execution
of 'is duty, as you might put it. Consequently, I was interested when
the sentry informs me while I was passin' on my lawful occasions that
Click had asked to see the captain. As a general rule warrant-officers
don't dissipate much of the owner's time, but Click put in an hour

and more be'ind that door. My duties kep' me within eyeshot of it.
Vickery came out first, an' 'e actually nodded at me an' smiled. This
knocked me out o' the boat, because, havin' seen 'is face for five
consecutive nights, I didn't anticipate any change there more than a
condenser in Hell, so to speak. The owner emerged later. His face
didn't read off at all, so I fell back on 'is cox, 'oo'd been eight years
with 'im and knew 'im better than boat-signals. Lamson – that was
the cox's name – crossed 'is bows once or twice at low speeds an'
dropped down to me visibly concerned. "He's shipped 'is court-martial
face," says Lamson. "Someone's goin' to be 'ung. I've never seen that
look but once before, when they chucked the gun-sights overboard
in the *Fantastic*." Throwin' gun-sights overboard, Mr Hooper, is the
equivalent for mutiny in these degenerate days. It's done to attract
the notice of the authorities an' the *Western Mornin' News* – generally
by a stoker. Naturally, word went round the lower deck an' we had
a private overaul of our little consciences. But, barrin' a shirt which
a second-class stoker said 'ad walked into 'is bag from the Marines'
flat by itself, nothin' vital transpired. The owner went about flyin' the
signal for "attend public execution", so to say, but there was no corpse
at the yard-arm. 'E lunched on the beach an' 'e returned with 'is
regulation harbour-routine face about 3 p.m. Thus Lamson lost
prestige for raising false alarms. The only person 'oo might 'ave
connected the epicycloidal gears correctly was one Pyecroft, when 'e
was told that Mr Vickery would go up-country that same evening to
take over certain naval ammunition left after the war in Bloemfontein
Fort. No details was ordered to accompany Master Vickery. He was
told off first person singular – as unit – by himself.'

The Marine whistled penetratingly.

'That's what I thought,' said Pyecroft. 'I went ashore with him in
the cutter an' 'e asked me to walk through the station. He was clickin'
audibly, but otherwise seemed happy-ish.

'"You might like to know," 'e says, stoppin' just opposite the
Admiral's front gate, "that Phyllis's Circus will be performin' at
Worcester to-morrow night. So I shall see 'er yet once again. You've
been very patient with me," 'e says.

'"Look here, Vickery," I said, "this thing's come to be just as much
as I can stand. Consume your own smoke. I don't want to know any
more."

'"You!" 'e said. "What have *you* got to complain of? – you've only
'ad to watch. I'm *it*," 'e says, "but that's neither here nor there," 'e says.
"I've one thing to say before shakin' 'ands. Remember," 'e says – we
were just by the Admiral's garden-gate then – "remember that I am *not*

a murderer, because my lawful wife died in childbed six weeks after
I came out. That much at least I am clear of," 'e says.

'"Then what have you done that signifies?" I said. "What's the rest
of it?"

'"The rest," 'e says, "is silence,"[24] an' he shook 'ands and went
clickin' into Simon's Town station.'

'Did he stop to see Mrs Bathurst at Worcester?' I asked.

'It's not known. He reported at Bloemfontein, saw the ammunition
into the trucks, and then 'e disappeared. Went out – deserted, if you
care to put it so – within eighteen months of his pension, an' if what
'e said about 'is wife was true he was a free man as 'e then stood. How
do you read it off?'

'Poor devil!' said Hooper. 'To see her that way every night! I wonder
what it was.'

'I've made my 'ead ache in that direction many a long night.'

'But I'll swear Mrs B. 'ad no 'and in it,' said the Sergeant, unshaken.

'No. Whatever the wrong or deceit was, he did it, I'm sure o' that.
I 'ad to look at 'is face for five consecutive nights. I'm not so fond o'
navigatin' about Cape Town with a South-Easter blowin' these days. I
can hear those teeth click, so to say.'

'Ah, those teeth,' said Hooper, and his hand went to his waistcoat-
pocket once more. 'Permanent things false teeth are! You read about
'em in all the murder trials.'

'What d'you suppose the captain knew – or did?' I asked.

'I've never turned my searchlight that way,' Pyecroft answered
unblushingly.

We all reflected together, and drummed on empty beer-bottles as the
picnic-party, sunburned, wet, and sandy, passed our door singing 'The
Honeysuckle and the Bee'.

'Pretty girl under that kapje,'[25] said Pyecroft.

'They never circulated his description?' said Pritchard.

'I was askin' you before these gentlemen came,' said Hooper to me,
'whether you knew Wankies – on the way to the Zambesi – beyond
Bulawayo?'

'Would he pass there – tryin' to get to that Lake what's 'is name?'
said Pritchard.

Hooper shook his head and went on: 'There's a curious bit o' line
there, you see. It runs through solid teak forest – a sort o' mahogany
really – seventy-two miles without a curve. I've had a train derailed
there twenty-three times in forty miles. I was up there a month ago
relievin' a sick inspector, you see. He told me to look out for a couple
of tramps in the teak.'

'Two?' Pyecroft said. 'I don't envy that other man if – '

'We get heaps of tramps up there since the war. The inspector told me I'd find 'em at M'Bindwe siding waiting to go North. He'd given 'em some grub and quinine, you see. I went up on a construction train. I looked out for 'em. I saw them miles ahead along the straight, waiting in the teak. One of 'em was standin' up by the dead-end of the siding an' the other was squattin' down lookin' up at 'im, you see.'

'What did you do for 'em?' said Pritchard.

'There wasn't much I could do, except bury 'em. There'd been a bit of a thunderstorm in the teak, you see, and they were both stone dead and as black as charcoal. That's what they really were, you see – charcoal. They fell to bits when we tried to shift 'em. The man who was standin' up had the false teeth. I saw 'em shinin' against the black. Fell to bits, he did too, like his mate squatting down an' watchin' him, both of 'em all wet in the rain. Both burned to charcoal, you see. And – that's what made me ask about marks just now – the false-toother was tattooed on the arms and chest – a crown and foul anchor with M. V. above.'

'I've seen that,' said Pyecroft quickly. 'It was so.'

'But if he was all charcoal, like?' said Pritchard, shuddering.

'You know how writing shows up white on a burned letter? Well, it was like that, you see. We buried 'em in the teak and I kept . . . But he was a friend of you two gentlemen, you see.'

Mr Hooper brought his hand away from his waistcoat-pocket – empty.

Pritchard covered his face with his hands for a moment, like a child shutting out an ugliness.

'And to think of her at Hauraki!' he murmured – 'with 'er 'air-ribbon on my beer. "Ada," she said to her niece . . . Oh, my Gawd!' . . .

> 'On a summer afternoon, when the honeysuckle blooms,
>   And all Nature seems at rest,
> Underneath the bower, 'mid the perfume of the flower,
>   Sat a maiden with the one she loves the best – '[26]

sang the picnic-party waiting for their train at Glengariff.

'Well, I don't know how you feel about it,' said Pyecroft, 'but 'avin' seen 'is face for five consecutive nights on end, I'm inclined to finish what's left of the beer an' thank Gawd he's dead!'

'THEY'

One view called me to another; one hill-top to its fellow, half across the county, and since I could answer at no more trouble than the snapping forward of a lever, I let the county flow under my wheels. The orchid-studded flats of the East gave way to the thyme, ilex, and grey grass of the Downs; these again to the rich cornland and fig-trees of the lower coast, where you carry the beat of the tide on your left hand for fifteen level miles; and when at last I turned inland through a huddle of rounded hills and woods I had run myself clean out of my known marks. Beyond that precise hamlet which stands godmother to the capital of the United States,[1] I found hidden villages where bees, the only things awake, boomed in eighty-foot lindens that overhung grey Norman churches; miraculous brooks diving under stone bridges built for heavier traffic than would ever vex them again; tithe-barns larger than their churches, and an old smithy that cried out aloud how it had once been a hall of the Knights of the Temple. Gipsies I found on a common where the gorse, bracken, and heath fought it out together up a mile of Roman road; and a little farther on I disturbed a red fox rolling dog-fashion in the naked sunlight.

As the wooded hills closed about me I stood up in the car to take the bearings of that great Down[2] whose ringed head is a landmark for fifty miles across the low countries. I judged that the lie of the country would bring me across some westward-running road that went to his feet, but I did not allow for the confusing veils of the woods. A quick turn plunged me first into a green cutting brim-full of liquid sunshine, next into a gloomy tunnel where last year's dead leaves whispered and scuffled about my tyres. The strong hazel stuff meeting overhead had not been cut for a couple of generations at least, nor had any axe helped the moss-cankered oak and beech to spring above them. Here the road changed frankly into a carpeted ride on whose brown velvet spent primrose-clumps showed like jade, and a few sickly, white-stalked bluebells nodded together. As the slope favoured I shut off the power and slid over the whirled leaves, expecting every moment to meet a keeper; but I only heard a jay, far off, arguing against the silence under the twilight of the trees.

Still the track descended. I was on the point of reversing and working my way back on the second speed ere I ended in some swamp, when I saw sunshine through the tangle ahead and lifted the brake.

It was down again at once. As the light beat across my face my fore-wheels took the turf of a great still lawn from which sprang horsemen ten feet high with levelled lances, monstrous peacocks, and sleek round-headed maids of honour – blue, black, and glistening – all of clipped yew. Across the lawn – the marshalled woods besieged it on three sides – stood an ancient house of lichened and weatherworn stone, with mullioned windows and roofs of rose-red tile. It was flanked by semi-circular walls, also rose-red, that closed the lawn on the fourth side, and at their feet a box hedge grew man-high. There were doves on the roof about the slim brick chimneys, and I caught a glimpse of an octagonal dove-house behind the screening wall.

Here, then, I stayed; a horseman's green spear laid at my breast; held by the exceeding beauty of that jewel in that setting.

'If I am not packed off for a trespasser, or if this knight does not ride a wallop at me,' thought I, 'Shakespeare and Queen Elizabeth at least must come out of that half-open garden door and ask me to tea.'

A child appeared at an upper window, and I thought the little thing waved a friendly hand. But it was to call a companion, for presently another bright head showed. Then I heard a laugh among the yew-peacocks, and turning to make sure (till then I had been watching the house only) I saw the silver of a fountain behind a hedge thrown up against the sun. The doves on the roof cooed to the cooing water; but between the two notes I caught the utterly happy chuckle of a child absorbed in some light mischief.

The garden door – heavy oak sunk deep in the thickness of the wall – opened further: a woman in a big garden hat set her foot slowly on the time-hollowed stone step and as slowly walked across the turf. I was forming some apology when she lifted up her head and I saw that she was blind.

'I heard you,' she said. 'Isn't that a motor-car?'

'I'm afraid I've made a mistake in my road. I should have turned off up above – I never dreamed – ' I began.

'But I'm very glad. Fancy a motor-car coming into the garden! It will be such a treat – ' She turned and made as though looking about her. 'You – you haven't seen any one, have you – perhaps?'

'No one to speak to, but the children seemed interested at a distance.'

'Which?'

'I saw a couple up at the window just now, and I think I heard a little chap in the grounds.'

'Oh, lucky you!' she cried, and her face brightened. 'I hear them, of course, but that's all. You've seen them and heard them?'

'Yes,' I answered. 'And if I know anything of children, one of them's having a beautiful time by the fountain yonder. Escaped, I should imagine.'

'You're fond of children?'

I gave her one or two reasons why I did not altogether hate them.

'Of course, of course,' she said. 'Then you understand. Then you won't think it foolish if I ask you to take your car through the gardens, once or twice – quite slowly. I'm sure they'd like to see it. They see so little, poor things. One tries to make their life pleasant, but –' she threw out her hands towards the woods. 'We're so out of the world here.'

'That will be splendid,' I said. 'But I can't cut up your grass.'

She faced to the right. 'Wait a minute,' she said. 'We're at the South gate, aren't we? Behind those peacocks there's a flagged path. We call it the Peacocks' Walk. You can't see it from here, they tell me, but if you squeeze along by the edge of the wood you can turn at the first peacock and get on to the flags.'

It was sacrilege to wake that dreaming house-front with the clatter of machinery, but I swung the car to clear the turf, brushed along the edge of the wood and turned in on the broad stone path where the fountain-basin lay like one star-sapphire.

'May I come too?' she cried. 'No, please don't help me. They'll like it better if they see me.'

She felt her way lightly to the front of the car, and with one foot on the step she called: 'Children, oh, children! Look and see what's going to happen!'

The voice would have drawn lost souls from the Pit, for the yearning that underlay its sweetness, and I was not surprised to hear an answering shout behind the yews. It must have been the child by the fountain, but he fled at our approach, leaving a little toy boat in the water. I saw the glint of his blue blouse among the still horsemen.

Very disposedly we paraded the length of the walk and at her request backed again. This time the child had got the better of his panic, but stood far off and doubting.

'The little fellow's watching us,' I said. 'I wonder if he'd like a ride.'

'They're very shy still. Very shy. But, oh, lucky you to be able to see them! Let's listen.'

I stopped the machine at once, and the humid stillness, heavy with the scent of box, cloaked us deep. Shears I could hear where some gardener was clipping; a mumble of bees and broken voices that might have been the doves.

'Oh, unkind!' she said weariedly.

'Perhaps they're only shy of the motor. The little maid at the window looks tremendously interested.'

'Yes?' She raised her head. 'It was wrong of me to say that. They are really fond of me. It's the only thing that makes life worth living – when they're fond of you, isn't it? I daren't think what the place would be without them. By the way, is it beautiful?'

'I think it is the most beautiful place I have ever seen.'

'So they all tell me. I can feel it, of course, but that isn't quite the same thing.'

'Then have you never – ?' I began, but stopped abashed.

'Not since I can remember. It happened when I was only a few months old, they tell me. And yet I must remember something, else how could I dream about colours. I see light in my dreams, and colours, but I never see *them*. I only hear them just as I do when I'm awake.'

'It's difficult to see faces in dreams. Some people can, but most of us haven't the gift,' I went on, looking up at the window where the child stood all but hidden.

'I've heard that too,' she said. 'And they tell me that one never sees a dead person's face in a dream. Is that true?'

'I believe it is – now I come to think of it.'

'But how is it with yourself – yourself?' The blind eyes turned towards me.

'I have never seen the faces of my dead in any dream,' I answered.

'Then it must be as bad as being blind.'

The sun had dipped behind the woods and the long shades were possessing the insolent horsemen one by one. I saw the light die from off the top of a glossy-leaved lance and all the brave hard green turn to soft black. The house, accepting another day at end, as it had accepted an hundred thousand gone, seemed to settle deeper into its rest among the shadows.

'Have you ever wanted to?' she said, after the silence.

'Very much sometimes,' I replied. The child had left the window as the shadows closed upon it.

'Ah! So've I, but I don't suppose it's allowed . . . Where d'you live?'

'Quite the other side of the county – sixty miles and more, and I must be going back. I've come without my big lamps.'

'But it's not dark yet. I can feel it.'

'I'm afraid it will be by the time I get home. Could you lend me someone to set me on my road at first? I've utterly lost myself.'

'I'll send Madden with you to the cross-roads. We are so out of the world, I don't wonder you were lost! I'll guide you round to the front of the house; but you will go slowly, won't you, till you're out of the grounds? It isn't foolish, do you think?'

'I promise you I'll go like this,' I said, and let the car start herself down the flagged path.

We skirted the left wing of the house, whose elaborately cast lead guttering alone was worth a day's journey; passed under a great rose-grown gate in the red wall, and so round to the high front of the house which in beauty and stateliness as much excelled the back as that all others I had seen.

'Is it so very beautiful?' she said wistfully when she heard my raptures. 'And you like the lead figures too? There's the old azalea garden behind. They say that this place must have been made for children. Will you help me out, please? I should like to come with you as far as the cross-roads, but I mustn't leave them. Is that you, Madden? I want you to show this gentleman the way to the cross-roads. He has lost his way, but – he has seen them.'

A butler appeared noiselessly at the miracle of old oak that must be called the front door, and slipped aside to put on his hat. She stood looking at me with open blue eyes in which no sight lay, and I saw for the first time that she was beautiful.

'Remember,' she said quietly, 'if you are fond of them you will come again,' and disappeared within the house.

The butler in the car said nothing till we were nearly at the lodge gates, where catching a glimpse of a blue blouse in a shrubbery I swerved amply lest the devil that leads little boys to play should drag me into child-murder.

'Excuse me,' he asked of a sudden, 'but why did you do that, sir?'

'The child yonder.'

'Our young gentleman in blue?'

'Of course.'

'He runs about a good deal. Did you see him by the fountain, sir?'

'Oh yes, several times. Do we turn here?'

'Yes, sir. And did you 'appen to see them upstairs too?'

'At the upper window? Yes.'

'Was that before the mistress come out to speak to you, sir?'

'A little before that. Why d'you want to know?'

He paused a little. 'Only to make sure that – that they had seen the

car, sir, because with children running about, though I'm sure you're
driving particularly careful, there might be an accident. That was all,
sir. Here are the cross-roads. You can't miss your way from now on.
Thank you, sir, but that isn't *our* custom, not with –'

'I beg your pardon,' I said, and thrust away the British silver.

'Oh, it's quite right with the rest of 'em as a rule. Good-bye, sir.'

He retired into the armour-plated conning-tower of his caste and
walked away. Evidently a butler solicitous for the honour of his house,
and interested, probably through a maid, in the nursery.

Once beyond the signposts at the cross-roads I looked back, but the
crumpled hills interlaced so jealously that I could not see where the house
had lain. When I asked its name at a cottage along the road, the fat
woman who sold sweetmeats there gave me to understand that people
with motor-cars had small right to live – much less to 'go about talking
like carriage folk'. They were not a pleasant-mannered community.

When I retraced my route on the map that evening I was little wiser.
Hawkin's Old Farm appeared to be the Survey title of the place, and
the old County Gazetteer, generally so ample, did not allude to it. The
big house of those parts was Hodnington Hall, Georgian with early
Victorian embellishments, as an atrocious steel engraving attested. I
carried my difficulty to a neighbour – a deep-rooted tree of that soil
– and he gave me a name of a family which conveyed no meaning.

A month or so later – I went again, or it may have been that my car
took the road of her own volition. She overran the fruitless Downs,
threaded every turn of the maze of lanes below the hills, drew through
the high-walled woods, impenetrable in their full leaf, came out at
the cross-roads where the butler had left me, and a little farther on
developed an internal trouble which forced me to turn her in on a grass
way-waste that cut into a summer-silent hazel wood. So far as I could
make sure by the sun and a six-inch Ordnance map,[3] this should be
the road flank of that wood which I had first explored from the heights
above. I made a mighty serious business of my repairs and a glittering
shop of my repair kit, spanners, pump, and the like, which I spread out
orderly upon a rug. It was a trap to catch all childhood, for on such a
day, I argued, the children would not be far off. When I paused in my
work I listened, but the wood was so full of the noises of summer
(though the birds had mated) that I could not at first distinguish these
from the tread of small cautious feet stealing across the dead leaves. I
rang my bell in an alluring manner, but the feet fled, and I repented,
for to a child a sudden noise is very real terror. I must have been at
work half an hour when I heard in the wood the voice of the blind
woman crying: 'Children, oh, children! Where are you?' and the stillness

made slow to close on the perfection of that cry. She came towards me, half feeling her way between the tree-boles, and though a child, it seemed, clung to her skirt, it swerved into the leafage like a rabbit as she drew nearer.

'Is that you?' she said, 'from the other side of the county?'

'Yes, it's me from the other side of the county.'

'Then why didn't you come through the upper woods? They were there just now.'

'They were here a few minutes ago. I expect they knew my car had broken down, and came to see the fun.'

'Nothing serious, I hope? How do cars break down?'

'In fifty different ways. Only mine has chosen the fifty-first.'

She laughed merrily at the tiny joke, cooed with delicious laughter, and pushed her hat back.

'Let me hear,' she said.

'Wait a moment,' I cried, 'and I'll get you a cushion.'

She set her foot on the rug all covered with spare parts, and stooped above it eagerly. 'What delightful things!' The hands through which she saw glanced in the chequered sunlight. 'A box here – another box! Why, you've arranged them like playing shop!'

'I confess now that I put it out to attract them. I don't need half those things really.'

'How nice of you! I heard your bell in the upper wood. You say they were here before that?'

'I'm sure of it. Why are they so shy? That little fellow in blue who was with you just now ought to have got over his fright. He's been watching me like a Red Indian.'

'It must have been your bell,' she said. 'I heard one of them go past me in trouble when I was coming down. They're shy – so shy even with me.' She turned her face over her shoulder and cried again: 'Children, oh, children! Look and see!'

'They must have gone off together on their own affairs,' I suggested, for there was a murmur behind us of lowered voices broken by the sudden squeaking giggles of childhood. I returned to my tinkerings and she leaned forward, her chin on her hand, listening interestedly.

'How many are they?' I said at last. The work was finished, but I saw no reason to go.

Her forehead puckered a little in thought. 'I don't quite know,' she said simply. 'Sometimes more – sometimes less. They come and stay with me because I love them, you see.'

'That must be very jolly,' I said, replacing a drawer, and as I spoke I heard the inanity of my answer.

'You – you aren't laughing at me?' she cried. 'I – I haven't any of my own. I never married. People laugh at me sometimes about them be-cause – because – '

'Because they're savages,' I returned. 'It's nothing to fret for. That sort laugh at everything that isn't in their own fat lives.'

'I don't know. How should I? I only don't like being laughed at about *them*. It hurts; and when one can't see . . . I don't want to seem silly,' – her chin quivered like a child's as she spoke – 'but we blindies have only one skin, I think. Everything outside hits straight at our souls. It's different with you. You've such good defences in your eyes – looking out – before anyone can really pain you in your soul. People forget that with us.'

I was silent, reviewing that inexhaustible matter – the more than inherited (since it is also carefully taught) brutality of the Christian peoples, beside which the mere heathendom of the West Coast nigger is clean and restrained. It led me a long distance into myself.

'Don't do that!' she said of a sudden, putting her hands before her eyes.

'What?'

She made a gesture with her hand.

'That! It's – it's all purple and black. Don't! That colour hurts.'

'But how in the world do you know about colours?' I exclaimed, for here was a revelation indeed.

'Colours as colours?' she asked.

'No. *Those* Colours which you saw just now.'

'You know as well as I do,' she laughed, 'else you wouldn't have asked that question. They aren't in the world at all. They're in *you* – when you went so angry.'

'D' you mean a dull purplish patch, like port wine mixed with ink?' I said.

'I've never seen ink or port wine, but the colours aren't mixed. They are separate – all separate.'

'Do you mean black streaks and jags across the purple?'

She nodded. 'Yes – if they are like this,' and zig-zagged her finger again, 'but it's more red than purple – that bad colour.'

'And what are the colours at the top of the – whatever you see?'

Slowly she leaned forward and traced on the rug the figure of the Egg itself.[4]

'I see them so,' she said, pointing with a grass-stem, 'white, green, yellow, red, purple, and when people are angry or bad, black across the red – as you were just now.'

'Who told you anything about it – in the beginning?' I demanded.

'About the Colours? No one. I used to ask what colours were when I was little – in table-covers and curtains and carpets, you see – because some colours hurt me and some made me happy. People told me; and when I got older that was how I saw people.' Again she traced the outline of the Egg which it is given to very few of us to see.

'All by yourself?' I repeated.

'All by myself. There wasn't any one else. I only found out afterwards that other people did not see the Colours.'

She leaned against the tree-bole plaiting and unplaiting chance-plucked grass-stems. The children in the wood had drawn nearer. I could see them with the tail of my eye frolicking like squirrels.

'Now I am sure you will never laugh at me,' she went on after a long silence. 'Nor at *them*.'

'Goodness! No!' I cried, jolted out of my train of thought. 'A man who laughs at a child – unless the child is laughing too – is a heathen!'

'I didn't mean that, of course. You'd never laugh *at* children, but I thought – I used to think – that perhaps you might laugh about *them*. So now I beg your pardon . . . What are you going to laugh at?'

I had made no sound, but she knew.

'At the notion of your begging my pardon. If you had done your duty as a pillar of the State and a landed proprietress you ought to have summoned me for trespass when I barged through your woods the other day. It was disgraceful of me – inexcusable.'

She looked at me, her head against the tree-trunk – long and stead-fastly – this woman who could see the naked soul.

'How curious!' she half whispered. 'How very curious!'

'Why, what have I done?'

'You don't understand . . . and yet you understood about the Colours. Don't you understand?'

She spoke with a passion that nothing had justified, and I faced her bewilderedly as she rose. The children had gathered themselves in a roundel behind a bramble bush. One sleek head bent over something smaller, and the set of the little shoulders told me that fingers were on lips. They, too, had some child's tremendous secret. I alone was hopelessly astray there in the broad sunlight.

'No,' I said, and shook my head as though the dead eyes could note. 'Whatever it is, I don't understand yet. Perhaps I shall later – if you'll let me come again.'

'You will come again,' she answered. 'You will surely come again and walk in the wood.'

'Perhaps the children will know me well enough by that time to let me play with them – as a favour. You know what children are like.'

'It isn't a matter of favour but of right,' she replied, and while I wondered what she meant, a dishevelled woman plunged round the bend of the road, loose-haired, purple, almost lowing with agony as she ran. It was my rude, fat friend of the sweetmeat shop. The blind woman heard and stepped forward. 'What is it, Mrs Madehurst?' she asked.

The woman flung her apron over her head and literally grovelled in the dust, crying that her grandchild was sick to death, that the local doctor was away fishing, that Jenny the mother was at her wits' end, and so forth, with repetitions and bellowings.

'Where's the next nearest doctor?' I asked between paroxysms.

'Madden will tell you. Go round to the house and take him with you. I'll attend to this. Be quick!' She half supported the fat woman into the shade. In two minutes I was blowing all the horns of Jericho under the front of the House Beautiful,[5] and Madden, in the pantry, rose to the crisis like a butler and a man.

A quarter of an hour at illegal speeds caught us a doctor five miles away. Within the half-hour we had decanted him, much interested in motors, at the door of the sweetmeat shop, and drew up the road to await the verdict.

'Useful things cars,' said Madden, all man and no butler. 'If I'd had one when mine took sick she wouldn't have died.'

'How was it?' I asked.

'Croup. Mrs Madden was away. No one knew what to do. I drove eight miles in a tax-cart[6] for the doctor. She was choked when we came back. This car'd ha' saved her. She'd have been close on ten now.'

'I'm sorry,' I said. 'I thought you were rather fond of children from what you told me going to the cross-roads the other day.'

'Have you seen 'em again, sir – this mornin'?'

'Yes, but they're well broke to cars. I couldn't get any of them within twenty yards of it.'

He looked at me carefully as a scout considers a stranger – not as a menial should lift his eyes to his divinely appointed superior.

'I wonder why,' he said just above the breath that he drew.

We waited on. A light wind from the sea wandered up and down the long lines of the woods, and the wayside grasses, whitened already with summer dust, rose and bowed in sallow waves.

A woman, wiping the suds off her arms, came out of the cottage next the sweetmeat shop.

'I've be'n listenin' in de back-yard,' she said cheerily. 'He says Arthur's unaccountable bad. Did ye hear him shruck[7] just now? Unaccountable bad. I reckon t'will come Jenny's turn to walk in de wood nex' week along, Mr Madden.'

'Excuse me, sir, but your lap-robe is slipping,' said Madden deferentially. The woman started, dropped a curtsey, and hurried away.

'What does she mean by "walking in the wood"?' I asked.

'It must be some saying they use hereabouts. I'm from Norfolk myself,' said Madden. 'They're an independent lot in this county. She took you for a chauffeur, sir.'

I saw the Doctor come out of the cottage followed by a draggletailed wench who clung to his arm as though he could make treaty for her with Death. 'Dat sort,' she wailed – 'dey're just as much to us dat has 'em as if dey was lawful born. Just as much – just as much! An' God, He'd be just as pleased if you saved 'un, Doctor. Don't take it from me. Miss Florence will tell ye de very same. Don't leave 'im, Doctor!'

'I know, I know,' said the man; 'but he'll be quiet for a while now. We'll get the nurse and the medicines as fast as we can.' He signalled me to come forward with the car, and I strove not to be privy to what followed; but I saw the girl's face, blotched and frozen with grief, and I felt the hand without a ring clutching at my knees when we moved away.

The Doctor was a man of some humour, for I remember he claimed my car under the Oath of Aesculapius, and used it and me without mercy. First we convoyed Mrs Madehurst and the blind woman to wait by the sick-bed till the nurse should come. Next we invaded a neat county town for prescriptions (the Doctor said the trouble was cerebro-spinal meningitis), and when the County Institute, banked and flanked with scared market cattle, reported itself out of nurses for the moment we literally flung ourselves loose upon the county. We conferred with the owners of great houses – magnates at the ends of overarching avenues whose big-boned womenfolk strode away from their tea-tables to listen to the imperious Doctor. At last a white-haired lady sitting under a cedar of Lebanon and surrounded by a court of magnificent Borzois – all hostile to motors – gave the Doctor, who received them as from a princess, written orders which we bore many miles at top speed, through a park, to a French nunnery, where we took over in exchange a pallid-faced and trembling Sister. She knelt at the bottom of the tonneau telling her beads without pause till, by short cuts of the Doctor's invention, we had her to the sweetmeat shop once more. It was a long afternoon crowded with mad episodes that rose and dissolved like the dust of our wheels; cross-sections of remote and incomprehensible lives through which we raced at right angles; and I went home in the dusk, wearied out, to dream of the clashing horns of cattle; round-eyed nuns walking in a garden of graves; pleasant tea-parties beneath shady trees; the carbolic-scented, grey-painted corridors of the County Institute; the steps of shy children in the wood, and the hands that clung to my knees as the motor began to move.

I had intended to return in a day or two, but it pleased Fate to hold me from that side of the county, on many pretexts, till the elder and the wild rose had fruited. There came at last a brilliant day, swept clear from the south-west, that brought the hills within hand's reach – a day of unstable airs and high filmy clouds. Through no merit of my own I was free, and set the car for the third time on that known road. As I reached the crest of the Downs I felt the soft air change, saw it glaze under the sun; and, looking down at the sea, in that instant beheld the blue of the Channel turn, through polished silver and dulled steel, to dingy pewter. A laden collier hugging the coast steered outward for deeper water, and, across copper-coloured haze, I saw sails rise one by one on the anchored fishing-fleet. In a deep dene behind me an eddy of sudden wind drummed through sheltered oaks, and spun aloft the first dry sample of autumn leaves. When I reached the beach road the sea-fog fumed over the brickfields, and the tide was telling all the groynes of the gale beyond Ushant.[8] In less than an hour summer England vanished in chill grey. We were again the shut island of the North, all the ships of the world bellowing at our perilous gates; and between their outcries ran the piping of bewildered gulls. My cap dripped moisture, the folds of the rug held it in pools or sluiced it away in runnels, and the salt-rime stuck to my lips.

Inland the smell of autumn loaded the thickened fog among the trees, and the drip became a continuous shower. Yet the late flowers – mallow of the wayside, scabious of the field, and dahlia of the garden – showed gay in the mist, and beyond the sea's breath there was little sign of decay in the leaf. Yet in the villages the house doors were all open, and bare-legged, bare-headed children sat at ease on the damp doorsteps to shout 'pip-pip' at the stranger.

I made bold to call at the sweetmeat shop, where Mrs Madehurst met me with a fat woman's hospitable tears. Jenny's child, she said, had died two days after the nun had come. It was, she felt, best out of the way, even though insurance offices, for reasons which she did not pretend to follow, would not willingly insure such stray lives. 'Not but what Jenny didn't tend to Arthur as though he'd come all proper at de end of de first year – like Jenny herself.' Thanks to Miss Florence, the child had been buried with a pomp which, in Mrs Madehurst's opinion, more than covered the small irregularity of its birth. She described the coffin, within and without, the glass hearse, and the evergreen lining of the grave.

'But how's the mother?' I asked.

'Jenny? Oh, she'll get over it. I've felt dat way with one or two o' my own. She'll get over. She's walkin' in de wood now.'

'In this weather?'

Mrs Madehurst looked at me with narrowed eyes across the counter.

'I dunno but it opens de 'eart like. Yes, it opens de 'eart. Dat's where losin' and bearin' comes so alike in de long run, we do say.'

Now the wisdom of the old wives is greater than that of all the Fathers, and this last oracle sent me thinking so extendedly as I went up the road, that I nearly ran over a woman and a child at the wooded corner by the lodge gates of the House Beautiful.

'Awful weather!' I cried, as I slowed dead for the turn.

'Not so bad,' she answered placidly out of the fog. 'Mine's used to 'un. You'll find yours indoors, I reckon.'

Indoors, Madden received me with professional courtesy, and kind inquiries for the health of the motor, which he would put under cover.

I waited in a still, nut-brown hall, pleasant with late flowers and warmed with a delicious wood fire – a place of good influence and great peace. (Men and women may sometimes, after great effort, achieve a creditable lie; but the house, which is their temple, cannot tell anything save the truth of those who live in it.) A child's cart and a doll lay on the black-and-white floor, where a rug had been kicked back. I felt that the children had only just hurried away – to hide themselves, most like – in the many turns of the great adzed staircase that climbed statelily out of the hall, or to crouch at gaze behind the lions and roses of the carven gallery above. Then I heard her voice above me, singing as the blind sing – from the soul:

'In the pleasant orchard-closes.'[9]

And all my early summer came back at the call.

'In the pleasant orchard-closes,
  "God bless all our gains," say we –
But "May God bless all our losses,"
  Better suits with our degree.'

She dropped the marring fifth line, and repeated:

'Better suits with our degree!'

I saw her lean over the gallery, her linked hands white as pearl against the oak.

'Is that you – from the other side of the county?' she called.

'Yes, me – from the other side of the county,' I answered, laughing.

'What a long time before you had to come here again!' She ran down the stairs, one hand lightly touching the broad rail. 'It's two months and four days. Summer's gone!'

'I meant to come before, but Fate prevented.'

'I knew it. Please do something to that fire. They won't let me play with it, but I can feel it's behaving badly. Hit it!'

I looked on either side of the deep fireplace, and found but a half-charred hedge-stake with which I punched a black log into flame.

'It never goes out, day or night,' she said, as though explaining. 'In case anyone comes in with cold toes, you see.'

'It's even lovelier inside than it was out,' I murmured. The red light poured itself along the age-polished dusky panels till the Tudor roses and lions of the gallery took colour and motion. An old eagle-topped convex mirror gathered the picture into its mysterious heart, distorting afresh the distorted shadows, and curving the gallery lines into the curves of a ship. The day was shutting down in half a gale as the fog turned to stringy scud. Through the uncurtained mullions of the broad window I could see the valiant horsemen of the lawn rear and recover against the wind that taunted them with legions of dead leaves.

'Yes, it must be beautiful,' she said. 'Would you like to go over it? There's still light enough upstairs.'

I followed her up the unflinching, wagon-wide staircase to the gallery whence opened the thin fluted Elizabethan doors.

'Feel how they put the latch low down for the sake of the children.' She swung a light door inward.

'By the way, where are they?' I asked. 'I haven't even heard them to-day.'

She did not answer at once. Then, 'I can only hear them,' she replied softly. 'This is one of their rooms – everything ready, you see.'

She pointed into a heavily-timbered room. There were little low gate tables and children's chairs. A doll's house, its hooked front half open, faced a great dappled rocking-horse, from whose padded saddle it was but a child's scramble to the broad window-seat overlooking the lawn. A toy gun lay in a corner beside a gilt wooden cannon.

'Surely they've only just gone,' I whispered. In the failing light a

door creaked cautiously. I heard the rustle of a frock and the patter of
feet – quick feet through a room beyond.

'I heard that,' she cried triumphantly. 'Did you? Children, oh, children! Where are you?'

The voice filled the walls that held it lovingly to the last perfect
note, but there came no answering shout such as I had heard in the
garden. We hurried on from room to oak-floored room; up a step here,
down three steps there; among a maze of passages; always mocked by
our quarry. One might as well have tried to work an unstopped warren
with a single ferret. There were bolt-holes innumerable – recesses in
walls, embrasures of deep-slitten windows now darkened, whence they
could start up behind us; and abandoned fireplaces, six feet deep in
the masonry, as well as the tangle of communicating doors. Above all,
they had the twilight for their helper in our game. I had caught one
or two joyous chuckles of evasion, and once or twice had seen the
silhouette of a child's frock against some darkening window at the
end of a passage; but we returned empty-handed to the gallery, just as
a middle-aged woman was setting a lamp in its niche.

'No, I haven't seen her either this evening, Miss Florence,' I heard
her say, 'but that Turpin he says he wants to see you about his shed.'

'Oh, Mr Turpin must want to see me very badly. Tell him to come
to the hall, Mrs Madden.'

I looked down into the hall whose only light was the dulled fire, and
deep in the shadow I saw them at last. They must have slipped down
while we were in the passages, and now thought themselves perfectly
hidden behind an old gilt leather screen. By child's law, my fruitless
chase was as good as an introduction, but since I had taken so much
trouble I resolved to force them to come forward later by the simple
trick, which children detest, of pretending not to notice them. They lay
close, in a little huddle, no more than shadows except when a quick
flame betrayed an outline.

'And now we'll have some tea,' she said. 'I believe I ought to have
offered it you at first, but one doesn't arrive at manners somehow when
one lives alone and is considered – h'm – peculiar.' Then with very
pretty scorn, 'Would you like a lamp to see to eat by?'

'The firelight's much pleasanter, I think.' We descended into that
delicious gloom and Madden brought tea.

I took my chair in the direction of the screen ready to surprise or
be surprised as the game should go, and at her permission, since a
hearth is always sacred, bent forward to play with the fire.

'Where do you get these beautiful short faggots from?' I asked idly.
'Why, they are tallies!'

'Of course,' she said. 'As I can't read or write I'm driven back on the early English tally for my accounts. Give me one and I'll tell you what it meant.'

I passed her an unburned hazel-tally, about a foot long, and she ran her thumb down the nicks.

'This is the milk-record for the home farm for the month of April last year, in gallons,' said she. 'I don't know what I should have done without tallies. An old forester of mine taught me the system. It's out of date now for every one else, but my tenants respect it. One of them's coming now to see me. Oh, it doesn't matter. He has no business here out of office hours. He's a greedy, ignorant man – very greedy, or – he wouldn't come here after dark.'

'Have you much land then?'

'Only a couple of hundred acres in hand, thank goodness. The other six hundred are nearly all let to folk who knew my folk before me, but this Turpin is quite a new man – and a highway robber.'

'But are you sure I shan't be – ?'

'Certainly not. You have the right. He hasn't any children.'

'Ah, the children!' I said, and slid my low chair back till it nearly touched the screen that hid them. 'I wonder whether they'll come out for me.'

There was a murmur of voices – Madden's and a deeper note – at the low, dark side door, and a ginger-headed, canvas-gaitered giant of the unmistakable tenant-farmer type stumbled or was pushed in.

'Come to the fire, Mr Turpin,' she said.

'If – if you please, Miss, I'll – I'll be quite as well by the door.' He clung to the latch as he spoke like a frightened child. Of a sudden I realised that he was in the grip of some almost overpowering fear.

'Well?'

'About that new shed for the young stock – that was all. These first autumn storms settin' in . . . but I'll come again, Miss.' His teeth did not chatter much more than the door-latch.

'I think not,' she answered levelly. 'The new shed – m'm. What did my agent write you on the 15th?'

'I – fancied p'r'aps that if I came to see you – ma–man to man like, Miss. But – '

His eyes rolled into every corner of the room wide with horror. He half opened the door through which he had entered, but I noticed it shut again – from without and firmly.

'He wrote what I told him,' she went on. 'You are overstocked already. Dunnett's Farm never carried more than fifty bullocks – even in Mr Wright's time. And *he* used cake. You've sixty-seven and you don't cake. You've broken the lease in that respect. You're dragging the heart out of the farm.'

'I'm – I'm getting some minerals – superphosphates – next week. I've as good as ordered a truck-load already. I'll go down to the station to-morrow about 'em. Then I can come and see you man to man like, Miss, in the daylight . . . That gentleman's not going away, is he?' He almost shrieked.

I had only slid the chair a little farther back, reaching behind me to tap on the leather of the screen, but he jumped like a rat.

'No. Please attend to me, Mr Turpin.' She turned in her chair and faced him with his back to the door. It was an old and sordid little piece of scheming that she forced from him – his plea for the new cowshed at his landlady's expense, that he might with the covered manure pay his next year's rent out of the valuation after, as she made clear, he had bled the enriched pastures to the bone. I could not but admire the intensity of his greed, when I saw him outfacing for its sake whatever terror it was that ran wet on his forehead.

I ceased to tap the leather – was, indeed, calculating the cost of the shed – when I felt my relaxed hand taken and turned softly between the soft hands of a child. So at last I had triumphed. In a moment I would turn and acquaint myself with those quick-footed wanderers . . .

The little brushing kiss fell in the centre of my palm – as a gift on which the fingers were, once, expected to close: as the all-faithful half-reproachful signal of a waiting child not used to neglect even when grown-ups were busiest – a fragment of the mute code devised very long ago.

Then I knew. And it was as though I had known from the first day when I looked across the lawn at the high window.

I heard the door shut. The woman turned to me in silence, and I felt that she knew.

What time passed after this I cannot say. I was roused by the fall of a log, and mechanically rose to put it back. Then I returned to my place in the chair very close to the screen.

'Now you understand,' she whispered, across the packed shadows.

'Yes, I understand – now. Thank you.'

'I – I only hear them.' She bowed her head in her hands. 'I have no right, you know – no other right. I have neither borne nor lost – neither borne nor lost!'

'Be very glad then,' said I, for my soul was torn open within me.

'Forgive me!'

She was still, and I went back to my sorrow and my joy.

'It was because I loved them so,' she said at last, brokenly. '*That* was why it was, even from the first – even before I knew that they – they were all I should ever have. And I loved them so!'

She stretched out her arms to the shadows and the shadows within the shadow.

'They came because I loved them – because I needed them. I – I must have made them come. Was that wrong, think you?'

'No – no.'

'I – I grant you that the toys and – and all that sort of thing were nonsense, but – but I used to so hate empty rooms myself when I was little.' She pointed to the gallery. 'And the passages all empty. . . . And how could I ever bear the garden door shut? Suppose –'

'Don't! For pity's sake, don't!' I cried. The twilight had brought a cold rain with gusty squalls that plucked at the leaded windows.

'And the same thing with keeping the fire in all night. *I* don't think it so foolish – do you?'

I looked at the broad brick hearth, saw, through tears, I believe, that there was no unpassable iron[10] on or near it, and bowed my head.

'I did all that and lots of other things – just to make believe. Then they came. I heard them, but I didn't know that they were not mine by right till Mrs Madden told me – '

'The butler's wife? What?'

'One of them – I heard – she saw. And knew. Hers! *Not* for me. I didn't know at first. Perhaps I was jealous. Afterwards, I began to understand that it was only because I loved them, not because – . . . Oh, you *must* bear or lose,' she said piteously. 'There is no other way – and yet they love me. They must! Don't they?'

There was no sound in the room except the lapping voices of the fire, but we two listened intently, and she at least took comfort from what she heard. She recovered herself and half rose. I sat still in my chair by the screen.

'Don't think me a wretch to whine about myself like this, but – but I'm all in the dark, you know, and *you* can see.'

In truth I could see, and my vision confirmed me in my resolve, though that was like the very parting of spirit and flesh. Yet a little longer I would stay since it was the last time.

'You think it is wrong, then?' she cried sharply, though I had said nothing.

'Not for you. A thousand times no. For you it is right . . . I am grateful to you beyond words. For me it would be wrong. For me only . . .'

'Why?' she said, but passed her hand before her face as she had done at our second meeting in the wood. 'Oh, I see,' she went on simply as a child. 'For you it would be wrong.' Then with a little indrawn laugh, 'And, d'you remember, I called you lucky – once – at first. You who must never come here again!'

She left me to sit a little longer by the screen, and I heard the sound of her feet die out along the gallery above.

'WIRELESS'

'It's a funny thing, this Marconi business, isn't it?' said Mr Shaynor, coughing heavily. 'Nothing seems to make any difference, by what they tell me – storms, hills, or anything; but if that's true we shall know before morning.'

'Of course it's true,' I answered, stepping behind the counter. 'Where's old Mr Cashell?'

'He's had to go to bed on account of his influenza. He said you'd very likely drop in.'

'Where's his nephew?'

'Inside, getting the things ready. He told me that the last time they experimented they put the pole on the roof of one of the big hotels here, and the batteries electrified all the water-supply, and' – he giggled – 'the ladies got shocks when they took their baths.'

'I never heard of that.'

'The hotel wouldn't exactly advertise it, would it? Just now, by what Mr Cashell tells me, they're trying to signal from here to Poole, and they're using stronger batteries than ever. But, you see, he being the guv'nor's nephew and all that (and it will be in the papers too), it doesn't matter how they electrify things in this house. Are you going to watch?'

'Very much. I've never seen this game. Aren't you going to bed?'

'We don't close till ten on Saturdays. There's a good deal of influenza in town, too, and there'll be a dozen prescriptions coming in before morning. I generally sleep in the chair here. It's warmer than jumping out of bed every time. Bitter cold, isn't it?'

'Freezing hard. I'm sorry your cough's worse.'

'Thank you. I don't mind cold so much. It's this wind that fair cuts me to pieces.' He coughed again hard and hackingly, as an old lady came in for ammoniated quinine.[1] 'We've just run out of it in bottles, madam,' said Mr Shaynor, returning to the professional tone, 'but if you will wait two minutes, I'll make it up for you, madam.'

I had used the shop for some time, and my acquaintance with the proprietor had ripened into friendship. It was Mr Cashell who revealed to me the purpose and power of Apothecaries' Hall what time a fellow-chemist had made an error in a prescription of mine, had lied to cover his sloth, and when error and lie were brought home to him had written vain letters.

'A disgrace to our profession,' said the thin, mild-eyed man hotly, after studying the evidence. 'You couldn't do a better service to the profession than report him to Apothecaries' Hall.'

I did so, not knowing what djinns I should evoke; and the result was such an apology as one might make who had spent a night on the rack. I conceived great respect for Apothecaries' Hall, and esteem for Mr Cashell, a zealous craftsman who magnified his calling. Until Mr Shaynor came down from the North his assistants had by no means agreed with Mr Cashell. 'They forget,' said he, 'that, first and foremost, the compounder is a medicine-man. On him depends the physician's reputation. He holds it literally in the hollow of his hand, sir.'

Mr Shaynor's manners had not, perhaps, the polish of the grocery and Italian warehouse next door, but he knew and loved his dispensary work in every detail. For relaxation he seemed to go no further afield than the romance of drugs – their discovery, preparation, packing, and export – but it led him to the ends of the earth, and on this subject, and the Pharmaceutical Formulary,[2] and Nicholas Culpeper,[3] most confident of physicians, we met.

Little by little I grew to know something of his beginnings and his hopes – of his mother, who had been a school-teacher in one of the northern counties, and of his red-headed father, a small job-master at Kirby Moors, who died when he was a child; of the examinations he had passed and of their exceeding and increasing difficulty; of his dreams of a shop in London; of his hate for the price-cutting Co-operative stores; and, most interesting, of his mental attitude towards customers.

'There's a way you get into,' he told me, 'of serving them carefully, and, I hope, politely, without stopping your own thinking. I've been reading Christy's *New Commercial Plants* all this autumn, and that needs keeping your mind on it, I can tell you. So long as it isn't a prescription, of course, I can carry as much as half a page of Christy in my head, and at the same time I could sell out all that window twice over, and not a penny wrong at the end. As to prescriptions, I think I could make up the general run of 'em in my sleep, almost.'

For reasons of my own, I was deeply interested in Marconi experiments at their outset in England; and it was of a piece with Mr Cashell's unvarying thoughtfulness that, when his nephew the electrician appropriated the house for a long-range installation, he should, as I have said, invite me to see the result.

The old lady went away with her medicine, and Mr Shaynor and I stamped on the tiled floor behind the counter to keep ourselves warm. The shop, by the light of the many electrics, looked like a Paris-diamond mine, for Mr Cashell believed in all the ritual of his craft. Three superb glass jars – red, green, and blue – of the sort that led Rosamond to parting with her shoes[4] – blazed in the broad plate-glass windows, and there was a confused smell of orris,[5] Kodak films, vulcanite,[6] tooth-powder, sachets, and almond-cream in the air. Mr Shaynor fed the dispensary stove, and we sucked cayenne-pepper jujubes and menthol lozenges. The brutal east wind had cleared the streets, and the few passers-by were muffled to their puckered eyes. In the Italian warehouse next door some gay feathered birds and game, hung upon hooks, sagged to the wind[7] across the left edge of our window-frame.

'They ought to take these poultry in – all knocked about like that,' said Mr Shaynor. 'Doesn't it make you feel fair perishing? See that old hare![8] The wind's nearly blowing the fur off him.'

I saw the belly-fur of the dead beast blown apart in ridges and streaks as the wind caught it, showing bluish skin underneath. 'Bitter cold,' said Mr Shaynor, shuddering. 'Fancy going out on a night like this! Oh, here's young Mr Cashell.'

The door of the inner office behind the dispensary opened, and an energetic, spade-bearded man stepped forth, rubbing his hands.

'I want a bit of tin-foil, Shaynor,' he said. 'Good evening. My uncle told me you might be coming.' This to me, as I began the first of a hundred questions.

'I've everything in order,' he replied. 'We're only waiting until Poole calls us up. Excuse me a minute. You can come in whenever you like – but I'd better be with the instruments. Give me that tin-foil. Thanks.'

While we were talking, a girl – evidently no customer – had come into the shop, and the face and bearing of Mr Shaynor changed. She leaned confidently across the counter.

'But I can't,' I heard him whisper uneasily – the flush on his cheek was dull red, and his eyes shone like a drugged moth's. 'I can't. I tell you I'm alone in the place.'

'No, you aren't. Who's *that*? Let him look after it for half an hour. A brisk walk will do you good. Ah, come now, John.'

'But he isn't – '

'I don't care. I want you to; we'll only go round by St. Agnes'. If you don't – '

He crossed to where I stood in the shadow of the dispensary counter, and began some sort of broken apology about a lady-friend.

'Yes,' she interrupted. 'You take the shop for half an hour – to oblige *me*, won't you?'

She had a singularly rich and promising voice that well matched her outline.

'All right,' I said. 'I'll do it – but you'd better wrap yourself up, Mr Shaynor.'

'Oh, a brisk walk ought to help me. We're only going round by the church.' I heard him cough grievously as they went out together.

I refilled the stove, and, after reckless expenditure of Mr Cashell's coal, drove some warmth into the shop. I explored many of the glass-knobbed drawers that lined the walls, tasted some disconcerting drugs, and, by the aid of a few cardamoms, ground ginger, chloric-ether,[9] and dilute alcohol, manufactured a new and wildish drink, of which I bore a glassful to young Mr Cashell, busy in the back office. He laughed shortly when I told him that Mr Shaynor had stepped out – but a frail coil of wire held all his attention, and he had no word for me bewildered among the batteries and rods. The noise of the sea on the beach began to make itself heard as the traffic in the street ceased. Then briefly, but very lucidly, he gave me the names and uses of the mechanism that crowded the tables and the floor.

'When do you expect to get the message from Poole?' I demanded, sipping my liquor out of a graduated glass.

'About midnight, if everything is in order. We've got our installation-pole fixed to the roof of the house. I shouldn't advise you to turn on a tap or anything tonight. We've connected up with the plumbing, and all the water will be electrified.' He repeated to me the history of the agitated ladies at the hotel at the time of the first installation.

'But what *is* it?' I asked. 'Electricity is out of my beat altogether.'

'Ah, if you knew *that* you'd know something nobody knows. It's just It – what we call Electricity, but the magic – the manifestations – the Hertzian waves[10] – are all revealed by *this*. The coherer, we call it.'

He picked up a glass tube not much thicker than a thermometer, in which, almost touching, were two tiny silver plugs, and between them an infinitesimal pinch of metallic dust. 'That's all,' he said proudly, as though himself responsible for the wonder. 'That is the thing that will reveal to us the Powers – whatever the Powers may be – at work – through space – a long distance away.'

Just then Mr Shaynor returned alone and stood coughing his heart out on the mat.

'Serves you right for being such a fool,' said young Mr Cashell, as annoyed as myself at the interruption. 'Never mind – we've all the night before us to see wonders.'

Shaynor clutched the counter, his handkerchief to his lips. When he brought it away I saw two bright red stains.

'I – I've got a bit of a rasped throat from smoking cigarettes,' he panted. 'I think I'll try a cubeb.'[11]

'Better take some of this. I've been compounding while you've been away.' I handed him the brew.

''Twon't make me drunk, will it? I'm almost a teetotaller. My word! That's grateful and comforting.'

He set down the empty glass to cough afresh.

'Brr! But it was cold out there! I shouldn't care to be lying in my grave a night like this. Don't *you* ever have a sore throat from smoking?' He pocketed the handkerchief after a furtive peep.

'Oh yes, sometimes,' I replied, wondering, while I spoke, into what agonies of terror I should fall if ever I saw those bright-red danger-signals under my nose. Young Mr Cashell among the batteries coughed slightly to show that he was quite ready to continue his scientific explanations, but I was thinking still of the girl with the rich voice and the significantly cut mouth, at whose command I had taken charge of the shop. It flashed across me that she distantly resembled the seductive shape on a gold-framed toilet-water advertisement whose charms were unholily heightened by the glare from the red bottle in the window. Turning to make sure, I saw Mr Shaynor's eyes bent in the same direction, and by instinct recognised that the flamboyant thing was to him a shrine. 'What do you take for your – cough?' I asked.

'Well, I'm the wrong side of the counter to believe much in patent medicines. But there are asthma cigarettes and there are pastilles. To tell you the truth, if you don't object to the smell, which is very like incense, I believe, though I'm not a Roman Catholic, Blaudett's Cathedral Pastilles relieve me as much as anything.'

'Let's try.' I had never raided a chemist's shop before, so I was thorough. We unearthed the pastilles – brown, gummy cones of benzoin[12] – and set them alight under the toilet-water advertisement, where they fumed in thin blue spirals.

'Of course,' said Mr Shaynor, to my question, 'what one uses in the shop for one's self comes out of one's pocket. Why, stock-taking in our business is nearly the same as with jewellers – and I can't say more than that. But one gets them' – he pointed to the pastille-box – 'at trade prices.' Evidently the censing of the gay, seven-tinted wench with the teeth was an established ritual which cost something.

'And when do we shut up shop?'

'We stay like this all night. The guv – old Mr Cashell – doesn't believe in locks and shutters as compared with electric light. Besides, it brings trade. I'll just sit here in the chair by the stove and write a letter, if you don't mind. Electricity isn't my prescription.'

The energetic young Mr Cashell snorted within, and Shaynor settled himself up in his chair over which he had thrown a staring red, black, and yellow Austrian jute blanket, rather like a table-cover. I cast about, amid patent-medicine pamphlets, for something to read, but finding little, returned to the manufacture of the new drink. The Italian ware-house took down its game and went to bed. Across the street, blank shutters flung back the gaslight in cold smears; the dried pavement seemed to rough up in goose-flesh under the scouring of the savage wind, and we could hear, long ere he passed, the policeman flapping his arms to keep himself warm. Within, the flavours of cardamoms and chloric-ether disputed those of the pastilles and a score of drugs and perfume and soap scents. Our electric lights, set low down in the windows before the tun-bellied Rosamond jars, flung inward three monstrous daubs of red, blue, and green, that broke into kaleidoscopic lights on the faceted knobs of the drug-drawers, the cut-glass scent flagons, and the bulbs of the sparklet bottles. They flushed the white-tiled floor in gorgeous patches; splashed along the nickel-silver counter-rails, and turned the polished mahogany counter-panels to the likeness of intricate grained marbles – slabs of porphyry and malachite. Mr Shaynor unlocked a drawer, and ere he began to write, took out a meagre bundle of letters. From my place by the stove, I could see the scalloped edges of the paper with a flaring monogram in the corner and could even smell the reek of chypre.[13] At each page he turned toward the toilet-water lady of the advertisement and devoured her with over-luminous eyes. He had drawn the Austrian blanket over his shoulders, and among those warring lights he looked more than ever the incarnation of a drugged moth – a tiger-moth as I thought.

He put his letter into an envelope, stamped it with stiff mechanical movements, and dropped it in the drawer. Then I became aware of the silence of a great city asleep – the silence that underlay the even voice of the breakers along the sea-front – a thick, tingling quiet of warm life stilled down for its appointed time, and unconsciously I moved about the glittering shop as one moves in a sick-room. Young Mr Cashell was adjusting some wire that crackled from time to time with the tense, knuckle-stretching sound of the electric spark. Upstairs, where a door shut and opened swiftly, I could hear his uncle coughing abed.

'Here,' I said, when the drink was properly warmed, 'take some of this, Mr Shaynor.'

He jerked in his chair with a start and a wrench, and held out his hand for the glass. The mixture, of a rich port-wine colour, frothed at the top.

'It looks,' he said suddenly, 'it looks – those bubbles – like a string of pearls winking at you[14] – rather like the pearls round that young lady's neck.' He turned again to the advertisement where the female in the dove-coloured corset had seen fit to put on all her pearls before she cleaned her teeth.

'Not bad, is it?' I said.

'Eh?'

He rolled his eyes heavily full on me, and, as I stared, I beheld all meaning and consciousness die out of the swiftly dilating pupils. His figure lost its stark rigidity, softened into the chair, and, chin on chest, hands dropped before him, he rested open-eyed, absolutely still.

'I'm afraid I've rather cooked Shaynor's goose,' I said, bearing the fresh drink to young Mr Cashell. 'Perhaps it was the chloric-ether.'

'Oh, he's all right.' The spade-bearded man glanced at him pityingly. 'Consumptives go off in those sort of dozes very often. It's exhaustion . . . I don't wonder. I daresay the liquor will do him good. It's grand stuff.' He finished his share appreciatively. 'Well, as I was saying – before he interrupted – about this little coherer. The pinch of dust, you see, is nickel-filings. The Hertzian waves, you see, come out of space from the station that despatches 'em, and all these little particles are attracted together – cohere, we call it – for just so long as the current passes through them. Now, it's important to remember that the current is an induced current. There are a good many kinds of induction – '

'Yes, but what *is* induction?'

'That's rather hard to explain untechnically. But the long and the short of it is that when a current of electricity passes through a wire there's a lot of magnetism present round that wire; and if you put another wire parallel to, and within what we call its magnetic field – why, then the second wire will also become charged with electricity.'

'On its own account?'

'On its own account.'

'Then let's see if I've got it correctly. Miles off, at Poole, or wherever it is – '

'It will be anywhere in ten years.'

'You've got a charged wire – '

'Charged with Hertzian waves which vibrate, say, two hundred and thirty million times a second.' Mr Cashell snaked his forefinger rapidly through the air.

'All right – a charged wire at Poole, giving out these waves into space. Then this wire of yours sticking out into space – on the roof of the house – in some mysterious way gets charged with those waves from Poole – '

'Or anywhere – it only happens to be Poole to-night.'

'And those waves set the coherer at work, just like an ordinary telegraph-office ticker?'

'No! That's where so many people make the mistake. The Hertzian waves wouldn't be strong enough to work a great heavy Morse instrument like ours. They can only just make that dust cohere, and while it coheres (a little while for a dot and a longer while for a dash) the current from this battery – the home battery' – he laid his hand on the thing – 'can get through to the Morse printing-machine to record the dot or dash. Let me make it clearer. Do you know anything about steam?'

'Very little. But go on.'

'Well, the coherer is like a steam-valve. Any child can open a valve and start a steamer's engines, because a turn of the hand lets in the main steam, doesn't it? Now, this home battery here ready to print is the main steam. The coherer is the valve, always ready to be turned on. The Hertzian wave is the child's hand that turns it.'

'I see. That's marvellous.'

'Marvellous, isn't it? And, remember, we're only at the beginning. There's nothing we shan't be able to do in ten years. I want to live – my God, how I want to live, and see it develop!' He looked through the door at Shaynor breathing lightly in his chair. 'Poor beast! And he wants to keep company with Fanny Brand.'

'Fanny *who*?' I said, for the name struck an obscurely familiar chord in my brain – something connected with a stained handkerchief, and the word 'arterial'.

'Fanny Brand – the girl you kept shop for.' He laughed. 'That's all I know about her, and for the life of me I can't see what Shaynor sees in her, or she in him.'

'*Can't* you see what he sees in her?' I insisted.

'Oh yes, if *that's* what you mean. She's a great, big, fat lump of a girl, and so on. I suppose that's why he's so crazy after her. She isn't his sort. Well, it doesn't matter. My uncle says he's bound to die before the year's out. Your drink's given him a good sleep, at any rate.' Young Mr Cashell could not catch Mr Shaynor's face, which was half turned to the advertisement.

I stoked the stove anew, for the room was growing cold, and lighted another pastille. Mr Shaynor in his chair, never moving, looked through and over me with eyes as wide and lustreless as those of a dead hare.

'Poole's late,' said young Mr Cashell, when I stepped back. 'I'll just send them a call.'

He pressed a key in the semi-darkness, and with a rending crackle there leaped between two brass knobs a spark, streams of sparks, and sparks again.

'Grand, isn't it? *That's* the Power – our unknown Power – kicking and fighting to be let loose,' said young Mr Cashell. 'There she goes – kick – kick – kick into space. I never get over the strangeness of it when I work a sending-machine – waves going into space, you know. T. R. is our call. Poole ought to answer with L. L. L.'

We waited two, three, five minutes. In that silence, of which the boom of the tide was an orderly part, I caught the clear '*kiss – kiss – kiss*' of the halliards on the roof, as they were blown against the installation-pole.

'Poole is not ready. I'll stay here and call you when he is.'

I returned to the shop, and set down my glass on a marble slab with a careless clink. As I did so, Shaynor rose to his feet, his eyes fixed once more on the advertisement, where the young woman bathed in the light from the red jar simpered pinkly over her pearls. His lips moved without cessation. I stepped nearer to listen. 'And threw – and threw – and threw,' he repeated, his face all sharp with some inexplicable agony.

I moved forward astonished. But it was then he found words – delivered roundly and clearly. These: –

'And threw warm gules on Madeleine's young breast.'[15]

The trouble passed off his countenance, and he returned lightly to his place, rubbing his hands.

It had never occurred to me, though we had many times discussed reading and prize-competitions as a diversion, that Mr Shaynor ever read Keats, or could quote him at all appositely. There was, after all, a certain stained-glass effect of light on the high bosom of the highly-polished picture which might, by stretch of fancy, suggest, as a vile chromo[16] recalls some incomparable canvas, the line he had spoken. Night, my drink, and solitude were evidently turning Mr Shaynor into a poet. He sat down again and wrote swiftly on his villainous note-paper, his lips quivering.

I shut the door into the inner office and moved up behind him. He made no sign that he saw or heard. I looked over his shoulder, and read, amid half-formed words, sentences, and wild scratches:

' – Very cold it was. Very cold
The hare – the hare – the hare –
The birds – '

He raised his head sharply, and frowned toward the blank shutters of the poulterer's shop where they jutted out against our window. Then one clear line came:

> 'The hare, in spite of fur, was very cold.'

The head, moving machine-like, turned right to the advertisement where the Blaudett's Cathedral pastille reeked abominably. He grunted, and went on: –

> 'Incense in a censer –
> Before her darling picture framed in gold –
> Maiden's picture – angel's portrait – '

'Hsh!' said Mr Cashell guardedly from the inner office, as though in the presence of spirits. 'There's something coming through from somewhere; but it isn't Poole.' I heard the crackle of sparks as he depressed the keys of the transmitter. In my brain, too, something crackled, or it might have been the hair on my head. Then I heard my own voice, in a harsh whisper: 'Mr Cashell, there is something coming through here, too. Leave me alone till I tell you.'

'But I thought you'd come to see this wonderful thing – sir,' indignantly at the end.

'Leave me alone till I tell you. Be quiet.'

I watched – I waited. Under the blue-veined hand – the dry hand of the consumptive – came away clear, without erasure:

> 'And my weak spirit fails
> To think how the dead must freeze – '

he shivered as he wrote –

> 'Beneath the churchyard mould.'[17]

Then he stopped, laid the pen down, and leaned back.

For an instant, that was half an eternity, the shop spun before me in a rainbow-tinted whirl, in and through which my own soul most dispassionately considered my own soul as that fought with an overmastering fear. Then I smelt the strong smell of cigarettes from Mr Shaynor's clothing, and heard, as though it had been the rending of trumpets, the rattle of his breathing. I was still in my place of observation, much as one would watch a rifle-shot at the butts, half-bent, hands on my knees, and head within a few inches of the black, red, and yellow blanket of his shoulder. I was whispering encouragement, evidently to my other self, – sounding sentences, such as men pronounce in dreams.

'If he has read Keats, it proves nothing. If he hasn't – like causes *must* beget like effects. There is no escape from this law. *You* ought to be grateful that you know "St Agnes' Eve" without the book; because, given the circumstances, such as Fanny Brand, who is the key of the enigma, and approximately represents the latitude and longitude of Fanny Brawne; allowing also for the bright red colour of the arterial blood upon the handkerchief, which was just what you were puzzling over in the shop just now; and counting the effect of the professional environment, here almost perfectly duplicated – the result is logical and inevitable. As inevitable as induction.'

Still, the other half of my soul refused to be comforted. It was cowering in some minute and inadequate corner – at an immense distance.

Hereafter, I found myself one person again, my hands still gripping my knees, and my eyes glued on the page before Mr Shaynor. As dreamers accept and explain the upheaval of landscapes and the resurrection of the dead, with excerpts from the evening hymn or the multiplication-table, so I had accepted the facts, whatever they might be, that I should witness, and had devised a theory, sane and plausible to my mind, that explained them all. Nay, I was even in advance of my facts, walking hurriedly before them, assured that they would fit my theory. And all that I now recall of that epoch-making theory are the lofty words: 'If he has read Keats, it's the chloric-ether. If he hasn't, it's the identical bacillus, or Hertzian wave of tuberculosis, *plus* Fanny Brand and the professional status which, in conjunction with the main-stream of subconscious thought common to all mankind, has thrown up temporarily an induced Keats.'

Mr Shaynor returned to his work, erasing and re-writing as before with swiftness. Two or three blank pages he tossed aside. Then he wrote, muttering:

'The little smoke of a candle that goes out.'[18]

'No,' he muttered. 'Little smoke – little smoke – little smoke. What else?' He thrust his chin forward toward the advertisement, whereunder the last of the Blaudett's Cathedral pastilles fumed in its holder. 'Ah!' Then with relief:

'The little smoke that dies in moonlight cold.'

Evidently he was snared by the rhymes of his first verse, for he wrote
and rewrote 'gold – cold – mould' many times. Again he sought inspiration from the advertisement, and set down, without erasure, the
line I had overheard:

'And threw warm gules on Madeleine's young breast.'

As I remembered the original it is 'fair' – a trite word – instead of
'young,' and I found myself nodding approval, though I admitted that
the attempt to reproduce 'Its little smoke in pallid moonlight died' was
a failure.

Followed without a break ten or fifteen lines of bald prose – the
naked soul's confession of its physical yearning for its beloved – unclean
as we count uncleanliness; unwholesome, but human exceedingly; the
raw material, so it seemed to me in that hour and in that place, whence
Keats wove the twenty-sixth, seventh, and eighth stanzas of his poem.[19]
Shame I had none in overseeing this revelation; and my fear had gone
with the smoke of the pastille.

'That's it,' I murmured. 'That's how it's blocked out. Go on! Ink it
in, man. Ink it in!'

Mr Shaynor returned to broken verse wherein 'loveliness' was made to
rhyme with a desire to look upon 'her empty dress'. He picked up a fold
of the gay, soft blanket, spread it over one hand, caressed it with infinite
tenderness, thought, muttered, traced some snatches which I could not
decipher, shut his eyes drowsily, shook his head, and dropped the stuff.
Here I found myself at fault, for I could not then see (as I do now) in what
manner a red, black, and yellow Austrian blanket coloured his dreams.[20]

In a few minutes he laid aside his pen, and, chin on hand, considered
the shop with thoughtful and intelligent eyes. He threw down the
blanket, rose, passed along a line of drug-drawers, and read the names
on the labels aloud. Returning, he took from his desk Christy's *New
Commercial Plants* and the old Culpeper that I had given him, opened
and laid them side by side with a clerky air, all trace of passion gone
from his face, read first in one and then in the other, and paused with
pen behind his ear.

'What wonder of Heaven's coming now?' I thought.

'Manna – manna – manna,' he said at last, under wrinkled brows.
'That's what I wanted. Good! Now then! Now then! Good! Good! Oh,
by God, that's good!' His voice rose and he spoke rightly and fully
without a falter:

> 'Candied apple, quince and plum and gourd,
> With jellies smoother than the creamy curd,
> And lucent syrops tinct with cinnamon;
> Manna and dates in argosy transferred
> From Fez; and spiced dainties, every one,
> From silken Samarcand to cedared Lebanon.'[21]

He repeated it once more, using 'blander' for 'smoother' in the second line; then wrote it down without erasure, but this time (my set eyes missed no stroke of any word) he substituted 'soother' for his atrocious second thought, so that it came away under his hand as it is written in the book – as it is written in the book.

A wind went shouting down the street, and on the heels of the wind followed a spurt and rattle of rain.

After a smiling pause – and good right had he to smile – he began anew, always tossing the last sheet over his shoulder:

> 'The sharp rain falling on the window-pane,
> Rattling sleet – the wind-blown sleet.'[22]

Then prose: 'It is very cold of mornings when the wind brings rain and sleet with it. I heard the sleet on the window-pane outside, and thought of you, my darling. I am always thinking of you. I wish we could both run away like two lovers into the storm and get that little cottage by the sea which we are always thinking about, my own dear darling. We could sit and watch the sea beneath our windows. It would be a fairyland all of our own – a fairy sea – a fairy sea . . .'

He stopped, raised his head, and listened. The steady drone of the Channel along the sea-front that had borne us company so long leaped up a note to the sudden fuller surge that signals the change from ebb to flood. It beat in like the change of step throughout an army – this renewed pulse of the sea – and filled our ears till they, accepting it, marked it no longer.

> 'A fairyland for you and me
> Across the foam – beyond . . . .
> A magic foam, a perilous sea.'[23]

He grunted again with effort and bit his underlip. My throat dried, but I dared not gulp to moisten it lest I should break the spell that was drawing him nearer and nearer to the high-water mark but two of the sons of Adam have reached. Remember that in all the millions permitted there are no more than five – five little lines – of which one can say: 'These are the pure Magic. These are the clear Vision. The rest is only poetry.' And Mr Shaynor was playing hot and cold with two of them!

I vowed no unconscious thought of mine should influence the blindfold soul, and pinned myself desperately to the other three, re-peating and re-repeating:

> 'A savage place! as holy and enchanted
> As e'er beneath a waning moon was haunted
> By woman wailing for her demon-lover.'[24]

But though I believed my brain thus occupied, my every sense hung upon the writing under the dry, bony hand, all brown-fingered with chemicals and cigarette-smoke.

> 'Our windows fronting on the dangerous foam,'

(he wrote, after long, irresolute snatches), and then –

> 'Our open casements facing desolate seas
> Forlorn – forlorn –'

Here again his face grew peaked and anxious with that sense of loss I had first seen when the Power snatched him. But this time the agony was tenfold keener. As I watched, it mounted like mercury in the tube. It lighted his face from within till I thought the visibly scourged soul must leap forth naked between his jaws, unable to endure. A drop of sweat trickled from my forehead down my nose and splashed on the back of my hand.

> 'Our windows facing on the desolate seas
> And pearly foam of magic fairyland – '

'Not yet – not yet,' he muttered. 'Wait a minute. *Please* wait a minute. I shall get it then –

> 'Our magic windows fronting on the sea,
> The dangerous foam of desolate seas . . .
>   For aye.

Ouh, my God!'

From head to heel he shook – shook from the marrow of his bones outwards – then leaped to his feet with raised arms, and slid the chair screeching across the tiled floor where it struck the drawers behind and fell with a jar. Mechanically, I stooped to recover it.

As I rose, Mr Shaynor was stretching and yawning at leisure.

'I've had a bit of a doze,' he said. 'How did I come to knock the chair over? You look rather – '

'The chair startled me,' I answered. 'It was so sudden in this quiet.'

Young Mr Cashell behind his shut door was offendedly silent.

'I suppose I must have been dreaming,' said Mr Shaynor.

'I suppose you must,' I said. 'Talking of dreams – I – I noticed you writing – before – '

He flushed consciously.

'I meant to ask you if you've ever read anything written by a man called Keats.'

'Oh! I haven't much time to read poetry, and I can't say that I remember the name exactly. Is he a popular writer?'

'Middling. I thought you might know him because he's the only poet who was ever a druggist. And he's rather what's called the lover's poet.'

'Indeed. I must dip into him. What did he write about?'

'A lot of things. Here's a sample that may interest you.'

Then and there, carefully, I repeated the verse he had twice spoken and once written not ten minutes ago.

'Ah! Anybody could see he was a druggist from that line about the tinctures and syrups. It's a fine tribute to our profession.'

'I don't know,' said young Mr Cashell, with icy politeness, opening the door one half-inch, 'if you still happen to be interested in our trifling experiments. But, should such be the case – '

I drew him aside, whispering, 'Shaynor seemed going off into some sort of fit when I spoke to you just now. I thought, even at the risk of being rude, it wouldn't do to take you off your instruments just as the call was coming through. Don't you see?'

'Granted – granted as soon as asked,' he said, unbending. 'I *did* think it a shade odd at the time. So that was why he knocked the chair down?'

'I hope I haven't missed anything,' I said.

'I'm afraid I can't say that, but you're just in time for the end of a rather curious performance. You can come in too, Mr Shaynor. Listen, while I read it off.'

The Morse instrument was ticking furiously. Mr Cashell interpreted: '"*K.K.V. Can make nothing of your signals.*"' A pause. '"*M.M.V.*

M.M.V. Signals unintelligible. Purpose anchor Sandown Bay. Examine instruments to-morrow." Do you know what that means? It's a couple of men-o'-war working Marconi signals off the Isle of Wight. They are trying to talk to each other. Neither can read the other's messages, but all their messages are being taken in by our receiver here. They've been going on for ever so long. I wish you could have heard it.'

'How wonderful!' I said. 'Do you mean we're overhearing Portsmouth ships trying to talk to each other – that we're eavesdropping across half South England?'

'Just that. Their transmitters are all right, but their receivers are out of order, so they only get a dot here and a dash there. Nothing clear.'

'Why is that?'

'God knows – and Science will know to-morrow. Perhaps the induction is faulty; perhaps the receivers aren't tuned to receive just the number of vibrations per second that the transmitter sends. Only a word here and there. Just enough to tantalise.'

Again the Morse sprang to life.

'That's one of 'em complaining now. Listen: "*Disheartening – most disheartening.*" It's quite pathetic. Have you ever seen a spiritualistic séance? It reminds me of that sometimes – odds and ends of messages coming out of nowhere – a word here and there – no good at all.'

'But mediums are all impostors,' said Mr Shaynor, in the doorway, lighting an asthma cigarette. 'They only do it for the money they can make. I've seen 'em.'

'Here's Poole, at last – clear as a bell. L.L.L. *Now* we shan't be long.' Mr Cashell rattled the keys merrily. 'Anything you'd like to tell 'em?'

'No, I don't think so,' I said. 'I'll go home and get to bed. I'm feeling a little tired.'

THE VILLAGE THAT VOTED
THE EARTH WAS FLAT

Our drive till then had been quite a success. The other men in the car were my friend Woodhouse, young Ollyett, a distant connection of his, and Pallant, the MP. Woodhouse's business was the treatment and cure of sick journals. He knew by instinct the precise moment in a newspaper's life when the impetus of past good management is exhausted and it fetches up on the dead-centre between slow and expensive collapse and the new start which can be given by gold injections – and genius. He was wisely ignorant of journalism; but when he stooped on a carcass there was sure to be meat. He had that week added a half-dead, halfpenny evening paper to his collection, which consisted of a prosperous London daily, one provincial ditto, and a limp-bodied weekly of commercial leanings. He had also, that very hour, planted me with a large block of the evening paper's common shares, and was explaining the whole art of editorship to Ollyett, a young man three years from Oxford, with coir-matting-coloured hair[1] and a face harshly modelled by harsh experiences, who, I understood, was assisting in the new venture. Pallant, the long, wrinkled MP, whose voice is more like a crane's than a peacock's, took no shares, but gave us all advice.

'You'll find it rather a knacker's yard,'[2] Woodhouse was saying. 'Yes, I know they call me The Knacker; but it will pay inside a year. All my papers do. I've only one motto: Back your luck and back your staff. It'll come out all right.'

Then the car stopped, and a policeman asked our names and addresses for exceeding the speed-limit. We pointed out that the road ran absolutely straight for half a mile ahead without even a side-lane. 'That's just what we depend on,' said the policeman unpleasantly.

'The usual swindle,' said Woodhouse under his breath. 'What's the name of this place?'

'Huckley,' said the policeman. 'H-u-c-k-l-e-y,' and wrote something in his note-book at which young Ollyett protested. A large red man on a grey horse who had been watching us from the other side of the hedge shouted an order we could not catch. The policeman laid his hand on the rim of the right driving-door (Woodhouse carries his spare tyres aft[3]), and it closed on the button of the electric horn. The grey horse at once bolted, and we could hear the rider swearing all across the landscape.

'Damn it, man, you've got your silly fist on it! Take it off!' Woodhouse shouted.

'Ho!' said the constable, looking carefully at his fingers as though we had trapped them. 'That won't do you any good either,' and he wrote once more in his note-book before he allowed us to go.

This was Woodhouse's first brush with motor law, and since I expected no ill consequences to myself, I pointed out that it was very serious. I took the same view myself when in due time I found that I, too, was summonsed on charges ranging from the use of obscene language to endangering traffic.

Judgment was done in a little pale-yellow market-town with a small Jubilee clock-tower and a large Corn Exchange. Woodhouse drove us there in his car. Pallant, who had not been included in the summons, came with us as moral support. While we waited outside, the fat man on the grey horse rode up and entered into loud talk with his brother magistrates. He said to one of them – for I took the trouble to note it down – 'It falls away from my lodge-gates, dead straight, three-quarters of a mile. I'd defy any one to resist it. We rooked seventy pounds out of 'em last month. No car can resist the temptation. You ought to have one your side the county, Mike. They simply can't resist it.'

'Whew!' said Woodhouse. 'We're in for trouble. Don't you say a word – or Ollyett either! I'll pay the fines and we'll get it over as soon as possible. Where's Pallant?'

'At the back of the court somewhere,' said Ollyett. 'I saw him slip in just now.'

The fat man then took his seat on the Bench, of which he was chairman, and I gathered from a bystander that his name was Sir Thomas Ingell, Bart., MP, of Ingell Park, Huckley. He began with an allocution pitched in a tone that would have justified revolt throughout empires. Evidence, when the crowded little court did not drown it with applause, was given in the pauses of the address. They were all very proud of their Sir Thomas, and looked from him to us, wondering why we did not applaud too.

Taking its time from the chairman, the Bench rollicked with us for seventeen minutes. Sir Thomas explained that he was sick and tired of processions of cads of our type, who would be better employed breaking stones on the road than in frightening horses worth more than themselves or their ancestors. This was after it had been proved

that Woodhouse's man had turned on the horn purposely to annoy Sir
Thomas, who 'happened to be riding by'! There were other remarks
too – primitive enough, – but it was the unspeakable brutality of the
tone, even more than the quality of the justice, or the laughter of
the audience, that stung our souls out of all reason. When we were
dismissed – to the tune of twenty-three pounds, twelve shillings and
sixpence[4] – we waited for Pallant to join us, while we listened to the
next case – one of driving without a licence. Ollyett, with an eye to his
evening paper, had already taken very full notes of our own, but we
did not wish to seem prejudiced.

'It's all right,' said the reporter of the local paper soothingly. 'We
never report Sir Thomas *in extenso*. Only the fines and charges.'

'Oh, thank you,' Ollyett replied, and I heard him ask who everyone
in Court might be. The local reporter was very communicative.

The new victim, a large, flaxen-haired man in somewhat striking
clothes, to which Sir Thomas, now thoroughly warmed, drew public
attention, said that he had left his licence at home. Sir Thomas asked
him if he expected the police to go to his home address at Jerusalem[5]
to find it for him; and the court roared. Nor did Sir Thomas approve
of the man's name, but insisted on calling him 'Mr Masquerader', and
every time he did so, all his people shouted. Evidently this was their
established *auto-da-fé*.

'He didn't summons me – because I'm in the House, I suppose. I
think I shall have to ask a Question,' said Pallant, reappearing at the
close of the case.

'I think *I* shall have to give it a little publicity too,' said Woodhouse.
'We can't have this kind of thing going on, you know.' His face was set
and quite white. Pallant's, on the other hand, was black, and I know
that my very stomach had turned with rage. Ollyett was dumb.

'Well, let's have lunch,' Woodhouse said at last. 'Then we can get
away before the show breaks up.'

We drew Ollyett from the arms of the local reporter, crossed the
Market Square to the Red Lion and found Sir Thomas's 'Mr Masquerader' just sitting down to beer, beef, and pickles.

'Ah!' said he, in a large voice. 'Companions in misfortune. Won't
you gentlemen join me?'

'Delighted,' said Woodhouse. 'What did you get?'

'I haven't decided. It might make a good turn, but – the public aren't
educated up to it yet. It's beyond 'em. If it wasn't, that red dub[6] on the
Bench would be worth fifty a week.'

'Where?' said Woodhouse. The man looked at him with unaffected
surprise.

'At any one of My places,' he replied. 'But perhaps you live here?'

'Good heavens!' cried young Ollyett suddenly. 'You *are* Masquerier, then? I thought you were!'

'Bat Masquerier.' He let the words fall with the weight of an international ultimatum. 'Yes, that's all I am. But you have the advantage of me, gentlemen.'

For the moment, while we were introducing ourselves, I was puzzled. Then I recalled prismatic music-hall posters – of enormous acreage – that had been the unnoticed background of my visits to London for years past. Posters of men and women, singers, jongleurs, impersonators and audacities of every draped and undraped brand, all moved on and off in London and the Provinces by Bat Masquerier – with the long wedge-tailed flourish following the final 'r'.

'*I* knew at once,' said Pallant, the trained MP, and I promptly backed the lie. Woodhouse mumbled excuses. Bat Masquerier was not moved for or against us any more than the frontage of one of his own palaces.

'I always tell My people there's a limit to the size of the lettering,' he said. 'Overdo that and the ret'na doesn't take it in. Advertisin' is the most delicate of all the sciences.'

'There's one man in the world who is going to get a little of it if I live for the next twenty-four hours,' said Woodhouse, and explained how this would come about.

Masquerier stared at him lengthily with gun-metal-blue eyes.

'You mean it?' he drawled; the voice was as magnetic as the look.

'I *do*,' said Ollyett. 'That business of the horn alone ought to have him off the Bench in three months.' Masquerier looked at him even longer than he had looked at Woodhouse.

'He told *me*,' he said suddenly, 'that my home address was Jerusalem. You heard that?'

'But it was the tone – the tone,' Ollyett cried.

'You noticed that, too, did you?' said Masquerier. 'That's the artistic temperament. You can do a lot with it. And I'm Bat Masquerier,' he went on. He dropped his chin in his fists and scowled straight in front of him . . . 'I made the Silhouettes – I made the Trefoil and the Jocunda. I made 'Dal Benzaguen.' Here Ollyett sat straight up, for in common with the youth of that year he worshipped Miss Vidal Benzaguen of the Trefoil immensely and unreservedly. '"*Is* that a dressing-gown or an ulster you're supposed to be wearing?" You heard *that*? . . . "And I suppose you hadn't time to brush your hair either?" You heard *that*? . . . Now, you hear *me*!' His voice filled the coffee-room, then dropped to a whisper as dreadful as a surgeon's before an operation. He spoke for several minutes. Pallant muttered 'Hear! hear!' I saw Ollyett's eye flash – it was to Ollyett that Masquerier addressed himself chiefly, – and Woodhouse leaned forward with joined hands.

'Are you *with* me?' he went on, gathering us all up in one sweep of the arm. 'When I begin a thing I see it through, gentlemen. What Bat can't break, breaks him! But I haven't struck that thing yet. This is no one-turn turn-it-down show. This is business to the dead finish. Are you with me, gentlemen? Good! Now, we'll pool our assets. One London morning, and one provincial daily, didn't you say? One weekly commercial ditto and one MP.'

'Not much use, I'm afraid,' Pallant smirked.

'But privileged.[7] *But* privileged,' he returned. 'And we have also my little team – London, Blackburn, Liverpool, Leeds – I'll tell you about Manchester later – and Me! Bat Masquerier.' He breathed the name reverently into his tankard. 'Gentlemen, when our combination has finished with Sir Thomas Ingell, Bart., MP, and everything else that is his, Sodom and Gomorrah[8] will be a winsome bit of Merrie England beside 'em. I must go back to Town now, but I trust you gentlemen will give me the pleasure of your company at dinner to-night at the Chop Suey – the Red Amber Room – and we'll block out the scenario.' He laid his hand on young Ollyett's shoulder and added: 'It's your brains I want.' Then he left, in a good deal of astrakhan collar and nickel-plated limousine, and the place felt less crowded.

We ordered our car a few minutes later. As Woodhouse, Ollyett and I were getting in, Sir Thomas Ingell, Bart., MP, came out of the Hall of Justice across the square and mounted his horse. I have sometimes thought that if he had gone in silence he might even then have been saved, but as he settled himself in the saddle he caught sight of us and must needs shout: 'Not off yet? You'd better get away and you'd better be careful.' At that moment Pallant, who had been buying picture-postcards, came out of the inn, took Sir Thomas's eye and very leisurely entered the car. It seemed to me that for one instant there was a shade of uneasiness on the baronet's grey-whiskered face.

'I hope,' said Woodhouse after several miles, 'I hope he's a widower.'

'Yes,' said Pallant. 'For his poor, dear wife's sake I hope that, very much indeed. I suppose he didn't see me in Court. Oh, here's the parish history of Huckley written by the Rector and here's your share of the picture-postcards. Are we all dining with this Mr Masquerier to-night?'

'Yes!' said we all.

If Woodhouse knew nothing of journalism, young Ollyett, who had graduated in a hard school, knew a good deal. Our halfpenny evening

paper, which we will call *The Bun* to distinguish her from her prosperous morning sister, *The Cake*, was not only diseased but corrupt.
We found this out when a man brought us the prospectus of a new
oil-field and demanded sub-leaders on its prosperity. Ollyett talked pure
Brasenose[9] to him for three minutes. Otherwise he spoke and wrote
trade-English – a toothsome amalgam of Americanisms and epigrams.
But though the slang changes, the game never alters, and Ollyett and
I and, in the end, some others enjoyed it immensely. It was weeks ere
we could see the wood for the trees, but so soon as the staff realised
that they had proprietors who backed them right or wrong, and specially
when they were wrong (which is the sole secret of journalism), and
that their fate did not hang on any passing owner's passing mood, they
did miracles.

But we did not neglect Huckley. As Ollyett said, our first care was
to create an 'arresting atmosphere' round it. He used to visit the village
of week-ends, on a motor-bicycle with a side-car; for which reason I
left the actual place alone and dealt with it in the abstract. Yet it was
I who drew first blood. Two inhabitants of Huckley wrote to contradict
a small, quite solid paragraph in *The Bun* that a hoopoe had been seen
at Huckley and had, 'of course, been shot by the local sportsmen'. There
was some heat in their letters, both of which we published. Our version
of how the hoopoe got his crest from King Solomon was, I grieve to
say, so inaccurate that the Rector himself – no sportsman as he pointed
out, but a lover of accuracy – wrote to us to correct it. We gave his
letter good space and thanked him.

'This priest is going to be useful,' said Ollyett. 'He has the impartial
mind. I shall vitalise him.'

Forthwith he created M. L. Sigden, a recluse of refined tastes who
in *The Bun* demanded to know whether this Huckley-of-the-Hoopoe
was the Hugly of his boyhood and whether, by any chance, the fell
change of name had been wrought by collusion between a local magnate
and the railway, in the mistaken interests of spurious refinement. 'For
I knew it and loved it with the maidens of my day – *eheu ab angulo!*[10]
– as Hugly,' wrote M. L. Sigden from Oxford.

Though other papers scoffed, *The Bun* was gravely sympathetic.
Several people wrote to deny that Huckley had been changed at birth.
Only the Rector – no philosopher as he pointed out, but a lover of
accuracy – had his doubts, which he laid publicly before Mr M. L.
Sigden, who suggested, through *The Bun*, that the little place might
have begun life in Anglo-Saxon days as 'Hogslea' or among the Normans
as 'Argilé', on account of its much clay. The Rector had his own ideas
too (he said it was mostly gravel), and M. L. Sigden had a fund of

reminiscences. Oddly enough – which is seldom the case with free reading-matter – our subscribers rather relished the correspondence, and contemporaries quoted freely.

'The secret of power,' said Ollyett, 'is not the big stick. It's the liftable stick.' (This means the 'arresting' quotation of six or seven lines.) 'Did you see the *Spec.* had a middle[11] on "Rural Tenacities" last week? That was all Huckley. I'm doing a "Mobiquity" on Huckley next week.'

Our 'Mobiquities' were Friday evening accounts of easy motor-bike-*cum*-side-car trips round London, illustrated (we could never get that machine to work properly) by smudgy maps. Ollyett wrote the stuff with a fervour and a delicacy which I always ascribed to the side-car. His account of Epping Forest, for instance, was simply young love with its soul on its lips. But his Huckley 'Mobiquity' would have sickened a soap-boiler. It chemically combined loathsome familiarity, leering suggestion, slimy piety and rancid 'social service' in one fuming compost that fairly lifted me off my feet.

'Yes,' said he, after compliments. 'It's the most vital, arresting and dynamic bit of tump I've done up to date. *Non nobis gloria!*[12] I met Sir Thomas Ingell in his own park. He talked to me again. He inspired most of it.'

'Which? The "glutinous native drawl", or "the neglected adenoids[13] of the village children"?' I demanded.

'Oh no! That's only to bring in the panel doctor.[14] It's the last flight we – I'm proudest of.'

This dealt with 'the crepuscular penumbra spreading her dim limbs over the boskage'; with 'jolly rabbits'; with a herd of 'gravid polled Angus'; and with the 'arresting, gipsy-like face of their swart, scholarly owner – as well known at the Royal Agricultural Shows as that of our late King-Emperor'.

'"Swart" is good and so's "gravid",' said I, 'but the panel doctor will be annoyed about the adenoids.'

'Not half as much as Sir Thomas will about his face,' said Ollyett. 'And if you only knew what I've left out!'

He was right. The panel doctor spent his week-end (this is the advantage of Friday articles) in overwhelming us with a professional counterblast of no interest whatever to our subscribers. We told him so, and he, then and there, battered his way with it into the *Lancet*, where they are keen on glands, and forgot us altogether. But Sir Thomas Ingell was of sterner stuff. He must have spent a happy week-end too. The letter which we received from him on Monday proved him to be a kinless loon of upright life, for no woman, however remotely interested in a man, would have let it pass the home wastepaper-basket. He objected to our references to his own herd, to his own labours in his own village, which he said was a Model Village, and to our infernal insolence; but he objected most to our invoice of his features. We wrote him courteously to ask whether the letter was meant for publication. He, remembering, I presume, the Duke of Wellington, wrote back, 'publish and be damned.'

'Oh! This is too easy,' Ollyett said as he began heading the letter.

'Stop a minute,' I said. 'The game is getting a little beyond us. To-night's the Bat dinner.' (I may have forgotten to tell you that our dinner with Bat Masquerier in the Red Amber Room of the Chop Suey had come to be a weekly affair.) 'Hold it over till they've all seen it.'

'Perhaps you're right,' he said. 'You might waste it.'

At dinner, then, Sir Thomas's letter was handed round. Bat seemed to be thinking of other matters, but Pallant was very interested.

'I've got an idea,' he said presently. 'Could you put something into *The Bun* to-morrow about foot-and-mouth disease in that fellow's herd?'

'Oh, plague if you like,' Ollyett replied. 'They're only five measly Shorthorns. I saw one lying down in the park. She'll serve as a substratum of fact.'

'Then, do that; and hold the letter over meanwhile. I think *I* come in here,' said Pallant.

'Why?' said I.

'Because there's something coming up in the House about foot-and-mouth, and because he wrote me a letter after that little affair when he fined you. Took ten days to think it over. Here you are,' said Pallant. 'House of Commons paper, you see.'

We read:

'Dear Pallant – Although in the past our paths have not lain much together, I am sure you will agree with me that on the floor of the House all members are on a footing of equality. I make bold, therefore, to approach you in a matter which I think capable of a very different interpretation from that which perhaps was put upon it by your friends. Will you let them know that that was the case and that I was in no way swayed by animus in the exercise of my magisterial duties, which as you, as a brother magistrate, can imagine are frequently very distasteful to – Yours very sincerely, T. Ingell.

'PS. – I have seen to it that the motor vigilance to which your friends took exception has been considerably relaxed in my district.'

'What did you answer?' said Ollyett, when all our opinions had been expressed.

'I told him I couldn't do anything in the matter. And I couldn't – then. But you'll remember to put in that foot-and-mouth paragraph. I want something to work upon.'

'It seems to me *The Bun* has done all the work up to date,' I suggested. 'When does *The Cake* come in?'

'*The Cake*,' said Woodhouse, and I remembered afterwards that he spoke like a Cabinet Minister on the eve of a Budget, 'reserves to itself the fullest right to deal with situations as they arise.'

'Ye-eh!' Bat Masquerier shook himself out of his thoughts. '"Situations as they arise." I ain't idle either. But there's no use fishing till the swim's baited. You' – he turned to Ollyett – 'manufacture very good ground-bait . . . I always tell My people – What the deuce is that?'

There was a burst of song from another private dining-room across the landing. 'It ees some ladies from the Trefoil,' the waiter began.

'Oh, I know that. What are they singing, though?'

He rose and went out, to be greeted by shouts of applause from that merry company. Then there was silence, such as one hears in the form-room after a master's entry. Then a voice that we all loved began again: 'Here we go gathering nuts in May – nuts in May – nuts in May!'

'It's only 'Dal – and some nuts,' he explained when he returned. 'She says she's coming in to dessert.' He sat down, humming the old tune to himself, and till Miss Vidal Benzaguen entered, he held us speechless with tales of the artistic temperament.

We obeyed Pallant to the extent of slipping into *The Bun* a wary paragraph about cows lying down and dripping at the mouth, which might be read either as an unkind libel or, in the hands of a capable lawyer, as a piece of faithful nature-study.

'And besides,' said Ollyett, 'we allude to "gravid polled Angus". I am advised that no action can lie in respect of virgin Shorthorns. Pallant wants us to come to the House to-night. He's got us places for the Strangers' Gallery. I'm beginning to like Pallant.'

'Masquerier seems to like you,' I said.

'Yes, but I'm afraid of him,' Ollyett answered with perfect sincerity. 'I am. He's the Absolutely Amoral Soul. I've never met one before.'

We went to the House together. It happened to be an Irish afternoon,[15] and as soon as I had got the cries and the faces a little sorted out, I gathered there were grievances in the air, but how many of them was beyond me.

'It's all right,' said Ollyett of the trained ear. 'They've shut their ports against – oh yes – export of Irish cattle! Foot-and-mouth disease at Ballyhellion. *I* see Pallant's idea!'

The House was certainly all mouth for the moment, but, as I could feel, quite in earnest. A Minister with a piece of typewritten paper seemed to be fending off volleys of insults. He reminded me somehow of a nervous huntsman breaking up a fox in the face of rabid hounds.

'It's question-time. They're asking questions,' said Ollyett. 'Look! Pallant's up.'

There was no mistaking it. His voice, which his enemies said was his one parliamentary asset, silenced the hubbub as toothache silences mere singing in the ears. He said:

'Arising out of that, may I ask if any special consideration has recently been shown in regard to any suspected outbreak of this disease on *this* side of the Channel?'

He raised his hand; it held a noon edition of *The Bun*. We had thought it best to drop the paragraph out of the later ones. He would have continued, but something in a grey frock-coat roared and bounded on a bench opposite, and waved another *Bun*. It was Sir Thomas Ingell.

'As the owner of the herd so dastardly implicated – ' His voice was drowned in shouts of 'Order!' – the Irish leading.

'What's wrong?' I asked Ollyett. 'He's got his hat on his head, hasn't he?'

'Yes, but his wrath should have been put as a question.'

'Arising out of that, Mr Speaker, Sirrr!' Sir Thomas bellowed through a lull, 'are you aware that – that all this is a conspiracy – part of a dastardly conspiracy to make Huckley ridiculous – to make *us* ridiculous? Part of a deep-laid plot to make *me* ridiculous, Mr Speaker, Sir!'

The man's face showed almost black against his white whiskers, and he struck out swimmingly with his arms. His vehemence puzzled and held the House for an instant, and the Speaker took advantage of it to lift his pack from Ireland to a new scent. He addressed Sir Thomas Ingell in tones of measured rebuke, meant also, I imagine, for the whole House, which lowered its hackles at the word. Then Pallant, shocked and pained: 'I can only express my profound surprise that in response to my simple question the honourable member should have thought fit to indulge in a personal attack. If I have in any way offended – '

Again the Speaker intervened, for it appeared that he regulated these matters.

He, too, expressed surprise, and Sir Thomas sat back in a hush of reprobation that seemed to have the chill of the centuries behind it. The Empire's work was resumed.

'Beautiful!' said I, and I felt hot and cold up my back.

'And now we'll publish his letter,' said Ollyett.

We did – on the heels of his carefully reported outburst. We made no comment. With that rare instinct for grasping the heart of a situation which is the mark of the Anglo-Saxon, all our contemporaries and, I should say, two-thirds of our correspondents demanded how such a person could be made more ridiculous than he had already proved himself to be. But beyond spelling his name 'Injle', we alone refused to hit a man when he was down.

'There's no need,' said Ollyett. 'The whole Press is on the huckle from end to end.'

Even Woodhouse was a little astonished at the ease with which it had come about, and said as much.

'Rot!' said Ollyett. 'We haven't really begun. Huckley isn't news yet.'

'What do you mean?' said Woodhouse, who had grown to have great respect for his young but by no means distant connection.

'Mean? By the grace of God, Master Ridley,[16] I mean to have it so that when Huckley turns over in its sleep, Reuters and the Press Association jump out of bed to cable.' Then he went off at score[17] about certain restorations in Huckley Church which, he said – and he seemed to spend his every week-end there – had been perpetrated by the Rector's predecessor, who had abolished a 'leper-window' or a 'squinch-hole' (whatever these may be) to institute a lavatory in the vestry. It did not strike me as stuff for which Reuters or the Press Association would lose much sleep, and I left him declaiming to Woodhouse about a fourteenth-century font which, he said, he had unearthed in the sexton's tool-shed.

My methods were more on the lines of peaceful penetration. An odd copy, in *The Bun's* rag-and-bone library, of Hone's *Every-Day Book*[18] had revealed to me the existence of a village dance founded, like all village dances, on Druidical mysteries connected with the Summer Solstice (which is always unchallengeable) and Midsummer Morning, which is dewy and refreshing to the London eye. For this I take no credit – Hone being a mine anyone can work – but that I rechristened that dance, after I had revised it, 'The Gubby' is my title to immortal fame. It was still to be witnessed, I wrote, 'in all its poignant purity at Huckley, that last home of significant mediaeval survivals'; and I fell so in love with my creation that I kept it back for days, enamelling and burnishing.

'You'd better put it in,' said Ollyett at last. 'It's time we asserted ourselves again. The other fellows are beginning to poach. You saw that thing in the *Pinnacle* about Sir Thomas's Model Village? He must have got one of their chaps down to do it.'

'Nothing like the wounds of a friend,' I said. 'That account of the non-alcoholic pub alone was – '

'I liked the bit best about the white-tiled laundry and the Fallen Virgins who wash Sir Thomas's dress-shirts. Our side couldn't come within a mile of that, you know. We haven't the proper flair for sexual slobber.'

'That's what I'm always saying,' I retorted. 'Leave 'em alone. The other fellows are doing our work for us now. Besides I want to touch up my "Gubby Dance" a little more.'

'No. You'll spoil it. Let's shove it in to-day. For one thing it's Literature. I don't go in for compliments, as you know, but, etc. etc.'

I had a healthy suspicion of young Ollyett in every aspect, but though I knew that I should have to pay for it, I fell to his flattery, and my priceless article on the 'Gubby Dance' appeared. Next Saturday he asked me to bring out *The Bun* in his absence, which I naturally assumed would be connected with the little maroon side-car. I was wrong.

On the following Monday I glanced at *The Cake* at breakfast-time to make sure, as usual, of her inferiority to my beloved but unremunerative *Bun*. I opened on a heading: 'The Village that Voted the Earth was Flat'. I read . . . I read that the Geoplanarian Society – a Society devoted to the proposition that the Earth is flat – had held its Annual Banquet and Exercises at Huckley on Saturday, when after convincing addresses, amid scenes of the greatest enthusiasm, Huckley village had decided by an unanimous vote of 438 that the Earth was flat. I do not remember that I breathed again till I had finished the two columns of description that followed. Only one man could have written them. They were flawless – crisp, nervous, austere yet human, poignant, vital, arresting – most distinctly arresting – dynamic enough to shift a city – and quotable by whole sticks at a time. And there was a leader, a grave and poised leader, which tore me in two with mirth, until I remembered that I had been left out – infamously and unjustifiably dropped. I went to Ollyett's rooms. He was breakfasting, and, to do him justice, looked conscience-stricken.

'It wasn't my fault,' he began. 'It was Bat Masquerier. I swear *I* would have asked you to come if – '

'Never mind that,' I said. 'It's the best bit of work you've ever done or will do. Did any of it happen?'

'Happen? Heavens! D'you think even *I* could have invented it?'

'Is it exclusive to *The Cake*?' I cried.

'It cost Bat Masquerier two thousand,' Ollyett replied. 'D' you think he'd let anyone else in on that? But I give you my sacred word I knew nothing about it till he asked me to come down and cover it. He had Huckley posted in three colours, "The Geoplanarians' Annual Banquet and Exercises". Yes, he invented "Geoplanarians". He wanted Huckley to think it meant aeroplanes. Yes, I know that there is a real Society that thinks the world's flat – they ought to be grateful for the lift – but Bat made his own. He did! He created the whole show, I tell you. He swept out half his Halls for the job. Think of that – on a Saturday! They – we went down in motor char-à-bancs – three of 'em – one pink, one primrose, and one forget-me-not blue – twenty people in each one and "The Earth *is* Flat" on each side and across the back. I went with Teddy Rickets and Lafone from the Trefoil, and both the Silhouette Sisters, and – wait a minute! – the Crossleigh Trio. You know the Every-Day Dramas Trio at the Jocunda – Ada Crossleigh, "Bunt" Crossleigh, and little Victorine? Them. And there was Hoke Ramsden, the lightning-change chap in *Morgiana and Drexel* – and there was Billy Turpeen. Yes, you know him! The North London Star. "I'm the Referee that got himself disliked at Blackheath." *That* chap! And there was Mackaye – that one-eyed Scotch fellow that all Glasgow is crazy about. Talk of subordinating yourself for Art's sake! Mackaye was the earnest inquirer who got converted at the end of the meeting. And there was quite a lot of girls I didn't know, and – oh yes – there was 'Dal! 'Dal Benzaguen herself! We sat together, going and coming. She's all the darling there ever was. She sent you her love, and she told me to tell you that she won't forget about Nellie Farren.[19] She says you've given her an ideal to work for. She? Oh, she was the Lady Secretary to the Geoplanarians, of course. I forget who were in the other brakes – provincial stars mostly – but they played up gorgeously. The art of the music-hall's changed since your day. They didn't overdo it a bit. You see, people who believe the earth is flat don't dress quite like other people. You may have noticed that I hinted at that in my account. It's a rather flat-fronted Ionic style[20] – neo-Victorian, except for the bustles, 'Dal told me, – but 'Dal looked heavenly in it! So did little Victorine. And there was a girl in the blue brake – she's a provincial – but she's coming to Town this winter and she'll knock 'em – Winnie Deans. Remember that! She told Huckley how she had suffered for the Cause as a governess in a rich family where they believed that the world is round, and how she threw up her job sooner than teach immoral geography. That was at the overflow meeting outside the Baptist chapel. She knocked 'em to sawdust! We must look out for Winnie. . . . But Lafone! Lafone was beyond every-thing. Impact, personality – conviction – the whole bag o' tricks! He sweated conviction. Gad, he convinced *me* while he was speaking! (Him? He was President of the Geoplanarians, of course. Haven't you read my account?) It *is* an infernally plausible theory. After all, no one has actually proved the earth is round, have they?'

'Never mind the earth. What about Huckley?'

'Oh, Huckley got tight. That's the worst of these model villages if you let 'em smell fire-water. There's one alcoholic pub in the place that Sir Thomas can't get rid of. Bat made it his base. He sent down the banquet in two motor lorries – dinner for five hundred and drinks for ten thousand. Huckley voted all right. Don't you make any mistake about that. No vote, no dinner. A unanimous vote – exactly as I've said. At least, the Rector and the Doctor were the only dissentients. We didn't count them. Oh yes, Sir Thomas was there. He came and grinned at us through his park gates. He'll grin worse to-day. There's an aniline dye that you rub through a stencil-plate that eats about a foot into any stone and wears good to the last. Bat had both the lodge-gates stencilled "The Earth *is* flat!" and all the barns and walls they could get at . . . Oh Lord, but Huckley was drunk! We had to fill 'em up to make 'em forgive us for not being aeroplanes. Unthankful yokels! D'you realise that Emperors couldn't have commanded the talent Bat decanted on 'em? Why, 'Dal alone was . . . And by eight o'clock not even a bit of paper left! The whole show packed up and gone, and Huckley hoo-raying for the earth being flat.'

'Very good,' I began. 'I am, as you know, a one-third proprietor of *The Bun*.'

'I didn't forget that,' Ollyett interrupted. 'That was uppermost in my mind all the time. I've got a special account for *The Bun* to-day – it's an idyll – and just to show how I thought of you, I told 'Dal, coming home, about your Gubby Dance, and she told Winnie. Winnie came back in our char-à-banc. After a bit we had to get out and dance it in a field. It's quite a dance the way we did it – and Lafone invented a sort of gorilla lockstep[21] procession at the end. Bat had sent down a film-chap on the chance of getting something. He was the son of a clergyman – a most dynamic personality. He said there isn't anything for the cinema in meetings *qua* meetings – they lack action. Films are a branch of art by themselves. But he went wild over the Gubby. He said it was like Peter's vision at Joppa.[22] He took about a million feet of it. Then I photoed it exclusive for *The Bun*. I've sent 'em in already, only remember we must eliminate Winnie's left leg in the first figure. It's too arresting . . . And there you are! But I tell you I'm afraid of Bat. That man's the Personal Devil. He did it all. He didn't even come down himself. He said he'd distract his people.'

'Why didn't he ask me to come?' I persisted.

'Because he said you'd distract me. He said he wanted my brains on ice. He got 'em. I believe it's the best thing I've ever done.' He reached for *The Cake* and re-read it luxuriously. 'Yes, out and away the best – supremely quotable,' he concluded, and – after another survey – 'By God, what a genius I was yesterday!'

I would have been angry, but I had not the time. That morning, Press agencies grovelled to me in *The Bun* office for leave to use certain photos, which, they understood, I controlled, of a certain village dance. When I had sent the fifth man away on the edge of tears, my self-respect came back a little. Then there was *The Bun's* poster to get out. Art being elimination, I fined it down to two words (one too many, as it proved) – 'The Gubby!' in red, at which our manager protested; but by five o'clock he told me that I was *the* Napoleon of Fleet Street. Ollyett's account in *The Bun* of the Geoplanarians' Exercises and Love Feast lacked the supreme shock of his version in *The Cake*, but it bruised more; while the photos of 'The Gubby' (which, with Winnie's left leg, was why I had set our doubtful press to work so early) were beyond praise and, next day, beyond price. But even then I did not understand.

A week later, I think it was, Bat Masquerier telephoned to me to come to the Trefoil.

'It's your turn now,' he said. 'I'm not asking Ollyett. Come to the stage-box.'

I went, and, as Bat's guest, was received as Royalty is not. We sat well back and looked out on the packed thousands. It was *Morgiana and Drexel*, that fluid and electric review which Bat – though he gave Lafone the credit – really created.

'Ye-es,' said Bat dreamily, after Morgiana had given 'the nasty jar' to the Forty Thieves in their forty oil 'combinations'. 'As you say, I've got 'em and I can hold 'em. What a man does doesn't matter much; and how he does it don't matter either. It's the *when* – the psychological moment. Press can't make up for it; money can't; brains can't. A lot's luck, but all the rest is genius. I'm not speaking about My people now. I'm talking of Myself.'

Then 'Dal – she was the only one who dared – knocked at the door and stood behind us all alive and panting as Morgiana. Lafone was carrying the police-court scene, and the house was ripped up crossways with laughter.

'Ah! Tell a fellow now,' she asked me for the twentieth time, 'did you love Nellie Farren when you were young?'

'Did we love her?' I answered. '"If the earth and the sky and the sea" – There were three million of us, 'Dal, and we worshipped her.'

'How did she get it across?' 'Dal went on.

'She was Nellie. The houses used to coo over her when she came on.'

'I've had a good deal, but I've never been cooed over yet,' said 'Dal wistfully.

'It isn't the how, it's the when,' Bat repeated. 'Ah!'

He leaned forward as the house began to rock and peal full-throatedly. 'Dal fled. A sinuous and silent procession was filing into the police-court to a scarcely audible accompaniment. It was dressed – but the world and all its picture-palaces know how it was dressed. It danced and it danced, and it danced the dance which bit all humanity in the leg for half a year, and it wound up with the lockstep finale that mowed the house down in swathes, sobbing and aching. Somebody in the gallery moaned, 'Oh Gord, the Gubby!' and we heard the word run like a shudder, for they had not a full breath left among them. Then 'Dal came on, an electric star in her dark hair, the diamonds flashing in her three-inch heels – a vision that made no sign for thirty counted seconds while the police-court scene dissolved behind her into Morgiana's Manicure Palace, and they recovered themselves. The star on her forehead went out, and soft light bathed her as she took – slowly, slowly to the croon of adoring strings – the eighteen paces forward. We saw her first as a queen alone; next as a queen for the first time conscious of her subjects, and at the end, when her hands fluttered, as a woman delighted, awed not a little, but transfigured and illuminated with sheer, compelling affection and goodwill. I caught the broken mutter of welcome – the coo which is more than tornadoes of applause. It died and rose and died again lovingly.

'She's got it across,' Bat whispered. 'I've never seen her like this. I told her to light up the star, but I was wrong, and she knew it. She's an artist.'

''Dal, you darling!' someone spoke, not loudly, but it carried through the house.

'Thank *you*!' 'Dal answered, and in that broken tone one heard the last fetter riveted. 'Good evening, boys! I've just come from – now – where the dooce was it I *have* come from?' She turned to the impassive files of the Gubby dancers, and went on: 'Ah, *so* good of you to remind me, you dear, bun-faced things! I've just come from the village – The Village that Voted the Earth was Flat.'

She swept into that song with the full orchestra. It devastated the habitable earth for the next six months. Imagine, then, what its rage and pulse must have been at the incandescent hour of its birth! She only gave the chorus once. At the end of the second verse, 'Are you *with* me, boys?' she cried, and the house tore it clean away from her – '*Earth* was flat – *Earth* was flat. Flat as my hat – Flatter than that' – drowning all but the bassoons and double-basses that marked the word.

'Wonderful,' I said to Bat. 'And it's only "Nuts in May" with variations.'

'Yes – but *I* did the variations,' he replied.

At the last verse she gestured to Carlini the conductor, who threw her up his baton. She caught it with a boy's ease. 'Are you *with* me?' she cried once more, and – the maddened house behind her – abolished all the instruments except the guttural belch of the double-basses on '*Earth*' – 'The Village that voted the *Earth* was flat – *Earth* was flat!' It was delirium. Then she picked up the Gubby dancers and led them in a clattering improvised lockstep thrice round the stage till her last kick sent her diamond-hilted shoe catherine-wheeling to the electrolier.[23]

I saw the forest of hands raised to catch it, heard the roaring and stamping pass through hurricanes to full typhoon; heard the song, pinned down by the faithful double-basses as the bull-dog pins down the bellowing bull, overbear even those; till at last the curtain fell and Bat took me round to her dressing-room, where she lay spent after her seventh call. Still the song, through all those whitewashed walls, shook the reinforced concrete of the Trefoil as steam pile-drivers shake the flanks of a dock.

'I'm all out – first time in my life. Ah! Tell a fellow now, did I get it across?' she whispered huskily.

'You know you did,' I replied as she dipped her nose deep in a beaker of barley-water. 'They cooed over you.'

Bat nodded. 'And poor Nellie's dead – in Africa, ain't it?'

'I hope I'll die before they stop cooing,' said 'Dal.

'"*Earth* was flat – *Earth* was flat!"' Now it was more like mine-pumps in flood.

'They'll have the house down if you don't take another,' some one called.

'Bless 'em!' said 'Dal, and went out for her eighth, when in the face of that cataract she said, yawning, 'I don't know how *you* feel, children, but *I*'m dead. You be quiet.'

'Hold a minute,' said Bat to me. 'I've got to hear how it went in the Provinces. Winnie Deans had it in Manchester, and Ramsden at Glasgow – and there are all the films too. I had rather a heavy week-end.'

The telephones presently reassured him.

'It'll do,' said he. 'And *he* said my home address was Jerusalem.' He left me, humming the refrain of 'The Holy City'.[24] Like Ollyett I found myself afraid of that man.

When I got out into the street and met the disgorging picture-palaces capering on the pavements and humming it (for he had put the gramophones on with the films), and when I saw far to the south the red electrics flash 'Gubby' across the Thames, I feared more than ever.

A few days passed which were like nothing except, perhaps, a suspense of fever in which the sick man perceives the searchlights of the world's assembled navies in act to converge on one minute fragment of wreckage – one only in all the black and agony-strewn sea. Then those beams focussed themselves. Earth as we knew it – the full circuit of our orb – laid the weight of its impersonal and searing curiosity on this Huckley which had voted that it was flat. It asked for news about Huckley – where and what it might be, and how it talked – it knew how it danced – and how it thought in its wonderful soul. And then, in all the zealous, merciless Press, Huckley was laid out for it to look at, as a drop of pond water is exposed on the sheet of a magic-lantern show. But Huckley's sheet was only coterminous with the use of type among mankind. For the precise moment that was necessary, Fate ruled it that there should be nothing of first importance in the world's idle eye. One atrocious murder, a political crisis, an incautious or heady continental statesman, the mere catarrh of a king, would have wiped out the significance of our message, as a passing cloud annuls the urgent helio. But it was halcyon weather in every respect. Ollyett and I did not need to lift our little fingers any more than the Alpine climber whose last sentence has unkeyed the arch of the avalanche. The thing roared and pulverised and swept beyond eyesight all by itself – all by itself. And once well away, the fall of kingdoms could not have diverted it.

Ours is, after all, a kindly earth. While The Song ran and raped it with the cataleptic kick of 'Ta-ra-ra-boom-de-ay', multiplied by the West African significance of 'Everybody's doing it', plus twice the infernal elementality of a certain tune in *Dona et Gamma*; when for all practical purposes, literary, dramatic, artistic, social, municipal, political, commercial, and administrative, the Earth *was* flat, the Rector of Huckley wrote to us – again as a lover of accuracy – to point out that the Huckley vote on 'the alleged flatness of this scene of our labours here below' was *not* unanimous; he and the Doctor having voted against it. And the great Baron Reuter himself (I am sure it could have been none other) flashed that letter in full to the front, back, and both wings of this scene of our labours. For Huckley was News. *The Bun* also contributed a photograph which cost me some trouble to fake.

'We are a vital nation,' said Ollyett while we were discussing affairs at a Bat dinner. 'Only an Englishman could have written that letter at this present juncture.'

'It reminded me of a tourist in the Cave of the Winds under Niagara.

Just one figure in a mackintosh. But perhaps you saw our photo?' I said proudly.

'Yes,' Bat replied. 'I've been to Niagara, too. And how's Huckley taking it?'

'They don't quite understand, of course,' said Ollyett. 'But it's bringing pots of money into the place. Ever since the motor-bus excursions were started – '

'I didn't know they had been,' said Pallant.

'Oh yes. Motor char-à-bancs – uniformed guides and key-bugles included. They're getting a bit fed up with the tune there nowadays,' Ollyett added.

'They play it under his windows, don't they?' Bat asked. 'He can't stop the right of way across his park.'

'He cannot,' Ollyett answered. 'By the way, Woodhouse, I've bought that font for you from the sexton. I paid fifteen pounds for it.'

'What am I supposed to do with it?' asked Woodhouse.

'You give it to the Victoria and Albert Museum. It is fourteenth-century work all right. You can trust me.'

'Is it worth it – now?' said Pallant. 'Not that I'm weakening, but merely as a matter of tactics?'

'But this is true,' said Ollyett. 'Besides, it is my hobby. I always wanted to be an architect. I'll attend to it myself. It's too serious for *The Bun* and miles too good for *The Cake*.'

He broke ground in a ponderous architectural weekly, which had never heard of Huckley. There was no passion in his statement, but mere fact backed by a wide range of authorities. He established beyond doubt that the old font at Huckley had been thrown out, on Sir Thomas's instigation, twenty years ago, to make room for a new one of Bath stone adorned with Limoges enamels; and that it had lain ever since in a corner of the sexton's shed. He proved, with learned men to support him, that there was only one other font in all England to compare with it. So Woodhouse bought it and presented it to a grateful South Kensington[25] which said it would see the earth still flatter before it returned the treasure to purblind Huckley. Bishops by the benchful and most of the Royal Academy, not to mention 'Margaritas ante Porcos',[26] wrote fervently to the papers. *Punch* based a political cartoon on it; the *Times* a third leader, 'The Lust of Newness'; and the *Spectator* a scholarly and delightful middle, 'Village Haussmania'.[27] The vast amused outside world said in all its tongues and types: 'Of course! This is just what Huckley would do!' And neither Sir Thomas nor the Rector nor the sexton nor anyone else wrote to deny it.

'You see,' said Ollyett, 'this is much more of a blow to Huckley than it looks – because every word of it's true. Your Gubby Dance was inspiration, I admit, but it hadn't its roots in – '

'Two hemispheres and four continents so far,' I pointed out.

'Its roots in the hearts of Huckley was what I was going to say. Why don't you ever come down and look at the place? You've never seen it since we were stopped there.'

'I've only my week-ends free,' I said, 'and you seem to spend yours there pretty regularly – with the side-car. I was afraid – '

'Oh, *that*'s all right,' he said cheerily. 'We're quite an old engaged couple now. As a matter of fact, it happened after "the gravid polled Angus" business. Come along this Saturday. Woodhouse says he'll run us down after lunch. He wants to see Huckley too.'

Pallant could not accompany us, but Bat took his place.

'It's odd,' said Bat, 'that none of us except Ollyett has ever set eyes on Huckley since that time. That's what I always tell My people. Local colour is all right *after* you've got your idea. Before that, it's a mere nuisance.' He regaled us on the way down with panoramic views of the success – geographical and financial – of 'The Gubby' and The Song.

'By the way,' said he, 'I've assigned 'Dal all the gramophone rights of "The Earth". She's a born artist. Hadn't sense enough to hit me for triple-dubs the morning after. She'd have taken it out in coos.'

'Bless her! And what'll she make out of the gramophone rights?' I asked.

'Lord knows!' he replied. 'I've made fifty-four thousand my little end of the business, and it's only just beginning. Hear *that*!'

A shell-pink motor-brake roared up behind us to the music on a key-bugle of 'The Village that Voted the Earth was Flat'. In a few minutes we overtook another, in natural wood, whose occupants were singing it through their noses.

'I don't know that agency. It must be Cook's,' said Ollyett. 'They *do* suffer.' We were never out of ear-shot of the tune the rest of the way to Huckley.

Though I knew it would be so, I was disappointed with the actual aspect of the spot we had – it is not too much to say – created in the face of the nations. The alcoholic pub; the village green; the Baptist chapel; the church; the sexton's shed; the Rectory whence the so wonderful letters had come; Sir Thomas's park gate-pillars still violently declaring 'The Earth *is* flat', were as mean, as average, as ordinary as the photograph of a room where a murder has been committed. Ollyett, who, of course, knew the place specially well, made the most of it to us. Bat, who had employed it as a back-cloth to one of his own dramas, dismissed it as a thing used and emptied, but Woodhouse expressed my feelings when he said: 'Is that all – after all we've done?'

'*I* know,' said Ollyett soothingly. '"Like that strange song I heard Apollo sing: When Ilion like a mist rose into towers."[28] I've felt the same sometimes, though it has been Paradise for me. But they *do* suffer.'

The fourth brake in thirty minutes had just turned into Sir Thomas's park to tell the Hall that 'The *Earth* was flat'; a knot of obviously American tourists were kodaking his lodge-gates; while the tea-shop opposite the lych-gate was full of people buying postcards of the old font as it had lain twenty years in the sexton's shed. We went to the alcoholic pub and congratulated the proprietor.

'It's bringin' money to the place,' said he. 'But in a sense you can buy money too dear. It isn't doin' us any good. People are laughin' at us. That's what they're doin' . . . Now, with regard to that Vote of ours you may have heard talk about . . .'

'For Gorze sake, chuck that votin' business,' cried an elderly man at the door. 'Money-gettin' or no money-gettin', we're fed up with it.'

'Well, I do think,' said the publican, shifting his ground, 'I do think Sir Thomas might ha' managed better in some things.'

'He tole me,' – the elderly man shouldered his way to the bar – 'he tole me twenty years ago to take an' lay that font in my tool-shed. He *tole* me so himself. An' now, after twenty years, me own wife makin' me out little better than the common 'angman!'

'That's the sexton,' the publican explained. 'His good lady sells the postcards – if you 'aven't got some. But we feel Sir Thomas might ha' done better.'

'What's he got to do with it?' said Woodhouse.

'There's nothin' we can trace 'ome to 'im in so many words, but we think he might 'ave saved us the font business. Now, in regard to that votin' business – '

'Chuck it! Oh, chuck it!' the sexton roared, 'or you'll 'ave me cuttin' my throat at cock-crow. 'Ere's another parcel of fun-makers!'

A motor-brake had pulled up at the door and a multitude of men and women immediately descended. We went out to look. They bore rolled banners, a reading-desk in three pieces, and, I specially noticed, a collapsible harmonium, such as is used on ships at sea.

'Salvation Army!' I said, though I saw no uniforms.

Two of them unfurled a banner between poles which bore the legend: 'The Earth *is* flat.' Woodhouse and I turned to Bat. He shook his head. 'No, no! Not me . . . If I had only seen their costumes in advance!'

'Good Lord!' said Ollyett. 'It's the genuine Society!'

The company advanced on the green with the precision of people well broke to these movements. Scene-shifters could not have been quicker with the three-piece rostrum, nor stewards with the harmonium. Almost before its cross-legs had been kicked into their catches, certainly before the tourists by the lodge-gates had begun to move over, a woman sat down to it and struck up a hymn:

> 'Hear ther truth our tongues are telling,
> Spread ther light from shore to shore,
> God harth given man a dwelling
> Flat and flat for evermore.
>
> When ther Primal Dark retreated,
> When ther deeps were undesigned,
> He with rule and level meted
> Habitation for mankind!'

I saw sick envy on Bat's face. 'Curse Nature,' he muttered. 'She gets ahead of you every time. To think *I* forgot hymns and a harmonium!' Then came the chorus:

> 'Hear ther truth our tongues are telling,
> Spread ther light from shore to shore –
> Oh, be faithful! Oh, be truthful!
> Earth is flat for evermore!'

They sang several verses with the fervour of Christians awaiting their lions. Then there were growlings in the air. The sexton, embraced by the landlord, two-stepped out of the pub-door. Each was trying to outroar the other. 'Apologising in advance for what he says,' the landlord shouted, 'you'd better go away' (here the sexton began to speak words). 'This isn't the time nor yet the place for – for any more o' this chat.'

The crowd thickened. I saw the village police-sergeant come out of his cottage buckling his belt.

'But surely,' said the woman at the harmonium, 'there must be some mistake. We are not suffragettes.'[29]

'Damn it! They'd be a change,' cried the sexton. 'You get out of this! Don't talk! *I* can't stand it for one! Get right out, or we'll font you!'

The crowd, which was being recruited from every house in sight, echoed the invitation. The sergeant pushed forward. A man beside the reading-desk said: 'But surely we are among dear friends and sympathisers. Listen to me for a moment.'

It was the moment that a passing char-à-banc chose to strike into The Song. The effect was instantaneous. Bat, Ollyett, and I, who by divers roads have learned the psychology of crowds, retreated towards the tavern door. Woodhouse, the newspaper proprietor, anxious, I presume, to keep touch with the public, dived into the thick of it. Everyone else told the Society to go away at once. When the lady at the harmonium (I began to understand why it is sometimes necessary to kill women) pointed at the stencilled park pillars and called them 'the cromlechs of our common faith', there was a snarl and a rush. The police-sergeant checked it, but advised the Society to keep on going. The Society withdrew into the brake fighting, as it were, a rearguard action of oratory up each step. The collapsed harmonium was hauled in last, and with the perfect unreason of crowds, they cheered it loudly, till the chauffeur slipped in his clutch and sped away. Then the crowd broke up, congratulating all concerned except the sexton, who was held to have disgraced his office by having sworn at ladies. We strolled across the green towards Woodhouse, who was talking to the police-sergeant near the park-gates. We were not twenty yards from him when we saw Sir Thomas Ingell emerge from the lodge and rush furiously at Woodhouse with an uplifted stick, at the same time shrieking: 'I'll teach you to laugh, you – ' but Ollyett has the record of the language. By the time we reached them, Sir Thomas was on the ground; Woodhouse, very white, held the walking-stick and was saying to the sergeant:

'I give this person in charge for assault.'

'But, good Lord!' said the sergeant, whiter than Woodhouse. 'It's Sir Thomas.'

'Whoever it is, it isn't fit to be at large,' said Woodhouse. The crowd suspecting something wrong began to reassemble, and all the English horror of a row in public moved us, headed by the sergeant, inside the lodge. We shut both park-gates and lodge-door.

'You saw the assault, sergeant,' Woodhouse went on. 'You can testify I used no more force than was necessary to protect myself. You can testify that I have not even damaged this person's property. (Here! take your stick, you!) You heard the filthy language he used.'

'I – I can't say I did,' the sergeant stammered.

'Oh, but *we* did!' said Ollyett, and repeated it, to the apron-veiled horror of the lodge-keeper's wife.

Sir Thomas on a hard kitchen chair began to talk. He said he had 'stood enough of being photographed like a wild beast', and expressed loud regret that he had not killed 'that man', who was 'conspiring with the sergeant to laugh at him'.

''Ad you ever seen 'im before, Sir Thomas?' the sergeant asked.

'No! But it's time an example was made here. I've never seen the sweep in my life.'

I think it was Bat Masquerier's magnetic eye that recalled the past to him, for his face changed and his jaw dropped. 'But I have!' he groaned. 'I remember now.'

Here a writhing man entered by the back door. He was, he said, the local solicitor. I do not assert that he licked Woodhouse's boots, but we should have respected him more if he had and been done with it. His notion was that the matter could be accommodated, arranged, and compromised for gold, and yet more gold. The sergeant thought so too. Woodhouse undeceived them both. To the sergeant he said, 'Will you or will you not enter the charge?' To the local solicitor he gave the name of his lawyers, at which the man wrung his hands and cried, 'Oh, Sir T., Sir T.!' in a miserable falsetto, for it was a Bat Masquerier of a firm. They conferred together in tragic whispers.

'I don't dive after Dickens,' said Ollyett to Bat and me by the window, 'but every time *I* get into a row I notice the police-court always fills up with his characters.'

'I've noticed that too,' said Bat. 'But the odd thing is you mustn't give the public straight Dickens – not in My business. I wonder why that is.'

Then Sir Thomas got his second wind and cursed the day that he, or it may have been we, were born. I feared that though he was a Radical he might apologise and, since he was an MP, might lie his way out of the difficulty. But he was utterly and truthfully beside himself. He asked foolish questions – such as what we were doing in the village at all, and how much blackmail Woodhouse expected to make out of him. But neither Woodhouse nor the sergeant nor the writing solicitor listened. The upshot of their talk, in the chimney-corner, was that Sir Thomas stood engaged to appear next Monday before his brother magistrates on charges of assault, disorderly conduct, and language calculated, etc. Ollyett was specially careful about the language.

Then we left. The village looked very pretty in the late light – pretty and tuneful as a nest of nightingales.

'You'll turn up on Monday, I hope,' said Woodhouse, when we reached Town. That was his only allusion to the affair.

So we turned up – through a world still singing that the Earth was flat – at the little clay-coloured market-town with the large Corn Exchange and the small Jubilee memorial. We had some difficulty in getting seats in the court. Woodhouse's imported London lawyer was a man of commanding personality, with a voice trained to convey blasting imputations by tone. When the case was called, he rose and stated his client's intention not to proceed with the charge. His client, he went on to say, had not entertained, and, of course, in the circumstances could not have entertained, any suggestion of accepting on behalf of public charities any monies that might have been offered to him on the part of Sir Thomas's estate. At the same time, no one acknowledged more sincerely than his client the spirit in which those offers had been made by those entitled to make them. But, as a matter of fact – here he became the man of the world colloguing with his equals – certain – er – details had come to his client's knowledge *since* the lamentable outburst, which . . . He shrugged his shoulders. Nothing was served by going into them, but he ventured to say that, had those painful circumstances only been known earlier, his client would – again 'of course' – never have dreamed – A gesture concluded the sentence, and the ensnared Bench looked at Sir Thomas with new and withdrawing eyes. Frankly, as they could see, it would be nothing less than cruelty to proceed further with this – er – unfortunate affair. He asked leave, therefore, to withdraw the charge *in toto*, and at the same time to express his client's deepest sympathy with all who had been in any way distressed, as his client had been, by the fact and the publicity of proceedings which he could, of course, again assure them that his client would never have dreamed of instituting if, as he hoped he had made plain, certain facts had been before his client at the time when . . . But he had said enough. For his fee it seemed to me that he had.

Heaven inspired Sir Thomas's lawyer – all of a sweat lest his client's language should come out – to rise up and thank him. Then, Sir Thomas – not yet aware what leprosy had been laid upon him, but grateful to escape on any terms – followed suit. He was heard in interested silence, and people drew back a pace as Gehazi passed forth.[30]

'You hit hard,' said Bat to Woodhouse afterwards. 'His own people think he's mad.'

'You don't say so? I'll show you some of his letters to-night at dinner,' he replied.

He brought them to the Red Amber Room of the Chop Suey. We forgot to be amazed, as till then we had been amazed, over The Song or 'The Gubby', or the full tide of Fate that seemed to run only for our sakes. It did not even interest Ollyett that the verb 'to huckle' had passed into the English leader-writers' language. We were studying the interior of a soul, flash-lighted to its grimiest corners by the dread of 'losing its position'.

'And then it thanked you, didn't it, for dropping the case?' said Pallant.

'Yes, and it sent me a telegram to confirm.' Woodhouse turned to Bat. 'Now d' you think I hit too hard?' he asked.

'No – o!' said Bat. 'After all – I'm talking of everyone's business now – one can't ever do anything in Art that comes up to Nature in any game in life. Just think how this thing has – '

'Just let me run through that little case of yours again,' said Pallant, and picked up *The Bun* which had it set out in full.

'Any chance of 'Dal looking in on us to-night?' Ollyett began.

'She's occupied with her Art too,' Bat answered bitterly. 'What's the use of Art? Tell me, someone!' A barrel-organ outside promptly pointed out that the *Earth* was flat. 'The gramophone's killing street organs, but I let loose a hundred-and-seventy-four of those hurdygurdys twelve hours after The Song,' said Bat. 'Not counting the Provinces.' His face brightened a little.

'Look here!' said Pallant over the paper. 'I don't suppose you or those asinine JP's knew it – but your lawyer ought to have known that you've all put your foot in it most confoundedly over this assault case.'

'What's the matter?' said Woodhouse.

'It's ludicrous. It's insane. There isn't two penn'orth of legality in the whole thing. Of course, you could have withdrawn the charge, but the way you went about it is childish – besides being illegal. What on earth was the Chief Constable thinking of?'

'Oh, he was a friend of Sir Thomas's. They all were for that matter,' I replied.

'He ought to be hanged. So ought the Chairman of the Bench. I'm talking as a lawyer now.'

'Why, what have we been guilty of? Misprision of treason or compounding a felony – or what?' said Ollyett.

'I'll tell you later.' Pallant went back to the paper with knitted brows, smiling unpleasantly from time to time. At last he laughed.

'Thank you!' he said to Woodhouse. 'It ought to be pretty useful – for us.'

'What d'you mean?' said Ollyett.

'For our side. They are all Rads[31] who are mixed up in this – from the Chief Constable down. There must be a Question. There must be a Question.'

'Yes, but I wanted the charge withdrawn in my own way,' Woodhouse insisted.

'That's nothing to do with the case. It's the legality of your silly methods. You wouldn't understand if I talked till morning.' He began to pace the room, his hands behind him. 'I wonder if I can get it through our Whip's thick head that it's a chance . . . That comes of stuffing the Bench with Radical tinkers,' he muttered.

'Oh, sit down!' said Woodhouse.

'Where's your lawyer to be found now?' he jerked out.

'At the Trefoil,' said Bat promptly, 'I gave him the stage-box for to-night. He's an artist too.'

'Then I'm going to see him,' said Pallant. 'Properly handled this ought to be a godsend for our side.' He withdrew without apology.

'Certainly, this thing keeps on opening up, and up,' I remarked inanely.

'It's beyond me!' said Bat. 'I don't think if I'd known I'd have ever . . . Yes, I would, though. He said my home address was – '

'It was his tone – his tone!' Ollyett almost shouted. Woodhouse said nothing, but his face whitened as he brooded.

'Well, anyway,' Bat went on, 'I'm glad I always believed in God and Providence and all those things. Else I should lose my nerve. We've put it over the whole world – the full extent of the geographical globe. We couldn't stop it if we wanted to now. It's got to burn itself out. I'm not in charge any more. What d'you expect 'll happen next. Angels?'

I expected nothing. Nothing that I expected approached what I got. Politics are not my concern, but, for the moment, since it seemed that they were going to 'huckle' with the rest, I took an interest in them. They impressed me as a dog's life without a dog's decencies, and I was confirmed in this when an unshaven and unwashen Pallant called on me at ten o'clock one morning, begging for a bath and a couch.

'Bail too?' I asked. He was in evening dress and his eyes were sunk feet in his head.

'No,' he said hoarsely. 'All night sitting. Fifteen divisions. 'Nother to-night. Your place was nearer than mine, so – ' He began to undress in the hall.

When he awoke at one o'clock he gave me lurid accounts of what he said was history, but which was obviously collective hysteria. There had been a political crisis. He and his fellow MP's had 'done things' – I never quite got at the things – for eighteen hours on end, and the pitiless Whips were even then at the telephones to herd 'em up to another dog-fight. So he snorted and grew hot all over again while he might have been resting.

'I'm going to pitch in my question about that miscarriage of justice at Huckley this afternoon, if you care to listen to it,' he said. 'It'll be absolutely thrown away – in our present state. I told 'em so; but it's my only chance for weeks. P'r'aps Woodhouse would like to come.'

'I'm sure he would. Anything to do with Huckley interests us,' I said.

'It'll miss fire, I'm afraid. Both sides are absolutely cooked. The present situation has been working up for some time. You see the row was bound to come, etc. etc.,' and he flew off the handle once more.

I telephoned to Woodhouse, and we went to the House together. It was a dull, sticky afternoon with thunder in the air. For some reason or other, each side was determined to prove its virtue and endurance to the utmost. I heard men snarling about it all round me. 'If they won't spare us, we'll show 'em no mercy.' 'Break the brutes up from the start. They can't stand late hours.' 'Come on! No shirking! I know *you*'ve had a Turkish bath,' were some of the sentences I caught on our way. The House was packed already, and one could feel the negative electricity of a jaded crowd wrenching at one's own nerves, and depressing the afternoon soul.

'This is bad!' Woodhouse whispered. 'There'll be a row before they've finished. Look at the Front Benches!' And he pointed out little personal signs by which I was to know that each man was on edge. He might have spared himself. The House was ready to snap before a bone had been thrown. A sullen Minister rose to reply to a staccato question. His supporters cheered defiantly. 'None o' that! None o' that!' came from the back benches. I saw the Speaker's face stiffen like the face of a helmsman as he humours a hard-mouthed yacht after a sudden following sea. The trouble was barely met in time. There came a fresh, apparently causeless gust a few minutes later – savage, threatening, but futile. It died out – one could hear the sigh – in sudden wrathful realisation of the dreary hours ahead, and the ship of State drifted on.

Then Pallant – and the raw House winced at the torture of his voice – rose. It was a twenty-line question, studded with legal technicalities. The gist of it was that he wished to know whether the appropriate Minister was aware that there had been a grave miscarriage of justice on such and such a date, at such and such a place, before such and such justices of the peace, in regard to a case which arose –

I heard one desperate, weary 'damn!' float up from the pit of that torment. Pallant sawed on – 'out of certain events which occurred at the village of Huckley.'

The House came to attention with a parting of the lips like a hiccough, and it flashed through my mind . . . Pallant repeated, 'Huckley. The village – '

'That voted the *Earth* was flat.' A single voice from a back bench sang it once like a lone frog in a far pool.

'*Earth* was flat,' croaked another voice opposite.

'*Earth* was flat.' There were several. Then several more.

It was, you understand, the collective, overstrained nerve of the House, snapping, strand by strand to various notes, as the hawser parts from its moorings.

'The Village that voted the *Earth* was flat.' The tune was beginning to shape itself. More voices were raised and feet began to beat time. Even so it did not occur to me that the thing would –

'The Village that voted the *Earth* was flat!' It was easier now to see who were not singing. There were still a few. Of a sudden (and this proves the fundamental instability of the cross-bench mind) a cross-bencher[32] leaped on his seat and there played an imaginary double-bass with tremendous maestro-like wagglings of the elbow.

The last strand parted. The ship of State drifted out helpless on the rocking tide of melody.

'The Village that voted the *Earth* was flat!
The Village that voted the *Earth* was flat!'

The Irish first conceived the idea of using their order-papers as funnels wherewith to reach the correct '*vroom – vroom*' on '*Earth*'. Labour, always conservative and respectable at a crisis, stood out longer than any other section, but when it came in it was howling syndicalism.[33] Then, without distinction of Party, fear of constituents, desire for office, or hope of emolument, the House sang at the tops and at the bottoms of their voices, swaying their stale bodies and epileptically beating with their swelled feet. They sang 'The Village that voted the *Earth* was flat': first, because they wanted to, and secondly – which is the terror of that song – because they could not stop. For no consideration could they stop.

Pallant was still standing up. Someone pointed at him and they laughed. Others began to point, lunging, as it were, in time with the tune. At this moment two persons came in practically abreast from behind the Speaker's chair, and halted appalled. One happened to be the Prime Minister and the other a messenger. The House, with tears running down their cheeks, transferred their attention to the paralysed couple. They pointed six hundred forefingers at them. They rocked, they waved, and they rolled while they pointed; but still they sang. When they weakened for an instant, Ireland would yell: 'Are ye *with* me, bhoys?' and they all renewed their strength like Antaeus. No man could say afterwards what happened in the Press or the Strangers' Gallery. It was the House, the hysterical and abandoned House of

Commons that held all eyes, as it deafened all ears. I saw both Front Benches bend forward, some with their foreheads on their dispatch-boxes, the rest with their faces in their hands; and their moving shoulders jolted the House out of its last rag of decency. Only the Speaker remained unmoved. The entire Press of Great Britain bore witness next day that he had not even bowed his head. The Angel of the Constitution, for vain was the help of man, foretold him the exact moment at which the House would have broken into 'The Gubby'. He is reported to have said: 'I heard the Irish beginning to shuffle it. So I adjourned.' Pallant's version is that he added: 'And I was never so grateful to a private member in all my life as I was to Mr Pallant.'

He made no explanation. He did not refer to orders or disorders. He simply adjourned the House till six that evening. And the House adjourned – some of it nearly on all fours.

I was not correct when I said that the Speaker was the only man who did not laugh. Woodhouse was beside me all the time. His face was set and quite white – as white, they told me, as Sir Thomas Ingell's when he went, by request, to a private interview with his Chief Whip.[34]

THE HOUSE SURGEON

On an evening after Easter Day, I sat at a table in a homeward-bound steamer's smoking-room, where half-a-dozen of us told ghost stories. As our party broke up, a man, playing Patience in the next alcove, said to me: 'I didn't quite catch the end of that last story about the Curse on the family's first-born.'[1]

'It turned out to be drains,' I explained. 'As soon as new ones were put into the house the Curse was lifted, I believe. I never knew the people myself.'

'Ah! I've had *my* drains up twice; I'm on gravel too.'

'You don't mean to say you've a ghost in your house? Why didn't you join our party?'

'Any more orders, gentlemen, before the bar closes?' the steward interrupted.

'Sit down again and have one with me,' said the Patience player. 'No, it isn't a ghost. Our trouble is more depression than anything else.'

'How interesting! Then it's nothing anyone can see?'

'It's – it's nothing worse than a little depression. And the odd part is that there hasn't been a death in the house since it was built – in 1863. The lawyer said so. That decided me – my good lady, rather – and he made me pay an extra thousand for it.'

'How curious. Unusual, too!' I said.

'Yes, ain't it? It was built for three sisters – Moultrie was the name – three old maids. They all lived together; the eldest owned it. I bought it from her lawyer a few years ago, and if I've spent a pound on the place first and last, I must have spent five thousand. Electric light, new servants' wing, garden – all that sort of thing. A man and his family ought to be happy after so much expense, ain't it?' He looked at me through the bottom of his glass.

'Does it affect your family much?'

'My good lady – she's a Greek by the way – and myself are middle-aged. We can bear up against depression; but it's hard on my little girl.

I say little; but she's twenty. We send her visiting to escape it. She almost lived at hotels and hydros last year, but that isn't pleasant for her. She used to be a canary – a perfect canary – always singing. You ought to hear her. She doesn't sing now. That sort of thing's unwholesome for the young, ain't it?'

'Can't you get rid of the place?' I suggested.

'Not except at a sacrifice, and we are fond of it. Just suits us three. We'd love it if we were allowed.'

'What do you mean by not being allowed?'

'I mean because of the depression. It spoils everything.'

'What's it like exactly?'

'I couldn't very well explain. It must be seen to be appreciated, as the auctioneers say. Now, I was much impressed by the story you were telling just now.'

'It wasn't true,' I said.

'My tale is true. If you would do me the pleasure to come down and spend a night at my little place, you'd learn more than you would if I talked till morning. Very likely 'twouldn't touch your good self at all. You might be – immune, ain't it? On the other hand, if this influenza-influence *does* happen to affect you, why, I think it will be an experience.'

While he talked he gave me his card, and I read his name was L. Maxwell M'Leod, Esq., of Holmescroft. A City address was tucked away in a corner.

'My business,' he added, 'used to be furs. If you are interested in furs – I've given thirty years of my life to 'em.'

'You're very kind,' I murmured.

'Far from it, I assure you. I can meet you next Saturday afternoon anywhere in London you choose to name, and I'll be only too happy to motor you down. It ought to be a delightful run at this time of year – the rhododendrons will be out. I mean it. You don't know how truly I mean it. Very probably – it won't affect you at all. And – I think I may say I have the finest collection of narwhal tusks in the world. All the best skins and horns have to go through London, and L. Maxwell M'Leod, he knows where they come from, and where they go to. That's his business.'

For the rest of the voyage up-Channel Mr M'Leod talked to me of the assembling, preparation, and sale of the rarer furs; and told me things about the manufacture of fur-lined coats which quite shocked me. Somehow or other, when we landed on Wednesday, I found myself pledged to spend that week-end with him at Holmescroft.

On Saturday he met me with a well-groomed motor, and ran me

out in an hour and a half to an exclusive residential district of dustless roads and elegantly designed country villas, each standing in from three to five acres of perfectly appointed land. He told me land was selling at eight hundred pounds the acre, and the new golf links, whose Queen Anne pavilion[2] we passed, had cost nearly twenty-four thousand pounds to create.

Holmescroft was a large, two-storied, low, creeper-covered residence. A veranda at the south side gave on to a garden and two tennis courts, separated by a tasteful iron fence from a most park-like meadow of five or six acres, where two Jersey cows grazed. Tea was ready in the shade of a promising copper beech, and I could see groups on the lawn of young men and maidens appropriately clothed, playing lawn tennis in the sunshine.

'A pretty scene, ain't it?' said Mr M'Leod. 'My good lady's sitting under the tree, and that's my little girl in pink on the far court. But I'll take you to your room, and you can see 'em all later.'

He led me through a wide parquet-floored hall furnished in pale lemon, with huge cloisonné[3] vases, an ebonised and gold grand piano, and banks of pot flowers in Benares brass bowls, up a pale oak staircase to a spacious landing, where there was a green velvet settee trimmed with silver. The blinds were down, and the light lay in parallel lines on the floors.

He showed me my room, saying cheerfully: 'You may be a little tired. One often is without knowing it after a run through traffic. Don't come down till you feel quite restored. We shall all be in the garden.'

My room was rather close, and smelt of perfumed soap. I threw up the window at once, but it opened so close to the floor and worked so clumsily that I came within an ace of pitching out, where I should certainly have ruined a rather lopsided laburnum below. As I set about washing off the journey's dust, I began to feel a little tired. But, I reflected, I had not come down here in this weather and among these new surroundings to be depressed, so I began to whistle.

And it was just then that I was aware of a little grey shadow, as it might have been a snowflake seen against the light, floating at an immense distance in the background of my brain. It annoyed me, and I shook my head to get rid of it. Then my brain telegraphed that it was the forerunner of a swift-striding gloom which there was yet time to escape if I would force my thoughts away from it, as a man leaping for life forces his body forward and away from the fall of a wall. But the gloom overtook me before I could take in the meaning of the message. I moved toward the bed, every nerve already aching with the fore-knowledge of the pain that was to be dealt it, and sat down, while my amazed and angry soul dropped, gulf by gulf, into that Horror of great darkness[4] which is spoken of in the Bible, and which, as auctioneers say, must be experienced to be appreciated.

Despair upon despair, misery upon misery, fear after fear, each causing their distinct and separate woe, packed in upon me for an unrecorded length of time, until at last they blurred together, and I heard a click in my brain like the click in the ear when one descends in a diving-bell,[5] and I knew that the pressures were equalised within and without, and that, for the moment, the worst was at an end. But I knew also that at any moment the darkness might come down anew; and while I dwelt on this speculation precisely as a man torments a raging tooth with his tongue, it ebbed away into the little grey shadow on the brain of its first coming, and once more I heard my brain, which knew what would recur, telegraph to every quarter for help, release, or diversion.

The door opened, and M'Leod reappeared. I thanked him politely, saying I was charmed with my room, anxious to meet Mrs M'Leod, much refreshed with my wash, and so on and so forth. Beyond a little stickiness at the corners of my mouth, it seemed to me that I was managing my words admirably, the while that I myself cowered at the bottom of unclimbable pits. M'Leod laid his hand on my shoulder, and said: 'You've got it now already, ain't it?'

'Yes,' I answered, 'it's making me sick!'

'It will pass off when you come outside. I give you my word it will then pass off. Come!'

I shambled out behind him, and wiped my forehead in the hall.

'You mustn't mind,' he said. 'I expect the run tired you. My good lady is sitting there under the copper beech.'

She was a fat woman in an apricot-coloured gown, with a heavily powdered face, against which her black long-lashed eyes showed like currants in dough. I was introduced to many fine ladies and gentlemen of those parts. Magnificently appointed landaus and covered motors swept in and out of the drive, and the air was gay with the merry outcries of the tennis-players.

As twilight drew on they all went away, and I was left alone with Mr and Mrs M'Leod, while tall men-servants and maid-servants took away the tennis and tea things. Miss M'Leod had walked a little down the drive with a light-haired young man, who apparently knew everything about every South American railway stock. He had told me at tea that these were the days of financial specialisation.

'I think it went off beautifully, my dear,' said Mr M'Leod to his wife; and to me: 'You feel all right now, ain't it? Of course you do.'

Mrs M'Leod surged across the gravel. Her husband skipped nimbly before her into the south veranda, turned a switch, and all Holmescroft was flooded with light.

'You can do that from your room also,' he said as they went in. 'There is something in money, ain't it?'

Miss M'Leod came up behind me in the dusk. 'We have not yet been introduced,' she said, 'but I suppose you are staying the night?'

'Your father was kind enough to ask me,' I replied.

She nodded. 'Yes, *I* know; and you know too, don't you? I saw your face when you came to shake hands with mamma. You felt the depression very soon? It is simply frightful in that bedroom sometimes. What do you think it is – bewitchment? In Greece, where I was a little girl, it might have been; but not in England, do you think? Or *do* you?'

'I don't know what to think,' I replied. 'I never felt anything like it. Does it happen often?'

'Yes, sometimes. It comes and goes.'

'Pleasant!' I said, as we walked up and down the gravel at the lawn edge. 'What has been your experience of it?'

'That is difficult to say, but – sometimes that – that depression is like as it were' – she gesticulated in most un-English fashion – 'a light. Yes, like a light turned into a room – only a light of blackness, do you understand? – into a happy room. For sometimes we are so happy, all we three, – so *very* happy. Then this blackness, it is turned on us just like – ah, I know what I mean now – like the head-lamp of a motor, and we are eclips-ed. And there is another thing – '

The dressing-gong roared,[6] and we entered the overlighted hall. My dressing was a brisk athletic performance, varied with outbursts of song – careful attention paid to articulation and expression. But nothing happened. As I hurried downstairs, I thanked Heaven that nothing had happened.

Dinner was served breakfast-fashion; the dishes were placed on the sideboard over heaters, and we helped ourselves.

'We always do this when we are alone, so we talk better,' said Mr M'Leod.

'And we are always alone,' said the daughter.

'Cheer up, Thea. It will all come right,' he insisted.

'No, papa.' She shook her dark head. 'Nothing is right while *it* comes.'

'It is nothing that we ourselves have ever done in our lives – that I will swear to you,' said Mrs M'Leod suddenly. 'And we have changed our servants several times. So we know it is not *them*.'

'Never mind. Let us enjoy ourselves while we can,' said Mr M'Leod, opening the champagne.

But we did not enjoy ourselves. The talk failed. There were long silences.

'I beg your pardon,' I said, for I thought someone at my elbow was about to speak.

'Ah! That is the other thing!' said Miss M'Leod. Her mother groaned.

We were silent again, and, in a few seconds it must have been, a live grief beyond words – not ghostly dread or horror, but aching, helpless grief – overwhelmed us, each, I felt, according to his or her nature, and held steady like the beam of a burning-glass. Behind that pain I was conscious there was a desire on somebody's part to explain something on which some tremendously important issue hung.

Meantime I rolled bread pills and remembered my sins; M'Leod considered his own reflection in a spoon; his wife seemed to be praying, and the girl fidgeted desperately with hands and feet till the darkness passed on – as though the malignant rays of a burning-glass had been shifted from us.

'There,' said Miss M'Leod, half rising. 'Now you see what makes a happy home. Oh, sell it – sell it, father mine, and let us go away!'

'But I've spent thousands on it. You shall go to Harrogate next week, Thea dear.'

'I'm only just back from hotels. I am so tired of packing.'

'Cheer up, Thea. It is over. You know it does not often come here twice in the same night. I think we shall dare now to be comfortable.'

He lifted a dish-cover, and helped his wife and daughter. His face was lined and fallen like an old man's after a debauch, but his hand did not shake, and his voice was clear. As he worked to restore us by speech and action, he reminded me of a grey-muzzled collie herding demoralised sheep.

After dinner we sat round the dining-room fire – the drawing-room might have been under the Shadow for aught we knew – talking with the intimacy of gipsies by the wayside, or of wounded comparing notes after a skirmish. By eleven o'clock the three between them had given me every name and detail they could recall that in any way bore on the house, and what they knew of its history.

We went to bed in a fortifying blaze of electric light. My one fear was that the blasting gust of depression would return – the surest way, of course, to bring it. I lay awake till dawn, breathing quickly and sweating lightly, beneath what De Quincey inadequately describes as 'the oppression of inexpiable guilt'.[7] Now as soon as the lovely day was broken, I fell into the most terrible of all dreams – that joyous one in which all past evil has not only been wiped out of our lives, but has never been committed; and in the very bliss of our assured innocence, before our loves shriek and change countenance, we wake to the day we have earned.

It was a coolish morning, but we preferred to breakfast in the south veranda. The forenoon we spent in the garden, pretending to play games that come out of boxes, such as croquet and clock-golf. But most of the time we drew together and talked. The young man who knew all about South American railways took Miss M'Leod for a walk in the afternoon, and at five M'Leod thoughtfully whirled us all up to dine in town.

'Now, don't say you will tell the Psychological Society, and that you will come again,' said Miss M'Leod, as we parted. 'Because I know you will not.'

'You should not say that,' said her mother. 'You should say, "Goodbye, Mr Perseus. Come again."'

'Not him!' the girl cried. 'He has seen the Medusa's head!'[8]

Looking at myself in the restaurant's mirrors, it seemed to me that I had not much benefited by my week-end. Next morning I wrote out all my Holmescroft notes at fullest length, in the hope that by so doing I could put it all behind me. But the experience worked on my mind, as they say certain imperfectly understood rays work on the body.

I am less calculated to make a Sherlock Holmes than any man I know, for I lack both method and patience, yet the idea of following up the trouble to its source fascinated me. I had no theory to go on, except a vague idea that I had come between two poles of a discharge, and had taken a shock meant for someone else. This was followed by a feeling of intense irritation. I waited cautiously on myself, expecting to be overtaken by horror of the supernatural, but my self persisted in being humanly indignant, exactly as though it had been the victim of a practical joke. It was in great pains and upheavals – that I felt in every fibre – but its dominant idea, to put it coarsely, was to get back a bit of its own. By this I knew that I might go forward if I could find the way.

After a few days it occurred to me to go to the office of Mr J. M. M. Baxter – the solicitor who had sold Holmescroft to M'Leod. I explained I had some notion of buying the place. Would he act for me in the matter?

Mr Baxter, a large, greyish, throaty-voiced man, showed no enthusiasm. 'I sold it to Mr M'Leod,' he said. 'It 'ud scarcely do for me to start on the running-down tack now. But I can recommend – '

'I know he's asking an awful price,' I interrupted, 'and atop of it he wants an extra thousand for what he calls your clean bill of health.'

Mr Baxter sat up in his chair. I had all his attention.

'Your guarantee with the house. Don't you remember it?'

'Yes, yes. That no death had taken place in the house since it was built. I remember perfectly.'

He did not gulp as untrained men do when they lie, but his jaws moved stickily, and his eyes, turning towards the deed-boxes on the wall, dulled. I counted seconds, one, two, three – one, two, three – up to ten. A man, I knew, can live through ages of mental depression in that time.

'I remember perfectly.' His mouth opened a little as though it had tasted old bitterness.

'Of course *that* sort of thing doesn't appeal to me,' I went on. '*I* don't expect to buy a house free from death.'

'Certainly not. No one does. But it was Mr M'Leod's fancy – his wife's rather, I believe; and since we could meet it – it was my duty to my clients – at whatever cost to my own feelings – to make him pay.'

'That's really why I came to you. I understood from him you knew the place well.'

'Oh yes. Always did. It originally belonged to some connections of mine.'

'The Misses Moultrie, I suppose. How interesting! They must have loved the place before the country round about was built up.'

'They were very fond of it indeed.'

'I don't wonder. So restful and sunny. I don't see how they could have brought themselves to part with it.'

Now it is one of the most constant peculiarities of the English that in polite conversation – and I had striven to be polite – no one ever does or sells anything for mere money's sake.

'Miss Agnes – the youngest – fell ill' (he spaced his words a little), 'and, as they were very much attached to each other, that broke up the home.'

'Naturally. I fancied it must have been something of that kind. One doesn't associate the Staffordshire Moultries' (my Demon of Irresponsibility at that instant created 'em) 'with – with being hard up.'

'I don't know whether we're related to them,' he answered importantly. 'We may be, for our branch of the family comes from the Midlands.'

I give this talk at length, because I am so proud of my first attempt at detective work. When I left him, twenty minutes later, with instructions to move against the owner of Holmescroft with a view to purchase, I was more bewildered than any Doctor Watson at the opening of a story.

Why should a middle-aged solicitor turn plover's-egg colour and drop his jaw when reminded of so innocent and festal a matter as that no death had ever occurred in a house that he had sold? If I knew my English vocabulary at all, the tone in which he said the youngest sister 'fell ill' meant that she had gone out of her mind. That might explain his change of countenance, and it was just possible that her demented influence still hung about Holmescroft. But the rest was beyond me.

I was relieved when I reached M'Leod's City office, and could tell him what I had done – not what I thought.

M'Leod was quite willing to enter into the game of the pretended purchase, but did not see how it would help if I knew Baxter.

'He's the only living soul I can get at who was connected with Holmescroft,' I said.

'Ah! Living soul is good,' said M'Leod. 'At any rate our little girl will be pleased that you are still interested in us. Won't you come down some day this week?'

'How is it there now?' I asked.

He screwed up his face. 'Simply frightful!' he said. 'Thea is at Droitwich.'

'I should like it immensely, but I must cultivate Baxter for the present. You'll be sure and keep him busy your end, won't you?'

He looked at me with quiet contempt. 'Do not be afraid. I shall be a good Jew. I shall be my own solicitor.'

Before a fortnight was over, Baxter admitted ruefully that M'Leod was better than most firms in the business. We buyers were coy, argumentative, shocked at the price of Holmescroft, inquisitive, and cold by turns, but Mr M'Leod the seller easily met and surpassed us; and Mr Baxter entered every letter, telegram, and consultation at the proper rates in a cinematograph-film of a bill. At the end of a month he said it looked as though M'Leod, thanks to him, were really going to listen to reason. I was some pounds out of pocket, but I had learned something of Mr Baxter on the human side. I deserved it. Never in my life have I worked to conciliate, amuse, and flatter a human being as I worked over my solicitor.

It appeared that he golfed. Therefore, I was an enthusiastic beginner, anxious to learn. Twice I invaded his office with a bag (M'Leod lent it) full of the spelicans[9] needed in this detestable game, and a vocabulary to match. The third time the ice broke, and Mr Baxter took me to his links, quite ten miles off, where in a maze of tramway-lines, railroads, and nursery-maids, we skelped our divoted way[10] round nine holes like barges plunging through head seas. He played vilely and had never expected to meet anyone worse; but as he realised my form, I think he began to like me, for he took me in hand by the two hours together. After a fortnight he could give me no more than a stroke a hole, and when, with this allowance, I once managed to beat him by one, he was honestly glad, and assured me that I should be a golfer if I stuck to it. I was sticking to it for my own ends, but now and again my conscience pricked me; for the man was a nice man. Between games he supplied me with odd pieces of evidence, such as that he had known the Moultries all his life, being their cousin, and that Miss Mary, the eldest, was an unforgiving woman who would never let bygones be. I naturally wondered what she might have against him; and somehow connected him unfavourably with mad Agnes.

'People ought to forgive and forget,' he volunteered one day between rounds. 'Specially where, in the nature of things, they can't be sure of their deductions. Don't you think so?'

'It all depends on the nature of the evidence on which one forms one's judgment,' I answered.

'Nonsense!' he cried. 'I'm lawyer enough to know that there's nothing in the world so misleading as circumstantial evidence. Never was.'

'Why? Have you ever seen men hanged on it?'

'Hanged? People have been supposed to be eternally lost on it.' His face turned grey again. 'I don't know how it is with you, but my consolation is that God must know. He *must*! Things that seem on the face of 'em like murder, or say suicide, may appear different to God. Heh?'

'That's what the murderer and the suicide can always hope – I suppose.'

'I have expressed myself clumsily as usual. The facts as God knows 'em – may *be* different – even after the most clinching evidence. I've always said that – both as a lawyer and a man, but some people won't – I don't want to judge 'em – we'll say they can't – believe it; whereas *I* say there's always a working chance – a certainty – that the worst hasn't happened.' He stopped and cleared his throat. 'Now, let's come on! This time next week I shall be taking my holiday.'

'What links?' I asked carelessly, while twins in a perambulator got out of our line of fire.

'A potty little nine-hole affair at a Hydro in the Midlands. My cousins stay there. Always will. Not but what the fourth and the seventh holes take some doing. You could manage it, though,' he said encouragingly. 'You're doing much better. It's only your approach-shots that are weak.'

'You're right. I can't approach for nuts! I shall go to pieces while you're away – with no one to coach me,' I said mournfully.

'I haven't taught you anything,' he said, delighted with the compliment.

'I owe all I've learned to you, anyhow. When will you come back?'

'Look here,' he began. 'I don't know your engagements, but I've no one to play with at Burry Mills. Never have. Why couldn't you take a few days off and join me there? I warn you it will be rather dull. It's a throat and gout place – baths, massage, electricity, and so forth. But the fourth and the seventh holes really take some doing.'

'I'm for the game,' I answered valiantly, Heaven well knowing that I hated every stroke and word of it.

'That's the proper spirit. As their lawyer I must ask you not to say anything to my cousins about Holmescroft. It upsets 'em. Always did. But speaking as man to man, it would be very pleasant for me if you could see your way to – '

I saw it as soon as decency permitted, and thanked him sincerely. According to my now well-developed theory he had certainly misappropriated his aged cousins' monies under power of attorney, and had probably driven poor Agnes Moultrie out of her wits, but I wished that he was not so gentle, and good-tempered, and innocent-eyed.

Before I joined him at Burry Mills Hydro, I spent a night at Holmescroft. Miss M'Leod had returned from her Hydro, and first we made very merry on the open lawn in the sunshine over the manners and customs of the English resorting to such places. She knew dozens of Hydros, and warned me how to behave in them, while Mr and Mrs M'Leod stood aside and adored her.

'Ah! That's the way she always comes back to us,' he said. 'Pity it wears off so soon, ain't it? You ought to hear her sing "With mirth, thou pretty bird".'

We had the house to face through the evening, and there we neither laughed nor sang. The gloom fell on us as we entered, and did not shift till ten o'clock, when we crawled out, as it were, from beneath it.

'It has been bad this summer,' said Mrs M'Leod in a whisper after we realised that we were freed. 'Sometimes I think the house will get up and cry out – it is so bad.'

'How?'

'Have you forgotten what comes after the depression?'

So then we waited about the small fire, and the dead air in the room presently filled and pressed down upon us with the sensation (but words are useless here) as though some dumb and bound power were striving against gag and bond to deliver its soul of an articulate word. It passed in a few minutes, and I fell to thinking about Mr Baxter's conscience and Agnes Moultrie, gone mad in the well-lit bedroom that waited me.

These reflections secured me a night during which I rediscovered how, from purely mental causes, a man can be physically sick. But the sickness was bliss compared with my dreams when the birds waked. On my departure, M'Leod gave me a beautiful narwhal's horn much as a nurse gives a child sweets for being brave at a dentist's.

'There's no duplicate of it in the world,' he said, 'else it would have come to old Max M'Leod,' and he tucked it into the motor. Miss M'Leod on the far side of the car whispered, 'Have you found out anything, Mr Perseus?'

I shook my head.

'Then I shall be chained to my rock all my life,' she went on. 'Only don't tell papa.'

I supposed she was thinking of the young gentleman who specialised in South American rails, for I noticed a ring on the third finger of her left hand.

I went straight from that house to Burry Mills Hydro, keen for the first time in my life on playing golf, which is guaranteed to occupy the mind. Baxter had taken me a room communicating with his own, and after lunch introduced me to a tall, horse-headed elderly lady of decided manners, whom a white-haired maid pushed along in a bath-chair through the park-like grounds of the Hydro. She was Miss Mary Moultrie, and she coughed and cleared her throat just like Baxter. She suffered – she told me it was the Moultrie caste-mark – from some obscure form of chronic bronchitis, complicated with spasm of the glottis; and, in a dead flat voice, with a sunken eye that looked and saw not, told me what washes, gargles, pastilles, and inhalations she had proved most beneficial. From her I was passed on to her younger sister, Miss Elizabeth, a small and withered thing with twitching lips, victim, she told me, to very much the same sort of throat, but secretly devoted to another set of medicines. When she went away with Baxter and the bath-chair, I fell across a Major of the Indian Army with gout in his glassy eyes, and a stomach which he had taken all round the Continent. He laid everything before me; and him I escaped only to be confided in by a matron with a tendency to follicular tonsilitis and eczema. Baxter waited hand and foot on his cousins till five o'clock, trying, as I saw, to atone for his treatment of the dead sister. Miss Mary ordered him about like a dog.

'I warned you it would be dull,' he said when we met in the smoking-room.

'It's tremendously interesting,' I said. 'But how about a look round the links?'

'Unluckily damp always affects my eldest cousin. I've got to buy her a new bronchitis-kettle. Arthurs broke her old one yesterday.'

We slipped out to the chemist's shop in the town, and he bought a large glittering tin thing whose workings he explained.

'I'm used to this sort of work. I come up here pretty often,' he said. 'I've the family throat too.'

'You're a good man,' I said. 'A very good man.'

He turned toward me in the evening light among the beeches, and his face was changed to what it might have been a generation before.

'You see,' he said huskily, 'there was the youngest – Agnes. Before she fell ill, you know. But she didn't like leaving her sisters. Never would.' He hurried on with his odd-shaped load and left me among the ruins of my black theories. The man with that face had done Agnes Moultrie no wrong.

We never played our game. I was waked between two and three in the morning from my hygienic bed by Baxter in an ulster over orange-and-white pyjamas, which I should never have suspected from his character.

'My cousin has had some sort of a seizure,' he said. 'Will you come? I don't want to wake the doctor. Don't want to make a scandal. Quick!'

So I came quickly, and, led by the white-haired Arthurs in a jacket and petticoat, entered a double-bedded room reeking with steam and Friar's Balsam. The electrics were all on. Miss Mary – I knew her by her height – was at the open window, wrestling with Miss Elizabeth, who gripped her round the knees. Her hand was at her throat, which was streaked with blood.

'She's done it. She's done it too!' Miss Elizabeth panted. 'Hold her! Help me!'

'Oh, I say! Women don't cut their throats,' Baxter whispered.

'My God! Has she cut her throat?' the maid cried, and with no warning rolled over in a faint. Baxter pushed her under the wash-basins, and leaped to hold the gaunt woman who crowed and whistled as she struggled towards the window. He took her by the shoulder, and she struck out wildly.

'All right! She's only cut her hand,' he said. 'Wet towel – quick!'

While I got that he pushed her backward. Her strength seemed almost as great as his. I swabbed at her throat when I could, and found no mark; then helped him to control her a little. Miss Elizabeth leaped back to bed, wailing like a child.

'Tie up her hand somehow,' said Baxter. 'Don't let it drip about the place. She' – he stepped on broken glass in his slippers – 'she must have smashed a pane.'

Miss Mary lurched towards the open window again, dropped on

her knees, her head on the sill, and lay quiet, surrendering the cut hand to me.

'What did she do?' Baxter turned towards Miss Elizabeth in the far bed.

'She was going to throw herself out of the window,' was the answer. 'I stopped her, and sent Arthurs for you. Oh, we can never hold up our heads again!'

Miss Mary writhed and fought for breath. Baxter found a shawl which he threw over her shoulders.

'Nonsense!' said he. 'That isn't like Mary'; but his face worked when he said it.

'You wouldn't believe about Aggie, John. Perhaps you will now!' said Miss Elizabeth. 'I *saw* her do it, and she's cut her throat too!'

'She hasn't,' I said. 'It's only her hand.'

Miss Mary suddenly broke from us with an indescribable grunt, flew, rather than ran, to her sister's bed, and there shook her as one furious schoolgirl would shake another.

'No such thing,' she croaked. 'How dare you think so, you wicked little fool?'

'Get into bed, Mary,' said Baxter. 'You'll catch a chill.'

She obeyed, but sat up with the grey shawl round her lean shoulders, glaring at her sister. 'I'm better now,' she crowed. 'Arthurs let me sit out too long. Where's Arthurs? The kettle.'

'Never mind Arthurs,' said Baxter. '*You* get the kettle.' I hastened to bring it from the side-table. 'Now, Mary, as God sees you, tell me what you've done.'

His lips were dry, and he could not moisten them with his tongue.

Miss Mary applied herself to the mouth of the kettle, and between indraws of steam said: 'The spasm came on just now, while I was asleep. I was nearly choking to death. So I went to the window. I've done it often before, without waking any one. Bessie's such an old maid about draughts! I tell you I was choking to death. I couldn't manage the catch, and I nearly fell out. That window opens too low. I cut my hand trying to save myself. Who has tied it up in this filthy handkerchief? I wish you had had my throat, Bessie. I never was nearer dying!' She scowled on us all impartially, while her sister sobbed.

From the bottom of the bed we heard a quivering voice: 'Is she dead? Have they took her away? Oh, I never could bear the sight o' blood!'

'Arthurs,' said Miss Mary, 'you are an hireling.[11] Go away!'

It is my belief that Arthurs crawled out on all fours, but I was busy picking up broken glass from the carpet.

Then Baxter, seated by the side of the bed, began to cross-examine in a voice I scarcely recognised. No one could for an instant have doubted the genuine rage of Miss Mary against her sister, her cousin, or her maid; and that the doctor should have been called in – for she did me the honour of calling me doctor – was the last drop. She was choking with her throat; had rushed to the window for air; had nearly pitched out, and in catching at the window-bars had cut her hand. Over and over she made this clear to the intent Baxter. Then she turned on her sister and tongue-lashed her savagely.

'You mustn't blame me,' Miss Bessie faltered at last. 'You know what we think of night and day.'

'I'm coming to that,' said Baxter. 'Listen to me. What *you* did, Mary, misled four people into thinking you – you meant to do away with yourself.'

'Isn't one suicide in the family enough? Oh, God, help and pity us! You *couldn't* have believed that!' she cried.

'The evidence was complete. Now, don't you think,' – Baxter's finger wagged under her nose – '*can't* you think that poor Aggie did the same thing at Holmescroft when she fell out of the window?'

'She had the same throat,' said Miss Elizabeth. 'Exactly the same symptoms. Don't you remember, Mary?'

'Which was her bedroom?' I asked of Baxter in an undertone.

'Over the south veranda, looking on to the tennis lawn.'

'I nearly fell out of that very window when I was at Holmescroft – opening it to get some air. The sill doesn't come much above your knees,' I said.

'You hear that, Mary? Mary, do you hear what this gentleman says? Won't you believe that what nearly happened to you must have happened to poor Aggie that night? For God's sake – for her sake – Mary, *won't* you believe?'

There was a long silence while the steam-kettle puffed.

'If I could have proof – if I could have proof,' said she, and broke into most horrible tears.

Baxter motioned to me, and I crept away to my room, and lay awake till morning, thinking more specially of the dumb Thing at Holmescroft which wished to explain itself. I hated Miss Mary as perfectly as though I had known her for twenty years, but I felt that, alive or dead, I should not like her to condemn me.

Yet at mid-day, when I saw Miss Mary in her bath-chair, Arthurs behind and Baxter and Miss Elizabeth on either side, in the park-like grounds of the Hydro, I found it difficult to arrange my words.

'Now that you know all about it,' said Baxter aside, after the first strangeness of our meeting was over, 'it's only fair to tell you that my poor cousin did not die *in* Holmescroft at all. She was dead when they found her under the window in the morning. Just dead.'

'Under that laburnum outside the window?' I asked, for I suddenly remembered the crooked evil thing.

'Exactly. She broke the tree in falling. But no death has ever taken place *in* the house, so far as we were concerned. You can make yourself quite easy on that point. Mr M'Leod's extra thousand for what you called the "clean bill of health" was something towards my cousins' estate when we sold. It was my duty as their lawyer to get it for them – at any cost to my own feelings.'

I know better than to argue when the English talk about their duty. So I agreed with my solicitor.

'Their sister's death must have been a great blow to your cousins,' I went on. The bath-chair was behind me.

'Unspeakable,' Baxter whispered. 'They brooded on it day and night. No wonder. If their theory of poor Aggie making away with herself was correct, she was eternally lost!'

'Do you believe that she made away with herself?'

'No, thank God! Never have! And after what happened to Mary last night, I see perfectly what happened to poor Aggie. She had the family throat too. By the way, Mary thinks you are a doctor. Otherwise she wouldn't like your having been in her room.'

'Very good. Is she convinced now about her sister's death?'

'She'd give anything to be able to believe it, but she's a hard woman, and brooding along certain lines makes one groovy. I have sometimes been afraid for her reason – on the religious side, don't you know. Elizabeth doesn't matter. Brain of a hen. Always had.'

Here Arthurs summoned me to the bath-chair, and the ravaged face, beneath its knitted Shetland wool hood, of Miss Mary Moultrie.

'I need not remind you, I hope, of the seal of secrecy – absolute secrecy – in your profession,' she began. 'Thanks to my cousin's and my sister's stupidity, you have found out – ' She blew her nose.

'Please don't excite her, sir,' said Arthurs at the back.

'But, my dear Miss Moultrie, I only know what I've seen, of course, but it seems to me that what you thought was a tragedy in your sister's case, turns out, on your own evidence, so to speak, to have been an accident – a dreadfully sad one – but absolutely an accident.'

'Do you believe that too?' she cried. 'Or are you only saying it to comfort me?'

'I believe it from the bottom of my heart. Come down to Holmescroft for an hour – for half an hour – and satisfy yourself.'

'Of what? You don't understand. I see the house every day – every night. I am always there in spirit – waking or sleeping. I couldn't face it in reality.'

'But you must,' I said. 'If you go there in the spirit the greater need for you to go there in the flesh. Go to your sister's room once more, and see the window – I nearly fell out of it myself. It's – it's awfully low and dangerous. That would convince you,' I pleaded.

'Yet Aggie had slept in that room for years,' she interrupted.

'You've slept in your room here for a long time, haven't you? But you nearly fell out of the window when you were choking.'

'That is true. That is one thing true,' she nodded. 'And I might have been killed as – perhaps – Aggie was killed.'

'In that case your own sister and cousin and maid would have said you had committed suicide, Miss Moultrie. Come down to Holmescroft, and go over the place just once.'

'You are lying,' she said quite quietly. 'You don't want me to come down to see a window. It is something else. I warn you we are Evangelicals. We don't believe in prayers for the dead. "As the tree falls – "'[12]

'Yes. I daresay. But you persist in thinking that your sister committed suicide – '

'No! No! I have always prayed that I might have misjudged her.'

Arthurs at the bath-chair spoke up: 'Oh, Miss Mary! you *would* 'ave it from the first that poor Miss Aggie 'ad made away with herself; an', of course, Miss Bessie took the notion from you. Only Master – Mister John stood out, and – and I'd 'ave taken my Bible oath *you* was making away with yourself last night.'

Miss Mary leaned towards me, one finger on my sleeve.

'If going to Holmescroft kills me,' she said, 'you will have the murder of a fellow-creature on your conscience for all eternity.'

'I'll risk it,' I answered. Remembering what torment the mere reflection of her torments had cast on Holmescroft, and remembering, above all, the dumb Thing that filled the house with its desire to speak, I felt that there might be worse things.

Baxter was amazed at the proposed visit, but at a nod from that terrible woman went off to make arrangements. Then I sent a telegram to M'Leod bidding him and his vacate Holmescroft for that afternoon. Miss Mary should be alone with her dead, as I had been alone.

I expected untold trouble in transporting her, but to do her justice, her promise given for the journey, she underwent it without murmur, spasm, or unnecessary word. Miss Bessie, pressed in a corner by the window, wept behind her veil, and from time to time tried to take hold of her sister's hand. Baxter wrapped himself in his newly-found happiness as selfishly as a bridegroom, for he sat still and smiled.

'So long as I know that Aggie didn't make away with herself,' he explained, 'I tell you frankly I don't care what happened. She's as hard as a rock – Mary. Always was. *She* won't die.'

We led her out on to the platform like a blind woman, and so got her into the fly.[13] The half-hour crawl to Holmescroft was the most racking experience of the day. M'Leod had obeyed my instructions. There was no one visible in the house or the gardens; and the front door stood open.

Miss Mary rose from beside her sister, stepped forth first, and entered the hall.

'Come, Bessie,' she cried.

'I daren't. Oh, I daren't.'

'Come!' Her voice had altered. I felt Baxter start. 'There's nothing to be afraid of.'

'Good heavens!' said Baxter. 'She's running up the stairs. We'd better follow.'

'Let's wait below. She's going to the room.' We heard the door of the bedroom I knew open and shut, and we waited in the lemon-coloured hall, heavy with the scent of flowers.

'I've never been into it since it was sold,' Baxter sighed. 'What a lovely restful place it is! Poor Aggie used to arrange the flowers.'

'Restful?' I began, but stopped of a sudden, for I felt all over my bruised soul that Baxter was speaking truth. It was a light, spacious, airy house, full of the sense of well-being and peace – above all things, of peace. I ventured into the dining-room where the thoughtful M'Leods had left a small fire. There was no terror there present or lurking; and in the drawing-room, which for good reasons we had never cared to enter, the sun and the peace and the scent of the flowers worked together as is fit in an inhabited house. When I returned to the hall, Baxter was sweetly asleep on a couch, looking most unlike a middle-aged solicitor who had spent a broken night with an exacting cousin.

There was ample time for me to review it all – to felicitate myself upon my magnificent acumen (barring some errors about Baxter as a thief and possibly a murderer), before the door above opened, and Baxter, evidently a light sleeper, sprang awake.

'I've had a heavenly little nap,' he said, rubbing his eyes with the backs of his hands like a child. 'Good Lord! That's not *their* step!'

But it was. I had never before been privileged to see the Shadow turned backward on the dial – the years ripped bodily off poor human shoulders – old sunken eyes filled and alight – harsh lips moistened and human.

'John,' Miss Mary called, 'I know now. Aggie didn't do it!' and 'She didn't do it!' echoed Miss Bessie, and giggled.

'I did not think it wrong to say a prayer,' Miss Mary continued. 'Not for her soul, but for our peace. Then I was convinced.'

'Then we got conviction,' the younger sister piped.

'We've misjudged poor Aggie, John. But I feel she knows now. Wherever she is, she knows that we know she is guiltless.'

'Yes, she knows. I felt it too,' said Miss Elizabeth.

'I never doubted,' said John Baxter, whose face was beautiful at that hour. 'Not from the first. Never have!'

'You never offered me proof, John. Now, thank God, it will not be the same any more. I can think henceforward of Aggie without sorrow.' She tripped, absolutely tripped, across the hall. 'What ideas these Jews have of arranging furniture!' She spied me behind a big cloisonné vase.

'I've seen the window,' she said remotely. 'You took a great risk in advising me to undertake such a journey. However, as it turns out . . . I forgive you, and I pray you may never know what mental anguish means! Bessie! Look at this peculiar piano! Do you suppose, Doctor, these people would offer one tea? I miss mine.'

'I will go and see,' I said, and explored M'Leod's new-built servants' wing. It was in the servants' hall that I unearthed the M'Leod family bursting with anxiety.

'Tea for three, quick,' I said. 'If you ask me any questions now, I shall have a fit!' So Mrs M'Leod got it, and I was butler, amid murmured apologies from Baxter, still smiling and self-absorbed, and the cold disapproval of Miss Mary, who thought the pattern of the china vulgar. However, she ate well, and even asked me whether I would not like a cup of tea for myself.

They went away in the twilight – the twilight that I had once feared. They were going to an hotel in London to rest after the fatigues of the day, and as their fly turned down the drive, I capered on the doorstep, with the all-darkened house behind me.

Then I heard the uncertain feet of the M'Leods, and bade them not to turn on the lights, but to feel – to feel what I had done; for the Shadow was gone, with the dumb desire in the air. They drew short, but afterwards deeper, breaths, like bathers entering chill water, separated one from the other, moved about the hall, tiptoed upstairs, raced down, and then Miss M'Leod, and I believe her mother, though she denies this, embraced me. I know M'Leod did.

It was a disgraceful evening. To say we rioted through the house is to put it mildly. We played a sort of Blind Man's Buff along the darkest passages, in the unlighted drawing-room, and the little dining-room, calling cheerily to each other after each exploration that here, and here, and here, the trouble had removed itself. We came up to *the* bedroom

– mine for the night again – and sat, the women on the bed, and we men on chairs, drinking in blessed draughts of peace and comfort and cleanliness of soul, while I told them my tale in full, and received fresh praise, thanks, and blessing.

When the servants, returned from their day's outing, gave us a supper of cold fried fish, M'Leod had sense enough to open no wine. We had been practically drunk since nightfall, and grew incoherent on water and milk.

'I like that Baxter,' said M'Leod. 'He's a sharp man. The death wasn't *in* the house, but he ran it pretty close, ain't it?'

'And the joke of it is that he supposes I want to buy the place from you,' I said. 'Are you selling?'

'Not for twice what I paid for it – now,' said M'Leod. 'I'll keep you in furs all your life; but not our Holmescroft.'

'No – never our Holmescroft,' said Miss M'Leod. 'We'll ask *him* here on Tuesday, mamma.' They squeezed each other's hands.

'Now tell me,' said Mrs M'Leod – 'that tall one I saw out of the scullery window – did *she* tell you she was always here in the spirit? I hate her. She made all this trouble. It was *not* her house after she had sold it. What do you think?'

'I suppose,' I answered, 'she brooded over what she believed was her sister's suicide night and day – she confessed she did – and her thoughts being concentrated on this place, they felt like a – like a burning-glass.'

'Burning-glass is good,' said M'Leod.

'I said it was like a light of blackness turned on us,' cried the girl, twiddling her ring. 'That must have been when the tall one thought worst about her sister and the house.'

'Ah, the poor Aggie!' said Mrs M'Leod. 'The poor Aggie, trying to tell every one it was not so! No wonder we felt Something wished to say Something. Thea, Max, do you remember that night – '

'We need not remember any more,' M'Leod interrupted. 'It is not our trouble. They have told each other now.'

'Do you think, then,' said Miss M'Leod, 'that those two, the living ones, were actually told something – upstairs – in your – in the room?'

'I can't say. At any rate they were made happy, and they ate a big tea afterwards. As your father says, it is not our trouble any longer – thank God!'

'Amen!' said M'Leod. 'Now, Thea, let us have some music after all these months. "With mirth, thou pretty bird," ain't it? You ought to hear that.'

And in the half-lighted hall, Thea sang an old English song that I had never heard before:

> With mirth, thou pretty bird, rejoice
> Thy Maker's praise enhancèd;
> Lift up thy shrill and pleasant voice,
> Thy God is high advancèd!
> Thy food before He did provide,
> And gives it in a fitting side,
> Wherewith be thou sufficèd!
> Why shouldst thou now unpleasant be,
> Thy wrath against God venting,
> That He a little bird made thee,
> Thy silly head tormenting,
> Because He made thee not a man?
> Oh, Peace! He hath well thought thereon,
> Therewith be thou sufficèd!

MARY POSTGATE

Of Miss Mary Postgate, Lady McCausland wrote that she was 'thoroughly conscientious, tidy, companionable, and ladylike. I am very sorry to part with her, and shall always be interested in her welfare.'

Miss Fowler engaged her on this recommendation, and to her surprise, for she had had experience of companions, found that it was true. Miss Fowler was nearer sixty than fifty at the time, but though she needed care she did not exhaust her attendant's vitality. On the contrary, she gave out, stimulatingly and with reminiscences. Her father had been a minor Court official in the days when the Great Exhibition of 1851 had just set its seal on Civilisation made perfect. Some of Miss Fowler's tales, none the less, were not always for the young. Mary was not young, and though her speech was as colourless as her eyes or her hair, she was never shocked. She listened unflinchingly to every one; said at the end, 'How interesting!' or 'How shocking!' as the case might be, and never again referred to it, for she prided herself on a trained mind, which 'did not dwell on these things'. She was, too, a treasure at domestic accounts, for which the village tradesmen, with their weekly books, loved her not. Otherwise she had no enemies; provoked no jealousy even among the plainest; neither gossip nor slander had ever been traced to her; she supplied the odd place at the Rector's or the Doctor's table at half an hour's notice; she was a sort of public aunt to very many small children of the village street, whose parents, while accepting everything, would have been swift to resent what they called 'patronage'; she served on the Village Nursing Committee as Miss Fowler's nominee when Miss Fowler was crippled by rheumatoid arthritis, and came out of six months' fortnightly meetings equally respected by all the cliques.

And when Fate threw Miss Fowler's nephew, an unlovely orphan of eleven, on Miss Fowler's hands, Mary Postgate stood to her share of the business of education as practised in private and public schools. She checked printed clothes-lists, and unitemised bills of extras; wrote to Head and House masters, matrons, nurses, and doctors, and grieved or rejoiced over half-term reports. Young Wyndham Fowler repaid her in his holidays by calling her 'Gatepost', 'Postey', or 'Packthread', by thumping her between her narrow shoulders, or by chasing her bleating, round the garden, her large mouth open, her large nose high in air, at a stiff-necked shamble very like a camel's. Later on he filled the house with clamour, argument, and harangues as to his personal needs, likes, and dislikes, and the limitations of 'you women', reducing Mary to tears of physical fatigue, or, when he chose to be humorous, of helpless laughter. At crises, which multiplied as he grew older, she was his ambassadress and his interpretress to Miss Fowler, who had no large sympathy with the young; a vote in his interest at the councils on his future; his sewing-woman, strictly accountable for mislaid boots and garments; always his butt and his slave.

And when he decided to become a solicitor, and had entered an office in London; when his greeting had changed from 'Hullo, Postey, you old beast', to 'Mornin', Packthread', there came a war which, unlike all wars that Mary could remember, did not stay decently outside England and in the newspapers, but intruded on the lives of people whom she knew. As she said to Miss Fowler, it was 'most vexatious'. It took the Rector's son, who was going into business with his elder brother; it took the Colonel's nephew on the eve of fruit-farming in Canada; it took Mrs Grant's son, who, his mother said, was devoted to the ministry; and, very early indeed, it took Wynn Fowler, who announced on a postcard that he had joined the Flying Corps and wanted a cardigan waistcoat.

'He must go, and he must have the waistcoat,' said Miss Fowler. So Mary got the proper-sized needles and wool, while Miss Fowler told the men of her establishment – two gardeners and an odd man, aged sixty – that those who could join the Army had better do so. The gardeners left. Cheape, the odd man, stayed on, and was promoted to the gardener's cottage. The cook, scorning to be limited in luxuries, also left, after a spirited scene with Miss Fowler, and took the housemaid with her. Miss Fowler gazetted Nellie, Cheape's seventeen-year-old daughter, to the vacant post; Mrs Cheape to the rank of cook, with occasional cleaning bouts; and the reduced establishment moved forward smoothly.

Wynn demanded an increase in his allowance. Miss Fowler, who always looked facts in the face, said, 'He must have it. The chances are he won't live long to draw it, and if three hundred makes him happy – '

Wynn was grateful, and came over, in his tight-buttoned uniform, to say so. His training centre was not thirty miles away, and his talk was so technical that it had to be explained by charts of the various types of machines. He gave Mary such a chart.

'And you'd better study it, Postey,' he said. 'You'll be seeing a lot of 'em soon.' So Mary studied the chart, but when Wynn next arrived to swell and exalt himself before his womenfolk, she failed badly in cross-examination, and he rated her as in the old days.

'You *look* more or less like a human being,' he said in his new Service voice. 'You *must* have had a brain at some time in your past. What have you done with it? Where d'you keep it? A sheep would know more than you do, Postey. You're lamentable. You are less use than an empty tin can, you dowey old cassowary.'[1]

'I suppose that's how your superior officer talks to *you*?' said Miss Fowler from her chair.

'But Postey doesn't mind,' Wynn replied. 'Do you, Packthread?'

'Why? Was Wynn saying anything? I shall get this right next time you come,' she muttered, and knitted her pale eyebrows again over the diagrams of Taubes, Farmans, and Zeppelins.

In a few weeks the mere land and sea battles which she read to Miss Fowler after breakfast passed her like idle breath. Her heart and her interest were high in the air with Wynn, who had finished 'rolling' (whatever that might be) and had gone on from a 'taxi'[2] to a machine more or less his own. One morning it circled over their very chimneys, alighted on Vegg's Heath, almost outside the garden gate, and Wynn came in, blue with cold, shouting for food. He and she drew Miss Fowler's bath-chair, as they had often done, along the Heath foot-path to look at the biplane. Mary observed that 'it smelt very badly.'

'Postey, I believe you think with your nose,' said Wynn. 'I know you don't with your mind. Now, what type's that?'

'I'll go and get the chart,' said Mary.

'You're hopeless! You haven't the mental capacity of a white mouse,' he cried, and explained the dials and the sockets for bomb-dropping till it was time to mount and ride the wet clouds once more.

'Ah!' said Mary, as the stinking thing flared upward. 'Wait till our Flying Corps gets to work! Wynn says it's much safer than in the trenches.'

'I wonder,' said Miss Fowler. 'Tell Cheape to come and tow me home again.'

'It's all downhill. I can do it,' said Mary, 'if you put the brake on.' She laid her lean self against the pushing-bar and home they trundled.

'Now, be careful you aren't heated and catch a chill,' said overdressed Miss Fowler.

'Nothing makes me perspire,' said Mary. As she bumped the chair under the porch she straightened her long back. The exertion had given her a colour, and the wind had loosened a wisp of hair across her forehead. Miss Fowler glanced at her.

'What do you ever think of, Mary?' she demanded suddenly.

'Oh, Wynn says he wants another three pairs of stockings – as thick as we can make them.'

'Yes. But I mean the things that women think about. Here you are, more than forty – '

'Forty-four,' said truthful Mary.

'Well?'

'Well?' Mary offered Miss Fowler her shoulder as usual.

'And you've been with me ten years now.'

'Let's see,' said Mary. 'Wynn was eleven when he came. He's twenty now, and I came two years before that. It must be eleven.'

'Eleven! And you've never told me anything that matters in all that while. Looking back, it seems to me that *I*'ve done all the talking.'

'I'm afraid I'm not much of a conversationalist. As Wynn says, I haven't the mind. Let me take your hat.'

Miss Fowler, moving stiffly from the hip, stamped her rubber-tipped stick on the tiled hall floor. 'Mary, aren't you *anything* except a companion? Would you *ever* have been anything except a companion?'

Mary hung up the garden hat on its proper peg. 'No,' she said after consideration. 'I don't imagine I ever should. But I've no imagination, I'm afraid.'

She fetched Miss Fowler her eleven-o'clock glass of Contrexéville.[3]

That was the wet December when it rained six inches to the month, and the women went abroad as little as might be. Wynn's flying chariot visited them several times, and for two mornings (he had warned her by postcard) Mary heard the thresh of his propellers at dawn. The second time she ran to the window, and stared at the whitening sky. A little blur passed overhead. She lifted her lean arms towards it.

That evening at six o'clock there came an announcement in an official envelope that Second-Lieutenant W. Fowler had been killed during a trial flight. Death was instantaneous. She read it and carried it to Miss Fowler.

'I never expected anything else,' said Miss Fowler; 'but I'm sorry it happened before he had done anything.'

The room was whirling round Mary Postgate, but she found herself quite steady in the midst of it.

'Yes,' she said. 'It's a great pity he didn't die in action after he had killed somebody.'

'He was killed instantly. That's one comfort,' Miss Fowler went on.

'But Wynn says the shock of a fall kills a man at once – whatever happens to the tanks,' quoted Mary.

The room was coming to rest now. She heard Miss Fowler say impatiently, 'But why can't we cry, Mary?' and herself replying, 'There's nothing to cry for. He has done his duty as much as Mrs Grant's son did.'

'And when he died, *she* came and cried all the morning,' said Miss Fowler. 'This only makes me feel tired – terribly tired. Will you help me to bed, please, Mary? – And I think I'd like the hot-water bottle.'

So Mary helped her and sat beside, talking of Wynn in his riotous youth.

'I believe,' said Miss Fowler suddenly, 'that old people and young people slip from under a stroke like this. The middle-aged feel it most.'

'I expect that's true,' said Mary, rising. 'I'm going to put away the things in his room now. Shall we wear mourning?'

'Certainly not,' said Miss Fowler. 'Except, of course, at the funeral. I can't go. You will. I want you to arrange about his being buried here. What a blessing it didn't happen at Salisbury!'[4]

Everyone, from the Authorities of the Flying Corps to the Rector, was most kind and sympathetic. Mary found herself for the moment in a world where bodies were in the habit of being dispatched by all sorts of conveyances to all sorts of places. And at the funeral two young men in buttoned-up uniforms stood beside the grave and spoke to her afterwards.

'You're Miss Postgate, aren't you?' said one. 'Fowler told me about you. He was a good chap – a first-class fellow – a great loss.'

'Great loss!' growled his companion. 'We're all awfully sorry.'

'How high did he fall from?' Mary whispered.

'Pretty nearly four thousand feet, I should think, didn't he? You were up that day, Monkey?'

'All of that,' the other child replied. 'My bar made three thousand, and I wasn't as high as him by a lot.'

'Then *that*'s all right,' said Mary. 'Thank you very much.'

They moved away as Mrs Grant flung herself weeping on Mary's flat chest, under the lych-gate, and cried, '*I* know how it feels! *I* know how it feels!'

'But both his parents are dead,' Mary returned, as she fended her off. 'Perhaps they've all met by now,' she added vaguely as she escaped towards the coach.

'I've thought of that too,' wailed Mrs Grant; 'but then he'll be practically a stranger to them. Quite embarrassing!'

Mary faithfully reported every detail of the ceremony to Miss Fowler, who, when she described Mrs Grant's outburst, laughed aloud.

'Oh, how Wynn would have enjoyed it! He was always utterly unreliable at funerals. D'you remember – ' And they talked of him again, each piecing out the other's gaps. 'And now,' said Miss Fowler, 'we'll pull up the blinds and we'll have a general tidy. That always does us good. Have you seen to Wynn's things?'

'Everything – since he first came,' said Mary. 'He was never destructive – even with his toys.'

They faced that neat room.

'It can't be natural not to cry,' Mary said at last. 'I'm *so* afraid you'll have a reaction.'

'As I told you, we old people slip from under the stroke. It's you I'm afraid for. Have you cried yet?'

'I can't. It only makes me angry with the Germans.'

'That's sheer waste of vitality,' said Miss Fowler. 'We must live till the War's finished.' She opened a full wardrobe. 'Now, I've been thinking things over. This is my plan. All his civilian clothes can be given away – Belgian refugees, and so on.'

Mary nodded. 'Boots, collars, and gloves?'

'Yes. We don't need to keep anything except his cap and belt.'

'They came back yesterday with his Flying Corps clothes' – Mary pointed to a roll on the little iron bed.

'Ah, but keep his Service things. Someone may be glad of them later. Do you remember his sizes?'

'Five feet eight and a half; thirty-six inches round the chest. But he told me he's just put on an inch and a half. I'll mark it on a label and tie it on his sleeping-bag.'

'So that disposes of *that*,' said Miss Fowler, tapping the palm of one hand with the ringed third finger of the other. 'What waste it all is! We'll get his old school-trunks to-morrow and pack his civilian clothes.'

'And the rest?' said Mary. 'His books and pictures and the games and the toys – and – and the rest?'

'My plan is to burn every single thing,' said Miss Fowler. 'Then we shall know where they are and no one can handle them afterwards. What do you think?'

'I think that would be much the best,' said Mary. 'But there's such a lot of them.'

'We'll burn them in the destructor,' said Miss Fowler.

This was an open-air furnace for the consumption of refuse; a little circular four-foot tower of pierced brick over an iron grating. Miss

Fowler had noticed the design in a gardening journal years ago, and had had it built at the bottom of the garden. It suited her tidy soul, for it saved unsightly rubbish-heaps, and the ashes lightened the stiff clay soil.

Mary considered for a moment, saw her way clear, and nodded again. They spent the evening putting away well-remembered civilian suits, underclothes that Mary had marked, and the regiments of very gaudy socks and ties. A second trunk was needed, and, after that, a little packing-case, and it was late next day when Cheape and the local carrier lifted them to the cart. The Rector luckily knew of a friend's son, about five feet eight and a half inches high, to whom a complete Flying Corps outfit would be most acceptable, and sent his gardener's son down with a barrow to take delivery of it. The cap was hung up in Miss Fowler's bedroom, the belt in Miss Postgate's; for, as Miss Fowler said, they had no desire to make tea-party talk of them.

'That disposes of *that*,' said Miss Fowler. 'I'll leave the rest to you, Mary. *I* can't run up and down the garden. You'd better take the big clothes-basket and get Nellie to help you.'

'I shall take the wheelbarrow and do it myself,' said Mary, and for once in her life closed her mouth.

Miss Fowler, in moments of irritation, had called Mary deadly methodical. She put on her oldest waterproof and gardening-hat and her ever-slipping goloshes, for the weather was on the edge of more rain. She gathered fire-lighters from the kitchen, a half-scuttle of coals, and a faggot of brushwood. These she wheeled in the barrow down the mossed paths to the dank little laurel shrubbery where the destructor stood under the drip of three oaks. She climbed the wire fence into the Rector's glebe[5] just behind, and from his tenant's rick pulled two large armfuls of good hay, which she spread neatly on the fire-bars. Next, journey by journey, passing Miss Fowler's white face at the morning-room window each time, she brought down in the towel-covered clothes-basket, on the wheelbarrow, thumbed and used Hentys, Marryats, Levers, Stevensons, Baroness Orczys, Garvices,[6] school-books, and atlases, unrelated piles of the *Motor Cyclist*, the *Light Car*, and catalogues of Olympia Exhibitions; the remnants of a fleet of sailing-ships from ninepenny cutters to a three-guinea yacht; a prep.-school[7] dressing-gown; bats from three-and-sixpence to twenty-four shillings; cricket and tennis balls; disintegrated steam and clockwork locomotives with their twisted rails; a grey-and-red tin model of a submarine; a dumb gramophone and cracked records; golf-clubs that had to be broken across the knee, like his walking-sticks, and an assegai;[8] photographs of private and public school cricket and football

elevens, and his OTC[9] on the line of march; kodaks and film-rolls; some
pewters, and one real silver cup, for boxing competitions and Junior
Hurdles; sheaves of school photographs; Miss Fowler's photograph;
her own which he had borne off in fun and (good care she took not to
ask!) had never returned; a playbox with a secret drawer; a load of
flannels, belts, and jerseys, and a pair of spiked shoes unearthed in the
attic; a packet of all the letters that Miss Fowler and she had ever
written to him, kept for some absurd reason through all these years; a
five-day attempt at a diary; framed pictures of racing motors in full
Brooklands career, and load upon load of undistinguishable wreckage
of tool-boxes, rabbit-hutches, electric batteries, tin soldiers, fret-saw
outfits, and jig-saw puzzles.

Miss Fowler at the window watched her come and go, and said to
herself, 'Mary's an old woman. I never realised it before.'

After lunch she recommended her to rest.

'I'm not in the least tired,' said Mary. 'I've got it all arranged. I'm
going to the village at two o'clock for some paraffin. Nellie hasn't
enough, and the walk will do me good.'

She made one last quest round the house before she started, and
found that she had overlooked nothing. It began to mist as soon as she
had skirted Vegg's Heath, where Wynn used to descend – it seemed to
her that she could almost hear the beat of his propellers overhead, but
there was nothing to see. She hoisted her umbrella and lunged into the
blind wet till she had reached the shelter of the empty village. As she
came out of Mr Kidd's shop with a bottle full of paraffin in her string
shopping-bag, she met Nurse Eden, the village nurse, and fell into talk
with her, as usual, about the village children. They were just parting
opposite the 'Royal Oak', when a gun, they fancied, was fired immediately behind the house. It was followed by a child's shriek dying
into a wail.

'Accident!' said Nurse Eden promptly, and dashed through the
empty bar, followed by Mary. They found Mrs Gerritt, the publican's
wife, who could only gasp and point to the yard, where a little cart-
lodge[10] was sliding sideways amid a clatter of tiles. Nurse Eden
snatched up a sheet drying before the fire, ran out, lifted something
from the ground, and flung the sheet round it. The sheet turned scarlet
and half her uniform too, as she bore the load into the kitchen. It was
little Edna Gerritt, aged nine, whom Mary had known since her
perambulator days.

'Am I hurted bad?' Edna asked, and died between Nurse Eden's
dripping hands. The sheet fell aside and for an instant, before she could
shut her eyes, Mary saw the ripped and shredded body.

'It's a wonder she spoke at all,' said Nurse Eden. 'What in God's name was it?'

'A bomb,' said Mary.

'One o' the Zeppelins?'

'No. An aeroplane. I thought I heard it on the Heath, but I fancied it was one of ours. It must have shut off its engines as it came down. That's why we didn't notice it.'

'The filthy pigs!' said Nurse Eden, all white and shaken. 'See the pickle I'm in! Go and tell Dr Hennis, Miss Postgate.' Nurse looked at the mother, who had dropped face down on the floor. 'She's only in a fit. Turn her over.'

Mary heaved Mrs Gerritt right side up, and hurried off for the doctor. When she told her tale, he asked her to sit down in the surgery till he got her something.

'But I don't need it, I assure you,' said she. 'I don't think it would be wise to tell Miss Fowler about it, do you? Her heart is so irritable in this weather.'

Dr Hennis looked at her admiringly as he packed up his bag.

'No. Don't tell anybody till we're sure,' he said, and hastened to the 'Royal Oak', while Mary went on with the paraffin. The village behind her was as quiet as usual, for the news had not yet spread. She frowned a little to herself, her large nostrils expanded uglily, and from time to time she muttered a phrase which Wynn, who never restrained himself before his womenfolk, had applied to the enemy. 'Bloody pagans! They *are* bloody pagans. But,' she continued, falling back on the teaching that had made her what she was, 'one mustn't let one's mind dwell on these things.'

Before she reached the house Dr Hennis, who was also a special constable, overtook her in his car.

'Oh, Miss Postgate,' he said, 'I wanted to tell you that that accident at the "Royal Oak" was due to Gerritt's stable tumbling down. It's been dangerous for a long time. It ought to have been condemned.'

'I thought I heard an explosion too,' said Mary.

'You might have been misled by the beams snapping. I've been looking at 'em. They were dry-rotted through and through. Of course, as they broke, they would make a noise just like a gun.'

'Yes?' said Mary politely.

'Poor little Edna was playing underneath it,' he went on, still holding her with his eyes, 'and that and the tiles cut her to pieces, you see?'

'I saw it,' said Mary, shaking her head. 'I heard it too.'

'Well, we cannot be sure.' Dr Hennis changed his tone completely. 'I know both you and Nurse Eden (I've been speaking to her) are perfectly trustworthy, and I can rely on you not to say anything – yet, at least. It is no good to stir up people unless – '

'Oh, I never do – anyhow,' said Mary, and Dr Hennis went on to the county town.

After all, she told herself, it might, just possibly, have been the collapse of the old stable that had done all those things to poor little Edna. She was sorry she had even hinted at other things, but Nurse Eden was discretion itself. By the time she reached home the affair seemed increasingly remote by its very monstrosity. As she came in, Miss Fowler told her that a couple of aeroplanes had passed half an hour ago.

'I thought I heard them,' she replied. 'I'm going down to the garden now. I've got the paraffin.'

'Yes, but – what *have* you got on your boots? They're soaking wet. Change them at once.'

Not only did Mary obey but she wrapped the boots in a newspaper, and put them into the string bag with the bottle. So, armed with the longest kitchen poker, she left.

'It's raining again,' was Miss Fowler's last word, 'but – I know you won't be happy till that's disposed of.'

'It won't take long. I've got everything down there, and I've put the lid on the destructor to keep the wet out.'

The shrubbery was filling with twilight by the time she had completed her arrangements and sprinkled the sacrificial oil. As she lit the match that would burn her heart to ashes, she heard a groan or a grunt behind the dense Portugal laurels.

'Cheape?' she called impatiently, but Cheape, with his ancient lumbago, in his comfortable cottage would be the last man to profane the sanctuary. 'Sheep,' she concluded, and threw in the match. The pyre went up in a roar, and the immediate flames hastened night around her.

'How Wynn would have loved this!' she thought, stepping back from the blaze.

By its light she saw, half hidden behind a laurel not five paces away, a bareheaded man sitting very stiffly at the foot of one of the oaks. A broken branch lay across his lap – one booted leg protruding from beneath it. His head moved ceaselessly from side to side, but his body was as still as the tree's trunk. He was dressed – she moved sideways to look more closely – in a uniform something like Wynn's, with a flap buttoned across the chest. For an instant, she had some idea that it might be one of the young flying men she had met at the funeral. But their heads were dark and glossy. This man's was as pale as a baby's, and so closely cropped that she could see the disgusting pinky skin beneath. His lips moved.

'What do you say?' Mary moved towards him and stooped.

'Laty! Laty! Laty!' he muttered, while his hands picked at the dead wet leaves. There was no doubt as to his nationality. It made her so angry that she strode back to the destructor, though it was still too hot to use the poker there. Wynn's books seemed to be catching well. She looked up at the oak behind the man; several of the light upper and two or three rotten lower branches had broken and scattered their rubbish on the shrubbery path. On the lowest fork a helmet, with dependent strings, showed like a bird's-nest in the light of a long-tongued flame. Evidently this person had fallen through the tree. Wynn had told her that it was quite possible for people to fall out of aeroplanes. Wynn told her, too, that trees were useful things to break an aviator's fall, but in this case the aviator must have been broken or he would have moved from his queer position. He seemed helpless except for his horrible rolling head. On the other hand, she could see a pistol-case at his belt – and Mary loathed pistols. Months ago, after reading certain Belgian reports[11] together, she and Miss Fowler had had dealings with one – a huge revolver with flat-nosed bullets, which latter, Wynn said, were forbidden by the rules of war to be used against civilised enemies. 'They're good enough for us,' Miss Fowler had replied. 'Show Mary how it works.' And Wynn, laughing at the mere possibility of any such need, had led the craven winking Mary into the Rector's disused quarry, and had shown her how to fire the terrible machine. It lay now in the top left-hand drawer of her toilet-table – a memento not included in the burning. Wynn would be pleased to see how she was not afraid.

She slipped up to the house to get it. When she came through the rain, the eyes in the head were alive with expectation. The mouth even tried to smile. But at sight of the revolver its corners went down just like Edna Gerritt's. A tear trickled from one eye, and the head rolled from shoulder to shoulder as though trying to point out something.

'Cassée. Tout cassée,' it whimpered.

'What do you say?' said Mary disgustedly, keeping well to one side, though only the head moved.

'Cassée,' it repeated. 'Che me rends. Le médecin![12] Toctor!'

'Nein!' said she, bringing all her small German to bear with the big pistol. 'Ich haben der todt Kinder gesehn.'[13]

The head was still. Mary's hand dropped. She had been careful to keep her finger off the trigger for fear of accidents. After a few moments' waiting, she returned to the destructor, where the flames were falling, and churned up Wynn's charring books with the poker. Again the head groaned for the doctor.

'Stop that!' said Mary, and stamped her foot. 'Stop that, you bloody pagan!'

The words came quite smoothly and naturally. They were Wynn's own words, and Wynn was a gentleman who for no consideration on earth would have torn little Edna into those vividly coloured strips and strings. But this thing hunched under the oak-tree had done that thing. It was no question of reading horrors out of newspapers to Miss Fowler. Mary had seen it with her own eyes on the 'Royal Oak' kitchen table. She must not allow her mind to dwell upon it. Now Wynn was dead, and everything connected with him was lumping and rustling and tinkling under her busy poker into red-black dust and grey leaves of ash. The thing beneath the oak would die too. Mary had seen death more than once. She came of a family that had a knack of dying under, as she told Miss Fowler, 'most distressing circumstances'. She would stay where she was till she was entirely satisfied that It was dead – dead as dear papa in the late 'Eighties; aunt Mary in 'Eighty-nine; mama in 'Ninety-one; cousin Dickin 'Ninety-five; Lady McCausland's housemaid in 'Ninety-nine; Lady McCausland's sister in Nineteen Hundred and One; Wynn buried five days ago; and Edna Gerritt still waiting for decent earth to hide her. As she thought – her underlip caught up by one faded canine, brows knit and nostrils wide – she wielded the poker with lunges that jarred the grating at the bottom, and careful scrapes round the brick-work above. She looked at her wrist-watch. It was getting on to half-past four, and the rain was coming down in earnest. Tea would be at five. If It did not die before that time, she would be soaked and would have to change. Meantime, and this occupied her, Wynn's things were burning well in spite of the hissing wet, though now and again a book-back with a quite distinguishable title would be heaved up out of the mass. The exercise of stoking had given her a glow which seemed to reach to the marrow of her bones. She hummed – Mary never had a voice – to herself. She had never believed in all those advanced views – though Miss Fowler herself leaned a little that way – of woman's work in the world; but now she saw there was much to be said for them. This, for instance, was *her* work – work which no man, least of all Dr Hennis, would ever have done. A man, at such a crisis, would be what Wynn called a 'sportsman'; would leave everything to fetch help, and would certainly bring It into the house. Now, a woman's business was to make a happy home for – for a husband and children. Failing these – it was not a thing one should allow one's mind to dwell upon – but –

'Stop it!' Mary cried once more across the shadows. 'Nein, I tell you! Ich haben der todt Kinder gesehn.'

But it was a fact. A woman who had missed these things could still be useful – more useful than a man in certain respects. She thumped like a pavior[14] through the settling ashes at the secret thrill of it. The rain was damping the fire, but she could feel – it was too dark to see – that her work was done. There was a dull red glow at the bottom of the destructor, not enough to char the wooden lid if she slipped it half over against the driving wet. This arranged, she leaned on the poker and waited, while an increasing rapture laid hold on her. She ceased to think. She gave herself up to feel. Her long pleasure was broken by a sound that she had waited for in agony several times in her life. She leaned forward and listened, smiling. There could be no mistake. She closed her eyes and drank it in. Once it ceased abruptly.

'Go on,' she murmured, half aloud. 'That isn't the end.'

Then the end came very distinctly in a lull between two rain-gusts. Mary Postgate drew her breath short between her teeth and shivered from head to foot. '*That's* all right,' said she contentedly, and went up to the house, where she scandalised the whole routine by taking a luxurious hot bath before tea, and came down looking, as Miss Fowler said when she saw her lying all relaxed on the other sofa, 'quite handsome!'

A MADONNA OF
THE TRENCHES

Whatever a man of the sons of men
  Shall say to his heart of the lords above,
They have shown man, verily, once and again,
  Marvellous mercies and infinite love.

O sweet one love, O my life's delight,
  Dear, though the days have divided us,
Lost beyond hope, taken far out of sight,
  Not twice in the world shall the Gods do thus.
                    SWINBURNE, *Les Noyades*[1]

Seeing how many unstable ex-soldiers came to the Lodge of Instruction (attached to 'Faith and Works EC 5837'[2]) in the years after the War, the wonder is there was not more trouble from Brethren whom sudden meetings with old comrades jerked back into their still raw past. But our round, torpedo-bearded local Doctor – Brother Keede, Senior Warden – always stood ready to deal with hysteria before it got out of hand; and when I examined Brethren unknown or imperfectly vouched for on the Masonic side, I passed on to him anything that seemed doubtful. He had had his experience as medical officer of a South London Battalion, during the last two years of the War; and, naturally, often found friends and acquaintances among the visitors.

Brother C. Strangwick, a young, tallish, new-made Brother, hailed from some South London Lodge. His papers and his answers were above suspicion, but his red-rimmed eyes had a puzzled glare that might mean nerves. So I introduced him particularly to Keede, who discovered in him a Headquarters Orderly of his old Battalion, congratulated him on his return to fitness – he had been discharged for some infirmity or other – and plunged at once into Somme memories.

'I hope I did right, Keede,' I said when we were robing before Lodge.

'Oh, quite. He reminded me that I had him under my hands at Sampoux in 'Eighteen, when he went to bits. He was a Runner.'

'Was it shock?' I asked.

'Of sorts – but not what he wanted me to think it was. No, he wasn't shamming. He had Jumps to the limit – but he played up to mislead me about the reason of 'em . . . Well, if we could stop patients from lying, medicine would be too easy, I suppose.'

I noticed that, after Lodge-working, Keede gave him a seat a couple of rows in front of us, that he might enjoy a lecture on the Orientation of King Solomon's Temple, which an earnest Brother thought would be a nice interlude between Labour and the high tea that we called our 'Banquet'. Even helped by tobacco it was a dreary performance. About half-way through, Strangwick, who had been fidgeting and twitching for some minutes, rose, drove back his chair grinding across the tessellated floor, and yelped: 'Oh, My Aunt! I can't stand this any longer.' Under cover of a general laugh of assent he brushed past us and stumbled towards the door.

'I thought so!' Keede whispered to me. 'Come along!' We overtook him in the passage, crowing hysterically and wringing his hands. Keede led him into the Tyler's Room, a small office where we stored odds and ends of regalia and furniture, and locked the door.

'I'm – I'm all right,' the boy began piteously.

''Course you are.' Keede opened a small cupboard which I had seen called upon before, mixed sal volatile[3] and water in a graduated glass, and, as Strangwick drank, pushed him gently on to an old sofa. 'There,' he went on. 'It's nothing to write home about. I've seen you ten times worse. I expect our talk has brought things back.'

He hooked up a chair behind him with one foot, held the patient's hands in his own, and sat down. The chair creaked.

'Don't!' Strangwick squealed. 'I can't stand it! There's nothing on earth creaks like they do! And – and when it thaws we – we've got to slap 'em back with a spa-ade! Remember those Frenchmen's little boots under the duckboards? . . . What'll I do? What'll I do about it?'

Someone knocked at the door, to know if all were well.

'Oh, quite, thanks!' said Keede over his shoulder. 'But I shall need this room a while. Draw the curtains, please.'

We heard the rings of the hangings that drape the passage from Lodge to Banquet Room click along their poles, and what sound there had been, of feet and voices, was shut off.

Strangwick, retching impotently, complained of the frozen dead who creak in the frost.

'He's playing up still,' Keede whispered. '*That's* not his real trouble – any more than 'twas last time.'

'But surely,' I replied, 'men get those things on the brain pretty badly. Remember in October – '

'This chap hasn't, though. I wonder what's really helling him. What are you thinking of?' said Keede peremptorily.

'French End an' Butcher's Row,' Strangwick muttered.

'Yes, there were a few there. But suppose we face Bogey instead of giving him best every time.' Keede turned towards me with a hint in his eye that I was to play up to his leads.

'What was the trouble with French End?' I opened at a venture.

'It was a bit by Sampoux, that we had taken over from the French. They're tough, but you wouldn't call 'em tidy as a nation. They had faced both sides of it with dead to keep the mud back. All those trenches were like gruel in a thaw. Our people had to do the same sort of thing – elsewhere; but Butcher's Row in French End was the – er – show-piece. Luckily, we pinched a salient from Jerry just then, an' straightened things out – so we didn't need to use the Row after November. You remember, Strangwick?'

'My God, yes! When the duckboard-slats were missin' you'd tread on 'em, an' they'd creak.'

'They're bound to. Like leather,' said Keede. 'It gets on one's nerves a bit, but – '

'Nerves? It's real! It's real!' Strangwick gulped.

'But at your time of life, it'll all fall behind you in a year or so. I'll give you another sip of – paregoric,[4] an' we'll face it quietly. Shall we?'

Keede opened his cupboard again and administered a carefully dropped dark dose of something that was not sal volatile. 'This'll settle you in a few minutes,' he explained. 'Lie still, an' don't talk unless you feel like it.'

He faced me, fingering his beard.

'Ye-es. Butcher's Row wasn't pretty,' he volunteered. 'Seeing Strangwick here has brought it all back to me again. Funny thing! We had a Platoon Sergeant of Number Two – what the deuce was his name? – an elderly bird who must have lied like a patriot to get out to the Front at his age; but he was a first-class Non-Com., and the last person, you'd think, to make mistakes. Well, he was due for a fortnight's home leave in January, 'Eighteen. You were at BHQ[5] then, Strangwick, weren't you?'

'Yes. I was Orderly. It was January twenty-first'; Strangwick spoke with a thickish tongue, and his eyes burned. Whatever drug it was, had taken hold.

'About then,' Keede said. 'Well, this Sergeant, instead of coming down from the trenches the regular way an' joinin' Battalion Details after dark, an' takin' that funny little train for Arras, thinks he'll warm himself first. So he gets into a dug-out, in Butcher's Row, that used to be an old French dressing-station, and fugs up between a couple of braziers of pure charcoal! As luck 'ud have it, that was the only dug-out with an inside door opening inwards – some French anti-gas fitting, I expect – and, by what we could make out, the door must have swung to while he was warming. Anyhow, he didn't turn up at the train. There was a search at once. We couldn't afford to waste Platoon Sergeants. We found him in the morning. He'd got his gas all right. A machine-gunner reported him, didn't he, Strangwick?'

'No, sir. Corporal Grant – o' the Trench Mortars.'

'So it was. Yes, Grant – the man with that little wen on his neck. Nothing wrong with your memory, at any rate. What was the Sergeant's name?'

'Godsoe – John Godsoe,' Strangwick answered.

'Yes, that was it. I had to see him next mornin' – frozen stiff between the two braziers – and not a scrap of private papers on him. *That* was the only thing that made me think it mightn't have been – quite an accident.'

Strangwick's relaxing face set, and he threw back at once to the Orderly Room manner.

'I give my evidence – at the time – to you, sir. He passed – overtook me, I should say – comin' down from supports, after I'd warned him for leaf. I thought he was goin' through Parrot Trench as usual; but 'e must 'ave turned off into French End where the old bombed barricade was.'

'Yes. I remember now. You were the last man to see him alive. That was on the twenty-first of January, you say? Now, *when* was it that Dearlove and Billings brought you to me – clean out of your head?' . . . Keede dropped his hand, in the style of magazine detectives, on Strangwick's shoulder. The boy looked at him with cloudy wonder, and muttered: 'I was took to you on the evenin' of the twenty-fourth of January. But you don't think I did him in, do you?'

I could not help smiling at Keede's discomfiture; but he recovered himself. 'Then what the dickens *was* on your mind that evening – before I gave you the hypodermic?'

'The – the things in Butcher's Row. They kept on comin' over me. You've seen me like this before, sir.'

'But I knew that it was a lie. You'd no more got stiffs on the brain then than you have now. You've got something, but you're hiding it.'

''Ow do *you* know, Doctor?' Strangwick whimpered.

'D'you remember what you said to me, when Dearlove and Billings were holding you down that evening?'

'About the things in Butcher's Row?'

'Oh, no! You spun me a lot of stuff about corpses creaking; but you let yourself go in the middle of it – when you pushed that telegram at me. What did you mean, f'r instance, by asking what advantage it was for you to fight beasts of officers if the dead didn't rise?'

'Did I say "beasts of officers"?'

'You did. It's out of the Burial Service.'[6]

'I suppose, then, I must have heard it. As a matter of fact, I 'ave.' Strangwick shuddered extravagantly.

'Probably. And there's another thing – that hymn you were shouting till I put you under. It was something about Mercy and Love. Remember it?'

'I'll try,' said the boy obediently, and began to paraphrase, as nearly as possible thus: '"Whatever a man may say in his heart unto the Lord, yea, verily I say unto you – Gawd hath shown man,[7] again and again, marvellous mercy an' – an' somethin' or other love."' He screwed up his eyes and shook.

'Now where did you get *that* from?' Keede insisted.

'From Godsoe – on the twenty-first Jan.[8] . . . 'Ow could *I* tell what 'e meant to do?' he burst out in a high, unnatural key – 'Any more than I knew *she* was dead.'

'Who was dead?' said Keede.

'Me Auntie Armine.'

'The one the telegram came to you about, at Sampoux, that you wanted me to explain – the one that you were talking of in the passage out here just now when you began: "O Auntie," and changed it to "O Gawd," when I collared you?'

'That's her! I haven't a chance with you, Doctor. *I* didn't know there was anything wrong with those braziers. How could I? We're always usin' 'em. Honest to God, I thought at first go-off he might wish to warm himself before the leaf-train. I – I didn't know Uncle John meant to start – 'ouse-keepin'.' He laughed horribly, and then the dry tears came.

Keede waited for them to pass in sobs and hiccoughs before he continued: 'Why? Was Godsoe your uncle?'

'No,' said Strangwick, his head between his hands. 'Only we'd known him ever since we were born. Dad 'ad known him before that. He lived almost next street to us. Him an' Dad an' Ma an' – an' the rest had always been friends. So we called him Uncle – like children do.'

'What sort of man was he?'

'One o' *the* best, sir. Pensioned Sergeant with a little money left him – quite independent – and very superior. They had a sittin'-room full o' Indian curios that him and his wife used to let Sister an' me see when we'd been good.'

'Wasn't he rather old to join up?'

'That made no odds to him. He joined up as Sergeant Instructor at the first go-off, an' when the Battalion was ready he got 'imself sent along. He wangled me into 'is platoon when I went out – early in 'Seventeen. Because Ma wanted it, I suppose.'

'I'd no notion you knew him that well,' was Keede's comment.

'Oh, it made no odds to him. He 'ad no pets in the platoon, but 'e'd write 'ome to Ma about me an' all the doin's. You see,' – Strangwick stirred uneasily on the sofa – 'we'd known him all our lives – lived in the next street an' all . . . An' him well over fifty. Oh dear me! *Oh* dear me! What a bloody mix-up things are, when one's as young as me!' he wailed of a sudden.

But Keede held him to the point. 'He wrote to your mother about you?'

'Yes. Ma's eyes had gone bad followin' on air-raids. Blood-vessels broke behind 'em from sittin' in cellars an' bein' sick. She had to 'ave 'er letters read to her by Auntie. Now I think of it, that was the only thing that you might have called anything at all – '

'Was that the aunt that died, and that you got the wire about?' Keede drove on.

'Yes – Auntie Armine – Ma's younger sister, an' she nearer fifty than forty. What a mix-up! An' if I'd been asked any time about it, I'd 'ave sworn there wasn't a single sol'tary item concernin' her that everybody didn't know an' hadn't known all along. No more conceal to her doin's than – than so much shop-front. She'd looked after Sister an' me, when needful – whoopin' cough an' measles – just the same as Ma. We was in an' out of her house like rabbits. You see, Uncle Armine is a cabinet-maker, an' second-'and furniture, an' we liked playin' with the things. She 'ad no children, and when the War came, she said she was glad of it. But she never talked much of her feelin's. She kept herself to herself, you understand.' He stared most earnestly at us to help out our understandings.

'What was she like?' Keede inquired.

'A biggish woman, an' had been 'andsome, I believe, but, bein' used to her, we two didn't notice much – except, per'aps, for one thing. Ma called her 'er proper name, which was Bella; but Sis an' me always called 'er Auntie Armine. See?'

'What for?'

'We thought it sounded more like her – like somethin' movin' slow, in armour.'

'Oh! And she read your letters to your mother, did she?'

'Every time the post came in she'd slip across the road from opposite an' read 'em. An' – an' I'll go bail for it that that was all there was to it for as far back as *I* remember. Was I to swing to-morrow, I'd go bail for *that*! 'Tisn't fair of 'em to 'ave unloaded it all on me, because – because – if the dead *do* rise, why, what in 'ell becomes of me an' all I've believed all me life? I want to know *that*! I – I – '

But Keede would not be put off. 'Did the Sergeant give you away at all in his letters?' he demanded, very quietly.

'There was nothin' to give away – we was too busy – but his letters about me were a great comfort to Ma. I'm no good at writin'. I saved it all up for my leafs. I got me fourteen days every six months an' one over . . . I was luckier than most, that way.'

'And when you came home, used you to bring 'em news about the Sergeant?' said Keede.

'I expect I must have; but I didn't think much of it at the time. I was took up with me own affairs – naturally. Uncle John always wrote to me once each leaf, tellin' me what was doin' an' what I was li'ble to expect on return, an' Ma 'ud 'ave that read to her. Then o' course I had to slip over to his wife an' pass her the news. An' then there was the young lady that I'd thought of marryin' if I came through. We'd got as far as pricin' things in the windows together.'

'And you didn't marry her – after all?'

Another tremor shook the boy. '*No!*' he cried. ''Fore it ended, I knew what reel things reelly mean! I – I never dreamed such things could be! . . . An' she nearer fifty than forty an' me own Aunt! . . . But there wasn't a sign nor a hint from first to last, so 'ow *could* I tell? Don't you *see* it? All she said to me after me Christmas leaf in 'Eighteen, when I come to say good-bye – all Auntie Armine said to me was: "You'll be seein' Mister Godsoe soon?" "Too soon for my likings," I says. "Well, then, tell 'im from me," she says, "that I expect to be through with my little trouble by the twenty-first of next month, an' I'm dyin' to see him as soon as possible after that date."'

'What sort of trouble was it?' Keede turned professional at once.

'She'd 'ad a bit of a gatherin' in 'er breast, I believe. But she never talked of 'er body much to any one.'

'*I* see,' said Keede. 'And she said to you?'

Strangwick repeated: '"Tell Uncle John I hope to be finished of my drawback by the twenty-first, an' I'm dyin' to see 'im as soon as 'e can after that date." An' then she says, laughin': "But you've a head like a sieve. I'll write it down, an' you can give it him when you see 'im." So she wrote it on a bit o' paper an' I kissed 'er good-bye – I was always her favourite, you see – an' I went back to Sampoux. The thing hardly stayed in my mind at all, d'ye see? But the next time I was up in the front line – I was a Runner, d'ye see? – our platoon was in North Bay Trench an' I was up with a message to the Trench Mortar there that Corporal Grant was in charge of. Followin' on receipt of it, he borrowed a couple of men off the platoon, to slue 'er round or somethin'. I give Uncle John Auntie Armine's paper, an' I give Grant a fag, an' we warmed up a bit over a brazier. Then Grant says to me: "I don't like it"; an' he jerks 'is thumb at Uncle John in the bay studyin' Auntie's message. Well, *you* know, sir, you had to speak to Grant about 'is way of prophesyin' things – after Rankine shot himself with the Very light.'

'I did,' said Keede, and he explained to me: 'Grant had the Second Sight – confound him! It upset the men. I was glad when he got pipped.[9] What happened after that, Strangwick?'

'Grant whispers to me: "Look, you damned Englishman. 'E's for it." Uncle John was leanin' up against the bay, an' hummin' that hymn I was tryin' to tell you just now. He looked different all of a sudden – as if 'e'd got shaved. *I* don't know anything of these things, but I cautioned Grant as to his style of speakin', if an officer 'ad 'eard him, an' I went on. Passin' Uncle John in the bay, 'e nods an' smiles, which he didn't often, an' he says, pocketin' the paper: "This suits *me*. I'm for leaf on the twenty-first, too."'

'He said that to you, did he?' said Keede.

'*Pre*cisely the same as passin' the time o' day. O' course I returned the agreeable about hopin' he'd get it, an' in due course I returned to 'Eadquarters. The thing 'ardly stayed in my mind a minute. That was the eleventh January – three days after I'd come back from leaf. You remember, sir, there wasn't anythin' doin' either side round Sampoux the first part o' the month. Jerry was gettin' ready for his March Push, an' as long as he kept quiet, we didn't want to poke 'im up.'

'I remember that,' said Keede. 'But what about the Sergeant?'

'I must have met him, on an' off, I expect, goin' up an' down, through the ensuin' days, but it didn't stay in me mind. Why needed it? And on the twenty-first Jan., his name was on the leaf-paper when I went up to warn the leaf-men. I noticed *that*, o' course. Now that very afternoon Jerry 'ad been tryin' a new trench-mortar, an' before our 'Eavies could out it, he'd got a stinker into a bay an' mopped up 'alf-a-dozen. They were bringin' 'em down when I went up to the supports, an' that blocked Little Parrot, same as it always did. *You* remember, sir?'

'Rather! And there was that big machine-gun behind the Half-House waiting for you if you got out,' said Keede.

'I remembered that too. But it was just on dark an' the fog was comin' off the Canal, so I hopped out of Little Parrot an' cut across the open to where those four dead Warwicks are heaped up. But the fog turned me round, an' the next thing I knew I was knee-over in that old 'alf-trench that runs west o' Little Parrot into French End. I dropped into it – almost atop o' the machine-gun platform by the side o' the old sugar-boiler an' the two Zoo-ave skel'tons. That gave me my bearin's, an' so I went through French End, all up those missin' duckboards, into Butcher's Row where the *poy-looz*[10] was laid in six deep each side, an' stuffed under the duckboards. It had froze tight, an' the drippin's had stopped, an' the creakin's had begun.'

'Did that really worry you at the time?' Keede asked.

'No,' said the boy with professional scorn. 'If a Runner starts noticin' such things he'd better chuck. In the middle of the Row, just before the old dressin'-station you referred to, sir, it come over me that somethin' ahead on the duckboards was just like Auntie Armine, waitin' beside the door; an' I thought to meself 'ow truly comic it would be if she could be dumped where I was then. In 'alf a second I saw it was only the dark an' some rags o' gas-screen, 'angin' on a bit of board, 'ad played me the trick. So I went on up to the supports an' warned the leaf-men there, includin' Uncle John. Then I went up Rake Alley to warn 'em in the front line. I didn't hurry because I didn't want to get there till Jerry 'ad quieted down a bit. Well, then a Company Relief dropped in – an' the officer got the wind up over some lights on the flank, an' tied 'em into knots, an' I 'ad to hunt up me leaf-men all over the blinkin' shop. What with one thing an' another, it must 'ave been 'alf-past eight before I got back to the supports. There I run across Uncle John, scrapin' mud off himself, havin' shaved – quite the dandy. He asked about the Arras train, an' I said, if Jerry was quiet, it might be ten o'clock. "Good!" says 'e. "I'll come with you." So we started back down the old trench that used to run across Halnaker, back of the support dug-outs. *You* know, sir.'

Keede nodded.

'Then Uncle John says something to me about seein' Ma an' the rest of 'em in a few days, an' had I any messages for 'em? Gawd knows what made me do it, but I told 'im to tell Auntie Armine I never expected to see anything like *her* up in our part of the world. And while I told him I laughed. That's the last time I *'ave* laughed. "Oh – you've seen 'er, 'ave you?" says he, quite natural-like. Then I told 'im about the sand-bags an' rags in the dark playin' the trick. "Very likely," says he, brushin' the mud off his puttees. By this time, we'd got to the corner where the old barricade into French End was – before they bombed it down, sir. He turns right an' climbs across it. "No, thanks," says I. "I've been there once this evenin'." But he wasn't attendin' to me. He felt behind the rubbish an' bones just inside the barricade, an' when he straightened up, he had a full brazier in each hand.

'"Come on, Clem," he says, an' he very rarely give me me own name. "You aren't afraid, are you?" he says. "It's just as short, an' if Jerry starts up again he won't waste stuff here. He knows it's abandoned." "Who's afraid now?" I says. "Me for one," says he. "I don't want *my* leaf spoiled at the last minute." Then 'e wheels round an' speaks that bit you said come out o' the Burial Service.'

For some reason Keede repeated it in full, slowly: 'If after the manner of men I have fought with beasts at Ephesus, what advantageth it me, if the dead rise not?'

'That's it,' said Strangwick. 'So we went down French End together – everything froze up an' quiet, except for their creakin's. I remember thinkin' – ' His eyes began to flicker.

'Don't think. Tell what happened,' Keede ordered.

'Oh! Beg y' pardon! He went on with his braziers, hummin' his hymn, down Butcher's Row. Just before we got to the old dressin'-station he stops and sets 'em down an' says: "Where did you say she was, Clem? Me eyes ain't as good as they used to be."

'"In 'er bed at 'ome," I says. "Come on down. It's perishin' cold, an' *I'm* not due for leaf."

'"Well, I am," 'e says. "*I* am . . ." An' then – 'give you me word I didn't recognise the voice – he stretches out 'is neck a bit, in a way 'e 'ad, an' he says: "Why, Bella!" 'e says. "Oh, Bella!" 'e says. "Thank Gawd!" 'e says. Just like that! An' then I saw – I tell you I *saw* – Auntie Armine herself standin' by the old dressin'-station door where first I'd thought I'd seen her. He was lookin' at 'er an' she was lookin' at him. I saw it, an' me soul turned over inside me because – because it knocked out everything I'd believed in. I 'ad nothin' to lay 'old of, d'ye see? An' 'e was lookin' at 'er as though he could 'ave et 'er, an' she was lookin' at 'im the same way, out of 'er eyes. Then he says: "Why, Bella," 'e says, "this must be only the second time we've been alone together in all these years." An' I saw 'er half 'old out her arms to 'im in that perishin' cold. An' she nearer fifty than forty an' me own Aunt! You can shop me for a lunatic to-morrow, but I saw it – I *saw* 'er answerin' to his spoken word! . . . Then 'e made a snatch to unsling 'is rifle. Then 'e cuts 'is hand away saying: "No! Don't tempt me, Bella. We've all Eternity ahead of us. An hour or two won't make any odds." Then he picks up the braziers an' goes on to the dug-out door. He's finished with me. He pours petrol on 'em, an' lights it with a match, an' carries 'em inside, flarin'. All that time Auntie Armine stood with 'er arms out – an' a look in 'er face! *I* didn't know such things was or could be!

Then he comes out an' says: "Come in, my dear"; an' she stoops an' goes into the dug-out with that look on her face – that look on her face! An' then 'e shuts the door from inside an' starts wedgin' it up. So 'elp me Gawd, I saw an' 'eard all these things with my own eyes an' ears!'

He repeated his oath several times. After a long pause Keede asked him if he recalled what happened next.

'It was a bit of a mix-up, for me, from then on. I must have carried on – they told me I did, but – but I was – I felt a – a long way inside of meself, like – if you've ever had that feelin'. I wasn't rightly on the spot at all. They woke me up sometime next morning, because 'e 'adn't showed up at the train; an' someone had seen him with me. I wasn't 'alf cross-examined by all an' sundry till dinner-time.

'Then, I think, I volunteered for Dearlove, who 'ad a sore toe, for a front-line message. I 'ad to keep movin', you see, because I 'adn't anything to 'old on to. Whilst up there, Grant informed me how 'e'd found Uncle John with the door wedged an' sand-bags stuffed in the cracks. I hadn't waited for that. The knockin' when 'e wedged up was enough for me. Like Dad's coffin.'

'No one told *me* the door had been wedged.' Keede spoke severely.

'No need to black a dead man's name, sir.'

'What made Grant go to Butcher's Row?'

'Because he'd noticed Uncle John had been pinchin' charcoal for a week past an' layin' it up behind the old barricade there. So when the 'unt began, he went that way straight as a string, an' when he saw the door shut, he knew. He told me he picked the sand-bags out of the cracks an' shoved 'is 'and through and shifted the wedges before any one come along. It looked all right. You said yourself, sir, the door must 'ave blown to.'

'Grant knew what Godsoe meant, then?' Keede snapped.

'Grant knew Godsoe was for it, an' nothin' earthly could 'elp or 'inder. He told me so.'

'And then what did you do?'

'I expect I must 'ave kept on carryin' on, till 'Eadquarters give me that wire from Ma – about Auntie Armine dyin'.'

'When had your aunt died?'

'On the mornin' of the twenty-first. The mornin' of the twenty-first! That tore it, d'ye see? As long as I could think, I had kep' tellin' myself it was like those things you lectured about at Arras when we was billeted in the cellars – the Angels of Mons,[11] and so on. But that wire tore it.'

'Oh! Hallucinations! I remember. And that wire tore it?' said Keede.

'Yes! You see' – he half lifted himself off the sofa – 'there wasn't a single gor-dam' thing left abidin' for me to take hold of, 'ere or 'ereafter. If the dead *do* rise – and I saw 'em – why – why, *anything* can 'appen. Don't you understand?'

He was on his feet now, gesticulating stiffly.

'For I saw 'er,' he repeated. 'I saw 'im an' 'er – she dead since mornin' time, an' he killin' 'imself before my livin' eyes so's to carry on with 'er for all Eternity – an' she 'oldin' out 'er arms for it! I want to know where I'm *at*! Look 'ere, you two – why stand *we* in jeopardy every hour?'[12]

'God knows,' said Keede to himself.

'Hadn't we better ring for someone?' I suggested. 'He'll go off the handle in a second.'

'No, he won't. It's the last kick-up before it takes hold. I know how the stuff works. Hul-lo!'

Strangwick, his hands behind his back and his eyes set, gave tongue in the strained, cracked voice of a boy reciting. 'Not twice in the world shall the Gods do thus,' he cried again and again.

'And I'm damned if it's goin' to be even once for me!' he went on with sudden insane fury. '*I* don't care whether we *'ave* been pricin' things in the windows . . . *Let* 'er sue if she likes! She don't know what reel things mean. *I* do – I've 'ad occasion to notice 'em . . . *No* I tell you! I'll 'ave 'em when I want 'em, an' be done with 'em; but not till I see that look on a face . . . that look . . . I'm not takin' any. The reel thing's life an' death. It *begins* at death, d'ye see? *She* can't understand . . . Oh, go on an' push off to Hell, you an' your lawyers. I'm fed up with it – fed up!'

He stopped as abruptly as he had started, and the drawn face broke back to its natural irresolute lines. Keede, holding both his hands, led him back to the sofa, where he dropped like a wet towel, took out some flamboyant robe from a press, and drew it neatly over him.

'Ye-es. *That*'s the real thing at last,' said Keede. 'Now he's got it off his mind he'll sleep. By the way, who introduced him?'

'Shall I go and find out?' I suggested.

'Yes; and you might ask him to come here. There's no need for us to stand to all night.'

So I went to the Banquet, which was in full swing, and was seized by an elderly, precise Brother from a South London Lodge, who followed me, concerned and apologetic. Keede soon put him at his ease.

'The boy's had trouble,' our visitor explained. 'I'm most mortified he should have performed his bad turn here. I thought he'd put it be'ind him.'

'I expect talking about old days with me brought it all back,' said Keede. 'It does sometimes.'

'Maybe! Maybe! But over and above that, Clem's had post-war trouble, too.'

'Can't he get a job? He oughtn't to let that weigh on him, at his time of life,' said Keede cheerily.

''Tisn't that – he's provided for – but' – he coughed confidentially behind his dry hand – 'as a matter of fact, Worshipful Sir, he's – he's implicated for the present in a little breach of promise action.'

'Ah! That's a different thing,' said Keede.

'Yes. That's his reel trouble. No reason given, you understand. The young lady in every way suitable, an' she'd make him a good little wife too, if I'm any judge. But he says she ain't his ideel or something. No getting at what's in young people's minds these days, is there?'

'I'm afraid there isn't,' said Keede. 'But he's all right now. He'll sleep. You sit by him, and when he wakes, take him home quietly . . . Oh, we're used to men getting a little upset here. You've nothing to thank us for, Brother – Brother –'

'Armine,' said the old gentleman. 'He's my nephew by marriage.'

'That's all that's wanted!' said Keede.

Brother Armine looked a little puzzled. Keede hastened to explain. 'As I was saying, all he wants now is to be kept quiet till he wakes.'

THE JANEITES

Jane lies in Winchester – blessed be her shade!
Praise the Lord for making her, and her for all she made!
And while the stones of Winchester, or Milsom Street, remain,
Glory, love, and honour unto England's Jane![1]

In the Lodge of Instruction attached to 'Faith and Works No. 5837 EC', which has already been described, Saturday afternoon was appointed for the weekly clean-up, when all Visiting Brethren were welcome to help under the direction of the Lodge Officer of the day: their reward was light refreshment and the meeting of companions.

This particular afternoon – in the autumn of '20 – Brother Burges, PM,[2] was on duty and, finding a strong shift present, took advantage of it to strip and dust all hangings and curtains, to go over every inch of the Pavement – which was stone, not floorcloth – by hand; and to polish the Columns, Jewels, Working outfit and organ. I was given to clean some Officers' Jewels – beautiful bits of old Georgian silver-work humanised by generations of elbow-grease – and retired to the organ-loft, for the floor was like the quarter-deck of a battleship on the eve of a ball. Half-a-dozen brethren had already made the Pavement as glassy as the aisle of Greenwich Chapel; the brazen chapiters[3] winked like pure gold at the flashing Marks on the Chairs; and a morose one-legged Brother was attending to the Emblems of Mortality with, I think, rouge.

'They ought,' he volunteered to Brother Burges as we passed, 'to be betwixt the colour of ripe apricots an' a half-smoked meerschaum. That's how we kept 'em in *my* Mother-Lodge – a treat to look at.'

'I've never seen spit-and-polish to touch this,' I said.

'Wait till you see the organ,' Brother Burges replied. 'You could shave in it when they've done. Brother Anthony's in charge up there – the taxi-owner you met here last month. I don't think you've come across Brother Humberstall, have you?'

'I don't remember –' I began.

'You wouldn't have forgotten him if you had. He's a hairdresser now, somewhere at the back of Ebury Street. Was Garrison Artillery. Blown up twice.'

'Does he show it?' I asked at the foot of the organ-loft stairs.

'No-o. Not much more than Lazarus[4] did, I expect.' Brother Burges fled off to set someone else to a job.

Brother Anthony, small, dark, and hump-backed, was hissing groom-fashion while he treated the rich acacia-wood panels of the Lodge organ with some sacred, secret composition of his own. Under his guidance Humberstall, an enormous, flat-faced man, carrying the shoulders, ribs, and loins of the old Mark '14, Royal Garrison Artillery, and the eyes of a bewildered retriever, rubbed the stuff in. I sat down to my task on the organ-bench, whose purple velvet cushion was being vacuum-cleaned on the floor below.

'Now,' said Anthony, after five minutes' vigorous work on the part of Humberstall. '*Now* we're gettin' somethin' worth lookin' at! Take it easy, an' go on with what you was tellin' me about that Macklin man.'

'I – I 'adn't anything against 'im,' said Humberstall, 'excep' he'd been a toff by birth; but that never showed till he was bosko absoluto. Mere bein' drunk on'y made a common 'ound of 'im. But when bosko, it all came out. Otherwise, he showed me my duties as mess-waiter very well on the 'ole.'

'Yes, yes. But what in 'ell made you go *back* to your Circus? The Board gave you down-an'-out fair enough, you said, after the dump went up at Eatables?'[5]

'Board or no Board, *I* 'adn't the nerve to stay at 'ome – not with mother chuckin' 'erself round all three rooms like a rabbit every time the Gothas[6] tried to get Victoria;[7] an' sister writin' me aunts four pages about it next day. Not for *me*, thank you! till the War was over. So I slid out with a draft – they wasn't particular in 'Seventeen, so long as the tally was correct – and I joined up again with our Circus somewhere at the back of Lar Pug Noy,[8] I think it was.' Humberstall paused for some seconds and his brow wrinkled. 'Then I – I went sick, or somethin' or other, they told me; but I know *when* I reported for dooty, our Battery Sergeant-Major says that I wasn't expected back, an' – 'an, one thing leadin' to another – to cut a long story short – I went up before our Major – Major – I shall forget my own name next – Major –'

'Never mind,' Anthony interrupted. 'Go on! It'll come back in talk!'

''Alf a mo'. 'Twas on the tip o' my tongue then.'

Humberstall dropped the polishing-cloth and knitted his brows again in most profound thought. Anthony turned to me and suddenly launched into a sprightly tale of his taxi's collision with a Marble Arch refuge on a greasy day after a three-yard skid.

'Much damage?' I asked.

'Oh no! Ev'ry bolt an' screw an' nut on the chassis strained; *but* nothing carried away, you understand me, an' not a scratch on the body. You'd never 'ave guessed a thing wrong till you took 'er in hand. It *was* a wop too: 'ead-on – like this!' And he slapped his tactful little forehead to show what a knock it had been.

'Did your Major dish you up much?' he went on over his shoulder to Humberstall, who came out of his abstraction with a slow heave.

'We-ell! He told me I wasn't expected back either; an' he said 'e couldn't 'ang up the 'ole Circus till I'd rejoined; an' he said that my ten-inch Skoda which I'd been Number Three of, before the dump went up at Eatables, had 'er full crowd. But, 'e said, as soon as a casualty occurred he'd remember me. "Meantime," says he, "I particularly want you for actin' mess-waiter."

'"Beggin' your pardon, sir," I says, perfectly respectful; "but I didn't exactly come back for *that*, sir."

'"Beggin' *your* pardon, 'Umberstall," says 'e, "but I 'appen to command the Circus! Now, you're a sharp-witted man," he says, "an' what we've suffered from fool-waiters in Mess 'as been somethin' cruel. You'll take on, from now – under instruction to Macklin 'ere." So this man, Macklin, that I was tellin' you about, showed me my dooties . . . 'Ammick! I've got it! 'Ammick was our Major, an' Mosse was Captain!' Humberstall celebrated his recapture of the name by labouring at the organ-panel on his knee.

'Look out! You'll smash it,' Anthony protested.

'Sorry! Mother's often told me I didn't know my strength. Now, here's a curious thing. This Major of ours – it's all comin' back to me – was a high-up Divorce Court lawyer; an' Mosse, our Captain, was Number One o' Mosse's Private Detective Agency. You've heard of it? Wives watched while you wait, an' so on. Well, these two 'ad been registerin' together, so to speak, in the Civil line for years on end, but hadn't ever met till the War. Consequently, at Mess their talk was mostly about famous cases they'd been mixed up in. 'Ammick told the Law-courts' end o' the business, an' all what had been left out of the pleadin's; an' Mosse 'ad the actual facts concernin' the errin' parties – in hotels an' so on. I've heard better talk in our Mess than ever before or since. It comes o' the Gunners bein' a scientific corps.'

'That be damned!' said Anthony. 'If anythin' 'appens to 'em they've got it all down in a book. There's no book when your lorry dies on you in the 'Oly Land. *That's* brains.'

'Well, *then*,' Humberstall continued, 'come on this Secret Society business that I started tellin' you about. When those two – 'Ammick an' Mosse – 'ad finished about their matrimonial relations – and, mind you, they weren't radishes – they seldom or never repeated – they'd begin, as often as not, on this Secret Society woman I was tellin' you of – this Jane. She was the only woman I ever 'eard 'em say a good word for. 'Cordin' to them Jane was a none-such. *I* didn't know then she was a Society. Fact is, I only 'ung out 'arf an ear in their direction at first, on account of bein' under instruction for mess-dooty to this Macklin man. What drew *my* attention to her was a new Lieutenant joinin' up. We called 'im "Gander" on account of his profeel, which was the identical bird. 'E'd been a nactuary – workin' out 'ow long civilians 'ad to live. Neither 'Ammick nor Mosse wasted words on 'im at Mess. They went on talking as usual, an' in due time, *as* usual, they got back to Jane. Gander cocks one of his big chilblainy ears an' cracks his cold finger-joints. "By God! Jane?" says 'e. "Yes, Jane," says 'Ammick, pretty short an' senior. "Praise 'Eaven!" says Gander. "It was 'Bubbly' where I've come from down the line." (Some damn revue or other, I expect.) Well, neither 'Ammick nor Mosse was easy-mouthed, or for that matter mealy-mouthed; but no sooner 'ad Gander passed that remark than they both shook 'ands with the young squirt across the table an' called for the port back again. It *was* a password, all right! Then they went at it about Jane – all three, regardless of rank. That made me listen. Presently, I 'eard 'Ammick say –'

''Arf a mo',' Anthony cut in. 'But what was *you* doin' in Mess?'

'Me an' Macklin was refixin' the sand-bag screens to the dug-out passage in case o' gas. We never knew when we'd cop it in the 'Eavies, don't you see? But we knew we 'ad been looked for for some time, an' it might come any minute. But, as I was sayin', 'Ammick says what a pity 'twas Jane 'ad died barren. "I deny that," says Mosse. "I maintain she was fruitful in the 'ighest sense o' the word." An' Mosse knew about such things, too. "I'm inclined to agree with 'Ammick," says young Gander. "Any'ow, she's left no direct an' lawful prog'ny." I remember every word they said, on account o' what 'appened subsequently. I 'adn't noticed Macklin much, or I'd ha' seen he was bosko absoluto. Then 'e cut in, leanin' over a packin'-case with a face on 'im like a dead mackerel in the dark. "Pa-hardon me, gents," Macklin says, "but this *is* a matter on which I *do* 'appen to be moderately well-informed. She *did* leave lawful issue in the shape o' one son; an' 'is name was 'Enery James."[9]

'"By what sire? Prove it," says Gander, before 'is senior officers could get in a word.

'"I will," says Macklin, surgin' on 'is two thumbs. An', mark you, none of 'em spoke! I forget 'oom he said was the sire of this 'Enery James man; but 'e delivered 'em a lecture on this Jane woman for more than a quarter of an hour. I know the exact time, because my old Skoda was on dooty at ten-minute intervals reachin' after some Jerry formin'-up area; and her blast always put out the dug-out candles. I relit 'em once, an' again at the end. In conclusion, this Macklin fell flat forward on 'is face, which was how 'e generally wound up 'is notion of a perfect day. Bosko absoluto!

'"Take 'im away," says 'Ammick to me. "'E's sufferin' from shell-shock."

'To cut a long story short, *that* was what first put the notion into my 'ead. Wouldn't it you? Even 'ad Macklin been a 'igh-up Mason –'

'Wasn't 'e, then?' said Anthony, a little puzzled.

'"E'd never gone beyond the Blue Degrees, 'e told me. Any'ow, 'e'd lectured 'is superior officers up an' down; 'e'd as good as called 'em fools most o' the time, in 'is toff's voice. I 'eard 'im an' I saw 'im. An' all he got was – me told off to put 'im to bed! And all on account o' Jane! Would *you* have let a thing like that get past you? Nor me, either! Next mornin', when his stummick was settled, I was at him full-cry to find out 'ow it was worked. Toff or no toff, 'e knew his end of a bargain. First, 'e wasn't takin' any. He said I wasn't fit to be initiated into the Society of the Janeites. That only meant five bob more – fifteen up to date.

'"Make it one Bradbury," 'e says. "It's dirt-cheap. You saw me 'old the Circus in the 'ollow of me 'and?"

'No denyin' it. I 'ad. So, for one pound, he communicated me the Password of the First Degree,[10] which was *Tilniz an' trap-doors*.[11]

'"I know what a trap-door is," I says to 'im, "but what in 'ell's *Tilniz*?"

'"You obey orders," 'e says, "an' next time I ask you what you're thinkin' about you'll answer, '*Tilniz an' trap-doors*,' in a smart and soldierly manner. I'll spring that question at me own time. All you've got to do is to be distinck."

'We settled all this while we was skinnin' spuds for dinner at the back o' the rear-truck under our camouflage-screens. Gawd, 'ow that glue-paint did stink! Otherwise, 'twasn't so bad, with the sun comin' through our pantomime leaves, an' the wind marcellin'[12] the grasses in the cutting. Well, one thing leading to another, nothin' further 'appened in this direction till the afternoon. We 'ad a high standard o' livin' in Mess – an' in the Group, for that matter. I was takin' away Mosse's lunch – dinner 'e would never call it – an' Mosse was fillin' 'is cigarette-case previous to the afternoon's dooty. Macklin, in the passage, comin' in as if 'e didn't know Mosse was there, slings 'is question at me, an' I give the countersign in a low but quite distinck voice, makin' as if I 'adn't seen Mosse. Mosse looked at me through and through, with his cigarette-case in his 'and. Then 'e jerks out 'arf-a-dozen – best Turkish – on the table an' exits. I pinched 'em an' divvied with Macklin.

'"You see 'ow it works?" says Macklin. "Could you 'ave invested a Bradbury to better advantage?"

'"So far, no," I says. "Otherwise, though, if they start provin' an' tryin' me, I'm a dead bird. There must be a lot more to this Janeite game."

'"'Eaps an' 'eaps," he says. "But to show you the sort of 'eart I 'ave, I'll communicate you all the 'Igher Degrees among the Janeites, includin' the Charges,[13] for another Bradbury. But you'll 'ave to work, Dobbin."'

'Pretty free with your Bradburys, wasn't you?' Anthony grunted disapprovingly.

'What odds? *Ac*-tually, Gander told us, we couldn't expect to av'rage more than six weeks longer apiece, an', any'ow, *I* never regretted it. But make no mistake – the preparation was somethin' cruel. In the first place, I come under Macklin for direct instruction *re* Jane.'

'Oh! Jane *was* real, then?' Anthony glanced for an instant at me as he put the question. 'I couldn't quite make that out.'

'Real!' Humberstall's voice rose almost to a treble. 'Jane? Why, she was a little old maid 'oo'd written 'alf-a-dozen books about a hundred years ago. 'Twasn't as if there was anythin' *to* 'em, either. *I* know. I had to read 'em. They weren't adventurous, nor smutty, nor what you'd call even interestin' – all about girls o' seventeen (they begun young then, I tell you), not certain 'oom they'd like to marry; an' their dances an' card-parties an' picnics, and their young blokes goin' off to London on 'orseback for 'air-cuts an' shaves. It took a full day in those days, if you went to a proper barber. They wore wigs, too, when they was chemists or clergymen. All that interested me on account o' me profession, an' cuttin' the men's 'air every fortnight. Macklin used to chip me about bein' an 'airdresser. 'E *could* pass remarks, too!'

Humberstall recited with relish a fragment of what must have been a superb commination-service, ending with, 'You lazy-minded, lousy-headed, long-trousered, perfumed perookier.'

'An' you took it?' Anthony's quick eyes ran over the man.

'Yes. I was after my money's worth; an' Macklin, havin' put 'is 'and to the plough, wasn't one to withdraw it. Otherwise, if I'd pushed 'im, I'd ha' slew 'im. Our Battery Sergeant-Major nearly did. For Macklin had a wonderful way o' passing remarks on a man's civil life; an' he put it about that our BSM had run a dope an' dolly-shop

with a Chinee woman, the wrong end o' Southwark Bridge. Nothin'
you could lay 'old of, o' course; but – ' Humberstall let us draw our
own conclusions.

'That reminds me,' said Anthony, smacking his lips. 'I' ad a bit of a
fracas with a fare in the Fulham Road last month. He called me a
parastit-ic Forder. I informed 'im I was owner-driver, an' 'e could see
for 'imself the cab was quite clean. That didn't suit 'im. 'E said it was
crawlin'.'

'What happened?' I asked.

'One o' them blue-bellied Bolshies of post-war Police (neglectin'
point-duty, as usual) asked us to flirt a little quieter. My joker chucked
some Arabic at 'im. That was when we signed the Armistice. 'E'd been
a Yeoman – a perishin' Gloucestershire Yeoman – that I'd helped gather
in the orange crop with at Jaffa, in the 'Oly Land!'

'And after that?' I continued.

'It 'ud be 'ard to say. I know 'e lived at Hendon or Cricklewood. I
drove 'im there. We must 'ave talked Zionism or somethin', because at
seven next mornin' 'im an' me was tryin' to get petrol out of a milk-
shop at St Albans. They 'adn't any. In lots o' ways this War has been a
public noosance, as one might say, but there's no denyin' it 'elps you
slip through life easier. The dairyman's son 'ad done time on Jordan
with camels. So he stood us rum an' milk.'

'Just like 'avin' the Password, eh?' was Humberstall's comment.

'That's right. Ours was *Imshee kelb*.* Not so 'ard to remember as
your Jane stuff.'

'Jane wasn't so very 'ard – not the way Macklin used to put 'er,'
Humberstall resumed. 'I 'ad only six books to remember. I learned
the names by 'eart as Macklin placed 'em. There was one called
Persuasion, first; an' the rest in a bunch, except another about some
Abbey or other[14] – last by three lengths. But, as I was sayin', what
beat me was there was nothin' *to* 'em nor *in* 'em. Nothin' at all, believe
me.'

'You seem good an' full of 'em, any'ow,' said Anthony.

'I mean that 'er characters was no *use*! They was only just like people
you'd run across any day. One of 'em was a curate – the Reverend
Collins – always on the make an' lookin' to marry money. Well, when
I was a Boy Scout, 'im or 'is twin brother was our troop-leader. An'
there was an upstandin' 'ard-mouthed Duchess or a Baronet's wife that
didn't give a curse for anyone 'oo wouldn't do what she told 'em to;
the Lady – Lady Catherine (I'll get it in a minute) De Bugg.[15] Before

---

* 'Get out, you dog.'

Ma bought the 'airdressin' business in London I used to know of an 'olesale grocer's wife near Leicester (I'm Leicestershire myself) that might 'ave been 'er duplicate. And – oh yes – there was a Miss Bates;[16] just an old maid runnin' about like a hen with 'er 'ead cut off, an' her tongue loose at both ends. I've got an aunt like 'er. Good as gold – but, *you* know.'

'Lord, yes!' said Anthony, with feeling. 'An' did you find out what *Tilniz* meant? I'm always huntin' after the meanin' of things meself.'

'Yes, 'e was a swine of a Major-General, retired, and on the make. They're all on the make, in a quiet way, in Jane. 'E was so much of a gentleman by 'is own estimation that 'e was always be'avin' like a hound. *You* know the sort. Turned a girl out of 'is own 'ouse because she 'adn't any money – *after*, mark you, encouragin' 'er to set 'er cap at his son, because 'e thought she had.'

'But that 'appens all the time,' said Anthony. 'Why, me own mother – '

'That's right. So would mine. But this Tilney was a man, an' some'ow Jane put it down all so naked it made you ashamed. I told Macklin that, an' he said I was shapin' to be a good Janeite. 'Twasn't *his* fault if I wasn't. 'Nother thing, too; 'avin' been at the Bath Mineral Waters 'Ospital in 'Sixteen, with trench-feet, was a great advantage to me, because I knew the names o' the streets where Jane 'ad lived. There was one of 'em – Laura,[17] I think, or some other girl's name – which Macklin said was 'oly ground. "If you'd been initiated *then*," he says, "you'd ha' felt your flat feet tingle every time you walked over those sacred pavin'-stones."

'"My feet tingled right enough," I said, "but not on account of Jane. Nothin' remarkable about that," I says.

'"'Eaven lend me patience!" he says, combin' 'is 'air with 'is little 'ands. "Every dam' thing about Jane is remarkable to a pukka[18] Janeite! It was there," he says, "that Miss What's-her-Name" (he had the name; I've forgotten it) "made up 'er engagement again, after nine years, with Captain T'other Bloke." An' he dished me out a page an' a half of one of the books to learn by 'eart – *Persuasion*, I think it was.'

'You quick at gettin' things off by 'eart?' Anthony demanded.

'Not as a rule. I was then, though, or else Macklin knew 'ow to deliver the Charges properly. 'E said 'e'd been some sort o' school-master once, and he'd make my mind resume work or break 'imself. That was just before the Battery Sergeant-Major 'ad it in for him on account o' what he'd been sayin' about the Chinee wife an' the dolly-shop.'

'What did Macklin really say?' Anthony and I asked together.

Humberstall gave us a fragment. It was hardly the stuff to let loose on
a pious post-war world without revision.

'And what had your BSM been in civil life?' I asked at the end.

"'Ead-embalmer to an 'olesale undertaker in the Midlands,' said
Humberstall; 'but, o' course, *when* he thought 'e saw his chance he
naturally took it. He come along one mornin' lickin' 'is lips. "You don't
get past me this time," 'e says to Macklin. "You're for it, Professor."

"'Ow so, me gallant Major," says Macklin; "an' what for?"

"'For writin' obese words on the breech o' the ten-inch," says the
BSM. She was our old Skoda that I've been tellin' you about. We called
'er "Bloody Eliza". She 'ad a badly wore obturator an' blew through
a fair treat. I knew by Macklin's face the BSM 'ad dropped it somewhere,
but all he vow'-saifed was, "Very good, Major. We will consider it in
Common Room." The BSM couldn't ever stand Macklin's toff's way
o' puttin' things; so he goes off rumblin' like 'ell's bells in an 'urricane,
as the Marines say. Macklin put it to me at once, what had I been doin'?
Some'ow he could read me like a book.

'Well, all *I*'d done – an' I told 'im *he* was responsible for it – was to
chalk the guns. 'Ammick never minded what the men wrote up on 'em.
'E said it gave 'em an interest in their job. You'd see all sorts of remarks
chalked on the side-plates or the gear-casin's.'

'What sort of remarks?' said Anthony keenly.

'Oh! 'Ow Bloody Eliza, or Spittin' Jim – that was our old Mark Five
Nine-point-two – felt that morning, an' such things. But it 'ad come
over me – more to please Macklin than anythin' else – that it was time
we Janeites 'ad a look in. So, as I was tellin' you, I'd taken an' rechristened all three of 'em, on my own, early that mornin'. Spittin' Jim
I 'ad chalked "The Reverend Collins" – that curate I was tellin' you
about; an' our cut-down Navy Twelve, "General Tilney", because it
was worse wore in the groovin' than anything *I*'d ever seen. The Skoda
(an' that was where *I* dropped it) I 'ad chalked up "The Lady Catherine
De Bugg". I made a clean breast of it all to Macklin. He reached up
an' patted me on the shoulder. "You done nobly," he says. "You're
bringin' forth abundant fruit,[19] like a good Janeite. But I'm afraid your
spellin' has misled our worthy BSM. *That's* what it is," 'e says, slappin'
'is little leg. "'Ow might you 'ave spelt De Bourgh for example?"

'I told 'im. 'Twasn't right; an' 'e nips off to the Skoda to make it so.
When 'e comes back, 'e says that the Gander 'ad been before 'im an'
corrected the error. But we two come up before the Major, just the
same, that afternoon after lunch; 'Ammick in the chair, so to speak,
Mosse in another, an' the BSM chargin' Macklin with writin' obese
words on His Majesty's property, on active service. When it transpired

that me an' not Macklin was the offendin' party, the BSM turned 'is hand in an' sulked like a baby. 'E as good as told 'Ammick 'e couldn't hope to preserve discipline unless examples was made – meanin', o' course, Macklin.'

'Yes, I've heard all that,' said Anthony, with a contemptuous grunt. 'The worst of it is, a lot of it's true.'

''Ammick took 'im up sharp about Military Law, which he said was even more fair than the civilian article.'

'My Gawd!' This came from Anthony's scornful midmost bosom.

'"Accordin' to the unwritten law of the 'Eavies," says 'Ammick, "there's no objection to the men chalkin' the guns, if decency is preserved. On the other 'and," says he, "we 'aven't yet settled the precise status of individuals entitled so to do. *I* 'old that the privilege is confined to combatants only."

'"With the permission of the Court," says Mosse, who was another born lawyer, "I'd like to be allowed to join issue on that point. Prisoner's position is very delicate an' doubtful, an' he has no legal representative."

'"Very good," says 'Ammick. "Macklin bein' acquitted – "

'"With submission, me lud," says Mosse. "I hope to prove 'e was accessory before the fact."

'"*As* you please," says 'Ammick. "But in that case, 'oo the 'ell's goin' to get the port I'm tryin' to stand the Court?"

'"I submit," says Mosse, "prisoner, bein' under direct observation o' the Court, could be temporarily enlarged for that duty."

'So Macklin went an' got it, an' the BSM had 'is glass with the rest. Then they argued whether mess-servants an' non-combatants was entitled to chalk the guns ('Ammick *versus* Mosse). After a bit, 'Ammick as CO give 'imself best, an' me an' Macklin was severely admonished for trespassin' on combatants' rights, an' the BSM was warned that if we repeated the offence 'e could deal with us summ'rily. He 'ad some glasses o' port an' went out quite 'appy. Then my turn come, while Macklin was gettin' them their tea; an' one thing leadin' to another, 'Ammick put me through all the Janeite Degrees, you might say. Never 'ad such a doin' in my life.'

'Yes, but what did you tell 'em?' said Anthony. 'I can't ever *think* my lies quick enough when I'm for it.'

'No need to lie. I told 'em that the backside view o' the Skoda, when she was run up, put Lady de Bugg into my 'ead. They gave me right there, but they said I was wrong about General Tilney. 'Cordin' to them, our Navy twelve-inch ought to 'ave been christened Miss Bates. I said the same idea 'ad crossed my mind, till I'd seen the General's groovin'.

Then I felt it had to be the General or nothin'. But they give me full marks for the Reverend Collins – our Nine-point-two.'

'An' you fed 'em *that* sort o' talk?' Anthony's fox-coloured eyebrows climbed almost into his hair.

'While I was assistin' Macklin to get tea – yes. Seein' it was an examination, I wanted to do 'im credit as a Janeite.'

'An' – an' what did they say?'

'They said it was 'ighly creditable to us both. I don't drink, so they give me about a hundred fags.'

'Gawd! What a Circus you must 'ave been!' was Anthony's gasping comment.

'It *was* a 'appy little Group. I wouldn't 'a changed with any other.'

Humberstall sighed heavily as he helped Anthony slide back the organ-panel. We all admired it in silence, while Anthony repocketed his secret polishing mixture, which lived in a tin tobacco-box. I had neglected my work for listening to Humberstall. Anthony reached out quietly and took over a Secretary's Jewel and a rag. Humberstall studied his reflection in the glossy wood.

'Almost,' he said critically, holding his head to one side.

'Not with an Army. You could with a Safety, though,' said Anthony. And, indeed, as Brother Burges had foretold, one might have shaved in it with comfort.

'Did you ever run across any of 'em afterwards, any time?' Anthony asked presently.

'Not so many of 'em left to run after, now. With the 'Eavies it's mostly neck or nothin'. We copped it. In the neck. In due time.'

'Well, *you* come out of it all right.' Anthony spoke both stoutly and soothingly; but Humberstall would not be comforted.

'That's right; but I almost wish I 'adn't,' he sighed. 'I was 'appier there than ever before or since. Jerry's March push in 'Eighteen did us in; an' yet, 'ow could we 'ave expected it? 'Ow *could* we 'ave expected it? We'd been sent back for rest an' runnin'-repairs, back pretty near our base; an' our old loco[20] that used to shift us about o' nights, she'd gone down the line for repairs. But for 'Ammick we wouldn't even 'ave 'ad our camouflage-screens up. He told our Brigadier that, whatever 'e might be in the Gunnery line, as a leadin' Divorce lawyer he never threw away a point in argument. So 'e 'ad us all screened in over in a cuttin' on a little spur-line near a wood, an' 'e saw to the screens 'imself. The leaves weren't more than comin' out then, an' the sun used to make our glue-paint stink. Just like actin' in a theatre, it was! But 'appy. *But* 'appy! I expect if we'd been caterpillars, like the new big six-inch hows, they'd ha' remembered us. But we was the old La Bassee '15 Mark o'

Heavies that ran on rails – not much more good than scrap-iron that
late in the War. An', believe me, gents – or Brethren, as I should say – we
copped it cruel. Look 'ere! It was in the afternoon, an' I was watchin'
Gander instructin' a class in new sights at Lady Catherine. All of a
sudden I 'eard our screens rip overhead, an' a runner on a motor-bike
come sailin', sailin' through the air – like that bloke that used to bicycle
off Brighton Pier – and landed one awful wop almost atop o' the class.
"'Old 'ard," says Gander. "That's no way to report. What's the fuss?"
"Your screens 'ave broke my back, for one thing," says the bloke on
the ground; "an' for another, the 'ole Front's gone." "Nonsense," says
Gander. 'E 'adn't more than passed the remark when the man was
vi'lently sick an' conked out. 'E 'ad plenty papers on 'im from Brigadiers
and CO's reporting 'emselves cut off an' askin' for orders. 'E was right
both ways – his back an' our Front. The 'ole Somme Front washed
out as clean as kiss-me-'and!' His huge hand smashed down open on
his knee.

'We 'eard about it at the time in the 'Oly Land. Was it reelly as quick
as all that?' said Anthony.

'Quicker! Look 'ere! The motor-bike dropped in on us about four
pip-emma. After that, we tried to get orders o' some kind or other, but
nothin' came through excep' that all available transport was in use an'
not likely to be released. *That* didn't 'elp us any. About nine o'clock
comes along a young Brass 'At in brown gloves. We was quite a surprise
to 'im. 'E said they were evacuating the area and we'd better shift.
"Where to?" says 'Ammick, rather short.

"'Oh, somewhere Amiens way," he says. "Not that I'd guarantee
Amiens for any length o' time; but Amiens might do to begin with."
I'm giving you the very words. Then 'e goes off swingin' 'is brown
gloves, and 'Ammick sends for Gander an' orders 'im to march the
men through Amiens to Dieppe; book thence to New'aven, take up
positions be'ind Seaford, an' carry on the War. Gander said he'd see
'im damned first. 'Ammick says 'e'd see 'im court-martialled after.
Gander says what 'e meant to say was that the men 'ud see all an'
sundry damned before they went into Amiens with their gun-sights
wrapped up in their puttees. 'Ammick says 'e 'adn't said a word about
puttees, an' carryin' off the gun-sights was purely optional. "Well,
anyhow," says Gander, "puttees *or* drawers, they ain't goin' to shift a
step unless you lead the procession."

"'Mutinous 'ounds," says 'Ammick. "But we live in a democratic
age. D'you suppose they'd object to kindly diggin' 'emselves in a bit?"
"Not at all," says Gander. "The BSM's kept 'em at it like terriers for
the last three hours." "That bein' so," says 'Ammick, "Macklin'll now

fetch us small glasses o' port." Then Mosse comes in – he could smell port a mile off – an' he submits we'd only add to the congestion in Amiens if we took our crowd there, whereas, if we lay doggo where we was, Jerry might miss us, though he didn't seem to be missin' much that evenin'.

'The 'ole country was pretty noisy, an' our dumps we'd lit ourselves flarin' heavens-high as far as you could see. Lyin' doggo was our best chance. I believe we might ha' pulled it off, if we'd been left alone, but along towards midnight – there was some small stuff swishin' about, but nothin' particular – a nice little bald-headed old gentleman in uniform pushes into the dug-out wipin' his glasses an' sayin' 'e was thinkin' o' formin' a defensive flank on our left with 'is battalion which 'ad just come up. 'Ammick says 'e wouldn't form much if 'e was 'im. "Oh, don't say *that*," says the old gentleman, very shocked. "One must support the Guns, mustn't one?" 'Ammick says we was refittin' an' about as effective, just then, as a public lav'tory. "Go into Amiens," he says, "an' defend 'em there." "Oh no," says the old gentleman, "me an' my laddies *must* make a defensive flank for you," an' he flips out of the dug-out like a performin' bullfinch, chirruppin' for his "laddies". Gawd in 'Eaven knows what sort o' push they was – little boys mostly – but they 'ung on to 'is coat-tails like a Sunday-school treat, an' we 'eard 'em muckin' about in the open for a bit. Then a pretty tight barrage was slapped down for ten minutes, an' 'Ammick thought the laddies had copped it already. "It'll be our turn next," says Mosse. "There's been a covey o' Gothas messin' about for the last 'alf-hour – lookin' for the Railway Shops, I expect. They're just as likely to take us." "Arisin' out o' that," says 'Ammick, "one of 'em sounds pretty low down now. We're for it, me learned colleagues!" "Jesus!" says Gander, "I believe you're right, sir." And that was the last word *I* 'eard on the matter.'

'Did they cop you then?' said Anthony.

'They did. I expect Mosse was right, an' they took us for the Railway Shops. When I come to, I was lyin' outside the cuttin', which was pretty well filled up. The Reverend Collins was all right; but Lady Catherine and the General was past prayin' for. I lay there, takin' it in, till I felt cold an' I looked at meself. Otherwise, I 'adn't much on excep' me boots. So I got up an' walked about to keep warm. Then I saw somethin' like a mushroom in the moonlight. It was the nice old gentleman's bald 'ead. I patted it. 'Im and 'is laddies 'ad copped it right enough. Some battalion run out in a 'urry from England, I suppose. They 'adn't even begun to dig in – pore little perishers! I dressed myself off 'em there, an' topped off with a British warm.[21] Then I went back to the cuttin', an' someone says to me: "Dig, you ox, dig! Gander's under." So I 'elped shift things till I threw up blood an' bile mixed. Then I dropped, an' they brought Gander out – dead – an' laid 'im next me. 'Ammick 'ad gone too – fair tore in 'alf, the BSM said; but the funny thing was, he talked quite a lot before 'e died, an' nothin' to 'im below 'is stummick, they told me. Mosse we never found. 'E'd been standing by Lady Catherine. She'd up-ended an' gone back on 'em, with 'alf the cuttin' atop of 'er, by the look of things.'

'And what come to Macklin?' said Anthony.

'Dunno . . . 'E was with 'Ammick. I expect I must ha' been blown clear of all by the first bomb; for I was the on'y Janeite left. We lost about half our crowd, either under, or after we'd got 'em out. The BSM went off 'is rocker when mornin' came, an' he ran about from one to another sayin': "That was a good push! That was a great crowd! Did ye ever know any push to touch 'em?" An' then 'e'd cry. So what was left of us made off for ourselves, an' I came across a lorry, pretty full, but they took me in.'

'Ah!' said Anthony with pride. '"They all take a taxi when it's rainin'." Ever 'eard that song?'

'They went a long way back. Then I walked a bit, an' there was a hospital-train fillin' up, an' one of the Sisters – a grey-headed one – ran at me wavin' 'er red 'ands an' sayin' there wasn't room for a louse in it. I was past carin'. But she went on talkin' an' talkin' about the War, an' her pa in Ladbroke Grove, an' 'ow strange for 'er at 'er time of life to be doin' this work with a lot o' men, an' next war, 'ow the nurses 'ud 'ave to wear khaki breeches on account o' the mud, like the Land Girls; an' that reminded 'er, she'd boil me an egg if she could lay 'ands on one, for she'd run a chicken-farm once. You never 'eard anythin' like it – outside o' Jane. It set me off laughin' again. Then a woman with a nose an' teeth on 'er marched up. "What's all this?" she says. "What do you want?" "Nothing," I says, "only make Miss Bates, there, stop talkin' or I'll die." "Miss Bates?" she says. "What in 'Eaven's name makes you call 'er that?" "Because she is," I says. "D' you know what you're sayin'?" she says, an' slings her bony arm round me to get me off the ground. "'Course I do," I says, "an' if you knew Jane you'd know too." "That's enough," says she. "You're comin' on this train if I have to kill a Brigadier for you," an' she an' an ord'ly fair hove me into the train, on to a stretcher close to the cookers. That beef-tea went down well! Then she shook 'ands with me an' said I'd hit off Sister Molyneux in one, an' then she pinched me an extra blanket. It was 'er own 'ospital pretty much. I expect she was the Lady Catherine de Bourgh of the area. Well, an' so, to cut a long story short, nothing further transpired.'

"Adn't you 'ad enough by then?' asked Anthony.

'I expect so. Otherwise, if the old Circus 'ad been carryin' on, I might 'ave 'ad another turn with 'em before Armistice. Our BSM was right. There never was an 'appier push. 'Ammick an' Mosse an' Gander an' the BSM an' that pore little Macklin man makin' an' passin' an' raisin' me an' gettin' me on to the 'ospital train after 'e was dead, all for a couple of Bradburys. I lie awake nights still, reviewing matters. There never was a push to touch ours – never!'

Anthony handed me back the Secretary's Jewel resplendent.

'Ah,' said he. 'No denyin' that Jane business was more useful to you than the Roman Eagles or the Star an' Garter.[22] Pity there wasn't any of you Janeites in the 'Oly Land. *I* never come across 'em.'

'Well, as pore Macklin said, it's a very select Society, an' you've got to be a Janeite in your 'eart, or you won't have any success. An' yet he made *me* a Janeite! I read all her six books now for pleasure 'tween times in the shop; an' it brings it all back – down to the smell of the glue-paint on the screens. You take it from me, Brethren, there's no one to touch Jane when you're in a tight place. Gawd bless 'er, whoever she was.'

Worshipful Brother Burges, from the floor of the Lodge, called us all from Labour to Refreshment. Humberstall hove himself up – so very a cart-horse of a man one almost expected to hear the harness creak on his back – and descended the steps.

He said he could not stay for tea because he had promised his mother to come home for it, and she would most probably be waiting for him now at the Lodge door.

'One or other of 'em always comes for 'im. He's apt to miss 'is gears sometimes,' Anthony explained to me, as we followed.

'Goes on a bust, d'you mean?'

''Im! He's no more touched liquor than 'e 'as women since 'e was born. No, 'e's liable to a sort o' quiet fits, like. They came on after the dump blew up at Eatables. But for them, 'e'd ha' been Battery Sergeant-Major.'

'Oh!' I said. 'I couldn't make out why he took on as mess-waiter when he got back to his guns. That explains things a bit.'

''Is sister told me the dump goin' up knocked all 'is Gunnery instruction clean out of 'im. The only thing 'e stuck to was to get back to 'is old crowd. Gawd knows 'ow 'e worked it, but 'e did. He fair deserted out of England to 'em, she says; an' when they saw the state 'e was in, they 'adn't the 'eart to send 'im back or into 'ospital. They kep' 'im for a mascot, as you might say. That's *all* dead-true. 'Is sister told me so. But I can't guarantee that Janeite business, excep' 'e never told a lie since 'e was six. 'Is sister told me so. What do *you* think?'

'He isn't likely to have made it up out of his own head,' I replied.

'But people don't get so crazy-fond o' books as all that, do they? 'E's made 'is sister try to read 'em. She'd do anythin' to please him. But, as I keep tellin' 'er, so'd 'is mother. D'you 'appen to know anything about Jane?'

'I believe Jane was a bit of a match-maker in a quiet way when she was alive, and I know all her books are full of match-making,' I said. '*You*'d better look out.'

'Oh, *that*'s as good as settled,' Anthony replied, blushing.

HIS GIFT

His Scoutmaster and his comrades, who disagreed on several points, were united in one conviction – that William Glasse Sawyer was, without exception, the most unprofitable person, not merely in the Pelican Troop, who lived in the wilderness of the 47th Postal District, London, SE, but in the whole body of Boy Scouts throughout the world.

No one, except a ferocious uncle who was also a French-polisher,[1] seemed responsible for his beginnings. There was a legend that he had been entered as a Wolf-Cub[2] at the age of eight, under Miss Doughty, whom the uncle had either bribed or terrorised to accept him; and that after six months Miss Doughty confessed that she could make nothing of him and retired to teach school in the Yorkshire moors. There is also a red-headed ex-cub of that Troop (he is now in a shipping-office) who asserts proudly that he used to bite William Glasse Sawyer on the leg in the hope of waking him up, and takes most of the credit for William's present success. But when William moved into the larger life of the Pelicans, who were gay birds, he was not what you might call alert. In shape he resembled the ace of diamonds; in colour he was an oily sallow.

He could accomplish nothing that required one glimmer of reason, thought, or common sense. He cleaned himself only under bitter compulsion. He lost his bearings equally in town or country after a five-minutes' stroll. He could track nothing smaller than a tram-car on a single line, and that only if there were no traffic. He could neither hammer a nail, carry an order, tie a knot, light a fire, notice any natural object, except food, nor use any edged tool except a table-knife. To crown all, his innumerable errors and omissions were not even funny.

But it is an old law of human nature that if you hold to one known course of conduct – good or evil – you end by becoming an institution; and when he was fifteen or thereabouts William achieved that position. The Pelicans gradually took pride in the notorious fact that they possessed the only Sealed Pattern, Mark A, Ass – an unique jewel, so to speak, of Absolute, Unalterable Incapacity. The poet of a neighbouring Troop used to write verses about him, and recite them from public places, such as the tops of passing trams. William made no comment, but wrapped himself up in long silences that he seldom broke till the juniors of the Troop (the elders had given it up long before) tried to do him good turns with their Scout-staves.

In private life he assisted his uncle at the mystery of French-polishing, which, he said, was 'boiling up things in pots and rubbing down bits of wood'. The boiling-up, he said, he did not mind so much. The rubbing-down he hated. Once, too, he volunteered that his uncle and only relative had been in the Navy, and 'did not like to be played with'; and the vision of William playing with any human being upset even his Scoutmaster.

Now it happened, upon a certain summer that was really a summer with heat to it, the Pelicans had been lent a dream of a summer camp in a dream of a park, which offered opportunities for every form of diversion, including bridging muddy-banked streams and unlimited cutting into young alders and undergrowth at large. A convenient village lay just outside the Park wall, and the ferny slopes round the camp were rich in rabbits, not to mention hedgehogs and other fascinating vermin. It was reached – Mr Hale their Scoutmaster saw to that – after two days' hard labour, with the Troop trek-cart, along sunny roads.

William's share in the affair was – what it had always been. First he lost most of his kit; next his uncle talked to him after the fashion of the Navy of '96 before refitting him; thirdly he went lame behind the trek-cart by reason of a stone in his shoe, and on arrival in camp dropped – not for the first, second, or third time – into his unhonoured office as Camp Orderly, and was placed at the disposal of The Prawn, whose light blue eyes stuck out from his freckled face, and whose long skinny arm was covered with badges. From that point on, the procedure was as usual. Once again did The Prawn assure his Scoutmaster that he would take enormous care of William and give him work suited to his capacity and intelligence. Once again did William grunt and wriggle at the news, and once again in the silence of the deserted camp next morning, while the rest of the Pelicans were joyously mucking themselves up to their young bills at bridging brooks, did he bow his neck to The Prawn's many orders. For The Prawn was a born organiser. He set William to unpack the trek-cart and then to neatly and exactly replace all parcels, bags, tins, and boxes. He despatched him thrice in the forenoon across the hot Park to fetch water from a distant well equipped with a stiff-necked windlass and a split handle that pinched William's fat palms. He bade him collect sticks, thorny for choice, out of the flanks of a hedge full of ripe nettles against which Scout uniforms offer small protection.³ He then made him lay them in the camp cooking-place, carefully rejecting the green ones, for most sticks were alike to William; and when everything else failed, he set him to pick up stray papers and rubbish the length and breadth of the camp. All that while, he not only chased him with comments but expected that William would show gratitude to him for forming his young mind.

"'Tisn't every one 'ud take this amount o' trouble with you, Mug,' said The Prawn virtuously, when even his energetic soul could make no further work for his vassal. 'Now you open that bully-beef tin and we'll have something to eat, and then you're off duty – for a bit. I shall try my hand at a little camp-cooking.'

William found the tin – at the very bottom, of course, of the trek-cart; cut himself generously over the knuckles in opening it (till The Prawn showed him how this should be done), and in due course, being full of bread and bully, withdrew towards a grateful clump of high fern that he had had his eye on for some time, wriggled deep into it, and on a little rabbit-browsed clearing of turf stretched out and slept the sleep of the weary who have been up and under strict orders since six a.m. Till that hour of that day, be it remembered, William had given no proof either of intelligence or initiative in any direction.

He waked, slowly as was his habit, and noticed that the shadows were stretching a little, even as he stretched himself. Then he heard The Prawn clanking pot-lids, between soft bursts of song. William sniffed. The Prawn was cooking – was probably qualifying for something or other. The Prawn did nothing but qualify for badges. On reflection William discovered that he loved The Prawn even less this camp than the last, or the one before that. Then he heard the voice of a stranger.

'Yes,' was The Prawn's reply. 'I'm in charge of the camp. Would you like to look at it, sir?'

'Seen 'em – seen heaps of 'em,' said the unknown. 'My son was in 'em once – Buffaloes, out Hendon way. What are *you*?'

'Well, just now I'm a sort of temporary Cook,' said The Prawn, whose manners were far better than William's.

'Temp'ry! Temp'ry!' the stranger puffed. 'Can't be a temp'ry Cook any more'n you can be a temp'ry Parson. Not so much. Cookin's cookin'! Let's see *your* notions of cookin'.'

William had never heard any one address The Prawn in these tones, and somehow it cheered him. In the silence that followed he turned on his face and wriggled unostentatiously through the fern, as a Scout should, till he could see that bold man without attracting The Prawn's notice. And this, too, was the first time that William had ever profited by the instruction of his Scoutmaster or the example of his comrades.

Heavenly sights rewarded him. The Prawn, visibly ill at ease, was shifting from one sinewy leg to the other, while an enormously fat little man with a pointed grey beard and arms like the fins of a fish investigated a couple of pots that hung on properly crutched sticks over the small fire that William had lighted in the cooking-place. He did not seem to approve of what he saw or smelt. And yet it was the impeccable Prawn's own cookery!

'Lor'!' said he at last after more sniffs of contempt, as he replaced the lid. 'If you hot up things in tins, *that* ain't cookery. That's vittles⁴ – mere vittles! And the way you've set that pot on, you're drawing all the nesty wood-smoke into the water. The spuds won't take much harm of it, but you've ruined the meat. That *is* meat, ain't it? Get me a fork.'

William hugged himself. The Prawn, looking exactly like his name-sake well boiled, fetched a big fork. The little man prodded into the pot.

'It's stew!' The Prawn explained, but his voice shook.

'Lor'!' said the man again. 'It's boilin'! It's boilin'! You don't boil when you stew, my son; an' as for *this*' – up came a grey slab of mutton – 'there's no odds between this and motor-tyres. Well! Well! As I was sayin' – ' He joined his hands behind his globular back and shook his head in silence. After a while, The Prawn tried to assert himself.

'Cookin' isn't my strong point,' began The Prawn, 'but – '

'Pore boys! Pore boys!' the stranger soliloquised, looking straight in front of him. '*Pore* little boys! Wicked, *I* call it. They don't ever let you make bread, do they, my son?'

The Prawn said they generally bought their bread at a shop.

'Ah! I'm a shopkeeper meself. Marsh, the Baker here, is me. *Pore* boys! Well! Well! . . . Though it's against me own interest to say so, *I* think shops are wicked. They sell people things out o' tins which save 'em trouble, an' fill the 'ospitals with stummick-cases afterwards. An' the muck that's sold for flour . . . ' His voice faded away and he meditated again. 'Well! Well! *As* I was sayin' – Pore boys! *Pore* boys! I'm glad you ain't askin' me to dinner. Good-bye.'

He rolled away across the fern, leaving The Prawn dumb behind him.

It seemed to William best to wriggle back in his cover as far as he could, ere The Prawn should call him to work again. He was not a Scout by instinct, but his uncle had shown him that when things went wrong in the world, someone generally passed it on to someone else.

Very soon he heard his name called, acidly, several times. He crawled out from the far end of the fern-patch, rubbing his eyes, and The Prawn re-enslaved him on the spot. For once in his life William was alert and intelligent, but The Prawn paid him no compliments, nor when the very muddy Pelicans came back from the bridging did The Prawn refer in any way to the visit of Messrs. E. M. Marsh & Son, Bakers and Confectioners in the village street just outside the Park wall. Nor, for that matter, did he serve the Pelicans much besides tinned meats for their evening meal.

To say that William did not sleep a wink that night would be what has been called 'nature-faking';[5] which is a sin. His system demanded at least nine hours' rest but he lay awake for quite twenty minutes, during which he thought intensely, rapidly, and joyously. Had he been asked he would have said that his thoughts dealt solely with The Prawn and the judgment that had fallen upon him; but William was no psychologist. He did not know that hate – raging hate against a too-badged, too-virtuous senior – had shot him into a new world, exactly as the large blunt shell is heaved through space and dropped into a factory, a garden, or a barracks by the charge behind it. And, as the shell, which is but metal and mixed chemicals, needs the mere graze on the fuse to spread itself all over the landscape, so did his mind need but the touch of that hate to flare up and illuminate not only all his world, but his own way through it.

Next morning, something sang in his ear that it was long since he had done good turns to any one except his uncle, who was slow to appreciate them. He would amend that error; and the more safely since The Prawn would be off all that day with the Troop on a tramp in the natural history line, and his place as Camp Warden and Provost-Marshal would be filled by the placid and easy-going Walrus, whose proper name was Carpenter,[6] who never tried for badges, but who could not see a rabbit without going after him. And the owner of the Park had given full leave to the Pelicans to slay by any means, except by gun, any rabbits they could. So William ingratiated himself with his Superior Officer as soon as the Pelicans had left . . .

No, the excellent Carpenter did not see that he needed William by his side all day. He might take himself and his bruised foot pretty much where he chose. He went, and this new and active mind of his that he did not realise, accompanied him – straight up the path of duty which, poetry tells us, is so often the road to glory.[7]

He began by cleaning himself and his kit at seven o'clock in the morning, long before the village shops were open. This he did near a postern gate with a crack in it, in the Park wall, commanding a limited but quite sufficient view of the establishment of E.M. Marsh & Son across the street. It was perfect weather, and about eight o'clock Mr Marsh himself in his shirt-sleeves rolled out to enjoy it before he took down the shutters. Hardly had he shifted the first of them when a fattish Boy Scout with a flat face and a slight limp laid hold of the second and began to slide it towards him.

'Well! Well!' said Mr Marsh. 'Ah! Your good turn, eh?'

'Yes,' said William briefly.

'That's right! Handsomely now, handsomely,' for the shutter was jamming in its groove. William knew from his uncle that 'handsomely' meant slowly and with care. The shutter responded to the coaxing. The others followed.

'Belay!' said Mr Marsh, wiping his forehead, for, like William, he perspired easily. When he turned round William had gone. The Movies had taught him, though he knew it not, the value of dramatic effect. He continued to watch Mr Marsh through the crack in the postern – it was the little wooden door at the end of the right of way through the Park – and when, an hour or so later, Mr Marsh came out of his shop and headed towards it, William retired backwards into the high fern and brambles. The manoeuvre would have rejoiced Mr Hale's heart, for generally William moved like an elephant with her young. He turned up, quite casually, when Mr Marsh had puffed his way again into the empty camp. Carpenter was off in pursuit of rabbits, with a pocket full of fine picture-wire. It was the first time William had ever done the honours of any establishment. He came to attention and smiled.

'Well! Well!' Mr Marsh nodded friendlily. 'What are *you*?'

'Camp-Guard,' said William, improvising for the first time in his life. 'Can I show you anything, sir?'

'No, thank'ee. My son was a Scout once. I've just come to look round at things. No one tryin' any cookin' to-day?'

'No, sir.'

''Bout's well. *Pore* boys! What you goin' to have for dinner? Tinned stuff?'

'I expect so, sir.'

'D' you like it?'

'Used to it.' William rather approved of this round person who wasted no time on abstract ideas.

'*Pore* boys! Well! Well! It saves trouble – for the present. Knots and splices in your stummick afterwards – in 'ospital.' Mr Marsh looked at the cold camp cooking-place and its three big stones, and sniffed.

'Would you like it lit?' said William suddenly.

'What for?'

'To cook with.'

'What d'*you* know about cookin'?' Mr Marsh's little eyes opened wide.

'Nothing, sir.'

'What makes you think *I*'m a cook?'

'By the way you looked at our cooking-place,' the mendacious William answered. The Prawn had always urged him to cultivate habits of observation. They seemed easy – after you had observed the things.

'Well! Well! Quite a young Sherlock, you are. Don't think much o' *this*, though.' Mr Marsh began to stoop to rearrange the open-air hearth to his liking.

'Show me how and I'll do it,' said William.

'Shove that stone a little more to the left then. Steady – So! That'll do! Got any wood? No? You slip across to the shop and ask them to give you some small brush-stuff from the oven.[8] Stop! *And* my apron, too. Marsh is the name.'

William left him chuckling wheezily. When he returned Mr Marsh clad himself in a long white apron of office which showed so clearly that Carpenter from far off returned at once.

'H'sh! H'sh!' said Mr Marsh before he could speak. 'You carry on with what you're doing. Marsh is my name. My son was a Scout once. Buffaloes – Hendon way. It's all right. Don't you grudge an old man enjoying himself.'

The Walrus looked amazedly at William moving in three directions at once with his face aflame.

'It's all right,' said William. 'He's giving us cooking-lessons.' Then – the words came into his mouth by themselves – 'I'll take the responsibility.'

'Yes, yes! He knew I could cook. Quite a young Sherlock he is! *You* carry on.' Mr Marsh turned his back on The Walrus and despatched William again with some orders to his shop across the road. 'And you'd better tell 'em to put 'em all in a basket,' he cried after him.

William returned with a fair assortment of mixed material, including eggs, two rashers of bacon, and a packet of patent flour, concerning which last Mr Marsh said things no baker should say about his own goods. The frying-pan came out of the trek-cart, with some other oddments, and it was not till after it was greased that Mr Marsh demanded William's name. He got it in full, and it produced strange effects on the little fat man.

'An' 'ow do you spell your middle name?' he asked.

'G-l-a-double-s-e,' said William.

'Might that be your mother's?' William nodded. 'Well! Well! I wonder now! I *do* wonder. It's a great name. There was a Sawyer in the cooking line once, but 'e was a Frenchman and spelt it different. Glasse[9] is serious though. And you say it was your ma's?' He fell into an abstraction, frying-pan in hand. Anon, as he cracked an egg miraculously on its edge: 'Whether you're a descendant or not, it's worth livin' up to, a name like that.'

'Why?' said William, as the egg slid into the pan and spread as evenly as paint under an expert's hand.

'I'll tell you some day. She was a very great cook – but she'd have come expensive at to-day's prices. Now, you take the pan an' I'll draw me own conclusions.'

The boy worked the pan over the level red fire with a motion that he had learned somehow or other while 'boiling up' things for his uncle. It seemed to him natural and easy. Mr Marsh watched in unbroken silence for at least two minutes.

'It's early to say – yet,' was his verdict. 'But I 'ave 'opes. You 'ave good 'ands, an' your knowin' I was a cook shows you 'ave the instinck. *If* you 'ave got the Touch – mark you, I only say if – but *if* you 'ave anything like the Genuine Touch, you're provided for for life. *An'* further – don't tilt her that way! – you 'old your neighbours, friends, and employers in the 'ollow of your 'and.'

'How do you mean?' said William, intent on his egg. 'Everything which a man *is* depends on what 'e puts inside 'im,' was the reply. 'A good cook's a King of men – besides being thunderin' well off if 'e don't drink. It's the only sure business in the whole round world; and I've been round it eight times, in the Mercantile Marine, before I married the second Mrs M.'

William, more interested in the pan than Mr Marsh's marriages, made no reply. 'Yes, a good cook,' Mr Marsh went on reminiscently, 'even on Board o' Trade allowance, 'as brought many a ship to port that 'ud otherwise 'ave mut'nied on the 'igh seas.'

The eggs and bacon mellowed together. Mr Marsh supplied some wonderful last touches and the result was eaten, with The Walrus's help, sizzling out of the pan and washed down with some stone ginger-beer from the convenient establishment of Mr E. M. Marsh outside the Park wall.

'I've ruined me dinner,' Mr Marsh confided to the boys, 'but I 'aven't enjoyed myself like this, not since Noah was an able seaman. You wash up, young Sherlock, an' I'll tell you something.'

He filled an ancient pipe with eloquent tobacco, and while William scoured the pan, he held forth on the art and science and mystery of cooking as inspiredly as Mr Jorrocks, Master of Foxhounds,[10] had lectured upon the Chase. The burden of his song was Power – power which, striking directly at the stomach of man, makes the rudest polite, not to say sycophantic, towards a good cook, whether at sea, in camp, in the face of war, or (here he embellished his text with personal experiences) the crowded competitive cities where a good meal was as rare, he declared, as silk pyjamas in a pig-sty. 'An' mark you,' he concluded, 'three times a day the 'aughtiest and most overbearin' of 'em all 'ave to come crawling to you for a round belly-full. Put *that* in your pipe and smoke it out, young Sherlock!'

He unloosed his sacrificial apron and rolled away.

The Boy Scout is used to strangers who give him good advice on the smallest provocation; but strangers who fill you up with bacon and eggs and ginger-beer are few.

'What started it all?' The Walrus demanded.

'Well, I can't exactly say,' William answered, and as he had never been known to give a coherent account of anything, The Walrus returned to his wires, and William lay out and dreamed in the fern among the cattle-flies. He had dismissed The Prawn altogether from his miraculously enlarging mind. Very soon he was on the High Seas, a locality which till that instant had never appealed to him, in a gale, issuing bacon and eggs to crews on the edge of mutiny. Next, he was at war, turning the tides of it to victory for his own land by meals of bacon and eggs that brought bemedalled Generals in troops like Pelicans, to his fireplace. Then he was sustaining his uncle, at the door of an enormous restaurant, with plates of bacon and eggs sent out by gilded commissionaires such as guard the cinemas, while his uncle wept with gratitude and remorse, and The Prawn, badges and all, begged for the scraps.

His chin struck his chest and half waked him to fresh flights of glory. He might have the Genuine Touch, Mr Marsh had said it. Moreover, he, The Mug, had a middle name which had filled that great man with respect. All the 47th Postal District should ring with that name, even to the exclusion of the racing-news, in its evening papers. And on his return from camp, or perhaps a day or two later, he would defy his very uncle and escape for ever from the foul business of French-polishing.

Here he slept generously and dreamlessly till evening, when the Pelicans returned, their pouches full of samples of uncookable vegetables and insects, and The Walrus made his report of the day's Camp doings to the Scoutmaster.

'Wait a minute, Walrus. You say The Mug actually *did* the cooking.'

'Mr Marsh had him under instruction, sir. But The Mug did a lot of it – he held the pan over the fire. I saw him, sir. And he washed up afterwards.'

'Did he?' said the Scoutmaster lightly. 'Well, that's something.' But when The Walrus had gone Mr Hale smote thrice upon his bare knees and laughed, as a Scout should, without noise.

He thanked Mr Marsh next morning for the interest he had shown in the camp, and suggested (this was while he was buying many very solid buns for a route-march) that nothing would delight the Pelicans more than a few words from Mr Marsh on the subject of cookery, if he could see his way to it.

'Quite so,' said Mr Marsh. '*I'm* worth listenin' to. Well! Well! I'll be along this evening, and, maybe, I'll bring some odds an' ends with me. Send over young Sherlock-Glasse to 'elp me fetch 'em. *That*'s a boy with 'is stummick in the proper place. Know anything about 'im?'

Mr Hale knew a good deal, but he did not tell it all. He suggested that William himself should be approached, and would excuse him from the route-march for that purpose.

'Route-march!' said Mr Marsh in horror. 'Lor'! The very worst use you can make of your feet is walkin' on 'em. Gives you bunions. Besides, 'e ain't got the figure for marches. 'E's a cook by build as well as instinck. 'Eavy in the run, oily in the skin, broad in the beam, short in the arm, *but*, mark you, light on the feet. That's the way cooks ought to be issued. You never 'eard of a really good *thin* cook yet, did you? No. Nor me. An' I've known millions that called 'emselves cooks.'

Mr Hale regretted that he had not studied the natural history of cooks, and sent William over early in the day.

Mr Marsh spoke to the Pelicans for an hour that evening beside an open wood fire, from the ashes of which he drew forth (talking all the while) wonderful hot cakes called 'dampers'; while from its top he drew off pans full of 'lobscouse', which he said was not to be confounded with 'salmagundi',[11] and a hair-raising compound of bacon, cheese, and onions all melted together. And while the Pelicans ate, he convulsed them with mirth or held them breathless with anecdotes of the High Seas and the World, so that the vote of thanks they passed him at the end waked all the cows in the Park. But William sat wrapped in visions, his hands twitching sympathetically to Mr Marsh's wizardry among the pots and pans. He knew now what the name of Glasse signified; for he had spent an hour at the back of the baker's shop reading in a brown-leather book dated AD 1767 and called *The Art of Cookery Made Plain and Easy by a Lady*, and that lady's name, as it appeared in facsimile at the head of Chap. I, was 'H. Glasse'. Torture would not have persuaded him (or Mr Marsh), by that time, that she was not his direct ancestress; but, as a matter of form, he intended to ask his uncle.

When The Prawn, very grateful that Mr Marsh had made no reference to his notions of cookery, asked William what he thought of the lecture and exhibition, William came out of his dreams with a start, and 'Oh, all right, I suppose, but I wasn't listening much.' Then The Prawn, who always improved an occasion, lectured him on lack of attention; and William missed all that too. The question in his mind was whether his uncle would let him stay with Mr Marsh for a couple of days after Camp broke up, or whether he would use the reply-paid telegram, which Mr Marsh had sent him, for his own French-polishing concerns. When The Prawn's voice ceased, he not only promised to do better next time, but added, out of a vast and inexplicable pity that suddenly rose up inside him, 'And I'm grateful to you, Prawn. I am reelly.'

On his return to Town from that wonder-revealing visit, he found the Pelicans treating him with a new respect. For one thing, The Walrus had talked about the bacon and eggs; for another, The Prawn, who when he let himself go could be really funny, had given some artistic imitations of Mr Marsh's comments on his cookery. Lastly, Mr Hale had laid down that William's future employ would be to cook for the Pelicans when they camped abroad. 'And look out that you don't poison us too much,' he added.

There were occasional mistakes and some very flat failures, but the Pelicans swallowed them all loyally; no one had even a stomach-ache, and the office of Cook's mate to William was in great demand. The Prawn himself sought it next spring when the Troop stole a couple of fair May days on the outskirts of a brick-field, and were very happy. But William set him aside in favour of a new and specially hopeless recruit; oily-skinned, fat, short-armed, but light on his feet, and with some notion of lifting pot-lids without wrecking or flooding the whole fireplace.

'You see, Prawn,' he explained, 'cookin' isn't a thing one can just pick up.'

'Yes, I could – watchin' you,' The Prawn insisted.

'No. Mr Marsh says it's a Gift – same as a Talent.'

'D'you mean to tell me Rickworth's got it, then?'

'Dunno. It's *my* job to find that out – Mr Marsh says. Anyway, Rickworth told me he liked cleaning out a fryin'-pan because it made him think of what it might be cookin' next time.'

'Well, if that isn't silliness, it's just greediness,' said The Prawn. 'What about those dampers you were talking of when I bought the fire-lighters for you this morning?'

William drew one out of the ashes, tapped it lightly with his small hazel-wand of office, and slid it over, puffed and perfect, towards The Prawn.

Once again the wave of pity – the Master's pity for the mere consuming Public – swept over him as he watched The Prawn wolf it down.

'I'm grateful to you. I reely *am*, Prawn,' said William Glasse Sawyer.

After all, as he was used to say in later years, if it hadn't been for The Prawn, where would he have been?

THE WISH HOUSE

The new church visitor had just left after a twenty minutes' call. During that time, Mrs Ashcroft had used such English as an elderly, experienced, and pensioned cook should, who had seen life in London. She was the readier, therefore, to slip back into easy, ancient Sussex ('t's softening to 'd's as one warmed) when the 'bus brought Mrs Fettley from thirty miles away for a visit, that pleasant March Saturday. The two had been friends since childhood, but, of late, destiny had separated their meetings by long intervals.

Much was to be said, and many ends, loose since last time, to be ravelled up on both sides, before Mrs Fettley, with her bag of quilt-patches, took the couch beneath the window commanding the garden, and the football-ground in the valley below.

'Most folk got out at Bush Tye for the match there,' she explained, 'so there weren't no one for me to cushion agin, the last five mile. An' she *do* just-about bounce ye.'

'You've took no hurt,' said her hostess. 'You don't brittle by agein', Liz.'

Mrs Fettley chuckled and made to match a couple of patches to her liking. 'No, or I'd ha' broke twenty year back. You can't ever mind when I was so's to be called round, can ye?'

Mrs Ashcroft shook her head slowly – she never hurried – and went on stitching a sack-cloth lining into a list-bound rush tool-basket. Mrs Fettley laid out more patches in the spring light through the geraniums on the window-sill, and they were silent a while.

'What like's this new Visitor o' yourn?' Mrs Fettley inquired, with a nod towards the door. Being very short-sighted, she had, on her entrance, almost bumped into the lady.

Mrs Ashcroft suspended the big packing-needle judicially on high, ere she stabbed home. 'Settin' aside she don't bring much news with her yet, I dunno as I've anythin' special agin her.'

'Ourn, at Keyneslade,' said Mrs Fettley, 'she's full o' words an' pity, but she don't stay for answers. Ye can get on with your thoughts while she clacks.'

'This 'un don't clack. She's aimin' to be one o' those High Church nuns, like.'

'Ourn's married, but, by what they say, she've made no great gains of it . . . ' Mrs Fettley threw up her sharp chin. 'Lord! How they dam' cherubim do shake the very bones o' the place!'

The tile-sided cottage trembled at the passage of two specially chartered forty-seat charabancs on their way to the Bush Tye match; a regular Saturday 'shopping' 'bus, for the county's capital, fumed behind them; while, from one of the crowded inns, a fourth car backed out to join the procession, and held up the stream of through pleasure-traffic.

'You're as free-tongued as ever, Liz,' Mrs Ashcroft observed.

'Only when I'm with you. Otherwhiles, I'm Granny – three times over. I lay that basket's for one o' your gran'chiller – ain't it?'

''Tis for Arthur – my Jane's eldest.'

'But he ain't workin' nowheres, is he?'

'No. 'Tis a picnic-basket.'

'You're let off light. My Willie, he's allus at me for money for them aireated wash-poles[1] folk puts up in their gardens to draw the music from Lunnon, like. An' I give it 'im – pore fool me!'

'An' he forgets to give you the promise-kiss after, don't he?' Mrs Ashcroft's heavy smile seemed to strike inwards.

'He do. No odds 'twixt boys now an' forty year back. Take all an' give naught – an we to put up with it! Pore fool we! Three shillin' at a time Willie'll ask me for!'

'They don't make nothin' o' money these days,' Mrs Ashcroft said.

'An' on'y last week,' the other went on, 'me daughter she ordered a quarter-pound suet at the butchers's; an' she sent it back to 'im to be chopped. She said she couldn't bother with choppin' it.'

'I lay he charged her, then.'

'I lay he did. She told me there was a whisk-drive[2] that afternoon at the Institute, an' she couldn't bother to do the choppin'.'

'Tck!'

Mrs Ashcroft put the last firm touches to the basket-lining. She had scarcely finished when her sixteen-year-old grandson, a maiden of the moment in attendance, hurried up the garden-path shouting to know if the thing were ready, snatched it, and made off without acknowledgment. Mrs Fettley peered at him closely.

'They're goin' picnickin' somewheres,' Mrs Ashcroft explained.

'Ah,' said the other, with narrowed eyes. 'I lay *he* won't show much mercy to any he comes across, either. Now 'oo the dooce do he remind me of, all of a sudden?'

'They must look arter theirselves – same as we did.' Mrs Ashcroft began to set out the tea.

'No denyin' *you* could, Gracie,' said Mrs Fettley.

'What's in your head now?'

'Dunno . . . But it come over me, sudden-like – about dat woman from Rye – I've slipped the name – Barnsley, wadn't it?'

'Batten – Polly Batten, you're thinkin' of.'

'That's it – Polly Batten. That day she had it in for you with a hay-fork – time we was all hayin' at Smalldene – for stealin' her man.'

'But you heered me tell her she had my leave to keep him?' Mrs Ashcroft's voice and smile were smoother than ever.

'I did – an' we was all looking that she'd prod the fork spang through your breastës when you said it.'

'No-oo. She'd never go beyond bounds – Polly. She shruck[3] too much for reel doin's.'

'Allus seems to *me*,' Mrs Fettley said after a pause, 'that a man 'twixt two fightin' women is the foolishest thing on earth. Like a dog bein' called two ways.'

'Mebbe. But what set ye off on those times, Liz?'

'That boy's fashion o' carryin' his head an' arms. I haven't rightly looked at him since he's growed. Your Jane never showed it, but – *him*! Why, 'tis Jim Batten and his tricks come to life again! . . . Eh?'

'Mebbe. There's some that would ha' made it out so – bein' barren-like, themselves.'

'Oho! Ah well! Dearie, dearie me, now! . . . An' Jim Batten's been dead this –'

'Seven-and-twenty year,' Mrs Ashcroft answered briefly. 'Won't ye draw up, Liz?'

Mrs Fettley drew up to buttered toast, currant bread, stewed tea, bitter as leather, some home-preserved pears, and a cold boiled pig's tail to help down the muffins. She paid all the proper compliments.

'Yes. I dunno as I've ever owed me belly much,' said Mrs Ashcroft thoughtfully. 'We only go through this world once.'

'But don't it lay heavy on ye, sometimes?' her guest suggested.

'Nurse says I'm a sight liker to die o' me indigestion than me leg.' For Mrs Ashcroft had a long-standing ulcer on her shin,[4] which needed regular care from the Village Nurse, who boasted (or others did, for her) that she had dressed it one hundred and three times already during her term of office.

'An' you that *was* so able, too! It's all come on ye before your full time, like. I've watched ye goin'.' Mrs Fettley spoke with real affection.

'Somethin's bound to find ye sometime. I've me 'eart left me still,' Mrs Ashcroft returned.

'You was always big-hearted enough for three. That's somethin' to look back on at the day's eend.'

'I reckon you've *your* back-lookin's, too,' was Mrs Ashcroft's answer.

'You know it. But I don't think much regardin' such matters excep' when I'm along with you, Gra'. Takes two sticks to make a fire.'

Mrs Fettley stared, with jaw half-dropped, at the grocer's bright calendar on the wall. The cottage shook again to the roar of the motor-traffic, and the crowded football-ground below the garden roared almost as loudly; for the village was well set to its Saturday leisure.

Mrs Fettley had spoken very precisely for some time without interruption, before she wiped her eyes. 'And,' she concluded, 'they read 'is death-notice to me, out o' the paper last month. O' course it wadn't any o' *my* becomin' concerns – let be I 'adn't set eyes on him for so long. O' course *I* couldn't say nor show nothin'. Nor I've no rightful call to go to Eastbourne to see 'is grave, either. I've been schemin' to slip over there by the 'bus some day; but they'd ask questions at 'ome past endurance. So I 'aven't even *that* to stay me.'

'But you've 'ad your satisfactions?'

'Godd! Yess! Those four years 'e was workin' on the rail near us. An' the other drivers they gave him a brave funeral, too.'

'Then you've naught to cast-up about. 'Nother cup o' tea?'

The light and air had changed a little with the sun's descent, and the two elderly ladies closed the kitchen-door against chill. A couple of jays squealed and skirmished through the undraped apple-trees in the garden. This time, the word was with Mrs Ashcroft, her elbows on the tea-table, and her sick leg propped on a stool . . .

'Well, I never! But what did your 'usband say to that?' Mrs Fettley asked, when the deep-toned recital halted.

"E said I might go where I pleased for all of 'im. But seein' 'e was bedrid, I said I'd 'tend 'im out. 'E knowed I wouldn't take no advantage of 'im in that state. 'E lasted eight or nine week. Then he was took with a seizure-like; an' laid stone-still for days. Then 'e propped 'imself up abed an' says: "You pray no man'll ever deal with you like you've dealed with some." "An' you?" I says, for *you* know, Liz, what a rover 'e was. "It cuts both ways," says 'e, "but I'm death-wise, an' I can see what's comin' to you." He died a-Sunday an' was buried a-Thursday . . . An' yet I'd set a heap by him – one time, or – did I ever?'

'You never told me that before,' Mrs Fettley ventured.

'I'm payin' ye for what ye told me just now. Him bein' dead, I wrote up, sayin' I was free for good, to that Mrs Marshall in Lunnon – which gave me my first place as kitchen-maid – Lord, how long ago! She was well pleased, for they two was both gettin' on, an' I knowed their ways. You remember, Liz, I used to go to 'em in service between whiles, for years – when we wanted money, or – or my 'usband was away – on occasion.'

''E *did* get that six months at Chichester, didn't 'e?' Mrs Fettley whispered. 'We never rightly won to the bottom of it.'

''E'd ha' got more, but the man didn't die.'

'None o' your doin's, was it, Gra'?'

'No! 'Twas the woman's 'usband this time. An' so, my man bein' dead, I went back to them Marshalls, as cook, to get me legs under a gentleman's table again, and be called with a handle to me name.[5] That was the year you shifted to Portsmouth.'

'Cosham,' Mrs Fettley corrected. 'There was a middlin' lot o' new buildin' bein' done there. My man went first, an' got the room, an' I follered.'

'Well, then, I was a year-abouts in Lunnon, all at a breath, like, four meals a day an' livin' easy. Then, 'long towards autumn, they two went travellin', like, to France; keepin' me on, for they couldn't do without me. I put the house to rights for the caretaker, an' then I slipped down 'ere to me sister Bessie – me wages in me pockets, an' all 'ands glad to be 'old of me.'

'That would be when I was at Cosham,' said Mrs Fettley.

'*You* know, Liz, there wasn't no cheap-dog pride to folk, those days, no more than there was cinemas nor whisk-drives. Man or woman 'ud lay hold o' any job that promised a shillin' to the backside of it, didn't they? I was all peaked up after Lunnon, an' I thought the fresh airs 'ud serve me. So I took on at Smalldene, obligin' with a hand at the early potato-liftin', stubbin' hens,[6] an' such-like. They'd ha' mocked me sore in my kitchen in Lunnon, to see me in men's boots, an' me petticoats all shorted.'

'Did it bring ye any good?' Mrs Fettley asked.

''Twadn't for that I went. You know, 's well 's me, that na'un happens to ye till it *'as* 'appened. Your mind don't warn ye before 'and of the road ye've took, till you're at the far eend of it. We've only a backwent view of our proceedin's.'

''Oo was it?'

''Arry Mockler.' Mrs Ashcroft's face puckered to the pain of her sick leg.

Mrs Fettley gasped. ''Arry? Bert Mockler's son! An' *I* never guessed!'

Mrs Ashcroft nodded. 'An' I told myself – *an'* I beleft it – that I wanted field-work.'

'What did ye get out of it?'

'The usuals. Everythin' at first – worse than naught after. I had signs an' warnings a-plenty, but I took no heed of 'em. For we was burnin' rubbish one day, just when we'd come to know how 'twas with – with both of us. 'Twas early in the year for burnin', an' I said so. "No!" says he. "The sooner dat old stuff's off an' done with,"' he says, "the better." 'Is face was harder'n rocks when he spoke. Then it come over me that I'd found me master, which I 'adn't ever before. I'd allus owned 'em, like.'

'Yes! Yes! They're yourn or you're theirn,' the other sighed. 'I like the right way best.'

'I didn't. But 'Arry did . . . 'Long then, it come time for me to go back to Lunnon. I couldn't. I clean couldn't! So I took an' tipped a dollop o' scaldin' water out o' the copper one Monday mornin' over me left 'and and arm. Dat stayed me where I was for another fortnight.'

'Was it worth it?' said Mrs Fettley, looking at the silvery scar on the wrinkled fore-arm.

Mrs Ashcroft nodded. 'An' after that, we two made it up 'twixt us so's 'e could come to Lunnon for a job in a liv'ry-stable not far from me. 'E got it. *I* 'tended to that. There wadn't no talk nowhere. His own mother never suspicioned how 'twas. He just slipped up to Lunnon, an' there we abode that winter, not 'alf a mile 'tother from each.'

'Ye paid 'is fare an' all, though.' Mrs Fettley spoke convincedly.

Again Mrs Ashcroft nodded. 'Dere wadn't much I didn't do for him. 'E was me master, an' – O God, help us! – we'd laugh over it walkin' together after dark in them paved streets, an' me corns fair wrenchin' in me boots! I'd never been like that before. Ner he! Ner he!'

Mrs Fettley clucked sympathetically.

'An' when did ye come to the eend?' she asked.

'When 'e paid it all back again, every penny. Then I knowed, but I wouldn't *suffer* meself to know. "You've been mortal kind to me," he says. "Kind!" I said. "'Twixt *us?*" But 'e kep' all on tellin' me 'ow kind I'd been an' 'e'd never forget it all his days. I held it from off o' me for three evenin's, because I would *not* believe. Then 'e talked about not bein' satisfied with 'is job in the stables, an' the men there puttin' tricks on 'im, an' all they lies which a man tells when 'e's leavin' ye. I heard 'im out, neither 'elpin' nor 'inderin'. At the last, I took off a liddle brooch which he'd give me an' I says: "Dat'll do. *I* ain't askin' na'un." An' I turned me round an' walked off to me own sufferin's. 'E didn't make 'em worse. 'E didn't come nor write after that. 'E slipped off 'ere back 'ome to 'is mother again.'

'An' 'ow often did ye look for 'en to come back?' Mrs Fettley demanded mercilessly.

'More'n once – more'n once! Goin' over the streets we'd used, I thought de very pave-stones 'ud shruck out under me feet.'

'Yes,' said Mrs Fettley. 'I dunno but dat don't 'urt as much as aught else. An' dat was all ye got?'

'No. 'Twadn't. That's the curious part, if you'll believe it, Liz.'

'I do. I lay you're further off lyin' now than in all your life, Gra'.'

'I am . . . An' I suffered, like I'd not wish my most arrantest enemies to. God's Own Name! I went through the hoop that spring! One part of it was 'eddicks which I'd never known all me days before. Think o' *me* with an 'eddick! But I come to be grateful for 'em. They kep' me from thinkin' . . .'

''Tis like a tooth,' Mrs Fettley commented. 'It must rage an' rugg[7] till it tortures itself quiet on ye; an' then – then there's na'un left.'

'*I* got enough lef' to last me all *my* days on earth. It come about through our charwoman's liddle girl – Sophy Ellis was 'er name – all eyes an' elbers an' hunger. I used to give 'er vittles. Otherwiles, I took no special notice of 'er, an' a sight less, o' course, when me trouble about 'Arry was on me. But – you know how liddle maids first feel it sometimes – she come to be crazy-fond o' me, pawin' an' cuddlin' all whiles; an' I 'adn't the 'eart to beat 'er off . . . One afternoon, early in spring 'twas, 'er mother 'ad sent 'er round to scutchel up[8] what vittles she could off of us. I was settin' by the fire, me apern over me head, half-mad with the 'eddick, when she slips in. I reckon I was middlin' short with 'er. "Lor'!" she says. "Is *that* all? I'll take it off you in two-twos!" I told her not to lay a finger on me, for I thought she'd want to stroke my forehead; an' – I ain't that make. "I won't tech ye," she says, an' slips out again. She 'adn't been gone ten minutes 'fore me old 'eddick took off quick as bein' kicked. So I went about my work. Prasin'ly, Sophy comes back, an' creeps into my chair quiet as a mouse. 'Er eyes was deep in 'er 'ead an' 'er face all drawed. I asked 'er what 'ad 'appened. "Nothin'," she says. "On'y I've got it now." "Got what?" I says. "Your 'eddick," she says, all hoarse an' sticky-lipped. "I've took it on me." "Nonsense," I says, "it went of itself when you was out. Lay still an' I'll make ye a cup o' tea." "'Twon't do no good," she says, "till your time's up. 'Ow long do *your* 'eddicks last?" "Don't talk silly," I says, "or I'll send for the Doctor." It looked to me like she might be hatchin' de measles. "Oh, Mrs Ashcroft," she says, stretchin' out 'er liddle thin arms. "I *do* love ye." There wasn't any holdin' again that. I took 'er into me lap an' made much of 'er. "Is it truly gone?" she says. "Yes," I says, "an' if 'twas you took it away, I'm truly grateful." "'*Twas* me," she says, layin' 'er cheek to mine. "No one but me knows how." An' then she said she'd changed me 'eddick for me at a Wish 'Ouse.'

'Whatt?' Mrs Fettley spoke sharply.

'A Wish House. No! I 'adn't 'eard o' such things, either. I couldn't get it straight at first, but, puttin' all together, I made out that a Wish 'Ouse 'ad to be a house which 'ad stood unlet an' empty long enough for Some One, like, to come an' in'abit there. She said a liddle girl that she'd played with in the livery-stables where 'Arry worked 'ad told 'er so. She said the girl 'ad belonged in a caravan that laid up, o' winters, in Lunnon. Gipsy, I judge.'

'Ooh! There's no sayin' what Gippos know, but I've never 'eard of a Wish 'Ouse, an' I know – some things,' said Mrs Fettley.

'Sophy said there was a Wish 'Ouse in Wadloes Road – just a few streets off, on the way to our green-grocer's. All you 'ad to do, she said, was to ring the bell an' wish your wish through the slit o' the letter-box. I asked 'er if the fairies give it 'er. "Don't ye know," she says, "there's no fairies in a Wish 'Ouse? There's on'y a Token."'

'Goo' Lord A'mighty! Where did she come by *that* word?' cried Mrs Fettley; for a Token is a wraith of the dead or, worse still, of the living.

'The caravan-girl 'ad told 'er, she said. Well, Liz, it troubled me to 'ear 'er, an' lyin' in me arms she must ha' felt it. "That's very kind o' you," I says, holdin' 'er tight, "to wish me 'eddick away. But why didn't ye ask somethin' nice for yourself?" "You can't do that," she says. "All you'll get at a Wish 'Ouse is leave to take someone else's trouble. I've took Ma's 'eddicks, when she's been kind to me; but this is the first time I've been able to do aught for you. Oh, *Mrs* Ashcroft, I *do* justabout love you." An' she goes on all like that. Liz, I tell you my 'air e'en a'most stood on end to 'ear 'er. I asked 'er what like a Token was. "I dunno," she says, "but after you've ringed the bell, you'll 'ear it run up from the basement, to the front door. Then say your wish," she says, "an' go away." "The Token don't open de door to ye, then?" I says. "Oh no," she says. "You on'y 'ear gigglin', like, be'ind the front door. Then you say you'll take the trouble off of 'ooever 'tis you've chose for your love; an' ye'll get it," she says. I didn't ask no more – she was too 'ot an' fevered. I made much of 'er till it come time to light de gas, an' a liddle after that 'er 'eddick – mine, I suppose – took off, an' she got down an' played with the cat.'

'Well, I never!' said Mrs Fettley. 'Did – did ye foller it up, anyways?'

'She askt me to, but I wouldn't 'ave no such dealin's with a child.'

'What *did* ye do, then?'

'Sat in me own room 'stid o the kitchen when me 'eddicks come on. But it lay at de back o' me mind.'

''Twould. Did she tell ye more, ever?'

'No. Besides what the Gippo girl 'ad told 'er, she knew naught, 'cept that the charm worked. An', next after that – in May 'twas – I suffered the summer out in Lunnon. 'Twas hot an' windy for weeks, an' the streets stinkin' o' dried 'orse-dung blowin' from side to side an' lyin' level with the kerb. We don't get that nowadays. I 'ad my 'ol'day just before hoppin',*[9] an' come down 'ere to stay with Bessie again. She noticed I'd lost flesh, an' was all poochy under the eyes.'

'Did ye see 'Arry?'

Mrs Ashcroft nodded. 'The fourth – no, the fifth day. Wednesday 'twas. I knowed 'e was workin' at Smalldene again. I asked 'is mother in the street, bold as brass. She 'adn't room to say much, for Bessie – you know 'er tongue – was talkin' full-clack. But that Wednesday, I was walkin' with one o' Bessie's chillern hangin' on me skirts, at de back o' Chanter's Tot. Prasin'ly, I felt 'e was be'ind me on the footpath, an' I knowed by 'is tread 'e'd changed 'is nature. I slowed, an' I heard 'im slow. Then I fussed a piece with the child, to force him past me, like. So 'e *'ad* to come past. 'E just says "Good-evenin'," and goes on, tryin' to pull 'isself together.'

'Drunk, was he?' Mrs Fettley asked.

'Never! S'runk an' wizen; 'is clothes 'angin' on 'im like bags, an' the back of 'is neck whiter'n chalk. 'Twas all I could do not to oppen my arms an' cry after him. But I swallered me spittle till I was back 'ome again an' the chillern abed. Then I says to Bessie, after supper, "What in de world's come to 'Arry Mockler?" Bessie told me 'e'd been a-Hospital for two months, 'long o' cuttin' 'is foot wid a spade, muckin' out de old pond at Smalldene. There was poison in de dirt, an' it rooshed up 'is leg, like, an' come out all over him. 'E 'adn't been back to 'is job – carterin' at Smalldene – more'n a fortnight. She told me the Doctor said he'd go off, likely, with the November frostës; an' 'is mother 'ad told 'er that 'e didn't rightly eat nor sleep, an' sweated 'imself into pools, no odds 'ow chill 'e lay. *An'* spit terrible o' mornin's. "Dearie me," I says. "But, mebbe, hoppin' 'll set 'im right again," an' I licked me thread-point, an' I fetched me needle's eye up to it an' I threads me needle under de lamp, steady as rocks. An' dat night (me bed was in de wash-house) I cried an' I cried. An' *you* know, Liz – for you've been

* Hop-picking

with me in me throes – it takes summat to make me cry.'

'Yes; but chile-bearin' is on'y just pain,' said Mrs Fettley.

'I come round by cock-crow, an' dabbed cold tea on me eyes to take away the signs. Long towards nex' evenin' – I was settin' out to lay some flowers on me 'usband's grave, for the look o' the thing – I met 'Arry over against where the War Memorial is now. 'E was comin' back from 'is 'orses, so 'e couldn't *not* see me. I looked 'im all over, an' "'Arry," I says twix' me teeth, "come back an' rest-up in Lunnon." "I won't take it," he says, "for I can give ye naught." "I don't ask it," I says. "By God's Own Name, I don't ask na'un! On'y come up an' see a Lunnon doctor." 'E lifts 'is two 'eavy eyes at me: "'Tis past that, Gra'," 'e says. "I've but a few months left." "'Arry!" I says. "*My* man!" I says. I couldn't say no more. 'Twas all up in me throat. "Thank ye kindly, Gra'," 'e says (but 'e never says "my woman"), an' 'e went on up-street, an' 'is mother – Oh, damn 'er! – she was watchin' for 'im, an' she shut de door be'ind 'im.'

Mrs Fettley stretched an arm across the table, and made to finger Mrs Ashcroft's sleeve at the wrist, but the other moved it out of reach.

'So I went on to the churchyard with me flowers, an' I remembered me 'usband's warnin' that night he spoke. 'E *was* death-wise, an' it 'ad 'appened as 'e said. But as I was settin' down de jam-pot on the grave-mound, it come over me there was one thing I *could* do for 'Arry. Doctor or no Doctor, I thought I'd make a trial of it. So I did. Nex' mornin', a bill came down from our Lunnon greengrocer. Mrs Marshall she'd lef' me petty cash for suchlike – o' course – but I tole Bess 'twas for me to come an' open the 'ouse. So I went up, afternoon train.'

'An' – but I know you 'adn't – 'adn't you no fear?'

'What for? There was nothin' front o' me but me own shame an' God's croolty. I couldn't ever get 'Arry – 'ow *could* I? I knowed it must go on burnin' till it burned me out.'

'Aie!' said Mrs Fettley, reaching for the wrist again, and this time Mrs Ashcroft permitted it.

'Yit 'twas a comfort to know I could try *this* for 'im. So I went an' I paid the greengrocer's bill, an' put 'is receipt in me hand-bag, an' then I stepped round to Mrs Ellis – our char – an' got the 'ouse-keys an' opened the 'ouse. First, I made me bed to come back to (God's Own Name! Me bed to lie upon!). Nex' I made me a cup o' tea an' sat down in the kitchen thinkin', till 'long towards dusk. Terrible close, 'twas. Then I dressed me an' went out with the receipt in me 'and-bag, feignin' to study it for an address, like. Fourteen, Wadloes Road, was the place – a liddle basement-kitchen 'ouse, in a row of twenty-thirty such, an'

tiddy strips o' walled garden in front – the paint off the front doors,
an' na'un done to na'un since ever so long. There wasn't 'ardly no one
in the streets 'cept the cats. *'Twas* 'ot, too! I turned into the gate bold
as brass; up de steps I went an' I ringed the front-door bell. She pealed
loud, like it do in an empty house. When she'd all ceased, I 'eard a cheer,
like, pushed back on de floor o' the kitchen. Then I 'eard feet on de
kitchen-stairs, like it might ha' been a heavy woman in slippers. Dey
come up to de stair-head, acrost the hall – I 'eard the bare boards creak
under 'em – an' at de front door dey stopped. I stooped me to the
letter-box slit, an' I says: "Let me take everythin' bad that's in store for
my man, 'Arry Mockler, for love's sake." Then, whatever it was 'tother
side the door let its breath out, like, as if it 'ad been holdin' it for to
'ear better.'

'Nothin' was *said* to ye?' Mrs Fettley demanded.

'Na'un. She just breathed out – a sort of *A-ah*, like. Then the steps
went back an' downstairs to the kitchen – all draggy – an' I heard the
cheer drawed up again.'

'An' you abode on de doorstep, throughout all, Gra'?'

Mrs Ashcroft nodded.

'Then I went away, an' a man passin' says to me: "Didn't you know
that house was empty?" "No," I says. "I must ha' been give the wrong
number." An' I went back to our 'ouse, an' I went to bed; for I was fair
flogged out. 'Twas too 'ot to sleep more'n snatches, so I walked me
about, layin' down betweens, till crack o' dawn. Then I went to the
kitchen to make me a cup o' tea, an' I hitted meself just above the ankle
on an old roastin'-jack[10] o' mine that Mrs Ellis had moved out from
the corner, her last cleanin'. An' so – nex' after that – I waited till the
Marshalls come back o' their holiday.'

'Alone there? I'd ha' thought you'd 'ad enough of empty houses,'
said Mrs Fettley, horrified.

'Oh, Mrs Ellis an' Sophy was runnin' in an' out soon's I was back,
an' 'twixt us we cleaned de house again top-to-bottom. There's allus a
hand's turn more to do in every house. An' that's 'ow 'twas with me
that autumn an' winter, in Lunnon.'

'Then na'un hap – overtook ye for your doin's?'

Mrs Ashcroft smiled. 'No. Not then. 'Long in November I sent Bessie
ten shillin's.'

'You was allus free-'anded,' Mrs Fettley interrupted.

'An' I got what I paid for, with the rest o' the news. She said the
hoppin' 'ad set 'im up wonderful. 'E'd 'ad six weeks of it, and now 'e
was back again carterin' at Smalldene. No odds to me *'ow* it 'ad
'appened – 's long's it *'ad*. But I dunno as my ten shillin's eased me

much. 'Arry bein' *dead*, like, 'e'd ha' been mine, till Judgment. 'Arry
bein' alive, 'e'd like as not pick up with some woman middlin' quick.
I raged over that. Come spring, I 'ad somethin' else to rage for. I'd
growed a nasty little weepin' boil, like, on me shin, just above the boot-
top, that wouldn't heal no shape. It made me sick to look at it, for I'm
clean-fleshed by nature. Chop me all over with a spade, an' I'd heal
like turf. Then Mrs Marshall she set 'er own doctor at me. 'E said I
ought to ha' come to him at first go-off, 'stead o' drawin' all manner
o' dyed stockin's over it for months. 'E said I'd stood up too much to
me work,[11] for it was settin' very close atop of a big swelled vein, like,
behither the small o' me ankle. "Slow come, slow go," 'e says. "Lay
your leg up on high an' rest it," he says, "an' 'twill ease off. Don't let
it close up too soon. You've got a very fine leg, Mrs Ashcroft," 'e says.
An' he put wet dressin's on it.'

''E done right.' Mrs Fettley spoke firmly. 'Wet dressin's to wet
wounds. They draw de humours, same's a lamp-wick draws de oil.'

'That's true. An' Mrs Marshall was allus at me to make me set down
more, an' dat nigh healed it up. An' then after a while they packed me
off down to Bessie's to finish the cure; for I ain't the sort to sit down
when I ought to stand up. You was back in the village then, Liz.'

'I was. I was, but – never did I guess!'

'I didn't desire ye to.' Mrs Ashcroft smiled. 'I saw 'Arry once or twice
in de street, wonnerful fleshed up an' restored back. Then, one day I
didn't see 'im, an' 'is mother told me one of 'is 'orses 'ad lashed out an'
caught 'im on the 'ip. So 'e was abed an' middlin' painful. An' Bessie,
she says to his mother, 'twas a pity 'Arry 'adn't a woman of 'is own to
take the nursin' off 'er. And the old lady *was* mad! She told us that 'Arry
'ad never looked after any woman in 'is born days, an' as long as she
was atop the mowlds, she'd contrive for 'im till 'er two 'ands dropped
off. So I knowed she'd do watch-dog for me, 'thout askin' for bones.'

Mrs Fettley rocked with small laughter.

'That day,' Mrs Ashcroft went on, 'I'd stood on me feet nigh all the
time, watchin' the doctor go in an' out; for they thought it might be 'is
ribs, too. That made my boil break again, issuin' an' weepin'. But it
turned out 'twadn't ribs at all, an' 'Arry 'ad a good night. When I heard
that, nex' mornin', I says to meself, "I won't lay two an' two together
yit. I'll keep me leg down a week, an' see what comes of it." It didn't
hurt me that day, to speak of – seemed more to draw the strength out
o' me like – an' 'Arry 'ad another good night. That made me persevere;
but I didn't dare lay two an' two together till the week-end, an' then,
'Arry come forth e'en a'most 'imself again – na'un hurt outside ner in
of him. I nigh fell on me knees in de wash-house when Bessie was

upstreet. "I've got ye now, my man," I says. "You'll take your good from me 'thout knowin' it till my life's end. O God, send me long to live for 'Arry's sake!" I says. An' I dunno that didn't still me ragin's.'

'For good?' Mrs Fettley asked.

'They come back, plenty times, but, let be how 'twould, I knowed I was doin' for 'im. I *knowed* it. I took an' worked me pains on an' off, like regulatin' me own range, till I learned to 'ave 'em at my commandments. An' that was funny, too. There was times, Liz, when my trouble 'ud all s'rink an' dry up, like. First, I used to try an' fetch it on again; bein' fearful to leave 'Arry alone too long for anythin' to lay 'old of. Prasin'ly I come to see that was a sign he'd do all right awhile, an' so I saved myself.'

''Ow long for?' Mrs Fettley asked, with deepest interest.

'I've gone de better part of a year onct or twice with na'un more to show than the liddle weepin' core of it, like. *All* s'rinked up an' dried off. Then he'd inflame up – for a warnin' – an' I'd suffer it. When I couldn't no more – an' I *ad* to keep on goin' with my Lunnon work – I'd lay me leg high on a cheer till it eased. Not too quick. I knowed by the feel of it, those times, dat 'Arry was in need. Then I'd send another five shillin's to Bess, or somethin' for the chillern, to find out if, mebbe, 'e'd took any hurt through my neglects. 'Twas *so*! Year in, year out, I worked it dat way, Liz, an' 'e got 'is good from me 'thout knowin' – for years and years.'

'But what did *you* get out of it, Gra'?' Mrs Fettley almost wailed. 'Did ye see 'im reg'lar?'

'Times – when I was 'ere on me 'ol'days. An' more, now that I'm 'ere for good. But 'e's never looked at me, ner any other woman 'cept 'is mother. 'Ow I used to watch an' listen! So did she.'

'Years an' years!' Mrs Fettley repeated. 'An' where's 'e workin' at now?'

'Oh, 'e's give up carterin' quite a while. He's workin' for one o' them big tractorisin' firms – plowin' sometimes, an' sometimes off with lorries – fur as Wales, I've 'eard. He comes 'ome to 'is mother 'tween whiles; but I don't set eyes on him now, fer weeks on end. No odds! 'Is job keeps 'im from continuin' in one stay anywheres.'

'But – just for de sake o' sayin' somethin' – s'pose 'Arry *did* get married?' said Mrs Fettley.

Mrs Ashcroft drew her breath sharply between her still even and natural teeth. '*Dat* ain't been required of me,' she answered. 'I reckon my pains 'ull be counted agin that. Don't *you*, Liz?'

'It ought to be, dearie. It ought to be.'

'It *do* 'urt sometimes. You shall see it when Nurse comes. She thinks I don't know it's turned.'

Mrs Fettley understood. Human nature seldom walks up to the word 'cancer'.

'Be ye certain sure, Gra'?' she asked.

'I was sure of it when old Mr Marshall 'ad me up to 'is study an' spoke a long piece about my faithful service. I've obliged 'em on an' off for a goodish time, but not enough for a pension. But they give me a weekly 'lowance for life. I knew what *that* sinnified – as long as three years ago.'

'Dat don't *prove* it, Gra'.'

'To give fifteen bob a week[12] to a woman 'oo'd live twenty year in the course o' nature? It *do*!'

'You're mistook! You're mistook!' Mrs Fettley insisted.

'Liz, there's *no* mistakin' when the edges are all heaped up,[13] like – same as a collar. You'll see it. An' I laid out Dora Wickwood, too. *She* 'ad it under the arm-pit, like.'

Mrs Fettley considered awhile, and bowed her head in finality.

"Ow long d'you reckon 'twill allow ye, countin' from now, dearie?'

'Slow come, slow go. But if I don't set eyes on ye 'fore next hoppin', this'll be good-bye, Liz.'

'Dunno as I'll be able to manage by then – not 'thout I have a liddle dog to lead me. For de chillern, dey won't be troubled, an' – O Gra'! – I'm blindin' up – I'm blindin' up!'

'Oh, *dat* was why you didn't more'n finger with your quilt-patches all this while! I was wonderin' . . . But the pain *do* count, don't ye think, Liz? The pain *do* count to keep 'Arry – where I want 'im. Say it can't be wasted, like.'

'I'm sure of it – sure of it, dearie. You'll 'ave your reward.'

'I don't want no more'n this – *if* de pain is taken into de reckonin'.'

"Twill be – 'twill be, Gra'.'

There was a knock on the door.

'That's Nurse. She's before 'er time,' said Mrs Ashcroft. 'Open to 'er.'

The young lady entered briskly, all the bottles in her bag clicking. 'Evenin', Mrs Ashcroft,' she began. 'I've come raound a little earlier than usual because of the Institute dance to-na-ite. You won't ma-ind, will you?'

'Oh no. Me dancin' days are over.' Mrs Ashcroft was the self-contained domestic at once. 'My old friend, Mrs Fettley 'ere, has been settin' talkin' with me a while.'

'I hope she 'asn't been fatiguing you,' said the Nurse a little frostily.

'Quite the contrary. It 'as been a pleasure. Only – only – just at the end I felt a bit – a bit flogged out, like.'

'Yes, yes.' The Nurse was on her knees already, with the washes to hand. 'When old ladies get together they talk a deal too much, I've noticed.'

'Mebbe we do,' said Mrs Fettley, rising. 'So now I'll make myself scarce.'

'Look at it first, though,' said Mrs Ashcroft feebly. 'I'd like ye to look at it.'

Mrs Fettley looked, and shivered. Then she leaned over, and kissed Mrs Ashcroft once on the waxy yellow forehead, and again on the faded grey eyes.

'It *do* count, don't it – de pain?' The lips that still kept trace of their original moulding hardly more than breathed the words.

Mrs Fettley kissed them and moved toward the door.

THE GARDENER

One grave to me was given,
   One watch till Judgment Day;
And God looked down from Heaven
   And rolled the stone away.

One day in all the years,
   One hour in that one day,
His Angel saw my tears,
   And rolled the stone away![1]

Everyone in the village knew that Helen Turrell did her duty by all her world, and by none more honourably than by her only brother's unfortunate child. The village knew, too, that George Turrell had tried his family severely since early youth, and were not surprised to be told that, after many fresh starts given and thrown away, he, an Inspector of Indian Police, had entangled himself with the daughter of a retired non-commissioned officer, and had died of a fall from a horse a few weeks before his child was born. Mercifully, George's father and mother were both dead, and though Helen, thirty-five and independent, might well have washed her hands of the whole disgraceful affair, she most nobly took charge, though she was, at the time, under threat of lung trouble which had driven her to the South of France. She arranged for the passage of the child and a nurse from Bombay, met them at Marseilles, nursed the baby through an attack of infantile dysentery due to the carelessness of the nurse, whom she had had to dismiss, and at last, thin and worn but triumphant, brought the boy late in the autumn, wholly restored, to her Hampshire home.

All these details were public property, for Helen was as open as the day, and held that scandals are only increased by hushing them up. She admitted that George had always been rather a black sheep, but things might have been much worse if the mother had insisted on her right to keep the boy. Luckily, it seemed that people of that class would do almost anything for money, and, as George had always turned to her in his scrapes, she felt herself justified – her friends agreed with her – in cutting the whole non-commissioned officer connection, and giving the child every advantage. A christening, by the Rector, under the name of Michael, was the first step. So far as she knew herself, she was not, she said, a child-lover, but, for all his faults, she had been very fond of George, and she pointed out that little Michael had his father's mouth to a line; which made something to build upon.

As a matter of fact, it was the Turrell forehead, broad, low, and well-shaped, with the widely spaced eyes beneath it, that Michael had most faithfully reproduced. His mouth was somewhat better cut than the family type. But Helen, who would concede nothing good to his mother's side, vowed he was a Turrell all over, and, there being no one to contradict, the likeness was established.

In a few years Michael took his place, as accepted as Helen had always been – fearless, philosophical, and fairly good-looking. At six, he wished to know why he could not call her 'Mummy', as other boys called their mothers. She explained that she was only his auntie, and that aunties were not quite the same as mummies, but that, if it gave him pleasure, he might call her 'Mummy' at bedtime, for a pet-name between themselves.

Michael kept his secret most loyally, but Helen, as usual, explained the fact to her friends; which when Michael heard, he raged.

'Why did you tell? *Why* did you tell?' came at the end of the storm.

'Because it's always best to tell the truth,' Helen answered, her arm round him as he shook in his cot.

'All right, but when the troof's ugly I don't think it's nice.'

'Don't you, dear?'

'No, I don't, and' – she felt the small body stiffen – 'now you've told, I won't call you "Mummy" any more – not even at bedtimes.'

'But isn't that rather unkind?' said Helen softly.

'I don't care! I don't care! You've hurted me in my insides and I'll hurt you back. I'll hurt you as long as I live!'

'Don't, oh, don't talk like that, dear! You don't know what – '

'I will! And when I'm dead I'll hurt you worse!'

'Thank goodness, I shall be dead long before you, darling.'

'Huh! Emma says, "Never know your luck."' (Michael had been talking to Helen's elderly, flat-faced maid.) 'Lots of little boys die quite soon. So'll I. *Then* you'll see!'

Helen caught her breath and moved towards the door, but the wail of 'Mummy! Mummy!' drew her back again, and the two wept together.

At ten years old, after two terms at a prep. school,[2] something or somebody gave him the idea that his civil status was not quite regular.

He attacked Helen on the subject, breaking down her stammered defences with the family directness.

"Don't believe a word of it,' he said, cheerily, at the end. 'People wouldn't have talked like they did if my people had been married. But don't you bother, Auntie. I've found out all about my sort in English Hist'ry and the Shakespeare bits. There was William the Conqueror[3] to begin with, and – oh, heaps more, and they all got on first-rate. 'Twon't make any difference to you, my being *that* – will it?'

'As if anything could – ,' she began.

'All right. We won't talk about it any more if it makes you cry.' He never mentioned the thing again of his own will, but when, two years later, he skilfully managed to have measles in the holidays, as his temperature went up to the appointed one hundred and four he muttered of nothing else, till Helen's voice, piercing at last his delirium, reached him with assurance that nothing on earth or beyond could make any difference between them.

The terms at his public school and the wonderful Christmas, Easter, and Summer holidays followed each other, variegated and glorious as jewels on a string; and as jewels Helen treasured them. In due time Michael developed his own interests, which ran their courses and gave way to others; but his interest in Helen was constant and increasing throughout. She repaid it with all that she had of affection or could command of counsel and money; and since Michael was no fool, the War took him just before what was like to have been a most promising career.

He was to have gone up to Oxford, with a scholarship, in October. At the end of August he was on the edge of joining the first holocaust of public-school boys who threw themselves into the Line; but the Captain of his OTC,[4] where he had been sergeant for nearly a year, headed him off and steered him directly to a commission in a battalion so new that half of it still wore the old Army red, and the other half was breeding meningitis through living overcrowdedly in damp tents. Helen had been shocked at the idea of direct enlistment.

'But it's in the family,' Michael laughed.

'You don't mean to tell me that you believed that old story all this time?' said Helen. (Emma, her maid, had been dead now several years.) 'I gave you my word of honour – and I give it again – that – that it's all right. It is indeed.'

'Oh, *that* doesn't worry me. It never did,' he replied valiantly. 'What I meant was, I should have got into the show earlier if I'd enlisted – like my grandfather.'

'Don't talk like that! Are you afraid of its ending so soon, then?'

'No such luck. You know what K.[5] says.'

'Yes. But my banker told me last Monday it couldn't *possibly* last beyond Christmas – for financial reasons.'

'Hope he's right, but our Colonel – and he's a Regular – says it's going to be a long job.'

Michael's battalion was fortunate in that, by some chance which meant several 'leaves', it was used for coast-defence among shallow trenches on the Norfolk coast; thence sent north to watch the mouth of a Scotch estuary, and, lastly, held for weeks on a baseless rumour of distant service. But, the very day that Michael was to have met Helen for four whole hours at a railway-junction up the line, it was hurled out, to help make good the wastage of Loos,[6] and he had only just time to send her a wire of farewell.

In France luck again helped the battalion. It was put down near the Salient, where it led a meritorious and unexacting life, while the Somme[7] was being manufactured; and enjoyed the peace of the Armentières and Laventie sectors when that battle began. Finding that it had sound views on protecting its own flanks and could dig, a prudent Commander stole it out of its own Division, under pretence of helping to lay telegraphs, and used it round Ypres at large.

A month later, and just after Michael had written Helen that there was nothing special doing and therefore no need to worry, a shell-splinter dropping out of a wet dawn killed him at once. The next shell uprooted and laid down over the body what had been the foundation of a barn wall, so neatly that none but an expert would have guessed that anything unpleasant had happened.

By this time the village was old in experience of war, and, English-fashion, had evolved a ritual to meet it. When the postmistress handed her seven-year-old daughter the official telegram to take to Miss Turrell, she observed to the Rector's gardener: 'It's Miss Helen's turn now.' He replied, thinking of his own son: 'Well, he's lasted longer than some.' The child herself came to the front-door weeping aloud, because Master Michael had often given her sweets. Helen, presently, found herself pulling down the house-blinds one after one with great care, and saying earnestly to each: 'Missing *always* means dead.' Then she took her place in the dreary procession that was impelled to go through an inevitable series of unprofitable emotions. The Rector, of course, preached hope and prophesied word, very soon, from a prison camp. Several friends, too, told her perfectly truthful tales, but always about other women, to whom, after months and months of silence, their missing had been miraculously restored. Other people urged her to communicate with infallible Secretaries of organisations who could communicate with benevolent neutrals, who could extract accurate information from the most secretive of Hun prison commandants. Helen did and wrote and signed everything that was suggested or put before her.

Once, on one of Michael's leaves, he had taken her over a munition factory, where she saw the progress of a shell from blank-iron to the all but finished article. It struck her at the time that the wretched thing was never left alone for a single second; and 'I'm being manufactured into a bereaved next of kin,' she told herself, as she prepared her documents.

In due course, when all the organisations had deeply or sincerely regretted their inability to trace, etc., something gave way within her and all sensation – save of thankfulness for the release – came to an end in blessed passivity. Michael had died and her world had stood still and she had been one with the full shock of that arrest. Now she was standing still and the world was going forward, but it did not concern her – in no way or relation did it touch her. She knew this by the ease with which she could slip Michael's name into talk and incline her head to the proper angle, at the proper murmur of sympathy.

In the blessed realisation of that relief, the Armistice[8] with all its bells broke over her and passed unheeded. At the end of another year she had overcome her physical loathing of the living and returned young, so that she could take them by the hand and almost sincerely wish them well. She had no interest in any aftermath, national or personal, of the War, but, moving at an immense distance, she sat on various relief committees and held strong views – she heard herself delivering them – about the site of the proposed village War Memorial.

Then there came to her, as next of kin, an official intimation, backed by a page of a letter to her in indelible pencil, a silver identity-disc, and a watch, to the effect that the body of Lieutenant Michael Turrell had been found, identified, and re-interred in Hagenzeele Third Military Cemetery – the letter of the row and the grave's number in that row duly given.

So Helen found herself moved on to another process of the manufacture – to a world full of exultant or broken relatives, now strong in the certainty that there was an altar upon earth where they might lay their love. These soon told her, and by means of time-tables made clear, how easy it was and how little it interfered with life's affairs to go and see one's grave.

'So different,' as the Rector's wife said, 'if he'd been killed in Mesopotamia, or even Gallipoli.'

The agony of being waked up to some sort of second life drove Helen across the Channel, where, in a new world of abbreviated titles, she learnt that Hagenzeele Third could be comfortably reached by an afternoon train which fitted in with the morning boat, and that there was a comfortable little hotel not three kilometres from Hagenzeele itself, where one could spend quite a comfortable night and see one's grave next morning. All this she had from a Central Authority who lived in a board and tar-paper shed on the skirts of a razed city full of whirling lime-dust and blown papers.

'By the way,' said he, 'you know your grave, of course?'

'Yes, thank you,' said Helen, and showed its row and number typed on Michael's own little typewriter. The officer would have checked it, out of one of his many books; but a large Lancashire woman thrust between them and bade him tell her where she might find her son, who had been corporal in the ASC.[9] His proper name, she sobbed, was Anderson, but, coming of respectable folk, he had of course enlisted under the name of Smith; and had been killed at Dickiebush, in early 'Fifteen. She had not his number, nor did she know which of his two Christian names he might have used with his alias; but her Cook's[10] tourist ticket expired at the end of Easter week, and if by then she could not find her child she should go mad. Whereupon she fell forward on Helen's breast; but the officer's wife came out quickly from a little bedroom behind the office, and the three of them lifted the woman on to the cot.

'They are often like this,' said the officer's wife, loosening the tight bonnet-strings. 'Yesterday she said he'd been killed at Hooge.[11] Are you sure you know your grave? It makes such a difference?'

'Yes, thank you,' said Helen, and hurried out before the woman on the bed should begin to lament again.

Tea in a crowded mauve-and-blue-striped wooden structure, with a false front, carried her still further into the nightmare. She paid her bill beside a stolid, plain-featured Englishwoman, who, hearing her inquire about the train to Hagenzeele, volunteered to come with her.

'I'm going to Hagenzeele myself,' she explained. 'Not to Hagenzeele Third; mine is Sugar Factory, but they call it La Rosière now. It's just south of Hagenzeele Three. Have you got your room at the hotel there?'

'Oh yes, thank you. I've wired.'

'That's better. Sometimes the place is quite full, and at others there's hardly a soul. But they've put bathrooms into the old Lion d'Or – that's the hotel on the west side of Sugar Factory – and it draws off a lot of people, luckily.'

'It's all new to me. This is the first time I've been over.'

'Indeed! This is my ninth time since the Armistice. Not on my own account. I haven't lost any one, thank God – but, like everyone else, I've a lot of friends at home who have. Coming over as often as I do, I find it helps them to have someone just look at the – the place and tell them about it afterwards. And one can take photos for them, too. I get quite a list of commissions to execute.' She laughed nervously and tapped her slung kodak. 'There are two or three to see at Sugar Factory this time, and plenty of others in the cemeteries all about. My system is to save them up, and arrange them, you know. And when I've got enough commissions for one area to make it worth while, I pop over and execute them. It *does* comfort people.'

'I suppose so,' Helen answered, shivering as they entered the little train.

'Of course it does. (Isn't it lucky we've got window-seats?) It must do or they wouldn't ask one to do it, would they? I've a list of quite twelve or fifteen commissions here' – she tapped the kodak again – 'I must sort them out to-night. Oh, I forgot to ask you. What's yours?'

'My nephew,' said Helen. 'But I was very fond of him.'

'Ah, yes! I sometimes wonder whether *they* know after death? What do you think?'

'Oh, I don't – I haven't dared to think much about that sort of thing,' said Helen, almost lifting her hands to keep her off.

'Perhaps that's better,' the woman answered. 'The sense of loss must be enough, I expect. Well, I won't worry you any more.'

Helen was grateful, but when they reached the hotel Mrs Scarsworth (they had exchanged names) insisted on dining at the same table with her, and after the meal, in the little, hideous salon full of low-voiced relatives, took Helen through her 'commissions' with biographies of the dead, where she happened to know them, and sketches of their next of kin. Helen endured till nearly half-past nine, ere she fled to her room.

Almost at once there was a knock at her door and Mrs Scarsworth entered; her hands, holding the dreadful list, clasped before her.

'Yes – yes – *I* know,' she began. 'You're sick of me, but I want to tell you something. You – you aren't married, are you? Then perhaps you won't . . . But it doesn't matter. I've *got* to tell someone. I can't go on any longer like this.'

'But please – ' Mrs Scarsworth had backed against the shut door, and her mouth worked dryly.

'In a minute,' she said. 'You – you know about these graves of mine I was telling you about downstairs, just now? They really *are* commissions. At least several of them are.' Her eye wandered round the room. 'What extraordinary wall-papers they have in Belgium, don't you think? . . . Yes. I swear they are commissions. But there's *one,* d'you see, and – and he was more to me than anything else in the world. Do you understand?'

Helen nodded.

'More than anyone else. And, of course, he oughtn't to have been. He ought to have been nothing to me. But he *was*. He *is*. That's why I do the commissions, you see. That's all.'

'But why do you tell me?' Helen asked desperately.

'Because I'm *so* tired of lying. Tired of lying – always lying – year in and year out. When I don't tell lies I've got to act 'em and I've got to think 'em, always. *You* don't know what that means. He was everything to me that he oughtn't to have been – the one real thing – the only thing – that ever happened to me in all my life; and I've had to pretend he wasn't. I've had to watch every word I said, and think out what lie I'd tell next, for years and years!'

'How many years?' Helen asked.

'Six years and four months before, and two and three-quarters after. I've gone to him eight times, since. To-morrow'll make the ninth, and – and I can't – I *can't* go to him again with nobody in the world knowing. I want to be honest with someone before I go. Do you understand? It doesn't matter about *me*. I was never truthful, even as a girl. But it isn't worthy of *him*. So – so I – I had to tell you. I can't keep it up any longer. Oh, I can't!'

She lifted her joined hands almost to the level of her mouth, and brought them down sharply, still joined, to full arms' length below her waist. Helen reached forward, caught them, bowed her head over them, and murmured: 'Oh, my dear! My dear!' Mrs Scarsworth stepped back, her face all mottled.

'My God!' said she. 'Is *that* how you take it?'

Helen could not speak, and the woman went out; but it was a long while before Helen was able to sleep.

Next morning Mrs Scarsworth left early on her round of commissions, and Helen walked alone to Hagenzeele Third. The place was still in the making, and stood some five or six feet above the metalled road, which it flanked for hundreds of yards. Culverts across a deep ditch served for entrances through the unfinished boundary wall. She climbed a few wooden-faced earthen steps and then met the entire crowded level of the thing in one held breath. She did not know that Hagenzeele Third counted twenty-one thousand dead already. All she saw was a merciless sea of black crosses, bearing little strips of stamped tin at all angles across their faces. She could distinguish no order or arrangement in their mass; nothing but a waist-high wilderness as of weeds stricken dead, rushing at her. She went forward, moved to the left and the right hopelessly, wondering by what guidance she should ever come to her own. A great distance away there was a line of whiteness. It proved to be a block of some two or three hundred graves whose headstones had already been set, whose flowers were planted out, and whose new-sown grass showed green. Here she could see clear-cut letters at the ends of the rows, and, referring to her slip, realised that it was not here she must look.

A man knelt behind a line of headstones – evidently a gardener, for he was firming a young plant in the soft earth. She went towards him, her paper in her hand. He rose at her approach and without prelude or salutation asked: 'Who are you looking for?'

'Lieutenant Michael Turrell – my nephew,' said Helen slowly and word for word, as she had many thousands of times in her life.

The man lifted his eyes and looked at her with infinite compassion before he turned from the fresh-sown grass toward the naked black crosses.

'Come with me,' he said, 'and I will show you where your son lies.'

When Helen left the Cemetery she turned for a last look. In the distance she saw the man bending over his young plants; and she went away, supposing him to be the gardener.[12]

DAYSPRING MISHANDLED

C'est moi, c'est moi, c'est moi!
Je suis la Mandragore!
La fille des beaux jours qui s'éveille à l'aurore –
Et qui chante pour toi![1]

C. NODIER

In the days beyond compare and before the Judgments, a genius called Graydon foresaw that the advance of education and the standard of living would submerge all mind-marks in one mudrush of standardised reading-matter, and so created the Fictional Supply Syndicate to meet the demand.

Since a few days' work for him brought them more money than a week's elsewhere, he drew many young men – some now eminent – into his employ. He bade them keep their eyes on the Sixpenny Dream Book, the Army and Navy Stores Catalogue (this for backgrounds and furniture as they changed), and *The Hearthstone Friend*, a weekly publication which specialised unrivalledly in the domestic emotions. Yet, even so, youth would not be denied, and some of the collaborated love-talk in 'Passion Hath Peril', and 'Ena's Lost Lovers', and the account of the murder of the Earl in 'The Wickwire Tragedies' – to name but a few masterpieces now never mentioned for fear of blackmail – was as good as anything to which their authors signed their real names in more distinguished years.

Among the young ravens driven to roost awhile on Graydon's ark was James Andrew Manallace – a darkish, slow Northerner of the type that does not ignite, but must be detonated. Given written or verbal outlines of a plot, he was useless; but, with a half-dozen pictures round which to write his tale, he could astonish.

And he adored that woman who afterwards became the mother of Vidal Benzaguen,* and who suffered and died because she loved one unworthy. There was, also, among the company a mannered, bellied person called Alured Castorley, who talked and wrote about 'Bohemia', but was always afraid of being 'compromised' by the weekly suppers at Neminaka's Café in Hestern Square, where the Syndicate's work was

* 'The Village that Voted the Earth was Flat.' *A Diversity of Creatures.*

apportioned, and where everyone looked out for himself. He, too, for a time, had loved Vidal's mother, in his own way.

Now, one Saturday at Neminaka's, Graydon, who had given Manallace a sheaf of prints – torn from an extinct children's book called *Philippa's Queen* – on which to improvise, asked for results. Manallace went down into his ulster-pockets, hesitated a moment, and said the stuff had turned into poetry on his hands.

'Bosh!'

'That's what it isn't,' the boy retorted. 'It's rather good.'

'Then it's no use to us.' Graydon laughed. 'Have you brought back the cuts?'[2]

Manallace handed them over. There was a castle in the series; a knight or so in armour; an old lady in a horned head-dress; a young ditto; a very obvious Hebrew; a clerk, with pen and inkhorn, checking wine-barrels on a wharf; and a Crusader. On the back of one of the prints was a note, 'If he doesn't want to go, why can't he be captured and held to ransom?' Graydon asked what it all meant.

'I don't know yet. A comic opera, perhaps,' said Manallace.

Graydon, who seldom wasted time, passed the cuts on to some-one else, and advanced Manallace a couple of sovereigns[3] to carry on with, as usual; at which Castorley was angry and would have said something unpleasant but was suppressed. Half-way through supper, Castorley told the company that a relative had died and left him an independence; and that he now withdrew from 'hackwork' to follow 'Literature'. Generally, the Syndicate rejoiced in a comrade's good fortune, but Castorley had the gift of waking dislike. So the news was received with a vote of thanks, and he went out before the end, and, it was said, proposed to 'Dal Benzaguen's mother, who refused him. He did not come back. Manallace, who had arrived a little exalted, got so drunk before midnight that a man had to stay and see him home. But liquor never touched him above the belt, and when he had slept awhile, he recited to the gas-chandelier the poetry he had made out of the pictures; said that, on second thoughts, he would convert it into comic opera; deplored the Upas-tree[4] Influence of Gilbert and Sullivan; sang somewhat to illustrate his point; and – after words, by the way, with a negress in yellow satin – was steered to his rooms.

In the course of a few years, Graydon's foresight and genius were rewarded. The public began to read and reason upon higher planes, and the Syndicate grew rich. Later still, people demanded of their printed matter what they expected in their clothing and furniture. So, precisely as the three-guinea[5] hand-bag is followed in three weeks by its thirteen-and-seven-pence-ha'penny[6] indistinguishable sister, they enjoyed perfect synthetic substitutes for Plot, Sentiment, and Emotion. Graydon died before the Cinema-caption school came in, but he left his widow twenty-seven thousand pounds.

Manallace made a reputation, and, more important money for Vidal's mother after her husband ran away and the first symptoms of her paralysis showed. His line was the jocundly-sentimental Wardour Street[7] brand of adventure, told in a style that exactly met, but never exceeded, every expectation.

As he once said when urged to 'write a real book,' 'I've got my label, and I'm not going to chew it off. If you save people thinking, you can do anything with 'em.' His output apart, he was genuinely a man of letters. He rented a small cottage in the country and economised on everything, except the care and charges of Vidal's mother.

Castorley flew higher. When his legacy freed him from 'hackwork', he became first a critic – in which calling he loyally scalped all his old associates as they came up – and then looked for some speciality. Having found it (Chaucer was the prey), he consolidated his position before he occupied it, by his careful speech, his cultivated bearing, and the whispered words of his friends whom he, too, had saved the trouble of thinking. It followed that, when he published his first serious articles on Chaucer, all the world which is interested in Chaucer said: 'This is an authority.' But he was no impostor. He learned and knew the poet and his age; and in a month-long dog-fight in an austere literary weekly, met and mangled a recognised Chaucer expert of the day. He also, 'for old sake's sake', as he wrote to a friend, went out of his way to review one of Manallace's books with an intimacy of unclean deduction (this was before the days of Freud) which long stood as a record. Some member of the extinct Syndicate took occasion to ask him if he would – for old sake's sake – help Vidal's mother to a new treatment. He answered that he had 'known the lady very slightly and the calls on his purse were so heavy that', etc. The writer showed the letter to Manallace, who said he was glad Castorley hadn't interfered. Vidal's mother was then wholly paralysed. Only her eyes could move, and those always looked for the husband who had left her. She died thus in Manallace's arms in April of the first year of the War.

During the War he and Castorley worked as some sort of departmental dishwashers in the Office of Co-ordinated Supervisals. Here Manallace came to know Castorley again. Castorley, having a sweet tooth, cadged lumps of sugar for his tea from a typist, and when she took to giving them to a younger man, arranged that she should be reported for smoking in unauthorised apartments. Manallace possessed himself of every detail of the affair, as compensation for the review of his book. Then there came a night when, waiting for a big air-raid, the two men had talked humanly, and Manallace spoke of Vidal's mother. Castorley said something in reply, and from that hour – as was learned several years later – Manallace's real life-work and interests began.

The War over, Castorley set about to make himself Supreme Pontiff[8] on Chaucer by methods not far removed from the employment of poison-gas. The English Pope was silent, through private griefs, and influenza had carried off the learned Hun[9] who claimed Continental allegiance. Thus Castorley crowed unchallenged from Upsala to Seville,[10] while Manallace went back to his cottage with the photo of Vidal's mother over the mantelpiece. She seemed to have emptied out his life, and left him only fleeting interests in trifles. His private diversions were experiments of uncertain outcome, which, he said, rested him after a day's gadzooking and vitalstapping.[11] I found him, for instance, one week-end, in his toolshed-scullery, boiling a brew of slimy barks which were, if mixed with oak-galls, vitriol and wine, to become an ink-powder. We boiled it till the Monday, and it turned into an adhesive stronger than birdlime, and entangled us both.

At other times, he would carry me off, once in a few weeks, to sit at Castorley's feet, and hear him talk about Chaucer. Castorley's voice, bad enough in youth, when it could be shouted down, had, with culture and tact, grown almost insupportable. His mannerisms, too, had multiplied and set. He minced and mouthed, postured and chewed his words throughout those terrible evenings; and poisoned not only Chaucer, but every shred of English literature which he used to embellish him. He was shameless, too, as regarded self-advertisement and 'recognition' – weaving elaborate intrigues; forming petty friendships and confederacies, to be dissolved next week in favour of more promising alliances; fawning, snubbing, lecturing, organising, and lying as unrestingly as a politician, in chase of the Knighthood due not to him (he always called on his Maker to forbid such a thought) but as tribute to Chaucer. Yet, sometimes, he could break from his obsession and prove how a man's work will try to save the soul of him. He would tell us charmingly of copyists of the fifteenth century in England and the Low Countries, who had multiplied the Chaucer MSS, of which there remained – he gave us the exact number – and how each scribe could by him (and, he implied, by him alone) be distinguished from every other by some peculiarity of letter-formation, spacing or like trick of pen-work; and how he could fix the dates of their work within five years. Sometimes he would give us an hour of really interesting stuff and then return to his overdue 'recognition'. The changes sickened me, but Manallace defended him, as a master in his own line who had revealed Chaucer to at least one grateful soul.

This, as far as I remember, was the autumn when Manallace holidayed in the Shetlands or the Faroes, and came back with a stone 'quern' – a hand corn-grinder. He said it interested him from the ethnological standpoint. His whim lasted till next harvest, and was followed by a religious spasm which, naturally, translated itself into literature. He showed me a battered and mutilated Vulgate[12] of 1485, patched up the back with bits of legal parchments, which he had bought for thirty-five shillings.[13] Some monk's attempt to rubricate chapter-initials had caught, it seemed, his forlorn fancy, and he dabbled in shells of gold and silver paint for weeks.

That also faded out, and he went to the Continent to get 'local colour' for a love-story about Alva and the Dutch,[14] and the next year I saw practically nothing of him. This released me from seeing much of Castorley, but, at intervals, I would go there to dine with him, when his wife – an unappetising, ash-coloured woman – made no secret that his friends wearied her almost as much as he did. But at a later meeting, not long after Manallace had finished his 'Low Countries' novel, I found Castorley charged to bursting-point with triumph and high information hardly withheld. He confided to me that a time was at hand when great matters would be made plain, and 'recognition' would be inevitable. I assumed, naturally, that there was fresh scandal or heresy afoot in Chaucer circles, and kept my curiosity within bounds.

In time, New York cabled that a fragment of a hitherto unknown Canterbury Tale lay safe in the steel-walled vaults of the seven-million-dollar Sunnapia Collection. It was news on an international scale – the New World exultant – the Old deploring the 'burden of British taxation which drove such treasures, etc.', and the lighter-minded journals disporting themselves according to their publics; for 'our Dan',[15] as one earnest Sunday editor observed, 'lies closer to the national heart than we wot of.' Common decency made me call on Castorley, who, to my surprise, had not yet descended into the arena. I found him, made young again by joy, deep in just-passed proofs.

Yes, he said, it was all true. He had, of course, been in it from the first. There had been found one hundred and seven new lines of Chaucer tacked on to an abridged end of *The Persone's Tale*, the whole the work of Abraham Mentzius, better known as Mentzel of Antwerp (1388–1438/9) – I might remember he had talked about him – whose distinguishing peculiarities were a certain Byzantine formation of his *g*'s, the use of a 'sickle-slanted' reed-pen, which cut into the vellum at certain letters; and, above all, a tendency to spell English words on Dutch lines, whereof the manuscript carried one convincing proof. For instance (he wrote it out for me), a girl praying against an undesired marriage says:

'Ah! Jesu-Moder, pitie my oe paine.
Daiespringe mishandeelt cometh nat agayne.'

Would I, please, note the spelling of 'mishandeelt'? Stark Dutch and Mentzel's besetting sin! But in *his* position one took nothing for granted. The page had been part of the stiffening of the side of an old Bible, bought in a parcel by Dredd, the big dealer, because it had some rubricated chapter-initials, and by Dredd shipped, with a consignment of similar odds and ends, to the Sunnapia Collection, where they were making a glass-cased exhibit of the whole history of illumination and did not care how many books they gutted for that purpose. There, someone who noticed a crack in the back of the volume had unearthed it. He went on: 'They didn't know what to make of the thing at first. But they knew about *me*! They kept quiet till I'd been consulted. You might have noticed I was out of England for three months.

'I was over there, of course. It was what is called a "spoil" – a page Mentzel had spoiled with his Dutch spelling – I expect he had had the English dictated to him – then had evidently used the vellum for trying out his reeds; and then, I suppose, had put it away. The "spoil" had been doubled, pasted together, and slipped in as stiffening to the old book-cover. I had it steamed open, and analysed the wash. It gave the flour-grains in the paste – coarse, because of the old millstone – and there were traces of the grit itself. What? Oh, possibly a handmill of Mentzel's own time. He may have doubled the spoilt page and used it for part of a pad to steady wood-cuts on. It may have knocked about his workshop for years. That, indeed, is practically certain because a beginner from the Low Countries has tried his reed on a few lines of some monkish hymn – not a bad lilt tho' – which must have been common form. Oh yes, the page may have been used in other books before it was used for the Vulgate. That doesn't matter, but *this* does. Listen! I took a wash, for analysis, from a blot in one corner – that would be after Mentzel had given up trying to make a possible page of it, and had grown careless – and I got the actual *ink* of the period! It's a practically eternal stuff compounded on – I've forgotten his name for the minute – the scribe at Bury St Edmunds, of course! – hawthorn bark and wine. Anyhow, on *his* formula. *That* wouldn't interest you either, but, taken with all the other testimony, it clinches the thing. (You'll see it all in my Statement to the Press on Monday.) Overwhelming, isn't it?'

'Overwhelming,' I said, with sincerity. 'Tell me what the tale was about, though. That's more in my line.'

'I know it; but *I* have to be equipped on all sides. The verses are relatively easy for one to pronounce on. The freshness, the fun, the humanity, the fragrance of it all, cries – no, shouts – itself as Dan's work. Why "Daiespringe mishandled" alone stamps it from Dan's mint. Plangent as doom, my dear boy – plangent as doom! It's all in my Statement. Well, substantially, the fragment deals with a girl whose parents wish her to marry an elderly suitor. The mother isn't so keen on it, but the father, an old Knight, is. The girl, of course, is in love with a younger and a poorer man. Common form? Granted. Then the father, who doesn't in the least want to, is ordered off to a Crusade and, by way of passing on the kick, as we used to say during the War, orders the girl to be kept in duresse till his return or her consent to the old suitor. Common form, again? Quite so. That's too much for her mother. She reminds the old Knight of his age and infirmities, and the discomforts of Crusading. Are you sure I'm not boring you?'

'Not at all,' I said, though time had begun to whirl backward through my brain to a red-velvet, pomatum-scented side-room at Neminaka's and Manallace's set face intoning to the gas.[16]

'You'll read it all in my Statement next week. The sum is that the old lady tells him of a certain Knight-adventurer on the French coast, who, for a consideration, waylays Knights who don't relish Crusading and holds them to impossible ransoms till the trooping season is over, or they are returned sick. He keeps a ship in the Channel to pick 'em up and transfers his birds to his castle ashore, where he has a reputation for doing 'em well. As the old lady points out:

> "And if perchance thou fall into his honde,
> By God, how canstow ride to Holilonde?"

'You see? Modern in essence as Gilbert and Sullivan, but handled as only Dan could! And she reminds him that "Honour and olde bones" parted company long ago. He makes one splendid appeal for the spirit of chivalry:

> "Lat all men change as Fortune may send,
> But Knighthood beareth service to the end,"

and *then*, of course, he gives in:

> "For what his woman willeth to be don
> Her manne must or wauken Hell anon."

'Then she hints that the daughter's young lover, who is in the Bordeaux wine-trade, could open negotiations for a kidnapping without compromising him. And *then* that careless brute Mentzel spoils his page and chucks it! But there's enough to show what's going to happen. You'll see it all in my Statement. Was there ever anything in literary finds to hold a candle to it? . . . And they give grocers Knighthoods for selling cheese!'

I went away before he could get into his stride on that course. I wanted to think, and to see Manallace. But I waited till Castorley's Statement came out. He had left himself no loophole. And when, a little later, his (nominally the Sunnapia people's) 'scientific' account of their analyses and tests appeared, criticism ceased, and some journals began to demand 'public recognition'. Manallace wrote me on this subject, and I went down to his cottage, where he at once asked me to sign a Memorial on Castorley's behalf. With luck, he said, we might get him a KBE[17] in the next Honours List. Had I read his Statement?

'I have,' I replied. 'But I want to ask you something first. Do you remember the night you got drunk at Neminaka's, and I stayed behind to look after you?'

'Oh, *that* time,' said he, pondering. 'Wait a minute! I remember Graydon advancing me two quid. He was a generous paymaster. And I remember – now, who the devil rolled me under the sofa – and what for?'

'We all did,' I replied. 'You wanted to read us what you'd written to those Chaucer cuts.'

'I don't remember that. No! I don't remember anything after the sofa episode . . . *You* always said that you took me home – didn't you?'

'I did, and you told Kentucky Kate outside the old Empire that you had been faithful, Cynara, in your fashion.'[18]

'Did I?' said he. 'My God! Well, I suppose I have.' He stared into the fire. 'What else?'

'Before we left Neminaka's you recited me what you had made out of the cuts – the whole tale! So – you see?'

'Ye-es.' He nodded. 'What are you going to do about it?'

'What are *you*?'

'I'm going to help him get his Knighthood – first.'

'Why?'

'I'll tell you what he said about 'Dal's mother – the night there was that air-raid on the offices.'

He told it.

'That's why,' he said. 'Am I justified?'

He seemed to me entirely so.

'But after he gets his Knighthood?' I went on.

'That depends. There are several things I can think of. It interests me.'

'Good Heavens! I've always imagined you a man without interests.'

'So I was. I owe my interests to Castorley. He gave me every one of 'em except the tale itself.'

'How did *that* come?'

'Something in those ghastly cuts touched off something in me – a sort of possession, I suppose. I was in love too. No wonder I got drunk that night. I'd *been* Chaucer for a week! Then I thought the notion might make a comic opera. But Gilbert and Sullivan were too strong.'

'So I remember you told me at the time.'

'I kept it by me, and it made me interested in Chaucer – philologically and so on. I worked on it on those lines for years. There wasn't a flaw in the wording even in 'Fourteen. I hardly had to touch it after.'

'Did you ever tell it to anyone except me?'

'No, only 'Dal's mother – when she could listen to anything – to put her to sleep. But when Castorley said – what he did about her, I thought I might use it. 'Twasn't difficult. *He* taught me. D'you remember my birdlime experiments, and the stuff on our hands? I'd been trying to get that ink for more than a year. Castorley told me where I'd find the formula. And your falling over the quern, too?'

'That accounted for the stone-dust under the microscope?'

'Yes. I grew the wheat in the garden here, and ground it myself. Castorley gave me Mentzel complete. He put me on to an MS in the British Museum which he said was the finest sample of his work. I copied his "Byzantine *g*'s" for months.'

'And what's a "sickle-slanted" pen?' I asked.

'You nick one edge of your reed till it drags and scratches on the curves of the letters. Castorley told me about Mentzel's spacing and margining. I only had to get the hang of his script.'

'How long did that take you?'

'On and off – some years. I was too ambitious at first – I wanted to give the whole poem. That would have been risky. Then Castorley told me about spoiled pages and I took the hint. I spelt "Daiespringe mishandeelt" Mentzel's way – to make sure of him. It's not a bad couplet in itself. Did you see how he admires the "plangency" of it?'

'Never mind him. Go on!' I said.

He did. Castorley had been his unfailing guide throughout, specifying in minutest detail every trap to be set later for his own feet. The actual vellum was an Antwerp find, and its introduction into the cover of the Vulgate was begun after a long course of amateur bookbinding. At last, he bedded it under pieces of an old deed, and a printed page (1686) of Horace's *Odes*, legitimately used for repairs by different owners in the seventeenth and eighteenth centuries; and at the last moment, to meet Castorley's theory that spoiled pages were used in workshops by beginners, he had written a few Latin words in fifteenth-century script – the Statement gave the exact date – across an open part of the fragment. The thing ran: '*Illa alma Mater ecca, secum afferens me acceptum. Nicolaus Atrib.*'[19] The disposal of the thing was easiest of all. He had merely hung about Dredd's dark bookshop of fifteen rooms, where he was well known, occasionally buying but generally browsing, till, one day, Dredd Senior showed him a case of cheap black-letter[20] stuff, English and Continental – being packed for the Sunnapia people – into which Manallace tucked his contribution, taking care to wrench the back enough to give a lead to an earnest seeker.

'And then?' I demanded.

'After six months or so Castorley sent for me. Sunnapia had found it, and as Dredd had missed it, and there was no money-motive sticking out, they were half convinced it was genuine from the start. But they invited him over. He conferred with their experts, and suggested the scientific tests. *I* put that into his head, before he sailed. That's all. And now, will you sign our Memorial?'

I signed. Before we had finished hawking it round there was a host of influential names to help us, as well as the impetus of all the literary discussion which arose over every detail of the glorious trove. The upshot was a KBE* for Castorley in the next Honours List; and Lady Castorley, her cards duly printed, called on friends that same afternoon.

Manallace invited me to come with him, a day or so later, to convey our pleasure and satisfaction to them both. We were rewarded by the sight of a man relaxed and ungirt – not to say wallowing naked – on the crest of Success. He assured us that 'The Title' should not make any difference to our future relations, seeing it was in no sense personal, but, as he had often said, a tribute to Chaucer. 'And, after all,' he pointed out, with a glance at the mirror over the mantelpiece, 'Chaucer was the prototype of the "verray parfit, gentil Knyght"[21] of the British Empire so far as that then existed.'

---

*Officially it was on account of his good work in the Department of Co-ordinated Supervisals, but many true lovers of Literature knew the real reason, and told the papers so.

On the way back, Manallace told me he was considering either an unheralded revelation in the baser Press which should bring Castorley's reputation about his own ears some breakfast-time, or a private conversation, when he would make clear to Castorley that he must now back the forgery as long as he lived, under threat of Manallace's betraying it if he flinched.

He favoured the second plan. 'If I pull the string of the shower-bath in the papers,' he said, 'Castorley might go off his verray parfit, gentil nut. I want to keep his intellect.'

'What about your own position? The forgery doesn't matter so much. But if you tell this you'll kill him,' I said.

'I intend that. Oh – my position? I've been dead since – April, 'Fourteen, it was. But there's no hurry. What was it *she* was saying to you just as we left?'

'She told me how much your sympathy and understanding had meant to him. She said she thought that even Sir Alured did not realise the full extent of his obligations to you.'

'She's right, but I don't like her putting it that way.'

'It's only common form – as Castorley's always saying.'

'Not with *her*. She can hear a man think.'

'She never struck me in that light.'

'*You* aren't playing against her.'

'Guilty conscience, Manallace?'

'H'm! I wonder. Mine or hers? I *wish* she hadn't said that. "More even than *he* realises." I won't call again for a while.'

He kept away till we read that Sir Alured, owing to slight indisposition, had been unable to attend a dinner given in his honour.

Inquiries brought word that it was but natural reaction, after strain, which, for the moment, took the form of nervous dyspepsia, and he would be glad to see Manallace at any time. Manallace reported him as rather pulled and drawn, but full of his new life and position, and proud that his efforts should have martyred him so much. He was going to collect, collate, and expand all his pronouncements and inferences into one authoritative volume.

'I must make an effort of my own,' said Manallace. 'I've collected nearly all his stuff about the Find that has appeared in the papers, and he's promised me everything that's missing. I'm going to help him. It will be a new interest.'

'How will you treat it?' I asked.

'I expect I shall quote his deductions on the evidence, and parallel 'em with my experiments – the ink and the paste and the rest of it. It ought to be rather interesting.'

'But even then there will only be your word. It's hard to catch up with an established lie,' I said. 'Especially when you've started it yourself.'

He laughed. 'I've arranged for *that* – in case anything happens to me. Do you remember the "Monkish Hymn"?'

'Oh yes! There's quite a literature about it already.'

'Well, you write those ten words above each other, and read down the first and second letters of 'em; and see what you get.* My Bank has the formula.'

He wrapped himself lovingly and leisurely round his new task, and Castorley was as good as his word in giving him help. The two practically collaborated, for Manallace suggested that all Castorley's strictly scientific evidence should be in one place, with his deductions and dithyrambs as appendices. He assured him that the public would prefer this arrangement, and, after grave consideration, Castorley agreed.

'That's better,' said Manallace to me. 'Now I shan't have so many hiatuses in my extracts. Dots always give the reader the idea you aren't dealing fairly with your man. I shall merely quote him solid, and rip him up, proof for proof, and date for date, in parallel columns. His book's taking more out of him than I like, though. He's been doubled up twice with tummy attacks since I've worked with him. And he's just the sort of flatulent beast who may go down with appendicitis.'

We learned before long that the attacks were due to gall-stones, which would necessitate an operation. Castorley bore the blow very well. He had full confidence in his surgeon, an old friend of theirs; great faith in his own constitution; a strong conviction that nothing would happen to him till the book was finished; and, above all, the 'Will to Live'.

He dwelt on these assets with a voice at times a little out of pitch and eyes brighter than usual beside a slightly-sharpening nose.

I had only met Gleeag, the surgeon, once or twice at Castorley's

*Illa
alma
Mater
ecca
secum
afferens
me
acceptum
Nicolaus
Atrib.

house, but had always heard him spoken of as a most capable man. He told Castorley that his trouble was the price exacted, in some shape or other, from all who had served their country; and that, measured in units of strain, Castorley had practically been at the Front through those three years he had served in the Office of Co-ordinated Supervisals. However, the thing had been taken betimes, and in a few weeks he would worry no more about it.

'But suppose he dies?' I suggested to Manallace.

'He won't. I've been talking to Gleeag. He says he's all right.'

'Wouldn't Gleeag's talk be common form?'

'I *wish* you hadn't said that. But, surely, Gleeag wouldn't have the face to play with me – or her.'

'Why not? I expect it's been done before.'

But Manallace insisted that, in this case, it would be impossible.

The operation was a success and, some weeks later, Castorley began to recast the arrangement and most of the material of his book. 'Let me have my way,' he said, when Manallace protested. 'They are making too much of a baby of me. I really don't need Gleeag looking in every day now.' But Lady Castorley told us that he required careful watching. His heart had felt the strain, and fret or disappointment of any kind must be avoided. 'Even' – she turned to Manallace – 'though you know ever so much better how his book should be arranged than he does himself.'

'But really,' Manallace began, 'I'm very careful not to fuss – '

She shook her finger at him playfully. 'You don't think you do; but, remember, he tells me everything that you tell him, just the same as he told me everything that he used to tell *you*. Oh, I don't mean the things that men talk about. I mean about his Chaucer.'

'I didn't realise that,' said Manallace, weakly.

'I thought you didn't. He never spares me anything; but *I* don't mind,' she replied with a laugh, and went off to Gleeag, who was paying his daily visit. Gleeag said he had no objection to Manallace working with Castorley on the book for a given time – say, twice a week – but supported Lady Castorley's demand that he should not be over-taxed in what she called 'the sacred hours'. The man grew more and more difficult to work with, and the little check he had heretofore set on his self-praise went altogether.

'He says there has never been anything in the History of Letters to compare with it,' Manallace groaned. 'He wants now to inscribe – he never dedicates, you know – inscribe it to me, as his "most valued assistant". The devil of it is that *she* backs him up in getting it out soon. Why? How much do you think she knows?'

'Why should she know anything at all?'

'You heard her say he had told her everything that he had told me about Chaucer? (I *wish* she hadn't said that!) If she puts two and two together, she can't help seeing that every one of his notions and theories has been played up to. But then – but then . . . Why is she trying to hurry publication? She talks about *me* fretting him. *She*'s at him, all the time, to be quick.'

Castorley must have over-worked, for, after a couple of months, he complained of a stitch in his right side, which Gleeag said was a slight sequel, a little incident of the operation. It threw him back a while, but he returned to his work undefeated.

The book was due in the autumn. Summer was passing, and his publisher urgent, and – he said to me, when after a longish interval I called – Manallace had chosen this time, of all, to take a holiday. He was not pleased with Manallace, once his indefatigable *aide*, but now dilatory, and full of time-wasting objections. Lady Castorley, he said, had noticed it, too.

Meantime, with Lady Castorley's help, he himself was doing the best he could to expedite the book; but Manallace had mislaid (did I think through jealousy?) some essential stuff which had been dictated to him. And Lady Castorley wrote Manallace, who had been delayed by a slight motor accident abroad, that the fret of waiting was prejudicial to her husband's health. Manallace, on his return from the Continent, showed me that letter.

'He has fretted a little, I believe,' I said.

Manallace shuddered. 'If I stay abroad, I'm helping to kill him. If I help him to hurry up the book, I'm expected to kill him. *She* knows,' he said.

'You're mad. You've got this thing on the brain.'

'I have not! Look here! You remember that Gleeag gave me from four to six, twice a week, to work with him. She called them "the sacred hours". You heard her? Well, they *are*! They are Gleeag's and hers. But she's so infernally plain, and I'm such a fool, it took me weeks to find it out.'

'That's their affair,' I answered. 'It doesn't prove she knows anything about the Chaucer.'

'She *does*! He told her everything that he had told me when I was pumping him, all those years. She put two and two together when the thing came out. She saw exactly how I had set my traps. I know it! She's been trying to make me admit it.'

'What did you do?'

'Didn't understand what she was driving at, of course. And then she asked Gleeag, before me, if he didn't think the delay over the book was

fretting Sir Alured. He didn't think so. He said getting it out might deprive
him of an interest. He had that much decency. *She*'s the devil!'

'What do you suppose is her game, then?'

'If Castorley knows he's been had, it'll kill him. She's at me all the
time, indirectly, to let it out. I've told you she wants to make it a sort
of joke between us. Gleeag's willing to wait. He knows Castorley's a
dead man. It slips out when they talk. They say "He was", not "He is".
Both of 'em know it. But *she* wants him finished sooner.'

'I don't believe it. What are you going to do?'

'What *can* I? I'm not going to have him killed, though.'

Manlike, he invented compromises whereby Castorley might be
lured up by-paths of interest, to delay publication. This was not a
success. As autumn advanced Castorley fretted more, and suffered from
returns of his distressing colics. At last, Gleeag told him that he thought
they might be due to an overlooked gall-stone working down. A second
comparatively trivial operation would eliminate the bother once and
for all. If Castorley cared for another opinion, Gleeag named a surgeon
of eminence. 'And then,' said he, cheerily, 'the two of us can talk you
over.' Castorley did not want to be talked over. He was oppressed by
pains in his side, which, at first, had yielded to the liver-tonics Gleeag
prescribed; but now they stayed – like a toothache – behind everything.
He felt most at ease in his bedroom-study, with his proofs round him.
If he had more pain than he could stand, he would consider the second
operation. Meantime Manallace – 'the meticulous Manallace', he called
him – agreed with him in thinking that the Mentzel page-facsimile,
done by the Sunnapia Library, was not quite good enough for the
great book, and the Sunnapia people were, very decently, having it
re-processed. This would hold things back till early spring, which had
its advantages, for he could run a fresh eye over all in the interval.

One gathered these things in the course of stray visits as the days
shortened. He insisted on Manallace keeping to 'the sacred hours', and
Manallace insisted on my accompanying him when possible. On these
occasions he and Castorley would confer apart for half an hour or so,
while I listened to an unendurable clock in the drawing-room. Then I
would join them and help wear out the rest of the time, while Castorley
rambled. His speech, now, was often clouded and uncertain – the result
of the 'liver-tonics'; and his face came to look like old vellum.[22]

It was a few days after Christmas – the operation had been postponed
till the following Friday – that we called together. She met us with word
that Sir Alured had picked up an irritating little winter cough, due to
a cold wave, but we were not, therefore, to abridge our visit. We found
him in steam perfumed with Friar's Balsam. He waved the old Sunnapia

facsimile at us. We agreed that it ought to have been more worthy. He took a dose of his mixture, lay back and asked us to lock the door. There was, he whispered, something wrong somewhere. He could not lay his finger on it, but it was in the air. He felt he was being played with. He did not like it. There was something wrong all round him. Had we noticed it? Manallace and I severally and slowly denied that we had noticed anything of the sort.

With no longer break than a light fit of coughing, he fell into the hideous, helpless panic of the sick – those worse than captives who lie at the judgment and mercy of the hale for every office and hope. He wanted to go away. Would we help him to pack his Gladstone?[23] Or, if that would attract too much attention in certain quarters, help him to dress and go out? There was an urgent matter to be set right, and now that he had The Title and knew his own mind it would all end happily and he would be well again. *Please* would we let him go out, just to speak to – he named her; he named her by her 'little name' out of the old Neminaka days? Manallace quite agreed, and recommended a pull at the 'liver-tonic' to brace him after so long in the house. He took it, and Manallace suggested that it would be better if, after his walk, he came down to the cottage for a week-end and brought the revise with him. They could then re-touch the last chapter. He answered to that drug and to some praise of his work, and presently simpered drowsily. Yes, it *was* good – though he said it who should not. He praised himself awhile till, with a puzzled forehead and shut eyes, he told us that *she* had been saying lately that it was too good – the whole thing, if we understood, was *too* good. He wished us to get the exact shade of her meaning. She had suggested, or rather implied, this doubt. She had said – he would let us draw our own inferences – that the Chaucer find had 'anticipated the wants of humanity'. Johnson, of course. No need to tell *him* that. But what the hell was her implication? Oh, God! Life had always been one long innuendo! *And* she had said that a man could do anything with any one if he saved him the trouble of thinking. What did she mean by that? *He* had never shirked thought. He had thought sustainedly all his life. It *wasn't* too good, was it? Manallace didn't think it was too good – did he? But this pick-pick-picking at a man's brain and work was too bad, wasn't it? *What* did she mean? Why did she always bring in Manallace, who was only a friend – no scholar, but a lover of the game – Eh? – Manallace could confirm this if he were here, instead of loafing on the Continent just when he was most needed.

'I've come back,' Manallace interrupted, unsteadily. 'I can confirm every word you've said. You've nothing to worry about. It's *your* find – *your* credit – *your* glory and – all the rest of it.'

'Swear you'll tell her so then,' said Castorley. 'She doesn't believe a word I say. She told me she never has since before we were married. Promise!'

Manallace promised, and Castorley added that he had named him his literary executor, the proceeds of the book to go to his wife. 'All profits without deduction,' he gasped. 'Big sales if it's properly handled. *You* don't need money . . . Graydon'll trust *you* to any extent. It 'ud be a long . . .'

He coughed, and, as he caught breath, his pain broke through all the drugs, and the outcry filled the room. Manallace rose to fetch Gleeag, when a full, high, affected voice, unheard for a generation, accompanied, as it seemed, the clamour of a beast in agony, saying: 'I wish to God someone would stop that old swine howling down there! *I* can't . . . I was going to tell you fellows that it would be a dam' long time before Graydon advanced *me* two quid . . .'

We escaped together, and found Gleeag waiting, with Lady Castorley, on the landing. He telephoned me, next morning, that Castorley had died of bronchitis, which his weak state made it impossible for him to throw off. 'Perhaps it's just as well,' he added, in reply to the condolences I asked him to convey to the widow. 'We might have come across something we couldn't have coped with.'

Distance from that house made me bold.

'You knew all along, I suppose? What was it, really?'

'Malignant kidney-trouble – generalised at the end. No use worrying him about it. We let him through as easily as possible. Yes! A happy release . . . What? . . . Oh! Cremation. Friday, at eleven.'

There, then, Manallace and I met. He told me that she had asked him whether the book need now be published; and he had told her this was more than ever necessary, in her interests as well as Castorley's.

'She is going to be known as his widow – for a while, at any rate. Did I perjure myself much with him?'

'Not explicitly,' I answered.

'Well, I have now – with *her* – explicitly,' said he, and took out his black gloves . . .

As, on the appointed words, the coffin crawled sideways through the noiselessly-closing door-flaps, I saw Lady Castorley's eyes turn towards Gleeag.

THE MANNER OF MEN

If after the manner of men I have fought with beasts.
St Paul's First Epistle to the Corinthians, xv. 32

Her cinnabar-tinted[1] topsail, nicking the hot-blue horizon, showed she was a Spanish wheat-boat hours before she reached Marseilles mole. There, her mainsail brailed itself, a spritsail broke out forward, and a handy driver aft; and she threaded her way through the shipping to her berth at the quay as quietly as a veiled woman slips through a bazar.

The blare of her horns told her name to the port. An elderly hook-nosed Inspector came aboard to see if her cargo had suffered in the run from the South, and the senior ship-cat purred round her captain's legs as the after-hatch was opened.

'If the rest is like this – ' the Inspector sniffed – 'you had better run out again to the mole and dump it.'

'That's nothing,' the captain replied. 'All Spanish wheat heats a little. They reap it very dry.'

'Pity you don't keep it so, then. What would you call *that* – crop or pasture?'

The Inspector pointed downwards. The grain was in bulk, and deck-leakage, combined with warm weather, had sprouted it here and there in sickly green films.

'So much the better,' said the captain brazenly. 'That makes it waterproof. Pare off the top two inches, and the rest is as sweet as a nut.'

'*I* told that lie, too, when I was your age. And how does she happen to be loaded?'

The young Spaniard flushed, but kept his temper.

'She happens to be ballasted, under my eye, on lead-pigs and bagged copper-ores.'

'I don't know that they much care for verdigris in their dole-bread[2] at Rome. But – you were saying?'

'I was trying to tell you that the bins happen to be grain-tight, two-inch chestnut, floored and sided with hides.'

'Meaning dressed African leathers on your private account?'[3]

'What has that got to do with you? We discharge at Port of Rome, not here.'

'So your papers show. And what might you have stowed in the wings[4] of her?'

'Oh, apes! Circumcised apes – just like you!'

'Young monkey! Well, if you are not above taking an old ape's advice, next time you happen to top off with wool and screw in more bales than are good for her, get your ship undergirt before you sail. I know it doesn't look smart coming into Port of Rome, but it'll save your decks from lifting worse than they do.'

There was no denying that the planking and water-ways round the after-hatch had lifted a little. The captain lost his temper.

'I know your breed!' he stormed. 'You promenade the quays all summer at Caesar's expense, jamming your Jew-bow into everybody's business; and when the Norther blows, you squat over your brazier and let us skippers hang in the wind for a week!'

'You have it! Just that sort of a man am I now,' the other answered. 'That'll do, the quarter-hatch!'

As he lifted his hand the falling sleeve showed the broad gold armlet with the triple vertical gouges which is only worn by master mariners who have used all three seas – Middle, Western, and Eastern.

'Gods!' The captain saluted. 'I thought you were – '

'A Jew, of course. Haven't you used Eastern ports long enough to know a Red Sidonian when you see one?'

'Mine the fault – yours be the pardon, my father!' said the Spaniard impetuously. 'Her topsides *are* a trifle strained. There was a three days' blow coming up. I meant to have had her undergirt off the Islands, but hawsers slow a ship so – and one hates to spoil a good run.'

'To whom do you say it?' The Inspector looked the young man over between horny sun-and salt-creased eyelids like a brooding pelican. 'But if you care to get up your girt-hawsers to-morrow, I can find men to put 'em overside. It's no work for open sea. Now! Main-hatch, there! . . . I thought so. She'll need another girt abaft the foremast.' He motioned to one of his staff, who hurried up the quay to where the port Guard-boat basked at her mooring-ring. She was a stoutly built single-banker, eleven a side,[5] with a short punching ram; her duty being to stop riots in harbour and piracy along the coast.

'Who commands her?' the captain asked.

'An old shipmate of mine, Sulinor – a River man. We'll get his opinion.'

In the Mediterranean (Nile keeping always her name) there is but one River – that shifty-mouthed Danube, where she works through her deltas into the Black Sea. Up went the young man's eyebrows.

'Is he any kin to a Sulinor of Tomi, who used to be in the flesh-traffic[6] – and a Free Trader?[7] My uncle has told me of him. He calls him Mango.'

'That man. He was my second in the wheat-trade my last five voyages, after the Euxine[8] grew too hot to hold him. But he's in the Fleet now . . . You know your ship best. Where do you think the after-girts ought to come?'

The captain was explaining, when a huge dish-faced Dacian, in short naval cuirass, rolled up the gang-plank, carefully saluting the bust of Caesar on the poop, and asked the captain's name.

'Baeticus, for choice,' was the answer.

They all laughed, for the sea, which Rome mans with foreigners, washes out many shore-names.

'My trouble is this – ' Baeticus began, and they went into committee, which lasted a full hour. At the end, he led them to the poop, where an awning had been stretched, and wines set out with fruits and sweet shore water.

They drank to the Gods of the Sea, Trade, and Good Fortune, spilling those small cups overside, and then settled at ease.

'Girting's an all-day job, if it's done properly,' said the Inspector. 'Can you spare a real working-party by dawn to-morrow, Mango?'

'But surely – for you, Red.'

'I'm thinking of the wheat,' said Quabil curtly. He did not like nicknames so early.

'Full meals *and* drinks,' the Spanish captain put in.

'Good! Don't return 'em too full. By the way' – Sulinor lifted a level cup – 'where do you get this liquor, Spaniard?'

'From our Islands [the Balearics]. Is it to your taste?'

'It is.' The big man unclasped his gorget in solemn preparation.

Their talk ran professionally, for though each end of the Mediterranean scoffs at the other, both unite to mock landward, wooden-headed Rome and her stiff-jointed officials.

Sulinor told a tale of taking the Prefect of the Port, on a breezy day, to Forum Julii, to see a lady, and of his lamentable condition when landed.

'Yes,' Quabil sneered. 'Rome's mistress of the world – as far as the foreshore.'

'If Caesar ever came on patrol with me,' said Sulinor, 'he might understand there was such a thing as the Fleet.'

'Then he'd officer it with well-born young Romans,' said Quabil.

'Be grateful you are left alone. *You* are the last man in the world to
want to see Caesar.'

'Except one,' said Sulinor, and he and Quabil laughed.

'What's the joke?' the Spaniard asked. Sulinor explained.

'We had a passenger, our last trip together, who wanted to see
Caesar.[9] It cost us our ship and freight. That's all.'

'Was he a warlock – a wind-raiser?'

'Only a Jew philosopher. But he *had* to see Caesar. He said he had;
and he piled up the *Eirene* on his way.'

'Be fair,' said Quabil. 'I don't like the Jews – they lie too close to my
own hold – but it was Caesar lost me my ship.' He turned to Baeticus.
'There was a proclamation, our end of the world, two seasons back,
that Caesar wished the Eastern wheat-boats to run through the winter,
and he'd guarantee all loss. Did *you* get it, youngster?'

'No. Our stuff is all in by September. I wager Caesar never paid you!
How late did you start?'

'I left Alexandria across the bows of the Equinox – well down in
the pickle, with Egyptian wheat – half pigeon's-dung – and the usual
load of Greek sutlers[10] and their women. The second day out the sou'-
wester caught me. I made across it north for the Lycian coast, and
slipped into Myra[11] till the wind should let me get back into the regular
grain-track again.'

Sailor-fashion, Quabil began to illustrate his voyage with date and
olive stones from the table.

'The wind went into the north, as I knew it would, and I got under
way. You remember, Mango? My anchors were apeak when a Lycian
patrol threshed in with Rome's order to us to wait on a Sidon packet
with prisoners and officers. Mother of Carthage, I cursed him!'

'Shouldn't swear at Rome's Fleet. Weatherly craft, those Lycian
racers! Fast, too. I've been hunted by 'em! Never thought I'd command
one,' said Sulinor, half aloud.

'And now I'm coming to the leak in *my* decks, young man,' Quabil
eyed Baeticus sternly. 'Our slant north had strained her, and I should
have undergirt her at Myra. Gods know why I didn't! I set up the
chain-staples in the cable-tier for the prisoners. I even had the girt-
hawsers on deck – which saved time later; but the thing I should have
done, that I did *not*.'

'Luck of the Gods!' Sulinor laughed. 'It was because our little
philosopher wanted to see Caesar in his own way at our expense.'

'Why did he want to see him?' said Baeticus.

'As far as I ever made out from him and the centurion, he wanted
to argue with Caesar – about philosophy.'

'He was a prisoner, then?'

'A political suspect – with a Jew's taste for going to law,' Quabil interrupted. 'No orders for irons. Oh, a little shrimp of a man, but – but he seemed to take it for granted that he led everywhere. He messed with us.'

'And he was worth talking to, Red,' said Sulinor.

'*You* thought so; but he had the woman's trick of taking the tone and colour of whoever he talked to. Now – as I was saying . . .'

There followed another illustrated lecture on the difficulties that beset them after leaving Myra. There was always too much west in the autumn winds, and the *Eirene* tacked against it as far as Cnidus. Then there came a northerly slant, on which she ran through the Aegean Islands, for the tail of Crete; rounded that, and began tacking up the south coast.

'Just darning the water again, as we had done from Myra to Cnidus,' said Quabil ruefully. 'I daren't stand out. There was the bone-yard of all the Gulf of Africa under my lee. But at last we worked into Fairhaven[12] – by that cork yonder. Late as it was, I should have taken her on, but I had to call a ship-council as to lying up for the winter. That Rhodian law may have suited open boats and cock-crow coasters,'* but it's childish for ocean-traffic.'

'*I* never allow it in any command of mine,' Baeticus spoke quietly. 'The cowards give the order, and the captain bears the blame.'

Quabil looked at him keenly. Sulinor took advantage of the pause.

'We were in harbour, you see. So our Greeks tumbled out and voted to stay where we were. It was my business to show them that the place was open to many winds, and that if it came on to blow we should drive ashore.'

'Then I,' broke in Quabil, with a large and formidable smile, 'advised pushing on to Phenike, round the cape, only forty miles across the bay. My mind was that, if I could get her undergirt there, I might later – er – coax them out again on a fair wind, and hit Sicily. But the undergirting came first. She was beginning to talk too much – like me now.'

Sulinor chafed a wrist with his hand.

'She was a hard-mouthed old water-bruiser in any sea,' he murmured.

'She could lie within six points of any wind,' Quabil retorted, and hurried on. 'What made Paul vote with those Greeks? He said we'd be sorry if we left harbour.'

---

*Quabil meant the coasters who worked their way by listening to the cocks crowing on the beaches they passed. The insult is nearly as old as sail.

'Every passenger says that, if a bucketful comes aboard,' Baeticus observed.

Sulinor refilled his cup, and looked at them over the brim, under brows as candid as a child's, ere he set it down.

'Not Paul. He did not know fear. He gave me a dose of my own medicine once. It was a morning watch coming down through the Islands. We had been talking about the cut of our topsail – he was right – it held too much lee wind – and then he went to wash before he prayed. I said to him: "You seem to have both ends and the bight[13] of most things coiled down in your little head, Paul. If it's a fair question, what *is* your trade ashore?" And he said: "I've been a man-hunter – Gods forgive me! – and now that I think The God has forgiven me, I am man-hunting again." Then he pulled his shirt over his head, and I saw his back. Did *you* ever see his back, Quabil?'

'I expect I did – that last morning, when we all stripped; but I don't remember.'

'*I* shan't forget it! There was good, sound lictor's work and criss-cross Jew scourgings[14] like gratings; and a stab or two; and, besides those, old dry bites – when they get good hold and rugg you. That showed he must have dealt with the Beasts. So, whatever he'd done, he'd paid for. I was just wondering what he *had* done, when he said: "No; not your sort of man-hunting." "It's your own affair," I said: "but I shouldn't care to see Caesar with a back like that. I should hear the Beasts asking for me." "I may that, too, some day," he said, and began sluicing himself, and – then – What's brought the girls out so early? Oh, I remember!'

There was music up the quay, and a wreathed shoreboat put forth full of Arlesian women. A long-snouted three-banker[15] was hauling from a slip till her trumpets warned the benches to take hold. As they gave way, the *hrmph-hrmph* of the oars in the oar-ports reminded Sulinor, he said, of an elephant choosing his man in the Circus.

'She has been here re-masting. They've no good rough-tree at Forum Julii,' Quabil explained to Baeticus. 'The girls are singing her out.'

The shallop ranged alongside her, and the banks held water, while a girl's voice came across the clock-calm harbour-face:

'Ah, would swift ships had never been about the seas to rove!
For then these eyes had never seen nor ever wept their love.
Over the ocean-rim he came – beyond that verge he passed,
And I who never knew his name must mourn him to the last!'

'And you'd think they meant it,' said Baeticus half to himself.

'That's a pretty stick,' was Quabil's comment as the man-of-war opened the island athwart the harbour. 'But she's overmasted by ten foot. A trireme's only a bird-cage.'

'Luck of the Gods I'm not singing in one now,' Sulinor muttered. They heard the yelp of a bank being speeded[16] up to the short sea-stroke.

'I wish there was some way to save mainmasts from racking.' Baeticus looked up at his own, bangled with copper wire.

'The more reason to undergirt, my son,' said Quabil. '*I* was going to undergirt that morning at Fairhaven. You remember, Sulinor? I'd given orders to overhaul the hawsers the night before. My fault! Never say "To-morrow". The Gods hear you. And then the wind came out of the south, mild as milk. All we had to do was to slip round the headland to Phenike – and be safe.'

Baeticus made some small motion, which Quabil noticed, for he stopped.

'My father – ' the young man spread apologetic palms – 'is not that lying wind the in-draught of Mount Ida? It comes up with the sun, but later – '

'You need not tell *me*! We rounded the cape, our decks like a fair (it was only half a day's sail), and then, out of Ida's bosom the full north-easter stamped on us! Run? What else? I needed a lee to clean up in. Clauda was a few miles down wind; but whether the old lady would bear up when she got there, I was not so sure.'

'She did.' Sulinor rubbed his wrist again. 'We were towing our longboat half-full. I steered somewhat that day.'

'What sail were you showing?' Baeticus demanded.

'None – and twice too much at that. But she came round when Sulinor asked her, and we kept her jogging in the lee of the island. I said, didn't I, that my girt-hawsers were on deck?'

Baeticus nodded. Quabil plunged into his campaign at long and large, telling every shift and device he had employed. 'It was scanting daylight,' he wound up, 'but I daren't slur the job. Then we streamed our boat alongside, baled her, sweated her up, and secured. You ought to have seen our decks!'

'Panic?' said Baeticus.

'A little. But the whips were out early. The centurion – Julius – lent us his soldiers.'

'How did your prisoners behave?' the young man went on.

Sulinor answered him. 'Even when a man is being shipped to the Beasts, he does not like drowning in irons. They tried to rive the chain-staples out of her timbers.'

'I got the main-yard on deck' – this was Quabil. 'That eased her a little. They stopped yelling after a while, didn't they?'

'They did,' Sulinor replied. 'Paul went down and told them there was no danger. And they believed him! Those scoundrels believed him! He asked me for the keys of the leg-bars to make them easier. "*I've* been through this sort of thing before," he said, "but they are new to it down below. Give me the keys." I told him there was no order for him to have any keys; and I recommended him to line his hold for a week in advance,[17] because we were in the hands of the Gods. "And when are we ever out of them?" he asked. He looked at me like an old gull lounging just astern of one's taffrail in a full gale. *You* know that eye, Spaniard?'

'Well do I!'

'By that time' – Quabil took the story again – 'we had drifted out of the lee of Clauda, and our one hope was to run for it and pray we weren't pooped.[18] None the less, I could have made Sicily with luck. As a gale I have known worse, but the wind never shifted a point, d'ye see? We were flogged along like a tired ox.'

'Any sights?' Baeticus asked.

'For ten days not a blink.'

'Nearer two weeks,' Sulinor corrected. 'We cleared the decks of everything except our ground-tackle, and put six hands at the tillers. She seemed to answer her helm – sometimes. Well, it kept *me* warm for one.'

'How did your philosopher take it?'

'Like the gull I spoke of. He was there, but outside it all. *You* never got on with him, Quabil?'

'Confessed! I came to be afraid at last. It was not my office to show fear, but I was. He was fearless, although I knew that he knew the peril as well as I. When he saw that trying to – er – cheer me made me angry, he dropped it. Like a woman, again. You saw more of him, Mango?'

'Much. When I was at the rudders he would hop up to the steerage, with the lower-deck ladders lifting and lunging a foot at a time, and the timbers groaning like men beneath the Beasts. We used to talk, hanging on till the roll jerked us into the scuppers. Then we'd begin again. What about? Oh! Kings and Cities and Gods and Caesar. He was sure he'd see Caesar. I told him I had noticed that people who worried Those Up Above' – Sulinor jerked his thumb towards the awning – 'were mostly sent for in a hurry.'

'Hadn't you wit to see he never wanted you for yourself, but to get something out of you?' Quabil snapped.

'Most Jews are like that – and all Sidonians!' Sulinor grinned. 'But what *could* he have hoped to get from anyone? We were doomed men all. You said it, Red.'

'Only when I was at my emptiest. Otherwise I *knew* that with any luck I could have fetched Sicily! But I broke – we broke. Yes, we got ready – you too – for the Wet Prayer.'

'How does that run with you?' Baeticus asked, for all men are curious concerning the bride-bed of Death.

'With us of the River,' Sulinor volunteered, 'we say: "I sleep; presently I row again."'

'Ah! At our end of the world we cry: "Gods, judge me not as a God, but a man whom the Ocean has broken."' Baeticus looked at Quabil, who answered, raising his cup: 'We Sidonians say, "Mother of Carthage, I return my oar!" But it all comes to the one in the end.' He wiped his beard, which gave Sulinor his chance to cut in.

'Yes, we were on the edge of the Prayer when – do you remember, Quabil? – *he* clawed his way up the ladders and said: "No need to call on what isn't there. My God sends me sure word that I shall see Caesar. *And* he has pledged me all your lives to boot. Listen! No man will be lost." And Quabil said: "But what about my ship?"' Sulinor grinned again.

'That's true. I had forgotten the cursed passengers,' Quabil confirmed. 'But he spoke as though my *Eirene* were a fig-basket. "Oh, she's bound to go ashore, somewhere," he said, "but not a life will be lost. Take this from me, the Servant of the One God." Mad! Mad as a magician on market-day!'

'No,' said Sulinor. 'Madmen see smooth harbours and full meals. I have had to – soothe that sort.'

'After all,' said Quabil, 'he was only saying what had been in my head for a long time. I had no way to judge our drift, but we likely might hit something somewhere. Then he went away to spread his cook-house yarn among the crew. It did no harm, or I should have stopped him.'

Sulinor coughed, and drawled:

'I don't see anyone stopping Paul from what he fancied he ought to do. But it was curious that, on the change of watch, I – '

'No – I!' said Quabil.

'Make it so, then, Red. Between us, at any rate, we felt that the sea had changed. There was a trip and a kick to her dance. *You* know, Spaniard. And then – I *will* say that, for a man half-dead, Quabil here did well.'

'I'm a bo' sun-captain,[19] and not ashamed of it. I went to get a cast of the lead. (Black dark and raining marlinspikes!) The first cast warned me, and I told Sulinor to clear all aft for anchoring by the stern. The next – shoaling like a slip-way – sent me back with all hands, and we dropped both bowers and the spare and the stream.'

'He'd have taken the kedge[20] as well, but I stopped him,' said Sulinor.

'I had to stop *her*! They nearly jerked her stern out, but they held. And everywhere I could peer or hear were breakers, or the noise of tall seas against cliffs. We were trapped! But our people had been starved, soaked, and half-stunned for ten days, and now they were close to a beach. That was enough! They must land on the instant; and was I going to let them drown within reach of safety? *Was* there panic? I spoke to Julius, and his soldiers (give Rome her due!) schooled them till I could hear my orders again. But on the kiss-of-dawn some of the crew said that Sulinor had told them to lay out the kedge in the longboat.'

'I let 'em swing her out,' Sulinor confessed. 'I wanted 'em for warnings. But Paul told me his God had promised their lives to him along with ours, and any private sacrifice would spoil the luck. So, as soon as she touched water, I cut the rope before a man could get in. She was ashore – stove – in ten minutes.'

'Could you make out where you were by then?' Baeticus asked Quabil.

'As soon as I saw the people on the beach – yes. They are my sort – a little removed. Phoenicians by blood. It was Malta – *one* day's run from Syracuse, where I would have been safe! Yes, Malta and my wheat gruel. Good port-of-discharge, eh?'

They smiled, for Melita may mean 'mash' as well as 'Malta'.

'It puddled the sea all round us, while I was trying to get my bearings. But my lids were salt-gummed, and I hiccoughed like a drunkard.'

'And drunk you most gloriously were, Red, half an hour later!'

'Praise the Gods – and for once your pet Paul! That little man came to me on the fore-bitts, puffed like a pigeon, and pulled out a breastful of bread, and salt fish, and the wine – the good new wine. "Eat," he said, "and make all your people eat, too. Nothing will come to them except another wetting. They won't notice that, after they're full. Don't worry about *your* work either," he said. "You *can't* go wrong today. You are promised to me." And then he went off to Sulinor.'

'He did. He came to me with bread and wine and bacon – good they were! But first he said words over them, and then rubbed his hands with his wet sleeves. I asked him if he were a magician. "Gods forbid!" he said. "I am so poor a soul that I flinch from touching dead pig." As a Jew, he wouldn't like pork, naturally. Was that before or after our people broke into the store-room, Red?'

'Had *I* time to wait on them?' Quabil snorted. 'I know they gutted my stores full-hand, and a double blessing of wine atop. But we all

took that – deep. Now this is how we lay.' Quabil smeared a ragged
loop on the table with a wine-wet finger. 'Reefs – see, my son – and
overfalls to leeward here; something that loomed like a point of land
on our right there; and, ahead, the blind gut of a bay with a Cyclops
surf hammering it. How we had got in was a miracle. Beaching was
our only chance, and meantime she was settling like a tired camel.
Every foot I could lighten her meant that she'd take ground closer
in at the last. I told Julius. He understood. "I'll keep order," he
aid. "Get the passengers to shift the wheat as long as you judge
it's safe."'

'Did those Alexandrian achatours[21] really work?' said Baeticus.

'*I*'ve never seen cargo discharged quicker. It was time. The wind was
taking off in gusts, and the rain was putting down the swells. I made
out a patch of beach that looked less like death than the rest of the
arena, and I decided to drive in on a gust under the spitfire-sprit – and,
if she answered her helm before she died on us, to humour her a shade
to starboard, where the water looked better. I stayed the foremast; set
the spritsail fore and aft, as though we were boarding; told Sulinor to
have the rudders down directly he cut the cables; waited till a gust
came; squared away the sprit, and drove.'

Sulinor carried on promptly: –

'I had two hands with axes on each cable, and one on each rudder-
lift; and, believe me, when Quabil's pipe went, both blades were down
and turned before the cable-ends had fizzed under! She jumped like a
stung cow! She drove. She sheared. I think the swell lifted her, and
overran. She came down, and struck aft. Her stern broke off under my
toes, and all the guts of her at that end slid out like a man's paunched
by a lion. I jumped forward, and told Quabil there was nothing but
small kindlings abaft the quarter-hatch, and he shouted: "Never mind!
Look how beautifully I've laid her!"'

'I had. What I took for a point of land to starboard, y'see, turned
out to be almost a bridge-islet, with a swell of sea 'twixt it and the
main. And that meeting-swill, d'you see, surging in as she drove, gave
her four or five foot more to cushion on. I'd hit the exact instant.'

'Luck of the Gods, *I* think! Then we began to bustle our people
over the bows before she went to pieces. You'll admit Paul was a help
there, Red?'

'I dare say he herded the old judies well enough; but he should have
lined up with his own gang.'

'He did that, too,' said Sulinor. 'Some fool of an under-officer had
discovered that prisoners must be killed if they look like escaping; and
he chose that time and place to put it to Julius – sword drawn. Think

of hunting a hundred prisoners to death on those decks! It would have been worse than the Beasts!'

'But Julius saw – Julius saw it,' Quabil spoke testily. 'I heard him tell the man not to be a fool. They couldn't escape further than the beach.'

'And how did your philosopher take *that*?' said Baeticus.

'As usual,' said Sulinor. 'But, you see, we two had dipped our hands in the same dish for weeks; and, on the River, that makes an obligation between man and man.'

'In my country also,' said Baeticus, rather stiffly.

'So I cleared my dirk – in case I had to argue. Iron always draws iron with me. But *he* said: "Put it back. They are a little scared." I said: "Aren't *you*?" "What?" he said; "of being killed, you mean? No. Nothing can touch me till I've seen Caesar." Then he carried on steadying the ironed men (some were slavering-mad) till it was time to unshackle them by fives, and give 'em their chance. The natives made a chain through the surf, and snatched them out breast-high.'

'Not a life lost! Like stepping off a jetty,' Quabil proclaimed.

'Not quite. But he had promised no one should drown.'

'How *could* they – the way I had laid her – gust and swell and swill together?'

'And was there any salvage?'

'Neither stick nor string, my son. We had time to look, too. We stayed on the island till the first spring ship sailed for Port of Rome. They hadn't finished Ostia breakwater that year.'

'And, of course, Caesar paid you for your ship?'

'I made no claim. I saw it would be hopeless; and Julius, who knew Rome, was against any appeal to the authorities. He said that was the mistake Paul was making. And, I suppose, because I did not trouble them, and knew a little about the sea, they offered me the Port Inspectorship here. There's no money in it – if I were a poor man. Marseilles will never be a port again. Narbo has ruined her for good.'

'But Marseilles is far from under-Lebanon,'[22] Baeticus suggested.

'The further the better. I lost my boy three years ago in Foul Bay, off Berenice, with the Eastern Fleet. He was rather like you about the eyes, too. You and your circumcised apes!'

'But – honoured one! My Master! Admiral! – Father mine – how *could* I have guessed?'

The young man leaned forward to the other's knee in act to kiss it. Quabil made as though to cuff him, but his hand came to rest lightly on the bowed head.

'Nah! Sit, lad! Sit back. It's just the thing the Boy would have said himself. You didn't hear it, Sulinor?'

'I guessed it had something to do with the likeness as soon as I set eyes on him. You don't so often go out of your way to help lame ducks.'

'You can see for yourself she needs undergirting, Mango!'

'So did that Tyrian tub last month. And you told her she might bear up for Narbo or bilge for all of you! But he shall have his working-party to-morrow, Red.'

Baeticus renewed his thanks. The River man cut him short.

'Luck of the Gods,' he said. 'Five – four – years ago I might have been waiting for you anywhere in the Long Puddle with fifty River men – and no moon.'

Baeticus lifted a moist eye to the slip-hooks on his yard-arm, that could hoist and drop weights at a sign.

'You might have had a pig or two of ballast through your benches coming alongside,' he said dreamily.

'And where would my overhead-nettings have been?' the other chuckled.

'Blazing – at fifty yards. What are fire-arrows for?'

'To fizzle and stink on my wet seaweed blindages. Try again.'

They were shooting their fingers at each other, like the little boys gambling for olive-stones on the quay beside them.

'Go on – go on, my son! Don't let that pirate board,' cried Quabil.

Baeticus twirled his right hand very loosely at the wrist.

'In that case,' he countered, 'I should have fallen back on my foster-kin – my father's island horsemen.'

Sulinor threw up an open palm.

'Take the nuts,' he said. 'Tell me, is it true that those infernal Balearic slingers of yours can turn a bull by hitting him on the horns?'

'On either horn you choose. My father farms near New Carthage. They come over to us for the summer to work. There are ten in my crew now.'

Sulinor hiccoughed and folded his hands magisterially over his stomach.

'Quite proper. Piracy *must* be put down! Rome says so. I do so,' said he.

'I see,' the younger man smiled. 'But tell me, why did you leave the slave – the Euxine trade, O Strategos?'

'That sea is too like a wine-skin. Only one neck. It made mine ache. So I went into the Egyptian run with Quabil here.'

'But why take service in the Fleet? Surely the Wheat pays better?'

'I intended to. But I had dysentery at Malta that winter, and Paul looked after me.'

'Too much muttering and laying-on of hands for *me*,' said Quabil; himself muttering about some Thessalian jugglery with a snake[23] on the island.

'*You* weren't sick, Quabil. When I was getting better, and Paul was washing me off once, he asked if my citizenship were in order. He was a citizen himself. Well, it was and it was not. As second of a wheat-ship I was *ex officio* Roman citizen – for signing bills and so forth. But on the beach, my ship perished, he said I reverted to my original shtay – status – of an extra-provinshal Dacian by a Sich – Sish – Scythian – I think she was – mother. Awkward – what? All the Middle Sea echoes like a public bath if a man is wanted.'

Sulinor reached out again and filled. The wine had touched his huge bulk at last.

'But, as I was saying, once *in* the Fleet nowadays one is a Roman with authority – no waiting twenty years for your papers. And Paul said to me: "Serve Caesar. You are not canvas I can cut[24] to advantage at present. But if you serve Caesar you will be obeying at least some sort of law." He talked as though I were a barbarian. Weak as I was, I could have snapped his back with my bare hands. I told him so. "I don't doubt it," he said. "But that is neither here nor there. If you take refuge under Caesar at sea, you may have time to think. Then I may meet you again, and we can go on with our talks. But that is as The God wills. What concerns you *now* is that, by taking service, you will be free from the fear that has ridden you all your life."'

'Was he right?' asked Baeticus after a silence.

'He was. I had never spoken to him of it, but he knew it. *He* knew! Fire – sword – the sea – torture even – one does not think of them too often. But not the Beasts! Aie! *Not* the Beasts! I fought two dog-wolves for the life on a sand-bar when I was a youngster. Look!'

Sulinor showed his neck and chest.

'They set the sheep-dogs on Paul at some place or other once – because of his philosophy! And he was going to see Caesar – going to see Caesar! And he – he had washed me clean after dysentery!'

'Mother of Carthage, you never told me that!' said Quabil.

'Nor should I now, had the wine been weaker.'

Notes

In compiling these notes, I have frequently consulted *The New Reader's Guide to the Works of Rudyard Kipling* (abbreviated as *NRG*), general editor, John Radcliffe (http://www.kipling.org.uk/): and E. W. Martindell's *Bibliography of the Works of Rudyard Kipling 1881–1923* (Bodley Head, 1923). For the early stories, I have also used Henry Yule and A. C. Burnell (eds.), *Hobson-Jobson: A Glossary of Anglo-Indian Colloquial Words and Phrases* (1886; repr. 1996) a useful guide for Anglo-Indian terms of Kipling's time in India. I am also deeply grateful to John Walker, librarian of the Kipling Society, for his help.

THE GATE OF THE HUNDRED SORROWS

First published in the *Civil and Military Gazette*, 26 September 1884; collected in *Plain Tales from the Hills* (1888).

1. *pice*: Smallest Indian coin: one-quarter of an anna, one-sixty-fourth of a rupee (*Hobson-Jobson*); equivalent to about 3p today.
2. *Gabral Misquitta, the half-caste*: A Eurasian of Portuguese descent.
3. *the Mosque of Wazir Khan*: A seventeenth-century mosque near Delhi Gate, Lahore.
4. *pukka*: Substantial, first-class (from Hindi *pakka*; *Hobson-Jobson*).
5. *chandoo-khanas*: Opium dens, from *chandoo*: extract or preparation of opium; *khana* house or room (*NRG*).
6. *Joss*: Idol or household god (pidgin, from Portuguese *Deus*; *Hobson-Jobson*).
7. *Babus*: 'Baboo: a native clerk who writes English' (*Hobson-Jobson*).
8. *bazar-woman*: Prostitute.
9. *MacSomebody*: McIntosh Jelulladin, who appears in 'To Be Filed For Reference' (*Plain Tales from the Hills*).
10. *'first-chop'*: Best quality (pidgin; *Hobson-Jobson*).

IN THE HOUSE OF SUDDHOO

First published in the *Civil and Military Gazette*, 30 April 1886; collected in
Plain Tales from the Hills (1888).

1.   *Churel*: The malignant ghost of a woman who died in childbed.
2.   *ghoul*: Goblin or man-devouring demon (*Hobson-Jobson*).
3.   *Taksali Gate*: Gate in the West Wall of Lahore (*NRG*).
4.   *seal-cutting*: Engraving signet rings and seals.
5.   *Bareilly*: Town 150 miles east of Delhi (*NRG*).
6.   *adulterator*: Man who dilutes goods with something inferior.
7.   *ekka*: Unsprung cart pulled by one pony (*Hobson-Jobson*).
8.   *Ranjit Singh's Tomb*: Outside Lahore fort (*NRG*).
9.   *Huzuri Bagh*: Garden nearby (*NRG*).
10. *Sirkar*: Government of India (*NRG*).
11. *the Empress of India*: Queen Victoria.
12. *jadoo*: Conjuring (*Hobson-Jobson*).
13. *between one hundred and two hundred rupees*: A substantial sum, about
     six months' pay for a house servant. Kipling's starting salary on the *Civil
     and Military Gazette* was 150 rupees per month.
14. *hookahs*: Water-cooled tobacco pipes (*Hobson-Jobson*).
15. *a thermantidote-paddle*: Blade of a rotating fan fitted in a window-opening
     and encased in wet cloths, used in British India to drive in a current of
     cooled air.
16. *Poe's account of the voice that came from the mesmerised dying man*:
     See Edgar Allan Poe, 'The Facts of the Case of M. Valdemar' (1845).
17. *teraphim*: Idols and images: objects of reverence or divination.
18. *Lazarus*: Dead man brought to life by Jesus (John 11: 1–46).
19. *bunnia*: Money-lender (*banyan, Hobson-Jobson*).

THE STRANGE RIDE OF MORROWBIE JUKES

First published in *Quartette*, a 'Christmas annual' supplement of work by
Kipling, his parents and sister, in the *Civil and Military Gazette*, December 1885;
collected in *The Phantom 'Rickshaw*, no. 5 of the Indian Railway Library series
(1888), and in *Wee Willie Winkie and Other Stories* (1895).

1.   *Bikanir*: Rajput state, much of which is desert.
2.   *C-spring barouches*: Luxurious sprung carriages.
3.   *Minton tiles*: An expensive brand of ceramic tiles manufactured by the
     firm of Minton, Stoke-on-Trent.

4. *Pakpattan*: Capital of a small province in the Punjab, now part of Pakistan (*NRG*).
5. *Mubarakpur*: City in Uttar Pradesh, India (*NRG*).
6. *in terrorem*: 'In order to frighten': to warn (Latin).
7. *persuaders*: Spurs.
8. *cob*: A short-legged, stout horse.
9. *ant-lion*: Insect of the genus *Myrmelon*, whose larva hunts by digging a pit in sand and waiting there for ants to fall in.
10. *terra firma*: firm ground, dry land (Latin).
11. *Martini-Henry 'picket'*: Long bullet fired by breech-loading 'Martini-Henry' rifle, used by the British Army from 1871 to 1888.
12. *fakirs*: Ascetic beggar-priests (*Hobson-Jobson*).
13. *Sahib*: Lord, Master: honorific used by colonial Indians to address Europeans.
14. *a Deccanee Brahmin*: Member of a priestly caste, from the south (*Hobson-Jobson*).
15. *Caste-mark*: Mark on the forehead indicating caste.
16. *continuations*: Trousers (slang).
17. *ghat*: Hindu funeral pyre (*Hobson-Jobson*).
18. *Okara Station*: City in the Punjab, now Pakistan (*NRG*).
19. *tiffin*: Light luncheon (*Hobson-Jobson*).
20. *Rs.9-8-5*: Equivalent to £33.37 today. A rupee was a silver coin, the equivalent of one shilling in Victorian England, worth £3.50 or $ US 5 in contemporary currency. The anna is one-sixteenth of a rupee; a pie (pl. pice) one-quarter of an anna.
21. *as bakshish*: For tipping.
22. *chapatti*: Flat Indian bread.
23. *nausea of the Channel passage*: Seasickness when crossing the English Channel, which can be very rough.
24. *women aged to all appearance as the Fates themselves*: In Greek mythology, the Fates were represented as old women.
25. *videlicet*: Namely (Latin).
26. *canon*: Law.
27. *The crew of the ill-fated Mignonette*: In July 1884 the three-man crew of the wrecked yacht *Mignonette*, having escaped in a dinghy without water, cut the cabin-boy's throat and drank his blood. They were later convicted of murder.
28. *bents*: Reeds.
29. *greatest good of greatest number is political maxim*: 'The greatest happiness of the greatest number is the foundation of morals and legislation': Jeremy Bentham, utilitarian philosopher (1748–1832).
30. *Feringhi*: A derogatory term for an European in India (*Hobson-Jobson*).

31. *Vishnu*: 'The Preserver'; Hindu deity, second in the triad Brahma, Vishnu and Shiva, representing the supreme spirit.
32. *punkah-ropes*: A punkah was a large swinging fan suspended from a ceiling, pulled by a coolie.

LISPETH

First published in *Civil and Military Gazette*, 29 November 1886; collected in *Plain Tales from the Hills* (1888).

1. *Kotgarh*: Town 30 miles east of Simla on the Tibet road (*NRG*).
2. *pahari*: Mountainous or hilly, sometimes 'hard' (*NRG*).
3. *Moravian missionaries*: The Moravians were a Protestant sect from Saxony, responsible for the first large-scale Protestant missionary movement.
4. *Diana of the Romans*: Roman goddess of virginity and hunting.
5. '*globe-trotters*': Derogatory term for tourists.
6. *The P. & O. fleet*: The Peninsular and Orient Fleet, sailing regularly between Britain and India, often mentioned by Kipling.
7. *Simla*: The summer capital of the British in India from 1864.
8. *Narkanda*: A beauty spot 12 miles from Kotgarh (*NRG*).
9. *Tarka Devi*: Goddess of the dawn (*NRG*).

BEYOND THE PALE

First published in *Plain Tales from the Hills* (1888). The title means 'out of bounds'. In the Middle Ages the 'Pale' divided a strip of eastern Ireland under English jurisdiction from the mainland where English laws did not hold.

1. *bustee*: Inhabited quarter, village (*NRG*).
2. *Gully*: A narrow alley.
3. *cow-byre*: The cows or buffaloes kept for milk in Indian cities were kept in their sheds.
4. *dhak*: East Indian tree bearing a profusion of intense vermilion velvet-textured blooms, sometimes called 'Flame of the Forest' (*Hobson-Jobson*).
5. *boorka*: Or 'burka', a veil covering a Muslim woman from the head down, with holes for the eyes.

DRAY WARA YOW DEE

First published in *The Week's News*, Allahabad, 28 April 1888; reprinted in *In Black and White*, no. 3 of the Indian Railway Library (1888); collected in

Soldiers Three and Other Stories (1895). The title (as translated in the text) means. 'All three are one'.

1. *Tirah*: Valley south-west of the Khyber Pass.
2. *trulls*: Trollops, prostitutes.
3. *Peshawur*: Peshawar; ancient capital and garrison of the north-west province of Pakistan.
4. *Amir*: Emir of Afghanistan.
5. *Pubbi*: Town on the Grand Trunk Road near Peshawar (*NRG*).
6. *Bokhariot belt*: Belt manufactured in Bokhara, Uzbekistan.
7. *Thana*: police station (*Hobson-Jobson*).
8. *a sweeper . . . lizard-men*: low-caste men, lizard-eaters.
9. *eight annas*: Half a rupee, worth about sixpence in Victorian currency, *c*. £1.50 today.
10. *an Afridi*: Member of a Pathan tribe.
11. *Abazai*: Another Pathan tribe.
12. *Rahman*: Abdul Rahman Baba (1653–1711), Pushtu and member of the Sufis, a mystical Muslim sect.
13. *Uzbegs*: Cavalry lancers in the Afghan army (*NRG*).
14. *from the Fakr to the Isha*: From the dawn prayer to the sunset prayer (*NRG*).
15. *Cherat*: Hill station and cantonment in the Peshawar district.
16. *matchlock*: Musket using a fuse to light the gunpowder.
17. *Kabul river*: Rises in the Hindu Kush, joins the Swat east of the city and the Indus at Attock or Uttock (*NRG*).
18. *charpoy*: Bedstead (*Hobson-Jobson*).
19. *Dora*: Darra, the pass between Peshawar and Kohat (*NRG*, which also identifies the other places in the Punjab where the speaker journeys before he loses his bearings when he goes south of Delhi, not glossed here).
20. *Black Water*: The ocean, also the penal colony in the Andaman Islands.
21. *Jamun*: Sweet fruit (*Hobson-Jobson*).
22. *Ak*: Thorn-tree (*Hobson-Jobson*).
23. *Alghias! Alghias!*: Exclamation of sorrow.
24. *Djinns*: Spirits.

AT THE PIT'S MOUTH

First published in *Under the Deodars*, no.4 of the Indian Railway Library (1888); collected in *Wee Willie Winkie and Other Stories* (1895).

1. *Men say . . . 'Enderby'*: 'The High Tide on the Coast of Lincolnshire (1571)' by Jean Ingelow (1820–97). In this Victorian ballad, which Kipling

also quotes in the later story 'My Son's Wife', (*A Diversity of Creatures*, 1917), a totally unexpected flood brings death to the unwary 'Elizabeth' and her children. Probably quoting from memory, Kipling here edits and rearranges lines 1–4 of Ingelow's stanza 2 and lines 6–7 of stanza 17 into a single stanza.

2. *Tertium Quid*: 'Third Something'; also the speaker of Book 4 of Robert Browning's *The Ring and the Book* (1869), a long poem dramatizing conflicting perspectives on a drama of adultery and death. Here, the wife's lover is implied.

3. *Jakko or Observatory Hill*: On the outskirts of Simla (*NRG*).

4. *four-hundred-rupee bracelets*: Expensive bracelets; 400 rupees represents more than £1,000 today.

5. *Elysium*: North of the Mashobra Tunnel, which is 5 miles east of Simla (*NRG*).

6. *as far as the Tara Devi gap*: Four miles south of Simla (*NRG*).

7. *ayahs*: Indian nannies (*Hobson-Jobson*).

8. *cantonments*: Military stations.

9. *ulster*: Overcoat.

10. *Fagoo*: Fagu, 5 miles east of Mashobra Tunnel on the Simla–Tibet road (*NRG*).

11. *snaffle*: Jointed bit, giving less control of a horse than a curb bit.

12. *Indian corn*: maize.

13. *Medusa*: In Greek mythology, a monstrous woman with serpents in her hair, whose glaring eyes turned live things to stone.

A WAYSIDE COMEDY

First published in *The Week's News*, 21 January 1888; issued in *Under the Deodars*, no.4 of the Indian Railway Library (1888); collected in *Wee Willie Winkie and Other Stories* (1895).

1. *jhils*: Ponds (*Hobson-Jobson*).

2. *Kashima . . . Dosehri hills . . . Narkarra*: Fictitious places.

3. *masonry platform*: Terrace.

4. *Samson broke the pillars of Gaza*: Samson, after being captured, chained and blinded by the Philistines, was brought into their palace at Gaza, containing three thousand men and women, and pulled down its pillars 'So the dead which he slew at his death were more than they which he slew in his life': Judges 16: 21–30.

5. *two days' dâk*: Two days' travel. A *dak* or *dawk* is a relay of men or horses carrying post (*Hobson-Jobson*).

6.   *terai hat*: Wide-brimmed hat with ventilation holes worn by Anglo-Indians (*Hobson-Jobson*).

7.   *purdah*: Curtain, often separating women's quarters in Hindu or Muslim homes (*Hobson-Jobson*).

8.   *mashing*: Flirting with.

9.   *to give 'satisfaction'*: To allow the injured husband to avenge the insult by fighting a duel.

10.   *sais*: Groom (*Hobson-Jobson*).

THE STORY OF MUHAMMAD DIN

First published in the *Civil and Military Gazette*, 8 September 1886; collected in *Plain Tales from the Hills* (1888).

1.   *Munichandra*: Believed to be from the Sanskrit 'Hymns of the Saints', trans. Peter Peterson (*NRG*).

2.   *khitmutgar*: Butler (*Hobson-Jobson*).

3.   *budmash*: Criminal (*Hobson-Jobson*).

4.   *jail-khana*: Prison.

5.   *Salaam*: Greeting.

6.   *rude*: Roughly drawn.

LITTLE TOBRAH

First published in the *Civil and Military Gazette*, 17 July 1888, collected in *Life's Handicap* (1891). A 'tobrah' is the leather nosebag in which a horse's feed is administered (*Hobson-Jobson*).

1.   *voyage across the other Black Water*: Little Tobrah fears that if he survives, he could be sent to the Andaman Islands used after the 1857 Mutiny as a much-feared penal colony.

2.   *net*: Slung beneath a cart to hold forage, etc.

3.   *Telis*: Members of a business caste, makers of edible oil (*NRG*). The oil would be pressed from seeds, crushed in a simple mill worked by a bullock harnessed to a central beam.

4.   *Bapri-bap*: Exclamation of surprise.

5.   *bunnia-folk*: Corn-dealers, money-lenders.

6.   *seven annas and six pies*: Equivalent to about £2 in today's currency.

THE FINANCES OF THE GODS

First published in *Life's Handicap* (1891). This story of the god Ganesh is also told in John Lockwood Kipling's *Beast and Man in India: A Popular Sketch of Indian Animals in Their Relations with the People* (Macmillan, 1892), pp. 211–13.

1. *Dhunni Bhagat's Chubara*: Monastery in north India, affectionately described in Kipling's 'Preface' to *Life's Handicap*, a centre for wandering mendicants and for ancient holy men.
2. *Gobind*: Holy mendicant and storyteller who has retired to the Chubara, described in the same 'Preface'.
3. *cow-dung cakes*: Dried cow-dung used for fuel.
4. *slate*: A piece of slate framed in wood, on which school exercises were written and erased, used in Victorian schools.
5. *Perlay-ball. Ow-at! Ran, ran, ran!*: Hindi approximation of the cricketing phrases 'Play the ball', 'How's that?' 'Run, run, run!'
6. *Arré, arré, arré!*: Words of encouragement.
7. *jujube-trees*: *Zikzyphus* trees bearing edible berries.
8. *Ganesh of the elephant head*: Hindu god of good luck and prosperity, represented with an elephant's head.
9. *lakh*: One hundred thousand (*Hobson-Jobson*).

BAA BAA, BLACK SHEEP

First published in the Christmas supplement to *The Week's News*, 21 December 1888; collected in *Wee Willie Winkie and Other Stories* (1895).

This autobiographical story closely corresponds to Kipling's briefer but equally bitter account of the experiences which he and his sister Alice, 'Punch' and 'Judy' of this story, endured in the 'House of Desolation' (Lorne Lodge, Southsea) in his posthumous memoir *Something of Myself*. It is also borne out by his sister's memoir, 'Some Childhood Memories of Rudyard Kipling', Mrs A. M. Fleming, *Chambers' Journal*, March 1939.

1. *'When I was in my father's house, I was in a better place'*: *As You Like It*, Act 2, scene 4: 'When I was at home, I was in a better place.'
2. *ayah*: Nanny.
3. *hamal*: Bath attendant (*NRG*).
4. *Meeta, the big Surti boy*: In *Something of Myself*, Kipling names 'Meeta' as his own 'bearer' (*Something of Myself and Other Autobiographical Writings*, ed. Thomas Pinney (Cambridge University Press 1985), p.3). *Surti*: from Surat (*NRG*).

5. *Punch-baba*: 'Baba', from Turki 'father', was used as affectionate diminutive to children (*Hobson-Jobson*).

6. *give me put-put*: Smack me.

7. *Ghauts*: Landing-places (*Hobson-Jobson*).

8. *Belait*: Britain (*Hobson-Jobson*).

9. *brougham*: Carriage.

10. *Apollo Bunder*: Main quay at Bombay, now Mumbai (*NRG*).

11. *broom-gharri*: That is, a smart carriage or brougham, from Hindi *gharri*, carriage (*Hobson-Jobson*).

12. *rune*: In this context, a charm or spell.

13. *'Sonny, my soul'*: 'Sun of my soul, Thou Saviour dear/ It is not night if thou be near': no. 24 of *Hymns Ancient and Modern: for use in Church Services with the Accompanying Tunes*, ed. H. Monk (1861).

14. *Downe Lodge*: Fictionalized name of Lorne Lodge, home of the foster-parents, the Holloways.

15. *a woman in black*: The original of 'Antirosa' was Sarah Holloway.

16. *a man, big, bony, grey, and lame as to one leg*: The original of 'Uncle Harry' was Captain Pryse Agar Holloway.

17. *a boy of twelve*: The original of 'Harry' was Henry Thomas Pryse Holloway, b. 1860.

18. *Navarino*: Site of a naval battle in 1824.

19. *curse God and die*: Job 2: 9.

20. *Rocklington*: Fictionalized Southsea.

21. *The City of Dreadful Night*: Misattribution for the verses slightly mis-quoted from A. H. Clough's poem 'Easter Day, Naples 1849': 'Eat, drink and die, for we are souls bereaved'.

22. *harbours where ships lay at anchor*: Southsea is close to Portsmouth, a major naval base.

23. *sovereigns*: gold coins worth £1, roughly £70 today.

24. *the wadding of a bullet*: Bullets for muzzle-loading rifles were rammed down on the gunpowder with a piece of cloth called 'wadding', a fragment of which might be driven into a wound.

25. *a 'falchion'*: A broad curved sword.

26. *pot-hooks*: curved lines made by children learning to write.

27. *Tilbury*: Two-wheeled horse-drawn vehicle.

28. *Black Sheep*: A bad character, disreputable member of the family.

29. *Cometh up as a Flower*: Novel by Rhoda Broughton (1840–1920).

30. *Journeys end . . . doth know*: From Feste's song 'O mistress mine', *Twelfth Night*, Act 2, scene 3.

31. *hubshi*: A black man, African (*Hobson-Jobson*).

32. *tout court*: Simply; that is, without any further name.

33. *the offence of Cain*: Cain who killed his brother Abel was accursed as the first murderer. See Genesis 4: 1–15.
34. *board-wages*: Wages allowed to servants to pay for their food.
35. *the Fear of the Lord was . . . the beginning of falsehood*: Apt misquotation from Psalm 111: 10: 'The fear of the Lord is the beginning of wisdom.'

THE MAN WHO WOULD BE KING

First published in *The Phantom 'Rickshaw*, no. 5 of the Indian Railway Library (1888); collected in *Wee Willie Winkie and Other Stories* (1895).

1. *'Brother to a Prince . . . worthy'*: From Kipling's own poem 'Banquet Night'.
2. *The Law*: The Masonic Law.
3. *upon the road to Mhow from Ajmir*: The line from Ajmir on which Kipling himself had travelled to reach Udaipur, when in 1887 the *Pioneer* newspaper sent him to travel in the Native States of Rajputana and report what he saw. These travel articles, entitled 'Letters of Marque', were published in the *Pioneer* and later collected in *From Sea to Sea* (1899). Mhow is a town and cantonment and Ajmir is the capital of Rajputana (*NRG*).

    Kipling wrote a long letter describing his experiences on this assignment to his cousin Margaret Burne-Jones, including the incident when he was asked by an unknown fellow Mason to deliver a mysterious message to another Mason, also unknown, who was travelling through a desert by a night express (see *The Letters of Rudyard Kipling*, ed. Thomas Pinney (Macmillan, 1990), vol. 1, p. 153), just as in this story.
4. *Eurasian*: Person of mixed Indian and European race, regarded as inferior by the colonial English.
5. *Backwoodsman*: Nickname of the *Pioneer* newspaper.
6. *going to the West . . . From the East . . . for the sake of my Mother*: phrases from the Masonic ritual of the Third Degree (NRG).
7. *Harun-al-Raschid*: (763–809), Caliph of Baghdad, hero of the *Arabian Nights*.
8. *I did business with divers Kings*: Cf. Kipling's letter to Margaret Burne-Jones: 'I railed and rode and drove and tramped and slept in Kings' palaces or under the stars themselves . . . and came to stately Residences where I feasted in fine linen and came to desolate way stations where I slept with natives upon cotton bales' (*Letters*, ed. Pinney, vol. 1, p. 151).
9. *Princes and Politicals*: Rulers of independent Native States and the resident British officials advising them.
10. *Zenana-mission ladies*: Missionaries to Indian women secluded in the women's quarters.

11. *Mister Gladstone*: Liberal Prime Minister, disliked by Kipling.

12. *as blank as Modred's shield*: This was 'blank as death': Tennyson, 'Gareth and Lynette', line 409.

13. *two strong men can Sar-a-whack*: Allusion to James Brooke, who became Rajah of Sarawak, Borneo, in 1841.

14. *Kafiristan*: remote area in north-east of Hindu Kush Afghanistan, inhabited by polytheistic tribes who were subdued and Islamicized by the Emir of Afghanistan in 1895–6, after the date of this story.

15. *Roberts' Army*: In the Second Afghan War (1878–80), the British forces were commanded by Sir Frederick (subsequently Lord) Roberts.

16. *Wood on the Sources of the Oxus*: Captain John Wood, *A Journey to the Source of the Oxus* (1841).

17. *United Services' Institute*: The Royal United Services Institute for Defence and Security Studies, Whitehall, which had a branch in Simla (*NRG*).

18. *Bellew*: Henry Walter Bellew, *Our Punjab Frontier, being a concise account of the various tribes* (1868).

19. *Raverty*: Major Henry George Raverty, *Notes of Afghanistan and Baluchistan* (1888).

20. *Roum*: Istanbul.

21. *Protected of God*: Madman (*NRG*).

22. *King of the Roos*: Tsar of the Russians.

23. *Pir Khan*: A political and religious leader: *Pir* is the descendant of a saint and *Khan* the leader of a clan (*NRG*).

24. *Huzrut*: Sir (*NRG*).

25. *Hazar*: Get ready (*NRG*).

26. *Martini*: See 'The Strange Ride of Morrowbie Jukes', n. 11, above.

27. *through the Khyber*: Through the Khyber Pass to Afghanistan.

28. *small charm compass*: A Masonic emblem.

29. *Imbra*: Chief god of Kafiristan (*NRG*).

30. *jim-jams*: In this context, idols.

31. *be fruitful and multiply*: Genesis 8: 17.

32. *matchlocks*: See 'Dray Wara Yow Dee', n.16, above.

33. *"Occupy till I come"*: Luke 19: 13.

34. *son of Alexander by Queen Semiramis*: That is, the descendant of ancient heroes: Alexander the Great and the legendary Semiramis, Assyrian queen of Babylon.

35. *The Craft's the trick*: Freemasonry.

36. *Mach on the Bolan*: Railway station on the Bolan Pass leading to Quetta (*NRG*).

37. *Fellow Craft Grip*: Masonic handshake.

38. *they've cut the marks on the rocks*: Masonic emblems, such as square and compasses (*NRG*).

39. *"It's against all the law"*: Masonic law requires a new Lodge to have a warrant from the Grand Lodge to the registered (*NRG*).

40. *apron*: Ornamental wear at Masonic ceremonies.

41. *sons of Alexander*: In the mythology of Freemasonry, Alexander the Great was once considered a Masonic Grand Master.

42. *Master's Mark*: The apron of the Master of a Lodge shows three inverted T signs, unlike ordinary ones, which have turquoise rosettes (*NRG*).

43. *By virtue of the authority vested in me by my own right hand*: This too is 'against the law', as a Master Mason must be installed by his predecessor (*NRG*).

44. *Communication*: Regular meeting held by a Grand Lodge, usually quarterly (*NRG*).

45. *jezails*: Long, heavy Afghan muskets.

46. *Rajah Brooke:* See n. 13 above.

47. *Sniders*: The Enfield Snider was a breech-loading rifle, issued to the British Army from 1893 to 1871 after which it was superseded for white troops (though not 'natives') by the Martini-Henry.

48. *The Bible says that Kings ain't to waste their strength on women*: Proverbs 31: 3.

49. *our 'Fifty-Seven*: Our Indian Rebellion (the Mutiny of 1857).

50. *'The Son of God . . . in his train'*: Hymn by Bishop R. Heber, *Hymns Ancient and Modern*, no. 439.

NABOTH

First published in the *Civil and Military Gazette*, 26 August 1886; collected in *Life's Handicap* (1891).

The title is from 1 Kings 21. Naboth possessed a vineyard close to the palace of King Ahab who wanted it for his garden. When Naboth refused to sell 'the inheritance of my fathers', Ahab's wife Jezebel had him stoned to death on a false charge of blasphemy, for which she and Ahab were cursed by the prophet Elijah ('Hast thou killed, and also taken possession?'). 'Naboth's vineyard' used to be a proverbial term for a poor man's small possession coveted by the wealthy and unscrupulous.

1. *an allegory of Empire*: A cynical allegory, since 'Naboth' is a would-be empire-builder preying on the narrator's weakness, while the narrator himself plays the role of the bad king Ahab who destroys the poor man's small property.

2. *sap*: Undermining.

3. *Isabella-coloured*: Yellowish-grey.

4. *feudatory*: Vassal.

5. *illicit still*: A means of illegally manufacturing spirits. 'Naboth' is running an illicit spirit-shop.

6. *Suzerain*: Sovereign.

7. *phaeton*: A light open carriage drawn by one horse.

8. *sweetmeats instead of salt*: In the ancient world, the lands of defeated enemies might be sown with salt to prevent anyone from tilling them again. The victorious Abimelech does this to the fields of Shechem (Judges 9:45), and the Romans were said to have salted the land around Carthage when they destroyed the city in 146 BC after the Third Punic War.

9. *how Ahab felt*: Kipling's reversal of Scripture in making Ahab the injured party contests, not quite convincingly, Ahab's reputation for greed and violence.

ON THE CITY WALL

First published in *In Black and White*, no. 3 of the Indian Railway Library (1888); collected in *Soldiers Three* (1892).

1. *she*: Rahab the harlot, who hid two Israelite spies in her house on Jericho wall and helped them to escape by letting them down from her window: Joshua 2: 1–16.

2. *Lilith*: Mythical first wife of Adam.

3. *jujube-tree*: *Zizyphus* trees bearing edible berries.

4. *Pax Britannica*: 'British peace': the peace imposed by the Empire (Latin, cf. *Pax Romana*).

5. *Peshawur and Cape Comorin*: The most northerly and southerly points of British India (*NRG*).

6. *chunam*: Lime made of burnt shells (*Hobson-Jobson*).

7. *Shiahs*: Adherents of the Muslim Shia denomination who reverence Mohammed's cousin Ali and his successors the Eleven Imams.

8. *Sufis*: Muslim mystics.

9. *Golden Temple*: Sikh temple at Amritsar, the headquarters of Sikh religion.

10. *electic*: Wali Dad's slip for 'eclectic'.

11. *the Athenians – always hearing and telling some new thing*: Acts 17: 21.

12. *a Demnition Product*: Alludes to the idiom of Mr Mantalini, a comic character in Charles Dickens's *Nicholas Nickleby* (1838).

13. *sitar*: Stringed instrument like a guitar.

14. *kites*: Scavenging birds of prey.

15. *Sivaji*: (1627–80) founder of the Mahratta empire (*NRG*).

16. *Mahratta laonee*: Maratha ballad.

17. *in '46 . . . in '57 . . . in '71*: In the Sutlej campaign (1845–6), the Mutiny

(1857) and the Kuka rising (1871–2), all Sikh rebellions suppressed by the British.

18. *Wahabi*: Follower of violent fundamentalist Islam sect, founded by ibn-al-Wahab (1703–93).

19. *whoring after strange gods*: Exodus 34: 15.

20. *Subadar Sahib*: Respectful address; 'Sahib' means 'Sir' and *subadar* was the highest rank of Native officers, equivalent of a Regimental Sergeant-Major (see also *Drums of the Fore and Aft*, n. 40, below).

21. *Sobraon*: Battle in the Sutlej campaign where the Sikhs were defeated.

22. *'niggers', which besides being extreme bad form, shows gross ignorance*: The narrator objects both to the rudeness of the derogatory word and to the confusion of Indians with Africans.

23. *'Sikhs?'*: The Subaltern hints that it is unwise to have Khem Singh guarded by men of his own faith.

24. *Sikhs, Pathans, Dogras*: Different peoples of north India.

25. *heterodox women*: Hetairas, ancient Greek courtesans.

26. *Vizier*: High state official.

27. *Mohurrum, the great mourning-festival*: Annual Shia festival commemorating the death of Hassan and his brother Husain, heirs of the Prophet. Their heroic death at the hands of usurpers is staged every year in plays and processions by Shia peoples (as in the medieval European 'mystery plays' enacting the Passion of Christ).

28. *tazias*: wood and fabric replicas of the tomb of Imam Husain carried in the 'Mohurrum' procession.

29. *Ladakh*: province of northern India.

30. *Vox Populi is Vox Dei*: 'The voice of the people is the voice of God' (dog-Latin).

31. *"Ya Hasan! Ya Hussain!"*: Ritual invocation of martyred heroes, accompanied by breast-beating.

32. *'Into thy hands, O Lord!'*: Luke 23: 41: Christ's last words from the cross.

33. *Sirkar*: Government of India.

34. *killing kine in their temples*: Slaughtering cattle sacred to Hindus.

35. *the iron bangle of the Sikhs*: Sikhs are required at all times to wear an iron bangle, together with uncut hair, a small comb, a dagger and a special undergarment (David Simmonds, *Believers All: A Study of Six World Religions* (Nelson Thomas, 1992), p. 120).

36. *A lakh*: One hundred thousand.

37. *bunnias*: money-lenders.

38. *'It is expedient that one man should die for the people'*: The words of Caiaphas planning the death of Jesus (John 18: 14).

39. *'Two Lovely Black Eyes'*: Music-hall song.

'THE CITY OF DREADFUL NIGHT'

First published in the *Civil and Military Gazette*, 10 September 1885; collected in *Life's Handicap* (1891). The title is taken from the title of a poem by James Thomson (1834–82).

1. *ekka-ponies*: See 'In the House of Suddhoo', n. 7, above.
2. *gunny-bags*: Jute sacks (*Hobson-Jobson*).
3. *pariahs*: Stray dogs (*Hobson-Jobson*).
4. *grampuses*: Whales.
5. *the Mosque of Wazir Khan*: See 'The Gate of the Hundred Sorrows', n. 3, above.
6. *Minars*: Towers of the mosque (minarets).
7. *kite*: Scavenging bird of prey.
8. *Doré . . . Zola*: Gustave Doré (1833–83), French black-and-white artist and engraver, whose 1871 engravings of London scenes were criticized for dwelling on poverty. He also engraved the darkly numinous illustrations for an edition of Dante's *Divine Comedy* (1868). Emile Zola (1840–1902), author of powerful naturalist novels considered shocking by contemporaries.
9. *Ravee*: River by which Lahore stands.
10. *heliographic signals*: A heliograph is an early telegraph using mirrors to flash messages in Morse code. It was employed by the British army in the 1880s.
11. *Muezzin*: Crier calling Muslims to prayer.
12. *'Allah ho Akbar!'*: God is great.
13. *'La ilaha Illallah!'*: There is no God but Allah.
14. *ram*: Instrument for compressing bales of fabric.

AT THE END OF THE PASSAGE

First published in the USA in *Lippincott's Monthly Magazine*, August 1890; collected in *Life's Handicap* (1891).

1. *Himalayan*: The epigraph is the first stanza of Kipling's poem 'Himalaya'.
2. *'life, liberty, and the pursuit of happiness'*: Quoted from the American Declaration of Independence, 1776.
3. *The room was darkened*: The curtains were drawn to keep out the sun.
4. *punkah*: Swinging fan.
5. *apoplexy*: Heatstroke.
6. *Indian Survey*: The institution responsible for mapping India.

7. *on special duty in the Political Department*: Lowndes was a resident official advising the prince of a Native State (see above, head-note to 'The Man Who Would Be King').

8. *bumble-puppy*: Any game played unscientifically; in this context, whist.

9. *vestrymen*: Members of a parish council, responsible for local government.

10. *drag*: Four-wheeled coach.

11. *Heidsieck*: Champagne.

12. *Chlorodyne*: A mixture of chloroform and opium (*NRG*).

13. *nitre*: Potassium nitrate, diluted to use as a saline diuretic, so unlikely to benefit dehydrated cholera patients (*NRG*).

14. *black cholera*: Turning a patient's face blue from lack of oxygen.

15. *sextant*: Instrument used by land surveyors for calculating angles of altitude.

16. *ophthalmia*: Inflammation of the eyes.

17. *the Graphic*: Illustrated magazine, similar to the *Illustrated London News*.

18. *Chucks*: Character from the novel *Peter Simple* by Frederick Marryat (1792–1842).

19. *Babu*: See 'The Gate of the Hundred Sorrows', n. 7, above.

20. *Job*: Proverbially unfortunate protagonist of the Old Testament Book of Job. A good man persecuted by Satan, Job loses his wealth, his children all die, and he is covered with boils 'from the sole of his foot to the crown of his head'.

21. *a gold mohur on the rub*: A mohur was the highest value coin in British India, worth 16 rupees; 'rub' is a rubber, meaning a set of three or five games (*NRG*).

22. *prestissimo*: Very quickly, a musical direction.

23. *'Glory to thee . . . light'*: From the Evening Hymn of Bishop Ken (1637–1711), no. 23 of *Hymns Ancient and Modern*; Hummil's version of the fifth stanza, probably quoted from memory, is not quite accurate. It should run 'When in the night I sleepless lie, / My soul with heavenly thoughts supply; Let no ill dreams disturb my rest, / No powers of darkness me molest.' Kipling also uses the numinous phrase 'powers of darkness', in 'The Phantom 'Rickshaw' and in *Kim*.

24. *cockchafer*: Large flying beetle.

25. *bandbox*: Large circular box for women's hats.

26. *seven fathom*: Forty-two feet (one fathom = six feet).

27. *'Well done, David!' 'Look after Saul, then'*: King Saul was possessed by an evil spirit which left him when David played the harp: 1 Samuel 16: 23.

28. *where I dines I sleeps*: Quotation from *Handley Cross* by Robert Surtees (1803–64), featuring Mr Jorrocks, grocer and Master of Foxhounds.

29. *Heaven-born*: Deferential title addressed to an English officer.

30. *the reeving and unreeving of the bed-tapes*: Pulling tapes through and out of holes in the sheets.

31. *the tremendous words*: The funeral service in the Book of Common Prayer begins, 'I am the Resurrection and the Life'.

32. *'There may be Heaven . . . We-ell?'*: Robert Browning, 'Time's Revenges', *Bells and Pomegranates* (1845): 'There may be heaven; there must be hell; / Meantime there is our earth here – well!'

THE DRUMS OF THE FORE AND AFT

First published in *Wee Willie Winkie*, no. 6 of the Indian Railway Library (1888); collected in *Wee Willie Winkie and Other Stories* (1895).

1.   *above proof*: 'Proof spirit' contains 58 per cent alcohol; spirits 'above proof' are extremely strong.

2.   *to encourage the others*: Captain John Byng was shot for cowardice; Voltaire wryly commented that this was done 'pour encourager les autres'.

3.   *the Pocket-book*: This was *The Soldier's Pocket-book* by General Sir Garnet Wolseley (1833–1913), first published 1869 and frequently reprinted in the nineteenth century (*NRG*).

4.   *drummer-boys*: Boys enrolled at 12, under command of the Drum-Major. They could enter the regular army at 18 (*NRG*).

5.   *through Dr Barnardo's hands*: Dr Barnardo was the founder of the orphanages named after him, which are still functioning.

6.   *Ishmaels*: Outcasts. Ishmael was the son of Abraham and Hagar: 'his hand will be against every man, and every man's hand against him' (Genesis 16: 12).

7.   *plug tobacco*: Strong tobacco pressed into bricks or plugs.

8.   *the Bazar-Sergeant's son*: A Bazar-Sergeant was an NCO responsible for supervising the local bazaar or shopping district (*NRG*).

9.   *jarnwar*: Soldier's pronounciation of Hindi *janwar*, animal (*NRG*).

10. *Lance*: Lance-corporal: lowest rank of NCO (*NRG*).

11. *'The War of the Lost Tribes'*: The Afghan War: the Afghans were supposed to be the 'Lost Tribes of Israel' (*NRG*).

12. *the Cape*: Cape of Good Hope.

13. *Colours*: The regimental flag, regarded as sacred.

14. *batta*: Field allowance (*Hobson-Jobson*).

15. *CB . . . KCB*: Commander or Knight Commander of the Bath.

16. *'coutrements*: Accoutrements: a soldier's belt, pouches, haversack, etc. (*NRG*).

17. *housewife*: A rolled cloth case for needle and scissors, pronounced 'hussif'.

18. *Commissariat*: Officers and men in charge of food supplies.

19. *steers*: Bullocks (for slaughter).

20. *Hussars*: Light cavalry.

21. *sons of the Beni-Israel*: Members of one of the Lost Tribes of Israel.

22. *puckrowed*: Seized (*Hobson-Jobson*).

23. *Kiswasti?*: Why? (*NRG*).

24. *Khana get, peenikapanee get – live like a bloomin' Rajah ke marfik ... bundobust*: 'You will have food, drinking water, and will live as luxuriously as a Rajah' (*NRG*).

25. *kushy*: Easy, soft (cushy).

26. *EP tent*: European Privates' tent (*NRG*).

27. *wither-wrung*: Sore-shouldered.

28. *hammered iron slug*: Handmade bullet (*NRG*).

29. *big men dressed in women's clothes*: Highland regiments, wearing kilts.

30. *a driven donkey*: A donkey driven towards the enemy to draw his fire.

31. *'two o'clock in the morning courage'*: Unprepared courage.

32. *screw-guns*: Small field artillery that could be dismantled and carried by mules.

33. *zymotic*: Infectious.

34. *ill taking the breeks off a Highlander*: An allusion to Sir Walter Scott's *The Fortunes of Nigel* (ch. 5). 'Breeks' are breeches or trousers.

35. *regiments attired in red coats*: The Afghan army.

36. *Martini-Henry bullets*: Martini-Henry guns, issued to the British Army (see 'The Strange Ride of Morrowbie Jukes', n. 11, above), presumably looted or stolen.

37. *brazed*: Soldered.

38. *Ghazis*: Fanatical Muslims who have sworn to kill unbelievers (*NRG*).

39. *kukris*: Curved Nepalese knives used by Gurkha regiments (*Hobson-Jobson*).

40. *Subadar-Major*: Highest rank of 'Native' officer, equivalent to Regimental Sergeant-Major (*NRG*).

41. *Senior Jemadar*: 'Native' officer, ranking below 'Subadar' (*Hobson-Jobson*).

42. *Snider bullets*: See 'The Man Who Would Be King', n. 47, above.

43. *'stung by the splendour of a sudden thought'*: Browning, 'A Death in the Desert', line 59.

44. *fife*: Shrill military flute.

45. *'British Grenadiers'*: A famous military marching song.

46. *Rissaldar*: Cavalry equivalent of Subadar or sergeant (NRG)

47. *carbine*: Gun, shorter and lighter than a rifle (*NRG*).

48. *doolies*: Cots used as litters (*Hobson-Jobson*).

49. *blooded*: Alludes to the fox-hunting ceremony of smearing children with blood from the dead beast's tail at their first hunt.

WITH THE MAIN GUARD

First published in *The Week's News*, 28 July 1888, issued in *Soldiers Three*, no.
1 of the Indian Railway Library (1888); collected in *Soldiers Three* (1895).

1. *C. G. Leland*: From 'Breitmann in Bivouac', *Hans Breitmann Ballads* (1884).
2. *skinful of water*: From a goat-skin bag.
3. *glacis*: Ground sloping upwards to a fort.
4. *mess-kid*: Tin for holding food.
5. *Faynians*: Fenians, precursors of the IRA.
6. *the Widdy*: Queen Victoria, the 'Widow of Windsor'.
7. *tattered Colours*: Flags embroidered with regimental arms and battle honours.
8. *fell acrost*: Bumped into.
9. *"Knee to knee!" . . . "Breast to breast!" . . . "hand over back!"*: Phrases from the Masonic Third Degree Ritual, hence the colonel's thanks to 'Brother Inner Guard'.
10. *"We've seen our dead"*: The corpses had been mutilated by the Afghans.
11. *lockin'-ring*: Ring securing bayonet to rifle-muzzle.
12. *asp on a leaf*: Leaf of the aspen, also called the Trembling Poplar.
13. *holted*: Halted.
14. *Roshus*: Roscius, a famous Roman actor.
15. *"Blood the young whelp!"*: Alludes to ceremony of 'blooding' (see 'The Drums of the Fore and Aft', n. 49, above). A whelp is a puppy.
16. *batman*: Soldier acting as officer's servant.

ON GREENHOW HILL

First published in *Harper's Magazine* and *Macmillan's Magazine*, September 1890; collected in *Life's Handicap* (1891).

1. *Rivals*: A poem by Alice Kipling, Rudyard's mother.
2. *Snider*: See 'The Man Who Would Be King', n. 47, above.
3. *a hound on a broken trail*: A foxhound trotting to and fro in search of scent.
4. *'list*: Enlist.
5. *Don Juan . . . Lotharius*: Don Juan is a legendary seducer; Lothario a heartless libertine in Rowe's *The Fair Penitent* (Mulvaney has been a theatre-goer).
6. *bight*: Loop.

7.   *drift*: Passage in a mine.
8.   *sumph*: sump, drainage-pit.
9.   *agaate*: Doing.
10.   *jealoused*: Scottish jaloused; suspected.
11.   *class-meetin's*: A 'class' was a small devotional group within the larger congregation. Active Methodists were expected to attend their weekly class-meeting.
12.   *shebeen*: Drinking-shop.
13.   *Sitha*: (Yorkshire) See here.
14.   *white choaker*: Slang for a clergyman's white collar.
15.   *"Th' sword o' th' Lord and o' Gideon"*: Judges 7: 18.
16.   *th' whole armour o' righteousness*: Echoes both Ephesians 6: 11 and 2 Corinthians 6: 7.
17.   *fightin' the good fight*: 1 Timothy 6: 12.
18.   *Forders*: Cabmen (slang).
19.   *boggart*: Ghost.

WITHOUT BENEFIT OF CLERGY

First published in *Macmillan's Magazine*, June 1890; collected in *Life's Handicap* (1891).

1.   *Bitter Waters*: Poem by Kipling.
2.   *of the Faith . . . born upon a Friday*: A Muslim born on the day of prayer.
3.   *Aré koko, Jaré koko!*: This cradle-song is also quoted in Lockwood Kipling's *Beast and Man in India*, p. 30.
4.   *Ya illah!*: O God!
5.   *Tobah, tobah!*: Exclamation of reproof: Shame!
6.   *sitar*: Stringed instrument like a guitar.
7.   *Rajah Rasalu*: Ancient semi-legendary king of Sialkot in Punjab (*NRG*).
8.   *dhak-tree*: Tree bearing red flowers.
9.   *vestrymen*: Members of a parish council.
10.   *scald-head*: Head diseased with ringworm.
11.   *janee*: Beloved (*NRG*).
12.   *black cholera*: See 'At the End of the Passage', n. 14, above.
13.   *there is no God but – thee, beloved!*: Adapts the Muslim declaration: 'There is no God but Allah'.
14.   *burning-ghat*: Platform by the river where Hindu corpses are cremated.

THE BRIDGE-BUILDERS

First published in the *Illustrated London News*, Christmas number, December 1893; collected in *The Day's Work* (1898)

1. *CIE . . . CSI*: Companion of the Indian Empire, Companion of the Star of India.
2. *Kashi*: Benares.
3. *CE*: Civil Engineer.
4. *spile-pier*: Pier built on timbers driven into the ground.
5. *pukka*: Good.
6. *Cooper's Hill*: Site of the Royal Indian College of Engineering in Surrey, closed in 1906.
7. *freshets*: Streams of water, here caused by small floods.
8. *Lascar*: Sailor from India.
9. *A Kharva from Bulsar*: Bulsar is a Gujerati town; the Kharva are a Hindu people from Gujerat.
10. *Rockhampton*: Port in Queensland, northern Australia.
11. *serang*: Native boatswain in charge of Lascar crew (*Hobson-Jobson*).
12. *donkey-engines*: Auxiliary engines.
13. *Mother Gunga*: Gunga (or Ganga) is the Hindi name of the Ganges, worshipped as a goddess because its water is said to wash away sin. She is sometimes represented as a crocodile (*NRG*).
14. *Kutch Mandvi*: Mandvi is on the Gulf of Cutch, 200 miles from Bulsar (*NRG*).
15. *Black Water*: The ocean.
16. *blue dungaree*: coarse blue cotton cloth (*Hobson-Jobson*).
17. *Chota Sahib*: The 'small master', Hitchcock, as opposed to the 'Burra Sahib' or 'big master', Findlayson (*NRG*).
18. *Quetta*: Cargo ship of British India Associated Steamers, wrecked in 1890.
19. *jiboonwallah*: A made-up word to mean 'baboon man'.
20. *pujah*: Worship, obeisance (*Hobson-Jobson*).
21. *tar*: A wire, telegram.
22. *cribs*: Timber supports on which the iron girders were mounted.
23. *wire-rope colt*: Wire whip.
24. *pegged, and stitched craft*: Boat fastened together without metal.
25. *peepul*: Pipal or sacred fig tree.
26. *Bull*: Ridden by Shiva, third in the Hindu Trinity of Brahma the Creator, Vishnu the Preserver, Shiva the Destroyer (*NRG*).
27. *A green Parrot*: A bird sacred to Krishna (*NRG*).

28. *Mugger*: 'The destructive broad-snouted crocodile of the Ganges' (*Hobson-Jobson*), a manifestation of the goddess Gunga.

29. *Punchayet*: council meeting (*Hobson-Jobson*).

30. *Kali*: Consort of Shiva who rides a tiger.

31. *Kotwal*: guardian (*NRG*).

32. *A nose-slitten . . . Ass*: Sitala or Mata, the goddess of smallpox. The 'near universal' Indian practice of slitting asses' nostrils to minimize their braying is deplored in Lockwood Kipling's *Beast and Man in India*, p. 77.

33. *no small bridge*: An allusion to Hanuman's feat of building a bridge across the Palk Strait dividing Sri Lanka from the Indian land-mass, described in the Hindu epic, *Ramayana*.

34. *the wreck of thy armies, Hanuman*: 'A notion exists among Hindus that the English may be his descendants . . . others, again, say that the English came from the "monkey army"'; Lockwood Kipling, *Beast and Man in India*, pp. 56–7.

35. *mahajuns*: Bankers (*Hobson-Jobson*).

36. *Prayag*: Hindi name for Allahabad (*NRG*).

37. *Puri, under the Image there*: The statue of Jagan-nath ('Juggernaut') in the temple at Puri, Orissa (*NRG*).

38. *Gopis*: Milkmaids (*NRG*).

39. *Krishna the Well-beloved*: Symbol of beauty, often represented as a handsome boy and associated with Vishnu (*NRG*).

40. *Karma*: Kama, Hindu god of love (*NRG*).

41. *lotahs*: Water-vessels (*Hobson-Jobson*).

42. *Goorkha*: The *Gurkha*, a British steamship.

43. *Brahm*: Brahma the Creator, representing the divine eternity beyond the apparent universe of matter and mind, first in the great Hindu trinity (see n. 26 above).

44. *pug*: Paw-mark (*Hobson-Jobson*).

45. *tufan*: Storm, typhoon.

46. *bear-led*: Taken on tour.

47. *seven koss*: Approximately 14 miles.

48. *Morphus*: Mispronunciation of Morpheus, Roman god of sleep and dreams.

THE MALTESE CAT

First published in *Pall Mall Gazette*, 26 June 1895; collected in *The Day's Work* (1898).

1. *neat-fitting boot*: Protection for the pony's cannon bone and fetlock above the hoof (*NRG*).

2.   *drags, and dog-carts*: Horse-drawn heavy coaches and two-wheeled vehicles.
3.   *tiffin*: Light luncheon.
4.   *blinkers*: Leather pieces attached to a horse's bridle to make it see only straight ahead.
5.   *flea-bitten*: light grey spotted or streaked with darker colour.
6.   *ekka*: One-horse cart.
7.   *vulcanite*: A preparation of India rubber and sulphur hardened by intense heat.

'THE FINEST STORY IN THE WORLD'

First published in *Contemporary Review*, July 1891; collected in *Many Inventions* (1893).

1.   *twenty-five shillings*: £1.25; equivalent to about £75 today.
2.   *the edge of his washstand*: Charlie is obliged to write in his bedroom.
3.   *Longfellow*: Henry Wadsworth Longfellow (1807–82), American poet. The lines Charlie quotes are taken from, successively, 'The Secret of the Sea', 'My Lost Youth' and 'Seaweed'.
4.   *'Pollock, Erckmann, Tauchnitz, Henniker'*: A transliteration of Greek, *pollak' ekamon tou kniz' heneka*, which the narrator mistakes for actual names; the literal translation is 'Often have I been weary, the rasping (or chafing) on account of'. Tauchnitz was a well-known German publisher.
5.   *metempsychosis*: Transmigration of souls.
6.   *'Lara'*: Like 'The Bride of Abydos', 'The Corsair', 'Cain' and 'Manfred', mentioned below, poems by Lord Byron.
7.   *'The Saga of King Olaf'*: From the 'Musician's Tale' in Longfellow's *Tales of a Wayside Inn*.
8.   *cockchafer*: Flying beetle.
9.   *Transmigration*: Novel by Collins (1827–76), published 1874.
10. *Furdurstrandi*: Viking name for the 'Long Beaches' of 'Vinland'.
11. *"But Othere . . . Behold this walrus-tooth!"*: From Longfellow's 'The Discovery of the North Sea'. Also quoted in 'Knights of the Joyous Venture', *Puck of Pook's Hill* (1905).
12. *playing knuckle-bones*: Idly throwing and catching small objects.
13. *Thorfinn Karlsefne's sailing to Wineland*: Narrated in Paul Henri Mallet (trans. Bishop Thomas Percy), *Northern Antiquities* (1770, repr. 1857), the source Kipling used for this story (*NRG*).
14. *Bohn volume*: Cheap edition of the classics.
15. *bill-book*: Leather wallet for holding bills flat.

16.   *Clive*: Robert Clive (1725–74), key figure in the conquest of India.

17.   *Aquarium poster*: For the Aquarium Theatre in London, demolished in 1908.

18.   *Northbrook Club*: Founded in 1879 for gentlemen from India.

19.   *tulsi*: Sweet basil, sacred to Vishnu (*NRG*).

20.   *purohit*: Family priest (*NRG*).

21.   *khuttri*: Merchant (*NRG*).

22.   *desi*: South Asian (*NRG*).

23.   *Mlech*: A Hindu term for a contemptible person. Hinduism divides people into a complex hierarchy of hereditary ranks or 'castes', each with its allotted duties and rights, from Brahmins at the top, from whose ranks come priests, to the 'Dalits' or 'Untouchables' at the bottom who deal with refuse. A 'mlech' comes very low in this order, 'just above the *Dalits*' according to *NRG*.

24.   *Wordsworth*: Grish Chunder is alluding to stanza V of Wordsworth's ode, 'Intimations of Immortality from Recollections of Early Childhood': 'Our birth is but a sleep and a forgetting, The Soul that rises with us, our life's star Hath had elsewhere its setting And cometh from afar.'

25.   *bus – hogya*: Stop – at once (*NRG*).

26.   *Tit-Bits*: Popular weekly magazine.

27.   *Argo*: In Greek myth, the ship on which Jason sailed to recover the Golden Fleece.

28.   *Wardour Street work*: Sham antique. In the nineteenth century this Soho street contained second-hand furniture shops.

29.   *centipede metres*: Metres with too many 'feet'. Charlie favours long lines rather than blank verse or ballad stanzas.

THE SHIP THAT FOUND HERSELF

First published in *The Idler*, December 1895; collected in *The Day's Work* (1898).

1.   *Lucania*: An ocean liner launched from Liverpool in 1893.

2.   *well found*: Well equipped.

3.   *knees*: L-shaped pieces securing the deck beams to their frames.

4.   *Cape Hatteras*: Eastern point of North Carolina coast.

5.   *broken falls whipped the davits*: Broken ropes struck the derrick from which the boat had hung.

6.   *Arizona*: A ship which collided with an iceberg in 1879 but was saved by its bulkhead holding together (*NRG*).

7.   *the Paris's engine-room*: The *City of Paris* suffered a flooded engine-room when a propeller cracked in 1890 (*NRG*).

MRS BATHURST

First published in *Windsor Magazine*, September 1904; collected in *Traffics and Discoveries* (1904):

1. *Simon's Bay*: Simonstown was the principal British naval base in South Africa.
2. *coaling*: Engaged in filling their ships' coal bunkers.
3. *Inspector Hooper*: He is a railway inspector, not a detective.
4. *tickey beer*: Cheap beer. A 'tickey' was a silver threepenny piece, equivalent to 1p, worth about 70p today.
5. *False Bay*: Deeply indented coastline east of Cape of Good Hope.
6. *Wankies*: coal-mining town, now in Zimbabwe.
7. *Belmont*: Site of naval battle in 1899.
8. *quart bottle*: Two pints, 1.36 litres.
9. *verbatim*: Word for word (Latin); here, 'verbally'.
10. *Number One rig*: Best uniform.
11. *"purr Mary, on the terrace"*: Joking allusion to *Per Mare, Per Terram*, 'by land and sea', Latin motto of the Royal Marines (*NRG*).
12. *Vancouver*: Vancouver Island, where the Royal Navy had its Pacific base.
13. *steerin'-flat*: Compartment in the stern of the ship housing the steering-gear.
14. *within eighteen months of his pension*: That is, throwing away his accumulated pension rights.
15. *Salisbury*: Now Harare, capital of Zimbabwe.
16. *casus belli*: Act occasioning war (Latin).
17. *status quo*: Short for *status quo ante*, 'the situation as before', here connoting 'backside' (Latin).
18. *warrants and non-coms*: Warrant and non-commissioned officers: minor navy officers.
19. *peeris*: Fairies, i.e. beautiful women.
20. *Pusser*: Purser, paymaster.
21. *an enteric at the last kick*: A person dying of typhoid fever.
22. *the mornin' an' the evenin' were the first day*: Genesis 1: 5.
23. *a Marconi ticker*: A radio receiver recording Morse code.
24. *"The rest . . . is silence"*: Hamlet's last words; *Hamlet*, Act 5, Scene 2.
25. *kapje*: Bonnet (Afrikaans).
26. 'On a summer afternoon . . . the one she loves the best – ': Opening stanza of 'The Honey-Suckle and the Bee', a popular late-Victorian song by Albert H. Fitz (1864–1922), with the once famous refrain, 'You are my honey,

honeysuckle / I am the bee / I'd like to taste the honey sweet / From those
red lips, you see'. The quotation from this song, familiar to Kipling's
original readers in 1904, is the story's final grim stroke.

'THEY'

First published in *Scribner's Magazine*, August 1904; collected in *Traffics and Discoveries* (1904).

1. *hamlet which stands godmother to the capital of the United States*: Washington, a Sussex village.
2. *that great Down*: Chanctonbury Ring, near the village of Washington.
3. *six-inch Ordnance map*: A map drawn to the scale of six inches to a mile, and therefore highly detailed.
4. *the figure of the Egg*: Allusion to the ancient belief that the world was egg-shaped; here, a mystic symbol of transcendence.
5. *House Beautiful*: in Bunyan's *Pilgrim's Progress*, the 'House called Beautiful' is a refuge and sanctuary for pilgrims.
6. *tax-cart*: A light two-wheeled cart, under taxable value (*NRG*).
7. *shruck*: Shriek (Sussex dialect).
8. *Ushant*: Ouessant, most westerly of French ports.
9. *'In the pleasant orchard-closes'*: From Elizabeth Barrett Browning's poem 'The Lost Bower'. The 'marring fifth line' is: 'Listen, gentle – ay, and simple! listen, children at the knee.'
10. *no unpassable iron*: Alludes to the folk belief that spirits could not endure the presence of iron – cf the story 'Cold Iron' in *Rewards and Fairies* (1910).

'WIRELESS'

First published in *Scribner's Magazine*, August 1902; collected in *Traffics and Discoveries* (1904).

1. *ammoniated quinine*: Once a popular remedy for colds.
2. *Pharmaceutical Formulary*: A handbook of drugs.
3. *Nicholas Culpeper*: Seventeenth-century herbalist and physician.
4. *glass jars . . . of the sort that led Rosamond to parting with her shoes*: In 'The Purple Jar', a story in Maria Edgeworth's *Early Lessons* (1804), Rosamond chooses to buy an enticing purple jar which turns out to contain coloured water, instead of new shoes.
5. *orris*: Dried iris root.

6. *vulcanite*: A preparation of India rubber and sulphur hardened by intense heat.

7. *some gay feathered birds and game, hung upon hooks, sagged to the wind*: A detail later used by Hemingway's 'In Another Country': 'There was much game hanging outside the shops . . . and small birds blew in the wind, and the wind turned their feathers.'

8. *See that old hare!*: An allusion to the opening lines of Keats's '*The Eve of St Agnes*': 'St Agnes' eve – Ah, bitter chill it was! / The owl, for all his feathers, was a-cold / The hare limped trembling through the frozen grass'.

9. *chloric-ether*: Spirits of chloroform.

10. *Hertzian waves*: Electromagnetic waves, the basis of radio.

11. *cubeb*: Spicy dried berry from a plant known as 'Java pepper' (*Piper cubeba*).

12. *benzoin*: Incense.

13. *chypre*: Cheap scent.

14. *like a string of pearls winking at you*: Cf. 'with beaded bubbles winking at the brim', Keats, 'Ode to a Nightingale', stanza 2.

15. '*And threw warm gules on Madeleine's young breast*': 'And threw warm gules on Madeleine's fair breast', Keats, 'The Eve of St Agnes', stanza 25.

16. *chromo*: Chromolithograph, a coloured reproduction.

17. '*And my weak spirit fails . . . Beneath the churchyard mould*': 'And his weak spirit fails / To think how they may ache in icy hoods and mails', Keats, 'The Eve of St Agnes', stanza 2.

18. '*The little smoke of a candle that goes out*': 'Its little smoke in pallid moonlight died', ibid., stanza 23.

19. *the raw material . . . of his poem*: In the stanzas mentioned, Porphyro watches Madeleine undress and lie down in bed.

20. *in what manner a red, black, and yellow Austrian blanket coloured his dreams*: See 'a cloth of woven crimson, gold and jet', ibid., stanza 29.

21. '*Candied apple, quince and plum and gourd . . . to cedared Lebanon*': Ibid., 30.

22. '*The sharp rain falling on the window-pane . . . the wind-blown sleet*': 'Meantime the frost-wind blows / Like Love's alarum pattering the sharp sleet / Against the window-panes', ibid., stanza 36.

23. '*A fairyland for you and me . . . a perilous sea*': Cf. 'magic casements, opening on the foam / Of perilous seas, in faery lands forlorn', Keats, 'Ode to a Nightingale', stanza 7.

24. '*A savage place! . . . her demon-lover*': Coleridge, 'Kubla Khan', lines 14–16.

THE VILLAGE THAT VOTED THE
EARTH WAS FLAT

First published in *A Diversity of Creatures* (1917).

1.   *coir-matting-coloured hair*: Hair the colour of brown coconut matting.

2.   *knacker's yard*: Slaughterhouse.

3.   *aft*: At the back.

4.   *twenty-three pounds, twelve shillings and sixpence*: The equivalent of more than £1,000 in today's currency, therefore a very large fine for speeding.

5.   *his home address at Jerusalem*: Anti-Semitic gibe, implying that Masquerier does not belong in England.

6.   *dub*: Puddle, meaning that Sir Thomas is a red-faced dullard (*NRG*).

7.   *privileged*: Members of Parliament are exempt from prosecution.

8.   *Sodom and Gomorrah*: Cities devastated by fire and brimstone; Genesis 19: 24–5.

9.   *Brasenose*: Oxford college, founded 1509.

10.   *eheu ab angulo!*: Alas for the nook (Latin).

11.   *the Spec. had a middle*: The *Spectator* had an article in the middle portion.

12.   *Non nobis gloria!*: Not unto us the glory (Latin).

13.   *adenoids*: Glands in the throat.

14.   *panel doctor*: A doctor prepared to accept as patients those registered under the National Insurance Act, 1911; here, the village doctor.

15.   *an Irish afternoon*: The House of Commons was dealing with Irish matters, a hot topic for Irish MPs elected to Westminster. This story was written before Irish independence.

16.   *By the grace of God, Master Ridley*: Alluding to Hugh Latimer's famous remark to Nicholas Ridley as they went to be burnt at the stake in 1555: 'By the grace of God, Master Ridley, we have lit such a candle in England this day as shall never be put out.'

17.   *went off at score*: Broke out suddenly into impetuous speech.

18.   *Hone's Every-Day Book*: William Hone's *Everlasting Calendar of Popular Sports and Pastimes* (1827).

19.   *Nellie Farren*: A genuine music-hall star (1848–1904). The other names and plays are invented.

20.   *Ionic style*: As in Greek robes.

21.   *lockstep*: Step in which the heel of one dancer is struck by the toe of the dancer behind.

22.   *Peter's vision at Joppa*: 'a certain vessel descending . . . wherein were all

manner of four-footed beasts of the earth, and wild beasts, and creeping things'; Acts of the Apostles 10: 11–12.

23. *electrolier*: Electric lamp.

24. *'The Holy City'*: Song by F. E. Weatherley, with the refrain 'Jerusalem! Jerusalem! Lift up your voice and sing / Hosanna in the highest! Hosanna to your King!' (*NRG*).

25. *a grateful South Kensington*: The Victoria and Albert Museum in London.

26. *'Margaritas ante Porcos'*: 'Pearls before swine', a Latin pen name.

27. *Haussmania*: Craze for modernizing, after Haussmann's remodelling of Paris, 1853–70.

28. *"Like that strange song ... When Ilion like a mist rose into towers"*: Tennyson, 'Tithonus', lines 62–3.

29. *suffragettes*: Women vigorously campaigning for the vote.

30. *Gehazi passed forth*: Gehazi was a servant of Elisha, punished for lying by being afflicted with leprosy; 2 Kings 5:20–27; cf. Kipling's own 1912 poem 'Gehazi', violently attacking Sir Rufus Isaacs for corruption.

31. *Rads*: Radicals.

32. *cross-bencher*: Used here, incorrectly, to mean one who changes his party allegiance. In the House of Lords, cross-benchers are members who have renounced party ties.

33. *syndicalism*: Left-wing extremism.

34. *private interview with his Chief Whip*: Probably to request Sir Thomas to resign his seat.

THE HOUSE SURGEON

First published in *Harper's Magazine*, September 1909; collected in *Actions and Reactions* (1909).

1. *the Curse on the family's first-born*: Alludes to the final plague sent on Egypt, in the death of first-born children and animals: Exodus 11:5.

2. *Queen Anne pavilion*: Built in the Queen Anne Revival style of the 1860s.

3. *cloisonné*: Decorated with coloured enamels separated by metal wires and fired, an expensive process.

4. *Horror of great darkness*: Genesis 15:12.

5. *diving-bell*: Vessel for descending into deep water.

6. *The dressing-gong roared*: Reminding ladies and gentlemen to put on evening dress for dinner.

7. *what De Quincey ... 'the oppression of inexpiable guilt'*: De Quincey says he dreamed that 'the weight of twenty Atlantics was upon me, or the oppression of inexpiable guilt'; *Confessions of an English Opium-Eater* (1822; Penguin Classics edition, 2006, p. 113).

8. *Mr Perseus ... 'He has seen the Medusa's head!'*: Perseus was a mythical Greek hero who rescued the princess Andromeda from a devouring monster. He had previously escaped the Medusa, avoiding being turned to stone as he did so.

9. *spelicans*: Spillikins, a belittling term for golf-clubs. In the game of spillikins, players must detach small rods from a pile one by one, without disturbing the others.

10. *skelped our divoted way*: Whacked our way hitting bits (divots) from the turf.

11. *Arthurs ... you are an hireling*: Miss Baxter, addressing her maid by her surname only, alludes contemptuously to John 10:12: 'he that is an hireling ... seeth the wolf coming, and leaveth the sheep'.

12. *"As the tree falls – "*: Allusion to Ecclesiastes 11:3: 'As the tree falleth, there it shall be.'

13. *fly*: Cab drawn by one horse.

MARY POSTGATE

First published in *Nash's Magazine*, September 1915; collected in *A Diversity of Creatures* (1917).

1. *cassowary*: A tall flightless bird; 'dowey' means dismal.

2. *'rolling' ... 'taxi'*: Mary muddles the terms here. Wynn has evidently progressed from 'rolling' or 'taxi-ing' the machine on the ground to a solo flight.

3. *Contrexéville*: French mineral water.

4. *Salisbury*: The Central Flying School was then at Netheravon, Wiltshire, on the edge of Salisbury Plain (*NRG*).

5. *glebe*: Land assigned to the Rector.

6. *used Hentys ... Garvices*: Books by G.A. Henty, Captain F. Marryat, Charles Lever, R. L. Stevenson and Charles Garvice: authors of adventure-stories popular with Edwardian British schoolboys.

7. *prep. school*: Fee-paying boarding school for boys aged 8 to 14, preparing them for entrance examinations to public schools.

8. *assegai*: Zulu spear.

9. *OTC*: Officers' Training Corps.

10. *cart-lodge*: A shed for carts. This scene may owe something to Kipling's own experience of being required as a young reporter to investigate and write up the deaths of three schoolboys who were crushed when the roof of Lahore High School collapsed at midnight on 28 May 1886. Kipling, who had known one of the dead boys, vividly described the horror of the experience and his nightmares afterwards in a letter to Margaret Burne

Jones (*Letters*, ed. Pinney, vol.1, pp.131–2). Dr Hennis's suggestion that Edna has suffered from a similar accident is contradicted by her 'ripped and shredded body', which indicates blast damage.

11.   *certain Belgian reports*: Newspaper reports of atrocities committed by the German army in Belgium: often exaggerated, but atrocities, such as the sacking of Louvain in 1914, did take place.

12.   '*Cassée. . . . Che me rends. Le médecin!*': 'Broken, all broken . . . I surrender. Doctor!'

13.   '*Nein! . . . Ich haben der todt Kinder gesehn*': Ungrammatical version of 'Nein, ich habe das todt Kind gesehn': 'No, I have seen the dead child.' As an educated lady, Mary has a smattering of French and German.

14.   *pavior*: One who rams down paving stones.

A MADONNA OF THE TRENCHES

First published in *MacLean's Magazine*, August 1924; collected in *Debits and Credits* (1926). In *Debits and Credits* and the Sussex edition, this story is preceded by the poem 'Gipsy Van' and followed by Act 5 Scene 3 of Kipling's unfinished Browningesque play 'Gow's Watch', revealing Gow's lifelong fidelity to his hidden love.

1.   *Swinburne, Les Noyades*: The first and sixteenth stanzas of A. C. Swinburne's poem, a hauntingly sexy and perverse ballad about socially divided lovers bound 'bosom to bosom, to drown and die' (stanza 5).

2.   '*Faith and Works EC 5837*': Masonic Lodge invented by Kipling.

3.   *sal volatile*: Solution of ammonium carbonate in alcohol or water, a restorative after fainting-fits.

4.   *paregoric*: A soothing mixture.

5.   *BHQ*: Battalion Headquarters.

6.   *beasts of officers . . . out of the Burial Service*: A garbled quotation from I Corinthians 15:32: 'If after the manner of men I have fought with beasts at Ephesus, what advantageth it me, if the dead rise not?', part of the Order for the Burial of the Dead in the *Book of Common Prayer*. Keede quotes the same text later in the story.

7.   *Whatever a man shall say in his heart . . . Gawd hath shown man*: Strangwick, who thinks of the Swinburne poem as a 'hymn', turns it into a scriptural-sounding paraphrase, conflating Swinburne's 'they have shown man, verily' with Jesus saying 'Yea, verily, I say unto you, Whatsoever you shall ask the Father in my name, he shall give it you': John 16:23.

8.   *the twenty-first Jan.*: St Agnes' Day (cf. Keats's 'The Eve of St Agnes', also quoted widely in 'Wireless').

9.   *pipped*: Hit by a shot.

10. *poy-looz*: That is, *poilus*, French private soldiers.

11. *the Angels of Mons*: A popular myth that angels had appeared to save two divisions of the British Expeditionary Force during the retreat from Mons, 26–7 August 1914.

12. *'why stand we in jeopardy every hour?'*: 1 Corinthians 15:30; also in the Burial Service.

THE JANEITES

First published in *MacLean's Magazine*, May 1924; collected in *Debits and Credits* (1926).

1. *Jane lies in Winchester . . . England's Jane!*: This verse became the last verse of Kipling's poem 'Jane's Marriage'.

2. *PM*: Past Master, i.e. a former Master of the Lodge.

3. *chapiters*: A biblical term referring to the Masonic pillars.

4. *Lazarus*: Raised from the dead by Jesus, John 11: 1–46.

5. *Eatables*: British army slang for Étaples.

6. *Gothas*: German bombing planes.

7. *Victoria*: London terminus, targeted because of troop-trains leaving it for the Western Front.

8. *Lar Pug Noy*: Larpugnoy, near Arras (British army slang; *NRG*).

9. *'Enery James*: The novelist Henry James (1843–1916), much admired and respected by Kipling. Macklin's literary genealogy anticipates the famous opening sentence of F. R. Leavis's *The Great Tradition* (Chatto & Windus, 1962): 'The great English novelists and Jane Austen, George Eliot, Joseph Conrad and Henry James' (p. 9).

10. *Password of the First Degree*: Humberstall thinks of Jane Austen fans as a Masonic order.

11. *Tilniz an' trap-doors*: In chapter XI of *Northanger Abbey*, Catherine's mind is full of 'Tilneys and trap-doors'.

12. *marcellin'*: Waving. Hairdressers called an artificial wave a 'marcel' after the Paris hairdresser Marcel Grateau (*NRG*).

13. *Charges*: Ritual exhortations read to a Mason on initiation (*NRG*).

14. *some Abbey or other*: That is, *Northanger Abbey*.

15. *Reverend Collins . . . Lady Catherine . . . De Bugg*: Mr Collins and Lady Catherine de Bourgh, in *Pride and Prejudice*.

16. *Miss Bates*: A character from *Emma*, 'a great talker upon little matters'.

17. *Laura*: Laura Place in Bath, mentioned in both *Northanger Abbey* and *Persuasion*.

18. *pukka*: Solid.

19. *bringin' forth abundant fruit*: See Matthew 13: 18–23 the parable of the sower.

20. *our old loco'*: Heavy guns were moved about by railway locomotives (*NRG*).

21. *British warm*: A woollen overcoat worn by British officers.

22. *Roman Eagles or the Star an' Garter*: Alludes to Masonic investiture ceremony (*NRG*).

HIS GIFT

First published in *Land and Sea Tales for Scouts and Guides* (1923).

1. *French-polisher*: French-polish is a solution of resin in alcohol used for polishing furniture.

2. *Wolf-Cub*: Junior Scout.

3. *against which Scout uniforms offer small protection*: Scouts wore shorts.

4. *vittles*: A phonetic pronunciation of 'victuals', or food.

5. *'nature-faking'*: A joking allusion to Theodore Roosevelt's 1907 attack on Jack London's animal stories as exaggerated 'nature-faking', a media cause célèbre.

6. *Walrus, whose proper name was Carpenter*: Alludes to 'The Walrus and the Carpenter' in Lewis Carroll's *Through the Looking-Glass*; probably also to this 'placid and easy-going' boy's large size.

7. *the path of duty . . . the road to glory*: A joking allusion to Tennyson's patriotic 'Ode on the Death of the Duke of Wellington': 'Not once or twice in our rough island's story / The path to duty was the way to glory' (lines 201–2).

8. *small brush-stuff from the oven*: Mr Marsh bakes in a traditional brick oven heated by firing with brushwood or furze.

9. *Sawyer . . . Glasse*: Alexis Soyer (1809–58), famous chef who reorganized army cooking in the Crimean War (1854–6); Hannah Glasse (1709–70), eighteenth-century cookery writer best known for *The Art of Cookery* (1747).

10. *Mr Jorrocks, Master of Foxhounds*: See 'At the End of the Passage', n.28, above.

11. *'dampers' . . . 'lobscouse' . . . 'salmagundi'*: Dampers are flour-and-water cakes baked in wood ashes; lobscouse is a stew of salt meat, potatoes and onions simmered together; salmagundi is a stew including salt fish and onions.

THE WISH HOUSE

First published in *MacLean's Magazine*, October 1924; collected in *Debits and Credits* (1926).

1. *aireated wash-poles*: Outdoor aerials.
2. *whisk-drive*: Whist-drive, an evening of competitive whist (card game), a form of village entertainment.
3. *shruck*: Shrieked.
4. *a long-standing ulcer on her shin*: Kipling relates in *Something of Myself* that a reviewer noted Grace Ashcroft's resemblance to the Chaucer's Wife of Bath 'even to the mormal [sore] on her shinne', at which 'I gave myself "out – caught to leg"' (*Something of Myself*, ed. Pinney, p.124). It is in fact Chaucer's Cook who has the 'mormal'; but as Nora Crook has pointed out, Grace Ashcroft does resemble the Wife of Bath in her candid recounting of sexual liaisons culminating with the struggle for 'mastery' with a much younger man (*Kipling's Myths of Love and Death*, Macmillan, 1990, p. 120); moreover, she is a retired cook.
5. *be called with a handle to me name*: A maid would be called by her surname (cf. 'The House Surgeon', n.11, above), whereas a cook was entitled to be called 'Mrs'.
6. *stubbin' hens*: Plucking chickens.
7. *rugg*: Tug violently (dialect).
8. *scutchel up*: Gather hurriedly (dialect).
9. *hoppin'*: Hops, which ripen in September, were picked by hand until 1959. It used to be common for working-class Londoners to take part in the annual hop-picking in Kent and Sussex as a working holiday.
10. *roastin'-jack*: Metal roasting spit.
11. *I'd stood up too much to me work*: Mrs Ashcroft suffers from varicose veins in her legs. Her wound, being close to a swollen vein, has turned to a varicose ulcer, which should be treated by raising and resting the leg (*NRG*).
12. *fifteen bob a week*: Fifteen shillings weekly, a generous pension for a servant in 1926. It is five shillings more than the Old Age Pension, then ten shillings weekly, and amounts to nearly four times the annual allowance of £10 which Virginia Woolf gave the Stephens family cook Nellie Farrell in 1930 (Alison Light, *Mrs Woolf and the Servants*, Penguin Fig Tree, 2007).
13. *when the edges are all heaped up*: A classic sign of an ulcer turned cancerous (*NRG*).

THE GARDENER

First published in *McCall's Magazine*, April 1924; collected in *Debits and Credits* (1926).

1. *One grave . . . And rolled the stone away!*: From Kipling's poem 'The Burden', the complete text of which follows this story in the Sussex Edition of *Debits and Credits*. The last line recalls the angel who 'descended from heaven and rolled the stone from the door' of Christ's tomb; Matthew 28: 2.
2. *prep. school*: See 'Mary Postgate', n. 7, above.
3. *William the Conqueror*: King William I of England.
4. *OTC*: Officers' Training Corps.
5. *K.*: Kitchener of Khartoum.
6. *the wastage of Loos*: The Battle of Loos 1915, notorious for heavy losses, including Kipling's son John.
7. *Somme*: The Battle of the Somme, July 1916.
8. *the Armistice*: Signed 11 November 1918.
9. *ASC*: Army Service Corps.
10. *Cook's*: Thomas Cook, the travel agent.
11. *Hooge*: Between Ypres and the Menin Gate in northern France (*NRG*).
12. *supposing him to be the gardener*: Quoted directly from John 20: 14–15, when the distraught Mary Magdalene meets the risen Chirst and 'saw Jesus standing, and knew not that it was Jesus . . . supposing him to be the gardener'.

DAYSPRING MISHANDLED

First published in *McCall's Magazine*, March 1928; collected in *Limits and Renewals* (1932).

1. *C'estmoi . . . Et qui chante pour toi!*: From the 'gothic' French writer Charles Nodier (1780–1844): 'It is I, it is I, it is I! I am the Mandragora! The daughter of the good days who wakes at dawn / And who sings for you!' Mandragora (mandrake) is a plant of the nightshade family with narcotic and poisonous properties.
2. *cuts*: Woodcut illustrations.
3. *a couple of sovereigns*: gold coins worth £1, roughly £70 today.
4. *Upas-tree*: Legendary poisonous tree said to kill everything underneath it (*Hobson-Jobson*).

5. *three-guinea*: Three pounds and three shillings (£3.15), worth about £200 today.

6. *thirteen-and-sevenpence ha'penny*: Thirteen shillings and seven and a half pence (67 p); roughly equivalent to £24.50 today.

7. *Wardour Street*: See 'The Finest Story in the World', n.28, above.

8. *Supreme Pontiff*: The Pope of Chaucer studies.

9. *learned Hun*: German scholar.

10. *from Upsala to Seville*: From Sweden to Spain.

11. *gadzooking and vitalstapping*: Writing dialogue full of sham archaisms: 'Gadzooks!' and 'Stap my vitals!'

12. *Vulgate*: Latin translation of the Bible by St Jerome, used throughout the Middle Ages.

13. *thirty-five shillings*: one pound fifteen shillings (£1.75), roughly £120 today.

14. *Alva and the Dutch*: The Duke of Alva suppressed the Dutch Protestant rebellion against Roman Catholic Spanish rule in the Netherlands in 1567, with notorious brutality.

15. *our Dan*: Cf. 'Dan Chaucer, well of English undefiled / On Fame's eternal beadroll worthy to be filed': Edward Spenser, *Faerie Queene*, book iv, canto ii, line 23.

16. *intoning to the gas*: Declaiming to an empty room. Victorian rooms were commonly illuminated by gaslight.

17. *KBE*: Knight Commander of the Most Excellent Order of the British Empire.

18. *you had been faithful, Cynara, in your fashion*: From Ernest Dowson's *fin de siècle* poem 'Non sum qualis eram': 'But I was desolate and sick of an old passion / I have been faithful to thee, Cynara! in my fashion.'

19. *'Illa alma Mater ecca, secum afferens me acceptum. Nicolus Atrib.'*: 'Lo that bounteous Mother who accepts me and takes me with her. Nicolas Atrib[us].' As shown in Kipling's footnote on p. 517, reading the first letters of each word and then the second gives the acrostic 'IAMES A MANALLACE FECIT': 'James A Manallace made [it]'. 'Fecit' is, appropriately, pro-nounced 'fake it'.

20. *black-letter*: Gothic minuscule, used throughout Europe in the Middle Ages.

21. *"verray parfit, gentil Knyght"*: 'true, perfect, gentle knight'; Chaucer, 'Prologue' to *The Canterbury Tales*, line 72.

22. *old vellum*: Old parchment.

23. *his Gladstone*: His suitcase.

THE MANNER OF MEN

First published in the *London Magazine*, September 1930; collected in *Limits and Renewals* (1932).

1. *cinnabar-tinted*: Coloured with red mercuric sulphate, used for dressing Roman sails (*NRG*).

2. *verdigris in their dole-bread*: The grain meant for distribution to the Roman people will be tainted by the copper ballast.

3. *dressed African leathers on your private account*: The captain is getting free transport for his private cargo of hides, used as bin-linings (*NRG*).

4. *wings*: Spaces between the grain-bins and the ship's sides (*NRG*).

5. *single-banker, eleven a side*: A rowing-galley of twenty-two oars.

6. *flesh-traffic*: Slave trade.

7. *Free Trader*: Pirate.

8. *Euxine*: Black Sea.

9. *a passenger, our last trip together, who wanted to see Caesar*: The apostle Paul, whose shipwreck on his journey to Rome is related in Acts of the Apostles 27. Quabil's account closely follows the Bible story.

10. *sutlers*: Sellers of provisions to the army.

11. *Myra*: Ancient port on the Lycian (Turkish) coast, now named Dembre: cf. Acts 27: 5.

12. *Fairhaven*: Acts 27: 8: 'a place which is called the fair havens: nigh whereunto was the city of Lasea.'

13. *bight*: Loop of rope. Paul has things neatly sorted out.

14. *lictor's work . . . Jew scourgings*: For Paul's record of punishment, see 2 Corinthians 11: 24–5.

15. *three-banker*: Trireme galley.

16. *the yelp of a bank being speeded up*: Cries of oarsmen being whipped to row faster.

17. *line his hold for a week in advance*: Eat heartily while he still could.

18. *pooped*: Overwhelmed by a wave breaking over the poop (after-deck) from behind.

19. *bo'sun-captain*: One who has risen from seaman to captain.

20. *kedge*: Lightest ship's anchor.

21. *achatours*: Purveyors.

22. *under-Lebanon*: Quabil's home.

23. *Thessalian jugglery with a snake*: Acts 28: 3–6.

24. *canvas I can cut*: Paul was trained as a tent-maker (*NRG*).

PENGUIN CLASSICS

PLAIN TALES FROM THE HILLS
RUDYARD KIPLING

'You are all liars, you English'

Plain Tales from the Hills, Rudyard Kipling's first collection of short stories, established his reputation and brought India to the British imagination. Including the stories 'Lispeth', 'Beyond the Pale' and 'In the Pride of His Youth', they tell of soldiers, wise children, exiles, forbidden romances and divided identities, creating a rich portrait of Anglo-Indian society. Originally published for a newspaper in Lahore when Kipling was a journalist, the tales were later revised by him to re-create as vividly as possible the sights and smells of India for readers at home. Far from being a celebration of empire, these stories explore the barriers between races, classes and sexes, and convey all the tensions and contradictions of colonial life.

Part of a series of new editions of Kipling's works in Penguin Classics, this volume contains a General Preface by Jan Montefiore and an introduction by Kaori Nagai discussing Kipling's portrayal of the relationship between India and England, the role of the narrator in his *Plain Tales*, and the revisions that he made to them.

Edited with an introduction by Kaori Nagai
Series Editor Jan Montefiore

PENGUIN CLASSICS

JUST SO STORIES
RUDYARD KIPLING

'The rhinoceros took off his skin and carried it over his shoulder as he came down to the beach to bathe'

The Camel gets his Hump, the Whale his Throat and the Leopard his Spots in these bewitching stories which conjure up distant lands, the beautiful gardens of splendid palaces, the sea, the deserts, the jungle and its creatures. Inspired by Kipling's delight in human eccentricities and the animal world, and based on bedtime stories he told to his daughter, these strikingly imaginative fables explore the myths of creation, the nature of beasts and the origins of language and writing. They are linked by poems and scattered with Kipling's illustrations, which contain hidden jokes, symbols and puzzles. Among Kipling's most loved works, the *Just So Stories* have been continually in print since 1902.

Part of a series of new editions of Kipling's works in Penguin Classics, this volume contains a General Preface by Jan Montefiore and an introduction by Judith Plotz exploring the origins of the stories in Kipling's own life and in folklore, their place in classic children's literature and their extraordinary language.

Edited with an introduction by Judith Plotz
Series Editor Jan Montefiore

PENGUIN CLASSICS

SPUNYARN: SEA POETRY AND PROSE
JOHN MASEFIELD

'I must down to the seas again, to the lonely sky and sea'

John Masefield was sent to join a training ship at a young age, his aunt hoping the experience would cure him of his addiction to books. Instead, Masefield was to become one of the greatest writers on life at sea. In this collection of short stories, extracts from novels, poetry (including 'Sea-Fever' and 'Cargoes') and autobiography, he writes of the hardship, romance and adventure of seafaring with a sailor's way with language and sense of a good yarn: of life in dock and on the swelling seas, of salt spray, mutiny, great storms, the spirits beneath the waves, and the devil and Davy Jones playing dice for souls.

This edition includes an introduction by Philip W. Errington on Masefield's reputation, his mistreatment of his own youthful work, and his conflicted attitude to his colourful life story. It also includes a chronology, further reading and notes.

Edited with an introduction and notes by Philip W. Errington

PENGUIN CLASSICS

KING SOLOMIN'S MINES
H. RIDER HAGGARD

'There at the end of the long stone table ... sat Death himself'

Onboard a ship bound for Natal, adventurer Allan Quartermain meets Sir Henry Curtis and Captain John Good. His new friends have set out to find Sir Henry's younger brother, who vanished seeking King Solomon's legendary diamond mines in the African interior. By strange chance, Quartermain has a map to the mines, drawn in blood, and agrees to join the others on their perilous journey. The travellers face many dangers on their quest – the baking desert heat, the hostile lost tribe they discover and the evil 'wise woman' who holds the secret of the diamond mines. *King Solomon's Mines* (1885) is a brilliant work of adventure romance that has gripped readers for generations.

In his preface Giles Foden considers Haggard's treatment of the cultural stereotypes of the time, while Robert Hampson's introduction discusses the explorations and empire building that inspired Haggard's writing. This edition also includes further reading, an appendix and notes.

'Enchantment is just what Rider Haggard exercised ... his books live today with undiminished vitality' Graham Greene

Edited with an introduction and notes by Robert Hampson
Preface by Giles Foden

PENGUIN CLASSICS

TYPHOON/AMY FOSTER/FALK/TO-MORROW
JOSEPH CONRAD

'The wind howled, hummed, whistled, with sudden booming gusts that rattled the doors and shutters in the vicious patter of sprays'

In these four stories Joseph Conrad explores alienation, danger and exploitation in strange worlds, at sea and on land. 'Typhoon' portrays a captain and his first mate as they face a deadly storm, while 'Falk', the companion sea-story, is a tale of love and the struggle for survival amid hideous moral disintegration. With his two stories set on land, Conrad explores the isolation of an Eastern European immigrant in a Kent village in 'Amy Foster', and expresses the plight of a woman trapped by two retired widowers in 'To-morrow'. All these works, written between 1900 and 1902, show individuals hemmed in by circumstances beyond their control in rigid, enclosed societies.

Part of a major series of new editions of Conrad's most famous works in Penguin Classics, this volume contains a chronology, further reading, notes, a glossary and an introduction discussing the background, themes and technique of each story and highlighting the contrasts and continuities between them.

Edited with an introduction by J. H. Stape
General editor J. H. Stape

PENGUIN CLASSICS

A DEAD MAN'S MEMOIR (A THEATRICAL NOVEL)
MIKHAIL BULGAKOV

'I confess quite frankly that what I produced was some kind of gibberish'

Sergei Maksudov has failed as a novelist and made a farce of a suicide attempt, but only after a surprise break as a playwright on the Moscow stage does his turmoil truly begin. Thrown uncomprehending into theatre life, he soon sees his beloved play dragged into chaos by inflated egos, jealous critics, literary double-dealers, communist censors and insanely bad acting. Full of affectionately drawn characters, *A Dead Man's Memoir* is a brilliant, absurdist tale of the exhilaration and black desperation wrought on one man by his turbulent love affair with the theatre. Based on his own experiences at the famous Moscow Art Theatre of the 1920s and 30s, it reaches its comic height in a merciless lampooning of Stanislavsky's fashionable stage techniques.

Andrew Bromfield's powerful new translation is accompanied by an introduction by Keith Gessen, which discusses the autobiographical basis of these fictionalized memoirs and Bulgakov's artistic integrity in the face of Soviet repression. This edition also contains notes and a chronology.

Translated with notes by Andrew Bromfield

With a new introduction by Keith Gessen

PENGUIN CLASSICS

A MODERN UTOPIA
H. G. WELLS

'There is no justice in Nature perhaps, but the idea of justice must be sacred'

While walking in the Swiss Alps, two English travellers fall into a space-warp, and suddenly find themselves in another world. In many ways the same as our own – even down to the characters that inhabit it – this new planet is still radically different, for the two walkers are now upon a Utopian Earth controlled by a single World Government. Here, as they soon learn, all share a common language, there is sexual, economic and racial equality, and society is ruled by socialist ideals enforced by an austere, voluntary elite: the 'Samurai'. But what will the Utopians make of these new visitors from a less perfect world?

A compelling blend of philosophical discussion and imaginative narrative, A Modern Utopia is one of Wells's most positive visions of a possible world. Part of a brand new Penguin series of H. G. Wells's works, this edition includes a newly established text, a full biographical reading list and detailed notes. The introduction, by Francis Wheen, considers the virtues and flaws of Wells's ideal society.

Introduced by Francis Wheen

Textual Editing by Gregory Claeys

Notes by Gregory Claeys

PENGUIN CLASSICS

ANN VERONICA
H. G. WELLS

'There was a pause, and then the front door slammed ... Ann Veronica realised that she was alone with the world'

Twenty-one, passionate and headstrong, Ann Veronica Stanley is determined to live her own life. When her father forbids her from attending a fashionable Ball, she decides she has no choice but to leave her family home and make a fresh start in London. There, she finds a world of intellectuals, socialists and suffragettes – a place where, as a student in Biology at Imperial College, she can be truly free. But when she meets the brilliant Capes, a married academic, and quickly falls in love, she soon finds that freedom comes at a price.

A fascinating description of the women's suffrage movement, *Ann Veronica* offers an optimistic depiction of one woman's sexual awakening and search for independence. Part of a brand-new Penguin series of H. G. Wells's works, this edition includes a newly-established text, a full biographical essay on Wells, a further reading list and detailed notes. The introduction, by Margaret Drabble, considers the relevance of the novel to Wells's personal life.

Introduction by Margaret Drabble

Textual Editing by Sita Schutt

Notes by Sita Schutt

Penguin Classics

TONO-BUNGAY H. G. WELLS

'I never really determined whether my uncle regarded Tono-Bungay as a fraud'

Presented as a miraculous cure-all, Tono-Bungay is in fact nothing other than a pleasant-tasting liquid with no positive effects. Nonetheless, when the young George Ponderevo is employed by his Uncle Edward to help market this ineffective medicine, he finds his life overwhelmed by its sudden success. Soon, the worthless substance is turned into a formidable fortune, as society becomes convinced of the merits of Tono-Bungay through a combination of skilled advertising and public credulity. As the newly rich George discovers, however, there is far more to class in England than merely the possession of wealth.

An acerbic account of human gullibility and a damning indictment of the British class-system, *Tono-Bungay* remains one of the greatest of all satires on the power of advertising and the press. Part of a brand new Penguin series of H. G. Wells's works, this edition includes a newly established text, a full biographical reading list and detailed notes. The introduction, by Edward Mendelson, explores the many ways in which the work satirises the fictions and delusions that shape modern life.

Introduced by Edward Mendelson

Textual Editing by Edward Mendelson and Patrick Parrinder

Notes by Edward Mendelson

PENGUIN CLASSICS

MAURICE
E. M. FORSTER

'People were all around them, but with eyes that were intensely blue he whispered, "I love you"'

Maurice Hall is a young man who grows up confident in his privileged status and well aware of his role in society. Modest and generally conformist, he nevertheless finds himself increasingly attracted to his own sex. Through Clive, whom he encounters at Cambridge, and through Alec, the gamekeeper on Clive's country estate, Maurice gradually experiences a profound emotional and sexual awakening. A tale of passion, bravery and defiance, this intensely personal novel was completed in 1914 but remained unpublished until after Forster's death in 1970. Compellingly honest and beautifully written, it offers a powerful condemnation of the repressive attitudes of British society, and is at once a moving love story and an intimate tale of one man's erotic and political self-discovery.

The introduction, by David Leavitt, explores the significance of the novel in relation to Forster's own life and as a founding work of modern gay literature. This edition reproduces the Abinger text of the novel, and includes new notes, a chronology and further reading.

Edited with an introduction and notes by David Leavitt

PENGUIN CLASSICS

A PASSAGE TO INDIA
E. M. FORSTER

'Shrines are fascinating, especially when rarely opened'

When Adela and her elderly companion Mrs Moore arrive in the Indian town of Chandrapore, they quickly feel trapped by its insular and prejudiced British community. Determined to explore the 'real India', they seek the guidance of the charming and mercurial Dr Aziz, a cultivated Indian Muslim. But a mysterious incident occurs while they are exploring the Marabar caves with Aziz, and the well-respected doctor soon finds himself at the centre of a scandal that rouses violent passions among both the British and their Indian subjects. A masterly portrait of a society in the grip of imperialism,

A Passage to India compellingly depicts the fate of individuals caught between the great political and cultural conflicts of the modern world.

The introduction, by Pankaj Mishra, outlines Forster's complex engagement with Indian society and culture. This edition reproduces the Abinger text and notes, and also includes four of Forster's essays on India, a chronology and further reading.

'His great book ... masterly in its prescience and its lucidity' Anita Desai

Edited by Oliver Stallybrass

With an introduction by Pankaj Mishra

PENGUIN CLASSICS

TRAVELS WITH A DONKEY AND THE AMATEUR EMIGRANT
ROBERT LOUIS STEVENSON

'I was not only travelling out of my country in latitude and longitude, but out of myself in diet, associates, and consideration'

In 1878, Robert Louis Stevenson escaped from his numerous troubles – poor health, tormented love, inadequate funds – by embarking on a journey through the Cévennes in France, accompanied by Modestine, a rather single-minded donkey. The notebook Stevenson kept during this time became *Travels with a Donkey*, a highly entertaining account of the French people and their country. *The Amateur Emigrant* is a vivid journal of his travels to and in America – describing the crowded weeks in steerage with the poor and sick, as well as stowaways – and the train journey he took across the country. Filled with sharp-eyed observations, this work brilliantly conveys Stevenson's perceptions of America and the Americans. Together, these two pieces are fascinating examples of nineteenth-century travel writing, revealing as much about the traveller as the places he travels to.

Christopher MacLachlan's introduction places the works in their biographical and literary context. This edition also includes pieces from Stevenson's original notebooks, a chronology, further reading, notes and maps of the journeys.

Edited with an introduction by Christopher MacLachlan

PENGUIN CLASSICS

THE FOX/THE CAPTAIN'S DOLL/THE LADYBIRD
D. H. LAWRENCE

These three novellas show D. H. Lawrence's brilliant and insightful evocation of human relationships – both tender and cruel – and the devastating results of war. In 'The Fox', two young women living on a small farm during the First World War find their solitary life interrupted. As a fox preys on their poultry, a human predator has the women in his sights. 'The Captain's Doll' explores the complex relationship between a German countess and a married Scottish soldier in occupied Germany, while in 'The Ladybird', a wounded prisoner of war has a disturbing influence on the Englishwoman who visits him in hospital.

In her introduction, Helen Dunmore discusses the profound effect the First World War had on Lawrence's writing. Using the restored texts of the Cambridge edition, this volume includes a new chronology and further reading by Paul Poplawski.

'As wonderful to read as they are disturbing ... Lawrence's prose is breath-taking'
Helen Dunmore

'A marvellous writer ... bold and witty' Claire Tomalin

Edited by Dieter Mehl
With an introduction by Helen Dunmore